LET THE
GALAXY BURN

IN THE NIGHTMARE future of the 41st millennium, mankind teeters upon the brink of extinction. The galaxy-spanning Imperium of Man is beset on all sides by ravening aliens, and threatened from within by malevolent creatures and heretic rebels. Only the strength of the immortal Emperor of Terra stands between humanity and its annihilation. Dedicated to His service are the countless warriors, agents and myriad servants of the Imperium. Foremost amongst them stand the Space Marines, mentally and physically engineered to be the supreme fighting force.

By popular demand, we've gathered up the best SF short stories ever written for the Black Library into one massive volume, and added some brand new tales! Warhammer 40,000 fans will once again be able to get their hands on classic stories that have long been unavailable.

More Warhammer 40,000 from the Black Library

• **WARHAMMER 40,000 SHORT STORIES** •

WHAT PRICE VICTORY
edited by Marc Gascoigne & Christian Dunn

BRINGERS OF DEATH
edited by Marc Gascoigne & Christian Dunn

• **GAUNT'S GHOSTS** *by Dan Abnett* •

The Founding
FIRST & ONLY
GHOSTMAKER • NECROPOLIS

The Saint
HONOUR GUARD • THE GUNS OF TANITH
STRAIGHT SILVER • SABBAT MARTYR

The Lost
TRAITOR GENERAL • HIS LAST COMMAND

• **ULTRAMARINES** *by Graham McNeill* •

NIGHTBRINGER • WARRIORS OF ULTRAMAR
DEAD SKY, BLACK SUN

• **CIAPHAS CAIN** *by Sandy Mitchell* •

FOR THE EMPEROR • CAVES OF ICE
THE TRAITOR'S HAND

• **SOUL DRINKERS** *by Ben Counter* •

SOUL DRINKER • THE BLEEDING CHALICE
CRIMSON TEARS

• **SPACE WOLVES** *by William King* •

SPACE WOLF • RAGNAR'S CLAW
GREY HUNTER • WOLFBLADE

A WARHAMMER 40,000 STORIES

LET THE GALAXY BURN

Edited by
Marc Gascoigne
& Christian Dunn

A Black Library Publication

The majority of these stories appeared in the following anthologies: *Into the Maelstrom* (© 1999, Games Workshop Ltd), *Dark Imperium* (© 2001, Games Workshop Ltd) and *Words of Blood* (© 2002, Games Workshop Ltd).
Playing Patience, The Tower and *The Fall of Malvolion* have not before appeared in print.

This omnibus edition published in Great Britain in 2006 by
BL Publishing,
Games Workshop Ltd.,
Willow Road, Nottingham,
NG7 2WS, UK.

10 9 8 7 6 5 4 3 2 1

Cover illustration by Jim Burns.

A CIP record for this book is available from the British Library.

ISBN 13: 978 1 84416 342 7
ISBN 10: 1 84416 342 3

Distributed in the US by Simon & Schuster
1230 Avenue of the Americas, New York, NY 10020, US.

See the Black Library on the Internet at
www.blacklibrary.com

Find out more about Games Workshop
and the world of Warhammer 40,000 at
www.games-workshop.com

Printed and bound in the US.

IT IS THE 41st millennium. For more than a hundred centuries the Emperor has sat immobile on the Golden Throne of Earth. He is the master of mankind by the will of the gods, and master of a million worlds by the might of his inexhaustible armies. He is a rotting carcass writhing invisibly with power from the Dark Age of Technology. He is the Carrion Lord of the Imperium for whom a thousand souls are sacrificed every day, so that he may never truly die.

YET EVEN IN his deathless state, the Emperor continues his eternal vigilance. Mighty battlefleets cross the daemon-infested miasma of the warp, the only route between distant stars, their way lit by the Astronomican, the psychic manifestation of the Emperor's will. Vast armies give battle in his name on uncounted worlds. Greatest amongst His soldiers are the Adeptus Astartes, the Space Marines, bio-engineered super-warriors. Their comrades in arms are legion: the Imperial Guard and countless planetary defence forces, the ever-vigilant Inquisition and the tech-priests of the Adeptus Mechanicus to name only a few. But for all their multitudes, they are barely enough to hold off the ever-present threat from aliens, heretics, mutants – and worse.

TO BE A man in such times is to be one amongst untold billions. It is to live in the cruellest and most bloody regime imaginable. These are the tales of those times. Forget the power of technology and science, for so much has been forgotten, never to be re-learned. Forget the promise of progress and understanding, for in the grim dark future there is only war. There is no peace amongst the stars, only an eternity of carnage and slaughter, and the laughter of thirsting gods.

CONTENTS

Editor's Introduction

Marc Gascoigne

PREPARE FOR IMPACT!

Brace yourselves. Splints at the ready. Hot towels and narthecium on standby. This is the big one. Let's face it, you really need power armour to haul this sucker around for very long. Because inside this ultra-hefty, Imperial Titan-sized collection you'll find a full thirty-eight great stories* from the decaying future nightmare that is Warhammer 40,000. We'll take you from the crenellated battle barges of the heretic Traitor Marines to the forgotten asylums of the Imperium, bolter at the ready and thirsting for alien blood. ·

So just what is it that makes a Warhammer 40,000 short story a great one? It's a question we asked ourselves every day, as we sifted through the piles of stories submitted for the Black Library range over the years, and it's one we continue to employ as we assess potential novels for our thriving fiction line. In our writers' guides, we go into great length, but when pushed to summarise we tend to boil it down to two basic rules: be true to the Warhammer universe, and be any good. And to be blunt, we think the various stories collected in this mammoth brick of a book fulfil both of those criteria.

Of course, there's a mass of expertise and sheer hard work behind hitting both of those criteria. The 40K universe is a complicated and detailed one, and anyone reporting back from the front lines better know what they are talking about. But more than that it has a certain true feel, a texture of dark despair and ceaseless conflict, a galaxy where mankind knows that pure survival is worth any sacrifice, even its humanity.

There is also the comforting (if such a word can ever be used for such a devastated and wartorn time) knowledge that the 40K universe is such a rich and varied one. Let's face it, it's a big galaxy out there. Over two decades, Warhammer 40,000 has transcended its influences and taken on a living, breathing and above all fighting life of its own. This wide selection of tales from this rich setting pokes an inquisitive eye into all corners, from the front lines where countless warriors battle under blazing skies, to the dusty, most heretical corners where only the Inquisition dare to crawl. In the grim darkness of the future, we say, there is only war. But what a war, fought on so many different battlefields, both traditional and obscure.

The traditional definition of any rattling good short story, as opposed to something longer and with complication such as a novel, tends to involve the suggestion of a problem to be solved, or a twist away from the norm – a classic "but what if…" question. To single out just one, there is a story you will soon be reading, one of my own favourites, that combines that approach with a knowing piece of Warhammer 40,000 detail. In "Words of Blood", the set-up is a classic one. The noble Space Marine warriors, the Black Templars, it is said, never retreat. Normally that's not a problem, says author Ben Counter, more a statement of their underlying ethos as the galaxy's toughest elite – but what if they absolutely have to, what if retreat is the only possible way to defeat their enemy? As you'll see shortly, it's not without a good deal of soul-searching and dissension.

There's a Thunderhawk's payload worth of "what if…" in this collection and it's ready for take-off. Let the galaxy burn? You heard what the great man said. Pull that lever.

– Marc Gascoigne
The Inner Chambers of the Black Library, 2006

---

* Please believe us, we really did try to squeeze in forty. (Sorry.)

WE ARE THE SPACE MARINES, THE CHAMPIONS OF HUMANITY

WORDS OF BLOOD
Ben Counter

DAY HAD NEARLY broken on Empyrion IX. Commander Athellenas glanced above him at the stars fading against the light of the planet's sun. He could still just see the silver dagger hanging in orbit, the renegade ship that was waiting to drop down onto the lone spaceport and rescue the heathen horde that was stranded here.

He had thirty Marines. Thirty Marines to halt an army that never gave up, never felt pain, who existed only to draw blood from the holy Imperium of man.

But Athellenas knew he must succeed. This temple on the outskirts of the planet's lone abandoned city dated back from the Great Crusade, when the people of the Imperium spontaneously elevated the Emperor to Godhood before His worship was taken over by the bureaucrats of the Ecclesiarchy – and it was by the faith that had built this temple that he swore no heretic would leave this planet alive.

Sergeant Valerian scrambled over the ruined outer wall of the temple, keeping low to avoid detection. 'Commander, they are sighted. They have left their ship.'

'Damage?'

'They came down shallow. Most of them survived.'

'Numbers?'

Valerian paused, a frown passing over his old, gnarled features. 'It is better that you see for yourself, commander.'

The devastator sergeant handed Athellenas the scope from the squad's lascannon. Athellenas made his way to the temple perimeter, from where the great smoking hulk of the crashed renegade craft could be seen, scarred and pitted, against the grey, pre-dawn sky.

He looked through the scope and saw the enemy for the first time. He counted them automatically – one batch stripping the dead, another, cavalry, dragging stubborn horses from the ship's hold, and a third group, the largest, surrounding the leader. They were cultists, and far gone – most of them shirtless and wearing the jackets of their uniforms tied around their waists; barefoot, their skins scarred and painted with blood, armed with whatever they had salvaged. Lasguns, knives, shards of twisted metal, a couple of heavy weapons on carriages pulled by the riders' horses. Every cultist had that same wide-eyed look, the look of rage mixed with desperation and unacknowledged fear, the emotions of treachery waiting to boil over at any second. Athellenas added up their numbers. Six thousand, give or take.

And the leader. If proof was needed that this was the work of the Blood God, he was it. Tall, not massively muscular, but wiry and powerful, almost glowing with pent-up energy. Dressed only in bloodstained cloth wrapped around his waist, black straggly hair, a violent, unshaven face, his skin covered in scars and branded with heathen symbols. One arm was gone, replaced with a pair of hydraulic industrial shears so big the tips reached the ground. The blades were pitted and worn, but even in the weak light the savagely sharp edge shone silver. He was talking animatedly to the heretics who surrounded him, his eyes flashing, his words so charged and evil that even though he was out of earshot, Athellenas could feel their power.

'Valerian?'

'Commander?'

'Take note. We have found the Gathalamor 24th.'

'The Manskinner? But he's–'

'He's a lot more than a rumour, Valerian. He's real, and he's here. He has the four thousand from Gathalamor and more. Probably the Guryan mutineers, and some cavalry.' Athellenas handed back the scope. 'Prepare a defensive position. The Manskinner will know we are here. He will attack with the sun.'

As Valerian gave instruction to the dug-in devastators, and the tactical and assault squads checked their weapons again for the fight that was to come, Athellenas ran over the rumours and official denials. That the famously pious planet of Gathalamor should supply the renegades for the Manskinner's army was too much for the Ecclesiarchy to admit. They had insisted the Manskinner was a rumour dreamed up by their enemies in the Administratum.

Athellenas's loyalty lay with Terra, not the Ecclesiarchy, but he, for one, would be happy to do them a favour and quell this rumour for good. And what rumours...

They said the Manskinner was nothing more than a criminal. He was being transported from a hive world – some said Necromunda, others Lastrati – when he broke out somehow. A bulkhead used to seal the brig had taken his arm off during the attempt, but the massive shock and blood loss had not killed him; he survived and fought on, and the last entries in the log of the drifting, burnt-out prison ship recorded how the plasma reactor was being tampered with and was about to go critical. The charred bodies of all those on board were recovered, save one.

It was on Gathalamor that the Manskinner turned up next and earned his name. Those officers in the regiment he infiltrated who opposed him were butchered in the night and their flayed skins run up the barrack's flag poles. Within three days of his arrival, it was said, several thousand of the planet's most trusted Guardsmen had disappeared, taking a troop transport ship from orbit as they did so, leaving a blood-soaked altar of skulls in the centre of their parade ground as if to mock those who stayed behind.

These were the tales that seemed to have substance. Others were just anecdotes and stories, about how the Manskinner could turn men to Chaos with his words alone, about the strange omens that accompanied him, and the abnormalities in the Astronomican which had confounded the spacecraft attempting to pursue his army.

Athellenas had been a commander for a long time, and a Space Marine for longer. He had learned that when cautious men believe nothing they have not seen, a true leader can sift truth from lies.

And there was a truth here, of the sheer monstrosity of the Manskinner, a force that corrupted the staunchest of men with horrifying ease. From foes such as him the Imperium had the most to fear – for it was built on the souls of its subjects, those same souls that the Manskinner was making his own.

'BROTHERS! SONS OF blood! This day, we face the final enemy. Some amongst you may believe the Blood God has seen fit to test us once more before we can truly worship him with the sacrifice of a million Macharian lives.'

The words of blood cut right into their minds, driving them to further heights of bloodlust. The Manskinner had never felt more grateful for the gift of the words – no army, no Marine, could stand before men who knew nothing but the joy of carnage.

'But the truth, sons of blood, is that such have we pleased him that he has given us yet more skulls to take! And what skulls! The Marines, the scum of humanity, the Imperium's blind machines, are here, to die in His name and prove His power to the weak!'

The Manskinner raised his remaining arm high, and the crowd around him cheered madly, screaming their insane joy at the battle to come.

Many had died in the crash, and still more were wounded or weak – their very bloodlust would kill them. Still, they were many. They would charge across the planet's lone city and take the spaceport, and their brothers in orbit would carry them the rest of their journey to Macharia, and on that world of thirty billion souls, his army would die in an orgy of carnage in the name of the Blood God. It was impossible to imagine the numbers that would die, the mindless hordes of the weak put to the sword before the last cultist died.

Such would be the pleasure of the Blood God, that he, the Manskinner, would become his chosen, an immortal champion murdering the very stars in His name.

'Brothers!' he called again over the din. 'Tend to your arms! the Imperial filth will die at the rising of the sun!'

The cultists scattered to prepare themselves: to load guns and sharpen blades, scar themselves, and contemplate the glorious acts of murder to come. Recoba, once a corporal, now commanding the four thousand Gathalamor rebels, bellowed orders and cracked heads. Kireeah, who had joined the Manskinner with over two thousand men from the Planetary Defence Force on Guryan, was rather more subtle, making sure his men could see his finger on the trigger of his duelling laspistol at all times.

'Diess!' yelled the Manskinner.

The rider galloped up on his jet-black horse. The beast's nostrils were flecked with foaming blood and its eyes bulged, but even this animal was infected by the power of the words of blood. Diess himself, young and breathlessly eager, sat bolt upright, cavalry sword raised in salute, still wearing his tattered officer's uniform.

'Sir! My Lord Manskinner!'

'Diess, to you goes the honour of first blood. You and your men will be the first to hit the Marines' position. Hit hard. If you can take some alive, do so. They will provide sport for the rest. If not, let nothing survive.'

Even Diess smiled at this. 'Thank you, my lord! This is a glorious day for Colcha!'

'Everyone on Colcha wants you dead, Diess. This is a glorious day for the Blood God.'

'Sir, yes sir!' Diess galloped off, infused with that strange joy that only the Blood God could give a man in the moments before battle.

The Manskinner could taste his victory on the air. The dry ground of Empyrion IX would run red before the day was out.

The first rays of the sun broke around the hulk of the cultists' spacecraft. Diess's horsemen, three hundred strong, spurred their mounts into motion as one and thundered across the plain towards the broken obsidian shell of the temple. Many of the foot troops followed them, waving their salvaged weapons and screaming with bloodlust, hoping that when they reached the temple there would be some Marines left alive for them.

Even as the first lasgun shots cut through the air, the Manskinner could feel the Blood God smiling down upon him from His throne of skulls in the warp.

Blood, keened a familiar voice in his head.

Blood for the Blood God.

'FIRE!' YELLED VALERIAN, his old, battered face creased with rage and indignation. The devastator squad's weapons sprouted sudden blossoms of flame and the first wave of heretic cavalry fell, some men shot off the backs of their mounts, some with their horses cut in half, all falling to the ground in clouds of dust.

But the horsemen kept on coming, their horses' hides smeared black with engine oil, beast and rider branded and scarred, the eyes both black with blood-madness. Those who had weapons which could shoot returned fire and a score of lasgun shots impacted against the black stone of the temple. Some hit the armour of the dug-in tactical and assault squads. None penetrated.

Athellenas flexed his hand encased in his power glove, feeling its power field leap into life around it. He raised his uncased hand, and brought it down in a swift chopping motion – at the signal, the tactical squad's bolters spat a rain of explosive steel.

Another wave of cavalry went down but they were closer now – and their leader, an officer in a ragged, stained parody of a uniform, still lived, holding his sabre high, leading his troops into the fray.

Shots kept coming and the assault squad sergeant, Kytellias, took a hit on the arm.

'Status, Kytellias?'

'Not serious,' replied the sergeant. 'Lost a couple of fingers. Ready for your order.'

'Hold, Kytellias. Hold.'

Another volley from the devastator and tactical squads cut down a swathe more horsemen, but the enemy were within laspistol range now. Athellenas's auto-sense warning icons flashed against his retina as one shot rang off his shoulder pad. He aimed his bolt pistol and took revenge for the firer's presumption, the shot taking a cultist in the neck and sending him somersaulting backwards off his horse.

They were close. Their horses were foaming. The officer raised his sword, ready to bring it down on the first Marine in his path.

'Charge!' yelled Athellenas. Before the word was out of his throat, Kytellias and his men had rocketed out of their dugouts, jump packs roaring. They came down on the heads of the nearest riders and each one cut down his opposite man. Kytellias himself sought his next target without breaking stride. Ignoring the cultists whose blades and clubs were turned aside by his armour, the sergeant ran at full pelt towards the officer.

He wants revenge, thought Athellenas. Revenge for his fingers. In any other army it would be considered ill-discipline – but for the Black Templars, for all Space Marines, everything they did was revenge.

Athellenas led the second charge himself, driving into the confused horsemen with the tactical squad. Plunging into the swirling dust and screams of the dying, he ducked the first blade and struck back with his power fist, a great pendulous blow that lifted rider and horse and threw them seven metres in a shower of blue sparks from the power field.

'Again!' yelled the officer. 'Again! Hit them again!' But his horsemen were too scattered and confused to regroup and counter-charge. Those who still had mounts were trying to wrestle their horses back under control through the hail of bolt pistol shells and the screeching walls of chainsword blades that lanced out of the dust and cut down a cultist with every stroke.

Athellenas's auto-senses picked out Kytellias, duelling with the officer. The officer was good, using his height advantage on his horse to keep Kytellias's power sword at bay. An aristocrat, thought Athellenas, raised in the saddle just as Athellenas and his Marines had been raised on the battlefield. He met Kytellias's every thrust, turning the blade so its power field didn't shatter his own.

Then Kytellias stopped toying with him and brought the power sword down so fast that the officer didn't have time to cry out as its point came down on his shoulder and carved him open. The officer dropped his sword, convulsed as his blood flooded out onto the dry earth, then toppled to the ground. His horse bolted and took many of the surviving animals with it. Those who were without mounts still fought, but they were so consumed with madness and confusion that the Assault and Tactical Marines picked them off at will with the chainsword tooth or the bolter shell.

'Sergeant Kytellias, report,' said Athellenas over his communicator.

'Seventy per cent enemy casualties, sir, no losses. Injuries nominal.'

Athellenas hurried forward through the clouds of dust and gunsmoke. He looked in the direction of the cultist spacecraft, auto-senses magnifying the image and picking out the sounds of the approaching horde.

The rest of the cultists were following. The Manskinner was acting true to form: the cavalry had been sent to draw out a counter-charge and break up the Marines' position, so the main body of cultists would hit a compromised Marine line.

'Valerian?'

'Sir.'

'Take your squad and fall back to the city's outskirts. Prepare another defensive position. Kytellias and I will join you there.'

Silence. Then...

'Sir, we cannot fall back. We cannot surrender this position.'

There was a quality in Valerian's voice that every commander came to know. The sound of rebellion.

'Valerian, you will fall back immediately. The enemy is too great. We cannot face them here.' Athellenas could see the Manskinner, claw swinging as he ran, the mass of cultists swarming around him.

'Sir, I cannot retreat in the face of the enemy. The Inititate Doctoris states as much–'

'Questions of doctrine will be dealt with on Terra. For now you will follow orders.'

Again, silence.

'Yes, sir.' But this time, rebellion was clear in Valerian's voice.

Athellenas signalled to the tactical and assault squads, and they moved as one back through the temple towards the outskirts of the city, leaving behind them a field of two hundred dead and an enemy who would not give up.

THE MANSKINNER KICKED over the worn marble icon of the Imperial eagle and watched it shatter on the ground. All around him, his men were taking out their rage on the fabric of the temple, firing shots into the carved walls, defiling the altars with their own blood.

'Where are they?' yelled Recoba. 'Where are the dogs? Cowardly dogs! Too afraid to face Khorne's wrath!' An untrained eye would see Recoba as a burned-out corporal running to fat, now turned to madness with the worship of the Blood God. But the truth was that he was strong – that his bulk was muscle, not fat, and he held the minds of his men in bonds of iron that the Blood God's worship had only forged tighter.

He spoke for all his men, and the Manskinner knew all his men were angry.

They had run. These Marines, these defenders of humanity, who should have died a hundred times over rather than yield one inch of ground to the Blood God's followers: they had retreated. They had fallen back in the face of heretics. They had surrendered this place, a symbol of their Emperor's false godhood, a place that was as holy as could be.

This was wrong. This was not the way of the Imperium. They were supposed to underestimate the Blood God's power in their arrogance, and die beneath the blades of His army as it swept them aside.

And his men, they all felt the same. They had been robbed of their battle, the ultimate deceit. The bloodlust was building up in them unchecked, a destroying hunger that only violence would satisfy.

'Brothers!' The Manskinner felt the words of blood hot in his mind. He had to use them wisely, and mould the minds of his men just as he wished. 'The enemy has shown its true face! Not merely weak, but cowardly! Deceitful! With their trickery they defy all that the Blood God has shown you! But we will not fall prey to their lies. We will wait here, in this, the very place they hold as a symbol of their weakling Emperor, and gather our strength before we strike and brand our victory against the spirit of the Imperium!'

Recoba strode forward, out of the gathered crowd. 'We cannot wait! By the Blood God's throne, the enemy are in flight! We must pursue them and run them down, not cower like children!'

The Manskinner fixed Recoba with a glare. The man was as dangerous as he was useful. He, amongst all the cultists, must be brought to heel. The Manskinner raised his claw so the steel tips hovered in front of Recoba's face.

'Recoba, my brother, you know nothing of the ways of the enemy. The Blood God has shown me the truth about the feeble ways of Man. The Marines wish to draw us out in pursuit so they can destroy one part of our force at a time, until finally there are none left to take to Macharia and begin the slaughter. They will use the commands of the Blood God against us, knowing we will become blind with bloodlust. Even now, when you wish to pursue, Kireeah's forces and half of your men have yet to arrive here. You would take on the Marines with a third, with a quarter, of your forces, only to let them run once more when the rest come to avenge them?'

The Manskinner turned once more to the rest of the cultists, who listened to his every word as if they were those of the Blood God himself. 'We will not let them, my brothers! We will all strike as one, so they will not break the back of this army before we reach the spaceport! Blood for the Blood God!'

Even now, the Manskinner could see a cohort of Gathalamor men gathering around Recoba, the old corporal's face twisted further with hate. He would break off, and lead them right into the Marines' trap.

Well, let him die, thought the Manskinner. Maybe his men would inflict some suffering on the Marines before the rest of the horde could reach them. It was for the good. To stop Recoba would be to fight him and his men, and he could not afford to have his army fall apart now. Let the Marines think their plan is working, that they will eliminate the Blood God's army piece by piece.

It will be all the more joyous when the enemy's skulls litter the ground of Empyrion IX, and our army is on its way to begin the holy slaughter. Let him die.

THE MIDDAY SUN cast few shadows through the outskirts of the deserted town. Empyrion IX's only settlement had been abandoned, along with the rest of the planet, when it was realised that its mineral deposits were far scarcer than the Adeptus Mechanicus Geologis had thought. And so it had stayed, for hundreds of years, until today, when the fates had chosen it for the conflict that would decide the fate of a billion lives.

Athellanas had chosen to set up the second Space Marine line in a string of decrepit residential blocks, ugly grey blank plascrete. His squad was in the upper floors of one block, with the devastators in the neighbouring building. Below them, the broad streets, designed to take mining machines and trucks of ore, were empty, scattered with fallen masonry and fragments of broken glass. Everything was quiet. Even the air was still. It was only Athellenas's enhanced auto-senses that registered the scent of blood.

'They haven't actually... said anything, sir.' Kytellias, speaking to his commander face-to-face, was choosing his words carefully, for this was an area a Marine would normally never encounter. The area of rebellion. It was a dark, unfamiliar taste in the air. 'But I can tell. The way they move, their voices. They... they're not happy, sir. Not happy with you.'

Commander Athellenas looked at his assault sergeant. Like all the Black Templars, he had been tested without his knowledge back on Terra for the risk of disobedience – and Kytellias had been designated the most likely to rebel in Athellenas's whole command. Kytellias's capacity for initiative and self-reliance, that made him an ideal assault sergeant, at the same time made him headstrong and potentially dangerous. Yet he was the Marine Athellenas could most trust here.

This was not a question of a Marine being required to sell his life for the fraction of a victory. This danger was not born of cowardice or malice. Valerian, and perhaps others, were being ordered to abandon their whole system of values, to change the way they saw right and wrong. Retreat in the face of the enemy – in the face of Chaos – was a fundamental evil to a Marine.

He was asking his men to do wrong. What commander, what Space Marine, had that right?

'You have done well to tell me this, Kytellias,' he said. 'What of your squad?'

'They are sound, but no more.'

'And your hand?'

Kytellias looked down at his wounded hand. His blood had crystallised quickly around the plasteel, where the lasgun blast had sheared off three fingers. 'I still have my trigger finger, sir. No operational concerns.'

'Good. The next wave will be poorly led, but larger. We will use the streets. You will use your squad to draw the enemy in, funnel them into the street below. My squad and Valerian's will open fire on them from above. Understood?'

'Understood, sir.'

Kytellias's jump pack flared and he leapt through the wide, glassless window, across to the roof of the opposite building to enact the equipment rituals with his squad.

'Valerian?'

'Sir?' Valerian's voice was clear with suppressed anger over the communicator.

'Have your squad move into position. The second wave is here.'

'Nothing on the auspex, sir.'

'They're close. They will be hard to break at first, but soon their formation will disperse. When Kytellias withdraws, you will open fire. Kytellias will chase down enemy stragglers.'

'And then, sir? The next wave?'

'You have your orders, sergeant.'

Athellenas and his squad gathered on the fourth floor, bolters checked, ready to turn the street below into a river of fire.

The horizon shifted, turned dark, and began to spread through the outskirts towards them.

The second wave.

'FOR EVERY GREEN and sainted isle, of Gathalamor's blue sea, for the sake of every man that's lost, we'll die or we'll be free!'

Recoba's spirit rose with pride. His men, his personal command within the Gathalamor army, had sided with him to a man – fully a third of the cultists in number. As they marched in time, as they had been drilled, it was like they were back on fair Gathalamor, before they had lost so many brothers and friends to the idiocy of the Guard's commanders, before they had first encountered that madman with the voice of a god who took them at their lowest hour and changed them into his own private army.

They didn't need the Imperium. But they didn't need the Manskinner either. He was just another fool who would throw away the lives of Recoba's men. Well, if they must die, they would die face-to-face with the enemy, the Marines.

Space Marines. When the Guard threw billions of men to be chewed up by whichever foe their wrath fell upon, it was the Marines who survived, who delivered the killing blow to an enemy the Guardsmen's deaths had laid open.

They would know what it was like to feel that utter despair. Recoba would see to that.

At the front of the marching formation some of the men were falling out of step, breaking into a run to get to grips with the Marines who lurked in the residential blocks around them. As they headed down the town's main road, lasguns ready, still singing, the men were breaking off, kicking down doors, hunting for the enemy.

His men. Recoba was proud. They were still his men, even after all the Imperium and the Manskinner had put them through.

The smell came first, the burning, metallic reek of fuel. Then the white noise as they descended from the sky on their exhaust jets, dropping down right on top of the formation.

'Fire!' yelled Recoba. 'Open fire!'

But many of the men had no time to pull the triggers before the Black Templars were upon them, their black armour gleaming in the bright midday sun, black crosses on their white shoulder pads flashing, chainsword teeth tearing through the cultists, bolt pistols blazing.

Recoba saw one of the Marines, no, two, swamped by cultists who, having lost their weapons in the crash, threw themselves at the assault squad and dragged them down under the weight of the mob. The cultists grabbed the only thing at hand that could be used as a weapon – chunks of plascrete torn from the ground by heavy weapons fire – and set to work on the Marines. Recoba himself opened fire with his bolter, even as the two Marines' ceramite armour gave way beneath the pounding of plascrete. He heard them crack open, and felt it, too, as it gave all his men the heart not to break, to stand and fight.

The Marines were used to enemies running from them. Not this time. These were Gathalamor men. Gathalamor men could never be beaten.

The rest of the assault squad fell back towards the nearest building, leaving a trail of broken bodies behind them, but ever more cultists – no, not cultists, Guardsmen once more – closed in behind them, volleys of lasgun shots sending up a wall of white-hot light around the Marines. Another fell, sparks cascading from his ruptured armour, still firing even as he died beneath the rifle butts and bare fists of the Guardsmen.

Recoba joined his men as they poured forward after the Marines, formation forgotten, some still singing, all of them eager for the fight now that blood had been tasted at last.

'All troops, rapid fire. Target saturation pattern.' Athellenas watched as incandescent death lanced down from the upper floors of the building overlooking the street, tearing a hole through the main body of cultists. Lascannon blasts gouged furrows in the broken road surface, and frag missiles burst into clouds of fire, sweeping across the road, engulfing a dozen cultists at a time. Heavy bolter shots stitched a bloody path through the cultists, and the heavy plasma blasts fell like huge drops of liquid fire that flowed as water but melted anything they touched. The noise was immense, a vast roar of explosive, mechanical rage, mixed with the screams of the dying and the hiss of burning flesh. But Athellenas's auto-senses filtered out the din, leaving only the communicator channels clear.

'Kytellias here. Taking fire, three men down. Counter-attacking.' The first losses, then. Now Athellenas's tactics had cost the lives of Marines. Rebellion would be an even sterner foe now.

The bolters of Athellenas's tactical squad added their own fire, each Marine picking a cultist target and spearing him with a bolt of screaming steel. The formation was nothing now and the streets were full of a swirling, burning mass of men, caught up in equal measures of panic and hate, scrambling over one another, howling, dying by the dozen. The cultists didn't fall back, but they were weak and broken.

'Kytellias, charge.'

Through a haze of static and battle-din, Kytellias's voice came over the communicator. 'Yes, sir! Squad, by sections! Charge!'

The blades of Kytellias's squad tasted blood once more as the Marines carved their way through the panicked cultists. A few of the heathens ran; others fought on half-blind, and died without ceremony. They stood their ground in knots of resistance, but the Marines showed nothing but disgust for their broken enemies, cutting them down like reeds in a thunderstorm.

Kytellias's power sword accounted for most, flashing like a harnessed bolt of lightning, every stroke taking a pagan's head.

The Space Marines strode across the burning, bloodstained road, killing anything that still lived, until there was nothing there but death.

'Sir?' Valerian's voice, full of hidden tension. 'What now, sir?'

'We fall back,' replied Athellenas. 'Kytellias, cover our retreat and look out for enemy stragglers. Retreat to the spaceport–'

'Sir,' said Valerian, 'I cannot follow such an order.'

'Sergeant, fall back and maintain a defensive position.'

'I can see what you are trying to do, commander. If we fall back and destroy the cultists a wave at a time then they would be finished, but their objective is the spaceport. We cannot absorb one wave and then fall back again, or the spaceport will be taken. We must destroy them all, at once, immediately, and that objective can only be achieved if we stand and fight.'

There was silence. Athellenas could hear the gunsmoke coiling in the air and the blood running down the walls, the last licks of flame playing over the charred bodies of the cultists.

'That is why you object?' asked Athellenas carefully. 'Because you believe the tactic will fail?'

Silence.

'No, sir. That is not why I object. Perhaps we can defeat this army, commander. But if we cannot, then we must sell our lives for as many heathen souls as we can.'

Valerian was almost lost, realised Athellenas. He was trying to hide it, but his whole belief system was breaking down. Everything he had been taught, as a child, and as a Marine, had told him that to retreat was to die a million deaths, to give up his honour as well as his life, to betray his Emperor, his primarch, his very species.

'Either way, we must stand and fight, commander,' Valerian continued. 'It is both our duty and our privilege.'

'Fall back, Valerian.'

'Damnation, commander, this is madness! Does this Chapter mean nothing to you? Have you no duty to the souls of your lost brothers?

Already we have lost men here, do you wish to defile their memories with your cowardice? This is madness, sir, nothing but madness! I will not retreat, not ever, not for anyone or anything! I will not turn away from the fight, I will die by fire and by the sword, for if the only other option is to run like a child alongside you then I have no choice to make.'

This was where the battle was won. Athellenas knew he was right. He knew he would win. It was required of him. The enemy was nothing, he told himself. But his own men, they were the dangerous ones. They could break the back of this whole operation. If he ever had to be a leader of men, it was now.

'Valerian, you will fall back and maintain a defensive line at the spaceport. If you do not you will be shot and your name will be struck from the Liber Honarium. Your soul will have no mention at the Feast of the Departed. Your gene-seed will not be taken and given to a new initiate, because you will not be fit to have a Marine follow you into this 7. The faces of Rogal Dorn and of the eternal Emperor will be turned from you forever. You will not be in the Emperor's army at the end of time when the final battle is fought.

'You fear dishonour, Sergeant Valerian? If you disobey me now, if you place duty to yourself above duties to your Chapter and your Imperium, then I will show you truly what dishonour is.'

Silence again. And through the silence, Athellenas could hear the echoes of that power – the words of the Manskinner, rallying his troops. The cultists knew they had to strike as one to break through the Marine line. This wave had been a dissident group, enraged at being denied their battle.

If Athellenas could only hold his own force together in the face of the enemy of dishonour, then the Templars would win. He knew it, with every part of his soul. If he could just hold them together.

'I do this under protest, sir,' came Valerian's voice. 'When we return to Terra, if we return, I shall bring a Protest Iudicarum to the Chapter Master in person. I shall see you tried and excommunicated. But for now, I retreat.'

Even as the power of the Manskinner's heresy built up in the air, Athellenas led his Marines back through the abandoned streets of Empyrion IX, towards the spaceport. Above them hovered unseen the traitor ship, always a reminder of what would happen if the Manskinner took the spaceport.

How many would die? Billions?

Athellenas wiped the question from his mind. Not one cultist would escape into orbit while a Black Templar still lived.

'RECOBA IS DEAD!' yelled Kireeah, his Guryan troops gathered around him. 'No more of this! The Marines may cower and deceive us, but nothing can survive us! We are still four thousand strong, and they are but a handful! Now, Lord Manskinner, now we must strike!'

By the gods, the Space Marine commander was clever, thought the Manskinner. Lying and cowardly, perhaps, but clever. The Manskinner was losing his cultists. The seeds of hatred he had sown in them with the words of blood were blossoming, and their bloodlust was drowning everything else in their minds. Without battle, deprived of the joy of facing this enemy who retreated constantly and destroyed his army piece by piece, the Manskinner's men were devolving beyond his control.

The Manskinner faced his underling. Kireeah had been dangerous even before the Manskinner had found him, a young, driven officer with a reputation for savagery amongst the rest of the Guard, who had done much of the Manskinner's work beforehand in dismantling the humanity of his men. Of all the cultists, Kireeah would be feeling that seductive hatred most keenly.

'Kireeah,' said the Manskinner darkly, 'this foe is like no other. We cannot simply charge them without a thought, for they will take us apart piece by piece. They have shown that well enough already.'

Kireeah stepped closer. The Manskinner could see the veins standing out on the side of the Guryan officer's shaven head, flecks of spittle flying as he spoke, undiluted rage filling up the darkness behind his eyes. 'Lord Manskinner, many of us may die, but we will out! Even now they cower in the spaceport. If they retreat again we shall have won! They must stand or fall, and if they stand they cannot but die! No matter what, we will take the spaceport, and within the hour we shall be on our way to Macharia. If we should die, then our skulls shall honour the Blood God! If we hold back, and fight with shadows and lies, like our enemy, then he will be disgusted at our weakness!'

The Manskinner knew he had only one choice. He had used the words of blood many times to turn men into animals, now they had to turn animals into men. He felt their power growing within him as he spoke, his voice speaking to the very souls of Kireeah and every cultist there.

'Brothers! My brothers, this is the Blood God's final test! For we fight now not to win, or to die, but for revenge! Revenge, for Diess and Recoba and all those slain by deceit! Revenge, for the violation of the Blood God's holy rites of battle by a foe who will not face us! Revenge, like murder and massacre, is an aspect of His teaching – but unlike them, it is cold, fought by men purged of all emotion who fight not like animals thirsty for blood but as men acting as one, not charging blindly into the fray but marching side by side, a machine of destruction. This is the Blood God's way, to show us all the joys that bloodshed can bring, the sane alongside the savage, the cold-blooded along–'

Kireeah thrust his face close, his very breath like tongues of flame, teeth bared, heart pounding so strongly that a trickle of blood ran from one nostril and the vessels in one eye had burst into a crimson cloud spreading across the eyeball. 'Lies!' he screamed. 'This is not the Blood God's way! Now, when His worship needs him most, our lord has faltered! He has given way to cowardice! He is no better than the enemy, a coward who fights with lies instead of fists!'

Kireeah turned to the cultists. 'Charge with me, Brothers of the Blood God! Kill them! Kill them all!'

And as one, the cultists changed. The hateful loyalty the words of blood created was unpicked in a moment and the soul of every man belonged to Khireeah, to the bloodstained madness that was bursting across their minds.

The Manskinner didn't think, he just acted. He swung back the shears that hulked in place of his long-dead arm and brought them shrieking through the air, a hydraulic stab snapping the great blades shut around Khireeah's neck, slicing his head from his shoulders so quickly that the officer's mouth still moved as it fell to the ground.

The body swayed, fountaining blood as it fell.

It was too late. The men were already turning and breaking away, across the plain towards the city, yelling their homeworld's battle-cries or just keening like animals if they were too enraged to speak, the blood on their skin gleaming in the sun.

'Stop!' yelled the Manskinner as his entire army began to plunge towards the ruined city. 'Damn you, stop!' The words of blood shook the very air as he spoke but it seemed to have no effect. These were men whose souls had been drowned by their bloodlust, and it was to the soul that the words spoke.

The Manskinner's claw lashed out and carved the nearest few cultists into pieces, but the others ignored him, clambering over one another to get out of the confines of the temple and join the mad stampede.

'Stop! The Blood God commands you!'

The Manskinner strode amongst his frenzied men, butchering any within range, taking off heads, limbs, shearing torsos in two, his skin and the metal of the shears slick with blood. It had come to this, raged his thoughts. They had abandoned him. The words had abandoned him. If he could murder every single one of them, he would, if he could bring together every single living human being and put their necks between the blades of his claw, if he could climb to the top of the Throne of Skulls itself and face the God who had betrayed him...

The army was gone now, and the Manskinner was alone in the temple, with only the bodies of the dead left under his command.

No. His men were not the ones he hated. The enemy...

The Space Marines. They had done this. They had hidden like children and denied his men the bloodletting they lived for. Their trickery had broken even the power of the words, defiled the authority of the Manskinner, and of the Blood God above him.

'Kill them!' yelled the words, speaking to him as clearly as they had to any of his men. 'Kill them all!'

Suddenly, he was running in the thick of his men, surrounded by the bare torsos and tattered uniforms of his cultists, back with the men who owed him everything. He knew now what he must do. He must strike like a thunderbolt into the Marines, tear them limb from limb, and give him a taste of the slaughter to come.

Beyond it all, beyond the baying of his men and the thunder of their feet, the clouds of dust billowing around them and the stench of sweat and fire, drowning everything out, were the words of blood.

'Blood!' they called. 'Blood for the Blood God!'

THEY POURED THROUGH the streets, sweeping through the town like a flash flood across a plain, bringing with them the stench of sweat and blood and the din of four thousand men driven to insanity.

The cavernous, decaying spaceport loomed all around the Marines, but the vast series of half-collapsed domes offered few defensive positions amongst the debris and abandoned docking equipment. The devastator squad had set up as best it could, shielded by a set of docking clamps corroded to lumps of rust, while Kytellias's battered Assault Marines were high up amongst the support struts of the nearest dome, looking down at the horde that charged headlong towards them. Athellenas and the tactical squad were effectively in the open, positioned at the edge of the great open expanse of smooth plascrete on which the cultists' ship would land if they took the spaceport.

This was the end, thought Athellenas. *Even if I tried to retreat, Valerian wouldn't go, and neither would most of the others. It is by our actions here that we will be judged.*

Or remembered, if we fail.

'Take aim.' Though the cultists were still out of range, the Black Templars took aim as one, ready to loose their firepower as soon as the heathens charged too close. Through the scope of his bolter, Athellenas could see the Manskinner himself, at the front of the horde, the massive industrial shears swinging heavily as he ran, eyes no longer those of a leader, but of a fanatical follower. That was the key. No one led this horde any more.

The scream grew louder as the cultists scrambled over the remains of fallen buildings and streamed down the main road towards the spaceport, blood running from thousands of abrasions caused by their headlong, heedless charge. They had no sense of pain. They were blind and deaf to anything other than battle. They were the true children of their god, insane and self-destructive.

'Ready to go, sir,' came Valerian's voice over the communicator.

'Hold, sergeant,' replied Athellenas. 'We wait.'

* * *

'BLOOD!' SCREAMED THE voice, over and over again, as the Manskinner's untiring limbs carried him closer and closer to where the domes of the spaceport rose above the residential blocks. There was a savage joy on the faces of his men, and in that moment he was happy, knowing that there would be a twofold slaughter ahead: the Marines first, then across the stars to Macharia.

The Manskinner was happy at last. This was why he had been born. This was why the Blood God had picked him out. To kill, to shed blood in his name.

He was at the head of the horde as it crossed the threshold of the spaceport, roaring towards the Marine lines.

'Nothing lives!' he yelled. He could see the black-armoured figures crouching amongst the debris, trying to hide, but no one could hide from the Blood God's chosen. 'No quarter! No mercy! Blood for the Blood God!'

He could see their commander, lying in wait armed with a power fist he was too cowardly to use, trying to catch them in an ambush of fire as he had done with Recoba's men. Up above them, an assault squad, under-strength, lurked – but they would drop down not onto confused weaklings but a boiling sea of men made godlike by rage. They would melt away. They all would. They were nothing.

His claw blades held open ready for the kill, the words of blood screaming in his ears to match the pounding of his heart, the Manskinner led the final charge towards the spaceport.

'No quarter! No mercy! Blood for the Blood God!'

'HOLD, SERGEANT.' THEY were so close that Athellenas could feel the heat coming off them even before his auto-senses registered it. A tidal wave of men was roaring towards them, a wall of incandescent hate that would destroy anything in its way, half-naked blood-stained animals of men, with a raging daemon at their head, around which played a halo of dark power.

They were within range. He could order the devastators to open fire but he did not. There were two battles here. The cultists must die, and along with them the stain of rebellion amongst his men.

'Hold your fire,' he ordered again. He could feel the agitation of his men, the urge to open fire on the horde battling with their respect for his command. That respect might not last much longer if Athellenas did not do everything right.

Then, it happened.

The first men across the spaceport perimeter began to falter, losing direction, eyes wild as their focus was taken off the waiting Marines. One swung his makeshift club wildly as if wishing an enemy to appear next to him – full of lust for battle, he could no longer wait to reach the enemy and sought out his nearest comrade. He struck the man across the back of the head. The victim fought back with his teeth, lunging for the first man's throat, dragging him to the ground. The violence spread like a flash fire and suddenly thrashing, kicking, biting bodies were piling up on the threshold, thick dark blood running across the plascrete, ankle-deep.

The leader tried to drag his men apart and then joined them in their carnage, his flailing shears cutting men apart, two or three at a time. The noise was awesome. None of these men felt pain any more, and they screamed not with pain, but with rage at the violence done to their bodies and the wounds they inflicted with their own hands.

This army, this river of liquid fire, foundered a pistol shot away from Athellenas's Marines, its members tearing each other apart. Denied the taste of blood for so long, they sought it in the only place they could find it: in their fellow heretics.

'BLOOD! BLOOD! No mercy! No quarter!' The Manskinner didn't realise he was screaming. He felt nothing any more, just the thirst at the back of his throat and in the hollow at the centre of his soul, the hollow that could only be filled with death. The payment for the Blood God's favour was that they must feel his thirst, the lust for battle, the intense and all-conquering desperation that madness brought.

His claw sheared through the press of men around him. Weaklings! he thought. Idiots! To fail when they were this close! To deny the Blood God his final honour by wasting their lives! The Marines had won, their deceit denying his men battle for so long that they would butcher one another rather than wait a moment longer.

The part of his mind that could still think was dwarfed by the boiling cauldron of rage that made up the rest of him. The Manskinner killed and killed and killed, each man slain a drop of relief in the chasm of thirst. Even as the writhing, screaming, bleeding bodies closed over him, he killed. When the press became too close for him to breathe, he killed. When night came down across his eyes and his heart finally gave up its frenzied beating, he still killed. The instinct to murder was not dulled by death alone, and the shears still snapped at the walls of flesh around him until every last scrap of the Manskinner's energy was spent.

As the life finally bled from the Manskinner, the Blood God turned his back on his champion.

WHEN THE MADNESS was over, there were perhaps three dozen that still lived, wandering dazed and battered between mounds of broken bodies. The Manskinner's army was nothing more than four thousand mangled corpses and a lake of blood that was slowly draining away between the cracks in the plascrete. Flies were beginning to descend and the heat of the cultists' rage was dissipating as the bodies turned cold. The sky above began to darken as evening fell, the lumpen shadows cast by the corpses growing longer.

'Templars, advance,' ordered Athellenas. The assault squad dropped from high up in the dome, their landings cushioned by jets from their jump packs. Chainswords flashed and surviving cultists, blind and insensible, died without a struggle. Athellenas moved forward with his tactical squad, bolters picking off the stragglers wandering in twos and threes through the human wreckage. Athellenas levelled his bolt pistol and another heretic fell.

They didn't need the devastators. Soon the last few survivors were dead and the Manskinner's threat was truly over.

'Why didn't you tell us, sir?' asked Valerian over the communicator. 'If you knew this would happen?'

'Because, Valerian, I do not have to explain my actions to you. As your commander my word is law. I have not achieved this rank through chance. I have been judged by my Chapter to be the individual whose leadership is most likely to result in victory. My purpose is to lead you, and your purpose is to follow. If this breaks down, then all is lost. You will do what you are told, Valerian, and you will not argue. We are Marines. We are Black Templars.'

The assault squad was making a sweep of the bodies, checking for survivors. Athellenas knew even now that they would not find any.

'Some of you,' he said, 'will rise to a position where you, too, will command others from this Chapter. And then you will remember the lesson you have learned here. Above everything, above procedure and mercy, and even above the honour that Valerian held so sacred, there is victory. It is only through victory that you can truly honour the Emperor and your fellow man. To fail is the greatest shame. We have retreated in the face of the enemy, but there is no shame in that, for by doing so we have defeated them. The shame belongs to the Manskinner, for throwing away his chance of victory by fighting alongside animals, not soldiers. '

The sky above was dark, the sun of Empyrion IX dipping below the horizon. 'Kytellias, what is the ETA of our support craft?'

'Nineteen days, sir. Two of our strike cruisers. They'll destroy the heretics' ship before they know they're there.'

Nineteen days, thought Athellenas. If they had failed, no Imperial forces would have been close enough to intercept the heathen ship. How deep a wound, in lives lost and damage to the spirit of the Imperium, had they prevented from being struck here? Deep indeed.

'Then let us bury our dead,' he said, 'and prepare their wargear and geneseed for transport back to Terra. Valerian, you and your squad will set up a trophy here to mark our victory, so that none who set foot on this world will go ignorant of what happened here. You have your orders. Fall out.'

Athellenas's auto-senses switched automatically to night vision as the sun finally set on Empyrion IX.

THE BLACK PEARL

Chris Pramas

THE ENGINES OF the gunship roared as the Thunderhawk tore through the atmosphere. Inside, Interrogator-Chaplain Uzziel of the Dark Angels led four squads of Space Marines in the Litany of Battle. As he chanted the sacred words to prepare them for the imminent combat, Uzziel ran his fingers over his rosarius but today he did not pray in the prescribed Imperial manner. Today his fingers kept returning to the single black pearl on his string, the only pearl that really mattered. He had earned it by coaxing one of the Fallen Angels to repent and receive the Emperor's mercy.

That wretch was much on his mind as he finished the prayer, the enthusiastic voices of his twenty Marines joining him to boom the final refrain. As their voices faded, Uzziel pushed back his cowl. Filled with his faith in the Emperor, he launched into his sermon.

'Brethren,' he began, 'it has been a long journey and now, at last, battle is upon us. Before we engage the enemy, I want to tell you all something. This is no ordinary mission.' He paused to let this sink in. 'My brothers, this is a quest, a most holy quest to bring back to the Rock... a sacred artefact, long-missed.' Uzziel stared intently at the Marines. He saw men of varied origins, but they were all united in their blazing faith in the Emperor, in their oath as Dark Angels and in the Sacrifice of the Lion. He wished they could understand the full meaning of their mission but knew such a revelation could shake their faith. Today, he needed that faith.

'Should we succeed,' he continued, 'your names and deeds will long be praised in the halls of the Rock. We will sit in the company of the Chapter's greatest heroes. So fill your heart with the grace of the Emperor, remember the sacrifice of our blessed primarch, Lion El'Jonson, and gird yourself with the righteousness of faith!' Uzziel leapt up, possessed by holy fury, and slammed his fist to his chest. 'For Jonson and the Emperor! Victory or death!'

'Victory or death!' the Dark Angels returned his salute with barely suppressed savagery.

Uzziel smiled. With such men at this back, how could he fail?

IT WAS NOT so long ago that Uzziel, newly-promoted to the position of interrogator-chaplain after his inspirational leadership on the Bylini campaign, had walked the halls of the Rock, the giant space fortress that was home to the Dark Angels. He remembered the looks of envy on the faces of his comrades when he brought back his first Fallen Angel for interrogation. They couldn't believe that one so young had succeeded where they had failed. Many had dismissed it as pure luck but Uzziel knew better. To prove it, he swore to extract the confession due from the renegade himself.

It was not the first oath Uzziel had ever sworn, but it proved the most difficult to fulfil. The traitor had roundly mocked Uzziel, the Dark Angels and the Emperor. He told gleeful stories of his hundreds of campaigns as a mercenary, an endless catalogue of rape, murder and torture. Uzziel was not a man who shrank from violence, but he believed that it needed to serve a greater, righteous purpose. The wanton slaughter of the Fallen Angel's tales had sickened him, and he had to suppress a powerful urge to rip the wretch before him limb from limb, to pay him back in kind for each of his deeds.

Uzziel had fought off his immediate desire for vengeance. First, the confession. The Fallen Angel had seen the hatred in Uzziel's eyes and laughed. 'What's the matter, whelp, do my stories frighten you? Can't you stand to hear how a real Marine goes to war? You can keep your cowls and your prayer beads, monk. A true warrior goes into battle with lust in his heart, lust to spill the red blood of victory and taste the glory of war. That's what you lack and that's why you'll always lose!'

Those haunting words were with Uzziel even now, echoing sickeningly inside his mind as the Thunderhawk screamed through the atmosphere. Despite the passing of time, the revulsion the chaplain felt recalling that moment was immediate and real. He relived his rage at the renegade's insolence and his desire to make him pay for that insolence.

Back there, in the interrogation cell, he had let his emotions overwhelm him for just a moment. Uzziel had backhanded the traitor, then grabbed him by the hair and slammed his head hard against the stone wall. 'You seem to have forgotten which one of us lies in chains, filth!' he had shouted. 'I've already won. We need only determine if the Emperor will have mercy on your soul!'

'You understand nothing!' the Fallen Angel spat back. 'After all you've heard, you still don't know why I fight, do you?'

Uzziel had stepped up close to his prisoner and the two had locked eyes, faith and faithlessness colliding with unmatched fury. 'You fight because you are tainted by Chaos,' Uzziel had begun. 'You had your chance to serve the Emperor and you failed him utterly. You, and Luther, and all of your wretched cohorts chose to betray he who gave you life!'

The Fallen Angel had stood firm in the face of these accusations, and stared back at Uzziel, his every feature screaming defiance. Snarling like an animal, the traitor had lashed out at his tormentor with venomous scorn. 'I was once like you, monk! Loyal, righteous, dutiful.' He paused to spit, as if the words themselves were poisonous. 'Despite my virtues, I was left behind on Caliban by Jonson while he went fighting across the galaxy.' The renegade's harsh voice became strained with emotions long-buried as he continued, 'While my brothers fought battle after battle, I was left at home with the invalids, the women and the children! What did I do to deserve such a fate? I was born to go to war, but the Lion and the Emperor turned their backs on me and the others.' His voice rose to a scream of pure hatred. 'That's why I've fought and killed my way over more worlds than you could even name. And now you think you have the right to judge me!'

The Dark Angel had said nothing at first, so shocked was he by the monstrousness of the traitor's replies. How the Fallen twisted the truth to hide their own failure! It would be tragic, had the traitor's hatred not driven him to a life of mindless butchery.

In sadness, the interrogator-chaplain had turned away and walked towards the heavy iron door that sealed the room shut. The rusted hinges gave out a tortured shriek as he forced it open, but he paused before leaving his prisoner alone to ponder his sins.

'Heretic,' he intoned, 'I had hoped for more from you. I prayed that some trace of the Lion still lurked in your soul, but I can see I was wrong. By your unrepentant actions you force me to use any method to save your soul. So let it be done.'

The door slammed shut, entombing the Fallen in the bowels of the Rock. Over the following days, Uzziel had displayed his expertise as he ground the Fallen Angel down. The weak would call it torture; Uzziel knew it to be justice. Eventually, when his tools were sticky with the traitor's blood and the screams had ceased, the Fallen Angel had broken. He had admitted his guilt, and that of the other Fallen Angels, and repented in full for his crimes. Ultimately it had been a pitiful spectacle, as the broken man, once one of the Emperor's elite, poured out his litany of evil deeds.

As Uzziel prepared to give the man the quick death his repentance had earned him, the Fallen Angel had spoken for the last time. 'Confessor,' he had whispered through broken teeth and swollen lips, 'there is one thing that I have yet to tell you.' His body was wracked by a coughing spell of such length and intensity that Uzziel had thought the repentant traitor might pass away. Hacking and wheezing to draw more of the stale air into his tortured lungs, the Fallen Angel was finally able to speak again. 'I'm sorry, confessor, but this deed fills me with regret as no other.'

'Go on, brother,' Uzziel had urged. 'Your repentance will not be complete until you tell everything.'

The Fallen Angel had nodded slowly before continuing. 'Confessor, three years ago I was in the Knight Worlds serving as a mercenary. My unit raided the eldar exodite worlds regularly and I relished the opportunity to spill the blood of such a spineless and decadent race. We went on countless sorties, hunting down the cowards and slaughtering them as they deserved.' At this point, the Fallen Angel's voice had become animated once more, talk of bloodletting seeming to arouse him from his pain. 'On one such raid, a band of eldar took refuge in an ancient place of power. They called on their gods, but the gods did not listen to their pathetic cries. We stormed the place and left not one of them alive.'

The Fallen Angel had paused, caught up in the memory. The obvious pleasure on his face had brought bile to the chaplain's lips. 'It was while we were sacking the place that I found it, confessor – an artefact of power lost since the breaking of Caliban.' The Fallen Angel had abruptly stopped again, overcome with another spasm. The spell did not pass until he had coughed up a wellspring of his own lifeblood.

Uzziel grew concerned, knowing the signs only too well. Even a Marine's body could take only so much punishment, and the chaplain had pushed this one past its breaking point.

Consumed with impatience, Uzziel shouted, 'What did you find, damn you? Tell me!'

The prisoner had pulled his body erect. Blood ran freely from his mouth, giving an evil cast to his grin. 'Fear not, confessor, I am not finished so easily.' The pain had washed over him again, but he fought it this time and forced out the words by willpower alone. 'In the temple, confessor, amongst the bodies of the slain… I found the Lion Sword.'

Uzziel had been stunned. The sword of Jonson, lost these ten thousand years? It could not be.

The Fallen Angel had seen the disbelief on Uzziel's face, but he was determined to be heard. 'I know it sounds fantastic, confessor, but I swear it is true. I could never forget the sword of Lion El'Jonson.' His confession delivered, the Fallen Angel's body had gone limp.

Uzziel's mind had swirled with confusion. How could he trust one of the Fallen? But if he didn't, the confession was meaningless. Still undecided, the chaplain had held up his prisoner's head, wiped the blood from his mouth, and spoken to him gently. 'Brother, what did you do with the Lion Sword?'

The Fallen Angel's life was near its end. He had struggled to talk, only a barely audible croak escaping from his lips. 'I was afraid… to face up to what I had done… so I left the sword where it lay.' His body had convulsed, blood gushing from his nose and mouth. Choking and spitting, his words ran together. 'I regret that I didn't take it. I could have returned it… to where it belongs, but I… failed again. Forgive me, confessor.'

Uzziel had almost been overcome in that moment. He could not deny the power or dignity of the confession, but neither could he forget the deeds that had brought his prisoner to the dungeons of the Rock. Holding the Fallen Angel's head, he had used his dagger to deliver the man's absolution. 'Brother, you are forgiven.'

THE JUDDERING OF the Thunderhawk snapped Uzziel from his reverie, and he shook his head to clear his mind, so clear and vivid were the images. Steeling his brow, Uzziel took his hand from his rosarius and returned his mind to the task at hand. They had a battle to fight, and he would not let himself be distracted when his men's lives were at stake. Striding the length of the command bay, Uzziel called the sergeants to go over the assault plan again, before checking his weapons one last time. Moments later, the Thunderhawk reared up suddenly, engines screeching like a bird of prey, before hitting the ground with a bone-jarring crash. The bay doors opened and the first squad rushed out, their bolters singing a song of death. The symphony of battle had begun.

AILEAN STOOD AT the Martyrs' Tomb, his fist clenched over the runes around his neck. Even now, days after the dream, the runes of divination gave him no clue to its meaning. He had dreamt of a bird of prey, a sword of power and a man with no soul. He looked for a pattern but saw only blood. He opened his senses but felt only a cold wind running through him, as if a great evil were about to awaken.

From the east came Dragonlord Martainn of the Seana. Tall, gaunt and wrapped in robes of black, Martainn looked like a wraith on his great steed. From the west rode Dragonlord Barra of the Eamann. Long hair flowing in the wind and brightly polished armour shining in the sun, Barra appeared blissfully unconcerned. Laughing and joking with his warriors, the Eamann leader signalled for a halt. His rival did the same. Leaving their retinues behind, the two chieftains rode up on their great stomping beasts. Their dragons hissed and spat at each other, raking their claws in the earth and lashing their tails in eager anticipation of battle. Both leaders dismounted, but did nothing to calm their beasts.

Ailean could see that their frosty exteriors belied the raging anger within. Let their hatred flow, he thought. They will need it this day.

Barra, so raucous amongst his men but now icily intent, spoke first. 'Warlock, why have you summoned us to this accursed place? Are not the living trouble enough?' he asked, shooting a vicious glance at Martainn. 'Why disturb the dead?'

'We meet here because the spirit runes demand it,' Ailean pronounced.

'I've no time for your cryptic comments, warlock,' Martainn growled. 'I fear neither the living nor the dead.' He looked meaningfully at Barra and the ancient temple ruins. 'I've only come here at your bidding and out of respect for our king. But Ailean, know this: the so-called knights of this coward cut down my son in cold blood and there will be no peace between us until the matter is settled.' He looked keenly at Ailean. 'Blood has been spilled, warlock, and blood will be spilled again before I am satisfied!'

Barra spat in disgust. 'Your son died because he was feeble and that is no fault of mine.'

Martainn bristled at the insult, gripping his sword so tightly that his knuckles cracked. He took one step forward and drew his blade half way out of its ornate scabbard. Before the warlords could take further action, Ailean was between them.

'Martainn,' shouted the warlock angrily, 'draw that sword now and I will banish you from Lughnasa!' He pointed his spear at the enraged Seana warlord and invoked the power of his office. 'None shall disturb the King's Peace until judgement has been passed. Now sheathe your sword and hear my judgement.'

The warlock and the Seana dragonlord faced each other while Barra watched with wry amusement. Martainn slowly pushed the sword back into its scabbard and removed his hand from the hilt. 'My quarrel is not with you,' he said. 'Pass your judgement.'

Ailean remained between the two dragonlords, and pondered a moment more before speaking. 'It pains me to see eldar lords consumed with hate,' he uttered, 'but sometimes our follies can still serve a higher purpose. I find the grievance of Dragonlord Martainn of the Seana to be legitimate and I decree that it should be settled on the field of battle.'

Both dragonlords smiled. Martainn stared past the warlock and addressed his rival. 'Barra, you have robbed me of my only son and for that I will make you pay.' With that, he strode off to his dragon. The mighty beast reared and gave out a roar of defiance, as Martainn pulled his laser lance free from his tall saddle levelling it at Barra. 'Prepare to die, Eamann scum!'

'The reckoning is indeed at hand, Seana,' Barra shot back, swinging up into his own saddle. 'Your mate will weep the tears of Isha before nightfall.'

'Both of you, cease your prattle!' Ailean ordered. 'The Seana and the Eamann do not fight each other this day.'

'What?' Martainn shouted. 'You promised me vengeance, you traitor!'

'I did not,' Ailean said icily. 'I said you would settle your grievance on the field of battle, and so you shall. But you will not fight each other.'

'What in Khaine's name are you talking about?' the bewildered Barra asked. 'Who are we to fight, if not each other?'

A deafening sonic boom rolled over the temple. Looking up, all could see the Thunderhawk gunship swooping down upon them. Ailean was immediately forgotten, as the two warlords whipped their beasts around savagely and returned to their men. War cries echoed across the field as the two veteran warriors prepared the exodites for battle.

Ailean, alone in the ruins, returned his attention to the runes. He did not hear Martainn's angry voice drift across the battlefield, proclaiming, 'Barra, this is not over!'

The runes were speaking to the warlock again and the critical moment bore down upon him. He reached for the runes of summoning and cleared his mind. 'The hawk,' Ailean whispered, 'we fight the hawk.'

In the Martyrs' Tomb, only the dead could hear him.

UZZIEL STOOD AT the top of the Thunderhawk's landing ramp, heedless of the shuriken that hissed all around him, and scanned the battlefield. Squad Beatus was in the vanguard and they had found cover behind a low stone wall some thirty paces ahead. To the right of the wall, there was a small copse of trees; Squad Strages was busy hauling its heavy weapons under the cover it promised. Beyond the Marines' makeshift line was the target of their attack: an ancient eldar temple.

Uzziel stared intently at the old ruins but could not see any defences. Good. The chaplain jogged down the ramp of the gunship, unhindered by the heavy jump pack strapped to his back. Squad Beatus was already receiving heavy fire from eldar warriors, who seemed determined to keep the Space Marines pinned down behind the stone wall. In the distance, Uzziel could see exodite dragon knights mounting their beasts and preparing for battle. It seemed that his surprise attack was barely a surprise at all. The eldar were obviously ready for them and Uzziel could only wonder how. Whether he liked it or not, however, the battle had been joined and was escalating rapidly. He could analyse it later; now he had decisions to make.

'Squad Beatus, stay in cover. Watch for a counter-attack,' Uzziel began. 'Squad Strages, on my signal, lay down a suppressing fire with your heavy weapons. Squad Redemptor, left flank and support Squad Beatus. Squad Ferus, you're with me!' He started forward, followed by the members of Squad Ferus, whom he had chosen specially for the mission. Armed with chainswords and plasma pistols, they had a well-earned reputation for savagery. Uzziel could see that only the tight leash of command prevented them from jumping forward to engage the enemy immediately.

Soon, my brethren, soon.

Behind them, the Thunderhawk fired its massive thrusters and clawed its way back into the sky. Uzziel activated his communicator again. 'Gunship Cestus, adopt Strafing Pattern Primus until the enemy is engaged. Then fire at available targets and be prepared for pick-up.'

The gunship's commander replied without pause, 'By the Emperor, it is done.'

Uzziel turned to Codicier Ahiezar, the librarian accompanying them on this mission. Uzziel had never fought with Ahiezar before, but he knew him by repute. Unfamiliarity in the heat of battle always worried Uzziel, and he prayed that his wavering of faith was unwarranted.

'Ahiezar, do you detect any psychic activity?' asked Uzziel.

'No, nothing yet, interrogator-chaplain.' The Librarian's voice was cool, as if he were unused to being questioned.

'Then remain vigilant, brother,' Uzziel ordered, 'and shield us from the witchery of the cursed eldar!' Turning his attention back to the enemy, the chaplain could see that the dragon knights were massing in two impressive formations.

As alien warriors frantically lashed their beasts into action, the Thunderhawk dropped back out of the clouds. Screaming low over the battlefield, the gunship swivelled its multi-lasers at the two clusters of mounted eldar. Deadly accurate pulses of white-hot energy swept over the dragon knights, blowing holes in their elaborate armour and slicing through their raging beasts. The Thunderhawk roared past the decimated eldar battle groups, its mighty engines kicking up dust and debris as it swung around for its next attack.

Even in the face of the withering fire from above, the eldar reformed their ranks with admirable discipline. The earth shook as the two eldar formations charged the Space Marine line. Filling the air with cacophonous battle cries, the alien warriors held their weapons high as their beasts' clawed feet propelled them violently towards the waiting Dark Angels.

Calmly, Uzziel noted that the ruined temple, clearly visible behind the streaming pennants and laser lances of the exodites, now seemed all but undefended. If Uzziel could break this charge, the Lion Sword would be his! 'Squads Beatus and Redemptor, hold fast and concentrate your fire on the left-hand group. Squad Strages, you take the right-hand. In the Emperor's name, fire!'

Guns erupted all across the Dark Angels' line. Standing firm, the Space Marines rained destruction on the charging knights. On the left, shell after shell slammed into the massed eldar ranks, sending knights tumbling from their saddles and riddling the dragons. At the same time, the heavy weapons of Squad Strages were blowing holes in the other eldar battle group with missiles and plasma.

Despite the rain of destruction, a few of the dragon knights on the left completed their charge. With wild shouts of 'Seana!' they smashed into the

Space Marines' line. The bolters, so effective just seconds before, were all but useless in close-quarter fighting. The eldar drove home their laser lances, blasting Dark Angel power armour open, sending them flying backwards or impaling them on their wicked tips. Others were trampled by dragons, torn apart under clawed feet.

Uzziel wasted no time. 'Squad Ferus, for Jonson and the Emperor, attack!' He immediately activated his jump pack and let the jets propel him towards the swirling melee. Codicier Ahiezar and the rest of the squad were a heart-beat behind, howling with delight now that they had finally been unleashed on the foe. As the Dark Angels arced over the battlefield, the remaining eldar foot troops brought their shuriken catapults to bear on them.

The air was immediately filled again with vicious discs of razor-sharp metal. Uzziel cursed aloud when Brother Alexius fell from the sky, his armour punctured in a dozen places. The chaplain commended his fallen soul to the Emperor, and added a prayer of thanks for the stout armour that had protected him from the hail of eldar fire.

Moments later, he landed, power sword in his right hand and bolt pistol in his left, scant feet from a bellowing dragon knight. Uzziel watched in hor-ror as the enraged eldar warrior plunged his laser lance through the visor of Brother Caleb, killing him instantly. Seeing Uzziel, the knight tried to pull his lance free, but he was already too late. Filled with righteous fury, Uzziel raised his bolt pistol and unloaded half a dozen shells into the eldar, blast-ing him right out of the saddle. The dragon opened its gaping jaws and howled a forlorn cry at the loss of its master. Uzziel swung his power sword in a mighty arc and silenced the beast with the bite of steel. The dragon's body collapsed to the ground, pumping steaming blood onto the scarred soil. Uzziel looked down at the lifeless body of Brother Caleb and whis-pered, 'Rest easy, brother. You are avenged.'

Looking about for fresh opponents, Uzziel saw that his assault squad had broken the charge of dragon knights. With deadly chainswords and white hot plasma, Squad Ferus had smashed the proud eldar and continued to rain death down on them as they fled. Codicier Ahiezar stood proudly over the smoking skeletons of two knights he had annihilated with crackling blue bolts of psychic energy.

Dead and dying eldar lay everywhere, their lovingly-etched armour shat-tered and useless, their loyal dragons quivering in death-throes and filling the air with the scent of charred meat, their brilliant pennons broken and trampled in the blood-stained grass. The pitiful survivors had turned their mounts around and were fleeing the battlefield in disarray, unable to defend themselves from the preying Thunderhawk that continued to harry them with death from above.

The chaplain quickly regained his wits. Realising that the eldar temple was now undefended, he turned to the librarian and yelled, 'Ahiezar! Follow me!'

Again the jets of his jump pack lifted him across the battlefield. As he flew through the air, aiming for the eldar temple, he saw that it had become mysteriously obscured. A dense and swirling mist covered the area where Uzziel knew the temple to be. Cursing, the chaplain cut his jump short and landed just outside the fog. The codicier landed behind him, force sword at the ready.

'What witchcraft is this?' Uzziel asked angrily.

The librarian licked his lips. 'I am unsure, interrogator-chaplain. Perhaps there is a warlock in the area. I sense something,' he said in a slow voice, 'but I've never felt its like before.'

Uzziel turned back towards the mist. He hardly needed Ahiezar to tell him that there might be an eldar witch in the temple. 'If there's a warlock in there,' the chaplain growled, 'he'll taste the Emperor's steel.'

Chanting the Lion Hymn quietly to himself, Uzziel stalked into the mist. An unearthly quiet immediately enveloped him and he quickly became disoriented. The chaplain couldn't hear himself praying – he couldn't even hear himself breathing. Surrounded by swirling darkness, the Dark Angel could barely see five feet in front of his hand. He felt he was floating in limbo.

Gritting his teeth against the sorcerous manifestation, Uzziel tried doggedly to keep walking forwards, but it was difficult to keep to any kind of bearing. Strange thoughts crept into his mind, and his concentration drifted. He saw the Emperor's Golden Throne, but the body inside was a decayed corpse. Twelve hooded figures surrounded the throne, laughing as they carved up the Emperor's corpse with cruel knives and issued edicts in his name. Nearly overcome with the force of the vision, Uzziel stopped and shook his head violently, willing the evil thoughts to cease. He was a Dark Angel and a chaplain, and nothing would shake his faith!

A startling flash of crimson lit up the miasma in front of him, illuminating an enormous serpentine mouth bearing down on him. Uzziel barely had time to fling himself out of the way, as row upon row of razored teeth lunged for his head. The beast loomed over him, its gargantuan body an indefinable shadow in the mist. As he tried to scramble away, a long tail snaked out of the darkness and thrashed him to the ground. The Dark Angel could see the beast's mouth, open as if screaming in rage, but in the all-enveloping dream-mist he heard nothing. He could only feel the awful shaking of the earth as the dragon drove its weighty bulk forward on monstrous limbs.

That dreadful head descended again, but this time Uzziel was ready. As the widening jaws plunged to engulf the chaplain, Uzziel rolled beneath the beast's slavering maw, jamming his power sword through the underside of its cavernous mouth. Black blood burst out of the wounded beast as the sword drove through scales to pinion the creature's jaws shut. The beast reared back in pain, clawing and lashing in fury. Uzziel tried to pull his sword free but it had become deeply embedded in the dragon's sinew and bone.

Desperate but determined, Uzziel refused to release his grip on the power sword, and found himself lifted bodily off the ground by the enraged monster. Suspended twenty feet off the ground, Uzziel struggled to use his bolt pistol as the crazed beast thrashed in agony. Straining his muscles almost to breaking point, he heaved himself upwards and planted the pistol against the skull of the monstrosity. Ignoring the searing pain in his tortured shoulder, he squeezed the trigger again and again until he had emptied the magazine. The mighty dragon fell to the ground with a soundless crash, the top of its head a bloody ruin. Using his last reserves of strength, Uzziel managed to twist his body away as the dragon fell, narrowly avoiding a crushing death under the monster's dead weight.

Heart singing with the joy of victory, Uzziel staggered to his feet. Planting his foot on what was left of the monster's head, the chaplain yanked his power sword from its fleshy sheath. He was alive!

Even as he stood panting and exhausted, the body faded into the mists and was gone.

The chaplain's sword arm was burning with pain, but Uzziel would not slow. Such sorcerous defences could only mean that the prize was near at hand.

'The Lion Sword!' The words were sweet upon his whispering lips.

Uzziel began chanting the Lion Hymn anew and strode forward. He would not be stopped. Suddenly, a wall emerged from the gloom in front of him – the temple, at last! Stumbling over the ruined remnants of the temple wall, Uzziel entered the Martyrs' Tomb. The mist was thinner here, mostly swirling about the floor and walls, and a pulsing red light illuminated the place. Uzziel stepped into the temple and immediately his boot sank into a deep sludge. Puzzled, he bent down and dipped his glove into the mire, raising it to his face through the fog so he could see its nature. He realised, to his revulsion, that his gauntlet was covered with congealed blood. He gasped. What cursed place was this? As if in answer, dim figures staggered from the mist.

Uzziel brought his sword up, ready to defend himself, until he saw them more distinctly. From all around him they came. Eldar men, women, and children, walking towards him, their bodies bearing terrible wounds. Here a man with no legs pulling himself across the floor, there a woman staggered with her shattered brain exposed. Uzziel's battle-trained eye could see the horrid tearing wounds of chainswords, the gaping holes that only bolter shells could make, flesh seared by boiling plasma. Countless victims with countless wounds, the eldar dead paced towards him. They said nothing to the chaplain, merely stared in silent condemnation.

With savage clarity, Uzziel realised what he beheld. These were the victims of the Fallen Angel and his cohorts, brutally murdered so many years ago.

Stunned, the chaplain could do nothing but stare back at their accusing faces. As the dead approached, Uzziel fought an overpowering urge to flee. The phantoms assaulted his mind, threatening to overwhelm him with madness. He cried out to the Emperor but his prayer was swallowed up by the hungry silence.

Surely nothing is worth facing this for? The seductive whisper snaked through his mind. Your wounds justify an honourable withdrawal.

Uzziel almost obeyed the voice in his head. Almost! Then he thought of his brethren, even now valiantly fighting and dying in the Emperor's name. Could he abandon his quest after his men had served him so well, giving up their very lives so that he might bring the Lion Sword back to the Rock? Of course not! He was compelled forward by his loyalty to the Emperor, by his oath as a Dark Angel, by the sacrifice of the dead. For Brother Caleb and all of his fallen brothers, he knew he must fight on.

'The Lion Sword will be mine, no matter the cost!' he roared in rage. Driven by will alone, Uzziel lifted his sword and slashed at the nearest of the walking dead. It melted to nothing before his blade. Relief flooded his mind as he banished the apparition. As a chaplain, he recognised too well that fear was the weapon of the dead, and he had proven himself fear's master.

With mounting confidence, Uzziel passed through the dead, their images fading before him, and strode purposefully towards a low slab of rock, an ancient altar. Uzziel paused for a moment, before raising his power sword high and bringing it down hard, cracking the time-worn stone in two. Something metallic glinted beneath the shattered stone. Uzziel pushed aside the rubble, revealing an ancient eldar box of intricate design. Cold sigils blazed on its surfaces. It had the look of some kind of weapons case and crackled with arcane energies. Maybe this was the stasis field generator that held the Lion Sword?

With trembling hands, Uzziel touched the box. As he did so, he heard an unearthly humming noise. Sound had returned to the world. Uzziel looked around to locate its source, but could see little despite the thinning mists. Even as he searched, the noise increased in pitch to a keening wail, followed by a gurgling scream. Spinning around, Uzziel saw Codicier Ahiezar framed in an emergent doorway, sharp metal sticking through his chest. The metal slowly withdrew and Ahiezar collapsed into the sludge of blood.

The fallen body of the slain librarian revealed a tall eldar wearing rune-encrusted armour and carrying a silvered spear. The eldar weapon was alive in the warlock's hand; it purred with pleasure now it had tasted the librarian's blood. The exodite spun the spear around and held it before him.

'I am Ailean, warlock of the King of Lughnasa. I know why you have come and I am here to deny you. You, human, have no right to disturb this place and you may not have what that stasis chest holds.'

Uzziel shook with rage. 'You speak so of the sword? No right? I have every right! That sword is the birthright of my Chapter and has been kept from us for ten thousand years. I will take it back to my brethren or die in the attempt. So I swore.' The chaplain removed his hand from the stasis box and gripped his power sword with both hands, wincing at the daggers of searing pain which streaked from his injured arm. He was ready to face the meddling warlock.

'You humans are strange,' Ailean said, seemingly unaware of the towering anger that filled the Dark Angel. 'You should thank us for keeping a sword such as this safe for as long as we have. Instead, you come to my world, kill my people and disturb the dead. Is the sword really worth all that? It would be better locked away for all eternity than loosed again upon the world.'

'Heretic!' Uzziel screamed. 'You will feel the Emperor's wrath for your insolence!' Uzziel charged, his power sword tracing a deadly arc. Ailean, apparently ready for such a manoeuvre, parried the blow swiftly. He tried to unleash a bolt of psychic energy at the Dark Angel, but found his power neutralised by the Space Marine's armour. Uzziel smiled inside his helmet, and silently mouthed a prayer of thanks for his Aegis suit. He would not fall to this warlock's witchcraft.

Ailean tried another psychic blast and this too was quashed. The warlock began to take the duel more seriously, shifting his spear into an offensive position and lunging with deadly intent at the raging Dark Angel. Uzziel met the spear stroke for stroke and the lance howled as it was thwarted time and again. The two were well-matched opponents, Ailean fighting with graceful elegance, Uzziel countering with berserk fervour.

Eventually, the sheer power of Uzziel's blows began to tell, and he drove the warlock back into a lichen-covered wall. Ailean still tried to pierce Uzziel with his hungry spear, but the Dark Angel grabbed the weapon's haft with his injured hand and held it fast.

The chaplain longed to sheath his blade in the eldar's flesh, but couldn't at such close quarters. Instead, he struck the warlock full in the face with the hilt of his power sword. The blow drove Ailean's head into the wall with an audible crack, and the warlock joined Ahiezar in the mire of blood.

Wasting no time, Uzziel sheathed his power sword and staggered towards the stasis chest. He was breathing heavily and bleeding from a number of spear wounds. Without further ceremony, the chaplain picked up the long box and all but ripped it in two. He could feel the energy dissipate as the alien device cracked open and the stasis field disappeared.

Reaching inside the shattered chest, Uzziel pulled out a sword encased in a ornate sheath. The shock near overwhelmed him, and he leaned on his own blade for support. Up to this moment, he had been prepared for disappointment and lies. A Fallen Angel could never really be trusted. But how could he have passed up any opportunity to recover the Lion Sword, no matter how remote the chance?

Now he, Uzziel, stood in this alien temple with the very sword in his hand! What a moment!

Uzziel began to pray fervently, thanking the Emperor and Lion El'Jonson for choosing him for this moment. The sword came free of the sheath and shone with a blinding brilliance. The remaining fog and mist burned away in seconds, exposing his surroundings for the first time. Uzziel was alone in the temple, save for the bodies of Ahiezar and Ailean. Now Uzziel could see that the once elegant temple was mostly a ruin. The towers that once flanked it had fallen and parts of the roof had caved in. Lichen covered the walls, which somehow glowed with an inner light.

A little calmer now, the chaplain examined the sword. The hilt was carved of gold, in the shape of an angel, its spreading wings forming the weapon's guard. Overcome by its beauty, Uzziel took the sword to a place where the sun shone through. There it gleamed in the light for the first time in ten thousand years. Uzziel hefted the blade and tried its balance. Perfection. This was a sword of kings, of conquerors. As if in a vision, he could see himself at the head of armies, wielding the unmatched blade and vanquishing the enemies of the Emperor.

His mind swam with heady visions of power and conquest. With this sword none could stand before him. Surely he was chosen! A weapon of greater power even than that wielded by Azrael, Supreme Master of the Dark Angels. Now Uzziel knew his time was upon them all! This was the evidence and the power to silence all his most jealous brethren back at the Rock.

Uzziel gasped involuntarily and laughed aloud that fate had sent him to this place! Soon he would be hailed as the greatest interrogator-chaplain in the Chapter's history, greater even than the legendary Molocia! All would fall before him, all would bow to him, and not just those of his Chapter.

No, now was the time to put away petty differences of Chapter and creed. The Imperium would be his. Swordbearer, conqueror, first of a new breed of primarch. Giddy with elation and power, Uzziel saw the universe laid bare for his legions, ready for the taking. This was decreed. It must be.

As Uzziel continued to gaze at the gleaming weapon, he noticed an inscription on the blade. This is below your notice, Lord Uzziel, an inner voice chided him, and so persuasive was its tone that he almost ignored the battle-worn lettering. But the small cold presence of his conscience pulled at his mind. Looking closer, he squinted to read the ancient letters. Each word pierced him like a dagger to his heart.

TO LUTHER, FRIEND AND COMRADE-IN-ARMS. MAY YOUR FAITH BE YOUR SHIELD. LEJ.

Uzziel staggered back and dropped the sword. Immediately, its treacherous power was broken, and he realised the full extent of his folly. This was not the Lion Sword, but the Sword of Luther, arch-traitor and most hated of the Fallen Angels. Once a noble weapon, it had been twisted by the power of Chaos as Luther led the Fallen Angels down their doomed path.

And had Uzziel not felt its power, listened to its lies and been ready to make it his own? How could he have been so blind? Tempted by the very sword that had killed the Lion! The chaplain shuddered with horror, thinking of the Lion's noble sacrifice. What folly! And so many noble eldar dead!

Thoroughly disgusted, steeped in self-loathing, Uzziel carefully sheathed the cursed blade. He would not be tempted again. He would not listen to the now-raging voice. He must, he *would* deny it!

Inside his helmet, his communicator crackled to life. 'Interrogator-chaplain, this is Gunship Cestus. Strong eldar reinforcements are heading towards us from the north. What are your orders?'

Uzziel paused a moment. He considered ordering his men away and staying to die at the hands of the eldar. 'I deserve no better!' he howled in torment at the sky.

But he could not. As a chaplain and a Dark Angel, he had to face up to his actions. Sighing heavily, he replied at last, activating his communicator link. 'Tell the troops to fall back by squads to rendezvous point secundus and meet there.'

'Yes, sir. By the Emperor, it is done.'

Uzziel walked to the stone doorway, where the prone form of the dead librarian lay. He looked out over the battlefield; more bodies lay everywhere. Many of his brethren had fallen today, their lives thrown away because of him and his pride. He had wanted to find the Lion Sword so much that he had let himself be fooled by one of the very traitors who had torn the Dark Angels asunder. Even the heretic had been given a merciful death as well!

Now there would be consequences, of that he was certain.

He considered leaving the sword in the temple, but too many had died for him to go home empty-handed. It was a part of the Chapter's history and as such belonged in the Rock. Perhaps Asmodai would know what to do with it.

Asmodai. He could not think of the aged Space Marine, the greatest living interrogator-chaplain, without touching his rosarius. Asmodai's rosarius had only two black pearls, and that was the work of hundreds of years. Uzziel looked at his own black pearl, the source of so much pride just hours ago. Now revulsion filled his soul at the sight of it.

Slowly, Uzziel unclasped his rosarius and slipped off the black gem. He placed it carefully on the hard rock of the temple floor before bringing the heavy boot of his power armour down upon it. The black pearl shattered and Uzziel ground it to bitter dust beneath his foot.

Next time, there would be no doubt.

ANGELS
Robert Earl

IT WAS ALMOST forty summers ago, but I still remember. Sometimes, though, the remembering is hard. In the warmth of a high summer's sun or in the smog of the inn, surrounded by familiar faces, it seems that it was only a dream or an old man's tale grown tall with the telling.

But when the wolves came last winter it was as clear as the summer's sky over the fields. And when Mary lay screaming in her first labour, the memory was the only thing that kept the fear from freezing me.

When it happened, Pasternach was smaller than it is now, much smaller. There was nothing north of the stream but the shadow of the mill, for all of the cottages, and even the workshops, were tucked safely behind the stockade. They huddled around the green, their backs to the world, but between their sturdy gables we could see the battle of distant treetops against the wind.

The stockade itself was higher back then. It had to be, for we had worse to worry about in those days than the prices come harvest time. The Emperor, may the gods protect him, had yet to start clearing the forest hereabouts. And the forest was near.

From time to time, lying in our beds, we would hear cries floating through the darkness of the night, savage cries that were neither human or animal. When they became too much to ignore, the council and the rest of the men would meet on the green.

There, amidst the comforting smells of smoke and stew and dung, they would drink and argue for a day or so. Then they would decide to do what they always decided to do – which was to send out a patrol. But always by daylight and never with very much enthusiasm. Sometimes the patrols would return in triumph carrying with them rabbits or even deer, but mostly they just returned hurriedly.

They were fools to avoid finding the enemy before he found us, but one cannot blame them, not really. Which of us wouldn't rather pull the blankets up over our heads and hope for the best?

One autumn the shadow of the forest grew longer. Rumours pulsed along the narrow tracks and open rivers of the land, rumours of northern sorcery and a hideous new progeny of the terrible art.

One of the scrawny, haunted-looking rangers who occasionally drifted through on the road to the city stopped for long enough in the village to frighten us all. He told a tale of lights in the sky, great fiery displays to rival the borealis, of villages found mysteriously deserted and gutted by fire, of horribly cloven two-footed tracks in the cooling ash.

After he had left, everybody told everyone else that he had been mad or a liar, and what else could you expect from a ranger? But even I noticed that after this the men of the patrols stayed nearer to home and kept their eyes more firmly shut. They even stopped bringing back game. Then, after Mullens was taken, the patrols from Pasternach stopped altogether.

MULLENS WAS A scarred old bull of a man. He had arrived at the village two years before, still dressed in his patched halberdier's uniform, and I think that my brother and I were only slightly more overawed by him than our parents were.

Even Alderman Fauser was at a loss for words when the old soldier took his hand in a painful, white knuckled grip and allowed the two massive war dogs that comprised the whole of his luggage to sniff his new neighbour's breeches.

In spite of his strange manners and southland accent, Mullens soon became popular in Pasternach. His hounds brought down many a wild boar which he would arrange to be roasted for the whole village in return for his fill of ale. When these feasts were finished apart from bones to gnaw and the dying embers of the fire, he would fill our imaginations with blood-curdling tales of death and glory from his time in the Emperor's great army.

Even more welcome was the fact that he was willing to hire any man who needed the coin. A couple of miles to the west of the village lay a derelict way station with a few neglected fields which Mullens had bought for his retirement. Because he always asked for the villagers' advice, as well as paying their sons to help him, the whole village took some pride in the way that Mullens rebuilt the crumbling stone walls of the gatehouse and cleared the land that it stood over.

It was some small measure of the affection in which he had become held, then, that when the old soldier didn't turn up at the village for two whole weeks a patrol went almost willingly to see if anything was amiss with him.

Though I was but young then, I will never forget the grim silence with which they returned to their families that afternoon and the sense of outrage that clung to them like the smell of the smoke. And the sight and sound of Gustav the blacksmith, iron-faced and iron-handed, suddenly choking and rushing into his hut. I tried to convince myself that the agony of sobbing we could all hear from within was the smith's wife. The thought of this, the hardest of men breaking down, was too unnerving.

None of the men who went to check on Mullens's farm, then burned it to the ground, ever did tell of what they had found there. Today, all being safely buried in the hallowed ground next to the village shrine, they never will. But over the years I have managed to piece together fragments of whispered conversations or the drunken rambling of men quickly hushed by their fellows. Not much, I grant you, but enough to give some idea of the bloody nightmare those men encountered.

I know that, amongst other things, they found Mullens at the farm – or at least what was left of him. He had been eaten right down to the bone, but even as he fell he had not abandoned his weapon. Skeletal fingers locked desperately around the heft of a bloodied spear. Even now, the image fills me with a kind of horrified wonder.

His dogs were found lying on either side of their master. Their ruined and convulsed bodies bore witness to the desperate resistance they had put up. They had died as they had lived, full of courage and · loyalty. Few men can hope for such an epitaph and my eyes sting even now at the memory of those fine animals.

Of the attackers who had committed this foul atrocity, there was scant sign. A few bones, a few fly-encrusted brown stains on the stone of the walls and the splintered wood of the door. It seems that their flesh had tasted as sweet to their companions as any other.

To witness such scenes at first hand must have been like stepping into a waking nightmare – and though it sounds almost perverse to say it, I thank the gods for it. The horror of Mullens's farm was enough to shock the whole village into wakefulness at last. It was no longer possible to ignore the danger, and all of our lives were changed and reordered overnight.

There was a meeting on the green the next morning. Nobody drank. The only argument was when Frau Henning, our young farrier's mother, tried to prevent his volunteering to ride to the nearest Empire town for help and men-at-arms. But Gulmar's father overruled her tears and protestations with a fervour that was close to rage. He was proud of his son's courage, I think, and didn't want to deny him the chance to prove it. That pride began to turn into a cancerous mixture of bitterness and regret a few short weeks later. Fuelled by grain alcohol and a nagging wife, it eventually killed him.

Of course we weren't to know that as we watched father and son bid each other farewell in the clear light of that bright morning. They were alive and together for the last time on this world and perhaps sensing it they shook hands as equals, maybe even friends, for the first time. Gulmar Henning never made it back but at least he didn't die a child.

As the hoofbeats of the farrier's borrowed horse faded into the distance, we all stood in a long, solemn silence, broken only by the accusing sobs of the boy's distraught and inconsolable mother. Then the discussion began and incredibly, insanely it seemed at the time, it was decided to do the unthinkable.

We abandoned the harvest.

THAT YEAR'S AUTUMN wheat was left to ripen then wither outside the palisade, a feast only for the teeming birds and vermin. While our golden lifeblood rotted back into the dark earth, the whole village worked at a fever pitch. The great mill wheel was lifted off its pole and wrestled through the gates, leaving a naked patch on the overgrown stone of the wall. Karsten the miller himself supervised this piece of necessary vandalism with shrill cries and fluttering hands. As he capered around he reminded me, despite his fleshy jowls and shiny head, of a hen that has lost its chicks. Even at that age, though, I had the sense to keep the thought to myself, as I did the private grievance that my brother and I would no longer be able to use the great wooden wheel as our private staircase over the wall into the village.

Most of the work was done in the forest, as more trees were felled to strengthen the stockade. By then I was confined to the village with the rest of the children, but even there I could hear the harsh cracks of axes biting into green wood and the occasional shocking crash of a falling tree. Throughout the next few weeks the sound of the men nibbling away at the edge of the forest became a constant rhythm that we all lived to.

Meanwhile Gulmar Henning's mother had taken to haunting the parapets in a painfully desperate vigil. She stood silently above the frenetic activity of the village, gaunt and crow-like in a windswept black cloak. She finally broke her silence after three days with a piercing shriek that sent us all rushing to the wall. My eyes followed the line of her trembling arm as it pointed to the east, and I saw it.

There was nothing much, just an orange glow on the horizon. Through the jagged arms of the black forest, the distant flames even looked a little comforting. The fire came from the direction of Groenveldt, thirty miles away, and I wondered aloud, quite innocently and without malice, if they were having a bonfire.

I turned to ask my father, but his tight-lipped expression of angry relief silenced me. I left the chill of the parapet and retreated to my bed, confused and afraid. The next day we began to work even harder.

I didn't have much time to reflect on the strange new turn our lives had taken, which was perhaps just as well. My days were spent with cleaning and splitting feathers for the growing bundles of arrows or spinning the sharpening stone at just the right pace to avoid Gustav the smith's wrath. My only break from all this was the occasional errand or, much to my disgust, doing the women's work and drawing the village's water.

Even though the work was hard, I do remember enjoying it, for the novelty made all of this excitement and panic a great game for a child as young as I was, albeit a slightly uneasy one. I couldn't understand why everyone was so gloomy and foul-tempered. Even Stanislav the brewer, usually the jolliest and certainly the reddest-faced man in the village, snarled at me when I knocked over a pile of hoops he was finding for the smith.

Then came the night, just as winter was starting to tighten its icy grip on Pasternach and all the land around it, when I did understand.

I WAS SHOCKED from my sleep in the steely grey hour before dawn by the awful sound of a man screaming, screaming and never ceasing. I clambered out of the cot I shared with my brother, still too groggy with sleep to be truly alarmed, when my father burst through the door half dressed and crazy-eyed.

Even in the gloom I could see his knuckles were white from the grip he had on his scythe, as sharp and gleaming now as it had ever been. He shouted at my brother and me to get under the bed, but the undercurrent of terror in his voice froze me where I stood. I'd never heard the like before.

As my father charged outside I saw the other villagers dashing to the north wall in the torchlight. Alderman Fauser was already high on the stockade with half a dozen other men, hacking down into the darkness beyond. I was almost as surprised to hear the alderman spitting out such obscene oaths as I was to see the blood that ran from his pitchfork as he pulled it from one of the shadows. My father had his foot on the lower rung of the ladder when he stopped, turned, and bellowed a warning.

Over the south wall, with a hideous snarling and squealing, poured a wave of dark, misshapen forms. They clambered over the eaves of the cottages and squeezed through the gaps between the walls like a boiling mass of gargoyles brought to life by the night's pale moon. When they reached the torchlit sanctuary of the village green I felt myself shrink at the sight of them.

The things were an obscene combination of man and beast, horribly melted and twisted together. But their deformities, far from weakening them, seemed to give them an abnormal strength. Their clothes were ragged strips, shredded and filthy, but the claws lashing at the end of their arms were sharp and bright enough to freeze me, my cry stopped in my gaping mouth.

The miller, who stood equally open-mouthed and incredulous in their path, was the first victim of this hellish tide. Without breaking their pace the twisted daemons tore him to pieces with a mercifully brief rending and shrieking. Even as they continued their charge I saw, with a rising gorge, shreds stripped from the man's separated limbs being crammed into their fanged, bestial mouths.

With a dreadful roar my father and the rest of the villagers turned to meet this vile onslaught. In the middle of the green, steel met claw in a nightmare of blood and savagery. The men of Pasternach fought with the burning madness of fear that night, but even so they were no match for the savage breeding and sheer weight of numbers of the enemy.

Gradually, remorselessly, the villagers were pushed back to the north wall by the ravenous horde before them. Every man who went down was fallen upon in a hideous feeding frenzy that merely seemed to fuel the enemies' bloodlust rather than sate it.

Then, in one terrible moment, two terrible things happened at once. The alderman, our appointed leader, was torn from his perch atop the wall by a second, slashing swarm of the monsters. And, infinitely worse, my father collapsed under a crushing blow. His opponent, a writhing bundle of fang, claw and muscle, roared in delighted triumph and lunged forward to feed.

There was no bravery in what I did, for without fear to overcome there can be no real courage. It's true that I had to plunge through the wave of horror which engulfed me to seize a rock and run yelling defiance at the beast-thing. There was no fear, though, only a sort of divine rage at the abomination before me.

Turning to face me, the beast let out a dreadful baying laugh. It towered above me, so close that I could smell the reek of it and see with crystal clarity a single drop of saliva roll down one curved yellow fang. Still, in the face of its laughter and in the face of its power I raised my feeble weapon and leapt towards its claws.

My blow never landed, nor did it need to. For in that dread moment, knowing my weakness and knowing my faith, the gods heard my raging prayers and struck for me! With a piercing whine and a blinding flash of light brighter than any storm, the corrupt beast in front of me burst apart in a spray of blood. The struggle around me stuttered into silence as man and monster alike looked in wonder at the astonishing, blinding death of my enemy.

Then the angels appeared.

THERE WERE FOUR of them, one on each wall of the village stockade, and they were both beautiful and terrible. They were clad as great armoured knights, and they moved as if they had the power of giants contained within them. Their huge, shining armour was of a strange and wondrous design, the sweeps and curves of it coloured in hues of blue and green. In their hands they held bizarre weapons: swords bearing teeth; ornate, carved metal wands; incomprehensible bundles of steel pipes which gleamed dully with a strange menace.

One of their number wore hugely distorted gauntlets, vast hands made of some worked metal which sparked and crackled with bound lightening. He lifted the flaring blue gloves above his armoured head and closed the steel fingers into a fist. It was the signal to begin.

In total silence, and in perfect harmony, three of the armoured figures plunged into the squalling mass of daemons below. The killing began as soon as their vast iron-shod feet hit the ground.

Fanged swords squealed and screamed like cats on a fire as they bit down into flesh and bone. They spat great gouts of blood and flesh high into the black vault of the night, and the shrieks of their victims added to the din.

I felt a curiously warm drizzle begin to fall and casually licked a droplet from my lips. It had the salty, coppery taste of fresh blood. Suddenly I was bent double, wracked and spasming, seized by a fit of vomiting.

Through my tears I saw the terrible blue fire of the steel fists. The being that wielded them strode amongst the shadows of his enemies with a hypnotic grace, a terrible dance of death. As he twisted and swung, the massive burning hands snatched at heads, limbs, torsos. Muscle and bone split asunder at his divine touch into hideous steaming wounds. The stink of burning carrion started to drift through the village.

At first the corrupt pack of abominations teeming within the stockade had reeled under the wrath of our saviours. They died like animals in a slaughter-house, shocked and bewildered, until an enraged roar cut through their stupor. The chilling cry was returned from another beast-thing, and then another, until it echoed back and forth from a score of deformed throats. It rose to a savage crescendo and once more the daemons flung themselves into the attack with a terrifying ferocity.

But as the fiends hurled themselves towards the blood-spattered angels, a staccato shriek from above suffocated their war cry. Hands clutched desperately over my ears, I looked up and saw the fourth of our saviours, still standing atop the wooden stockade, thrown into sharp and flickering relief by guttering flames. The bundle of steel pipes he held whirled and flared as they spat burning lances of fire into the charging forms of the enemy.

The living were lifted, torn into bloody ruins, and hurled to the ground. The dead were shredded further, their remains beaten deeply down into the wet soil. Jaws snapped open in rictus howls of agony, inaudible over the awesome noise of their execution.

Still the daemons fought. Despite the lines of holy, magical fire that sliced through them like a new scythe through ripe corn, despite the fresh meat afforded by the rising piles of the dead, despite everything they fought back against the angels. Their blood lust drove them to total annihilation. Claws and fangs cracked and splintered on celestial armour. Divine weapons ate eagerly through verminous hides into the twisted bones beneath. Tainted blood splashed, stinking and steaming, into the cold night air. It was a massacre.

Finally, some semblance of realisation must have come to the last few survivors from the warband, and the last of the monsters tried to flee. I watched the panic, the sheer terror, in their rolling yellow eyes with grim satisfaction, barely able to understand what I had witnessed. They rushed past the angel with the blazing steel fists, leaving two of their number slashed and dying at his feet, and leapt for the stockade.

There was to be no escape from the divine wrath of our saviours. Burning spears chased them, found them, and ripped them apart in arcs of blood and fire. The sizzling gore splattered across the splintered timber of the stockade in glistening sweeps and curves. I stared into the grisly patterns, my mind a shocked blank, and suddenly I imagined I could see the bloodied face of Gulmar, the young farrier, staring back out at me.

I began to shake and gag with dry heaves. My ears still shrilled and rang painfully from the noise of their deafening weapons. For a time I could do nothing but crouch and heave and cry. It was a long while before I realised that the battle was over.

The angels stood amongst great banks of corpses, silent and still in the gloom like terrible statues. Even then, covered in gore and stinking of burnt flesh, they were beautiful. For one long moment we stood together, angel and boy, in the midst of the carnage. Then, as silently as they had appeared, they faded from our sight and were gone.

I like to think I was the only one who saw the star rise from the forest that night. It was no more than a silent, distant flash of light and I would have missed it too if I hadn't looked up from the well at precisely the right moment. As I carried the water back to bathe my father's wounds I marvelled at the glimpse I had been afforded of their celestial chariot. And even now I still smile to myself when some travelling sage or other tries to tell us what the stars are.

IT WAS ALMOST forty summers ago, but still I remember. When the wolves came last winter the memory gave me the courage to find and destroy them in their own lair and when Mary lay screaming in her first labour the memory gave me the strength to break the taboos and deliver my son.

Now, as the voices of my people fade away and all I can hear is the ticking of the deathwatch in my ears, I remember the events of that singular night and I am not afraid. For I know that in the darkness that I soon must face, the gods will send their angels to watch over me again.

And this time they will not fade.

UNFORGIVEN

Graham McNeill

THE MIDNIGHT DARK closed on Brother-Sergeant Kaelen of the Dark Angels like a fist. The emission-reduced engines of the rapidly disappearing Thunderhawk were the only points of light he could see. His visor swum into a ghostly green hue and the outlines of the star shaped city below became clear as his auto-senses kicked in.

The altimeter reading on his visor was unravelling like a lunatic countdown, the shapes below him resolving into clearer, oblong forms. The speed of his descent was difficult to judge, the powered armour insulating Kaelen from the sensations of icy rushing air and roaring noise as he plummeted downwards.

With a pulse of thought, Kaelen overlaid the tactical schematics of the city onto his visor, noting with professional pride that the outline of the buildings below almost perfectly matched the image projected before him.

The altimeter rune flashed red and Kaelen pulled out of his drop position, smoothly bringing his legs around so that he was falling feet first. Glancing left and right he saw the same manoeuvre being repeated by his men and slammed the firing mechanism on his chest. He felt the huge deceleration as the powerful rocket motors ignited, slowing his headlong plunge into a controlled descent.

Kaelen's boots slammed into the marble flagged plaza, his jump pack flaring a wash of heated air around him as he landed. Streams of bright light licked up from the city, flak waving like undersea fronds as the rebels sought to down the departing Thunderhawk. But the heretic gunners were too late to prevent the gunship from completing its mission; its deadly cargo had already arrived.

Kaelen whispered a prayer for the transport's crew and transferred his gaze back to the landing zone. Their drop was perfect, the Thunderhawk's jumpmaster had delivered them dead on target. A target that was thronged with screaming, masked cultists.

Kaelen ducked a clumsy swing of a cultist's power maul and punched his power fist through his enemy's chest, the man shrieking and convulsing as the energised gauntlet smashed though his flesh and bone. He kicked the corpse off his fist and smashed his pistol butt into the throat of another. The man fell, clutching his shattered larynx and Kaelen spared a hurried glance to check the rest of his squad had dropped safely with him.

Stuttering blasts of heat and light flared in the darkness as the remaining nine men in Squad Leuctra landed within five metres of him, firing their bolters and making short dashes for cover.

A cultist ran towards him swinging a giant axe, his features twisted in hatred. Kaelen shot him in the head. By the Lion, these fools just didn't stop coming! He ducked behind a giant marble statue of some nameless cardinal as a heavy burst of gunfire stitched its way towards him from the gigantic cathedral at the end the plaza. Muzzle flashes came through smashed stained glass windows, the bullets tearing up the marble in jagged splinters and cutting down cultists indiscriminately. Kaelen knew that advancing into the teeth of those guns would be bloody work indeed.

Another body ducked into cover with him, the dark green of his armour partially obscured by his chaplain's robes. Interrogator Chaplain Bareus raised his bolt pistol. The weapon's barrel was intricately tooled and its muzzle smoked with recent firing.

'Squad form on me!' ordered Kaelen, 'Prepare to assault! Evens advance, odds covering fire!'

A PROPHET HAD risen on the cathedral world of Valedor and with him came the planet's doom. Within a year of his first oration, the temples of the divine Emperor had been cast down and his faithful servants, from the highest cardinal to the lowliest scribes, were cast into the charnel fire-pits. Millions were purged and choking clouds of human ash fell as grotesque snow for months after.

The nearest Imperial Guard regiment, the 43rd Carpathian Rifles, had fought through the temple precincts for nine months since the planet's secession, battling in vicious close combat with the fanatical servants of the Prophet. The pacification had progressed well, but now ground to a halt before the walls of the planet's capital city, Angellicus. The heavily fortified cathedral city had withstood every assault, but now it was the turn of the Adeptus Astartes to bring the rebellion to an end. For the Space Marines of the Dark Angels Chapter, more than just Imperial honour and retribution was at stake. Many centuries ago, Valedor had provided a clutch of fresh recruits for the Chapter and the planet's heresy was a personal affront to the Dark Angels. Honour must be satisfied. The Prophet must die.

DOZENS OF CULTISTS were pitched backwards by the Space Marines' first volley, blood bright on their robes. More died as the bolters fired again. Kaelen exploded from cover, a laser blast scoring a groove in his shoulder plate. The first cultist to bar his path died without even seeing the blow that killed him. The next saw Kaelen bearing down on him and the Marine sergeant relished the look of terror on his face. His power fist took his head off.

Gunfire sounded, louder than before, as more covering fire raked the robed cultists. Kaelen fought and killed his way towards the temple doors, gore spattering his armour bright red. All around him, Squad Leuctra killed with a grim efficiency. Short dashes for cover combined with deadly accurate bolter fire had brought them to within eighty metres of the temple doors with no casualties. In their wake, more than two hundred cultists lay dead or dying.

Powerful blasts of gunfire spat from the smashed windows. Too heavy to charge through, even for power armour, Kaelen knew. He activated his vox-com.

'Brother Lucius.'

'Yes, brother-sergeant?'

'You have a good throwing arm on you. You think you can get a couple of grenades through those windows?'

Lucius risked a quick glance over the rim of the fountain he was using for cover and nodded curtly. 'Yes, brother-sergeant. I believe I can, the Lion willing.'

'Then do so,' ordered Kaelen. 'The Emperor guide your aim.'

Kaelen shifted position and spoke to the rest of his squad. 'Be ready. We move on the grenade's detonation.'

Each tiny rune on his visor that represented one of his men blinked once as they acknowledged receipt of the order. Kaelen glanced round to check that Chaplain Bareus was ready too. The hulking figure of the chaplain was methodically examining the dead cultists, pulling back their robes like a common looter. Kaelen's lip curled in distaste before he quickly reprimanded himself for such disloyalty. But what was the chaplain doing?

'Brother-chaplain?' called Kaelen.

Bareus looked up, his helmeted face betraying nothing of his intent.

'We are ready,' Kaelen finished.

'Brother-sergeant,' began Bareus, moving to squat beside Kaelen. 'When we find this Prophet, we must not kill him. I wish him taken alive.'

'Alive? But our orders are to kill him.'

'Your orders have been changed, sergeant,' hissed the chaplain, his voice like cold flint. 'I want him alive. You understand?'

'Yes, brother-chaplain. I shall relay your orders.'

'We must expect heavy resistance within the temple. I will tell you now that I do not expect many, if any, of your men to survive,' advised Bareus, his voice laden with the promise of death.

'Why did you not brief me on this earlier?' snapped Kaelen. 'If the forces we are to face are so strong then we should hold here for now and call in support.'

'No,' stated Bareus. 'We do this alone or we die in the attempt.' His voice brooked no disagreement and Kaelen suddenly understood that there was more at stake with this mission than simple assassination. Regardless of the chaplain's true agenda, Kaelen was duty bound to obey.

He nodded, 'As you wish, chaplain.' He opened the vox-com to Lucius again. 'Now, Brother Lucius!'

Lucius stood, lithe as a jungle cat and powered a frag grenade through each of the windows either side of the cathedral doors. No sooner had the last grenade left his hand than the heavy blast of a lascannon disintegrated his torso. The heat of the laser blast flashed his super-oxygenated blood to a stinking red steam.

Twin thumps of detonation and screams. Flashing light and smoke poured from the cathedral windows like black tears.

'Now!' yelled Kaelen and the Marines rose from cover and sprinted towards the giant bronze doors. Scattered small arms fire impacted on their armour, but the Space Marines paid it no heed. To get inside was the only imperative.

Kaelen saw Brother Marius falter, a lucky shot blasting a chunk of armour and flesh from his upper thigh, staining the dark green of his armour bright red. Chaplain Bareus grabbed Marius as he staggered and dragged him on. Kaelen's powerful legs covered the distance to the temple in seconds and he flattened his back into the marble of the cathedral wall. Automatically, he snapped off a pair of grenades from his belt and hurled them through the smoking windows. The shockwave of detonation shook the cathedral doors and he vaulted through the shattered window frame, snapping shots left and right from his bolt pistol.

Inside was a blackened hell of smoke, blood and cooked flesh. Bodies lay sprawled, limbs torn off, skeletons pulverised and organs melted. The wounded gunners shrieked horribly.

Kaelen felt no pity for them. They were heretics and had betrayed the Emperor. They deserved a death a hundred times worse. The Dark Angels poured inside, moving into defensive positions, clearing the room and despatching the wounded. The vestibule was secure, but Kaelen's instincts told him that it wouldn't remain that way for long.

Marius propped himself up against the walls. The bleeding had already stopped, the wound already sealed. He would fight on, Kaelen knew. It took more than a shattered pelvis to stop a Dark Angel.

'We have to keep moving,' he snapped. Movement meant life.

Chaplain Bareus nodded, reloading his pistol and turned to face Kaelen's squad.

'Brothers,' he began, 'we are now in the fight of our lives. Within this desecrated temple you shall see such sights as you have never witnessed in your darkest nightmares. Degradation and heresy now make their home in our beloved Emperor's vastness and you must shield your souls against it.'

Bareus lifted his chaplain's symbol of office, the crozius arcanum, high. The blood red gem at its centre sparkled like a miniature ruby sun. 'Remember our primarch and the Lion shall watch over you!'

Kaelen muttered a brief prayer to the Emperor and they pressed on.

'THEY ARE WITHIN your sanctuary, my lord!' said Casta, worry plain in every syllable. 'What would you have us do to destroy them?'

'Nothing more than you are already, Casta.'

'Are you sure, lord? I do not doubt your wisdom, but they are the Adeptus Astartes. They will not give up easily.'

'I know. I am counting on it. Do you trust me, Casta?'

'Absolutely, lord. Without question.'

'Then trust me now. I shall permit the Angel of Blades to kill all the Marines, but I want their chaplain.'

'It will be as you say, lord,' replied Casta turning to leave.

The Prophet nodded and rose from his prayers to his full, towering height. He turned quickly, exposing a sliver of dark green beneath his voluminous robes.

'And Casta...' he hissed. 'I want him alive.'

CHAPLAIN BAREUS SWUNG the crozius in a brutal arc, crushing bone and brain. Fighting their way along a reliquary studded cloister, the Marines battled against more followers of the Prophet.

The Dark Angels fought in pairs, each warrior protecting the other's back. Kaelen fought alongside Bareus, chopping and firing. The slide on the bolt pistol racked back empty. He slammed the butt of the pistol across his opponent's neck, shattering his spine.

Bareus slew his foes with a deadly grace, ducking, kicking and stabbing. The true genius of a warrior was to create space, to flow between the blades where skill and instinct merged in lethal harmony. Enemy weapons sailed past him and Kaelen knew that Bareus was a warrior born. Kaelen felt as clumsy as a new recruit next to the exquisite skill of the interrogator chaplain.

Brother Marius fell, a power maul smashing into his injured hip. Hands held him down and an axe split his skull in two. Yet even though his head had been destroyed, he shot his killer dead.

Then it was over. The last heretic fell, his blood spilt across the tiled floor. As Kaelen slammed a new magazine into his pistol, Bareus knelt beside the corpse of Brother Marius and intoned the Prayer for the Fallen.

'You will be avenged, brother. Your sacrifice has brought us closer to expunging the darkness of the past. I thank you for it.'

Kaelen frowned. What did the chaplain mean by that? Bareus stood and pulled out a data slate, displaying the floor plans of the cathedral. While the chaplain confirmed their location, Kaelen surveyed his surroundings in more detail.

The walls were dressed stone, the fine carvings hacked off and replaced with crude etchings depicting worlds destroyed, angels on fire and a recurring motif of a broken sword. And a dying lion. The rendering was crude, but the origins of the imagery was unmistakable.

'What is this place?' he asked aloud. 'This is our Chapter's history on these walls. Lion El'Jonson, dead Caliban. The heretics daub their halls with mockeries of our past.'

He turned to Bareus. 'Why?'

Bareus looked up from the data slate. Before he could answer, roaring gunfire hammered through the cloisters. Brother Caiyne and Brother Guias fell, heavy calibre shells tearing through their breastplates and exploding within their chest cavities. Brother Septimus staggered, most of his shoulder torn away by a glancing hit, his arm hanging by gory threads of bone and sinew. He fired back with his good arm until another shot took his head off.

Kaelen snapped off a flurry of shots, diving into the cover of a fluted pillar. The concealed guns were pinning them in position and it would only be a matter of time until more cultists were sent against them. As if in answer to his thoughts, a studded timber door at the end of the cloister burst open and a mob of screaming warriors charged towards them. Kaelen's jaw hung open in disgust at the sight of the enemy.

They were clad in dark green mockeries of power armour, an abominable mirror of the Space Marines' glory. Crude copies of the Dark Angels' Chapter symbol, spread wings with a dagger through the centre, adorned their shoulder plates and Kaelen felt a terrible rage build in him at this heresy.

The Marines of Squad Leuctra screamed their battle cry and surged forward to tear these blasphemers apart and punish them for such effrontery. To mock the Dark Angels was to invite savage and terrible retribution. Fuelled by righteous anger, Squad Leuctra fought with savage skill. Blood, death and screams filled the air.

As the foes met in the centre of the cloister, the hidden guns opened fire again.

A storm of bullets and ricochets, cracked armour and smoke engulfed the combatants, striking Space Marines and their foes indiscriminately. A shell tore downwards through the side of Kaelen's helmet. Redness, pain and metallic stink filled his senses, driving him to his knees. He gasped and hit the release catch of his ruined helmet, wrenching it clear. The bullet had torn a bloody furrow in the side of his head and blasted the back of the helmet clear. But he was alive. The Emperor and the Lion had spared him.

A booted foot thundered into the side of his head. He rolled, lashing out with his power fist and a cultist fell screaming, his leg destroyed below the knee. He pushed himself to his feet and lashed out again, blood splashing his face as another foe died. Kaelen sprinted for the cover of the cloister, realising they had been lured out of cover by the fraudulent Dark Angels. He cursed his lack of detachment, angrily wiping sticky redness from his eyes.

The tactical situation was clear, they could not go back the way they had come. To reach the main vestibule was not an option; the gunfire would shred them before they got halfway. The only option was onwards and Kaelen had a gnawing suspicion that their enemies knew this and were channelling them towards something even more fearsome.

Bareus shouted his name over the stuttering blasts of shooting, indicating the timber door the armoured cultists had emerged from.

'I believe we have only one way out of this. Forwards, sergeant!'

Kaelen nodded, his face grim as the icon representing Brother Christos winked out. Another Space Marine dead for this mission. But Kaelen knew that they would all lay down their lives for the mission, no matter what it was. Chaplain Bareus had decided that it was worth all of them dying to achieve it and that was good enough for him.

Under cover of the cloisters, Bareus and the remaining five members of Squad Leuctra sprinted through the studded door that led out of this firetrap. Sergeant Kaelen just hoped that they weren't running into something worse.

'Is THE ANGEL ready to administer the Evisceral Blessing, Casta?' inquired the Prophet.

'It is my lord,' said Casta, his voice trembling with fear. The Prophet smiled, understanding the cause of his underling's unease.

'The Angel of Blades makes you uncomfortable, Casta?'

Casta fidgeted nervously, his bald head beaded with sweat. 'It frightens me, my lord. I fear that we count such a thing as our ally. It slaughtered ten of my acolytes as we released it from the crypts. It was horrible.'

'Horrible, Casta?' soothed the Prophet, placing both hands on the priest's shoulders, his gauntlets large enough to crush Casta's head. 'Was it any more horrible than what we did to take this world? Was it bloodier than the things we did when we stormed this temple? There is already blood on your hands, Casta, what matters a little more? Is what we do here not worthy of some spilt blood?'

'I know, but to actually see it, to taste and smell it... it was terrible!' The priest was shaking. The memory of the Angel had unmanned him completely.

'I know, Casta, I know,' acknowledged the Prophet. 'But all great things must first wear terrible masks in order that they may inscribe themselves on the mind of the common man.'

The Prophet shook his head sadly, 'It is the way of things.'

Casta nodded slowly, 'Yes, my lord. I understand.'

The Prophet said, 'We bring a new age of reason to this galaxy. The fire we begin here will ignite a thousand others that will engulf the False Emperor's realm in the flames of revolution. We shall be remembered as heroes, Casta. Do not forget that. Your name shall shine amongst men as the brightest star in the firmament.'

Casta smiled, his vanity and ego overcoming his momentary squeamishness. Fresh determination shone in his zealous eyes.

The Prophet turned away.

It was almost too easy.

SERGEANT KAELEN STALKED the darkened corridors of the cathedral like a feral world predator, eyes constantly on the move, hunting his prey. Flickering electro-flambeaux cast a dim glow that threw the carved walls into stark relief and he deliberately averted his gaze from them. Looking too carefully at the images carved into the walls left his eyes stinging and a nauseous rolling sensation in the pit of his stomach.

Since leaving the death trap of the cloisters they had snaked deeper into the cathedral and Kaelen couldn't help but feel that they were in terrible danger. Not the danger of dying, Kaelen had stared death in the face too many times to fear extinction.

But the dangers of temptation and blasphemy... they was another matter entirely. The paths to damnation were many and varied, and Kaelen knew that evil did not always wear horns and breathe fire. For if it did, all men would surely turn from it in disgust. No, evil came subtly in the night, as pride, as lust, as envy.

In his youth, Kaelen had known such feelings, had fought against all the whispered seductions that flesh and the dark could offer in the dead of night, but he had prayed and fasted, secure in his faith in the Divine Emperor of Mankind. He had achieved a balance in his soul, a tempering of the beast within him.

He understood that there were those who gave into their base desires and turned their faces from the Emperor's light. For them there could be no mercy. They were deviants of the worst kind. They were an infection, spreading their lies and abomination to others, whose weakened faith was an open doorway to them. If such forces were at work within these walls, then Kaelen would fight till the last drop of blood had been squeezed from his body to root it out and destroy it.

Bareus led the way, his strides long and sure. The passageway they followed dipped slightly and Kaelen could feel a cool breath of night air caress his skin. The stone walls gave way to a smooth, blackened glass, opaque and blemish free, widening to nearly ten metres across. The walls curved up into a rounded arch above them and were totally non-reflective. Doors constructed of the same material barred the way forward, the susurration of air coming from where the glass had been cracked near the top of the frame. An ominous stain dripped down the inside face of the door from where a torn fragment of white cloth was caught, flapping in the breeze on a jagged shard of broken glass.

'Blood,' said Bareus.

Kaelen nodded. He had smelt it before seeing it. An odd whickering mechanical sound came from the other side of the doors and Kaelen felt an instinctive dread send a hot jolt of fear into his system. Bareus stepped forwards and thundered his boot into the door, smashing it completely from the frame. Black glass flew outwards and Kaelen swept through the portal, bolter and power fist at the ready.

Kaelen entered a domed arena, its stone floor awash with blood and sliced chunks of flesh. The stink of the charnel house filled the air. The same non-reflective black substance that had formed the door enclosed the arena. He pounded down some steps and skidded to a halt, his blood thundering in horror at the sight before him.

A mad screaming echoed around the enclosed arena. A dome of utter darkness rose above them as the horrifying bulk of the creature before the Space Marines turned to face them with giant, slashing strides. Perhaps it had once been a dreadnought. Perhaps it had evolved or mutated in some vile parody of a dreadnought. But whatever it was, it was clearly a beast of pure evil. Even Bareus, who had fought monstrous abominations before, was shocked at the terrifying appearance of the bio-mechanical killing machine. Fully six metres high, the creature stood on four splayed, spider-like legs of scything blades, that cut the air with a deadly grace. A massive, mechanically muscled torso rose from the centre of the bladed legs and clawed arms, lightning sheathed, swung insanely from its shoulders, upon which was mounted an ornately carved heavy bolter. At its back, a pair of glittering, bladed wings flapped noisily, their lethal edges promising death to any who came near.

The bio-machine's head was a pulped mass of horribly disfigured flesh. Multiple eyes, milky and distended, protruded from enlarged and warped sockets. Its vicious gash of a slobbering mouth was filled with hundreds of serrated, chisel-like teeth and its skin was a grotesque, oily texture – the colour of rotten meat.

It was impossible to tell where the man ended and the machine began.

Its entire body was soaked in blood, gobbets of torn flesh still hanging from its claws and teeth. But the final horror, the most sickening thing of all was that where the metal of the dreadnought's hide was still visible, it was coloured an all too familiar shade of dark green.

And upon its shoulder was the symbol of the Dark Angels.

Whatever this creature was, it had once been a brother Space Marine.

Now it was the Angel of Blades and as the Space Marines recoiled in horror, the monster howled in mad triumph and stamped forwards on its scythe legs.

The speed of the Angel of Blades was astonishing for such a huge creature. Blood burst from its face as the Space Marines overcame their shock and began firing their bolters. Every shell found its mark, detonating wetly within the Angel's dead skin mask, but its lunatic screams continued unabated.

A silver blur lashed from the monster A casual flick of its bladed leg licked out and eviscerated Brother Mellius quicker than the eye could follow. His shorn halves collapsed in a flood of red, but his bellows of pain were drowned by the Angel's hateful shrieks. The baroque heavy bolter mounted on the beast's shoulder roared and blasted the remains of Mellius apart.

Kaelen knew it had to die. Now.

He sprinted across the courtyard as the rest of his squad spread out and leapt in front of the rampaging machine, a brilliant burst of blue-white lightning arcing from his power fist as he struck at the beast's face. A coruscating corona of burning fire enveloped its huge frame as the lethal power of Kaelen's gauntlet smashed home. Its deformed flesh blistered and sloughed from its face, exposing a twisted metallic bone structure beneath. The Angel struck back, unheeding of the terrible hurt done to it.

Kaelen dodged a swipe meant to remove his head and rolled beneath its flailing arms. He powered his crackling fist into its groin and ripped upwards.

The power fist scored deep grooves in the Angel's exterior, but Kaelen's strike failed to penetrate its armoured shell. The beast side-stepped and another leg slashed out at him. He ducked back, not quick enough, and the armoured knee joint thundered into his chest, hurling him backwards.

Kaelen's breastplate cracked wide open, crushing his ribs and shattering the Imperial eagle on his chest into a million fragments. Bright lights exploded before his eyes as he fought for breath and struggled to rise, reeling from the massive impact. Even as he fell, he knew he had been lucky. Had the cutting edge struck him, he would now be as dead as Mellius. Heavy bolter shells spat from the shoulder-mounted gun, hammering into his legs and belly, driving him to his knees.

One shell managed to penetrate the cracks in his armour and he screamed, white hot fire bathing his nerves as the shell blasted a fist-sized hole in his hip, blood washing in a river down his thigh. He fell to the ground as the Angel loomed above him, its bloody claws poised to deliver the death blow and tear Kaelen in two.

With a howling battle cry, Chaplain Bareus and the surviving members of Squad Leuctra rushed to attack the monstrosity from the flanks and rear. Brother Janus died instantly, decapitated by a huge sweep of the creature's claws. Another leg whipped out, impaling his corpse and lifting him high into the air. Brother Temion leapt upon the thing from behind, holding his sword in a reverse grip and driving it into the Angel's back with a yell of triumph. The monster screamed and bucked madly, casting the brave Space Marine from its back. Its wings glittered in the torchlight and powered wide with a ringing clash of metal. A discordant shriek of steel on steel sounded as the Angel's wings slashed the air and a storm of razor edged feathers flew from the beast's back and engulfed Temion as he raised his bolter. He had no time to scream as the whirlwind of blades slashed through him and tore his body to shreds. The bloody chunks of flesh and armour that fell to the ground were no longer recognisable as human.

Bareus smashed his crozius arcanum against the back of one of the Angel's knee joints, ducking a swipe of the beast's razor wings. Brother Urient and Brother Persus hammered the huge machine from the front while Kaelen pushed himself unsteadily to his feet.

Urient died as the Angel caught him with both sets of claws, ripping his body apart and tossing the pieces aside in contempt. The beast staggered as Bareus finally chopped through the silver steel of its leg. It tried to turn and slash at its diminutive assailant, but staggered as the severed leg joint collapsed under its weight. The huge arms spun as it fought for balance. Kaelen and Bareus were quick to press home their advantage.

Kaelen smashed his power fist into the monstrosity's mutated face, the huge gauntlet obliterating its features and tearing through its armoured sarcophagus. Kaelen kept pushing deeper and deeper inside the heart of the monster's body. The stench gusting from the rotted interior was the odour of a week old corpse. His fist closed around something greasy and horribly organic and the Angel shuddered in agony, lifting Kaelen from the ground. He grasped onto the beast's shell with his free hand, still struggling to tear the beast's heart out. Agony coursed through his body as the Angel's limbs spasmed on his wounded hip and chest. Kaelen's grip slid inside the Angel's body, glistening amniotic fluids pouring over his arm and preventing him from slaying the vile creature that lurked within its body. His grip finally found purchase. A writhing, pulsing thing with a grotesque peristaltic motion. He closed his fist on the fleshy substance of the monstrosity's heart and screamed as he released a burst of power within the bio-machine's shell.

The monster convulsed as the deadly energies of the power fist whiplashed inside its shell, blue fire geysering from its exhausts. Its legs wobbled and the massive beast collapsed, sliding slowly to its knees. A stinking black gore gushed from every joint and its daemonic wailing dimmed and at last fell silent. Kaelen wrenched clear his gauntlet, a grimace of pain and revulsion contorting his features as the lifeless Angel of Blades toppled forwards, a mangled heap of foetid meat and metal.

Kaelen slid down the Angel's shell and collapsed next to the foul creature, blood loss, shock and pain robbing him of his prodigious strength. Breathless, Chaplain Bareus grabbed Kaelen's arm and helped him to his feet. Brother Persus joined him, his dark green armour stained black with the monster's death fluids.

The three Dark Angels stood by the rotted corpse and tried to imagine how such a thing could possibly exist. Kaelen limped towards the remains of the beast and stared at the shattered carapace of the Angel's shell. The iconography on the sarcophagus was of a winged figure in a green robe carrying a scythe, its face shrouded in the darkness of its hood. Fluted scrollwork below the image on its chest bore a single word, partially obscured by black, oily blood. Kaelen reached down, wiping his hand across the carapace and felt as though his heart had been plucked from his chest. He sank to his knees as he stared at the word, willing it not to be true. But it remained the same, etched with an awful finality.

Caliban.

The Dark Angels' lost homeworld. Destroyed in the Great Heresy thousands of years ago. How this thing could have come from such a holy place, Kaelen did not know. He rose and turned to Bareus.

'You knew about this, didn't you?' he asked.

The chaplain shook his head. 'About that abomination, no. That we would face one of our brothers turned to the Dark Powers... yes. I did.'

Kaelen's face twisted in a mixture of anger and disbelief, 'The Dark Powers? How can that be possible? It cannot be true!'

A voice from the shadows, silky and seductive said, 'I'm afraid that it is, sergeant.'

Kaelen, Bareus and Persus spun to see a tall, hugely built figure in flowing white robes emerge from the shadows accompanied by a stoop shouldered man with a shaven head. The tall figure wore his black hair short, close cropped into his skull and three gold studs glittered on his forehead. His handsome features were smiling wryly. Bareus swiftly drew his bolt pistol and fired off the entire clip at the robed figure. As each shot struck, a burst of light flared around the man, but he remained unharmed. Kaelen could see the faint outline of a rosarius beneath his robes. The small amulet would protect the Prophet from their weapons and Kaelen knew that such protection would be almost impossible to defeat. All around the arena the opaque glass walls began to sink into the ground and a score of armed men stepped through, their weapons aimed at the three Space Marines. Bareus dropped the empty bolt pistol and reluctantly Kaelen and Persus did likewise.

'How can it be true?' asked Kaelen again. 'And who are you?'

'It is very simple, sergeant. My name was Cephesus and once I was a Dark Angel like you. When your dead husk of an Emperor still walked amongst you, we were betrayed by Lion El'Jonson. He abandoned our Chapter's true master, Luther, and left with the Emperor to conquer the galaxy. The primarch left him to rot on a backwater planet while he vaingloriously took the honour of battle that should have been ours! How could he have expected us not to fight him on his return?'

Bareus stepped forwards and removed his helm, tossing it aside as he stared at the tall figure with undisguised hatred. He raised his crozius arcanum to point at the other's chest.

'I know you, Cephesus. I have read of you and I will add your name to the Book of Salvation. It was necessary for Luther to remain behind on Caliban. His was a position of great responsibility!'

'Necessity, chaplain, is the plea for every act of ignorance your Imperium perpetrates. It is the argument of tyrants and the creed of slaves,' snapped the Prophet. 'Wipe the virtue from your eyes, we were cast aside! Scattered throughout time and space to become the Fallen. And for that I will kill you.'

He nodded towards the dead monstrosity, his earlier composure reasserting itself and said, 'You killed the Angel of Blades. I am impressed.'

The Prophet smiled and parted his robes, allowing them to fall at his feet. Beneath them, he wore a suit of powered armour, ancient and painted unmistakably in the colours and icons of the Dark Angels. The ornate form of a rosarius, similar to the one worn by Bareus, hung on a chain, nestling against the eagle on his breastplate. 'I was Cephesus, but that name no longer has any meaning for me. I foreswore it the day Lion El'Jonson betrayed us.'

'The primarch saved us!' roared Bareus, his face contorted in fury. 'You dare to blaspheme against his blessed name?'

Cephesus shook his head slowly. 'You are deluded, chaplain. I think that it is time you start looking at yourself and judge the lie you live. You can project it back at me, but I am only what lives inside each and every one of you. I am a reflection of you all.'

Sneering, he descended the steps to stand before the interrogator chaplain, pulling a thin chain from a pouch around his waist. Attached along its length were several small polished blades, each inlaid with a fine tracery of gold wire. Bareus's eyes widened in shock and he reached for his hip scabbard, drawing an identical blade.

'You call these weapons Blades of Reason. Such an irony. It is as much a badge of office to you as your crozius, is it not? I have eleven here, each taken from the corpse of a Dark Angel chaplain. I will take yours and make it an even dozen.'

Without warning he snapped a blade from the chain and spun on his heel, slashing it across Persus's throat. The Space Marine sank to the ground, arterial blood bathing his breastplate crimson.

Kaelen screamed and launched himself forwards, swinging his power fist at the Prophet's head. Cephesus swayed aside and smashed his bladed fist into Kaelen's ribs.

The neural wires inscribed in the blades shrieked fiery electric agony along Kaelen's nerves, and he howled as raw pain flooded every fibre in his body. His vision swam and he fell to the ground screaming, the blades still lodged in his side.

Bareus howled in fury and slashed with his crozius arcanum. Cephesus ducked and lunged in close, tearing the rosarius from around Bareus's neck. Silver and gold flashed; blood spurted. The chaplain fell to his knees, mouth open in mute horror as he felt his life blood pump from his ruined throat. He fell beside Kaelen and dropped his weapons beside the fallen sergeant.

Cephesus reached down and knelt beside the dying chaplain. He smiled indulgently and scooped up Bareus's intricate blade, threading the thin chain through its hilt.

'An even dozen. Thank you, chaplain,' hissed Cephesus.

Sergeant Kaelen gritted his teeth and fought to open his eyes. The Prophet's blades were lodged deep in his flesh. With a supreme effort of will, each tiny movement bringing a fresh spasm of agony, he reached down and dragged the weapon from his body. His vision cleared in time for him to see the Prophet leaning over Chaplain Bareus. He growled in anger and with strength born of desperation lunged forwards, throwing himself at the heretic.

Both hands outstretched, he slashed with the blades and tried to crush the Prophet's head with his power fist. But Cephesus was too quick and dodged back, but not before Kaelen's hand closed about an ornate chain around his neck and tore it free. He rolled forwards, falling at the Prophet's feet and gasped in pain.

Cephesus laughed and addressed the men around the arena. 'You see? The might of the Adeptus Astartes lies broken at my feet! What can we not achieve when we can humble their might with such ease?'

Kaelen could feel the pain ebbing from his body and glanced down to see what lay in his hand and smiled viciously. He lifted his gaze to look up into the shining, mad face of the Prophet and with a roar of primal hatred, struck out at the traitor Dark Angel, his power fist crackling with lethal energies.

He felt as though time slowed. He could see everything in exquisite detail. Every face in the arena was trained on him, every gun. But none of that mattered now. All he could focus on was killing his foe. His vision tunnelled until all he could see was Cephesus's face, smugly contemptuous. His power fist connected squarely on the Prophet's chest and Kaelen had a fleeting instant of pure pleasure when he saw the heretic's expression suddenly change as he saw what the sergeant held aloft in his other hand.

Cephesus's chest disintegrated, his armour split wide open by the force of the powerful blow. Kaelen's power fist exploded from his back, shards of bone and blood spraying the arena's floor. Kaelen lifted the impaled Prophet high and shouted to the assembled cultists.

'Such is the fate of those who would defy the will of the immortal Emperor!'

He hurled the body of Cephesus, no more than blood soaked rags, to the ground and bellowed in painful triumph. Kaelen was a terrifying figure, drenched in blood and howling with battle lust. As he stood in the centre of the arena, the black glass walls rapidly began to rise and the armed men vanished from sight, their fragile courage broken by the death of their leader.

Kaelen slumped to the ground and opened his other fist, letting the rosarius he had inadvertently torn from around the Prophet's neck fall to the ground. A hand brushed his shoulder and he turned to see the gasping face of Chaplain Bareus. The man struggled to speak, but could only wheeze breathlessly. His hand scrabbled around his body, searching.

Guessing Bareus's intention, Kaelen picked up the fallen crozius arcanum and placed it gently into the chaplain's hand. Bareus coughed a mouthful of blood and shook his head. He opened Kaelen's fist, pressed the crozius into the sergeant's hand and pointed towards the corpse of the Fallen Dark Angel.

'Deathwing...' hissed Bareus with his last breath and closed his eyes as death claimed him.

Kaelen understood. The burden of responsibility had been passed to him now. He held the symbol of office of a Dark Angels chaplain and though he knew that there was much for him yet to learn, he had taken the first step along a dark path.

NEWS OF THE Prophet's death spread rapidly throughout Angellicus and within the hour, the rebel forces broadcast their unconditional surrender. Kaelen slowly retraced his steps through the cathedral precincts, using the vox-comm to call in the gunship that had delivered their assault. He limped into the main square, squinting against the bright light of the breaking morning. The Thunderhawk sat in the centre of the plaza, engines whining and the forward ramp lowered. As he approached the gunship, a lone Terminator in bone white armour descended the ramp to meet him.

Kaelen stopped before the Terminator and offered him the crozius and a thin chain of twelve blades.

Kaelen said, 'The name of Cephesus can now be added to the Book of Salvation.'

The Terminator took the proffered items and said, 'Who are you?'

Kaelen considered the question for a moment before replying.

'I am Deathwing,' he answered.

IN THE BELLY OF THE BEAST
William King

THE ATMOSPHERE IN the steering chapel of the *Spiritus Sancti* was tense as the scouts pushed through the brocade-curtained archway into the cool basalt fastness of the command centre. Tech-adepts chanted, counting down the range. The machine language gibberish of shaven-headed monitors hummed in the background, a constant, incomprehensible babble. Above them, on the cat-walks, dark-robed figures strode from control-icon to control-icon, checking the purity seals of the major systems and wafting censers of burning incense. The chapel bustled with a controlled panic that Sven Pederson had never encountered before. The young Space Marine didn't need the red warning globes hovering on either side of the holo-pit to tell him that the starship was at battle-stations.

'Ah, gentlemen, there you are at last. I'm so pleased you could join us.' The measured tones of Karl Hauptman, commander of the vessel, cut easily through the noise.

'You summoned us, jarl. We are your bondsmen and we obey.' Sergeant Hakon spoke evenly but Sven could tell that the rogue trader's mockery had touched a nerve. Hakon was a proud old warrior, passed over for Terminator duty, and it rankled to have to serve under this foppish aristocrat, supervising a bunch of scouts on their first training mission. Still, he was a Space Wolf to the bone and had to obey.

Hauptman lounged easily behind the master lectern, projecting effortless authority, the one man present who seemed perfectly calm. He seemed more than Hakon's equal in stature although the giant Space Marine towered over him.

The shipmaster gestured to the holo-pit with one long, perfectly man-icured finger. Control runes flickered emerald on the lectern, underlighting his face and giving it a hollow, almost daemonic look. 'Give me the benefit of your wisdom, Brother-Sergeant Hakon – what do you make of that?'

One of the monitors closed his camera-eyes and intoned a mantra. Sven had a clear view of the cyberlink feeds that connected the man to his work-lectern. Each tiny fibre pulsed with light. The rhythm of the pulses slowed until they coincided with that of the chant. When the monitor opened his eyes again, their mirrored lenses caught the light, burning in the gloom like tiny red suns.

An object appeared in the pit: it was greyish and round, and looked like a small asteroid. Hauptman gestured again. The plainsong of the tech-priests swelled, echoing under the groined ceiling of the chapel. The smell of hallucinogenic incense grew sweeter and more sickly. Sven felt slightly nauseous as his system adjusted to the drug then neutralised it. The air blurred, lights flickered and the object expanded then came into better resolution.

For no reason he could think of, the sight filled Sven with dread. He glanced at Brother-Cadet Njal Bergstrom, his closest friend among the other Space Wolves. The ruddy light of the warning globes stained his pale face, making the look of horror there more intense. Njal had tested positive for psychic abilities and, if he survived his cadetship, might be trained as a librarian, just as Sven would be trained as a wolf-priest. What-ever, Sven had learned to respect his comrade's intuition.

'Extremely unusual. Are those doorways in the thing's side? Is it a base of some sort?' Hakon was clearly puzzled.

Hauptman stroked his beard, cocked his head to one side. 'Astropath Chandara assures me that it is alive. Sensor divination appears to confirm this.'

The man he had mentioned stood beside the command throne, clutch-ing at the arm-rest as if it were the only thing that held him upright. Sweat beaded his dark, pudgy face and formed deep circles under the armpits of his white robes. Chandara looked stricken, like a man in the latter stages of some fatal fever. His eyes had the fey, haunted look that Sven had seen in whalehunter shamans when the death-madness came upon them.

'I beg of you, shipmaster, destroy this abomination. Nothing but evil can come from preserving it a moment longer.' Chandara's husky voice carried a strange resonance, the certainty of prophesy.

Hauptman spoke reassuringly. 'Don't worry, my friend. If it proves necessary I will destroy it instantly. However it may be that this deviant artefact contains something of use to the Imperium. We must investi-gate, if only to increase the knowledge of the scholars of the Adeptus Terra.'

Sven could tell that Chandara disagreed but could not challenge the shipmaster's authority. The astropath shrugged in resignation. Like many of the crew he had become completely used to obeying orders.

Sergeant Hakon understood where all this was leading. 'You want my men to investigate this deviant nest.'

Hauptman smiled as if Hakon were a child who had been quick on the uptake. 'Yes, sergeant. I'm sure that you are competent enough to manage this.'

Sven saw how the statement trapped Hakon; to refuse would be to call his ability into question. He was manipulated only for a moment but that moment was long enough. Hakon responded instantly and with pride: 'Of course.'

Sven would have liked him to have asked more questions and he could see that once the words were out of his mouth the sergeant wished that he had done so. Now it was too late. They were committed.

'Prepare the boarding torpedo,' Hauptman said. 'Your squad can begin its investigations immediately.'

HELMETS READY, PRESERVER systems primed, the Space Marines sat in the cold, dark fuselage of the boarding torpedo. Sven studied each of his companions in turn, taking a last glimpse before they donned their almost insect-like breather masks, trying to fix their faces in his mind. Each ragged visage was obscured by war-paint. He was suddenly, painfully aware that this might be the last time he ever saw his comrades alive.

Sergeant Hakon sat still, his body tense. His bolt pistol held firmly against his chest. His taut-skinned, thin lipped features were set. The cold blue eyes peering out from beneath a skullcap of silver-grey hair. Unlike the cadets, Hakon did not keep his head shaved except for a single strip of hair. He was a full Space Marine.

Njal sat opposite Sven beneath a stained glass window that showed stars through a portrait of the apotheosis of the Emperor into the Throne of Eternal Life. Njal had his hands folded as if in prayer, his fine ascetic features were composed and calm. Sven guessed that he was sub-vocalising the Litany Against Fear.

'Why didn't Hauptman send in his house troops?' asked Egil, his bull-dog face set in its characteristic permanent sneer. Of all the Space Wolf cadets he was the most flawed. His eyes held the cold, frozen, madness so characteristic of troll-blooded berserkers. He had broken two of Sven's ribs during unarmed combat practice back on Fenris and smiled coldly as the younger scout was carried to the apothecarion. Sven had overheard Sergeant Hakon tell Brother-Captain Thorsen that he would be keeping a special eye on Egil. Whether that was good or bad, Sven had never decided.

'The guards were probably too scared to travel in this rust-bucket they call a boarding torpedo. By the ghost of Leman Russ, I can't say I blame them.' This came from Gunnar, the squad support man who grinned amiably as he said it. He smiled, revealing the specially lengthened incisors that were the mark of the Space Wolf gene-seed. There was something reassuring about Gunnar's broken-nosed, heavily pock-marked features, Sven thought.

Hakon let out a short bark of mirthless laughter. 'When you have seen as much combat in the Emperor's service as those Guardsmen have then you will be true Space Marines. Till then, mock them not. Simply thank the Emperor for providing you with this chance to show your own bravery.'

'I hope this thing is full of deviants,' Egil said with relish. 'I'll prove my bravery soon enough.'

Gunnar slapped a cartridge into his weapon. 'Don't worry, Njal, we'll see you're safe.'

Sven knew that Gunnar was just teasing. The worried expression on Njal's face made it plain that he did not.

'I can look after myself,' he said sharply.

Gunnar clapped him on the shoulder of his armour and laughed. 'I know you can, little brother. I know you can.'

'Final checks,' Sergeant Hakon said. Each Marine fell silent as he concentrated on the prayers necessary to activate his armour.

Sven knew that his suit was well-maintained. He had carried out all the maintenance rituals himself, washing the armour with scented oils while intoning the Litany Against Corrosion, greasing the articulated joints with blessed unguents, checking the pipes of the rebreather with coloured smoke from an auto-censer. He believed firmly in the old Space Marine saying, if you look after your equipment it will look after you.

Yet it went deeper than that. He knew that the armour he had been given was really only loaned to him. He felt a sense of reverence for the ancient artefact. It had been worn by a hundred generations of Space Wolves before his birth and would be worn by a hundred more after his death. He was part of a family of Wolves that stretched off into the fathomless future. When he touched the armour he touched the living history of his Chapter.

Now, as he touched each command rune in turn, he tried to imagine the previous wearers of the armour. Each, like him, had been chosen from the blond haired seafarer clans of the island chains of Nordheim. Each, like him, had undergone the years-long basic training of the Space Marine. Each, like him, had undergone the implantation of the various bio-systems that had transformed them into a superman far stronger, faster and more resilient than an ordinary mortal. Some had gone on to glory; others had died in this armour. Sven had often wondered which group he would belong to when his time came. Now the sense of fore-boding he had felt when he first saw the alien artefact returned.

He was aware how much he relied on this armour for protection. Its ceramite carapace to protect him from heat and cold and enemy fire. Its auto-sensory systems that let him see in the darkness. Its recycling mechanisms that let him breath in hard vacuum and survive for weeks on his own reconstituted excrement. As these thoughts filtered into his mind, his prayers moved from being an empty recital of a well-worn litany into something genuine and sincere. He did not want to die and perhaps his suit might save him.

He fitted the comm-net ear-bead into place and checked the position of the speaking circlet over his larynx. He bowed his head and prayed that the ship's Tech-Adepts had taken as much care of the equipment as his order's own lay-brothers would. Once inside the alien artefact it might be his only means of communication with his fellow scouts.

He pushed his hands together in prayer, feeling the muscle amplification of the suit's exoskeleton lend him the strength of dozens. He closed his eyes and let the pheromone traces of his companions be picked up by the suit's receptors. He knew that if the alien artefact was pressurised he could identify his companions, even in total darkness, by scent alone. With an act of will he switched his hearing from normal sound to comm-net pickup. The sub-vocalised activation litanies of his companions rang in his ears, interspersed with the comms chatter of the ship's crew.

'Helmets on,' the sergeant said. In turn the Space Marines donned their protective headgear. One by one, each gave the thumbs up sign. When his turn came Sven did the same. He felt the click of the helmet lock as it slid into place. Targeting icons appeared in his sight underneath the Gothic script of his head-up display. All the read-outs were fine. He gave the signal. The sergeant put his own helm on last.

'All clear. The Emperor is served,' Hakon said for them all.

'The Blessing of the Holy One upon you,' responded the ship's controller. There was a hiss and a fine mist filled the air as the cabin was depressurised. The external temperature dropped sharply; a frost-blue icon flashed an appropriate warning. It clicked for three heartbeats to indicate a lack of air-pressure. There was another click from the neckband of the armour. Sven knew that his helmet had locked into place and could not now be removed until his suit had checked the atmosphere and found it safe for breathing.

There was a faint kick of acceleration. For a moment Sven felt weightless as the boarding torpedo left the artificial gravity field of the Spiritus Sancti, then a fraction of his normal weight returned as the torpedo accelerated. In the view-monitors the starship showed first as a vast metal wall. As it receded, the turrets that studded its exterior became visible, then the whole ship from winged stern to dragon-beaked prow. The sheer size of the ship was obvious from the hundreds of great arched windows, each of which Sven knew was the length of a whaling ship and taller than its mast. The rogue trader's ancient vessel dwindled until it was nearly lost amid the stars, just one point of light among many. In the flickering green forward monitors, the alien object swelled ominously in size.

'There's no turning back now,' he heard Njal mutter.

'Good,' Egil said.

With a violent, lurching shudder, the boarding torpedo lodged itself in the wall of the alien artefact. Sven opened his eyes and ceased praying. He hit the quick release amulet on the restraining straps and floated free for a moment before the boarding torpedo's artificial gravity returned.

The squad had moved to ready positions covering the forward bulkhead doors with all their weapons. Vibration thrummed through the soles of Sven's boots as the boarding torpedo's drilling nose-cone bored into the other vessel's walls. After a moment the motion ceased.

+Squad, ready to disperse!+ Hakon's voice came clear over the comm-link.

+Opus Dei!+ the squad responded.

The bulkhead doors swung open and the scout's covered the area with their weapons, just as they had practised a thousand times in training. Sven braced himself as air rushed into the torpedo, misting as it hit the chill within the vehicle.

+Ghost of Russ!+ someone breathed. +I don't believe it.+

Their helmet lights revealed an awesome vista. They stared down into a vast corridor, as high as the chapel ceiling on the *Spiritus Sancti* and the colour of fresh meat. The walls were not smooth and regular; they looked rough and were covered in innumerable folds, like the exposed surface of the brain the medics had shown him during his novitiate. The walls glistened with pink mucous.

From each fold of the wall protruded thousands of multicoloured cilia, each metres long and as fine as titanite thread. They swayed like ferns in a breeze. Here and there huge, muscle-like sacs pulsed. Orifices in the wall opened and shut in time with their pulsing, making sounds like last laboured breaths. Sven guessed that they were circulating air. Fluid gurgled through transparent pipes that lined the walls like great veins.

+Looks like the place is inhabited+ Gunnar said. His voice sounded too loud over the comm-link.

Spores danced and glittered in the air, catching the light and twinkling like stars in the void of space. As they responded to the helmet lights, they seemed to ignite with phosphorescence, like fireflies, and the glow became dazzling. Sven blinked and his second, translucent eyelids dropped into place, filtering the light back to a manageable level. His armour's glowlamps dimmed automatically as the ambient light increased.

While Gunnar covered them, Egil and Njal moved forward, following a standard, well-drilled pattern. As they left the torpedo, their feet sank into the spongy floor of the alien vessel. They walked as if on a thick carpet, disturbing the waving cilia. Sven wondered whether the fronds were some sort of early warning device or whether they might even be poisonous.

The atmosphere icon on his display flashed green three times and then settled. There was a click as the neck-lock of his helmet released. Sven advanced into the alien vessel, flexing his knees to compensate for the gravity shift. The ship seemed to be generating its own internal gravity with centripetal force from its rotation. Even so, Sven felt as if he were only half his normal weight.

Sergeant Hakon had already undone his helmet, and stood taking several deep breaths. He grimaced as his bio-engineered system adapted to the local conditions. Sven knew that he would soon be acclimatised to the local conditions and immune to any toxins present in the atmosphere. After a long, tense minute, Hakon gestured for them all to remove their helms.

The first thing that surprised Sven was how warm it was. The air seemed almost blood heat. He started to sweat as his body compensated for the temperature and the humidity. He coughed as the membranes within his gullet filtered out the airborne spores. The sparkling colours of his surroundings filled his sight; the inside of the ship was a riot of hues glowing with phosphorescent fire in the vessel's warm, shadowy interior.

He was reminded of the coral reefs around the equator on Nordheim where the Space Wolves kept their summer palaces, far from the icy mountains and glaciers of Fenris. He had often gone swimming through the reefs after the battle exercises on the warmer tropical islands. The walls reminded him of certain formations of hard coral. He wondered whether this ship had been created from similar creatures, colonies of microscopic organisms joined to form one vast structure. Everything looked tranquil; it seemed safe and relaxing.

Suddenly, something lashed past him and stung his face. He flinched and reflexively swung his pistol up and fired. The bolter kicked in his hand as it released its missile. In the brief second between pulling the trigger and watching the thing explode, he caught sight of what looked like a metre-wide jellyfish, drifting parachute-like on the air currents. His face went numb as bio-systems moved to cope with the toxin.

'Careful,' said Sergeant Hakon. 'We don't know what we'll find here.' He moved over to Sven and passed a medical amulet over the wound. The small gargoyle headed talisman did not flicker. It gave no warning chime.

'You seem to be coping,' Hakon said calmly. At the sound of the shot the rest of the Space Wolves had taken up positions facing outward covering all lines of fire. Nothing obvious menaced them. No more floating jellyfish came in sight.

The ceiling had started to glow; long veins of bio-luminescent tubing had flickered to life as if in response to the presence of the scouts. They illuminated the corridor which curved downwards out of sight. Sven was reminded of the inside of a snail's shell.

Sven felt slightly nauseous as the tailored antibodies of his blood-stream dealt with whatever invaders the alien creature had injected. He was struck by a comparison. Perhaps the jellyfish thing had been an antibody responding to the appearance of the scouts.

He tried to dismiss the thought as mere fancy but the thought kept returning that perhaps the alien ship had other ways of dealing with intruders.

THEY ADVANCED CAUTIOUSLY through the pulsing dark. Their cat-like eyes had adjusted to the gloom. They kept their weapons ready to deal death. At every turn and junction they left comm-link relays. These kept them in touch with the Spiritus Sancti and served as navigation beacons.

'Ghost of Russ!' Sven cursed, slipping and falling on the mucus-covered floor. The spongy surface absorbed the impact as he rolled back into a crouch. Njal moved over to make sure he was all right. Sven could see the look of concern on his face. He waved his friend away, almost embarrassed by the fall.

'We are in the belly of leviathan,' Njal said, studying walls the colour of bruised flesh. Sven grimaced; the rotten meat stench of their surroundings made him want to gag. He glanced round.

In the dim light, the other Space Marines were spectral, ghostly figures. Gunnar was on point duty; the rest of the scouts straggled back in a long line behind him. The sergeant brought up the rear. Breathing sacs deflated and a stream of mist and spores erupted forth, refracting the light from the scouts' armour, turning it into rainbows.

'I never much cared for that story, brother,' Sven said quietly, wiping mucus from his armour. His father loved telling him the old tale: of the fisherman, Tor, who was swallowed by the giant sea-monster leviathan and lived in its vast belly for fifty days before being rescued by the original Space Wolf Terminators and being asked to join their order. His father had used it to frighten Sven and his brothers to keep them from stealing out to sea on their makeshift rafts. At least he had, until the day when he had set out on his dragonship and never returned. As a child, Sven had always suspected that leviathan had got him.

When he had finally become a cadet, he had laughed at such childish stories. He had consulted the archivum of the Order and discovered that the story of Tor and the leviathan was a truly ancient tale, one dating back to before the Imperium, to the distant, time-lost days of primordial Earth. It existed in one form or another on many Imperium worlds, a distant trace memory of a time before humanity colonised the galaxy. He had never thought to be troubled by it again.

Now, within the bowels of this alien ship, he found the horror of the ancient tale had returned to him. He could hear his father's rasping voice speaking in the darkness of the longhouse as the winter gales howled outside. He remembered the chill that filled him when the old man had dwelt on the nauseating things found in the sea monster's belly.

He recalled as well looking out to sea on stormy nights when gale-driven waves lashed the black rocks and imagining huge monsters, bigger than his home island lurking beneath the sea. It was the memory of his strongest boyhood fear and now it returned to haunt him. He felt the same way now; all around he sensed the presence of a huge, waiting monster.

All around him in the gloom he sensed presences. Overhead, he thought he heard the flapping of wings. When he glanced up he was startled to see dark forms like a shoal of manta rays, flapping along the ceiling. As he watched, they vanished into orifices in the flesh wall.

Fluids gurgled through the pipe-veins around him. He was within some vast living being and he knew it for certain now. And he was sure that it knew of his presence in some dim, instinctual way, sensed him and resented his intrusion. There was a sense of evil, malign intelligence about this alien vessel. It was a presence inimical to humanity and any other form of life.

Sven felt an almost claustrophobic terror. His heartbeat sounded like thunder in his ears. His breath seemed louder than the breathing of the valves of the ship. He fingered the hilt of his mono-molecular knife uneasily and recited the comforting words of the Imperial Litany to himself. In this place, at this time, the words sounded hollow, empty. He met Njal's gaze and saw the unvoiced fear there too. Neither of them had expected their first mission to be like this.

'Move on, brothers.' Hakon's voice seemed to come from far away. Sven forced himself to move deeper into the darkness.

FROM THE MOMENT he had set foot on this alien ship, Njal had known he was doomed to die. More than any of his companions, he was aware of the strangeness of this vessel and the fact that it was alive. He knew that it was dormant at present but it would take only the slightest of actions to waken it. It was only a matter of time. He felt it in his bones.

Ever since he had been a child, that feeling of unconquerable dread had continually been proved correct. Njal had never been wrong. He had watched Sven's father's ship, the *Waverider*, set sail that fatal morning knowing it would never return. He had wanted to warn them but he knew that it was useless. Each man aboard had been marked for death and it was unavoidable. And so it came to pass.

He had watched a party of hunters led by Ketil Strongarm disappear into the mountains above Orm's Fjord. The stink of death was upon them. He had wanted to warn them not to go. He knew without being able to explain why they would never return. Two days later, word came back that Ketil and all his brothers had been killed by an avalanche.

The night that his mother had died Njal had sensed the presence of death, swooping like an immense, midnight-black hawk to carry the old woman away. The whalehunter shaman had assured his father that the fever had broken. Njal knew differently and in the cold, mist-strangled morning he had been proved correct. He had not cried as the pall-bearers were summoned. He had said his farewells long before in the darkness.

He worried about his inability to speak, at what had locked his lips. He had been unable to talk about his forebodings even with his tutors in the Space Wolves' citadel. In later years he had worried that it was pride. His gift had set him apart from the others and if he had warned them, he would have proven it wrong. Perhaps the future was fixed and there was nothing any man could do about it; or perhaps he wanted to be correct, needed the secret, almost proud knowledge of his own uniqueness. He smiled bleakly to himself. Many and subtle were the traps of daemons.

He was a sensitive; the Space Wolf librarians in the Fortress Among the Glaciers had confirmed this. They said that, in time, his talent would mature and they would teach him how to channel it. All he had to do was ward himself from impure thoughts. But his time had run out and he knew it. He did not want to die so soon and all of the training he had received could not alter the fact. He was more scared than he had ever been.

Shocked by his own blasphemy, he cursed the old librarians. What could the old fools who ruled Fenris like gods from their cloud-girt citadel, know of how he felt? A single, sensitive youth isolated among people who might burn him as a daemon-spawned freak. Since the time of the ancient wars, the Sea Peoples had been wary of anything that smacked of the preternatural. Anger and resentment surged through him.

He felt more alone than ever surrounded by his fellow cadets, all of whom except Sven made fun of him. They reminded him of the older lads in his home village of Ormscrag who had mocked him until the day he had grown large enough to give them a good hiding. Marching here in the alien gloom, Njal felt his lifelong resentment of the others, the lesser mortals, the ungifted, return.

The intensity of the feeling surprised him. Why was he so filled with bitterness towards the comrades with whom he had gone through basic training? Why did he hate the patronising tutors of the order who had done nothing but good for him? Was it because they had circumscribed his choices, had forced him onto the dark path that had led to this terrible place of death?

Njal tried to calm himself. All roads lead to death eventually, he told himself. It is the manner in which you walk the path that is important. Somehow, at that moment, the noble sentiment of the old Chapter saying seemed cheap and tawdry.

Briefly, he considered that the thoughts might not be his own, that they might be being projected into his mind by some outside source. Then, abnormally quickly, he rejected the idea and decided that it was simply his lifelong feelings emerging in the face of death. He was being made uneasy by the strangeness of his surroundings and his own forebodings.

All around him, the things that slept in the darkness stirred towards wakefulness.

SVEN GLANCED DOWN the long corridor. The composition of the walls seemed to have changed as the scouts made their way deeper into the alien vessel. They were slicker, smoother and gave more impression of life. It seemed darker and more alive. Here and there, vein-pipes vanished beneath the flesh of the walls, leaving only smooth bulges.

'It seems to be getting more active the deeper we go,' he said into the comm-link. 'The walls seemed engorged with blood.'

'I think the beast stirs,' Njal said.

Sven stared back at him coldly. The last thing he wanted to be reminded of was that they were inside some vast living creature.

'I hope Hauptman is getting good pictures of this,' Gunnar said cheerfully. 'If I'm going to be swallowed alive I want it to be in a good cause.'

'That's enough,' Hakon said. His voice was edgy. He had obviously detected the undercurrent of fear in the scouts' nervous chatter and decided to put an end to it. The cadets fell silent for a while.

The corridor ended in a massive fleshy sphincter valve.

'It looks like an airlock,' Sven said, studying it. The doorway rippled moistly. The scout warily eyed the folds of flesh surrounding the valve.

'I'll open it,' Egil said and blasted away at it with his bolt pistol. The bolts tore into the flabby mass of flesh. The valve-door spasmed as if in pain, the whole floor shaking as underfloor muscles joined the action. The scouts were thrown flat, unable to keep their footing on the unstable floor. Sven's head struck something hard and his vision filled with stars for a moment.

'Is everyone all right?' Hakon asked after the floor settled back down again. Everyone nodded or murmured. Hakon glared at Egil. 'Don't ever do that again. Don't even think about doing anything like that ever again unless I specifically order you to!' Cold menace filled the sergeant's voice.

Egil looked away and shrugged.

Sven inspected the door. Great gobbets of flesh had been torn out of it but it still barred their way. Another shot would tear the ruptured muscle away. He didn't know whether they should risk another small earthquake.

He paused to think. The more they proceeded, the more the alien spaceship resembled two things: a giant living body, and the work of some alien technology. There was obviously some plan to its layout. The plan might be incomprehensible to the human mind but it was there. These sphincter valves were obviously airlocks of some kind but they were too far into the ship for them to open onto vacuum.

Perhaps they were a safety measure like the bulkheads on the *Spiritus Sancti*, designed to section off an area if decompression occurred. Or perhaps they were security systems barring access to certain areas.

Either way, there must be some means of opening them. Suddenly it dawned on Sven that he was thinking from a purely human perspective. It did not need to be true. Perhaps the doors sensed the presence of authorised personnel and opened automatically or perhaps they responded to scent cues the scouts could not duplicate. If either of these theories were the case then perhaps Egil's was the only way forward.

Sven noticed a small fleshy node near the valve. Acting on impulse he reached out and stroked it. The partially-torn door flapped open with a soft, almost animal sigh. Egil looked at the fingers of his gauntlet. They were covered in pink slime. It was scented like musk. He wiped his fingers against his chest piece, taking care to avoid touching the two-headed Imperial eagle on the breastplate.

Sergeant Hakon nodded at him in approval, then gestured for them all to proceed. Sven stepped through into the fleshy gloom.

EGIL GLARED EAGERLY out into the shadows. Murder-lust burned in his heart. He felt the same warm excitement as he had felt the night before his first great battle. Anticipation filled him. He could sense the danger here, the threat of the unknown. He relished it, confident in his ability to master whatever stepped into his path.

He glanced contemptuously at Sven and Njal and smiled to himself. Let the white-livered cowards be afraid, he thought. They were unworthy to be true Space Marines and in this test they would be found wanting. A born Space Wolf knew no fear. He lived only to slaughter the enemies of the Emperor and die a warrior's death, so that he might sit at the right hand of his god in the Hall of Eternal Heroes.

Seeing the worried look on Sven's face, he felt like laughing. The whelp was afraid; the prospect of death made him uneasy! Egil knew in his heart that death was a warrior's true and constant companion; he had done since he tore out an Ormscrag warrior's throat with his teeth during his first night-raid. Death was not something to inspire fear. Rather, it was the true measure of a man: how much death he could inflict and how he faced his own.

He did not expect anything better from Njal and Sven. He had always been astonished that the Space Wolves recruited from the islanders. They were a puny people, hardly worthy to be called warriors. They cringed on their islands and cruised only the coastlines of their tiny domains. His own people were much better kin to the Gods of the Glacier.

The Storm-riders took their ships to the four corners of the world, raiding where they pleased and following the ocean-going herds of leviathan. Yes, they were much more worthy. It took a true man to stare into the eye of a leviathan and still be able to throw a harpoon straight. It took a true man to sail the open sea where the only company was the mammoth shark, the leviathan and mightiest of all, the kraken. He felt almost pity towards the islanders. How could they understand the great truths of his people?

He glanced at the great hallway with its arch of bone white ribs visible through a tightly stretched ceiling the colour of putrefying meat. He looked at the cancerous growths that marred the floor and walls, at the strange pods of translucent membrane that expanded and contracted like a child's balloon. He looked at the puddles of rank, bile-like fluid that covered the floor. He wiped beads of sweat from his face and took another lungful of the acrid acidic air.

Egil knew that it did not matter to a true warrior whether he died here among the alien growths or at sea with storm winds tossing his hair and the salt spray lashing his face. Like the others, he sensed the presence of the hidden enemy – but unlike the others, he told himself, he longed to face it. To feel the cold supercharged frenzy of battle and the sweet satiation of his killing lust.

He knew he was a killer, had done ever since he butchered his first leviathan calf. Egil had enjoyed the sound the harpoon made as it plunged into flesh. The scent of warm blood had been perfume to his nostrils. Yes, he was a killer and he was proud of it. It did not matter to him whether his prey was a mindless animal, another man or some alien monstrosity. He welcomed the chance of combat. He knew that he would face whatever came like a true warrior and, if necessary, die like a true man.

He hefted his knife, admiring its fine balance, and touched the rune that activated the mono-filament element. Egil knew that it could slice the bonds between actual atoms if he wanted it to. In his secret heart he hoped that he would have a chance to use it. He felt that the true worth of a man was measured in breast-to-breast combat, when the action got close and deadly. Any fool could kill at a distance, with a bolt pistol. Egil liked to look into his foe's eyes when he killed them. He liked to watch the light go out of them.

Egil glared out into the warm dark, daring his foes to appear. In the distance he felt something respond.

* * *

Let the Galaxy Burn

SVEN SAW THE strange sneering smile appear on Egil's youthful face and he shuddered. He wondered what was going on. All of his companions seemed to be behaving a little oddly. He wondered whether it was simply the strangeness of the place combined with the feeling of danger that was bringing out hidden facets of their personality or whether there was some strange force at work here.

He could understand it if it were the eerie nature of the place. The deeper they went, the more sinister the place became. The air seemed thick with acrid stenches. Long columns of glistening flesh rose from floor to ceiling. Slime dripped from the ceiling to form phosphorescent puddles in the depressions of the floor. The slow drip-drip-drip kept pace with his own heartbeat. The noise mingled with the gurglings of the vein-pipes and the laboured gasping of the air-valves.

Occasionally, out of the corner of his eye, Sven would catch sight of small scuttling things, moving with the speed of spiders between the patches of shadow. The further the Space Marines proceeded, the more apparent it became that they had disturbed something. It seemed like the whole place was waking from a long period of hibernation.

Hakon gestured for them to be still. Everyone froze in place. The sergeant advanced, moving cautiously towards a patch of darkness. Sven brought his bolt pistol up to cover him, focusing down the sight. As the sergeant filled the cross-hairs it occurred to Sven how easy it would be to kill him. A life was such an easy thing to end. All he would have to do is squeeze the trigger…

Sven shook his head, wondering where the thought had come from. Had something outside tried to influence him or was some long con-cealed flaw in his own personality come to light. He pushed the thought aside and concentrated on his duty to provide support for Hakon.

The sergeant stood over something, looking down. He kicked it with his foot. A skull rolled into the light. Sven recognised the sloping brow and rows of protruding tusks from his comparative anatomy classes.

'Ork,' he said.

Egil gave a short, barking laugh that sounded harsh and shallow in this alien place. 'This place doesn't belong to orks,' the Space Wolf sneered.

'No… but maybe they've been here before us,' Hakon said. His expres-sion was grave as he considered the possibility of a new threat from this unexpected quarter.

'It's been dead a long time,' Njal pointed out. 'Maybe there are no more about.'

Sven bent down to examine it, noting the column of snapped vertebrae that depended from the neck. 'Then the question is: what killed it?'

The scouts exchanged worried looks.

'Perhaps we should return to the ship,' Njal suggested. 'We've seen enough, surely.'

'No,' Hakon said firmly. 'We've to perform a complete survey.'

'We've come too far to back out,' Egil added fiercely.

'Surely you're not scared, little brother,' Gunnar said. There was a hint of fear in his own voice.

'Enough,' Hakon said. He led them on down the path. His stride was determined and Sven knew that the sergeant was going to see this thing through to the bitter end, whatever it might be.

THE JOKE FROZE on Gunnar's lips as he looked down into the long hallway. Back when he was younger, he had seen the body of a leviathan washed up on the beach. His father's bondsmen had surrounded the great mammal, hacking open the creature and stripping off great flaps of blubber from its ribcage. The stink from the great cauldrons in which they were melting down oil mingled with the corrupt stench of the creature's innards. It rose from the beach to assail his nostrils even atop the cliff on which he stood.

He had gazed down into the thing's guts and seen, naked and exposed, the pulpy hidden workings of its guts. A bondsman had climbed in and was ploughing through the great ropes of the intestine with a knife. His hands and face and beard were smeared with blood and filth.

Looking down from the jaw-like ledge of flesh, the moment returned to him with sudden force. He felt simultaneously like his younger self and like the old fisherman ploughing through the disgusting meat. The full horror of their position rammed itself home in his mind. They were in the belly of the beast. They had been swallowed like the ancient seafarer, Tor, and for them there would be no Terminators to rip them free.

He rubbed at the slime that now coated his armour and fought down an urge to gag. Not for the first time, he wished he were back home in his father's longhouse, safe under his protection and lording it over the villagers.

He knew that was impossible. There was no going back. His father had exiled him for killing young Strybjorn Grimson in that fight. It did not matter that the death had been an accident. He hadn't really meant to throw the boy off the cliff; he had meant merely to frighten him. It did not matter either that his father had only sent him west-over-the-sea to avoid retribution at the hands of Strybjorn's kin, who had refused weregeld for his death. Gunnar still felt bitter about it, even if he hid his bitterness the same way as he hid his unease, behind a smile and a sarcastic joke.

He let his breath hiss out between his teeth; at least his reverie had distracted him from their predicament, trapped within this alien monster. He saw Njal looking at him and he restrained a taunt. It was too easy for him, the son of an upland jarl, to patronise Sven and Njal who were born freemen. He felt guilty about it. They were his battle-brothers, all equal in the eyes of the Emperor. If the Space Wolves had not chosen him after the great contest of arms at Skaggafjord then he would be a simple landless man, less even than a bondsman. He vowed that in the future he would do his best to contain his feeling of superiority, if only the Emperor would protect him this once.

And now he was attempting to bargain with his Lord and Emperor, a demeaning act for both the deity and a Fenris noble. He tried to clear his mind and make a most devout prayer of atonement but when he did so the only thing that sprang to mind was the picture of the dead beast lying on the shore, with the gore-streaked old man burrowing through its filthy innards.

'WHAT WAS THAT?' Sven asked in a hurried, panicky whisper, raising his bolt pistol to eye-level, readying it to fire.

'What was what?' Hakon asked. The sergeant looked tired and haggard, as if all the weight of command had suddenly pressed down upon him. He had the abstracted air of a man facing an insoluble problem.

'I thought I heard something.'

The sergeant paused for a moment, then shook his head.

'Sven's right. He did hear something,' Njal chipped in. 'I heard– There it is again!'

They all strained to listen. It was as if a great pump had started in the distance. The sound carried for a long way, seeming to echo down the rib-like arches of the corridors from far off. The sound was like the slow, measured beat of a massive drum. Sven shuddered, suddenly very cold within his ancient armour.

The scouts stood frozen. The breathing valves moved in time to the beat. The gurgle of liquids through the pipes rose to a rush. A waterfall of viscous fluid tumbled slowly from ledges halfway down the corridor. Steam rose from the stinking pools it created. Shapes seemed to writhe within the flesh of the walls. Sven was reminded of the movement of maggots within rotten meat.

'It's waking up,' Njal said softly, his voice trembling. 'We should go back.'

Egil sniggered. 'Are you a Marine or soft-skinned girl? Why should a little noise scare us?'

Sven whirled to confront the berserk. 'Can't you see the changes that are happening? Who knows what's going to occur next.'

'Why's this happening?' Hakon asked. 'Is it because we're here?'

Sven paused to consider. 'Yes, I think so. It's probably reacting to our presence. The whole ship seems to be alive. It's been rousing since we've come aboard. Think of the changes we've seen as we've come deeper. The outside walls were hard as rock. These ones still seem to be living flesh. Maybe we should go back, wait for reinforcements.'

'No,' Hakon said. 'Let's explore further. We've yet to find anything of real interest.'

He took the lead, leaping lightly over the steaming pools of bile. In the distance Sven thought he could hear a sound much like scuttling, or the clacking of giant pincers. The sound made him think uncomfortably of scorpions. Looking about him he knew the others had heard it too. The sound disappeared, drowned out by the slow thumping of that monstrous heartbeat.

Sven made the sign of the eagle across his chest and tried very hard not to think about the fisherman, Tor, and his sojourn within the innards of leviathan.

NJAL COULD SENSE the mind of the Beast. It was a slow, steady pressure in his head, perceptible as the vessel's heartbeat or the bellows breathing of the life support systems. He felt its oppressive weight bear down on him, adding to the claustrophobic feel of the long, intestinal corridors with their vile yellow floors and tiny digestive nodes whose acid scarred his armoured boots. He sensed the being's ancient might and the sheer, incomprehensible alienness of it.

He was caught in the cross-currents of its thoughts as he was caught within the coils of its body. Sometimes strange hungers and longings flickered through his mind and Njal felt himself roused by alien lusts and desires: flashes of bizarre, inhuman memories, views seen through a myriad infra-red receptors, sounds overheard by organic radio antennae, the incommunicable sight-smell of pheromone analysers.

Nausea had filled him. There were times when he felt human, long minutes in which he doubted his sanity. Then micro-second exposures to the alien impressions rocked his being to the core.

The strangest thing was that the thoughts appeared to be coming from all around him. There seemed to be no fixed source of consciousness, no psychic beacon radiating through the eternal night the way the will of the Emperor was said to be visible as the flare of the Astronomicon.

No, what he was picking up was coming from every direction, from myriad points of consciousness. It was like the chatter of many individuals over the comm-net. Yet there was a pattern, an organising structure to it. He could sense it but could not comprehend it fully. The thoughts simultaneously seemed to belong to one mind and many – as if thousands of telepathic nodes of consciousness surrounding him seemed to make up a single greater mind.

He caught sight of what he suddenly knew was himself through a tiny eyeball high in the corridor ceiling. He scuttled along the ledge, looking down on himself. At the same time he was aware of himself looking up to see the things scuttling in the shadows. He opened his mouth to scream a warning. He saw himself gazing up into the alien darkness, frozen in terror…

Several things happened near-simultaneously. The entity which had been overwhelming him became aware that it was being eavesdropped on and all contact ceased. He was himself once more. The warning left his lips, coming out in a long incoherent shriek in alien words.

And the scuttling things moving along the wall leapt to the attack.

WHEN NJAL SCREAMED, Sven reacted immediately, throwing himself down and rolling along the spongy floor, scanning his surroundings with a quick movement of his head. He caught sight of the segmented black objects descending from the ceiling. Their fall seemed strangely slow in the low gravity.

He lay on his back and braced his bolt pistol in both hands, blasting at the thing springing at him. It reminded him of a cross between a scorpion and a giant termite. It had an armoured, multi-segmented body and great claws. Eight evil eyes glittered in the gloom. Venom dripped from clicking mandibles.

The pistol roared and kicked in his hand. The monster exploded in front of him as the shells slammed into its alien body. Yellow phosphorous light limned its corpse as gobbets of meat were thrown everywhere by the explosion. He felt wetness on the back of his neck. At first he thought it was his target's blood then he realised it was fluid pumping from tiny broken capillaries in the fleshy floor. He scrambled to his feet, seeking another target.

The sergeant stood as still as a statue. His whole form flickered with the light from his blazing pistol. With every shot, an alien monster was destroyed.

'Fire at will,' Hakon shouted. 'Choose your targets carefully. Don't let them get too close.'

Sven sighted on a thing that moved across the floor like a great manta ray, its body undulating with every bump and depression in the carpet of alien flesh. His mind was paralysed with fear but his body seemed to respond like some mechanical automaton. The long hours of training where he repeated every combat action until it was ingrained like habit had paid off.

Without thinking he pulled the trigger and as his target flew apart, he re-aimed and fired, re-aimed and fired. The howl of bolt pistol fire filled the air as his companions did the same.

Nearby, Egil crouched in the slime, a feral snarl revealing his elongated incisors. The blue flare of his pistol flickered in the gloom. The light-trails of his bolter shells blazed towards their targets. The creepers were blown asunder, their shells cracked; burning meat oozed from within. Egil held his knife ready in his left hand in case any got too close; he would be ready to tear them to pieces.

Gunnar wheeled from the hip, his heavy bolter swivelling with him. His hand pumped furiously on the trigger mechanism. Short controlled bursts stitched across the oncoming tide of creepers, tearing them in two.

Only Njal stood frozen, a look of horror on his face. As Sven watched one of the aliens reached his face, claw extended, ready to snap into his neck. Quickly, heart racing Sven drew a bead and fired. The claw of the creeper was torn off, black blood spattered Njal's face. He shook his pale face and moved like a man waking from a trance. Sven felt hundreds of tiny legs tickle his neck, and a weight descended on his back. He wheeled and found himself staring into the tiny eyes of one of the monsters.

Filled with panic and horror he thrust it back one armed, bludgeoning it across the head with the barrel of his pistol. There was a sickening crunch as he broke its armour. A foul spray burned his flesh.

The memory of those small legs on his flesh, so like those of a centipede made him shudder. He flicked out his knife activating it and as the creature rushed at him, rearing to use its claws, he slashed it across the chest horizontally. Then, with a backhand sweep, he cut it again vertically. Its warm innards sprayed out uncontrollably, drenching him.

Sven looked around. The wave of attackers seemed to have broken on the Space Marines' defence. All of the scouts remained upright and seemingly unscathed.

'Any injuries?' Sergeant Hakon asked. Everyone shook their head. Sven noticed uneasily the fixed, hungry grin on Egil's face – and the pale horror on Njal's.

'Very well. We've seen enough. I think it's time to return.'

Thankfully, the scouts agreed.

Behind them, things moved in the darkness.

EGIL STRODE FORWARD confidently. This was more like it! No more skulking round in the darkness. No more waiting for the hammer to fall. Now he had a foe to face and what more could any true Space Wolf ask for? The only flaw was that they were heading in the wrong direction. Hakon should be leading them deeper into the alien vessel, towards the source of the evil that polluted it.

He paused at the junction, noting how unusual, near-spherical objects were moving through the vein-pipes in the wall. They looked for all the world like eggs that had been swallowed by a snake. Whatever new threat they represented, Egil welcomed it. Now was his chance to show his bravery, to prove his worth as a Space Marine.

The berserker fury burned within him, a dim coal ready to be fanned into bright flame. He clutched his knife tightly, feeling the inset runes even through the thick stuff of his gauntlet. He longed to plunge it into the breast of a foe. Killing the creepers had only whetted his appetite for bloodletting. Now he wanted worthier enemies for his blade to taste.

To the right, down the pale, flesh-walled corridor Egil picked up a sound. It sounded like the thrashing of something trapped. He moved to investigate, hoping that some new foe was almost upon him. As he passed, he slashed at the tiny arteries lacing the wall and laughed as black fluid ran down the central channel of his blade. Excitement filled him. Now he was truly alive, perched on the razor-edge between life and death. This was the place for a true warrior.

+Egil, where are you going? You are not following the beacon-path!+ Hakon's voice sounded worried, even through the distortion of the comm-net.

+There's something moving down here. I'm moving to secure the flank.+

+Hold your position. We'll send someone to support you.+

Egil smiled... and bounced his gauntleted palm against the comm-net circlet: +Say again. I can't hear you. There appears to be some comm-net distortion.+

He ignored the sergeant's orders just as he ignored the massive sphincter door closing behind him. He stood in a great chamber. The ceiling was as high as that of the great cathedral in the fortress among the glaciers. It was supported by immense, rib-like arches that met high overhead, where the bone of each rib emerged from the pink flesh. Great vein-pipes ran all around them, tangled into tight pleats. At the far end of the chamber was a huge mass of flesh that looked like a massive kidney, suspended by dozens of pumping, vein-like tubes, each thicker than Egil's leg.

Great blisters, twice the height of a man, covered the walls. The skin around them seemed near-translucent, like the shed skin of a snake. Within each, a massive figure seemed to struggle and squirm. There was a sound like tearing as whatever was within started to loosen its bonds.

Even as Egil watched, eyes as wide as saucers, one of the massive blisters split and from it something emerged, like a chicken new-born from an egg. It uncoiled rising unsteadily to its full height and it let out a triumphant scream that sent mucus blasting outward from its throat.

It looked almost like a dinosaur, one of the primeval sea-dragons who dwelled in the warmer seas around Fenris's equator. Its head was large and bulged back, its horny carapace protecting a hefty brain case. Its ribs seemed to be outside its body, like the exo-skeleton of an insect, and its internal organs were clearly visible. Egil could see its lungs pulse with breath and its heart beating underneath them.

It had four muscular arms, two of which terminated in long claws; the other pair clutched a long weapon that looked like a strange rifle. Its long legs ended in hoofs and raised it to over twice Egil's height. A lengthy stinger lay curled between its legs. The shape of the creature's structure reminded the scout of the ship. It was all long curves and exposed innards. It reminded him of pictures he had seen of genestealers, but from memories of archivum pictures, he recognised it as something even worse.

'Tyranid,' he breathed, barely daring to pronounce the word. 'We're in a tyranid ship.'

As he spoke the words into the comm-net, the thing swung the alien gun to bear on him. From all around there was the sound of other blisters ripping.

EGIL'S WORDS SENT a paralysing chill through Sven. He recalled studying the aliens in the archives of the order. The Space Wolves had come late to the campaign against Hive Fleet Behemoth and the records of the action had been scanty.

A company of assault troops had taken part in the ground action on Calth IV, facing the giant monsters and their legions of hideously mutated bio-killers. Afterwards, the tyranids had swiftly decomposed as mortuary micro-organisms devoured their bodies, preventing proper forensic analysis.

Most of what the archives contained was little more than speculation. The theory was that the tyranids were an immeasurably old, extra-galactic race; they drifted from system to system via a network of warp gates. They searched for new races to conquer and consume, breaking down their gene-runes to create their terrifying bio-engineered horrors.

The tyranids used bio-technology for every conceivable purpose. They had muscle-engined living chariots to carry them into battle. Their guns seemed to consist of clusters of symbiotic organisms that fired hard-shelled organic bullets or acids. Their starships were vast, living creatures, true space-going leviathans that swamed the unknowable currents of the warp.

They had an organised, powerful society, most of which worked on principles incomprehensible to or indecipherable by Imperial scholars. Hive Fleet Behemoth had been totally inimical to mankind. It devastated an entire sector in its sweep through the galaxy. It had shredded worlds. Legions of its creatures had dropped on plague-weakened planets, carrying entire populations into the maw of the motherships, never to be seen again. They had dropped asteroids on some worlds, and brought many others to their knees with deadly biological contaminations.

Some, more superstitious peoples had turned from the worship of the Emperor and abased themselves before the image of Behemoth. In the time of anarchy that the hive-fleet brought with it, Chaotic cults had gained power promising salvation from a threat against which the Imperium seemed powerless. Trade had been disrupted; nests of gen-estealers had been uncovered. A new Dark Age seemed about to fall.

It had taken a full military mobilisation of the Imperium to stop Hive Fleet Behemoth. More than orks, more than eldar, the tyranids were the most dangerous threat that humanity faced outside of the Eye of Terror. And even then, Sven speculated, another Behemoth might match even the threat of Chaos. He wondered whether this ship were perhaps some remnant of Behemoth, a straggler cut off from the main hive-fleet that had drifted powerless through space for centuries until the crew of the Spiritus Sancti had disturbed it. He prayed to the Emperor that this was the case.

The alternative – that this was the out-rider of a new hive-fleet, a successor to Behemoth – was just too dreadful to contemplate.

THROWING HIMSELF TO one side, Egil blasted the newly-hatched tyranid warrior. His bolter flared in his hand but his shot went wild. The gun in the tyranid's claws gave out a hideous grinding sound. The sacs at its base pulsed and then a stream of shrapnel and steaming acid belched forth. A terrible acrid stench filled the air. Something burned Egil's cheek as he dove aside. He gritted his teeth against the searing pain and rolled behind one of the nodes of cartilage protruding from the floor.

The ammunition warning rune of his pistol glowed red. He fumbled in his belt pouch for another clip. While he did so the alien monster lumbered closer. He could hear its hoof-beats and its slow, laboured breathing coming nearer and nearer. In his efforts he ignored the frantic comm-net chatter of his fellow Space Wolves.

His fingers were covered in mucus from the broken capillaries on the floor and the clip slid free. He grabbed it before it hit the floor and tried to ram it home. The shadow of the tyranid fell upon him. He felt its warm breath on his neck. Frantically he twisted to bring his bolter to bear. He glared up into blank, pupilless eyes. The thing's dinosaur-like head seemed to smile as it pointed its weapon towards him.

Egil looked upon the face of death and grinned back.

THE SCOUTS RACED down the corridor towards Egil's last known position. Sven's heartbeat was hammering in his ears, more from fear than exertion. He skipped over a pool of slime and saw the sphincter door ahead. He dreaded to think what lay beyond it. All of his childhood nightmares concerning monsters seemed to be coming true. He felt that if he had one more shock he would most likely go completely mad.

'Brother Egil, report! Report, damn you!' Sergeant Hakon was bellowing. 'What is your situation. Come in!'

Sven strained to hear any response. There was none. The Space Marines now stood by the door. They were ready to enter.

'Njal, watch the way we came, in case anything comes behind us! Gunnar, cover us! Sven, we're going in! Get ready. When I say the word, open the door!' Hakon's orders were crisp and clear. Sven nodded to show he understood. He swallowed again and again; his mouth felt so dry he thought he might choke at any moment.

'Go!' Hakon shouted and Sven stroked the bulbous protrusion that would open the door.

The scene that greeted them was a vision from Hell. From blisters in the walls of the vast, fleshy chamber, dozens of giant monsters were hatching, each clutching an obscene-looking weapon. Some carried two swords of bone, others long alien guns. The tyranids themselves looked as if they didn't need weapons. They were huge and their fighting claws looked deadly.

Egil lay behind a mound of flesh on the floor. His face had been horribly burned by acid, revealing bone and some scorched muscle. Near him lay a dead tyranid. Its ribcage had been torn open by the explosive blast of a bolt shell. Egil looked at them and gave a thumbs-up sign.

'Ghost of Russ!' Gunnar breathed.

'Fire at will,' Hakon shouted.

Sven sighted on a newly-hatching monstrosity. It stood, shaking the slime off its glittering carapace. He took careful aim and put a bolter shell through its head. The thing toppled like a felled tree. Sven heard Gunnar working the pump action of his heavy weapon and behind him the whole vast chamber was illuminated by the incandescent blast of a Hellfire shell. Shadows danced around the bony ridges. Two tyranids caught fire, seeming to perform a horrific dance of death in their final agonies.

Gunnar worked the Hellfire action repeatedly, laying a carpet of fire between the tyranids and Egil.

'Come on, let's get him!' Hakon ordered, setting off across the chamber, bolter spraying all around him. Sven raced after him. When he reached them, the sergeant had already raised Egil to his feet and was offering him support. Egil shook him off.

'Leave me alone! When I cannot stand on my own two feet it will be time to set me on my funeral pyre.' There was a wild, dangerous look in the berserk's eyes. He seemed half-crazed with pain and murder-lust. He reeled on his feet but stayed upright. 'I'm alright. It will take more than a little acid to finish me.'

Through the dying flames of the Hellfire curtain loomed the mighty figure of a tyranid warrior, a bio-sword held in each claw. The blades were surrounded by a sickly greenish light that reminded Sven of a festering wound. It raised its blades like scythes to cut down its chosen prey.

'Watch out!' Sven shouted leaping forward, swinging his knife left-handed. Its blade cut deeply into the tyranid, cleaving through bone and skin. Sven felt his hand and blade imbed themselves in the tyranid's alien flesh. He felt the soft clammy pressure of the thing's innards on his hand. As he withdrew his blade there was a vile sucking sound.

'Fall back!' Sven tugged Egil towards the door. For a moment the acid-burned man stood looking at the scene of the battle and Sven thought he wasn't going to come. Then Egil turned and loped to the door.

There was a hiss as the sphincter sealed behind them. Egil let out a horrible laugh. The sound seemed to bubble out from his ruined cheek. 'We showed them who the masters were,' he crowed.

Sven kept silent, wondering how many other such nightmarish hatcheries there were.

WHILE THE BATTLE raged, Njal fought down a growing feeling of panic. The sense of the alien presence had returned to his mind, a pressure as constant and morale-sapping as the unceasing, metronome-regular pulse of the distant heart. This time he sensed the alien was being more subtle. It sought to undermine his resolve. It saw him as the weak link in the squad.

And he feared that it was correct.

He felt the surge of its mighty alien mind about him, each thought emanating from a single creature, one small brain that housed a component of the group-mind.

It was hopeless, he knew. Why fight it? His premonition would come true, as it always did. Would it not be easier to simply give up? At least that would end the waiting and the fear. Why not simply lay down his weapon and welcome the inevitable? It was hopeless; he and his brethren could never escape from within the beast. It was a living world and everything in it would be aligned against them. Nothing could escape.

Even as Njal tried to dismiss these thoughts as coming from an inimical, external source, another idea filtered into his confused brain. Perhaps the group-mind might even spare them, welcome them as a slave-race, let them live and adapt them to dwelling within the breast of the hive-fleet. Then he would be safe, comfortable, welcome.

Had he not been lonely all of his life? Apart from the people around him, misunderstood, separate? If he joined the group-mind he need never be alone again. He would be part of a greater whole, a new and essential component to be sent forth and deal with other humans. The hive-fleet would nurture and protect him, make him its own. The day of humankind was done. A new order was rising in the universe. He could be a part of it, if he wished.

At first, Njal tried to dismiss the thoughts as fantasies created by his fear-crazed mind but as they continued he understood that he was not deluded. He was in touch with the hive-mind and the offer was perfectly sincere.

He was tempted. He did feel isolated and alone and had done all his life. He did not want to die, even though he knew that this was a blasphemy against his faith. A true Marine would choose death over dishonour or betrayal without thinking. The hive-mind was offering him not only a chance to live and be part of its community but perhaps even a form of immortality within itself.

For a moment he allowed himself the luxury of succumbing to temptation – then he stepped back from the brink.

He realised that he wanted to remain apart, to be himself. The loneliness that his gift brought was like the gift itself: it made him who he was.

It made him unique and he wanted that more than anything. His sense of self made him human, and made him alive. If he submerged it within something else he, the unique being, would cease to be as surely as if he had died.

More than that, being a Space Marine was part of his identity too. They had made him who he was. He was surprised to find that he did accept their way. He had spent too much time with his companions to betray them. Shared hardship and shared danger had forged bonds between them that sometimes, when he wanted it, caused his isolation to fade. They were his community. They allowed him to be himself and yet part of something greater.

For a second, though, he saw a parallel between the hive fleet and his Chapter. The Chapter was, in its own way, a living thing. Its flesh was the men who served it. Its traditions and obligations were its memories and its mind. It, too, demanded a loyalty and a submission of self – but it was of a different order to what the tyranid wanted. He could live with that.

As if sensing his rejection of it, he sensed the presence of the hive-mind withdraw. He stood alone, in an ominously empty corridor, while behind him battle raged.

SVEN FINISHED SPRAYING Egil's face with field dressing. He took a deep breath, revelling in the cool disinfectant tang of the stuff, a momentary release from the revolting stink of the place. He hoped that the antiseptic synthetic flesh would be enough to keep the berserk going till he could be got to an apothecarion.

Egil certainly seemed to think so. He lurched to his feet, beat on his huge chest with one fist and said, 'Ready!'

Hakon surveyed Sven's work critically. 'It'll do.'

Sven glanced at Njal. He was worried about his friend. Since this expedition had started he had seemed more and more distracted. Sven hoped that he had not crumbled under the strain of combat.

Gunnar finished checking his weapon and worked the loading action. It clicked loudly. He grinned from ear to ear, unnaturally jubilant.

'We're still alive. We showed them what Space Wolves can do, right enough.'

'We're not free of this place yet, lad,' Hakon said evenly. 'We've still got to follow the beacons home.'

'If we meet any more they'll taste my knife,' Egil sneered. Gunnar nodded emphatically and grinned again. The relief of surviving his first real combat was obviously getting to him, Sven thought.

'Don't be so cocky,' Hakon said. 'We beat a few half-awake monsters who'd been in suspended animation for only Russ knows how long. The next batch will be ready for us. We'd best move fast.'

His calm, commanding tone sobered the mood of all of the scouts except Egil. He continued grinning maniacally. 'Bring them on,' he muttered happily. 'Bring them on.'

GUNNAR WAS HAPPY, happier than he could ever remember being. His breath sang within him. Every heartbeat was a drumbeat of triumph. He was still alive.

His weapon felt light in his grip. He felt like kissing it. He had been so afraid when he saw the monsters but he had overcome his fear. He had kept firing and he had killed them before they could kill him or his companions.

For the very first time, he knew the thrill of triumph in real combat. There had been nothing accidental about the deaths he had caused. He had meant to kill the alien monstrosities. It had been either their lives or his. He felt no guilt about it, just a sweet sense of release and relief. The waiting was over. It had been the worst part. Sneaking down these loathsome, stinking corridors not knowing what was round the next bend. He had not realised how much the tension had played on his nerves, on all their nerves.

Now he knew what they faced and it was horrible. But now he could put a picture to the horror. It was not as frightening as the ghastly phantoms his imagination had populated the place with, nor ever would be again. They were mortal. They could die, just like any other living thing.

He felt vindicated. He knew that his action had saved the lives of his comrades. His covering fire had let the sergeant and Sven save Egil. It was the most important thing he had ever done, saving the lives of his friends. All his ambivalent feelings towards them had melted away. He knew that they were true brothers, relying on each other for their very lives in this hellish place. In the face of the awful alien menace of the tyranids, all men were brothers. Petty differences over race or class or colour meant nothing.

He smiled happily. Having faced death, he felt truly alive. He was glad simply to be able to draw another breath, see another stretch of corridor, feel the distance back to their own ship dwindle under his booted stride. He had never truly appreciated what a wonder it was to simply be.

Not even the ominous change in the beat of the distant heart or the scuttling sound in the distance could break into his mood of good cheer.

SVEN BRACED HIMSELF for another attack. Something was closing in. He could hear regular, padded footfalls on the fleshy floor behind him. He turned to look back – and saw something ducking slowly back into cover behind him.

He took a snap-shot but the shell slewed into the wall and exploded, sending gobbets of flesh everywhere. Ichor oozed from small broken blood vessels. The thing moved back into view. Sven saw it was small and dark-skinned, with six limbs – a termagant. It slowly raised its slime-dripping bio-weapon at him. He took careful aim and pumped a shell into its chest. The thing reeled backwards, squealing and scrabbling.

Sven wondered if these, too, were newly-awakened creatures, summoned forth to deal with the human trespassers. He shrugged the thought away and shot it again. His bolt burst through its target and out of the termagant's head, sending jelly-like bits of brain everywhere.

More termagants moved slowly into view from the shadows. From behind Sven, his battle-brothers' fire erupted into the advancing group. Sven fired again but the red 'empty' warning rune on his bolt pistol flickered and he realised he was out of shells. Caught in the crossfire between his own side and the oncoming termagants he threw himself flat to reload.

Shells whizzed all around him, lighting the gloom with their firework contrails. The roar of small arms echoed down the corridor, reverberating in the small space until it was deafening. As he slotted the new clip smoothly into place Sven wondered about how the termagants had got there. Were they captives taken as slaves on some alien world or were they some newly-evolved product of this vile craft? He thought the latter more likely. But how did that explain the ork skull they had found earlier?

Once more he opened fire, feeling the heavy bolt pistol kick in his hand with a kind of grim satisfaction. The withering fire of the Space Marines soon drove the termagants back into concealment. Sven knew they would be back though and wondered how many other nasty surprises the alien ship had in store.

NJAL TOOK POINT. He was happy to lead the way back. Having resisted the temptation to succumb to the hive-mind he felt so much stronger. His premonition of doom had receded. Perhaps, just this once, he would be proved wrong.

Slowly, he picked his way along the slime-covered floors, avoiding the strange circular valves at his feet. He pointed downward to indicate his fellow scouts should do the same. He heard them move to one side in response to his instruction and was glad. They were almost half-way to the boarding torpedo. Soon they could rest once more on the Spiritus Sancti and let Hauptman blow this alien nest to kingdom come.

Relief made him careless. He slid on the slippery floor and tumbled forward on top of one of the circles. He put his hand down to steady himself and the whole floor seemed to give way. He tumbled into darkness, feeling the walls squash shut round him. He reached back up through the valve to grab the edge and felt Sergeant Hakon's strong hand grasp his. Relief filled him. The sergeant could lift him back into the light.

The walls around him began to contract and then expand. He felt their glistening sides press on him. He was reminded of a man swallowing – and he was the tasty morsel. As a mindless panic rose within him, he tried to pull himself up frantically. Sergeant Hakon attempted to aid him. Njal felt him strain against the downward pull of the tunnel-throat. For a moment he was pulled upwards… then he felt the sergeant's grip falter and slip on his slime-covered gauntlet.

'No,' he screamed as he was sucked downward into the darkness. When the motion ceased he was in corrosive liquid. He could sense it eating away at the ceramite of his armour. One by one, the red emergency icons on his sleeve came on. Bathed in the eerie light from their useless warnings, he felt the warm digestive acid began to eat his flesh and etch his bones. As his life faded he seemed to hear the gloating thoughts of the hive-mind.

One way or another you will become part of me, it said.

'No. HE'S GONE. There's nothing you can do!' Sven felt Sergeant Hakon's hand on his shoulder pulling him away from the valve. He stopped beating futilely on it with his fist and prepared to blast it.

'Brother-Sergeant Hakon is right,' he heard Gunnar say. 'There's nothing we can do. Nothing. Njal is gone and we'll be joining him if we don't move.'

Slowly, sanity started to percolate into Sven's mind. His friend was gone, never to return. He was dead. The thought had such a terrible finality to it. Sven shut his eyes and gave out the terrible death-howl of his order. The feral wolf-cry echoed down the corridors and was swallowed. The distant heartbeat of the ship continued undisturbed.

'There will be time to grieve later,' Hakon said gently. 'Now we must return to the ship.'

'Don't worry,' Egil said, his eyes glittering with murder-lust. 'He will be avenged. I swear it.'

Sven nodded and pulled himself to his feet. He gripped his pistol firmly in one hand and his knife in the other. He crossed them across his chest in the ritual position and said a brief prayer to the Emperor for the soul of his battle brother. Then he followed the others on the long path back to the boarding torpedo.

SERGEANT HAKON WAS next to die. The thing uncoiling from the air-vent got him. A four-armed, fanged and clawed horror with hypnotic eyes tore his head off before he could even swing his chainsword.

Egil didn't wait for his turn. He launched himself at it, aiming his knife squarely at its back. The thing turned with eye-blurring speed and batted him aside effortlessly with one mighty hand. He felt ribs crack under the force of the blow. Even his ceramite breastplate did not protect him. If it had cut him with its pincer, Egil knew he would have died. He did not care.

A red haze was upon him. He ignored the pain, gathered his legs beneath him and prepared to spring again.

'Genestealer,' he heard Sven mutter. 'By Russ, is there no end to the horrors in this place?'

A red haze fell over Egil's vision. He howled his warcry and leapt. He knew he had made a mistake when the thing's claw swept up like a scythe. He knew he was about to receive a disembowelling stroke and he welcomed it with open eyes.

The stroke never fell.

Sven shot the genestealer twice in the head. It reeled backward under the impact. Shrieking with frustrated bloodlust, Egil tore it to shreds with his knife.

Behind him he heard Sven mutter: 'Two down. Three to go.'

'I can't believe the sergeant is dead,' Gunnar said. He tossed a Hellfire shell almost negligently in one hand. 'I mean, him and Njal both gone. It's– I–'

'Believe it,' Sven told him firmly. He felt a growing coldness in his heart. He was numb. He seemed to have gone beyond pain, beyond any feeling at all. All he felt was a growing hatred for his enemies and a cold determination to survive and present his report to the Imperium. It was the only way he could think of to give the deaths of his companions any meaning.

He studied the other two, trying to gauge how much use they would be. Egil looked gaunt and evil; a strange light was in his eyes and his loping stride suggested a blood-maddened beast. There was a coiled ferocity within the berserker just waiting to be unleashed. Sven knew that he could be counted on to fight – but could he be trusted to make a sensible decision?

Gunnar's mood seemed to have swung from near-insane cheerfulness to depressive gloom. He looked bewildered by the sudden deaths of his comrades. He seemed unable to come to terms with the fact they had died so suddenly.

Sven coldly assessed their chances and knew it was up to him to take charge. He was the only one who seemed capable of rational decision making. 'Right. We'd better go,' he said.

'But what about Hakon's body? We can't just leave it here.'

'He's dead, Gunnar. There's no point in encumbering ourselves with a corpse. I'll cut the gene-seed from him, for his successor. He won't go unremembered. I swear it.'

Fitting action to words, he set about reclaiming the sergeant's gene-seed, the control mechanism that transformed him into a Space Marine. It was gory work and soon Hakon's blood mingled with that of the enemy on Sven's knife.

* * *

THEY NEARLY MADE it. The tyranid ambushed them from behind the branches of a carcinoma tree. Sven leapt backward as acid spurted over the ground where he had stood. The shrapnel from the monster's vile living weapon gouged across his cheek, drawing blood. He ignored the notch torn from his ear and took aim at the monster. It lurched back into cover as Sven's shots raked its hiding place.

'Gunnar, burn that thing!' he yelled, but Gunnar stood stock still, not loading his weapon, not doing anything.

'More coming behind us,' Egil roared.

Sven cursed. He considered haranguing Gunnar but wasn't sure it would do any good. Instead he unclipped a grenade and lobbed it at the tyranid. The explosion sent the thing reeling into the open. Gunnar snapped out of his immobility and sent a blast of automatic fire dancing across its chest. Its top half suddenly separated from its legs, the tyranid collapsed, shrieking.

Sven risked a backwards glance. A line of tyranids was bounding up the corridor towards them. Their gait seemed slow and awkward but they covered the ground at a tremendous rate. Sven knew that the three of them could not outrun the monsters. He moved forward anyway. Perhaps they could make a last stand behind the carcinoma tree.

'Follow me,' he shouted and leapt forward into cover. Gunnar and Egil swiftly followed. The distant pounding of the ship's heart sounded as loud as thunder now and the air was thick with the acidic stench of tyranid blood. Sven sighted on the leading tyranid and fired. It pained him to have come so near to escape and to fail at the last. His shot glanced off its armoured hide. He aimed at the head.

'Gunnar. Use the Hellfire!' he shouted.

'I can't – the mechanism's jammed!' Gunnar yelled back.

Sven cursed. A spray of shots from the tyranid's weapon sent him ducking back into cover, the memory of claw-armed monstrosities leaping towards them burned into his mind. There were just too many of them. The scouts were doomed.

'You two – get out of here!' yelled Egil. 'I'll hold them off.'

'It's certain death, man.'

'Don't argue! Just do it!'

Sven swiftly weighed things up in his racing mind. He could stay here and die – or he could save the sergeant's gene-seed, himself and another Space Marine. The balance had already been tipped; there was no choice.'

'Goodbye,' he said, rushing towards the last beacon, the one belonging to the boarding torpedo.

'Farewell, landsman,' he heard Egil say. 'I'll show you what makes a true Space Wolf.'

* * *

EGIL HOWLED HIS laughter and fired again. He leapt to his feet and pumped the trigger of his pistol, blasting shots wildly at the tyranids. Their advance halted in the face of the withering fire. The Space Wolf scout unclipped a grenade and lobbed it at them. They ducked back behind a sphincter-door. The grenade exploded against it. The door buckled but didn't give.

Suddenly it was quiet. Egil risked a glance back over his shoulder towards where Sven and Gunnar had vanished. Briefly he considered following them. Yet he couldn't guarantee that the tyranids wouldn't follow him and overtake him. Better to keep them pinned down.

He caught a flicker of movement out of the corner of his eye. The tyranids had circled round and entered the chamber from the other side. Good, Egil thought, feeling the killing rage build within him. More enemies to take to Hell with him.

The tyranids rushed at him. He swung his pistol round but a blast from an organic gun tore into his arm, ripping the bolter from his grasp and shredding his flesh to the bone. He fought to keep from blacking out as unquenchable agony seared him. He gripped his knife tight and howled with rage. He lurched to his feet and ran towards them.

'I'll kill you! I'll kill you all!' he shouted, blood-specked froth staining his lips. The last thing he saw was the monster take careful, direct aim at him. He pulled back his knife to throw.

THE SOUND OF fighting stopped. Sven bundled Gunnar into the torpedo, slammed the hatch shut and hit the control icon.

As the alien craft shrank smaller and smaller in the flickering green view-screen, Sven commended Egil's soul to the Emperor. He noticed that Gunnar was weeping. Whether it was from sorrow or relief, Sven could not tell.

HAUPTMAN WATCHED AS the plasma-bombs raked the tyranid craft from end to end. Within scant moments the organic ship was utterly destroyed. As Hauptman stared in rapt fascination, the solar wings so recently unfurled tore off and drifted into space. The men in the *Spiritus Sancti*'s turrets used them for target practice. He saw the look of satisfaction on Sven's face as he watched the alien artefact being cleansed.

'Well,' he said. 'I think that ends that.'

'I think not,' Chandara the astropath said from next to the pair of them, pale faced and drawn. 'Before it died, it sent out a signal of enormous psychic power. It was tightly focused in the direction of the Magellanic Cloud but it was so powerful that I picked up its overspill.

'It was a signal, shipmaster. It was summoning something. Something big.'

An appalled hush fell over the steering chapel of the *Spiritus Sancti*.

Sven looked down at the gene-seed in his hand. He swore to be worthy of his dead comrades. If war with the tyranids was coming, he was ready to fight.

SUFFER NOT THE ALIEN TO LIVE

HELLBREAK

Ben Counter

'You WILL NEVER know, scum,' the mechanically translated voice hissed in Commissar von Klas's ear, 'just how lucky you are!'

An unseen hand thrust him up the last few stairs, out of the darkness and into the searing glare of the arena. He stumbled in the sudden light and slipped, hitting the coarse sand face-first, scouring a layer of skin off his cheek. From all around him there rose a cackling cheer. He looked up and a terror shot through him that his training couldn't banish.

An area the size of a landing field spread out before him, its sandy floor streaked with crescents of maroon that could only be the bloody traces of those who had come before him. Around the edge of the arena was a ring of spikes as tall as a man, with a head impaled on each tip. There were heads of men and orks, the long slender faces of eldar, the twisted alien features of a hundred different species.

Beyond them, the amphitheatre rose, huge and dark, forged of black iron into forms which seemed to have been pulled, fully formed, from a madman's imagination. Wicked spikes and curving galleries formed the mouths of leering faces; immense claws of iron held up the private boxes of the elite. The whole edifice rose to join the myriad black pinnacles and spires of Commorragh which speared upwards, a mockery of beauty, to puncture a sky the colour of a wound gone bad.

That was not the worst of it. As von Klas hauled himself to his feet, feeling his muscles complaining with the sudden release from the steel bonds which had held them for so long, he felt their eyes upon him, and he heard their laughter. The audience of eldar renegades, many hundreds of thousands strong, sat in great serried ranks, their pale alien faces shining like lanterns against the purples and blacks of their clothing. Silver blades gleamed everywhere, and he could hear them talking to one another in low voices – perhaps wagering on whether he would live or die, or just mocking a man who didn't know he was dead yet. In the prime position, right at the edge of the arena, sat a great dignitary, with a face that even from this distance von Klas could tell was as long and cruel as any he had ever seen. His purple robe only half-concealed ceremonial armour with great crescent-shaped shoulder guards. The dignitary was surrounded by a bodyguard who stood stone-still and carried spears tipped with bright silver blades, and any number of hangers-on and courtiers lounged nearby.

Von Klas had barely time to take all this in when the dignitary raised one slender hand to the crowd, who screamed their approval with a deafening rising screech. Von Klas looked around him to see what had just been signalled – but he was alone in the vast arena. The doorway through which he had been pitched had sunk back into the sand behind him.

Something flickered in the corner of his eye. In the time it took him to turn and face it, it had got much closer. As a storm of thoughts and fears rushed through his commissar's mind, his old, trained instincts took over and he tensed his aching muscles for the fight.

THE HUMAN HAD maybe a second and a half to see the wych as she back-flipped and cartwheeled her way across the sand towards him. She wore armour only to display her body, which was lithe and supple to an extent which no human could match. Her long red-black hair flowed out in a stormy trail behind her as she moved, along with the glistening metallic net that she held in one hand. In the other, twirling like a rotor blade, was a halberd, as long as she was tall and tipped with a broad, wickedly curved blade.

In his luxuriously fitted box at the front of the audience, the eldar who had signalled, Archon Kypselon, leaned across to Yae, who reclined next to him, her long, slim body draped over the seat, showing off her snake-like muscles. The leader of the Cult of Rage, Kypselon's most valuable ally, Yae looked every bit as formidable as her reputation, her dark hair braided with lengths of silver chain and her glassy, emerald eyes enough to intimidate any lesser eldar into submission.

'I hear this is one of the finest of your wyches,' he said off-handedly. 'Rather wasted on a single creature.'

'Perhaps, my archon,' she replied. 'But I hear it is one of their ruling class. It might provide some sport. They can breed them remarkably tough.'

Out in the arena, the human turned, holding its body low and hands high preparing for the wych's first strike. Through the blur of violent motion it would just be able to make out her face, twisted with exertion and hate, her eyes burning with the sacred narcotics which coursed joyfully through her veins. The delicately pointed eldar ears and large eyes would do nothing to offset the base savagery.

'I hope she is as fine as they say,' Kypselon continued. 'The Kabal of the Broken Spine needs fine warriors. There are others who would take away the authority that I have earned.'

'You know the Cult of Rage is with you,' Yae smiled. 'Power and wisdom such as yours is enough to secure our loyalty.'

Kypselon smirked indulgently. He had been around long enough to know such words were nothing more than a cipher on Commorragh – he had seen enough eldar die by treachery, his included, to know that. But Yae's wyches were truly vital to him. Uergax and the Kabal of the Blade's Edge were threatening to shatter the delicate savagery of his territory. But those were matters for his court. He tried to concentrate on the entertainment at hand; it had, after all, been put on specifically for him. Such honour was really born of fear, of course, but on Commorragh fear and honour were much the same thing.

The wych let out a piercing shriek of pleasure and rage as she whipped the halberd back over her shoulder, leaping high into the air and preparing to bring the blade down on the human in a shining arc.

Yae gave a sudden, sharp gasp of excitement, like a child, sitting up with a glint of rapture in her eyes. Kypselon smiled – an old eldar like him could still appreciate the simple pleasures. A dead human was a pleasure indeed.

The man drove one foot into the arena's sand and thrust himself sideways, away from the shimmering blur of the wych's limbs, just as her blade scythed down in a silver-white blur past his face. Anyone else would have lost their balance and pitched into the bloodsoaked sand, but the wych somersaulted elegantly, landing on her feet and turning on a heel to face her quarry. But the human was ready too, and quicker than most men could, it drove the palm of one hand into the wych's face, snapping her head back, splitting her nose open in a vermilion spray.

There was a dark, displeased hiss from the galleries. Kypselon heard low obscenities muttered around him. Yae stood up, her eyes still shining with glee – for a true wych loves combat whoever wins. But the rest of the audience were not so happy.

The wych in the arena rolled onto her front in a heartbeat, ready to rise and face the upstart human, but he stamped a booted foot into the small of her back, pinning her to the ground.

'Kill it!' yelled an incensed spectator. 'Kill the animal!'

A hundred other voices joined in, rising to a roar – that became a cheer as the wych caught one of the man's legs with her own and tipped him sprawling on his back. She sprang up for the kill, her net forgotten, ready to swipe off his head with her halberd.

The audience noticed before she did: she was no longer holding the weapon. Her opponent was. Before she had time to respond, he drove the blade towards her. She held up the net in front of her neck and face, knowing its metallic strands would parry the blow and keep her head on her shoulders.

But the human was not aiming for her neck, for it did not care for the elegant decapitation that was the most graceful of murders. Instead, the blade went right through her stomach and out between the wych's shoulders. As her lifeblood gouted upwards, she looked unutterably surprised, still coming to realise that her weapon had been stolen.

The man drew out the blade and pulled himself to his feet. The wych slumped to the ground, amidst a growing crimson stain upon the sand.

The yells from the audience became a wordless howl of rage that rang violently around the amphitheatre. Yae was still on her feet, breathing in sharp, shallow gasps, her eyes wide.

Kypselon rose to stand at her side.

'Never fear,' he whispered to her under the din, 'This is as grave an insult to me as it is to you. I shall have the human given to the haemonculi. Then I shall deliver the skin to you once I am sure it can take no more pain.'

Yae did not answer. Her eyes burned and a snarl grew on her face. With a silent gesture, Kypselon ordered his black-armoured bodyguards to fetch the man and remove the body of the wych.

Seeing the dark eldar approaching, the man dropped the wych's halberd, perhaps expecting a quick despatch as a reward for his victory. The crowd continue to howl its derision as one of the warriors knocked him unconscious with the butt of his spear, and the body was dragged away to a fate that it could never have imagined.

It was always the same with aliens, Kypselon reflected. They are simply too stupid to realise when they would be better off dead.

THE ROOM WAS mercilessly lit by a bright glowing ceiling. Two of the alien warriors stood guard at the back wall. The floor was of bare metal, sloping towards a drain in the centre through which his bodily fluids were supposed to drain away. The walls were hung with skins, complete human pelts, presumably the finest of those taken by the torturer over the years. Tattoos had been favoured, and von Klas could recognise the regimental insignia and devotional verses inscribed on the skins: Catachan, Stratix, Jurn, even his own Hydraphur. The words of the Ecclesiarchy in intricate script. Primitive tribal scars. Even a green-brown ork hide with kill tallies gouged into the chest.

He looked down at himself. He was not bound. Presumably they thought the fear alone would keep him here. They were probably right.

'I won't die,' von Klas said aloud, every word like a hammer blow to his aching head. 'I'm a difficult man to kill.'

The warriors said nothing. The door between them opened with a hiss, and the torturer shuffled in. Von Klas had heard rumours about the torture artists of the renegade eldar, but it was only now that he started to believe them.

The eldar looked at von Klas with eyes which had long since sunken out of sight, the sockets just deep, ravaged tunnels. His skin was a dead blue-grey, stretched and striated by age and untold torment, the lips drawn back like a corpse's, the nose crushed and misshapen, the scalp hairless and paper-thin so white bone showed through.

The robes that covered his shuffling frame were fashioned from skins too, and he had picked out the best designs for them: rare metallic tattoos, the elaborate medical scars of an Astartes veteran. From a belt of gnarled hide, perhaps from an ogryn, hung a multitude of implements, scalpels and syringes, strange arcane devices for lifting the skin or teasing out nerve endings like splinters from a finger. There was something else, too, an articulated silver gauntlet with a medical blade tipping each digit, so sharp that their edges caught the acidic light and scraped incandescent curves in the air.

Behind him was a slave, a young human female, dressed in rags with long, lank, once-blonde hair, who scampered along behind the torturer like a fearful pet. She bore few obvious scars, the torturer needing her alive and lucid, since she acted as his interpreter.

The torturer hissed some words in his own language, a tongue as dry as snakeskin slithering between the exposed teeth.

'Verredaek, haemonculus to Lord Archon Kypselon of the Broken Spine Kabal,' began the translator in hesitant Imperial Gothic, 'wishes his... his subject to know that he does not rely on mindless devices to perform his art. Some haemonculi employ cowardly machines which produce mediocre results in the art. Verredaek will only use the ancient talents passed on by the torturers of the Broken Spine. He is proud of this.'

Von Klas stood up, still aching. He was tall, as tall as the guards and far taller than the shrivelled haemonculus. 'I am not going to die here. I am going to kill every single one of you myself.' He kept his voice level, as if he was instructing his own men. 'I might not see it, and I might not even be there. But I will kill you.'

The terrified girl stammered his words back in the eldar language. Through her, Verredaek replied, 'It is good that you do not give up. The bodies and souls of creatures who do not believe themselves to be on the edge of death have long... fascinated me. The first cut will be sweet indeed.'

Without any discernible motion, a blade as long as an index finger, so sharp it disappeared when turned edge-on, appeared in Verredaek's hand. The torturer stepped forward, the skins of his robes hissing as they rubbed together. 'You will know fear, but know also that it is not in vain you die.

The art of pain continues through souls such as yours, their agony distilled and passed on, and one day you shall become part of a much greater work.'

Von Klas looked from the knife to Verredaek's sightless eye-sockets, and saw his mistake. This was how he managed to torture his victims without strapping them down or tying them up. Those desperately empty caverns, the ridges of desiccated skin picked out by the harsh light, seemed to bolt him to the ground and drain his limbs of strength.

His superiors had decided that von Klas was officer material, but he had never been a greatly distinguished officer, never led charges that shattered armies, never held the line against awesome odds. He had the medals they give commissars as a matter of course, and nothing more. He might have been in effective command of twenty thousand men, but in the Imperium that made him one amongst a million.

But he had survived the battle in the arena. He had proved to be something special to his captors, so much so that he had been given to Verredaek as a punishment. And now he would be something again. He would survive this, too. He didn't care if it was unknown. He would still do it.

For a second, Verredaek's hypnotic aura was broken as von Klas made his vow to survive. He closed his eyes, and his body was his own again. He would not get a second chance.

With all his strength, he punched, low and hard. His hand hit spongy flesh and drove deeper. The haemonculus gasped in astonishment. The commissar grabbed Verredaek so he would not fall, and spun both of them around, just as the eldar guards began to shoot. One shot sprayed Verredaek across the back, his skin splitting and bursting like a rotten fruit under the assault of a hundred splinters of crystal. The second caught von Klas on the shoulder, a glancing blow but one that drove a dozen splinters deep into the muscle.

The translator screamed and scampered across to the far side of the room, wrapping her arms around her head so she couldn't see.

Von Klas drove Verredaek's body forward into one guard, smashing the eldar into the back wall, knocking him senseless. The second eldar hesitated. It was enough. Von Klas scrabbled at Verredaek's belt until he felt the cold steel of his gauntlet. He thrust his hand into it, feeling the woven metal mesh close around his hand. With one motion he snapped it off the tendon that bound it to the belt and thrust it deep into the second guard's chest. The eldar let out a muffled cry, then slumped lifelessly to the floor.

Von Klas stood up once more, Verredaek's limp body sliding off his shoulders and down the wall. The first eldar lay motionless against the back wall where he had been rammed. He might have been dead, but behind the lifeless jade of the alien's helmet's eyes von Klas couldn't be sure. The second was certainly dead, though, his blood running down into the drain at the room's centre.

Verredaek shifted slightly and suddenly there was an alien gun pointing at von Klas, slender and strange, held in a gnarled blue-grey hand. Without thinking, von Klas slashed the torturer's gauntlet downwards as the eldar turned his head to aim. The blades swiped cleanly through his face, slicing the withered skin to ribbons. The haemonculus slumped to the floor at last.

He had been difficult to kill. But then so am I, thought Commissar von Klas.

He considered taking one of the guard's rifles, but he would have needed two hands to fire it and he wanted to keep hold of the razor-gauntlet. And the splinters that had hit him, though they were sending occasional flashes of pain through his muscles, had still left him alive. Not very efficient, he thought coldly. The torturer's gun might prove more useful. He prised it from Verredaek's dead hands. It was oddly light, and very strange to look at, with a barrel so slender only a needle, surely, could be fired out.

He turned to the translator slave still cowering in the corner behind one of the hanging skins.

'You coming?' he asked. 'We can escape from here if we hurry.'

The translator didn't seem to understand him, as if she wasn't used to having Imperial spoken directly to her and wasn't sure how to respond. She shook her head and redoubled her efforts to hide from him. Von Klas decided to leave her.

The door through which Verredaek had entered opened with a simple touch of his hand on a panel set into the wall. Beyond it, the corridors were made of the same polished metal, but bent and buckled into strange shapes, as if the whole place had been picked up and twisted by a giant. Von Klas jogged down the corridor, mind buzzing, trying to work out if the place had a pattern to it, one part of his brain keeping watch for signs of more guards.

He came to a row of cells, four of them, the doors again opening easily with a press of their inset panels. Behind the first was a human, an Imperial Guardsman, still dressed in his grime-grey uniform, his head shaved and his face aged beyond his years.

The man blinked in the sudden light, for the cells were pitch black inside, and looked up at what must have been von Klas's silhouette. 'You're one of us,' he said, surprised into stupidity.

'Come on. We're getting out,' von Klas replied.

The Guardsman smiled sadly and shook his head. 'They'll be here any moment. We won't stand a chance.'

'That's an order, soldier. I'm a commissar and I've got scores to settle. If I say we're leaving then we're out of here already. Now move!'

The Guardsman shrugged and shuffled unsteadily out of the cell – prisoners weren't manacled, Verredaek must have thought he was above that. Von Klas hurried to open the other three cells.

'Sir! Trouble!' yelled the Guardsman. A sketchy reflection of the approaching eldar warriors shimmered on the metal wall and splinters began shattering against the walls.

As three other Guardsmen emerged, stumbling and confused, von Klas levelled Verredaek's pistol to defend them. He fired at the first hint of purple and silver that came round the corner, tiny darts leaving a glittering trail as they raced for their target.

There was a strangled cry and the first renegade eldar pitched forward, clutching at the shattered mask of his helmet. As his cries became garbled howls, the warrior convulsed, his body splitting and twisting as it was ripped apart. Hot blood and shards of bone spattered and ricocheted across the walls. The Guardsmen – two in sand-coloured uniforms, Tallarn maybe; the last in the remains of a dark red uniform that could have been Adeptus Mechanicus – ducked back into the cells for cover. Von Klas might not have understood the eldar tongue but he knew fear when he heard it, and that was what he heard now, as the remaining eldar guards howled in fright or pain and fell back.

'Move!' von Klas said quickly. 'They're scared of us now!'

The first man he had released darted forwards and grabbed two rifles from where the guards had dropped them, throwing one to one of the Tallarn. After a moment to scrutinise the controls, they started pumping fire back down the corridor, before hurrying after the others.

Von Klas and his men – they were surely his men now, his unit – hurried away from the cells, von Klas leading, the two armed men jogging backwards with their rifles ready to offer covering fire. All the while von Klas could hear voices, the guards calling for help, trying to organise a pursuit, or perhaps just cursing the Guardsmen in their vile alien tongue.

The labyrinth of prison corridors rolled out in front of them in ever more tormented designs. As they stumbled along, von Klas was beginning to believe that surviving might be impossible after all, even for a commissar. But no more guards came. It was not the guards that were supposed to stop prisoners escaping – it was the torment and brutality that were meant to break their will. Von Klas and his men passed the threshold of scarred iron, and emerged, breathless, bloody and exhausted, hearts racing, into the open air, the bowels of Verredaek's torture machine behind them.

But von Klas knew with an officer's instinct that they were not safe. Because they had only freed themselves in order to enter the dark eldar world-city of Commorragh.

* * *

VERREDAEK LOOKED OLDER, thought Kypselon, older even than the shattered, wizened specimen that first came into the archon's employ. But, of course, it could just be the vile old creature's shredded face. It had been a long time since Kypselon had seen Verredaek – not since the haemonculus had first retreated into his underground complex to pursue the art of torturer at his command, in fact.

Verredaek shuffled pathetically across the floor of Kypselon's throne room, across the milky marble shot though with amethyst veins. He looked small and feeble under the gaze of the three hundred or so eldar warriors who stood around the room's edge, weapons held ready, constantly at attention.

'Fallen One's teeth, what happened to him?' slurred Exuma, Kypselon's dracon, who was lounging in a seat held aloft by anti-grav motors so he didn't have to walk anywhere. A quietly gurgling medical array pumped a steady stream of narcotics into Exuma's blood.

'He failed,' Kypselon replied with feeling. When he rose from his black iron throne, the wide window behind him cast the shadow of his shoulder guards across Verredaek in two great crescents. The torturer seemed to shrink, and though his eyes were hidden, Kypselon could detect fear in the dark sockets.

'Verredaek, you will recall that when you first entered my services, I had my servants take a little of your blood.' Kypselon's deep voice echoed faintly off the high, vaulted ceiling and purple-draped marble walls.

'Yethhh, archon,' Verredaek replied, his speech impeded by his newly-forked tongue.

'I still have what I took. The reason I keep it, and that of all my followers, is to make real the notion that I own you. You are mine, you are a part of my territory, just like the streets and palaces. Just like my temple. The price of belonging to the Broken Spine is total subservience to me. Yet you failed to carry out my commands.'

Verredaek tried to speak, but he too had been alive longer than most on Commorragh, and he knew that words would not save him here.

'I ordered you to bring the human here, skinless and broken, so I could watch him die. This you failed to do. The reasons are irrelevant. You failed. By definition, being a possession of mine, you must be discarded.'

Kypselon shot a glance at the front row of warriors and four of them strode forwards, grabbing Verredaek and holding him fast.

The haemonculus didn't struggle as Yae flipped her lithe body from the shadows into the centre of the room. Her eyes and smile flashed, as she drew twin hydraknives. They turned to lightning bolts in her hands as she danced – and killed.

As Yae twirled and slashed a thousand cuts into Verredaek's body, Kypselon turned to his dracon. 'What is the situation with the Blade's Edge?'

Exuma looked back with glazed eyes. 'Little has changed, my archon. Uergax has the mandrakes, and the incubi favour him as well. Some remain loyal to us, but what Uergax lacks in territory he makes up for with most admirable diplomacy.' The dracon paused to gasp with pleasure as another bolt of drugs shot through his veins.

Kypselon shook his head. 'It is not good. Uergax may soon crush us as I would wish to crush him. The Blade's Edge covets our corner of Commorragh and if incompetence like this persists he will get it. Yae!'

The wych span to a halt and let her lacerated handiwork collapse to the floor. 'Archon?'

'The human we wished to see dead is more resourceful than we thought. It is now loose on Commorragh. Find it.'

Yae smiled with genuine relish. 'It is a great honour to perform a task that would give me such pleasure in the name of one so great.'

'No time for blandishments, Yae. Uergax is bleeding us dry and I do not need this creature running loose to complicate matters. I fully expect you to succeed.'

'Yes, lord.'

'And be wary. This one has a colder heart than most. You may go.'

Yae flitted away, as only a wych could, to fulfil his commands. Kypselon turned to the great window behind him. It was a view of Commorragh, a riot of dark madness and broken spires, bridges that crossed to nothing, mutilated cathedrals to insanity and evil, a planet-wide city at once unfinished and ancient, swarming beneath a glorious swirling thunderstorm sky. And in the centre, obscene, bleached and pale, was Kypselon's temple. A temple to him, because living so long and rising to such power on Commorragh was such an impossible task it might as well be that of a god. A thousand pillars made of thigh bones held up a roof tiled with skulls. Whole skeletons acted out scenes of violation and murder on friezes and pediments.

'Every eldar, human, ork, every enemy I have ever killed stands there, Exuma. Every one. My temple is a testament to the fact that I will not give up, not ever. I have carved a path for myself through the very bodies of my foes.'

Exuma allowed himself to drift back into lucidity long enough to reply: 'Archon, none can say that you have failed in anything you have attempted.'

'That is the past. I have risen to power and I will not relinquish it to a boy like Uergax. I am not ashamed of fear, Exuma, even though young upstarts like Uergax and yourself are. And I feel fear now. But I will use that fear, and my temple will grow.'

Outside, the cancerous rain of Commorragh began to fall.

* * *

'IN THE CITY, you need those who want your money or your honour. On the plains, in the desert, you need brothers.' Rahimzadeh of Tallarn was a wiry, intense man, not long a soldier but already well versed in the hot fear and desperation of war. 'Though there are only two of us left, we are brothers still.'

Ibn, the second Tallarn, looked up from the ornate eldar splinter rifle he was examining. 'You would not understand. On your Hydraphur, a million men live within sight of one another. No room for true brothers.'

Von Klas winced as Scleros, the lexmechanic, pulled another shard from the commissar's raw shoulder. It felt like the razor-sharp crystals were doing as much damage coming out as they did going in. 'Brothers or not, we still have a chain of command. I am a commissar and you are now my men.'

'Why?' Ibn asked with a sneer. 'What good can orders and rank do here?' He waved an arm to indicate their surroundings – a shattered shell of a building, the carcass of some vast cathedral of soaring flutes and arches, now gutted and decrepit. It was deserted, which was why they had stopped here, but they all knew that there were malevolent eyes everywhere on Commorragh and they could soon be found wherever they hid.

'We can get out of here,' the commissar replied. 'There's a spaceport nearby, close to the temple.'

'Temple? This place has no gods,' Rahimzadeh said. 'Even the Emperor's light is faint upon us here.'

'It is consecrated to the foul leader of this part of the planet. The scum raised a temple to himself. The spaceport's nearby but it's garrisoned. We'd have to occupy the temple, draw in the garrison troops and make a break for the spaceport.'

'Death would claim us all before we reached it,' said Ibn.

'Not all of us. Not if there were enough. Would you rather let them recapture you? They wouldn't let you run away twice. If we try to escape we'll either make it or die trying. Whatever happens then, it's better than skulking here until one of them finds us.'

Rahimzadeh thought for a second. 'What you say is true. I think you are a good man. But we need others.'

'We'll need a whole damn army,' Ibn said.

Von Klas turned around. 'Scleros?'

The commissar had been right – the tattered dark rust-red uniform was that of the Adeptus Mechanicus. Scleros was a lexmechanic, his brain adapted to allow him to absorb a huge amount of information, produce calculations and battlefield reports. His augmentation was belied by the intricate web of silver tracery surrounding his artificial right eye. 'You said there is a chain of command. As commanding officer, the decision is yours.'

'Fine. And you?'

The fourth Guardsman had said little. His head was shaven and he wore the grey uniform that could be from one of a thousand regiments. 'Sure. Whatever. As long as I get a shot at some of those freaks.'

Von Klas studied the Imperial Guardsman: his hollow eyes, his scowl, the nose that had been broken two or three times. 'What's your name, soldier?'

'Kep. Necromundan Seventh.'

Ibn let out a short, barking laugh. 'Lucky Sevens? The sands do not lie so much. You are penal legions, my friend. The tattoo at the top of your arm, they can read it. You have the scar on your wrist where the machine makes your blood mad.'

Kep shrugged and held up his hand. Von Klas could see the scar where a frenzon dispenser had once been implanted. 'Guilty. I am from the First Penal Legion.'

'The First?' Rahimzadeh said with a hint of awe in his voice. 'The Big One?'

'What's your crime?' asked von Klas, his words straining as Scleros removed the last of the eldar shrapnel.

'Heresy. Third class. Standard practice – if eldar pirates show up you feed them the penal legion. They get their slaves, the Imperium ditches a few more scum, everyone's happy.'

The bruise-coloured clouds above had coagulated. Large, filthy grey raindrops started to fall, grey with pollutants. Kep and the Tallarn ran, hunched, into a corner of the old cathedral, where some of the roof remained and there was cover.

Von Klas looked round at Scleros, the remaining soldier. The lexmechanic, as he expected, had no expression. 'You had the surgery?'

The thick rain sent strange trails across the circuitry on Scleros's face. 'Emotional repression protocol, sir. It allows me to deal with information of an ideologically sensitive nature.'

'Thought so. Scleros, you realise that we're never going to get off this planet, don't you?'

'I was unable to understand how we could escape through a spaceport. We would not be able to use a spacecraft, even if we were able to understand eldar technology. We would be shot down. We can not escape this place.'

'I trust you not to tell the men. This mission's objective does not allow for our survival.'

Scleros held out a hand and let a little of the rain collect in his palm. It swam with grey trails of impurity. 'We should get out of the rain. This could infect us.'

The two headed for shelter, while all around them, the soul of Commorragh seethed for their blood.

* * *

SYBARITE LAEVEQ GAZED down from the gantry at the immense metallic beast, powered by the exertions of the many hundreds of deliciously emaciated human slaves that were chained to its pneumatic limbs. Great clouds of acrid smoke and steam from the huge cauldron of molten metal obscured their faces, and Laeveq felt as if he were striding in the clouds, a god looking down upon the wretches who both feared him and needed him to survive.

The eldar guard watched as another of them fell, limbs flopping loose as the clanking, screeching steel mill machinery carried on without it, head snapping back and forth as the machinery threw it about blindly. Soon Laeveq's eldar would go onto the factory floor and take away the battered corpse and replaced it with another faceless barbarian.

'Sybarite Laeveq,' a hasty voice came through his communicator. 'A problem has presented itself.'

'Elaborate, Xaron.'

'It's Kytellias. She didn't call in on her patrol so we went to find her. Her throat had been slit, ear to ear. Very pretty. Very clean.'

Laeveq cursed his fortune. 'Fugitives. Bring every armed eldar to me, on the gantry above the main hall. We will sweep this entire factory and disembowel them on top of the machinery so all these brute animals will see the cost of denial.'

'It may not be that simple, sybarite. Lady Yae has sent word of dangerous escaped arena slaves.'

'Then we will take much reward for bringing them in. Send everyone here. Is that understood?'

There was no answer. A dim static crackled where the warrior's voice should have been.

'I said, "Is that understood?" Xaron?'

Nothing. Laeveq looked around him at the web of gantries spanning the great space of the main factory hall. Through the billowing sheets of steam, he could see nothing. He felt suddenly alone.

When Laeveq caught sight of the human figure running towards his position along the gantry, he was sure he could take him. It was a tall and strong man, to be sure, with hair cut close and a muscled torso riven with many old scars. It had found a scissorhand and a stinger pistol from somewhere, too, but it would not be skilled with them.

Laeveq whipped out his own splinter pistol and took pleasure in the aiming, fancying he could take the animal in the lower abdomen, and watch it squeal in bestial pain before taking its head.

Before he could pull the trigger, however, the human leapt into the air, swiping the glittering blades of the scissorhand through one of the chains that suspended the gantries from the high ceiling. It landed again, almost falling onto its face. Laeveq smiled, knowing that he could not miss such a fallen target.

The room soared upwards around him as the gantry fell vertical, the chain holding it sliced through. The last things Laeveq saw were the pale, frightened upturned faces of the slaves swirling towards him through the smoke, and the violent red heat of the cauldron, before the liquid fire enveloped him.

VON KLAS ARRIVED at Kep's side. The Guardsman was just watching as the molten metal finally covered the top of the eldar's head.

'Your heresy might be third-class,' the commissar said, 'but you're a first-rate murderer.'

'It's what kept me alive.' Kep looked over the gantry rail, and the factory floor below. Hundreds of frightened eyes gazed back. 'So what now?'

Von Klas got to his feet. 'We start our little war. Get Rahimzadeh and Ibn and start unchaining those slaves. And send Scleros up here, we'll need his logistics. We've got an army now.'

THE MOST INTOLERABLE thing of all, thought Kypselon, was that he could see it from his own throne room. The beautiful cold temple of bone, the icon of perfection which would place the seal of immortality on his long and brutal life, now stained by the presence of two thousand barbaric aliens.

'How long have they occupied it?' he asked, his voice quiet and low, as it always was when Kypselon was at his most wrathful, and thus his most dangerous.

Exuma's eyes unclouded slightly. 'Since the turning of the second sun,' he replied. 'They attacked the temple and slaughtered the garrison. Some of them will be armed by now, they had quite an armoury there. It's your human all right. It must have recruited the slaves when it took over Laeveq's factory a few hours ago. Remember Laeveq? Bright boy.'

Kypselon waved a hand brusquely and the great window dimmed into shadow. He turned, his dark purple robes sweeping out behind him, and strode into the centre of the throne room. The eyes of his elite warriors followed his every move. He raised his arms as he spoke, his voice deep and resonant with hate.

'To your strike craft, my children!' he howled. 'This is an insult to you as it is to me. There will be no animals defiling my temple. There will be no barbarian aliens defying our natural dominion! Take up arms and we shall revel in the blood of slaves!'

The warriors held up their weapons and screamed. Their keening war cry drifted through the palace and out into Commorragh, echoing across the nightmarish spires, through the evil air.

FROM WITHIN, THE temple was a vast hollowed carcass, bleached white, monstrous vertebrae spanning the ceiling, an altar of skulls the size of a command bunker towering above them all. The slaves crouched behind the barricades they had made from the shattered architectural debris of Commorragh, fragments of broken arches, bouquets of iron spikes. Those that were armed had their rifles and pistols pointed at the horizon – those that were not found themselves jagged shards of metal or heavy bars to fight with at closer quarters.

Rahimzadeh and Kep were in the front line, the slaves formed up around them. It occurred to von Klas that the wasted, broken slaves were the first command the Guardsmen had ever had. Near the altar, Ibn was organising those slaves who seemed the strongest, the ones who had been given the few heavy weapons they had found.

'How many do we have?' Commissar von Klas asked Scleros.

'Eighteen hundred. Of two thousand we attacked with.'

'Armed?'

'Seven hundred.' Scleros seemed unmoved by the information.

Von Klas looked between the pillars at the churning sky. He saw something, vague flitting black spots like flies. He had seen them before, untold millions of miles away, on an insignificant moon of Hydraphur. They were devastating eldar attack craft: Raiders.

'No ALIEN MUST live. Bring me the head of the man-scum who dared defy my will.' Kypselon gave his order in a stern, quiet voice, knowing it would be transmitted into the very consciousness of every eldar under his control.

His ornate strike craft touched down and all around him flowed a tide of his followers, a wave that crashed against the makeshift barricades and swept over them. The first were absorbed by the slaves, those that were armed keeping low against their barricades and pouring splinter fire into their foes. Warriors fell broken to the floor, a hundred at a stroke, but they could be replaced.

From within the depths of the front lines a horde of slaves armed with little save fear and anger poured out. They were led by a shaven-headed maniac with a splinter pistol in each hand, the fury in his eyes infecting the slaves formed up around him, who attacked with crude blades and clubs.

Yae's wyches went to meet them, dancing gleefully between the barbarians, lashing out with their silver blades, slicing through the pale skinny bodies of the slaves. But the slaves still would not fall back, still they charged forward, even as their leader died under Yae's twin blades. Countless slaves died, slashed to pieces or riddled with splinter rounds. Heavy fire from stolen dark lances and splinter cannons scythed through the eldar warriors, but then Yae broke through, and again the slaves' blood swirled ankle-deep on the temple floor.

Kypselon ordered his craft forward through the carnage. Before him lay only one target: the human filth who had started it all, he of the colder heart, standing defiant by the great skull altar, still bearing the weapons he had stolen from Verredaek.

Alerting Verredaek's miserable translator slave with a cuff to the head, Kypselon landed within earshot of the human, where they could talk above the cries of the dead. The eldar bodyguard stood aside. Kypselon spoke.

'Who are you to defy my will?' he asked via the translator.

'I am Commissar von Klas, of Hydraphur,' replied the alien, almost as if he wasn't afraid. 'You may remember. When you took my command prisoner, you picked out a handful of us to kill at your leisure. Ten per cent.'

Kypselon thought for a second. He was old, he had killed so many...

Then he remembered.

'Of course,' he said with a smile of pride. 'You're the one in ten.'

The human, von Klas, smiled coldly. 'No, the one in a million.'

Kypselon noticed the young one too late, the one in a dirty dark red uniform, with the web of metal across the side of his face, skulking at the foot of the altar. It pressed down a plunger on the control it was holding.

A dozen explosive charges stolen from the factory went off at once. They blasted the bases out from the pillars, sending great shards of bone shearing down from the ceiling. They crushed eldar and slave alike, and punched through the hulls of the eldar Raiders. Only Kypselon's craft managed to dodge out between the pillars.

Half the warriors were buried as a cloud of dust rose to obscure the imploding mass of bone which had once represented Kypselon's endless career of murder and savage glory. Broken skulls rained down from a sky the colour of dead flesh.

Kypselon felt that emotion he had not felt for a very long time. The feeling that he had lost control.

'Death to men!' he hissed to anyone who could hear. 'I want no slave sullying my city! Kill them all! Every one! This disgusting species shall never again face me and live!'

WHEN VON KLAS awoke he was manacled to the cold metal floor of a cell. The skin on his back was raw from the lash. He was unable to focus properly; the taste of blood was in his mouth. In the minimal light he could see that his legs had been broken, and were lying out in front of him like useless twigs. He was probably dying. But had he won? He drifted into unconsciousness again.

Days or weeks later, he could no longer tell, the cell door was opened and another two prisoners were thrown in. One was human, a girl, with straggly hair that had once been blonde, who crawled like a beaten dog.

The other was an eldar, thin and feeble without his armour and his legions of elite guards, his eyes dull, his wrinkling skin bruised. He stared at von Klas and started with recognition. Then he spoke. The translator took up his dark sibilant language in Imperial Gothic automatically, working from an instinct that had been bored into her soul.

'I knew you had a cold heart, human,' Kypselon said, with something approaching admiration.

Von Klas laughed darkly, even though it hurt his raw throat. 'What was it in the end? What finished you?'

Kypselon shook his head gravely. 'Uergax. We had no slaves, we had no factories, no expendable troops. We were crippled. He had the mandrakes, the incubi. He carved the Broken Spine apart as if he had been born to it.' The archon slumped to the cell floor, and von Klas saw the old eldar's fires of ambition were out.

'Your Raiders turned up as blips on our scanners,' said the human who called himself a commissar. 'Seventy-two hours later, the only survivor of seventeen whole platoons was me, but I had my orders. I was to eliminate any threats and a commissar either fulfils his orders or dies. I fulfilled mine.'

He looked Kypselon deep in his unknowable alien eyes. 'We humans aren't as stupid as you eldar believe. Remember my words, when Uergax comes to execute us both. I know I'll get a blade through the neck, like any other animal.

'But I imagine that it will take far, far longer for you to die.'

SMALL COGS
Neil Rutledge

COLONEL SOTH BELIEVED in order, in preparation and attention to detail. But as he stood by the shining, silver doors of the Water Temple he felt far from prepared for the coming battle. True, his face was always somewhat drawn, his sparse flesh stretched tightly over his bones, his body all sinew and muscle; no more room for padding on his frame than there was for luxury in his austere life. And his dark eyes flickered restlessly around the rocky bowl in which the temple stood but this, too, was quite normal.

The colonel, rigid and controlled, did not readily display his emotions and only those who knew him well could have detected the slightest signs of anxiety. The sporadic running of his wiry fingers through his tight, grey-ing curls. The thin lips compressed even more tightly and the occasional barely audible sniff as he straightened his dress uniform.

His dress uniform! That indeed was one of his irritations. Perhaps it was fortunate that his unit of the Ulbaran VIIIth was on ceremonial guard duty for the Water Temple festival when the infernal eldar raided. At least they were able to deploy quickly to secure the area. But to be going to war in their dress uniforms, the splendid attire of a bygone era; clumping old-fashioned boots, the traditional white fibre-cloth itching at the neck and cuffs and the gleaming, lovingly polished pectorals, it was ridiculous! No helmets, no webbing. Praise be to the Emperor that they always paraded armed and with a full complement of heavy weapons! But a slight clench-ing of his long fingers was another clue to the colonel's worry as he reflected that ammunition was not plentiful. He trusted that Headquarters would get some reinforcements to them soon – and in the meantime they would manage with what they had.

The enemy worried him too, the mysterious eldar! What were they doing here on the agri-world of Luxoris Beta? Colonel Soth was an experienced and well-trained officer but other than the ork pirates his men had defeated to liberate this planet two years previously, he had never faced aliens before. Nor had any of the men. They had manuals, training materials and holo-exercises, but these were not reality. Even the supposedly simplistic orks had constantly produced harrowing surprises in action. What would the inhumanly sophisticated eldar do?

Routine, practice and experience produced confident warriors. This had long been one of Colonel Soth's basic maxims. But they had had no experience against this foe. Lack of practice and experience meant uncertainty – and uncertainty meant fear.

Soth remembered the nervous eyes of the young lasgunner catching his, and the boy's anxious question. 'Do they really skin their captives alive, sir?'

With an outward calm which did not entirely reflect his inner feelings, the colonel had reassured the Guardsman. Such barbarity he had explained, was not practised by these eldar and besides, if the Guardsmen followed orders and shot straight, no alien would capture them anyway. Colonel Soth was almost confident in his advice. From what he had gleaned, these were not the so-called dark eldar, the notorious piratical renegades, but then what was the difference? They were all aliens, all humanity's enemies.

He mentally castigated himself for such futile speculation and was about to return to his command post when a soft footfall behind him made him stop and turn. It was the priest from the temple, Jarendar. He was a tall man and, in his full ceremonial costume, he made a striking figure. Even in the shade of the temple portico, his long white kilt gleamed and the elaborate gold pectoral, set with rubies to form the symbols of the Ecclesiarchy, glinted brightly, catching the light reflected from the huge doors. As Soth looked into the priest's face he was struck by a similar effect. The man had a strong jaw and jutting nose and though his gaze was even, there was a sense of masked strength and confidence.

A strength more than spiritual, the colonel thought, as he noted how the heavy gold and red leather head-dress spread down across powerful shoulders more like those of a labourer or warrior than a priest.

'The Emperor's light shine upon you,' the priest greeted him formally. The worship of the Divine Emperor here on Luxoris had acquired its own unique trappings in the eighteen hundred years since it had first been settled, but its people were devoted servants nevertheless.

'And also on you,' Soth replied.

'Are your defences prepared, colonel? Is there more my servant or I can do to assist you?' The priest's voice was calm, Soth noted with approval. He had courage even on the verge of an alien attack.

'We are as ready as we can be.' The colonel gestured towards his gleaming parade boots with his gilded ceremonial baton. 'But we are not exactly conventionally attired for action.' There was another slight sniff.

'Who can fully understand the will of the Emperor?' Jarendar asked. 'Had it not been for the festival you would not have been here to deploy to protect us. As you said yourself, if the cursed eldar realise the irrigation controls are here and they can flood the levels to impede our reinforcements, they will certainly attempt to capture the temple.'

'It is not an orderly way to conduct a defence.' Soth spoke almost to himself. 'We are not properly attired or equipped.'

'Properly attired?' The priest smoothed his kilt. 'These garments go back to the dark days of our slavery to the orks, before the Emperor gathered us once more to his bosom, praise him always. Yet even in those terrible times some were able to resist.'

'And,' he added, pointing at the rubies on his pectoral, 'these garments are marked now with the symbols of the Emperor's constancy. Even when we struggled alone we were not forgotten. Why is this temple here, Colonel Soth? It is to thank the Emperor for his blessing, in giving us the means to control the irregular rains of this harsh land so that we may offer him this land's bounty. In the short term we may see difficulties. In the long term, the Emperor cares for his children.'

Soth was irritated – and was even more annoyed that he could not control his irritation in the presence of this calm priest. 'But how,' he asked sharply, 'can a commander exercise proper control without even adequate comm-links?' He tapped the low-powered wrist communicator he was wearing to emphasis his point.

The priest pointed to where his servant, a young novice, stood by one of the pillars of the portico. 'Rigeth, my servant, he understands. He knows he is only a novice, a servant, a minute component in the Emperor's divine plan. We priests in charge of temples, or colonels in charge of regiments, are inclined to forget that we are merely servants too; only one tiny piece in the Emperor's great whole. Would you allow your men to question–'

A sudden, shrieking whine and burst of laser fire from the great ridge above them cut off the priest's homily. 'The eldar!' Soth spat. 'It's begun! Get to safety. I must reach my command post!' Leaving the priest, he began sprinting up the slope to where he had set up his headquarters on the rocky edge.

The section of the ridge surrounding the depression in which the temple sat was not the steepest. To gain some cover, Soth kept off the road but the surrounding terrain was rough. He needed to concentrate on his footing and as he raced on, he dared only to glance around himself from time to time, sporadically catching sight of the blurs of red screaming along the edge of the crest, their progress marked by staccato spurts of rock dust. The ghastly screech of projectiles ricocheting off the boulders was audible even over the shriek of their engines. These, he assumed, were the eldar's notorious jetbikes, a first wave of attack to soften up his defences and keep his men's heads down.

He paused just before the lip of the great ridge, crouching against a boulder. The tumbled rocks of the ridge offered good cover and he could see the bright stab of lasgun fire as his troops offered up some form of defence. Praying that the eldar weren't trying some form of jamming against which his own dress-issue communicator would be useless, he barked into his wrist unit, 'Soth to Captain Hoddish.'

'Hoddish receiving, sir.' The captain's voice was crisp even over the vox-link.

'Pass the order to cease lasgun fire against the jetbikes. We haven't the ammunition to waste.'

The colonel continued up the slope, his teeth clenched. He could hear Hoddish using the command vox-link. 'Hoddish to all units: no lasgun fire on jetbikes. Don't waste power against those lightning spirits. Save it for the infantry.'

The jetbikes continued their attack passes and Soth had to hurl himself behind a boulder as one craft hurtled straight for him, its projectiles singing an unearthly war-cry as they fragmented the rocks all around him. He caught a split-second glimpse of the alien's helmet as its craft howled overhead. This was certainly a far cry from fighting orks. Even the very sounds of battle were different.

Now, as he approached the top of the ridge, the enemy fire was more intense – but the eldar were not having things all their own way. As one larger jet craft tore across the wide depression there was a flash and a spurt of smoke as a missile was launched by the fire-team posted on the ornate roof of the ancient temple. The eldar craft jerked sharply and dived for the far rim of the rocky bowl but Soth watched the flare of the missile as it blasted towards the enemy, guiding true to catch the vehicle and detonate with a thunderous explosion just short of the crest. The blazing wreckage seemed to fall in mesmerising slow motion and it was only with some effort that Soth managed to tear his eyes away and dash for the summit.

AMIDST A SERIES of blasts from some unseen enemy heavy weapon down the far side of the great slope, the colonel dived into his hastily improvised command post. There, amidst the slightly better shelter of the hurriedly piled rocks and scraped depressions (no text book trench could be dug in this terrain!), Colonel Soth rapidly appraised himself of the developing attack. He led sound troops and they held a strong defensive perimeter, commanding both the temple depression and its surrounding approaches. If it hadn't been for their lack of proper equipment and the unknown nature of their enemy he would have been as confident as any Imperial Guard officer should dare to be.

Crouched under the shadow of a huge sandy-coloured boulder, he hastily conferred with Hoddish and his other staff, while the command comm-link operator – a small, leathery skinned veteran of many anti-pirate operations with the Ulbaran VIIIth – coolly passed them updates from other sections as best as their limited equipment allowed.

'I do not think they are fully pressing us yet, sir,' Hoddish was saying when a deathly howl, followed by a rattling storm of shrapnel and rock fragments made all the men suddenly crouch even lower. Hoddish grinned as the noise subsided, patting a long tear in the still smartly-creased sleeve of his dress jacket. His round face had always struck Soth as peculiarly boyish, with his thin moustache only serving to further the impression of a youth trying to pass as a man. He had a cool head though and continued, unperturbed.

'The main attack has yet to develop. This is just to soften us up. There do not seem to be many enemy and they do not appear to have much armour or heavy weaponry. The best information we can gain from central command is that the whole assault is some form of raid rather than an invasion. I suggest our opponents are a force dispatched to attempt to flood the levels to stop our armour from getting into action. I expect they will press all our perimeter from the air but concentrate on the ground, attempting a breakthrough at just one point.'

'Here, perhaps?' Soth mused out loud. 'We have the widest view but it is the easiest section of the ridge to break through.'

'Yes, sir,' the captain agreed.

As if on cue, there was a shout from a nearby trooper: 'Enemy advancing, sir!'

Soth crawled forward cautiously. The slopes of the ridge raked back on both sides of the spur on which he had located his command post but the Guardsman who had called the warning gestured down the left slope. He was another younger man and he looked pale, his knuckles showing white where they gripped his meltagun. His cap was jammed down ridiculously tight on his head, perhaps to try to shield his ears from the ghastly racket of the jetbikes.

'Sir...' He looked nervously at the colonel.

'Yes, Guardsman?'

'They're not really spirits, are they sir?'

Soth was mystified. 'Explain yourself.'

'The flying eldar, sir. They're not... spirits, are they?'

Suddenly the words of Hoddish's warning not to waste ammunition against the flying craft came back to Soth. He looked the young Guardsman in the eye. 'No, they are not spirits. Captain Hoddish spoke only figuratively. Did you not see the one downed by the missile? And, Guardsman...'

'Yes, sir.'

'Straighten your cap!'

'Yes, sir!' The young man showed a slight smile as he carried out the colonel's order.

Soth scrutinised the scene down the slope. He didn't even have viewers but Hoddish passed him a lasgun with a targeter and he was able to search for the enemy more effectively. The slope was a mass of tumbled rock dotted with thorny scrub. It made good concealment for them but also offered the enemy ample cover for a cautious advance. Soth forced himself to concentrate carefully amidst the growing barrage along their section of ridge. They were coming all right! Overhead, the jetbike sweeps seemed to intensify yet further. The colonel doubted if they were causing many casualties but they were keeping the Guardsmen from grouping to counter the mounting attack.

'Pass the order to hold fire until range band amber,' he instructed Hoddish without taking his eye from the targeter. 'Heavy weapons to target armour or support troops only!'

He could pick out occasional movements but no clear targets. Suddenly, further along the ridge some form of dreadnought or similar fighting machine appeared from behind a tangle of thorns. There was the crackling whoosh of a lascannon shot from their left and beyond that the staccato tattoo of a heavy bolter, but with frightening speed the machine strode across some open ground and with a grace more organic than mechanised vaulted into a gully and out of sight.

The colonel could hear the young Guardsman swearing nervously beside him. In truth Soth could remember scant details of such machines but said clearly, loud enough for the meltagunner to hear, 'An eldar dreadnought. Fast but poorly armoured. They always suffer at shorter ranges.'

There were increasing signs of movement downslope and the eldar infantry were starting to open fire. The air was full of the whine of their strange projectiles and sharp cracks as they ricocheted off the rock. As they came closer the storm intensified and the Guardsmen began to reply. Soth nodded approval to himself at the disciplined nature of his men's firing. The eldar advance slowed but now under cover of the fire of their supporting infantry and the continuing, howling passes of the jetbikes, a new threat showed. In several places turrets were rising above scrub patches and rocky outcrops and a torrent of heavier fire was poured on the guards. A deadly duel began between the well-placed and concealed cannons of the guards and the bobbing and weaving grav-tanks of the eldar – and all the time the alien infantry pressed gradually closer.

The Guardsmen were taking casualties but the constant drill and practice that Colonel Soth had always insisted on, was paying off. One grav-tank exploded, setting ablaze the patch of scrub in which it had been inadequately concealed. The smoke drifted across their front and under this cover the strange dreadnought machine ventured out of the gully – only to be caught in a torrent of heavy bolter fire that buckled one of its legs, tumbling it back into the gulch.

The enemy continued to advance, however, and suddenly the storm of doom broke loose. The jetbikes broke off but the remainder of the aliens charged, firing their bizarre weapons as they came. The Guardsmen poured down a fusillade of fire but still the tide surged up the slope. One more grav-tank exploded away to the left but, almost directly in front of them, another whined forwards, weapons blazing as it outstripped its escorting infantry.

'In the Emperor's name: where is that lascannon?' Hoddish was shouting. The tank was getting closer, heading for a dip in the crest, the red-armoured alien troops storming after it.

Soth grabbed the meltagun off the young Guardsman beside him. 'Cover me!' he cried as he sprinted across the slope. He could hear shouts behind him and lasgun bolts echoing off the rocks but it was the sudden zing of eldar projectiles around him that he was most conscious of as he ran, desperate to cut across the advance of the grav-tank and get close enough for a shot. He was closing the range when something snatched at his leg and he fell, tumbling wildly down the slope. With a painful tearing he was brought up, caught fast in a thorn bush, staring at the red wall of the passing grav-tank. Too shocked even to aim properly, he raised the meltagun and fired. There was the distinctive hiss and then a crashing as the blast tore into the plates at the rear of the alien vehicle, which whined on by.

Soth could see an eldar approaching and struggled to free himself from the thorn bush to bring the meltagun to bear. The alien figure was raising its long, strangely-fashioned weapon, its tall, almost insectoid helmet a blank mask of menace. But before it could fire there was a flash on its chest as it was hit and it dropped.

There was a fusillade of fire from behind Soth as the Guardsmen counter-attacked. The colonel found his arm grabbed by the young Guardsman whose weapon he had snatched. The youth was shouting and waving his laspistol as, with his other hand, he helped Soth out of the bush. 'You got it, sir! You got the tank.'

But he had no time to say more before two of the red aliens charged them. Soth dropped back to his knees as a shot knocked the meltagun from his hands. His young companion managed to drop one eldar with his pistol and the other was dispatched by the bayonet of a huge sergeant with a bald and scarred head almost as inhuman as the aliens' helmets.

The firing and tumult of battle continued but it faded slightly and moved downhill. The enemy was being driven back. Soth, eagerly assisted by the young Guardsman, took cover behind a jagged boulder and examined his leg where he had been hit. There was a good deal of blood on his now less-than-pristine dress trousers but he had been fortunate and the wound was only a long gash across his calf. Lacking his webbing and full kit he had to improvise a dressing with cloth torn from his shirt. Even so, he managed to staunch the bleeding and prepared himself for action once more. The hiss and whine of the eldar infantry's weapons was less noticeable now but the air was once more filled with the awful howl of the jetbikes as they shrieked back to the attack.

'Back to the command post,' Soth ordered the men. 'And keep your heads down.'

It was a short stretch to cover but it was a tense dash as they raced back to the improvised headquarters. Captain Hoddish knew his commander too well to waste time on congratulating him on the destruction of the grav-tank. He merely grinned his boyish grin and, after a simple, 'Good to see you back, sir,' quickly updated the colonel on the situation. They had taken some casualties, ammunition was holding, for the present, but the eldar had probably only paused in their assault. If they were to impede the Imperial advance and gain any benefit from flooding the levels, their enemy would have to move fast.

THE SUN WAS beginning to sink and throw long, jagged shadows amongst the rocks and thorns. The low light brought an astonishing warmth to the reds, sand yellows and ochres of the broken terrain. It was a harsh land but under this light it achieved a mellow beauty that struck even the practical Soth.

But there was no time for pondering on such beauty now. The rich, blue sky of evening was suddenly full of the streaking red of the jetbikes once more and the colonel again had some anxious moments as he made his way to inspect their positions prior to the expected second alien attack. Of particular concern to him was the lascannon emplacement that had been silent. He had feared the crew were dead but finally, after crawling and sliding through jagged rocks and grasping thorns he reached their position and found the men alive.

Coated in sweat and dust, a stocky corporal was feverishly stripping the weapon mounting down. His fellow crewman, forearms and tunic front stained with oil, was examining the components closely.

'Praise the Throne, I have it!' he shouted, his proud face a picture of relief. Sighing and wiping the sweat from his forehead, he only succeeded in smearing his face with oil; wide-eyed with delight, he presented more the aspect of an ancient barbarian than a smart Guardsman. Both men looked up to notice Soth at the same time and simultaneously they moved to stand and salute him.

'At ease!' Soth ordered curtly, waving them to stay put. 'What have you got, trooper?'

'Grit, sir!' the oil-smeared gunner replied. 'It was jamming the traverse cog.'

'How did grit get in the traverse gears?' The colonel's voice was sharp and full of meaning.

'I don't know, sir. It must have been as we emplaced.' The gunner's voice had acquired a slightly nervous edge. Soth was a strict officer and the lascannon's failure to track the grav-tank had jeopardised both their own position and their colonel's life.

There was a short pause before Soth asked, 'Carelessness, gunner?'

'Yes, sir!' It was the corporal who spoke now. He was still on his knees but he had stiffened to a sort of attention. Eyes rigidly front, his strong jaw thrust out but caked in grime and his dark curls blonde with dust, he made a bizarre picture. He continued quickly, 'I must have rushed too much while emplacing the gun, sir.'

The colonel gave one of his soft sniffs of irritation. This whole action was so disorderly! 'These are difficult conditions, corporal, but that makes attention to detail even more important. It is often the smallest cogs that are the most important. Neatness, care, dedication, these are all as necessary to a Guardsman of the Emperor as being able to shoot straight!'

The slight flicker of a smile cracked the flat face of the other gunner. Soth swung on him at once. 'Yes, soldier?'

The man instantly stiffened too. 'Sorry, sir! I was just thinking that we are not too neat just now, sir.'

Soth clenched his fingers. 'No, soldier – but we can still maintain our weapons, even if our uniforms suffer. Get this cannon re-assembled and let me see your training pay off!'

'Yes, sir!' both men chorused and Soth continued his rounds with caution.

As THE COLONEL was heading carefully back to the command post the jetbike passes seemed to ease once more and a rising thunder of las-fire from over the ridge heralded a further eldar attack. Soth had climbed higher to just beyond the ridge top in an attempt to find a path where he could make faster progress. Now with the aerial attack switched to other sections of the ridge, he risked less cover and managed to jog and scramble along just below the crest. It was still tough going and the sting from his flesh wound made him wince as he scrabbled up out of a gully. Still, there was a smoother section ahead and he was prepared to chance a dash across it.

As he stood on the gully edge, he unconsciously moved to straighten his uniform, re-adjusting the bronze pectoral on his chest. It was a misplaced gesture of habit – but it saved the colonel's life. As he moved the bronze plate, something slammed into it with a sharp shock and hiss. It was more a reflex action than the impact that hurled Soth back over the lip of the gully.

A sniper! His brain whirled as he instinctively switched his position, sliding and slipping as carefully as he could, following the gully downhill again. How had an alien sniper penetrated their position?

As Soth pulled himself up to where an overhanging thorn bush offered some chance of concealment for a cautious reconnaissance, he glanced at the small, melted hole in the pectoral. He had no doubt that embedded in that hole was a deadly, toxic dart. When the attack had first started he had considered discarding the pectoral but his own sense of neatness and propriety had stopped him. After all, it was part of the regulation dress uniform. The Emperor be praised for his own fastidiousness!

All this spun through Soth's mind as, with the utmost caution, his laspistol ready in his hand, he pulled himself up behind the thorn bush. His view was restricted but he gained a reasonable grasp of the sweep of slope in front of him. The most likely place of concealment for the alien was another patch of stunted thorn slightly up slope from where he watched. The ground was relatively open, as he had noted previously. It would be hard for his adversary to move without being spotted, but then what of those cameleoline cloaks he recalled from long-past training? As he pondered, straining his eyes for any clue to the alien's whereabouts, a brief movement caught his eye, a quick reddish flick behind a rock. Soth's vision, long used to the arid terrain and hardened wildlife of his homeland, at once discounted it as one of the large chaser lizards that laired amongst these tumbled boulders.

Just a lizard… but what had startled it?

He carefully scoured the area around where he had seen the creature move. Each rock and tuft of dried vegetation was scrutinised. Every shadow evaluated.

Got it! Only Soth's long training and habitual discipline prevented a hiss of amazement from escaping his compressed lips. As it was, his grip tightened involuntarily on his laspistol. It seemed a rock had moved! Now that he had spotted the alien it was easier to track its wary progress. Its camouflage was truly incredible, making it almost impossible to spot as, crouching almost double, it crept across the rocks.

'Are they really spirits, sir?' The young Guardsman's words came back to him. It would be easy to believe it!

To be moving thus across the open, the alien probably thought him dead but it obviously retained some caution. It was too far away for Soth to risk a shot with his pistol. He would somehow have to get closer. One pistol-armed Guard colonel in ragged dress uniform against a near-invisible, needle rifle toting and possibly armoured alien? He didn't give much for his chances!

His best hope was to drop back into the gully, crawl higher up the slope and pray he could spot the eldar by peering from behind the larger boulders there. All the time he hadn't taken his eyes off the ghostly progress of the alien but now he was going to have to. He judged the sniper's line of progress as best he could and inched back into the gully. He felt the prickle of sweat on his palm where it gripped the laspistol and his heart thumped in his ribs as he moved, carefully judging each step, back up the small gorge.

It seemed agonisingly slow progress but eventually he was in place to risk a glimpse from behind the boulders. Setting his cap to one side and holding his breath he peered round. No dart pierced him but, look as he might, he could see no sign of the alien. A knot began to form in his stomach when there was a sudden crackle and voice beside him.

'Hoddish to Colonel Soth!' his communicator crackled.

There was a sudden confusion of the rocks almost directly ahead of him, as if his vision had blurred for a second. Reflexively Soth fired.

'Hoddish to Colonel Soth. Are you all right, sir? Hoddish to Colonel Soth.'

The colonel, somewhat shaken, raised his wrist communicator. 'Soth receiving. I'm fine, captain.'

'We are holding the enemy, sir, but ammunition is depleting.'

'I'll be with you shortly, captain. Take extreme care to be alert for infiltrating snipers and ensure the men are warned also. I've just bagged an alien scout. Soth out.'

The colonel had heard rather than seen the eldar fall but by looking carefully he could now make out the body, only partially covered by the concealing cloak. The needle rifle had fallen separately and he could see its oddly graceful stock protruding from some dried weeds. The alien appeared dead but Soth took no chances and, keeping his pistol trained on the body, he advanced carefully.

Soth stood over the body of the dead scout, staring down at the strangely flowing features of the alien's respirator mask. These eldar devils made him shudder. The neat hole in the creature's forehead, burned by his laspistol shot, seemed a more natural eye than the opalescent crystalline lenses beneath it. The lowering sun cast strong shadows amongst the harsh tumbled rocks and, even dead and prone at his feet, the cameleoline cloak broke up the eldar's outline in a most disconcerting fashion. The colonel concentrated on the more clearly defined respirator mask but the sun's rays, lacing over the yellow heights, made the iridescent lenses flicker with eerie life and he turned away.

Soth knew he should get back to the battle, the fury of which he heard just down-slope beyond the boulders. It had been a close run thing though and he was content to snatch a moment's rest. He was still breathing heavily, but more importantly something was nagging him, jabbing the back of his mind with anxiety and the pit of his stomach with persistent adrenaline.

How had the scout infiltrated their perimeter?

In an unconscious gesture of order, he straightened the life-saving pectoral on his chest and started as if a revelation had come directly from the metal itself. The grav-tank! Who had cleared it? A ghastly dread washed over him as he sprinted across the steep slope of the bowl towards the still gently smoking wreck. Dust and small stones skittered from under his boots as he gingerly negotiated the steep flow of the scree across which the enemy tank had ploughed before landing against a rock spire.

The Falcon was clearly a wreck. It had spun around to face up the slope and the front end was burnt out. The rear seemed less damaged however and it was to here that Soth carefully made his way, the sharp edges of the rocks scratching his hands, the stink from the burnt vehicle scouring his nostrils.

The door of the internal compartment hung slightly ajar. Prudence dictated proper clearance procedure but the colonel was on his own and besides, he reckoned it was too late now for prudence. He confidently expected to find something more awful, in its own way, than an armed and lurking eldar. Steadying himself against the rock spire, laspistol at the ready, he kicked the hanging door aside.

Cursing, he lost his balance as the door seemed to bounce from his foot. What hellish stuff did these aliens build their vehicles from? It certainly wasn't the weighty metal of their own Chimeras! But no attack from within caught him off guard. Instead he stared at the charred and twisted bodies of more eldar scouts. Most still sat strapped to their seats in death. One, torn free by the mad careering of the doomed vehicle, was flung mangled, against his comrades. This time Soth's eyes were not held by the blank stare of the alien respirator masks, they were riveted to the empty seats. He desperately counted and re-counted.

Five empty seats. One scout torn free. One killed by him… There were three of the devils alive out there. And he knew where they would be heading!

COLONEL SOTH GAZED down at the distant Water Temple, thinking furiously. Three camouflaged alien snipers! The temple, covered by the Guards' ridge top heavy weapons, was defended by only an anti-aircraft section. From his own experience with the alien heretic, Soth didn't doubt that the three remaining eldar could easily evade or dispatch the unwitting Guardsmen. He must act fast!

Quickly he radioed Hoddish. 'How pressed are you, captain?'

'It's quite tough, sir.' The statement was given in Hoddish's usual cheerful manner but Soth knew that this mild phrase meant that the Guards were under heavy attack. 'Ammunition is getting low but we're holding out.'

'Hoddish, I am sure our perimeter has been breached by three alien scouts and they will attempt to infiltrate the Water Temple. Use the command link to alert the missile teams there. Warn them that the enemy are extremely difficult to locate due to their camouflage cloaks, and that their weapons are silent. Spare me just three men, experienced Guardsmen, and I'll attempt to contain the situation. Get them to bring me an extra lasgun. I'm just over the ridge from you, holed up by the wrecked grav-tank.'

'Yes sir! I'll dispatch them at once.'

Soth racked his brains to try to think of how best to combat the alien scouts. As he pondered, he threw away his officer's cap and stripped some of the more prominent braid from the grimy tatters that had so recently been his best uniform. There was no point in providing the alien devils with an even more obvious target than he already was. Appearing like this and carrying a standard lasgun he hoped he would not stand out from the other men. Soth was no coward but he wanted to deal with the alien scum personally.

As he straightened up from checking the makeshift dressing on his leg, he caught sight of the men Hoddish had sent to assist him. They skittered and slid briskly down the loose scree, before jogging up and saluting.

'Sergeant Tarses reporting for duty, sir!'

It was the bald and scarred NCO who had led the counter-charge that had saved Soth that afternoon. This afternoon! It seemed an age ago! Soth was pleased with Hoddish's choice. The sergeant was a tough customer and a veteran of several operations against the orks. He was an expert in close combat and fairly bulged out of the white cloth of his uniform – which he had somehow managed to preserve in a far neater state than his comrades. Tarses had a reputation for ferocity that went beyond the wild looks given to him by his heavy brows, missing right ear and the pale scar that twisted across his cheek and chin. But, as he handed Soth a lasgun, his face was as calm as if on parade.

'Also, Corporal Nibbeth and Guardsman Sokkoth, sir. Guardsman Sokkoth specifically volunteered to assist you, sir.'

Both the other men saluted. Nibbeth was another veteran, a short man but of the same wiry build as Soth himself. He had a calm sureness in his stance and movement, even on the loose scree, and the colonel noted with interest the sniper's badge on the torn sleeve of his tunic. Sokkoth was the young meltagunner who had rescued Soth from the bush. He was inexperienced but he had certainly acquitted himself well on that occasion. There was an earnestness in his thin face and bright eyes as he saluted. Soth had seen such devotion before in many young recruits. He hoped the lad was not to pay heavily for his keenness.

They moved off as rapidly as they could over the difficult terrain, Soth issuing orders for the advance on the temple as they went. There was a plan but a sketchy one, the kind of plan Soth hated and had often chided junior officers for on exercise. Too much was being left to chance! But they had been caught on parade by this ghostly enemy and their options were severely limited. Not even Tarses had any form of comm-link and Soth judged it prudent that they should operate as one group to maintain contact.

Hoddish had alerted the missile teams and there was little else they could do other than proceed with caution and hope for the best. As they cleared the slopes and moved out onto the flat base of the depression, Soth attempted to use his wrist communicator to raise the Guards stationed at the temple but without success. The sun had dipped behind the ridge and he strained to see the temple clearly in the fading light. The missile team should have been contactable with even the short range unit by now and the colonel feared the worst. Several times as he was descending, he had thought he had heard the crack of a lasgun shot from the direction of their goal, once even a faint cry, but against the background noise of battle from over the ridge top it was impossible to be sure. Soth knew his fears of infiltration to be well-grounded but how much was his proper concern turning to feverish imagination? His mind's eyes locked in memory with the eerie stare of the dead sniper he had so luckily managed to defeat and a brief shiver, owing nothing to the evening chill, ran down his spine. Grimly he pushed the memory aside and signalled to the other men to increase their separation as they hastened on.

THE GROUND WAS flat at the bottom of the depression and, although still rocky and scattered with clumps of brush, offered little cover compared to the ridge walls. The colonel felt his heart beat faster as they reached the broad, paved ceremonial road which led to the temple. Sweat slicked his hands and his eyes scanned each boulder and bush as he prepared to dash across the road. Never had he felt so appallingly vulnerable. Was it even worthwhile attempting to find cover from these fiendish, invisible death dealers? He looked over to where Sokkoth was ready to cover his dash over the road, nodded and ran. The slap of his boots on the paving stones rung in his ears even over the noise of battle echoing from the ridge tops and it was with clear relief that he finally dropped into the broad drainage conduit at the far edge of the road.

At once, he sprinted further on and took up position to cover Nibbeth, who was to follow him, and Sokkoth and Tarses, who were to advance up the other ditch. The others were across in seconds. Nibbeth sprinted over the road and sprang into the trench with the speed and ease of a desert gazelle and Soth made a mental note to commend Hoddish on his choice of men.

The conduits, paved to carry and channel the surging flows of water that accompanied the irregular rains, offered the best chance of a covered approach to the temple. Now dry, their reddish stones warm in the afterglow that just reached them from the over rim of the bowl, they would provide at least the illusion of concealment while, closer to the temple, the towering sandstone statues, erected to the glory of the Emperor and the great amongst His children, would offer further cover.

Soth wiped his hands on the torn remnants of his tunic and cautiously jogged forward up the conduit. Suddenly he froze as there was a dull detonation from somewhere ahead. There was still a constant backdrop of noise from the fighting beyond the ridge behind them but this explosion had been to the front.

The colonel thought of the massive temple doors. A demolition charge? He knew clearly now they could expect no help from the missile team at the temple. What were these aliens? How could three of them wipe out an entire anti-aircraft squad with such ease and so silently? Soth had met one of these devils face-to-face and he knew only too well.

He attempted to hasten forward but he felt strangely weak. This was not war as he knew it, calmly facing the hulking brutality of the orks, meeting their primitive power and ferocity with nerve and disciplined firepower. Now it was he and his Guardsmen who seemed the primitives. The memory of the dead eldar's remarkable camouflage haunted Soth as he moved on, his eyes sweeping the rocks on either side. How could he hope to spot the enemy? Only luck had saved him before. There was a knot in his stomach quite different from the normal adrenaline he felt before combat. Soth was a veteran. A cool head, discipline and training had always carried him through but now, just as the sweat ran under the high collar of his ceremonial tunic, the first tingling of fear chafed under his normal tempered resolve. There was a sound ahead. All at once he leapt sideways, swinging up his lasgun. But it had only been the slight rustling of dead stems in the first stirrings of a light evening breeze. The colonel forced himself to breathe deeply, calm as he turned to signal the all-clear to Nibbeth who followed on behind.

THEY SOON REACHED the lines of colossal statues which flanked the roadway on its final approach to the temple. Soth had always found the giant figures, sculpted stiff in the style of the ancient, desert-dwelling ancestors of the Luxorisians, the first colonists, to be foreboding. Now, looking up at the august images of priests, commanders and dignitaries, he felt not that these pillars of the Empire were watching over him, but rather that they held a vague menace, frowning disapproval on his unkempt appearance and fast beating heart.

He paused under the enormous stylised feet of the statue of the Adeptus Astartes commander who had been the first person to set foot on this planet in the name of the Emperor. The evening breeze blew more steadily and as it ruffled through Soth's tight curls, drying his sweat, he felt chilled. What would that ancient commander have done here? He would have hardly come skulking up a drain! Soth had a sudden mental image of the Space Marine trying to manoeuvre his bulky power armour up the conduit and, oddly, it cheered him. He suddenly grinned to himself. After all, wasn't the kind of covert approach, lightly equipped, that he was performing exactly how his ancestors would have raided from the cold deserts back on his own homeworld? This land was his to protect now and he would deal with these alien devils yet! Tradition should be, must be, upheld.

He waved his men to continue and soon they were at the point where the conduit swung to go around the temple. He still felt vulnerable, still felt tense but the relief he had felt under the statue had not dissipated entirely. They had a plan, if only a rough one. This was the rear of the temple, the side opposite the building's only entrance. There were probably only three enemy scouts facing them. There was a chance they might all be able to dash to the relative shelter of the surrounding portico and make an attempt on the temple doors. Each of them had his duty and his part to play and, to Soth, duty and a clear role were sacred.

He was exceptionally careful as he moved into his covering position, crawling warily up the steep side of the conduit in the shadow of another giant statue. He felt calmer, though, and was thankful that his hands were no longer damp with nervous sweat. He checked to his right and saw Nibbeth silently inching himself into position alongside him. In front of them, across the flagged rear court, the massive octagonal columns of the temple portico rose out of the deep gloom at their base. Predictably perhaps, he could see no sign of the enemy but he tensed as he spotted the brutal evidence of their actions. Slumped on the broad steps of the raised portico, leaning back against one of the great, sandstone pillars was one of the missile team. In other circumstances, he might almost have been taken as asleep but Soth knew better. The aliens had reached the temple. But where were they?

The colonel found that his hands had tensed once more as he waited for Trooper Sokkoth to make his prearranged dash for the portico. The young soldier had volunteered to make the first advance and Soth had seen no reason to refuse him. Sokkoth himself had said, his eyes bright with ardour, that he was the least experienced and most expendable if the aliens had to be drawn into revealing themselves. He was correct, of course and the colonel wondered if this had been in Hoddish's mind as well when he let the recruit come in the first place. But there was no time for such melancholy thoughts.

A soft scrape of stone made Soth turn, to see Sokkoth vault out of the ditch on the other side of the road and sprint for the columns. The lad was fast and had almost reached the steps when he seemed to stumble and next second was face down, a small puff of dust rising with the soft thud of his fall, the clatter of his lasgun a brief underlining of his fate. Sokkoth himself made no sound. Of the alien sniper there had been not a trace.

Some of Soth's previous feeling of powerlessness returned as he scanned the shadows between the pillars. No sign! He scrutinised each section of the rim of the gently pitched, stone flagged roof. No sign! Their next, prearranged tactic in the event of the rear being guarded was to wait five minutes and make a concerted rush from three different directions. The colonel glanced to his right to check that Nibbeth was moving off, further down the conduit, prior to the charge but the wiry little man was standing pressed against the wall at the bottom of the ditch. He was signalling frantically for Soth to join him. In spite of his curiosity, Soth forced himself to descend with the greatest of care and crept along in the shadow of the wall, taking pains not to make any sound, until he was alongside the Guardsman. Nibbeth's soft whisper was quick but clear: 'The alien's not on the roof. It's by the end column on the far side.'

'Where? Can you see him?'

'No.'

'But… how can you know?'

'It's where I would be.'

Nibbeth's tone was very matter-of-fact and he slightly shrugged his shoulders as he spoke, as if to emphasise his own sniper's badge. He continued, 'The roof's not high enough for a decent view and to get any kind of shot it would have had to skyline itself. With that ghost suit it can just stand against a corner column and watch both ways. It's on the far side because Sokkoth was almost across before it had a clear shot and dropped him.' The Guardsman glanced briefly at the timepiece on his wrist, before looking his commanding officer straight in the eye. 'When the time to charge comes, sir, let Tarses go alone. It's a terrible risk for the sergeant but if we watch that end pillar, we'll have the best chance we'll get of nailing the devil.'

Soth thought back to when Sokkoth had saved his skin earlier that day. The young Guard had been aided by the determined charge led by the big NCO, who would even now be working himself into a position to charge the other side of the portico. One of the colonel's saviours was already dead. Was the other to perish too? And to die charging alone, without his expected support? All this flashed through the commander's mind but in the end all he said, glancing at his own watch, was, 'Very well. Into place, quickly!'

As fast as caution allowed, he took up his position again, wondering with every cautious movement of his lasgun if a silent death was about to follow. He carefully sighted on the end column and, seemingly immediately, he heard Tarses's stentorian shout as he charged from the conduit. A shadow bulged from the pillar and there was the crack of a lasgun from beside him even as he fired himself. He took two more shots at the column but Nibbeth was out of the ditch and charging the portico. After a moment Soth leapt forward too and the two men reached the columns together. As they dashed into the shadows they saw Tarses pulling his bayonet from the fallen eldar. He looked up, his long scar pale against his dark skin and the gloom. He had no questions, no reproach or surprise, his quiet 'Sir?' merely a request for orders.

Soth lost no time. 'Nibbeth, far side. Tarses with me, this side.'

Nibbeth's compact form vanished silently into the dimness of the further reaches of the portico while Soth crept along the temple wall and the sergeant dashed in short sprints between the outside columns. Two filthy alien scouts dead; two left to deal with. There would probably be one at the temple front. Could they somehow spot that alien too? The colonel moved quickly but kept close to the wall. Shaded by the portico it had captured none of the day's heat and felt chill where he brushed against it. It gave some sense of safety even if, as Soth grimly reflected, it was a purely illusory security.

As they approached the temple forecourt they moved far more cautiously. Soth crept around the corner column as Tarses moved to drop down the steps and crawl around the front of the building. It was quiet except for the barest rustle as the wind tumbled some dead thorn leaves across the flagstones.

Tarses died so quickly that his commander barely noticed. The colonel heard a slight hiss and then a series of thumps as the big sergeant's body tumbled down the steps. Heart in his mouth, Soth pressed his back to the pillar and stood, immobile.

Where was the devil? He dare not move and, tensed against the cold stone, he stared across at the shining doors of the temple. One had been blasted with some kind of alien demolition charge, a surprisingly neat hole blown clean through. The other remained intact, still glowing in all its glory, reflecting what little light there was left. Soth was surprised at how effective a mirror it made and, suddenly hopeful, he scanned it for any sign of the alien.

But he could see nothing other than the leaves, scraping in fits and starts over the stone as the wind caught them. They blew fitfully, barely moving, occasionally lodging against a column base or... Why had those leaves stopped, when others, close by, were still moving? There was no stone to stop them!

The colonel's heart skipped a beat. It must be the eldar scum! He stared at the reflection, desperately trying to make out even a hint of the shadowy outline he had been able to see up on the slopes when he had tackled the first scout. The reflection was too poor but he had a reasonable idea of where his enemy crouched. With a shock colder than the stone at his back Soth realised that in turn the eldar now knew exactly where he was! Even now his enemy was probably studying his reflection, waiting for him to move.

The commander had never felt so hopeless but the solid knot of anxiety in the pit of his stomach was hardening further to become a clenched mass of frustrated rage. He would have to try his luck. Perhaps his attempt would distract the alien enough for the wily Nibbeth to nail it. He stared at the reflection and prepared himself to move. Not normally religious, Soth surprised himself by mentally intoning a prayer to the Emperor that came back to him from his childhood – and then he lunged. Swinging around the column he let loose a volley of lasgun shots, their cracks echoing wildly off the stone and the vicious, red stabs tearing the gloom. There were further thuds and the clatter of falling arms.

Astonished, Soth realised he was still alive and that, from the outline he could now see sprawled on the flags, his enemy was dead. He fired a further shot into where he could see the fallen alien's head was and, as the echoes died, he cried out to Nibbeth. But there was no answer.

Where was the final scout? Deep within the temple or, alerted by the noise, hurrying to stalk them? Where for that matter was Nibbeth? There was another of the colonel's soft hisses of irritation as he strode forward. The irritation vanished in an instant as he stepped clear of a pillar and saw Nibbeth's body. The soldier lay face down, his lasgun under him. It was he, not Soth, who had distracted the alien at the crucial moment. Abruptly, the colonel turned on his heel and plunged through the blasted temple entrance.

IMMEDIATELY INSIDE THE great doorway, Soth leapt to one side and took cover behind one of the double row of pillars which mirrored those of the exterior. His eyes took a moment to adjust as the interior was brighter than the evening shade of the portico. It was not glaringly lit but soft lights, carefully hidden amongst the carved reliefs of the high walls, gave out a gentle glow. The long hall that comprised the bulk of the temple was flagged with the same worn sandstone as outside and seemed completely empty.

Cautiously Soth surveyed the chamber. It was a plain room, without furnishings, only the pillars breaking the view to the end. Even the carvings were subdued, seeming as natural as the grain in the stone itself. All seemed clear and he began to jog to the end where he knew an antechamber gave access to a staircase which led to the control room for the irrigation system, as well as to the passages and cells of the priest's quarters. He felt a curious confidence. He had always liked the building, not from any particular spiritual motivation but for its lack of ostentation and the manner in which it blended the Imperial discipline so dear to him, with the shadowy past of the desert peoples of this world. If he was to face such a lethal foe as these aliens, here was a suitable battleground.

That he was to face the third eldar was clear as he approached the antechamber. Its door had been forced and from somewhere down the stairs he could hear the sounds of a struggle. He quickened his pace, while still trying to move as quietly as possible.

The steps down were worn and steep but the lighting was now brighter and Soth took them two at a time. On the small landing, one doorway, its ancient wooden door closed, led to the priest's apartments. Another entrance, its modern steel door blasted through, led into the control chamber. Lasgun at the ready, the colonel charged through. His quick brain, tuned to action, took in the scene in an instant.

The priest, Jarendar, had obviously surprised the alien as it tried to manipulate the irrigation controls. The two were now locked in a desperate struggle. The slight form of the eldar was backed against the bank of instruments while the massive priest, his back towards Soth and blocking any chance of a shot, was attempting to crush his squirming adversary. The priest was a powerful man but, for all that, he was no fighter and just as Soth entered, the foul alien heretic managed to break his hold, draw its laspistol and fire. The priest died with a grunt, the shot blasting through his chest. His body shielded the alien and Soth caught only a glimpse of a raised pistol and ghastly, gem-like lenses before there was another spurt of las-fire and the world went black.

Soth was unsure how long he had been unconscious. It couldn't have been more than a few moments as, when he came painfully back to his senses, the alien was still working at the irrigation controls. His chest seemed a mass of searing agony as, with blurred eyes, he watched the eldar working. It was tall yet slight, and even its small movements, as it passed some glowing, crystal device over the control panel, seemed to have an inhuman grace about them. The other-worldly effect was heightened by its cameleoline cloak which even in the stark and brightly lit control room, still broke up its slender form to a remarkable degree.

Soth's thoughts were as fuzzy as his vision. He thought he saw Nibbeth's body lying next to the dead priest. Had they died, Sokkoth and Tarses, too, only for he, himself to fail? He must try to reach his lasgun. It was just beside him, its stock temptingly near. Could he retrieve it without alerting his enemy? The harrowing vision of the face of the first alien he had killed, the extra blank eye of the pistol wound staring from its forehead, seemed to superimpose itself on the back of the head of the scout working in front of him. It appeared to watch him, daring him to move. He screwed shut his eyes and tried to concentrate, driving the visions from his brain.

Wracked with pain, the colonel tensed himself and tried to move. The only result was even more agony somewhere under his ribs and an uncontrollable gasp that hissed from his lips. The alien turned, the strange crystal device still glowing, its strangely sensuous laspistol drawn in a movement of fluid grace. Soth stared helplessly up into the opalescent lenses of the blank mask as the creature walked lightly over, covering him with its weapon. It paused and almost in one movement, a quick flick from one of its gracile boots sent Soth's lasgun sliding well out of reach, and it was back working at the controls.

Soth trembled with agony and frustration but could do nothing. His head felt as if it was swimming from his body on a haze of pain and his vision seemed to be deteriorating further. He was sure he saw the ghost of Sokkoth creeping towards the alien from behind. He wanted to shout at the dead youth. To tell him it was all futile; that the lad had been correct, the aliens were spirits and they could not be thwarted.

His lips quivered but no sound came. Sokkoth's wraith was almost upon the eldar now and was raising his lasgun to club the scout. The colonel stared at the apparition, his hazy world hovering between dream and reality. Why was this ghost carrying a non-regulation weapon? He would have to discipline it!

But somewhere on a deeper, more rational level of his brain, Soth recognised that it was not Sokkoth's ghost but the young temple novice Jarendar had talked about earlier, the minor component in the Emperor's plan. The weapon was not a lasgun but a candlestick. The candlestick came crashing down just as darkness descended once more on the colonel.

THIS TIME HIS period of unconsciousness must have lasted longer for when Soth came to again he was floating up the temple stairs. His head swam. Was his spirit being carried off to the Emperor? A face looked down at him, pallid in the bright lights. Soth recognised the insignia around the face's collar. They were the badges of a Guard medic.

The colonel's eyes flickered and his lips moved soundlessly as he tried to speak. The medic, concern clear in his dark eyes, addressed him firmly: 'Don't try to talk, sir. You're badly wounded but we'll patch you up. The enemy have been driven back. The reinforcements are here as well and Captain Hoddish is organising the clean-up operations.'

Soth weakly shook his head. The pain was terrible but he felt he must speak. His lips shook, but this time a weak, croaking voice was audible, 'Warn him!'

'Warn who, sir?' the medic frowned, plainly not understanding.

'Warn Hoddish. Tell him… tell him to look out for the minor components. Tell him it's the small cogs that count.'

The medic looked forward to where his companion was lifting the front of the stretcher. 'I think the colonel's delirious,' he said.

THE FALL OF MALVOLION
Dan Abnett

By HIS WRIST-chronometer, it was not yet noon, but the air was warm and clammy. Trooper Karl Grauss of the Mordian Iron Guard 15th let his lasrifle swing loose on its harness strap, wiped the perspiration from his eyes, and pushed the angular nose of the wrench-bar into the rusty door lock.

He paused and glanced around at Major Hecht. The officer was tensed, his lasrifle pulled up tight with the butt in his armpit, ready to fire. Beads of sweat dotted his face too, and it wasn't just the heat.

'What are you waiting for?' he hissed.

Grauss shrugged. He didn't know, exactly. He didn't know anything except what Hecht had told him and the others of Zwie Company that morning: get out to that pumping station in the delta and find out why they hadn't checked in for three days.

Grauss jiggled the wrench-bar until the tool locked against the latch mechanism, and then began to wind the ratchet so that the door release slowly began to turn manually.

Down the low hallway behind him, the major and six other men from Zwie hugged the walls and braced lasguns. This was the job at its worst, thought Grauss as he cranked the tool. Sneaking into a mystery and opening doors blind when you had no idea what in the name of the God-Emperor lay on the other side.

But, dammit, they were Iron Guard! More disciplined, determined Imperial soldiers you couldn't find.

They'd reached the pumping station early that morning. A cluster of machine-barns and modular habitats, it stood at a confluence of irrigation channels which watered the entire delta area and fed over a dozen farm steads. The suns were low and cool. There had been no sign of life, not even the ever-present water birds that Grauss had seen everywhere in the marshes.

And once they had got inside, with no answers to their voice or vox calls, it had been so damned hot and humid, like someone had set the environment controls to 'tropical'.

The latch popped and Grauss kicked the door inwards, swinging aside so that the major could slide in, gun raised and aimed.

Before them lay some kind of hydroponics workshop, with a high, cera-glass roof and metal support pillars rusting in the steamy air. Samples of crops and yield-plants stood in labelled pots and trays and bins all around. The walkways between the bins were metal grille. Sappy moisture dripped from the transparent panes above.

The Mordians fanned out into the hothouse, dripping with sweat in their temperate zone-issue fatigues and tunics.

'What's this?' called Trooper Munce. Grauss moved over to him, and the major joined them too. Munce gestured with disgust at a rack of culture-trays set under some daylight lamps. Nutrient feeder sprays intermittently misted what was in the trays with chemical washes.

Major Hecht cursed. The things in the trays looked like rotting, globular fungi: puffy, swollen, the size of human heads. They pulsed irregularly. None of the Mordians had any horticultural training, and none had been on Malvolion long enough to get a feel for the local flora, but they all knew this stuff just wasn't right.

'Burn it. Get a flamer in here and burn it all.' Hecht looked away from the obscene crop.

Grauss was about to obey the command when they heard the las-fire. Close by, two or three buildings away. Six short, frantic bursts, then a longer report made by several guns on auto, firing together. Zwie Company's vox-intercoms spluttered out an overlapping, unintelligible series of ear-splitting cries and yells.

The platoon turned and ran towards the sounds, Hecht in the lead. Platoon Two, scouting to the left of them, was in trouble.

Hecht's men burst into the chamber that had been Two's last recorded position. It was a hangar barn, with several big-wheeled agricultural vehicles parked in it. The air was full of smoke from discharged weapons.

There were two bodies on the floor, both men from Two, both looking like they'd been dismembered by industrial crop-reapers.

Platoon One crept forward through the gloom, twitching for targets. Grauss found the headless corpse of another man from Two leaning against the wheel-arch of one of the agri-tractors.

Looking aside from the corpse in distaste, Grauss saw that the tractor was hitched to a big flatbed cargo truck, with something large and strange chain-lashed to it. Caked in the mud of the delta, it looked for all the world like some kind of ship: those bulbous projections at the rear could only be propulsion units. But... it was small, not large enough for any-thing more than a single human, and it made him sick to look at it. It wasn't made of metal. It wasn't technology as he understood it. It looked... organic. Fleshy, pod-like, akin to the things he had seen grow-ing in the hothouse but many, many times larger. Was this something the station crew had found out there in the delta and hauled back for study?

There was a cry and a burst of las-fire behind him. Grauss spun around, in time to see Trooper Munce's body sailing across the chamber in a welter of blood and torn flesh. Lasguns roared and flashed. Something was mov-ing through the gloom with terrifying rapidity. Something with claws. Four sets of claws.

It sliced through Major Hecht at the waist, and his body fell in two, still firing.

It was right on Grauss now. He howled and started to fire.

Genestealer...

GRAUSS WOKE WITH a start. He was wet and slippery with night-sweat and his head pounded. It had been two weeks since that nightmare in the pumping station, a nightmare that only he and three others from the Zwei Company detail had survived. And he could not shake it. He'd had battle-shock before, he was a veteran But the sheer alien horror of what he had seen, and smelled, and felt... it haunted his sleep and his waking mind.

Genestealers...

Grauss got off his barrack cot unsteadily and pulled on dirty combat fatigues. Outside it was daylight, and he could hear men and vehicles. He needed to get active. If he was going to get past the trauma, he had to keep his mind and body occupied.

He went outside, into the raw suns-light, and watched the troop trucks and cargo-machines rolling past in the mud. Unseasonal, warm rain hosed the street. The modular roofs and towers of Malvolion Collective farm-plex 132/5 glistened and their gutters drooled.

The evacuation was underway.

As he crossed between growling heavy transports, he tried to reassure himself. He'd killed the thing, blown it apart with his lasgun. It and two more like it. Then he and the other survivors of the search detail had blown the pumping station with krak mines. They'd kept their heads, true to the famed iron discipline of the Mordians. They'd got their report back to Guard Command, and thanks to them, the planet-wide advisory had been issued.

That had to make him feel better, didn't it?

Grauss spotted Colonel Tiegl supervising the loading of transports on a stretch of hardpan behind a row of produce barns. The colonel looked hot and flustered. Settlers thronged around him, begging for more of their valuable agri-machinery to be included on the evacuation manifest.

Tiegl broke off from them as he saw Grauss approach.

'By the Golden Throne,' he muttered under his breath to the trooper, 'these people will be the death of me! I just want to get them, their loved ones and their basic possessions out of here, and they're all too worried about their damned cultivators and multi-ploughs! I've half a mind to let you tell them what you saw.'

'And cause a mass panic, sir?' smiled Grauss sadly.

Tiegl sighed. 'No, no...'

'Is there anything I can do?'

'I thought you were on sick-rest? Medic's orders?'

'Making me crazy, sir. Give me something to do, and it might take my mind off the... the things in my head.'

The colonel nodded. 'Good man. Well, we need drivers. Can you handle a truck-rig?'

'Pretty much,' said Grauss.

Tiegl consulted his dataslate and pointed to a dirt-caked eight wheeler parked over by the side sheds. 'Unit 177. She's yours.'

'What's the program?'

'I want the main evacuation section out of here by 15.00. No excuses. Anything we haven't loaded by then is staying, and that includes these bloody farmers. Uplift point is the Nacine Plains, nineteen hours north of here. According to transmitted reports, we're expecting nearly sixty bulk transports to be waiting there to take us to the orbiting fleet units. There are eight other evac convoys like ours heading in from other collectives, so it'll pay to be on time. We want to get our place, and if things turn nasty, we don't want them leaving without us.'

'What if it does come to a fight, sir?'

'Then we'll show these alien freaks what Mordian fighting spirit is. There are seventy thousand men from our regiment deployed planetside, not to mention thirty thousand from the Phyrus regiments. General Caen has informed me that armour units are a few hours from landing, and there's even talk of help from the Chapters.'

'That's reassuring,' said Grauss. 'It may have been a little isolated outbreak we found down at the pump station, but it pays to be prepared.'

'More then prepared now,' said Tiegl, a little darkly. 'The alert's moved up a notch. Didn't anybody tell you?'

'Tell me what?'

'Off-world astropathic communications went down five hours ago. The Shadow has fallen across us. They're coming, Grauss, they're definitely coming.'

LIKE BEACHED LEVIATHANS with screaming, wide mouths, the vast battle-barges squatted on the dry, stony flats of the Nacine Plain, disgorging rivers of armour amid clouds of churned, pale dust. Even from the high observation mast of the command ship, three hundred metres above ground, General Caen could hear the clank and grumble of the Paladian tanks and fighting vehicles. He swept his magnoculars around and then nodded in satisfaction. Colonel Grizmund was deploying his armour as fast as ordered, faster perhaps. A good, clean dispersal. The sky was a clear blue, and they had visibility to ten kilometres. They wouldn't be caught napping.

Caen let the magnoculars dangle against the crisp, pressed front of his immaculate Mordian uniform. Beside him on the ship's watch-platform, two servitors and three Mordian adjutants manned the supervision consoles and vox-caster sets. A steady stream of radio traffic crackled in the background.

Hanff, one of the adjutants, approached him across the metal grille and handed the general a data-slate.

'Reports in from all the evacuation points, sir. Most of the collectives are underway to us in convoy. Tiegl at Collective farm-plex 132/5 informs you they will be underway by 15.00.'

'Why so slow?'

'That's where the outbreak occurred, sir. I think the colonel is being especially careful.'

Caen nodded. He knew Tiegl and trusted him well. The man would get the job done.

'And this?' he asked, pointing to the slate. 'Collective 344/9?'

'They haven't embarked either, General. Men from the Phyrus regiment are there. I... don't know what the hold up is.'

'Vox them. Find out. Tell them I'll skin them alive if they don't move soon.'

'Sir.'

The air trembled with subsonic, basso power. A shadow passed over them. Another ten thousand ton bulk transport swung down in to land on the plain, braking jets squirting blue flames.

'The *Ariadne*,' said Hanff. 'Right on time.'

Boots clanged up the mast ladder and Colonel Grizmund pulled himself up onto the platform. He was a tall, thick-set man wearing the crimson battledress of the Paladian armour brigade proudly. He saluted Caen.

'Reporting in person,' he said. 'We're ready to move out. Where do you want us?'

Caen shook the colonel's hand and showed him the chart table.

'We're playing watchdog right now, Grizmund. Some of my men down in the delta stirred up genestealers two weeks ago, and blew the whistle. From the reports, it looks like the locals found some kind of tyranid scout-drone or incursion probe and woke it up. Emperor alone knows how long its been sending its beacon, but since the Shadow fell this morning, we can be sure it's been heard. I'd like you to move south. The evac convoy from the delta collective may need support if trouble starts there, and they're lagging.'

'We'll embark at once, and meet them en route.'

'Good, good…' Caen turned to look at Hanff. 'Any joy with those damned Phryus idiots yet?'

THEY'D BEEN IN Farm Collective 344/9 only six hours and Trooper Nink was already banging on that something bad was coming.

The Phyrus troopers were packing crates into the pack of heavy transports behind the main maize silo and the suns, a matched pair, were coming up hard and bright. Sergeant Syra Gallo tossed another crate up into Nink's hands and told him to shut the hell up.

'Of course there's something bad coming, you moron! That's why we're here! That's why we were diverted nine days ago with express orders to head for Malvolion! That's why we're busting our humps getting a bunch of dirt-scratchers onto transports and away to the uplift! Something bad! Something really bad!'

Nink looked down at him as if the sergeant had just broken awful news about his wife.

'Don't look at me like that,' Gallo turned around to regard the other men of the Phyrus Fourth Regiment who had all paused in their work. 'None of you!'

'For the Emperor's sake, you moon-eyed bastards, we're Imperial Guard! We only go to places like this because something bad is coming! I mean, the Warmaster doesn't say "Oh, Malvolion, nothing bad's gonna happen there. Let's deploy thirty thousand of our brave Phyrus boys immediately!" does he? Eh? No he freaking doesn't! We're here because we are the Imperial freaking Guard and people give thanks and kiss our spotty butts in gratitude because we are there when that Something Bad arrives! Now get these crates stowed and tell yourselves this…'

Gallo dropped his voice and grinned at his men. 'We're the freaking Phyrus Fourth. We're stone-killers to a man. It had better be something really freaking bad because when it gets here, it's gonna find us, and we are gonna kill it so many times it's gonna wish it had never been born!'

There were cheers. Even Nink cheered. The Malvolion colonists trudging past to the waiting trucks further down the evacuation convoy line were silent and looked far too scared for Gallo's liking.

Silently, he just wished he knew what was coming, what they were up against, and why they were here.

'Repeated signals from Nacine Plain Command,' Vox-officer Binal called to Gallo.

'Yeah, yeah…'

'It's the general himself, sergeant. He wants to know why we're not moving yet.'

Gallo dropped a crate in contempt and turned to look at Binal. 'We're not moving because Major Hunnal hasn't given the order yet. Tell him that.'

'I did, sergeant. He wants to know why not.'

Wiping his sore, dusty palms, Gallo stalked away across the sunlit compound. 'Tell him I'll ask the major himself.'

Gallo entered the main hall of the collective, a dirty, zinc-panelled prefab that creaked in the heat. Air-scrubbers chattered fitfully. Gallo had seen the major and two other officers disappear inside an hour before to discuss the final evacuation conditions with the collective's selectmen.

'Major? Major Hunnal?'

Gallo checked a few rooms. The place was empty. Unnerved, he called in a squad to help him search. Five men, all in heavy Phyrus battledress, clattered in through the entryway to join him. One brought Gallo his lasgun. 'Spread out,' he told them.

Gallo and a trooper called Matlyg had the pleasure of finding Hunnal, the other two officers, and the six farm selectmen. What was left of them anyway. Reduced to blood and bone-meal, they coated the floor and walls of cargo bay behind the hall.

Matlyg threw up and fell over in the mess of bloody remains. Gallo tried to stammer into his vox-link.

Something tall and still that he had taken to be a roof support quivered and moved. Fast... so freaking fast! A scything talon the size of a grown man lashed out of the shadows and ripped the vomiting Matlyg into ribbons of flesh and a spume of airborne blood.

Gallo found his legs, retreating, screaming, firing. Purple plates knotted with whitish bone, iridescent green tendrils lapping between its jagged, filthy teeth, the mantis killer disengaged itself from the ultraviolet spectrum and shimmered into being, towering over him.

'Spook! Spook!' Gallo wailed.

His shots punching into the dark, bony plates of the thing's belly and chewed off some splinters of chitin. Then he was in through the doors and running.

The vox-channels were alive with panic. Gallo ran into two of his searchers and pulled them down into cover, backs against the prefab wall.

He was trying to tell them what he had seen when two metres of talon sliced in through the wall and one of the troopers. Blood boiled out of the trooper's sagging mouth as the talon withdrew and let him slide free. Gallo threw himself away as another bio-blade slammed through the wall and decapitated the other trooper, splitting his skull lengthways.

It can see us. Even through the walls, it can see our heat!

Gallo ran.

He reached the outside.

The evacuation convoy was where he had left it, still not underway. Now it would never get underway. Ever. Several trucks were overturned, and two were on fire. Phyrus troops ran in all directions, firing into the smoke. Farmers and their families stampeded in panic all around. Bodies littered the ground. None were remotely intact.

Stumbling forward, Gallo found Nink. From the belly down, Nink was nothing but tatters of bloody cloth, ropes of torn entrails and fragments of semi-articulated raw bone. But somehow, horribly, he was still alive. He clawed at Gallo, begging the sergeant to take him with him. Nink clutched at Gallo's leggings.

Gallo shot Nink through the forehead. A mercy, he considered.

He dropped into cover as a clutch of farmers tumbled by in extreme distress. Something darted after them, taller than a man, its armoured body swept forward over racing, bird-like limbs. The genestealer's primary limbs, hugely taloned, the uppermost of its four torso limbs, raked at the screaming settlers, disembowelling one. Its drooling tongue flapped between snapping teeth.

Like the mantis killer, it moved so fast....

It corralled the settlers, and two more abominations just like it chased in out of the fuel-oil smoke, stubby tails erect and wagging like excited dogs. Together, their limbs thrashed and ploughed, ripping the frantic people into offal.

Gallo realised two things with ghastly clarity. He would never forget the screams of the slaughtered farmers and their folk for as long as he lived. And that wasn't going to be very long.

He saw a mantis killer through the smoke, busy rending a truck apart. He ran, reaching one of the laden trucks at the edge of the compound. Binal lay dead by the rear wheels. Gallo knew it was Binal because the corpse still wore the vox-caster set, even if it didn't have a head any more.

He tore the vox-unit from the body and clambered into the truck's cab.

It took him a moment to find the emergency channel.

'344/9! 344/9!' he rasped. 'Incursion! Tyranid incursion! Repeat–'

There was no time to repeat. The genestealers were at the cab windows, on the bonnet, smashing the glass and reaching in.

Though unintelligible and more a sound of pain than real words, Gallo's last transmission was heard six hundred kilometres away at Nacine Plain.

THE CHANNEL WENT dead. Caen looked away, avoiding Hanff's face as he tried to compose himself. That sound. That scream...

He was about to signal Grizmund's armour brigade, which had left the plain just forty minutes before to turn on a bearing for 132/5, but the sky went abruptly black.

Wind-borne spores began to winnow down around them, burning flesh and thickening the air.

Caen ran to get below as the first of the atmospheric toxins began killing Mordian troops and navy personnel. Ship landing lights came on automatically as the natural light died, illuminating streams of pelting spores like a black blizzard.

Against the blackness high above, colossal shapes descended. Harridan brood-organisms, the tyranid main dispersal form. Caen had read about them. But to see them, to see their size, smell their downwashed stink... it ruined his mind.

Swarms of winged bat-forms swirled out of them like drifts of fallen leaves billowing on the wind. The gargoyles filled the air, shrieking, targeting individual men, membranous wings beating. They executed steep, perilous dives, raking the ground beneath them with the flesh borers they clutched to their leathery torsos. Plasma fire rained down, shrivelling and igniting men as they ran for cover.

Caen pulled out his power-sword, and slashed at a gargoyle that swooped towards him. He split it into two, and was drenched in its stinking ichor.

He fell.

Rising, the ground shaking, he saw how the corrosive spore-mines were collapsing the superstructure of most of the landing ships. Bulk transports were sagging and melting as they lost integrity. Parts of some exploded outwards.

Things no bigger than a man scuttled forward through the burning darkness and confusion. Termagants and the larger, bounding hormagaunts. There were thousands of them, Caen realised. So many, so many...

He sliced at the alien filth that closed on him. He cut the snout off one termagaunt, the forelimb off another. He was distracted by a liquid scream as Hanff, running for cover nearby, was destroyed by mycetic spores, both necrotic and corrosive. A fat, bubbly slick punctuated by corroding bone mass was all that remained of him after thirty seconds.

The fleshborer hit Caen in the chest. He writhed and wailed as it quivered and dug and turned the contents of his body cavity into mush.

THE EVAC CONVOY was two hours out from 132/5 when they saw the change in weather patterns a hundred kilometres ahead. A dark stain, like a wash of thunderheads, was bruising the distance, widening with every passing moment.

From the cab of unit 177, Grauss saw the blue skies fill with dark-bellied clouds. His guts tightened. Around the black stain in the distance, the weather was being tormented in an ever-expanding radius. Frothing clouds whirled cyclonically like blast ripples from the ominous darkness. Drizzles of rain, thick with dingy fluid and what seemed like seed-pods, pelted down. The two kilometre-long convoy switched on their headlights almost as one, and wipers began to beat.

'What the hell is this?' asked Trooper Femlyn, riding shotgun next to Grauss, an autogun across his lap.

'Turn west! Turn west!' Colonel Tiegl's voice rattled over the inter-vehicle comm. The convoy, ungainly and slow to respond, shunted and churned as it tried to make the new heading.

The air was sweet and hot, Grauss realised. It smelled like the pumping station hot-house.

Two trucks overturned on the trackway, slumping into revets as they tried to turn. Another three broke axles and were stranded. Tiegl left them and their screaming occupants behind.

'Nacine Plain has gone!' he yelled into his vox-horn. 'Our only hope is the main hive at Malvo Height! Turn west!'

Grauss looked at his chart-plate. Malvo Height was a thousand kilometres away to the west. They'd never reach it. Never.

He put his foot down anyway.

GRIZMUND'S ARMOUR WAS running hard from the filth storm that expanded ever outwards from the Nacine Plain. All hope of reaching the evac convoy from 132/5 was gone. All hope was gone, period.

He turned his vehicles to meet the onrush. It was a slow business, because the torrential rain had turned the dry, stony fields to mud and tangles of vegetation were growing up out of it even as he watched. In the space of fifteen minutes a dry, arid upland had turned into a mossy, fern-filled swamp. Another hour, and it would be a thick, impenetrable jungle of creepers and moulds, spilling outwards and consuming the dry land.

Grizmund didn't have an hour, and would never see that floral conquest. His tank guns roared up into the dense packs of flying things that swooped from the staining sky. Burning, membranous creatures dropped to the ground or were annihilated in the air.

Then his tanks started to die. Advancing tides of biovore engines spat spore mines into them, blowing armour units apart or melting them with acid and poison. Overwhelming floods of hormagaunts and termagants skittered forward out of the deluge, completely burying some vehicles under their writhing numbers. The air pulsed with the psychic throb of the tyranid warriors, tall and hideous, as they advanced amidst the smaller monsters. Zoanthropes, glistening like great floating brains, their atrophied limbs clutched to themselves, hovered over the swarms and flashed out lances of energy that blew tanks asunder.

Grizmund saw the twisting, lashing shapes of raveners approaching, and shouted down from his turret for the gun layer and aimer to increase fire.

Then the carnifex was on them. Shrieking, it lacerated two nearby tanks and flicked them aside. The last thing Grizmund saw was mouth of the venom cannon it raised towards his vehicle.

THE EVAC CONVOY from collective 132/5 was running west, hard, turbines roaring. They'd laboriously crossed a network of interfarm trackways and finally made it onto a metalled highway running east-west, the main overland arterial route used by the produce road-trains every harvest season to ship grain to the world hive at Malvo Heights. They were kicking dust in a trail four kilometres long from the dry white roadway, passing irrigation canals and wide, flooded field-basins lined with rows of growing frames. Then the rain caught up with them again, washing out the dust, glistening the roadway, until they were kicking up spray instead.

South of them, the sky was pale and blue; north, black and oily like pitch, a swirling, expanding bolus of dark cloud that blotted out the light.

Femlyn was rechecking his autogun's drum magazine. Keeping one hand on the steering wheel, Grauss pulled out his laspistol and tossed it to Femlyn.

'Check it,' he ordered. 'My rifle too.'

The wipers were thumping hard. Wind blew spume up over the road from the waterbeds like ocean spray. Grauss tried not to notice the wriggling black spores that were hitting the windshield and conglomerating like pus in his wipers.

Through the driving rain, he saw the braking lights of the truck in front come on suddenly, and slammed on his own brakes. Rig 177 slid violently from side to side on the wet road. Femlyn cried out and Grauss hauled on the wheel. They stopped hard, clipping the rear bars of the truck ahead.

The inter-cab vox was crackling with shouts. Grauss opened his door, about to get out, peering ahead to identify the obstruction.

Something came off the back of the truck ahead of them and landed on the bonnet of 177, denting the metal. It crouched there, for what was probably only a second but felt like an eternity, the rain dribbling down over its bared, smiling teeth.

Femlyn threw Grauss his laspistol, and Grauss fired it wildly. His salvo burst the termagant's neck open in a fountain of noxious fluid and it crumpled off the bonnet.

Settlers were streaming back down the road past them in blind panic.

The truck ahead started again, wheels spinning, drove ten metres and then plunged sideways off the road, rolling down the levee into the water-bed. Grauss saw four termagants scampering towards him. He stood on the throttle. Two of them were crushed under the heavy truck, another slammed away through the air after contact with the wheel arch.

Femlyn was firing out of the cab window. Shell cases tumbled down into the footwell.

The convoy ahead was now moving, though several trucks had slewed off the road and one was burning. Grauss had to drop speed to inch past them. Something grotesque and grinning appeared at the cab window beside Grauss and he dropped forward, allowing Femlyn to blast it through the glass.

A smaller vehicle drew level with them, matching their speed. It was one of the open, short wheel-base escorts mounting a Hydra battery. Grauss waved the driver past and then fell in behind. A moment later, the Hydra battery was pounding, firing directly ahead of the speeding machine. Grauss saw something big and iridescent explode under the anti-aircraft fire and collapse off the road. 177's wheels span in the ichor slick as they sped past.

Behind them, on the highway, the racing convoy was assailed by things that poured up out of the fields and irrigation channels to the north and into their hindquarters. The escort vehicles, mounting Hydras and heavy stub-guns, ran alongside the transports, raking the fields. Mantis killers reared and clacked their talons, disintegrating in drizzles of mucus and chitin as the guns found them. Swarming termagants were smashed under speeding wheels. Hit by multiple fleshborers, a Hydra truck span out of control and flew off the road, exploding in a drain canal. Biovore spore mines crumped down, blowing two of the fast-moving transports into fragments.

There were bat-shapes in the air above.

The convoy's heavier armour – four Chimeras and a half dozen standard-pattern Leman Russ tanks in Mordian camo, were lagging badly, and found themselves cut off from the fleeing convoy elements.

Hormagaunts overran two of the Chimeras, covering their hulls with squirming shapes as they opened them like seed cases. Two of the tanks stopped dead, traversed their turrets and began pounding at the wave of obscenities that rippled after the convoy. The crews knew they were as good as dead. Mordian discipline made them sell their lives as dearly as they could. Spitting bio-plasma destroyed one tank. The other was struck by some energised flash that looked like green lightning, and blew apart as its munitions ignited.

Caught by a trio of lictors, another Chimera tried to turn and was thrown end over end, torn track sections flying. Corrosive spores reduced another of the Leman Russes to tar and semi-solid lumps.

Standing in the back of a speeding escort truck, Colonel Tiegl manned the gun mount himself. Searing, frenzied, red tendrils had just turned his main gunner inside out. He swung the stub-gun on its pintle, squeezing the firing grip, spraying the road behind him with twin, dipping, dragging streams of heavy fire. He was drenched with rain.

There was something in his mouth, something crawling on his skin. Mycetic spores plastered him, eating him away.

By the time his driver fell to a barb-round and spun the vehicle into a transport's back wheels with splintering force, there was nothing left of Tiegl but some articulated limb bones dragging from the gun-grip.

TEN KILOMETRES ON, out of the irrigated arable spread and into the lowlands beyond, evac 132/5 found there was no going forward. The convoy was a ragged mess. The black, weeping sky had utterly overtaken what remained of the column and the tide of horror was upon them.

Femlyn was blasting from the cab window with his autogun, and Grauss was firing his lasrifle out the other side. There was no shifting truck 177 now. Vines, thorn-creepers and other fast-growing things had meshed the axles and ruptured the tyres.

'Look! Look!' cried Femlyn.

There were dots in the sky, burning dots that fast resolved themselves into drop-pods flaring in atmospheric entry. A dozen, two dozen, three.

'Oh, praise the Emperor!' Grauss breathed.

The first pods hit the ground, bouncing and tearing through the cushion of foliage.

Grauss saw the men clamber out. Adeptus Astartes. Space Marines, the Lamenters. They had come, as promised, yellow armour gleaming in the dying light. They had come despite the odds.

The giant armoured warriors, humanity's finest, deployed from their pods, blasting with boltguns, flamers and meltas. Termagants and hormagaunts exploded beneath the withering firepower. Flamers burned the stinking plant growth away. Gargoyles were blown, ruptured, out of the sky. Grauss saw a ravener convulse and die under a melta's kiss. He saw plasma-fire destroy a mantis killer.

There, a Marine with a power claw ripped a tyranid warrior in two, the corpse exploding with bile and psychic energy. Here, a Marine with a rocket launcher sent up a jinking missile that blew a zoanthrope into flaring specks of matter.

Grauss leapt from the truck's cab and ran into the fray, his lasgun blasting. Mordian troopers were with him now, enervated by the Lamenters' swinging assault. Grauss cut down a leaping termagaunt in mid-air, blowing it apart. He saw four Marines cripple and kill a lictor nearby.

We could live, we could live yet, he thought triumphantly!

He heard a keening behind him, and turned to face the horror of a carnifex charging, blades clicking, saliva flying from the cutting limbs. Femlyn tried to turn his autogun but became nothing more than a shower of meat.

A lamenter, two of them, hit the screamer-killer from the left side with bolt rounds, and as it turned, destroying its head with melta-fire. Its scything blades, still whickering lethally as it toppled, decapitated them both.

Grauss fell to his knees. He honestly didn't think it possible that Space Marines could die. They seemed to him invulnerable, god-like, the walking manifestations of the God-Emperor of Terra himself. But it was true. He looked down at the fallen, splintered helm of one Marine, the glassy, dull, dead face peering out of it.

He looked away, but saw another Lamenter ripped in two by a mantis killer fifty meters away. A ravener fell, twisting and flicking, onto three more and ground them into the soil, ripping open their armour with its chitinous mouth-parts.

Then Grauss saw the worst sight of all, the worst, most unmanning thing his eyes had ever witnessed. Four Lamenter Space Marines: falling back, overwhelmed.

They scrambled through the treacherous, matted ground-growth, trying to find cover from the zoanthrope that shimmered after them, spitting bolts of energised death. They turned, fired, ran on, to no avail. The hovering thing exploded one of them and then closed on the other three. One headed left and ran onto the keening bone-swords of a tyranid warrior. Another was felled by a glancing blast from the zoanthrope and was swiftly torn apart by a pack of termagants.

The last made it another twenty metres before the relentless zoanthrope hit him and exploded his armoured form with a vicious stab of energy.

Grauss couldn't believe was he was seeing.

In the first twenty minutes from drop, the Lamenters had cut a hole in the alien assault that had punished them cruelly. Now, in just five more minutes, they were being annihilated.

A spore mine from a biovore blew two more apart and sent a wash of mud and sap high into the air.

Two Lamenters faced down another carnifex and blew it apart with sustained bolt fire. A second later, they were both dismembered by hormagaunts before they could reload.

Grauss saw the hive tyrant advancing through the flaming greenery, slaughtering Space Marines with its massive blade. He saw the vast, obscene shapes of the bio-titans lurching forward in the distant smog.

The last Lamenter died thirty-nine minutes after the first had clambered from his drop-pod.

The convoy was ablaze, what parts of it weren't shredded or swarmed over.

Grauss dropped into a foxhole, feeling the undergrowth flourish and twist around him. His body was crawling with parasitic infection. He heard chattering.

On the horizon line, most nightmarish of all, the vile ripper swarms were moving in, consuming everything in their path, eating up the world.

Karl Grauss made his peace with the God-Emperor, with his long dead parents, with his long-lost homeworld, beloved, distant Mordia, praying it would never suffer this blasphemous fate.

He put the snout of his lasgun in his open mouth.

CHILDREN OF THE EMPEROR

Barrington J Bayley

HOARSE SCREAMS AND the screech of tortured hot metal filled the air. Massive laser blasts were punching into the spaceship. They superheated the air that men breathed, set fire to everything that could burn and sent fireballs exploding through the crowded passageways.

Imperial Guardsman Floscan Hartoum found himself in a crowd of jostling, panicking men. Minutes before, the men of the Aurelian IXth regiment had been ordered to the armoury to collect their lasguns and short-swords in case the enemy should manage to teleport aboard. They would never reach the armoury now. The crippled troopship *Emperor's Vengeance* was in a state of absolute chaos. Suddenly a great howl of collective terror rose up. Down the corridor a glowing, writhing red mass had appeared, rolling down the passageway towards them.

Like the others, Floscan turned and ran. He had been at the back of the crowd; now he was at the front. Pushed from behind, he fell, then managed to get his legs under him and leaped. Behind him he heard an automatic emergency bulkhead descend with a thump.

Staggering to his feet, he found that he was alone in an empty section of corridor. He had been the only one to slither under the bulkhead as it came down. Everyone else was trapped on the other side. Floscan stood, shaking, hearing the fireball slam against the steel partition, accompanied by the agonised shrieks of his comrades who were being incinerated. He pressed his hands to his ears to shut out the cries.

The *Emperor's Vengeance* was old, centuries old. Guardsman Hartoum firmly believed that only the holy rituals carried out daily by the ship's priests kept it in one piece. But it was meticulously tended. The burnished metal ribs of the arch-roofed passageway gleamed. Effigies and efficacious runes, etched at various times by mechanics and priests, adorned the walls. But right now Floscan was blind to all this. The dying screams of his comrades fading behind him, he stumbled to an oval porthole set in a brass surround, and stared blindly out.

He was looking into the star-strewn blackness of space. Unknown miles away, the sharp outlines of the attacking ships were visible. Even at this distance they were an extraordinary sight, a motley collection had set, of mongrelised and ramshackle craft, looking for all the galaxy as though they had each been constructed from two or three spacecraft crudely welded together. They had set upon the flotilla of troop transports, clumsy barges only lightly armed, as it emerged from the warp to take its bearings. The result was utter carnage. The makeshift character of the ships identi-fied their crews as orks, who did not build spacecraft themselves but used whatever they could capture or scavenge from other races. How they must have roared with savage delight to see units of the Imperial Navy materi-alise unsuspectingly before them!

Now the flotilla's escorting battlecruiser *Glorious Redeemer* hove into view, a massive structure with baroque, gargoyle-encrusted spires and weapons turrets which were gouting plasma as it attempted to defend the troopships. But it was heavily out-gunned and had been taken by surprise. Half a dozen ork ships had surrounded it and their armament was tearing it to pieces, great crenellated chunks spinning off into space.

From another of the ork craft something came flimmering. It was fol-lowed by a juddering shock that went right through the vitals of the *Emperor's Vengeance* with a roaring noise. The passageway buckled. From all around came the cacophony of a ship breaking up. They had been hit by a plasma torpedo!

'ABANDON SHIP! ABANDON SHIP!'

The order crackled through the antique ceiling speakers. Guardsman Hartoum however, needed no prompting. He was already dashing for the nearest escape pods, scrambling over the newly-made folds and rents in the floor.

'Belay that order, Guardsman! Fight to the end against the vile enemies of the Emperor!'

Floscan pulled up sharp. An intimidating figure in a black, square-shouldered longcoat was standing stiffly at the corridor's next bend. It was the commissar, Leminkanen. The grim expression beneath his peaked cap was nothing new. He wore it all the time, but especially during the fanati-cal morale-boosting lectures Floscan had been required to attend.

The order to abandon ship had come from the captain. Floscan had no idea who ranked higher in this situation, captain or commissar, but he did know that if he obeyed the latter he was unlikely to still be alive one minute from now. Instinctively he moved to the nearby pod.

'You will not run in the face of the enemy, Guardsman. Where is your lasgun?'

The last words were drowned out by an enormous squealing of metal being torn apart, followed by the terrifying hiss of air escaping from the ruptured hull. A lasgun suddenly appeared in the Commissar Leminkanen's hand. Its lethal beam zipped past Hartoum's ear as he hurled himself into the lifepod, in the same motion striking the rune-encrusted button that closed the hermetic seal. His hand trembling with panic, he pulled the lever to eject.

Fragments rattled against the pod as it rocketed away from the disintegrating troopship. The fierce acceleration drained the blood from Floscan's brain and he blacked out.

WHEN HE CAME TO, the total silence of the pod's close confines, in which there was barely room to move, was frightening. Even the sound of Floscan's breathing seemed unnaturally loud. He dragged himself to the tiny porthole and peered out.

If there was anything to be seen at all, it consisted of spread wreckage which occasionally drifted between himself and the stars, making them twinkle. The flotilla was destroyed, and with it the Aurelian IXth Regiment. Of the ork ships there was no sign.

Guardsman Hartoum fell back on the pod's couch, unable to bear the devastating sight.

Aurelia, where Floscan had been raised, was an agricultural world. He had joined the founding Imperial Guard regiment voluntarily, hoping for challenge and adventure. Now that he had found them, he was wishing for his quiet life back on the farm. He firmly believed in the Emperor, of course, but now he was beyond even His help. He was alone, and lost. Rescue was impossible. The navy would not even know where the flotilla had emerged from the warp. The pod would keep him alive for a few days, and then…

It would have been better to have died alongside his comrades.

Overcome with despair and even shame at his escape, Floscan buried his face in his hands and sobbed for a while. Then he took a grip on himself. He was an Imperial Guardsmen, he told himself. The Emperor would expect him to keep up his courage, no matter how bad things became. He steeled himself to face death calmly. Eventually, some dread curiosity drew him back to the porthole. He felt compelled to look again into the void which was to be his grave. When he did, he gasped, his jaw hanging.

There was a planet below him.

FLOSCAN HARTOUM'S HEART was beating wildly, thoughts racing through his brain. The planet might have a poisonous atmosphere; it might hold deadly horrors – or it might offer a chance of survival, though he would be marooned for life. It was beautiful, too, with dazzling blue oceans and shining white clouds.

The pod could already be falling towards the planet, or it could be in orbit around it, but most likely it was on a course that would take it out of range and unable to reach the shining world. Hartoum would have to act quickly. He studied the simple controls. Escape pods were manufactured cheaply, in huge numbers, and were best described as crude. Floscan's training in their use had lasted less than twenty minutes, and he barely knew what to do. Luckily, there was little to understand. There were none of the glowing icons and shining runes that would have embellished more sophisticated equipment. Instead there was, included in the moulding of the control panel, a simple prayer to the Emperor:

Fotens Terribilitas, adjuva me in extremis!
Mighty Terribilitas, aid me in my plight!

Fervently muttering the prayer, he took hold of the control levers. The gyro whined, rotating the pod to point its snub nose at the luminous world. The small rocket engine fired again, drawing on the scant amount of fuel. Floscan was sent hurtling into the planet's atmosphere.

Despite it being his only way to see outside, Floscan dogged down the porthole's cover once the buffeting began. He wasn't sure the glassite would be able to withstand the heat that would be generated by the friction of the atmosphere.

The rocket engine had soon ran out of fuel and was silent. Escape pods were supposed to be able to land on a planet automatically, but like everything else about them the arrangements were rudimentary at best, escape for defeated Guardsmen was scarcely high on the Imperium's list of priorities, and Floscan began to feel there was something wrong. Strapped into the acceleration couch, he was being spun around wildly, tossed up and down and jerked from side to side. It was getting very hot, too, making him wish he had cut off the rocket engine sooner. He had hit the atmosphere at too high a speed. The pod's outer layer was supposed to absorb heat and then shed it by peeling away in fragments, but how thick was it? When it was all gone he would be roasted alive. So violent became the descent that Floscan passed out again.

When he next opened his eyes, he did not know how much later, everything had become still. A breeze was on his face. He could hear a distant chirruping sound, as of unknown animal calls.

He had landed.

The acceleration couch had been torn from its moorings and his face had struck the control panel. He threw off the restraint straps and felt his aching cheek. It was bleeding. Automatically he consulted the survival meter under the mangled panel. It told him that the planet had a breathable atmosphere but then he already knew that, because he was already breathing the local air. Evidently the pod had cracked open on impact. He could see daylight through the gaping rent.

His limbs seemed to be made of lead and he was finding it difficult to move, making him fearful of having internal injuries. Several times he struck the rune-inscribed button that should have opened the hatch, but it was stuck. Then he tried to undo the hatch manually. The frame was warped and he was unable to shift it.

Finally, panting with effort, he attacked the rent in the pod's side, placing his feet on one edge and bracing his back against a stanchion. The surprisingly thin shell of the pod moved, making a gap large enough for him to squeeze through.

He tried to stand up and found that he couldn't. He had no internal injuries. It was simply that his body weighed three or four times more than it normally would. He was on a heavy gravity planet. How could he survive if he couldn't even stand up? Guardsman Hartoum struggled to come to his feet. Using his arms, he managed to push himself to a squatting position. Then he heaved with all the strength he could muster in his legs, until he thought the blood vessels would burst.

'God-Emperor, aid me!' Grimacing with effort, Floscan came upright, shaking, feeling the gravity drain him of muscle power and try to drag him down. How long could he maintain himself like this?

He looked around him. The sky was a shining, metallic blue-grey, casting the landscape in a sinister glow. The terrain consisted of rocky crags and low hills to which clung shrub-like trees and crimson reeds. Altogether it was a dismal, depressing environment, over which there seemed to hang a feeling of menace.

The escape pod had cracked open on striking a rocky outcropping. Thick white parachute cords straggled from it but the parachute itself had been torn off sometime during the descent, though presumably not far from the surface or the impact would have killed him.

A stiff cold wind was blowing making Floscan shiver. Grey clouds raced overhead. He felt dizzy, whether from the blow to his head or because the heavy gravity made it difficult for blood to reach his brain he did not know. And he felt frightened, filled with foreboding. It was hard to believe that only yesterday he had been cursing the monotony of the space journey to an equally unexciting posting.

He was about to sit down again and rest when a hoarse shout made him turn round. He was standing at one end of a shallow valley. Charging along it towards him was a troop of about twenty men. They were massively muscled, evidently well adapted to the heavy gravity, with shaggy hair which streamed behind them in the wind. Some brandished spears, others raised bows and were whipping arrows from quivers strapped to their backs. And. they were heading straight towards him.

Death now seemed both certain and sudden, and all of Guardsman Floscan Hartoum's gloom and uncertainty cleared from his mind. He was defenceless; escape pods carried no lasguns, which were too expensive to waste on men with little or no chance of survival. He doubted if he could run at all, let alone outdistance his pursuers, and if he took refuge in the pod he would only be left trapped like an animal.

He took a deep breath. Best take it like a soldier of the Aurelian IXth. He would go down fighting with his bare hands. But perhaps there was better than that. A flung spear clattered on the rock to his left. He managed to take a few steps, squatted down and lifted the thick wooden shaft off the ground. It was incredibly heavy in his hands, but somehow he heaved himself erect once more and turned to face the enemy, the spear-point held before him. If he could take just one of the attackers with him, he would have died with honour.

Another spear came hurtling by, together with a flock of arrows, but the aim was poor and all missed him by a wide berth. There seemed to be something strange about the oncoming natives' gait. As they came close enough for him to make them out clearly, he saw that he had been mistaken about them.

They were not men at all, they were four-footed aliens! Seen from the front they looked human enough, clad as they were in short smocks of coarse cloth belted at the waist, but from the side or the rear it was a different matter entirely. The lower back and rump were sloped and extended, and were supported by a second pair of legs. These were just like the front legs except that they were shorter, almost stubby. Both pairs seemed to work in unison, so that the creatures ran with a swift but swaying gait.

The strange spectacle startled Floscan. The induction address at his regiment's Founding flashed through his mind: 'You will be fighting aliens, mutants, monsters, heretics, all things abominable to the Emperor!' Now he was to die in fulfilment of those words!

But instead of rushing straight at him, the troop thundered past. It was charging, not at Floscan, but at something else. Floscan turned to look – and dropped his spear, paralysed with shock.

The quadruped aliens had been shouting warnings, not threats. The valley ended in a craggy hill, like many littering the broken landscape. Emerging over the brow was a monster combination of lobster, crab and armoured centipede – but of stupendous size. It almost covered the hill over which it was clambering, its bossed shell scraping on the rock, hissing sounds issuing from its oscillating mouth parts. As it descended, a giant claw reached out to seize the escape pod, crushing it like an eggshell before dropping it again.

The same claw reached for Floscan. He staggered back, struggling to maintain his footing. Yelling battle-cries, the natives sent spears and arrows clattering against the shiny carapace. They were aiming at the monster's soft parts: waving eyestalks and the broad, dripping mouth that could have taken them all in one go. Stone axes hacked at the claw that was about to pick up Floscan. Chitin splintered, purple ichor flowed and gouted, the limb was severed and lay twitching.

It was incredible to Floscan that the natives would take on this gigantic, fearsome beast with their primitive weapons. And yet they were winning. Two staring golden eyes were transfixed by arrows, a third by a spear. Hissing and screeching, the monster retreated and crawled back over the hill to whoops of victory from the four-footed warriors.

Now their attention turned to Floscan. The leader, a fierce-looking individual with fiery red hair and beard, pointed to him and bellowed an order in a guttural, unintelligible language. A second quadruped dashed forward and seized Floscan, flinging him violently across his well-muscled, smock-covered back and holding him there in a vice-like grip. The whole troop turned and raced back the way it had come, knocking the breath out of Floscan with every pace.

Once again he had been snatched from the jaws of death. Once again, most likely, to face something worse. He was in the hands of aliens.

ONCE THROUGH THE valley, Floscan managed to raise his head and was able to see just how strange and dangerous a world he had come into. It was a nightmare world with its glaring sky, tumbled landscape and gigantic lifeforms. The crab-centipede monstrosities seemed to be everywhere, ambling aimlessly in search of food. The quadrupeds managed to avoid them, but apparently there were more terrifying threats to their existence. They slowed before they had got very far, spreading out and jinking nervously.

Floscan spotted what he thought at first was a factory smokestack rearing high in the air in the distance, such as might be seen in Aurelia's industrial zone. It even belched smoke, or perhaps it was steam, and gave off vague hooting sounds. But it was not a factory chimney. It was alive. It was flexible. And it was bending over, its reeking mouth swooping across the terrain towards the troop. The quadrupeds scattered, taking cover in rock crevices. From there Floscan watched in fascination. Briefly he saw a ring of eyes around the 'chimney's' circular rim as it picked off a crab-centipede. The monster was sucked struggling into the tube as it whipped upright once more, presumably to be drawn into an enormous stomach.

Cautiously the quadrupeds set off once more. Once out of reach of the stack-beast they sought high ground. Floscan was puzzled as to why they would expose themselves so, but from the vantage point of a craggy ridge he got the answer. The low ground was dotted with a terrifying type of plant-like animal: a house-sized bulb, vaguely resembling a cactus, from which spread dozens of wriggling, searching tentacles, radiating in every direction. Any edible animal they found was whipped back to be devoured.

A quadruped, or anything roughly the size of a man, would have stood no chance trying to cross that deadly network. Floscan's mind whirled. Just how many alien horrors did this planet have to offer? Suddenly the quadrupeds seemed out of place, as if they did not really belong here. They were like hapless insects, ready to be picked off by a host of larger creatures.

But he could think no more, only concentrate on the agony of his rough ride on the back of the native. Though he dreaded what awaited him, it was almost a relief when the quadrupeds' village came in sight. It was fortified with a twenty foot tall hedge bristling with thorns and sharpened stakes. At a shouted signal, a section of hedge was dragged inward allowing them to enter.

The scene within was tumultuous, a throng of four-footed aliens surging among huts thatched with crimson reeds. A blazing fire burned in the centre of the compound, some sort of animal roasting over it on a spit. Floscan was tossed from his carrier and set on his feet, again struggling to stand against the dragging gravity.

Great excitement greeted his arrival. The natives jostled with one another, rearing on their hind legs and uttering exultant cries. Hands grabbed Floscan and pulled him towards the fire. He shrank back, his face slack. Terror coursed through his every nerve. He was destined for the spit! He lost control of himself and began struggling desperately as the flames scorched his face.

Suddenly he was released. A chunk of smoking cooked meat, torn from the roasting carcass, was thrust into his hand. For all the ecstasy of relief he felt, Guardsman Floscan Hartoum discovered that he was hungry. He sniffed the meat. It smelled good. He bit, chewed, then began to eat ravenously. The aliens cheered. While he satisfied his hunger, Floscan glanced from side to side. What was in their minds? Were they toying with him, treating him well, before killing him? He had heard that primitive tribes did that.

How strangely human these aliens looked, if one did not look below the waist. True, they were of fierce appearance, and were very broad-set. Floscan, who thought of himself as a burly youth, felt positively slim beside them. And of course he was weak as a child compared with their rippling muscles.

As he swallowed the last fragment of meat, the natives suddenly fell silent. Their ranks parted to allow the passage of one who had emerged from a nearby hut. He walked slowly and with dignity on his four legs. His face was craggy with age, and his hair and beard were white.

He halted before Floscan, regarding him with steady eyes. Then, to the Guardsman's total surprise, he spoke, not in the unintelligible local speech Floscan had heard earlier, but in a strangled version of Imperial

Gothic, so that he had to repeat his question twice before he made himself understood.

'Have you come to us from the Emperor?'

Floscan blinked. How could these primitives on an out-of-the-way planet speak Imperial Gothic and know of the God-Emperor? Aware that his life might well depend on his reply, he thought for a moment and then spoke in a clear voice. 'Yes! I am a warrior of the Emperor!'

The elder was clearly not impressed by these words. He looked Floscan up and down. 'You? Warrior? Warrior has weapons. Where are yours?'

Too late, Floscan realised he hardly counted as a fighting man by these natives' standards. He waved his arms defiantly and became theatrical. 'The Emperor sent me through the sky to fight his enemies. I was cast down to this land… but lost my weapons.'

'Then you were defeated,' the aged quadruped grunted. He beckoned. 'Follow.'

He turned and walked with his ambling gait back to the hut. Floscan tried to follow, but after only a few steps needed to be helped by another quadruped who put out a beefy hand to support him.

Inside the hut the elder gestured to a reed pallet on the floor. 'More comfortable lying down.'

Thankfully Floscan lowered himself to a sitting position. The old alien did likewise, folding both pairs of legs under him. 'I am Ochtar, the Remembering One of our tribe. My duty is to remember the ancient histories, make sure they are not forgotten.' Floscan could understand his thick accent a little better now. But the next words left him dumbfounded. 'Do you bring us a message from the Emperor? Is he going to take us into the Imperium and make us his children?'

To Guardsman Hartoum such an idea was not only bizarre and sinister, it was also impossible. He had been raised in the Imperial cult, and his childhood beliefs had been given additional fire during his short time in the Imperial Guard. Already the Aurelian IXth regiment had helped in the extermination of an alien race who for a while had shared their world with human colonists. Humans could not be expected to live indefinitely on a contaminated planet. He was grateful to the aliens for saving his life, but they were aliens.

'It is the Imperium of Man, no?' Ochtar insisted, when Floscan failed to answer. 'We are men.'

Floscan looked at the animal-like appearance of Ochtar's lower body. 'Men have two legs!' he burst out without thinking. 'You have four!'

Ochtar sprang to his feet, glaring angrily. 'We are humans with four legs!' Seeing that he had frightened Floscan he calmed down and seated himself again. 'Forgive my anger, Emissary. It is right that you should probe and question. Let me explain. Our ancestors were like you – two legs. Like you, they travelled the sky, searching for new worlds on which to live. Instead, they crashed here and became stranded. That was many, many years ago.

'You have seen what sort of world this is. Where you come from, objects do not weigh very much and one needs only two legs to stand up. Here, everything is heavy. Not only that, but our world is hostile to human life. The ancients who crashed here realised that they would not survive long. But they had powerful magic, and they used this to give their children four legs so that they could stand up. And they gave them stronger muscles so that they could fend for themselves. By this means, our people have conquered adversity and have lived for countless generations, even though we have lost the ancient magic. Surely the Emperor will be pleased with us, and bring us into his family?'

Floscan thought hard. If there was any truth in this tale then the quadrupeds' ancestors would have come from Mars. whose tech-priests sent countless ships out into the galaxy during the Dark Age. And yes, they would have had the ability to alter genes in the way Ochtar described as 'magic'. But the tale was wildly improbable. 'How did you learn the Imperial language?' Floscan asked. 'How do you even know of the Emperor?'

'You are not the first two-legs to come here recently. Magson came. He wanted gemstones. In return, he gave us this. Try it on. It will help you.'

Ochtar stood and drew aside a curtain. He brought out something made of a rubbery material. Floscan's eyes widened when he saw it. It was a heavy-gravity suit, designed to make life tolerable on just such a planet as this.

'Magson stayed long enough for me to learn his language,' Ochtar continued. 'He told us about the Imperium, and about the Emperor who is our God. All our legends were confirmed! We entrusted him with a petition to the Emperor, asking for his rule and guidance. That was years ago. Since then, we have been waiting for you.'

From the sound of it, this Magson was a Free Trader. It was most unlikely he had even reported the existence of the quadrupeds to the authorities, let alone forwarded the petition to the Administratum on Terra. Usually such traders heeded no one but themselves.

Floscan guessed he had the explanation of Ochtar's claim to be human too. Ochtar was obviously highly intelligent – to have learned Imperial Gothic from a passing stranger was no mean feat. But he must have concocted the myth on hearing of the marvels of the Imperium, perhaps confusing the Imperial Cult with some tribal beliefs and so believing it himself.

'I can prove what I said,' Ochtar added then, as if reading his thoughts. 'I will take you to the holy shrine of our ancestors. We will travel at night, when it is safer. Put on the cloth that takes away weight.'

Floscan accepted the h-g suit Ochtar handed to him. Inspecting the runic icons on the shoulder tabs, he could see why the trader Magson had been so ready to trade it. The suit's power was low. Also it seemed to be damaged, no doubt ready to cut out at any time. Just the same, he pulled it on and immediately felt relief from the crippling gravity. He stood up, stretched and smiled.

His smile vanished as he remembered that he was going to have to spend the rest of his life here.

OCHTAR LEFT HIM alone to let him rest. Floscan spent the hours before darkness deep in thought. For about an hour he became very depressed, realising that he was never to see another human being again. Whatever life was left to him would have to be spent with these four-footed villagers. Without them, he had no chance of surviving at all.

Then, once again, he rallied, and became determined to see things through. Some said the Emperor watched over all that he thought was worthy of the title Guardsman. He would prove his mettle.

He was going to have to humour Ochtar for the time being. It was essential that the quadrupeds accepted him. For the time being, he switched off the h-g suit to conserve its power. Besides, he needed to build up his muscles; eventually he would need to withstand the dreadful gravity.

Night fell abruptly, like a curtain. Soon Ochtar returned and explained the journey that lay ahead. 'We are going to visit the Temple of the Ancient Relics,' he said. 'It is deserted now, and we shall have to travel with caution, for it lies within the territory of the enemy.'

'You have enemies?' Floscan replied curiously.

Ochtar nodded curtly. 'The worshippers of the evil God of Blood. Once they were our friends, but now...'

He would say no more, and Floscan turned on the h-g suit once more. Guards pulled the hedge-gate open. They crept out, Ochtar looking to the left and right.

Within the defensive circle of the hedge, the fire was kept burning at all times so that even at night the village had a cheerful look. Outside was an eerie darkness relieved by a dim, silvery light cast by massed stars, though the sky boasted no moons. Floscan soon learned that Ochtar's description 'safer' at night did not mean 'safe' when a living tangle of hooks and barbs the size of a small armoured vehicle flew at them. Ochtar proved himself a master spearman, despite his age. Instead of trying to evade the barbs he lunged straight at them and struck home. The raving mass jerked wildly from side to side, then slumped. He had penetrated the creature's tiny brain.

Ochtar brushed a dozen sharp hooks from his skin, ignoring the trickling blood. 'They wait around villages hoping to catch children who stray,' he said. 'They're not much to worry about.'

Ochtar knew his world well. He took Floscan on a wandering route that avoided the haunts of night predators, though Floscan shivered to hear a chaos of grumbling, hissing and clacking noises all around them. After a while he evidently became dissatisfied with his companion's progress, and invited him to climb onto his back. With Floscan clinging to him he set off at a tireless gallop, the great shaft of his spear resting on his shoulder. Eventually he slowed, setting Floscan on his feet again. From then on he proceeded carefully, sliding from cover to cover and looking carefully about him as he went.

They came at last to a natural amphitheatre. At its bottom, a ruined stone temple glittered faintly in the starlight. Its shape was hard to make out. There was a circle of broken pillars, and within it the remains of a round building which might once have been domed. It must have been thousands of years old.

Alert for any savage beast which might be using the temple as a lair, Ochtar approached carefully, but all was quiet. They stepped within lichen-covered walls. The roof had gone long ago. Light from the star-clouds streamed into the circular enclosure, revealing an unexpected, wondrous display.

Strange machines! Ochtar stood in silence, allowing Floscan to take in the wondrous view. This was indeed a holy place! Floscan felt as though he had been transported to the ancient, ancient past, to the Dark Age of Technology and the days of the Cult Mechanicus. Plainly the machines had once been arranged with reverence so that they could be worshipped as a sacred shrine, but now they were scattered across the ruined chamber, some of them smashed to pieces while others had simply fallen apart. A few, however, appeared to be still intact, matt black surfaces gleaming, rectangular display screens reflecting the starlight. They were like no machines Floscan was familiar with, and their purpose was a mystery, but there were plain signs that they were designed to be operated by humans, in the form of keyboards, knobs and slides.

'The ancient ones from the sky came to our world with these sacred objects,' Ochtar told him in a hushed tone. 'By these means they could work magic, though how we do not know.'

Presumably the quadrupeds had thought better than to reveal the shrine to the trader, Magson. He would certainly have wanted to take them away with him. They represented arcane sciences superior even to those of the present-day Imperium. The shrine-machines might even contain examples of Standard Template Construction, sought throughout inhabited space!

And all this meant that Ochtar's claim was true. The quadrupeds were of human stock! During the two campaigns in which he had served, Floscan had seen abhumans. He had seen ogryns and beastmen, degenerate forms of human of low intelligence. He could not help but compare them with the noble Ochtar. But for his weird lower limbs, he was much more human than they had been. Furthermore, the physical difference had been arranged by the arts of the ancient tech-priests, not left to the vagaries of evolution. Did they not, then, deserve the Emperor's recognition? Yes they did!

While these thoughts whirled through his brain, a drumming sound came to Floscan's ears. Ochtar heard it too. He capered round on all four legs, glaring, spear at the ready. 'Worshippers of the Blood God! We were seen, emissary! Hide yourself!'

A savage roar rose up all around them. Swarming down the slope of the amphitheatre was a spear-bearing, axe-waving mob of quadrupeds clad in shaggy animal skins or armour fashioned from the shells of the crab-monsters. On their heads were helmets consisting of the emptied carapaces of smaller armoured creatures, complete with claws – or, in some cases, what appeared to be human skulls!

By the silvery starlight Floscan saw all this clearly through the gaps in the temple wall. When the quadrupeds got closer he saw, even more clearly, why they could not be of Ochtar's tribe. Their faces were tattooed, transforming them into hideous masks. The good-natured ferocity of Ochtar's people was completely absent; instead were the bestial snarls, hate-filled grimaces and blood-curdling shrieks of those bent on wanton murder and destruction. Floscan shrank back at first, thinking to hide as he had been instructed, but when he saw the old Remembering One dash from the temple, apparently determined to defend the Emperor's emissary to the last, he could not help himself. He looked around for something to use as a weapon.

Now the attackers were within the circle of pillars. Ochtar thrust his spear into the chest of the first to reach him, bringing the savage down. Floscan grabbed up a piece of fallen masonry, hefting it despite its weight, and ran to his aid. Ochtar had his back to one of the pillars, surrounded and sorely pressed. Floscan did not think he could throw the rock – it would simply fall from his hand. He ran forward and struck with all his might against a crab-protected head, aiming for the exposed cheek bone. The quadruped merely staggered a little and turned to give Floscan a look of outrage. Sour-smelling breath washed over Floscan from a snarling, tattooed and scarred face. He glimpsed a stone axe flashing down towards his skull.

Then the axe was miraculously stayed; another warrior had deflected it. Instead, rough hands seized him. In that same moment, sheer weight of numbers overcame the struggling Ochtar, three spears lunging into him at once, his legs buckling, so that he was brought down like some magnificent animal by a yapping pack of predators. He turned piteous eyes to the struggling Floscan.

'Tell the Emperor… we are human…'

Then Floscan, held in a steely grip, was forced to watch in horror as with jubilant screeches the killers continued to hack and stab at the body of the Remembering One until it was nothing but a bloody mass.

Eventually, leaving off their gruesome work, they turned to stare inquisitively at Floscan. As well as their elaborate tattoos, each face bore intricate tribal scars, so that it was difficult to discern any human features at all. Floscan stared straight back at the devilish masks, clenching his fists. For the moment rage burned all the fear out of him. Ignorant savages had murdered a brave worshipper of the Emperor. If only he could deliver the full vengeance of the Imperial Guard on them!

Mocking laughter arose among the quadrupeds. Did they perhaps regard him as a two-legged cripple, an object of mirth?

While this went on, something else was afoot. Roaring warriors charged into the temple and began smashing the precious ancient relics. Others collected bundles of a dry, mossy material that grew nearby, piling it over the mysterious machines. A spark was struck from two fragments of stone, setting the floss alight. Soon the machines themselves were burning, with a brilliant white, seething flame, forcing everyone out of the temple. Suddenly there was a loud explosion and an enormous glare, bringing down the remains of the ruin and hurtling stone chunks into the crowd. Something amongst the machinery – perhaps long-dead fuel cells – had ignited.

This turn of events seemed to scare the raiders. Floscan was dragged roughly on to a quadruped's back and the whole pack set off with alarmed howls, scrambling up out of the amphitheatre and streaming into the darkness.

The ride did not last long. The alien sun was rising when the village of the tattooed four-legs came into sight. Like Ochtar's, it was protected by a high thorn hedge, a section of which was dragged inward to allow them to enter.

Set on his feet, Floscan stared around him in fascination. There seemed to be a pattern to the quadrupeds' settlements. Within the compound was the same circle of reed-thatched huts and a central fire. But here the atmosphere vibrated with savagery and violence. Fighting was a way of life; several brawls seemed to be happening at any one time.

Except for females and the young, all faces were scarred and tattooed. Floscan's eyes were drawn to a huge totem pole towering over the huts near the central fire. Carved on it was a huge, crimson, maniacally glaring face, eyes bulging, teeth bared, seeming to radiate a lust for death and battle. The Blood God.

Floscan was dragged into a nearby hut and tied by his hands to a rough wooden post. After his captors left, and his eyes grew accustomed to the gloom, he realised that he was not alone. A second prisoner was slumped on the ground, tied to a wooden post wearing a thick black greatcoat.

It was Commissar Leminkanen!

FOR ALL HIS hunched dishevelled state, crushed as he was by the excessive gravity, Commissar Leminkanen was still formidable. His glinting, steely gaze directed itself at Floscan from beneath his peaked cap. Floscan realised that the heavy gravity suit hid his uniform.

'I am Guardsman Hartoum, commissar, from the *Emperor's Vengeance,*' he said quickly.

'Did you desert your post, Guardsman?' Leminkanen accused in a grating voice. Then, not waiting for an answer, he added, 'I, too, was on that ship. The last thing I remember is when the torpedo struck us. Someone must have put me in an escape pod. I was already falling through the atmosphere when I regained my senses – with my laspistol missing from its holster! Do you have yours, guardsman?'

It was a relief to Floscan that the commissar did not remember trying to 'absolve' a panicking trooper by executing him in the transport ship's last moments. 'No, commissar. I am unarmed.'

Leminkanen grunted. The commissar seemed eager to explain his presence on the planet. Could he have thrown himself into an escape pod out of self-preservation, just as Floscan had? But then he would still have his laspistol... unless the quadrupeds had taken it from him... in which case they would have searched Floscan for one too. So he had to be telling the truth. Floscan felt ashamed to have doubted him.

Leminkanen was frowning at him, perhaps puzzled to see him in an h-g suit. 'Did anyone but ourselves escape the battle?' he asked sharply.

Floscan shook his head. 'Not as far as I know The entire flotilla was destroyed. The Aurelian IXth is gone!' A sob came into his voice. 'I may be the only one left! And no one even knows where in space we came out of the warp...'

'You are an ignorant young fool, Guardsman. We are deep inside a planetary system! Ships cannot emerge from the warp this close to a star, except by means of a known and charted warp gate. The navy will be here to investigate when the flotilla fails to arrive. Not that you or I will benefit from it. We are in the hands of aliens, of the most savage and perverted type. In the next few hours they will torture us to death. You are lucky to have me with you. I will help you face the end with fortitude, keeping your faith in the Emperor.'

Floscan gulped, impressed though he was by Leminkanen's steadfastness. 'Are you sure, commissar?' he whispered.

'Of course I am sure! Have you seen that totem outside? I have seen that same image on half a dozen worlds. It is the emblem of a Chaos god, the god of slaughter and destruction. These aliens are its devotees.'

'The Blood God,' Floscan murmured. 'That's what they call it.'

'Then you have heard of it too. Yes, the Blood God! That's what it is called, all across the galaxy.'

'But surely the Emperor is the only true god?' Floscan had heard stories about the Chaos gods on Aurelia, but he had taken them to be fanciful superstitions. The commissar's words sounded strange to him.

'The Emperor is the only true god, but the Chaos gods are real, too,' Leminkanen assured him. 'They oppose the Emperor, and are responsible for every evil and depravity. Here we have two enemies of the Emperor together – aliens and a Chaos god!'

Floscan could not contain himself. 'These people are not aliens, commissar – they are human!' he cried out. 'And some of them worship the Emperor!' In a rush of words he related everything that had happened since he was deposited on the planet: his rescue from the crab-monster, the gift of the h-g suit, how Ochtar had proved his claim to be human. The commissar listened closely, growing more and more astounded.

'Standard Template?' he breathed in excitement. 'Are you sure it is all destroyed?'

'There can't be anything left after the fire and the explosion.'

'We shall see.'

Floscan was not really concerned with that. 'Will good tribes like Ochtar's be admitted into the Imperium?' he asked eagerly. 'After all, there are plenty of other abhumans.'

Leminkanen's voice rose in impassioned fury. 'How many times must I tell you that you are a fool, Guardsman; ogryns and the like are natural human types. A human being with four legs is an abomination! It is a mutant! And a mutant is a child of Chaos! It cannot be allowed to live!' His voice fell to an exhausted drone. 'It is a good thing we have discovered this. We must try to leave a record for the investigators. There is nothing here but twisted human mutation and the taint of Chaos. My report will recommend the cleansing of this entire planet.'

Floscan sank into an appalled silence. Had the quadrupeds been listed as aliens they would have been left alone – the Imperium could not exterminate every alien race in the galaxy, meritorious though that ideal was. But now he had doomed them to extinction!

The heavy gravity was clearly too much for Leminkanen. His frenzied speech seemed to have exhausted what was left of his strength. He fell into a fitful doze. Floscan was almost sorry he could not give him the h-g suit for a while.

The worshippers of the Blood God did not seem to be in any hurry. After several hours, the crude door opened and a bearded, tattooed quadruped, smelling like a goat and wearing a jerkin made from a bristling porcupine-like skin, entered and raised a bowl of water to Floscan's lips. Glancing at the sleeping commissar, he merely grunted and went out again.

The next time the door opened, a throng of leering, mocking faces crowded around the opening, then drew aside to reveal the result of the morning's work. It was a large oval container, shaped from clay. Floscan easily recognised it for what it was: an oven, able to take two men inside it. Beneath it was a fireplace already piled with wood. Jeering laughter greeted the look on Floscan's face as he stared at the thing.

He and the commissar were going to be baked alive.

The closing door shut out the horrid grimacing faces. Shortly it began to grow dark again. The brief day was ending, and outside it was growing quiet as the worshippers of the Blood God retired to their huts. Floscan could guess that the grisly death-rite, undoubtedly a sacrifice to their foul Blood God, was scheduled for the next day.

Leaning trembling against the post to which he was tied, he began thinking with terror of the excruciating death which was shortly to come upon him. Then he started thinking of his comrades of the Aurelian IXth who had suffered hardly less painful deaths on the *Emperor's Vengeance*. Some had been personal friends back in his home district of Aurelia.

He stopped shaking. Resolve formed in him. He owed a duty to his dead comrades, to his superior officer Commissar Leminkanen, and a debt of gratitude to Ochtar and his people. He had to change Leminkanen's mind about them. And above all, he wished to avoid the clay oven.

All day long Floscan had been working on his bonds, with little effect. Now an idea came to him. The h-g suit had metal ribs with squared off edges. He worked the braided cord to one of these and began to rub.

It was slow work, but in the end his patience was rewarded. The hut was in near darkness when he had worn down the cord enough so that he could break it. Finally he stood unfettered, and glanced at the sleeping form of Commissar Leminkanen. Briefly he considered trying to take the commissar with him, before realising that it would be impossible. Leminkanen's only hope – and it remained a faint one – was for Floscan to bring help.

He slipped from the hut, moving with the stealth of a shadow. As he had expected the village was sleeping, with sentinels posted atop the hedge fortification. But he spotted only two, and neither was looking his way. Floscan sidled to the hedge. The foot-long thorns made it perfectly easy to scale, and in moments he was over the top and down the other side. Crouching, he took stock. Tonight the sky was cloudy and few stars were visible. Of the terrain, there were only vague humps in the darkness. Still, he thought he could remember which way to go.

He pulled at one of the sharpened stakes which made the hedge bristle. It came out easily. Now he had a weapon. Silently, Imperial

Guardsman Hartoum loped off into the lightless unknown, intent on retrieving the honour of the Aurelian IXth.

ALL THAT NIGHT Floscan travelled, trying not to stray from his chosen direction, trying to suppress his fright. Clicking, buzzing, rattling noises sounded all around him. All too often he thought he felt a chill touch – a claw, a feeler, a rasp, a feathery antenna – causing him to lash out with the stake in a sidewise swipe or a jab with the point, often followed by the sound of something scuttling away. Dawn found him weary. Something else found him, too.

He first became aware of it as a sharp, acid smell. Then it charged from behind a rock to attack him. It was about twice the size of a horse, but in appearance like a cockroach whose head was a mass of razor-sharp sword blades sliding in and out with a scything sound, rubbing against one another. At their full extent they were as long as his stake.

He took a lesson from Ochtar. To retreat was death – therefore, attack! He ran at the animal, which in turn was scurrying towards him, eager to slice him to bits with its battery of blades. Go for the brain. Ochtar had taught him that too. A bubbling, whistling noise came from the creature as he pushed the stake in as hard as he could. Then it turned on its back, a dozen stubby legs waving in death agony.

As he withdrew the stake, from which a purple goo dripped, a sensation of irresistible weight seized him. He looked at the icons, and groaned. The h-g suit had lost power.

Floscan sank to his knees. Where was the village? The creature was but the first and smallest of the monsters that were likely to find him. Others would be gigantic, impossible to fight even with a fully functioning h-g suit. Abandoning the stake, he was reduced to crawling on all fours as his own weight settled on him, dragging him into a pit of despair. Soon even this was too much. He was forced to lie down and close his eyes in exhaustion.

The sound of a human voice awoke him with a start. A quadruped stood over him, clad in a cloth tunic, lacking facial scars and tattoos, and with no claw-bearing helmet. One of Ochtar's people! Floscan struggled to sit up. Had he made it out of the territory of the Blood God? Or were the Remembering One's tribe looking for him after he had failed to return?

'Ochtar is dead! Blood God! They have messenger from the Emperor! Going to kill him!' Floscan pleaded. Had Ochtar been the only one understand Imperial Gothic? Had he taught it to any of the others? The quadruped looked at him, frowning.

'Blood God? Emperor? Blood God kill Emperor?'

'Yes! Help Emperor!'

For the first time he noticed a large curved horn hanging from the four-leg's neck. The tribesmen raised it to his lips and blew a long, winding blast.

More warriors appeared among the crags and began making their way down to them. Floscan's guess seemed to have been correct: they were searching for Ochtar, and must already have been to the destroyed temple. The quadruped with the horn began bellowing commands, flinging out his arm in the direction Floscan had indicated. In moments a small horde was racing for the village of the Blood God. A hand came down, helping Floscan up and on to a sturdy back. Heart exulting, he hung on for all his worth – and realised that his limbs no longer seemed so heavy. Glancing at the h-g icons, he grinned. The suit's photoelectric stripes had been soaking up sunlight. The h-g field was re-energised!

For ferocity the assault on the village would have done the Imperial Guard credit. Taken by surprise, the devotees of the Blood God forayed through the gate at first, attempting to defend their settlement outside its bounds, but they were soon driven back. The attacking warriors swarmed up over the hedge and down into the compound, climbing it as Floscan had. He mounted it too and watched from the top as axes rose and fell, spears jabbed, blood flowed.

The Blood God's followers were fighting for their homes, fighting for their lives, fighting for their savage god, and they laid about them as if demented, their bestial roars filling the air. But Ochtar's people were fighting for a god, too – the Emperor! It was hard to say who would be the victor at this stage; it was as if the butchery would continue until there was almost no one left. Floscan chose his moment to drop into the compound and dodge his way to the prison hut near the newly-constructed oven, which he was glad to see had not been used yet.

In the dim interior, Leminkanen looked up at him in wonderment. He did not even speak as the Guardsman untied him and helped him to his feet, supporting his weight.

'We have been rescued, commissar!' Floscan yelled. 'By four-legged men who are loyal to the Emperor! Did I not tell you?'

Leminkanen's response was a look of sour disbelief and an emphatic shake of his head. Nevertheless, he allowed Floscan to guide him gingerly to the door.

There, an extraordinary sight met their eyes. The fighting had all but stopped. Something had wrapped itself around the village. It was like a millipede, many hundreds of paces long, which had coiled around the circular hedge-wall, though it overtopped it by nearly half its height again. From each of its countless segments sprouted a pair of tentacles tipped with eyes, lashing down into the compound to pick up defenders and attackers alike, whipping them over the hedge to be devoured.

Perhaps the smell of blood from the battle had attracted it. The spectacle seemed to send Leminkanen into a frenzy. He pushed Floscan away from him and staggered through the doorway, forcing himself to stand erect.

'I must make my report! Order the Exterminatus! Guardsman, if I am martyred you must deliver it into the right hands!'

From within his greatcoat he whipped out a flat grey plate with a keypad. It was his personal log. Feverishly he began typing, oblivious of what went on around him.

'Look out, commissar!' Floscan lunged to knock the commissar aside, but it was too late. A slithering tentacle had seized him, pinning his arms to his body.

With a barely heard gurgle, Leminkanen was gone.

Floscan snatched up the log-plate as it fell to the dusty ground, nimbly avoiding a flailing tentacle as he did so. By now the tribesmen were dealing with the millipede in their own fashion. They had set the hedge alight, but so intent was the beast on its feeding that it ignored the flames until it was too late. It, too, caught fire, writhing soundlessly, crushing huts in its agony while an indescribably foul smelling smoke filled the air.

Everything in the village was burning now, everything was being flattened as the blazing monster flexed and rolled, forcing villagers and invaders to flee as one for the exit or trample their way through the glowing cinders of the collapsing hedge, the battle forgotten. Floscan too was caught up in the stampeding rush.

Out in the open the two sides drew apart, glaring at one another. It was doubtful if they even remembered what they were fighting over, but they were ready to begin again.

Then a glinting movement high in the air made Floscan look up. His heart leaped. His prayer to the Emperor was answered. All around Floscan, four-legged men dropped to their knees. A large, shining metal shape was descending. It was an Imperial shuttle craft.

'THE AURELIAN IXTH's sole survivor handed this in, sir. It appears that Commissar Leminkanen was making his last report when he was killed.'

In his brass-ornamented cabin, Captain Gurtlieder, commander of the battleship *Ravenger*, took the commissar's data-slate from his officer's hand. He noticed that the log was not closed. Leminkanen had not even had time to finish the report or key in his code.

He tapped a key and began to read.

Emergency report by Commissar Lemuel Leminkanen LX/38974B on unnamed planet in Cluster FR/7891 in vicinity of Warp Gate 492.

This planet is of no value to the Imperium. It is a feral world of the most extreme violence and would be very difficult to colonise. It contains a primitive semi-intelligent alien species unlikely to advance further. Recommend no action particularly on account of

There it ended.

'Who is this survivor?' Captain Gurtlieder asked.

'Just a regular Guardsman, sir. He was with Commissar Leminkanen to the end. He appears to have acquitted himself well in difficult circumstances. I shall recommend his promotion when he is reassigned.'

The captain handed back the data-slate. 'Very well, see that this is passed on to the Administratum.'

DOWN IN THE crew quarters of the *Ravenger*, Guardsman Floscan Hartoum was feeling very nervous indeed. Once aboard the battleship, he had contrived to be alone for a while. He could not resist taking a look at Commissar Leminkanen's open log.

Leminkanen had opened the log using his personal code, but had got no further than the heading, stating time and place. The millipede-creature had eaten him at that point.

So Floscan, appalled at his own audacity, had made an entry of his own. He couldn't close the entry, of course, since he didn't know Leminkanen's code. So he had left it in mid-sentence, hoping that made it look all the more authentic.

He dreaded to think what would become of him if it was ever discovered that he had made a false entry in a commissar's log. But he had realised that neither Leminkanen nor any other agent of the Administratum would ever look favourably on the quadrupeds once their human ancestry was known.

A mutant is a mutant. They had altered themselves too much. Well, now they would be registered as aliens and left alone. Floscan had already heard that Warp Gate 492 was to be marked as unusable on the charts, a deadly trap now that it had been discovered by the orks, who must have been lurking nearby waiting for Imperial vessels to emerge. The planet would receive no more visitors.

For the hundredth time, he wondered if it was true that the Emperor saw everything. Did He know what Floscan had done? And did He approve or abhor Floscan for it? Floscan took it as a good sign that no one had questioned why he was wearing an h-g suit.

A war between good and evil was shaping up on the quadrupeds' planet. He hoped, of course, that the Blood God would be defeated. But whatever the outcome, it was going to be settled by the quadrupeds themselves. Though sadly, outside of the family of man.

DEUS EX MECHANICUS

Andy Chambers

THE SCREAM OF the engines fought against the howling winds in a terrifying crescendo of doom. Hyper-velocity mica particles skittered across the hull of the ship like skeletal fingers as it wallowed in the storm, shuddering and dropping by steps as the pilot struggled for control. In the midst of the tumult, Lakius Danzager, tech-priest engineer, Votaris Laudare, illuminant of Mars, adept of the Cult Mechanicus was struggling to open up the skull of that failing pilot, and cursing in a distinctly un-priestly fashion as he struggled to find the right tools for the job.

'Dammit! Osil, find me a hydro coupling, my boy. We'll need one if I can free these accursed fasteners. Look in the vestibule.' He tried to keep his voice calm so as not to frighten his acolyte, but Osil's face was pallid in his cowl as he nodded and hurried out through the rusty bulkhead hatch.

The ship's rattling, brassbound altimeter showed them at a height of nearly seven kilometres above the planet. They had already been dropping out of control for twelve. As Lakius turned back to the rune-etched panel enclosing the ship's pilot, another violent lurch smashed his shaven skull against it, triggering an emgram patch he had only recently divined from his auto-shrine. It was about their too-rapidly approaching destination, and ran in confusing counterpoint through his right optic viewer as he tried to focus on repairing the nav-spirit.

NAOGEDDON IS A DEAD WORLD.

The ringing impact of Lakius's metal-shod head had partially freed the rusting key-bolts. With a whispered prayer for forgiveness from the already distraught machine-spirit, he bent to the task. He carefully unscrewed the panel, murmuring the rite of unbinding and ensuring that he removed the keys in the correct cardinal directions. The ghostly image of a dun-coloured sphere hovered in his right eye. Red text scrolled past it.

Orbital distance: 0.78 AU.
Equatorial Diameter: 9,749 km.
Rotation: 34.6 hours.
Axial Tilt: 0.00.

As he'd feared, the coupling between the augur spike and the pilot-stone had ruptured, blinding the pilot to its landing beacon. He checked the altimeter as he began the ritual of dislocation to remove the charred remnants. Less than two kilometres of howling winds now lay beneath their rocking hull.

Weather: See storms*.

'Osil! Where's that coupling, boy?'

'Here, father. The first one was faulty and I had to go back for another.'

0% Precipitation. Wind speed: Constant 24 kts, Variance 76 kts.

Lakius took the twist of hydro-plastic without comment but silently gave praise to the Omnissiah that the lad had been attentive enough to spot the difference. Under current circumstances, a normally forgivable sin of oversight could prove fatal. Lakius took a breath to steady himself before beginning the ritual of insertion.

Lifeforms: Autochthonic: None.
Introduced: None.

Less than a league of free air remained before they would hurtle into solid rock. His servo-hand shook as he tried to apply the proscribed number of half-turns to the coupling mounts. He yearned to simply call the rite finished and resurrect the pilot. But years of discipline and doctrine drove him on as he completed the benediction against failure, applied the sacred unguents and retrieved the panel so he could begin the final rites of protection and sealing.

Archaeotech Resource: Limited/Xeno artifacts*/@ 600,000,000 yrs (pre.GA) Class: Omega.

'Father, I can see dust dunes below us. I think we're going to crash.'

Notes:

First Catalogued: 7/243.751.M32, Rogue trader Xiatal Parnevue. Orbital Augury Only*. Annexus Imperialus.

'Mechanism, I restore thy spirit! Let the God-Machine breathe half-life unto thy veins and render thee functional.' Lakius firmly depressed the activation rune on the pilot's casing and prayed.

Landed: 6/832.021.M35. Explorator Magos Dural Lavank. Expedition Lost.

Landed: 7/362.238.M37. Explorator Magos Prime Holisen Zi. Expedition Lost.

The ship's engines rose in a triumphant scream to drown out the rushing winds and skittering dust. Lakius and Osil felt the heavy weight of high-G deceleration as the ungainly craft steadied itself and slowed. Lakius could see dust dunes too now, through the curving port in the ship's prow, but the dunes with their trailing streamers of blowing dust were dwarfed by the serried ranks of sharp-angled black monoliths which rose up around the ship as it dipped between them. Osil let out an involuntary gasp as the scale of the structures became apparent. The monoliths were mountain-sized edifices of harsh, alien rock cutting the horizon into sawtooth edge, or a predator's maw.

Landed: 6/839.641.M41. Explorator magos Prime Reston Egal. Surface Survey*. Xeno Structures Catalogued*.

The ship changed course, angling towards a vast dark triangle which blotted out half the sky. The pilot-spirit was faithfully following the beacon, bringing them in towards a tiny ring of light in the shadows below it. There lay the Explorators' camp.

GRITTY SAND CRUNCHED underfoot and a cold, stinging wind blew more of it into their faces as they stepped down to the landing ground. Patchwork figures of steel and flesh were rolling towards them on armoured treads; Lakius and Osil waited by the ship and made no sudden moves.

'See there, Osil: the Explorators have invoked a laser mesh for the protection of the camp. How powerful would you say it is?'

'I see three transformation engines on this side of camp. Assuming the same number on the far side I would estimate 10 to 20 gigawatts, father.'

The figures came closer. They were Praetorians, bionically reconstructed warrior-servitors of the Machine God. Their cadaverous faces gazed stonily from a nest of targeting scopes and data-wires, gun barrels and energy tubes tracked Lakius and Osil until they halted. A chest-mounted speaker on one crackled into life.

'Two lifeforms identified. Classified non-hostile. Please follow, Father Lakius, Acolyte Osil.'

They followed a pair of the heavy servitors between low buildings of pre-fabricated armourplas panelling towards a central command sphere. Osil pointed to one of the smaller structures which had its panels folded back to create a workshop lit from within by welding arcs and showers of sparks.

'What works are being undertaken here, father?'

Lakius repressed a chill sensation of foreboding 'They are re-initiating servitors, Osil. Evidently there has been some accident or mishap which has rendered the units non-functional.' He forbore to comment on the row of ready caskets outside the workshop, containers for tech-priests whose biological components were fit only for incorporation into new servitors. Several priests must have died here already.

The Praetorians motioned them into the command-sphere and remained on guard outside. Inside was a scene of barely organised chaos. Wiring cascaded from panels and conduits, devices of a hundred types thrummed, buzzed and sparked, screenplates flickered and scrolled through endless lines of scripture. A robed priest detached himself from a group clustering around the central dais and addressed Lakius.

'Adept Danzager, your arrival has been greatly anticipated. I am Adept Noam, Lexmechanic Magos Tertius. I have the honour of analysing and compiling data on this expedition.' Noam was gaunt and emotionless, only his lack of bionic enhancement and priestly robes marking him apart from the servitors. Two other priests gathered behind him. Noam pointed to each in turn and pronounced their roles with toneless efficiency.

'Adept Santos, artisan, responsible for camp construction and maintenance.' A rotund man nodded. He was heavily rebuilt with a subsidiary lifting arm at his shoulder and a mass of diagnostic probes in place of his left hand and eye.

'Adept Borr, rune priest, extrapolation and theory.' Borr was slight and nervous-looking, and seemed to be on the edge of speaking when Noam cut him off. Noam and Borr evidently didn't get along. Noam gestured to the other robed figures within the chamber.

'Adepts Renallaird, Kostas and Adso are engineers like yourself, their areas of expertise covering the mysteries of generation, augury and metriculation. Adept Virtinnian is absentia, attending to the servitors at present.' Renaillard, Kostas and Adso looked up briefly as their names were mentioned and gave a perfunctory nod before bending back to their work.

'Blessings of the Omnissiah be upon you all,' Lakius said. 'Am I to assume that you are the leader of this expedition, Adept Noam?'

'No, Explorator Magos Prime Reston Egal has that blessing. He will be joining us shortly.'

'Can you tell me why I have been summoned here then? I know that this is an important undertaking; after all, it has already made me late for my own funeral.'

If Noam understood the joke he made no sign, but Borr grinned behind his hand. Noam replied, 'Yes, you were scheduled for dissemination at the termination of your last assignment. A post with the Officio Assassinorum, I understand. You must be disappointed that your emgrams cannot yet be joined with the Machine-God.'

'In truth, it is my belief that I serve better as a living being than a collection of memories and servitor wetware.'

'Understandable, and very biological.' Something close to disdain passed across Noam's features when he said biological. 'I see that you have never considered undertaking the unction of clear thought.'

'The unction of clear thought? What is that, father?' blurted Osil, forgetting that he should be seen and not heard amongst such adepts.

Noam replied smoothly, apparently not troubled by the acolyte's gaucheness. 'The full utilisation of cerebral mass is a simple matter of isolating our thoughts from the rigours and distractions of emotion – hunger, fear, joy, boredom and so forth. This we know as the unction of clear thought.'

'A common surgical practice among lexmechanics,' Lakius told Osil, 'whose renowned cognitive abilities are enhanced thereby.' At the price of becoming an emotionless automaton he thought to himself, before adding more diplomatically, 'In my own role as engineer I have always found crude emotions such as "fear" and "pain" to be useful motivators under the right circumstances.'

'Indeed?' Noam said, warming to his subject matter. 'Studies of stress–'

'Splendid! This must be our new expert in cryo-stasis!'

Noam was cut off by a newcomer who had lurched into the chamber like an animated scarecrow, all gangling arms and legs. His narrow, vulpine head, scrawny neck and thin body conspired to complete the illusion. He grinned voraciously at Lakius. 'Now you're finally here, we can get on with it! Splendid!'

Lakius bowed deeply. 'Magos Egal, I presume.'

'That's right. I see you've met the others and Noam's about to treat you to a sermon!' Magos Egal winked conspiratorially at Lakius, bouncing up and down on his heels as if he couldn't contain his delight. Lakius was astonished. He was used to a certain amount of... eccentricity among senior members of the Mechanicus, Explorators in particular, but Egal seemed to be verging on the edge of lunacy. 'You come highly commended, you know! Highly commended! Two centuries of experience!'

'Almost fifty years aboard a single craft, servicing a single sarcophagus, magos. Admittedly, that was of alien design and its failure would have brought about my immediate dissemination – but I cannot imagine how I may be of service here.' In truth, Lakius had a strong and unpleasant suspicion exactly why cryo-stasis was of interest to this famed Explorator, but he wished to hear it said out loud.

'You can't guess? I bet you can, but you want to hear it anyway! You're a sharp one! I like that.' Egal grinned lopsidedly, 'Do you know what this place is?' Egal thrust his arms outwards to encompass the whole world.

'Naogeddon... a dead world.'

'No!' Egal thrust up a finger to make his point. 'Not dead, sleeping! Sleeping these six hundred million years!' Lakius's stomach underwent a queasy lurch.

Egal composed himself a little and went on. 'Let me begin at the beginning. Over six hundred million years ago, a race we know as the necrontyr arose and spread across the galaxy. What little we know of these giants of prehistory has been learned from a handful of so-called dead worlds, like this one, scattered at the very fringes of the galaxy. On each world stand vast, monolithic structures which have remained all but impenetrable to every device at the hand of Man. The level of technology evident in their construction is almost incomprehensible to us and many Explorators have been lost winning the fragmentary knowledge we do have.

'On my first expedition to Naogeddon, we gained certain measurements and calibrations which are singular to the dead worlds of the outer rim, these ancient seats of the necrontyr. These have enabled myself and Adept Borr to fashion a device… a key, if you will, which can unlock these structures without awakening their occupants.'

Adept Borr had grown increasingly agitated as Magos Egal spoke and now he interjected, 'Magos, the last attempt caused an exponential jump in attacks–'

Noam cut him off smoothly. 'Adept Borr, those projections have not been verified. Adept Santos has confirmed the current threat is well within the capacity of our defences to contain.'

'The current threat, yes, but if things go wrong–'

Adept Santos seemed affronted by Borr's implied criticism. 'We have a fifteen gigawatt laser mesh, twenty armed servitors and storm-bunkers built out of cubit thick, Titan grade armourplas panels. What could possibly go wrong?'

Egal had passively watched the exchange with fatherly humour and a slight grin, but now he became animated again. 'Ah yes! Speaking of which, I believe they're due to attack any time now. Stations, everyone!'

Lakius's queasy stomach lurched up towards his mouth. Sirens wailed a second later.

'You mean they attack at the same time every day?'

'Well, every dusk. Strictly speaking.'

Lakius, Osil and Borr were in an observation gallery at the top of the command sphere. As a rune priest adept, Borr was trained to piece together fragmentary information and make a speculative theorem, something akin to black magic to most tech-priests. As such, Borr had explained, he was detailed to make observations of their attackers, try to understand their tactics, strengths and weaknesses and then feed effective protocols to the Praetorians.

'I thought it was already night,' Osil said.

'No, Osil, it's always this dark because of the dust in the atmosphere, most of the suns' light is reflected back into the void,' Lakius replied. 'Adept Borr, what are these attackers? Despite Adept Santos's reassurances, I note a number of casualties have already been incurred.'

'They appear to be mechanisms: humanoid, skeletal, most assuredly armed. We have not been able to secure one for study, despite strenuous efforts.'

'And I did not note an astropath adept among those spoken of so far.'

Hesitantly, Borr looked up at Lakius. His tattooed face was underlit by the greenly glowing glass of the augurs before him, but to Lakius the sickly pallor was underwritten by a deeper fear. 'Adept Arraius… disappeared prior to the very first attack. I–I fear Magos Egal has not fully thought through the implications of this site. There are machine spirits here which have functioned continuously for six hundred million years.'

Borr would have continued but an alarm began chiming, quietly but insistently.

The augur screen flashed and displayed a grid with moving icons, Borr glanced down and said, 'The Praetorians have spotted something. We should have it at any moment. There, eight energy sources, six hundred metres out on the west side. We'll have visual soon.' Another glass flashed and displayed icons. Borr was all business now, his fears forgotten in his devotion to his work. 'Eight more, at six hundred and closing from the south-east. They're tempting us to split our fire, I expect… yes here it is, a third group at six hundred metres north waiting to see which way we go.'

Outside, the dark skies had deepened to an impenetrable, inky blackness which the powerful arc lights of the camp barely kept at bay. Borr fed attack vectors and co-ordinates to the Praetorians while Lakius and Osil clustered around an augur glass. The laser mesh was shown as a ragged line of X's representing the ground based refraction spines. Red triangles approached in serried lines from two directions and held back on another angle. The Praetorians were represented by cog-shapes, in respect for their selfless devotion to the Machine-God. The Praetorians were moving southwest and an exchange of fire soon took place across the laser mesh. The tiny bolts flying back and forth on the glass were eerily echoed by the flashes visible through the observation ports. More frightening were the snaps and booms like distant lightning that came rolling across the compound.

The massed fire of the Praetorians was overwhelming the south-west group, the red triangles dimmed in quick succession, some disappearing altogether. Only two of the Praetorian-cogs showed the solid black of non-function, but even as Lakius watched one of the red triangles brightened momentarily and its shot turned another icon solid black. On the west the enemy was at the laser mesh, advancing through it in a tight wedge and destroying the spines with tightly controlled salvoes. Red lines flickered across the interloper's progress as detection beams were broken and the continuous energy flow of the mesh jumped to full output, searing through the ranks. Time and again the icons dimmed but recovered, they would soon break through. The northern group began to move.

'The north group are coming,' Lakius said.

'I see them.'

Most of the Praetorians turned west, leaving a small group to finish off the tattered southern group.

The artificial lightning storm was getting closer. Osil was not paying attention to the glass any more. The scenes unfolding outside in plain sight froze him. Stray shots flashed into the camp, exploding in sparks or gouging glittering welts in Santos's storm-bunkers. Several Praetorians were in view, driving parallel with the laser mesh and firing at something out of view. More came into view from the camp, closing in around the spectral alien cohort forcing its way in from the west. The foe was terrible to see, their shining metal skulls and skeletons too symbolic to be missed. Here is Death, they had been built to communicate, in any language, across any gulf of time and to any race.

That was not the worst of them. These harbingers seemed in some horrible sense to live. Each was a mechanism, to be sure, but one with a fierce anime, like the idol of some ferocious, primitive god. Not only were they death, but they manifested a horrible sense of passion, even joy in their work. As machine spirits they were the most obscene perversions Lakius had ever seen, and inwardly part of him wept to see such things could still exist.

'Father,' Osil said, 'the northern group…'

Lakius couldn't tear his eyes away from the battle between the Praetorians and death machines below. The energy weapons of the aliens were frightening in their potency, their actinic bolts visibly flaying through whatever they struck layer by layer like some obscene medical scan compressed into a heart beat. The warrior-servitors fought back with plasma fire and armour piercing missiles, cutting down the skeletal apparitions one by one, but four more servitors had been cut down by the enemies' deadly accurate fire.

Borr used the same tactic again, the bulk of Praetorians broke off and wheeled north. A small group was left to finish off the alien machines which kept stubbornly rising after hits that would have stopped a dreadnought. Lakius was grateful for Borr's obvious tactical skill. If either the western or southern groups were not completely eliminated the foe would undoubtedly get a foothold inside the camp. The trouble was the Praetorians moving north to parry the third thrust numbered only six; for the first time they would not outnumber the enemy.

'Borr, set the northern face of the mesh to maximum sensitivity,' Lakius said.

'But the spines will fire continuously, dissipate into the windblown dust!'

'Mica dust,' Lakius corrected.

Borr grinned and began a rite of supplication.

THE PRAETORIANS FOUGHT well on the northern side. They used a storm bunker to narrow the angles so they only fought part of the enemy at once. Clattering forward on armoured treads, a salvo of missiles scorched across the void-black sky and cut down two enemy machines as they emerged from the las-mesh. Lightning-crack discharges of plasma burned another, but a critical overheat damaged one of the servitors as his shoulder-mounted plasma cannon suffered meltdown. Five faced five. The storm bunker was being torn to pieces, its adamantium sheath impossibly burning with metal-fires. With a groan it collapsed in on itself, revealing more of the foe at the inner edge of the mesh. The Praetorians lost two of their number for only one of the enemy. Three armoured servitors were left against four skull-faced killers. The aliens grinned their hideous, fixed grins as they stepped forward.

Without warning the laser mesh crackled into a frenzy of discharges. Gigawatts of energy were dissipated into the swirling dust particles, pointlessly scattering their power in flashes of heat and light.

The flashes were harmless, but powerful enough to temporarily blind the optics of the nearby skeleto-machines. Their fire slackened momentarily and the Praetorians used the opportunity to halt and let rip with every weapon in their arsenals; bolter shells, missiles and plasma carved through the silhouetted enemy.

Osil gaped at the scopes. A moment ago he had thought he was going to be killed, but instead they had won.

They had won.

LAKIUS STOOD LOOKING at Magos Egal's 'key', a fifteen metre-long phase field generator, poised like some giant, complex syringe of steel and brass over the unyielding black stone of the alien structure. The smooth, blank wall sloped away to giddying heights, making an artificial horizon of solid black against the grey sky. Adept Renaillard was connecting power couplings at the nether region of the key-machine, quietly reciting catechisms as he anointed each socket and clamped the cables in place. Noam stood nearby, arguing with Borr about something. Four paces further along the key the magos himself was making fine adjustments to the its controls. Four Praetorians were arrayed nearby, their torsos swivelling back and forth as they scanned for danger.

Lakius had just completed a long shift restoring what Praetorians and servitors they could from the casualties sustained in the attack. The unseen Adept Virtinnian, whose duty it was to undertake such blessings, had been crushed to death along with Adept Adso and six servitors in one of Santos's Titan grade storm bunkers. Adept Santos himself had lost an arm when he attempted to secure an alien machine which had reactivated.

If the alien machine-spirits kept to their rigid timetable the next attack was due in six hours. The thought of it crawled at the back of Lakius's mind constantly, a nagging fear which grew minute by minute, hour by hour. He wished he could find some reason to dissuade the magos, stop him pursuing this patently dangerous study, but his authority was beyond question on an expedition like this. The doctrine of the Mechanicus was clear – entire planetary populations of tech-priests could be sacrificed in pursuit of sacred knowledge; the individual weighed nothing against the Cult Mechanicus. But was this sacred knowledge or something ancient and tainted?

'All set?' Magos Egal trilled to Renaillard, who nodded his assent. 'Places everyone! Lakius, you stand with me and we can all chant the liturgy of activation together.'

Chanting in choral tones, Egal made a series of connections and static started to jump from the generator, accompanied by a rising humming noise and the reek of ozone. The black stone shimmered, glittering like quicksilver as it started to deform away from the spiralled needle of the generator. An arch was appearing, tall and tapering, of perfect dimensions and straightness. Within its angles the stone writhed and coiled like a living thing before fading away like mist to reveal the mouth of a corridor. The perfect alien symmetry of it was marred only by the head and shoulder of a Praetorian which appeared to be sunk into the wall on the left hand side – mute testimony to the previously failed attempt to penetrate the structure.

Unperturbed by its silent brother, the first Praetorian moved into the corridor, its powerful floodlights piercing the darkness within. Osil gasped, the outer shell of the structure had made him imagine the inside to be the same, unadorned stone. But the lights picked out complex traceries of silvery metal set into every surface; walls, floor and ceiling twinkled with captured starlight. A murmur of wonder rose from the gathered tech-priests. Magos Egal grinned with delight.

'You see! A simple adjustment of three degrees was all it took! Quite, quite fascinating! I haven't seen anything quite like this since the moons of Proxima Hydratica!' he chuckled. Lakius felt relieved; the Magos was evidently more accomplished than he appeared. One by one, trailing sensor cables and power threads behind, the techno-magi entered the alien structure.

The corridor with its rich silver filigrees sloped down and away. After a dozen metres it dropped down in knee-high steps for another hundred. The Praetorians struggled to negotiate the giant steps, laboriously lowering themselves over each one. The slow progress gave Lakius ample time to examine the silver-traced corridor walls. They were undoubtedly depicting script in a language of some form. Spines and whorls marched in lines apparently formed from continuous individual strands. The lines and strands of script crossed and re-crossed up and down the walls, across the floor and on high in frozen sine waves, creating the sensation that the alien language was somehow conveyed by the totality of what was before him, rather than its individual elements.

Adept Noam was taking input from a cadaverous-looking scanning servitor, a long umbilical connecting its oversized eye-lenses to a socket in the lexmechanic's chest. Borr was nearby, puzzling over a hand-held auspex.

'Can you make anything of it, Adept Borr?' Lakius whispered to the rune priest. The sepulchral quiet of the necrontyr monolith seemed to demand silence, as if noise would manifest all of its invisible, crushing weight to punish the impudent interlopers.

By unspoken agreement none of the party had broken that brooding silence with more than a harsh whisper since they had entered.

'No, I'm not sure that it's supposed to be read in the human optic range. Set your view-piece to read magnetic resonance and you'll see what I mean.'

Lakius fumbled with the focusing knob on the rim of his artificial eye, tuning it to scan electromagnetic frequencies. The corridor was bathed in it, every whorl and spine was a tiny energy source which glowed with magnetic force. The overall effect was dizzying, like walking through a glass corridor over an infinite gulf full of stars. After a time Lakius had to reset his vision to blank it out.

After an hour of descent the corridor flattened out and then twisted sharply to the right before being blocked by a portal of black metal. The two lead Praetorians halted before it, their floodlights darkly reflected in the glossy metal of the obstacle. Three geometric symbols were marked on it at knee, waist and shoulder height.

'Should we use weapons fire, magos?' asked one of the Praetorians, its plasma cannon eagerly swivelling into the ready position. Magos Egal shook his head, stepping up to the door with Noam faithfully shadowing him with his trailing servitor.

'No, no,' Egal muttered 'I'm sure it's a simple matter of–' He touched the metal of the portal. Lakius flinched slightly, fearing some ancient necrontyr death trap. Nothing happened. 'Understanding how to trigger these symbols.'

A pregnant silence fell behind Egal's words. Noam began analysing the symbols, cross-referencing with all the data he stored in his machine-enhanced brain.

Lakius softly let out a breath he'd been holding until he heard a new sound, a low buzz which rose quickly to a high pitched whine. It sounded horribly like a weapon charging up, its capacitors being filled to maximum before it unleashed an atomising blast. Hairs rose on Lakius's neck. The sigils were flickering with their own light now; their ghostly fingers of energy could be felt tangibly. The Praetorians sensed it too and went to a threat response, readying and charging their own weapons with a hiss of servos and whine of capacitors.

Lakius felt a surge of panic, as if he stood beneath a giant hammer which would smash down at any second. He wanted to run back up the corridor but his way was blocked by the two rearmost Praetorians. They were swivelling back and forth with their baleful targeting eyes lit as they searched for enemies. One of them turned far enough to spot its companion and its ruby eye irised down into a pinpoint as it locked on target. The Praetorian's plasma cannon crackled up to a full charge, a compressed lightning bolt which would annihilate anything within metres of its impact point.

Osil was gibbering with fear.

Lakius was shouting out command dogma: 'Praetorians! Audio primus command! Deus ex Terminus est.'

The cannon fired, a searing flash and thunderclap which tore through the other Praetorian and sent white-hot shrapnel scything down the corridor. Osil bravely shouldered Lakius to one side, saving the old engineer from a fiery demise. Shouts and another roar echoed from near the portal, as a wave front of scorching heat washed back up the corridor. The nearby Praetorian swivelled round and trained its plasma cannon on Lakius and Osil, its eye glowed with single-minded determination to destroy as it narrowed at them.

'Ergos Veriat excommen!' Lakius shouted hoarsely. 'Shut down!'

The Praetorian sagged down on its chassis like a puppet with its strings cut and the crisis was over as suddenly as it had begun. The eerie silence fell like a curtain which was broken by the crackle of tiny fires, the plink of cooling metal and the groans of Osil as he writhed on the blood slick slabs. Metal splinters had struck him in his side when he saved Lakius. By the blessings of the Omnissiah, the wounds were not too deep and Adept Borr shrived them with a somatic welder.

Adept Renaillard had not been so lucky and a shard of smouldering casing had struck him in the throat, almost shearing his head off. Smoke rose from the smouldering remains of the two Praetorians nearest the portal. Noam's servitor had been destroyed in the exchange of fire as the two destroyed each other, but Magos Egal and the lexmechanic were unharmed.

'A sophisticated form of faeran field,' Noam explained dispassionately. 'It was cut off when I completed decryption of the portal locks.' A faeran field interfered with brain functions, inducing, among other things, extreme fear responses and seizures. Lakius couldn't help but think the lexmechanic sounded a little smug. Clear thought indeed.

Beyond the portal the corridor appeared to continue as before. Osil was sorely hurt in spite of Borr's ministration, and Lakius undertook the rituals to reboot the solitary remaining Praetorian so that it could carry him back to the surface. Osil protested weakly, but Lakius spoke a few quiet words to him before sending him on his way. The young acolyte looked very much like a child clinging to the Praetorian's wide back and Lakius prayed that nothing was waiting back there in the darkness for them. With only four tech-priests left in the expedition it seemed dangerous to

Lakius to push on, but the Magos insisted, convinced they were at the verge of a breakthrough.

EGAL'S BREAKTHROUGH PROVED to be a labyrinth. The corridor split and then split again and again to become many. The different ways sloped sharply up and down, some narrowing to slits too small for even a servomat to enter. Within three turns Lakius felt thoroughly disorientated. The marching hieroglyphs on the walls seemed to hint at other corridors lying just out of sight, showing outlines of other labyrinths, turnings, dead ends which were just out of phase with themselves. In the Mechanicus doctrine the faeran portal alone would have been the subject of months of careful study before further advance was made. The twistings of this alien maze would constitute a lifetime's work with studies of geometry and numerology.

Magos Egal was in no mood to linger, though, and he set Noam and Borr to calculating a path through. Adept Noam's vast analytic power was directed entirely onto building an accurate map of the interweaving passages they moved through using direct observation, phasic scanning, micropressure evaluation and tactile interrogation. Adept Borr used his carefully learned arts conjecture and intuition to understand the underlying structure of the maze, and to determine what kind of xenomorphic logic would guide them through it.

Lakius was reduced to doing the work of a servitor, spooling out power thread and invoking marker-points at each junction so that Noam could tick them off on his mental plan.

The spool's metriculator showed less than a thousand metres left of its five kilometre length when they found another portal, though the term seemed inappropriate for the gargantuan metal slabs confronting them.

The gleaming, baroquely etched metal stretched up into the darkness further than their hand lights could reach. The corridor angled away in either direction, following some inner wall but leaving a sizeable vestibule that the four Explorators now occupied. They were dwarfed by the new barrier, rendered so insignificant that the opening of those titanic gates could only foretell their doom at the hand of something ancient and monstrous. Adept Noam did not even flinch as he stepped forward to begin deciphering the locking-glyphs.

Lakius's mouth was dry with fear as the adept began tracing the first glyph. He looked back along the corridor, sure he had heard some scuttling noise. The twinkling silver traceries hurt his eyes, mechanical and organic. It took him a moment to realise that shapes were moving across them. Silvery, glittering shapes.

'Watch the rear!' Lakius shouted and hefted his personal weapon, an ancient and beautifully crafted laser made by Ortisian of Arkeness, whose spirit he had long tended to. Its angry red lash was sharp and true: it caught a shape, which blew apart in a blinding flash that spoke of minor atomics. The others crouched on their spindly legs and then leapt forward, buzzing down the corridor like a swarm of metallic insects.

Each was the size of a man's torso, flattened at the edges like scarabs and fringed with vicious looking hooks and claws. They were fast but so aggressive that they impeded each other's progress as they rattled and bounced over one another. Borr's bolt launcher joined its roaring song to the hiss of Lakius's laser. Their combined fire clawed down three more of the steely scarabs. Nonetheless, Lakius and Borr had to back towards the doors to keep their distance as more swarmed forward.

'Keep them back!' shouted Egal. 'Noam almost has it!'

Their backs were almost against the doors already. Lakius focused all his attention on tracking and eliminating the machine-scarabs, his laser flickering from one to another in a deadly dance of destruction. But they were still getting closer. One scarab ducked between two of its fellows at the point of their destruction, and surged forward while the tech-priests were half-blinded by the explosions. The machine's scrabbling claws ripped Borr's bolter from his hands before its momentum carried it over Lakius's head. It bounced off a wall and arrowed down amongst the priests. Lakius flinched away and saw it clamp on to Adept Noam's back even as he completed the last sigil. Surgical-sharp hooks ripped into the lexmechanic as the twin portals began to slowly separate.

'Could someone remove this?' Noam asked calmly, like a man being troubled by a wasp on a summer's day. 'I–'

The scarab exploded like a miniature nova and Adept Noam was gone, consumed in an actinic fireball which knocked Lakius flat. He rolled desperately, purple after-images flashing in his vision, ears filled with the roar of detonation. He expected to feel the dread weight of one of the machines landing on him at any second.

OSIL LAY GRIPPED to an operating table by steel bands, the arms of an auto chirurgeon delicately sliced at his skin, pulling forth steel splinters and suturing his torn flesh together. Pain blockers numbed his body but his mind was racing. Father Lakius had told him to prepare their sacred cargo for release. Such a dangerous undertaking was normally only made in response to a signal from the Adeptus Terra on distant Earth.

To begin the investiture of the living weapon the ship carried in cryostasis without the initiation code was tantamount to suicide. If the assassin's crypt was opened without receiving the preparatory mnemonics and engrams specifying its target it would kill everything it found until it was destroyed.

Father Lakius, he concluded, must privately believe things had gone very, very wrong indeed.

LAKIUS FLINCHED AS something gripped his shoulder and started dragging him backwards. He realised someone was trying to pull him to safety and kicked his legs to scramble across the floor.

Moments later, Lakius's vision cleared enough to see that he was beyond the doors and that they were closing. The dark slit of the corridor outside narrowed rapidly as they smoothly swept together. He pointed the laser still gripped in his shaking hand but no scarab-machines came through the gap before it sealed.

'Splendid! They are without and we are within,' Magos Egal's voice said, close to Lakius's ear.

He scrambled to his feet as quickly as he could, fearfully looking around. Egal stood nearby and beyond him the chamber they had entered could be seen in its full majesty. Huge, angular buttresses marched away down either wall, and the floor sloped gently downward. Frosty pillars of greenish light shone down from an unseen roof to reveal row upon row of tall blocks covered in angular alien script. The air held a chill and the silence of the labyrinth outside had given way to a gentle susurration like waves against a distant shore.

'Where's Adept Borr?' Lakius demanded. Egal turned away from his accusing gaze, looking off down the cyclopean chamber.

'I'm sorry, I had to shut the portal or the scarabs would have killed all of us,' Egal seemed genuinely repentant. He could not even meet Lakius's gaze.

'You just left him outside!' Lakius's angry words rang hollow even to him. The young rune priest was dead and recriminations would not bring him back. They were trapped at the centre of the monolith now, the heart of the ancient structure. The Mechanicus-trained academic in him was already studying the chamber, too awed by the storehouse of alien archaeotech to give thought to the cost already incurred. The rows of man-high blocks seemed familiar, something about them... understanding blossomed with a now-familiar tang of fear.

'These are cryo-stasis machines,' he whispered. Metriculation memochips in his optic viewer calmly extrapolated that the chamber held over a million of them.

'It's what I brought you to see. They resemble the cryo-crypt of the Assassinorum vessel you arrived in, do they not? The best is at the centre, these are just... servants. Come and we may look upon a sight no living thing has seen in six hundred million years.'

Egal moved off down the slope and Lakius numbly followed. They passed block after block, each glittering with a rime of ancient frost. The floor got steeper until they had to crawl on hands and knees, gripping the blocks to lower themselves down to a flat circular section dominated by an immense stasis crypt. It was a sarcophagus in form, its top moulded into a representation of what lay within. Lakius expected to see a mask of death like the machine warriors, but instead found vivid life rendered in polished metal, beautiful but inhuman and cruel. Rows of sigils around the lid shone with an inner light, and it felt warm to the touch.

'Its already been opened,' said Lakius. 'Help me move the lid. I need to see inside.'

Between them they managed to turn the huge, heavy lid, swivelling it to reveal the interior. The sarcophagus was empty.

Egal seemed unsurprised; in fact, he was delighted. 'Splendid! Just as I had hoped.' He reached a gangling arm into the sarcophagus and brought out a silvery, metallic staff.

'Lakonius described an artefact like this in the Apocrypha of Skarros. He spoke of a symbol of mastery born by the lords of the necrontyr, called the "staff of light".' He hefted the ornate device in both hands. As he did so, an intense blue-white light flared in the symbol at the top of the staff. 'With this, we need fear no denizen of this edifice; with time they can even be tamed and made to serve.'

'But what of the occupant of the crypt?' Lakius asked, nervously noting the maniacal gleam in Egal's eye. 'The lord and master of this place that we're plundering from? I fear in our current circumstances we could scarcely fend off any kind of attack and that artefact is more likely to draw one to us. We should go while we still can.'

'Very well, but the staff of light could be our salvation. It would be madness to leave it behind.'

OSIL LIMPED TOWARDS the landing field where their ship lay. He had agonised greatly about whether to accede to his mentor's request. By Imperial and Mechanicus law, the activation of one of the lethal members of the Officio Assassinorum without proper authorisation was treason of the highest order. Death of the flesh would be a secondary consideration beside the terrible punishments that would entail.

But Osil had spent almost twenty Terran years in the company of Lakius Danzager, studying the tasks he would one day continue when the father was gathered to the Librarium Omnissiah. He had imagined he would spend the rest of his life aboard the ageing cutter, maintaining its systems and preparing its cargo of Imperial vengeance when it was required. That was not going to be the case now. Osil had learned enough of Lakius's clarity to understand that the Explorator's expedition was woefully inadequate in the face of the alien terrors of Naogeddon. Father Lakius feared the worst, that they were about to unwittingly unleash something so terrible that he believed only an adept of the Eversor temple would have a chance of stopping it. And so the assassin must be prepared.

* * *

MAGOS EGAL STRODE ahead confidently through the labyrinth, thrusting out the staff like a torch, its fierce light burning back the shadows and setting the hieroglyphs aflame with blue-white flashes. Lakius scuttled along behind him, jumping at each new scraping, slithering noise, jabbing his pistol towards each new vagrant glitter of steel as it flicked out of sight behind a corner. The denizens of the labyrinth were dogging their heels, giving back before the circle of light from the staff and closing in behind.

After what seemed like an eternity they reached the first portal where they had fallen foul of the faeran field. The melted wreckage of the Praetorians and Renaillard's body were gone, the corridor clear except for the power threads trailing off into the darkness. Magos Egal wanted to stop and investigate but Lakius feared some assault would take place if they lingered, and urged him to press on. The soft scrapes and scratches of movement were behind them now, but following closely all the time. As they started to climb the steps Lakius looked back and caught sight of dozens of tiny lights floating in the gloom. They looked like blue fires, seemingly cold and distant, but drifting forward in pairs, the twin eye-lights of murder-machines on their trail.

The cool grey light of the outside seemed blinding after the blackness within. The edges of the phasic rift in the structure's outer sheath were wavering alarmingly and they ran past the entombed Praetorian to stumble out onto the gritty dust of the surface. It took Lakius a moment to gain his breath and he looked up to see Egal making adjustments to the phase generator.

'You're shutting it down, I trust,' said Lakius.

'Quite the contrary; I'm stabilising it so we can use the same entryway to go back in.'

'That's what I thought,' Lakius said, and fired his laser.

OSIL'S KNEES ALMOST failed him when he saw their ship. A living sheath of machines covered it, their silvery bodies shifting over one another as they sought a way inside. The ship carried a great many devices to prevent tampering, as Osil knew all too well. If the machines found a way in, or worse still tried to breach the hull, the results could be devastating. He turned and forced his torn legs to start back to the command sphere.

EGAL DARTED AWAY from Lakius's laser with inhuman quickness. But Lakius had been aiming at the phase generator's power couplings, and the hit was more spectacular than he had imagined. The key-machine detonated and then imploded, a halo of white-hot flame flashing outwards for a moment before it was dragged back. A ragged distortion-veil skated erratically over the machine, crushing it smaller and smaller as it tried to suck everything nearby into it. Egal had been blown clear, but was left wrestling to hold onto the alien staff of light as it was drawn inexorably towards the rift.

'Help me, Lakius. I can't hold it!' Egal shouted over the piercing shriek of air being annihilated in the void. Lakius levelled his laser at the magos and shot him in the head without replying. Egal fell back clutching his face. The staff plunged into the rift and exploded with a crack like lightning. Ozone hung heavy in the air as Lakius backed away through the laser mesh spines towards the camp. He spared a glance for his treasured weapon's indicator jewel, and saw it was dim. His last shot had been at full strength, enough to punch through plasteel. Magos Egal was still moving, standing up.

'Have you any idea how hard it was to get this texture right?' he demanded indignantly, indicating the side of his face that had been caressed by a steel-burning laser. Charred welts revealed glittering metal beneath, quicksilver curves that betrayed an inhuman, yet familiar, anatomy. Lakius kept moving back, the figure of the thing that had pretended to be Egal was getting reassuringly distant, dwarfed by the solid black base of the alien structure. A pair of Praetorians came rattling forward from amidst the stormbunkers, balefully scanning Lakius with their targeters.

'One life form identified. Classified non-hostile,' one concluded.

The magos-thing was at the laser mesh. It leapt suddenly, astoundingly covering the hundred metres to Lakius and the Praetorians in a single somersaulting bound.

'One life form identified. Classified non-hostile,' the other Praetorian stated.

'Surely you didn't believe these clattering toys would be able to identify me?' the Egal-thing smiled. 'I had thought you one of the more intelligent specimens.'

Lakius's mouth was dry with fear, but he managed a curt nod of acceptance before crying out 'Praetorians! Audio primus command! Overwatch!' The Praetorians locked their weapons onto the alien with eye-blurring speed, their simple brains entirely devoted to obliterating the first rapid movement they sensed.

'You forget that I spent time repairing servitors after the last battle. I took the liberty of updating their command protocols at the same time,' Lakius said with more courage than he felt.

The thing smiled more broadly still, and slowly cocked its head to one side. The Praetorians' weapons tracked the minute movement faithfully.

'Good for you, Lakius Danzager. You really are a clever one. How did you know I wasn't human?'

Lakius hesitated for a moment. The thing before him exuded an almost primal sense of power. It was at his mercy for the present, but his instincts told him it could pounce on him at any moment. The Mechanicus in him yearned to learn what he could about it while his humanity screamed out to destroy it. His curiosity overpowered his instincts for a moment.

'I wasn't sure, but either you were the thing from the crypt or an insane Explorator who was bent on unleashing something unspeakable upon the world. When I understood that, my choices became clear. How did you replace Egal? Did he wake you in there?' Icy daggers caressed Lakius's back as he talked to the thing. Its silver and flesh smile widened even further.

'What makes you think I replaced him at all? I have travelled a great distance since my first waking, walked in many places that have changed so very much since I saw them last.'

'What were you seeking?' whispered Lakius.

The thing's ferocious smile was spread almost ear to ear. 'Knowledge, mostly. I wanted to know how the galaxy had fared; who was left after the plague. You can't imagine my surprise on finding your kind and the krork scattered everywhere. I've seen you humans trying to forge an empire in the name of a corpse; I have seen your churches to the machine. Racially, your fear and superstition are most gratifying. You make excellent subjects.'

'You are necrontyr, then. You went into stasis to escape a disease.'

'No, your language is inefficient. The plague was not a disease and it couldn't harm us, but...' The necrontyr tilted its head back as if dreaming of long lost times. 'It was killing everything else.' It looked back at Lakius. 'And no, I am not a necron. You mistake the slave for the master. You'll understand better when I take you back inside.'

It leapt. The Praetorians blazed into it with lasers and plasma, their bolts lashing at the thin form. Lakius was momentarily blinded by the orgy of destruction, and he fled towards the command centre in the hope of finding reinforcements. He looked back to see a silvery figure ripping pieces out of one the Praetorians. The other battle-servitor was smouldering nearby. The figure waved a piece of carapace jauntily at Lakius.

'Sorry, Lakius, I couldn't resist it,' the thing called. 'My race raised what you call "melodrama" to a high art form before you were even evolved.' It chuckled and returned to eviscerating the Praetorian.

LAKIUS WAS SPINNING the locks shut on the command centre hatch when he sensed a presence behind him. He turned, too terrified and weary to fight but wanting to see his nemesis. He almost died of relief when he saw it was Osil.

'Osil, it's–'

'I know, father, I was watching on the monitor.'

'The assassin?' Lakius gasped as he sagged to the ground.

'I couldn't reach the ship, it was covered by a swarm of insect machines. I'm afraid they'll trigger its anti-tampering protocols sooner or later. I searched for something we could use to protect ourselves but there are only components, nothing complete.'

'I fear the thing out there may survive the blast anyway. If so it would be better to–'

A ringing blow sounded against the hatch, making both Osil and Lakius jump. Then another blow slammed into it, then a third. At the third blow a bulge appeared in the Titan-grade adamantium plate. Silence fell.

'I think we'd better look at those components, Osil.' Lakius said, struggling to his feet. Osil fussed around him, his fears assuaged by having someone else to think about. He showed Lakius the ready-caskets and crates he had brought.

'I've performed the rites of preparation on these pieces, and anointed the calibrators,' Osil said hopefully. A hissing, popping noise came from the hatch, and a bright heat-spot formed at its centre.

Lakius looked at the mass of unconnected components and despaired.

THE HEAT SPOT had made a complete orbit of the door, leaving a trail of molten fire behind it. As the circle was closed the metal fell inward of its own weight, clanging to the ground and sending up a cloud of reeking fumes. A tall, inhuman figure stepped through the gap.

'Mechanism, I restore thy spirit. Let the God-Machine breathe half-life unto thy veins and render thee functional,' muttered Lakius, scarcely looking up. Osil gaped at the apparition, sure that his life was over.

'Ah, splendid, both of you,' it grinned. 'Don't tell me you've been trying to make something to stop me? With all your chanting and bone-rattling it would take days, years!'

There was a flash outside, and seconds later a titanic roar. The blast wave from the assassinorum vessel's plasma reactor going critical was a second behind that.

'Don't worry, I can save you.' The thing grinned again.

'No need,' grated Lakius and closed the last connection.

A dome of shimmering, bluish light sprang into being. It filled the hatchway with the necron-master frozen at its centre. It was a charcoal-black silhouette in the glare of the plasma-flash beyond the field. The rest of the armoured command centre shook and rattled alarmingly but held, its vulnerable hatch protected by Lakius's improvised stasis bubble.

After the blast wave had passed there was a long moment of silence before Osil asked. 'Father, won't the Omnissiah be angry that you mistreated all those Machine Spirits making the field?'

'Let it be our secret, Osil. Deus Ex Mechanicus. The Emperor watches over us.'

BUSINESS AS USUAL

Graham McNeill

RIGHT AWAY, SNOWDOG could tell that these six, deadhead Jackboys were trying to pull one over on him. Sure, they talked the talk, walked the walk and apparently had some real heavy connections with the High Hive gangs, but his gut told him that this deal was going to hell. He couldn't put his finger on it, but something was definitely wrong. Maybe it was the location the Jackboys had chosen for the deal, too close to the tyranid nests for Snowdog's liking. Or maybe it was their attitude. They were too cocky, acting like he was some dumb squarejohn who didn't know the score and Snowdog didn't like that. Not one bit. It meant they thought they were holding all the cards.

Like all Jackboys, they wore plain grey boiler suits, pulled in at the waist with a broad leather belt. Every one of them had shaven heads, tattooed with crosses, guns and gang symbols. They wore knee-length, shining jackboots and two carried Arbites combat shotguns, no doubt looted from a couple of dead Bronzes. They looked a bit too ready to use them and if this deal did go ballistic, then he'd have to put those two down first.

'Well?' said one of the Jackboys. 'It's good stuff, yeah? Your boy looks like he's pretty happy with it.'

Snowdog had to agree, the Kalma was top notch. Lex was smacked out of his damn eyeballs, sedated by the euphoric drug and grinning inanely, thick ropes of drool dangling from his chin. If some shooting action went down here, Lex would be frag all use in the fight. Thank the Hive Spirit he'd decided to bring Silver and Tigerlily with him. The girls could take on any hardcase and make him wish he'd never been born. He'd seen their handiwork many times and was eternally grateful they ran with his gang.

Both were dressed in dark catsuits and pistol belts. Tigerlily kept her red hair cropped close to her skull in shaven stripes and wore a baldric of assorted throwing knives and daggers across her chest. Silver's albino-white hair was tied in a long ponytail and she was armed with two gleaming autopistols, holstered beneath a long, leather coat. The kind of firepower the Jackboys were packing was beginning to make him wish he'd brought Trask or Jonny Stomp along as well, but he'd wanted to make a point. He'd wanted the Jackboys to know he didn't need big guns to prove how much of a player he was.

'Yeah,' nodded Snowdog, conceding the point, 'it looks like good stuff, but Lex trips out on coffee and ain't payin' for it neither.'

'Hey, a free sample only goes so far, you know? You wanna deal or what?' said a second Jackboy, irritation in his voice. Snowdog's suspicions racked up a notch. They were too eager to deal. Jackboys usually felt the need to strut like damn peacocks before getting down to the dealing.

They sat in a junked out factory unit, on the northern edge of the Stank, one of the lowest and most dangerous badzones in Erebus Hive. Not even the Arbites Enforcers would come here without damn good reason. A hab unit had collapsed on the factory a couple of months back, killing all the workers and flattening most of the machinery. It had been abandoned and left to rot; another stinking, sedimentary layer of metal and flesh. There were still tunnels and chambers left in the unit, areas that had escaped the violence of the hab's collapse. The area they now sat in was low ceilinged and strewn with broken glass and twisted metal girders. The flattened hulk of a milling machine served as their business table.

A large, sealed petri dish sat on the machine, filled with tiny red capsules. Six hundred Kalma drops, worth a small fortune – enough to get some real heavy ordnance, haul themselves upwards and carve out some more stamping grounds.

'So, you wanna deal?' repeated the Jackboy.

'Maybe,' said Snowdog, nodding imperceptibly to Silver.

'Don't be givin' me no "maybe". Yes or no, that's all I wanna hear. I don't give out nothing for nothing. Understand, boy? You take our Kalma, we want something back.'

'Hey, I didn't say I wasn't gonna deal,' soothed Snowdog, 'let's all just flat-line and be cool. We're all here to do a little business, not bag 'n' tag each other.'

The Jackboys seemed to relax at this and moved their hands away from their pistols. They might be hardcases in the High Hive, but they didn't know jack about how negotiations were handled down here in the badzones.

Snowdog glanced at the petri dish again. Six hundred Kalma drops. It looked pure as well, the best, not cut with chalk or rock powder. This stuff would make you feel like the inside of your brain had been dipped in honey.

The cares of the world could all go to hell while you were on Kalma, at least for a while.

But the good stuff didn't come cheap.

No. These boys were setting him up for something and he sure as hell didn't like the feeling. He'd stayed alive in the Stank this long by trusting his instincts and right now there was a four alarm fire going off in his head. The Jackboys knew he had the connections and the hard cash to pay for this and he also knew they would probably try to keep the drugs and the money... which meant they wouldn't let him leave here alive.

Snowdog was not an especially tall man, but his compact body was rangy and muscled and he could fight like a cornered hellcat. His skin had an unhealthy pallor to it, the result of living in the darkness of the underhive and his full features were rugged and careworn. His head was crowned with short, bleached blond hair that was backcombed in short spikes and his brown eyes suspiciously checked out the Jackboys. He wore a pair of black, tiger striped trousers, tucked into a pair of enforcer's combat boots he'd pulled from a dead Bronze. At his belt hung a long bladed knife and a wire garrotte. His white shirt was printed with a faded holo-patch depicting a rippling explosion that expanded and contracted as he moved. Over this he wore a black leather waistcoat and shoulder holster containing a battered autopistol.

'Look, how much you want for this?' asked Snowdog. 'You got a lot of stuff here, probably more'n I can take in one go.'

'Hey, man. It's cool. We know we got a lot. But we need to get rid of it quick, you know?' said the lead Jackboy, his pitted face right in Snowdog's. Out of the corner of his eye, he saw the Jackboys with the shotguns quietly ease the safeties off their weapons.

Snowdog sat back, folded his arms and, unnoticed, loosened the catch on his autopistol's shoulder holster. He noticed Silver and Tigerlily tensing, readying their muscles for instant action. They knew the drill.

He locked eyes with the Jackboy and shrugged, 'Like I said, how much you want?'

'Ten thousand,' snapped the Jackboy without hesitation.

'Ten thousand–' said Snowdog, knowing what the next question would be. 'You got that kinda cash?'

'Yeah,' said Snowdog, sliding his hand towards his holster.

'Then I guess we'll take all you got!' shouted the Jackboy, snatching for his gun.

Snowdog was quicker.

He whipped out his autopistol and squeezed off a round full in the Jackboy's face. The ganger screamed foully, tumbling backwards, the top of his head blasted clear.

The Jackboys with the shotguns were moving. Chambering shells, they aimed and fired. Snowdog dropped, hitting the deck hard and rolling, firing off an entire clip of wild shots. Tigerlily leapt towards the second Jackboy and rammed her elbow into his throat. She spun low and hammered a slender-bladed dagger into his belly, slicing upwards in one fluid motion. The Jackboy gurgled and fell to the factory floor, dropping his shotgun and grasping his crushed larynx.

Silver calmly fired her pistols, double tapping the second shotgun-wielding Jackboy in the head. Snowdog slid another clip into the grip of his pistol and rose from behind his shelter.

Bullets stitched a path towards him. He spun quickly and fired twice towards a crouching Jackboy. The man grunted, shot in the chest and fell back, blood pouring from his wounds.

Snowdog felt a whipcrack sting to his cheek and dived forwards, reaching for the fallen shotgun. He scooped it up on the roll and rose smoothly to a crouch, firing off a succession of shots. The noise was tremendous and he whooped with excitement as the Jackboy who'd fired at him went down, his chest punched clean through by the close range blasts.

Silver and Tigerlily worked their way towards him, using every bit of cover available. Neither had even broken sweat. He smiled at them as silence descended on the factory.

'Time to split, girls,' he said.

'Damn straight,' said Silver. 'Bound to be some more Jackboys nearby waitin' for us.'

'Figured as much.'

'Only way outa here that ain't gonna take us into more of these guys is down past the 'nid nests,' pointed out Tigerlily, 'and that ain't gonna be a barrel of laughs.'

'Nope,' Silver agreed. She glanced over the debris they'd sheltered behind and said, 'What about Lex? We just gonna leave him for the Jackboys? They'll bag'n'tag him for sure, man.'

'Damn!' said Snowdog. He'd forgotten about Lex. He'd still be lying there thinking that this was some Kalma related trip-out. He could hear the Jackboy talking on a comm-unit. More would be here soon, that was for damn sure. He checked his pistol and also took Silver's gun, handing her the Arbites shotgun.

'I'll get Lex. You cover me with this. We'll be out of here and high n' dry before you know it.'

THE STANK DARKENED at their passing. The black, armour-clad warriors charged down the twisting halls, combat shotguns held at the ready across their broad chests. Dark cloaks trailed behind them, gusted by the sputtering oxy-recyc units. The six man Adeptus Arbites Enforcer squad, grim men in fully enclosed suits of carapace armour, cast a pall of fear as they passed the stinking hovels and battered habs of the lower hive.

The leader of the squad, Captain Jakob Gunderson, scanned from side to side, alert for a Skum sniper, Wyldern snuff gang or any one of the many other dangers that lurked in this place. Travelling in such numbers and at this speed made such an attack unlikely, but in the Stank, if you wanted to stay alive, you never took things like that for granted.

The Wall of the Dead in the Precinct House was carved with the names of those who had.

Gunderson was a feared man. His name was spoken in whispers by the denizens of the Stank. It was a name to quell the worst of riots, a reputation to tell over flickering fires by older, wiser heads which nonetheless glanced furtively over their shoulders as though the mere mention of his name would somehow conjure him from thin air.

At well over two metres, Gunderson was a giant of a man, radiating his authority and power like a threat. He was broad and powerfully built, with muscles like slabs of iron beneath his midnight blue carapace armour. He wore his non-reflective bronze captain's badge over his left breast and was helmetless, tiny vox-comm beads attached to his larynx and the canal of his ear. A black, protective eye visor shielded his vision.

The ragged residents ducked out of sight of the Enforcers, pulling rusted iron doors shut and hauling tattered strips of cloth over tears that served as windows in their prefabricated steel shacks. Children were dragged indoors, the adults fearing the soldiers of the Adeptus Arbites as much as the feral Stank gangs and tyranid monsters that roamed these regions of Erebus Hive.

They'd intercepted a radio call on an unlicensed frequency moments earlier as they patrolled the outskirts of District Quintus, almost half a kilometre away. Strictly speaking, this area wasn't within their patrol envelope, but a chance to nail that punk Snowdog was too good to pass up.

Snowdog had been a thorn in Jakob Gunderson's side for longer than he cared to remember. Several times Gunderson had almost had the diminutive ganger in his sights, but each time the slippery little fragger had managed to escape him.

He was known to front for a couple of heavy hitters up in the refinery city of Desirata who synthesised Kalma, Spook, Slaught and Throne knew what else in secret factories, shipped it to every hive on the planet and, it was rumoured, off-world.

Snowdog was a major player in the odious underworld of Erebus Hive. He ran a fair sized piece of turf with his gang, the Nightcrawlers, and supplied drugs and guns to the ever-hungry population of the hive. What was even more of an affront to Gunderson was that they knew portions of Snowdog's territory included his own Precinct House 13.

As well as being immensely satisfying, a bullet in Snowdog's head would put a sizeable dent in the drug traffic entering the lower hive from Desirata.

From the garbled communication his men had intercepted, it appeared that some kind of drug deal had gone wrong and there was a chance Snowdog was involved.

Gunderson carried his shotgun as though it were part of his own flesh, grasping it tight in a vice-like grip. It was set to fire Executioner rounds, hunting shells that would zero in on their target's location. He was taking no chances that Snowdog would get away this time.

He and his squad of five Enforcers reached the collapsed factory their vox-comms had identified as the source of the signal and began climbing the rugged, metal slope of girders and debris towards the entrance, no more than a rusted iron cave mouth.

From inside he could hear screams and gunfire, heavy shotgun blasts and the smaller crack of pistol fire. He racked the slide of his own shotgun, turned to face his men and said, 'No one kills Snowdog but me.'

SNOWDOG HOLLERED AND hurdled the crate, firing wildly. Silver rose with him and began pumping shells from the shotgun at the surviving Jackboy. He was well under cover and hopefully the fire she was laying down would keep it that way.

He'd almost reached Lex when he saw he'd made a mistake. A big mistake.

From his left, the light at the entrance to the factory was suddenly blocked as a team of Bronzes pushed their way inside. He swore to himself as he recognised the bulky form of their leader and twisted to snap off a couple of shots at him.

He saw them hit, but cursed as they were deflected by the Bronze's heavy carapace armour. Gunderson turned at the sound of the shots and a feral grin spread across his face as he recognised his prey before him. Snowdog veered off to find cover.

Gunderson lifted the shotgun to his shoulder and squeezed the trigger twice.

Snowdog saw the distinctive flashes of Body-Chaser shells as their tiny motors ignited. He knew he was a goner. Bagged 'n' tagged for sure. He kept running anyway, suddenly changing direction as an idea came to him.

He dived forwards, pulling Lex's doped-up body around and over him.

Sorry, Lex, it's you or me, buddy.

And let's face it. It's you.

He felt the double thump as the 'Chasers slammed into his human shield, blasting a plate sized-hole in him. Lex didn't even make a sound, and Snowdog knew he was so doped up that he probably hadn't even felt the shells hit. Snowdog winced, thinking that if Lex lived, it was going to hurt like a cast-iron bitch when the Kalma wore off. He pulled Lex's body closer as he heard more shotgun blasts. He tensed, expecting the agony of scatter shot flensing the flesh from his bones or a solid shot punching a giant crater in his chest.

But he felt nothing – then realised the shots had come from Silver's direction.

'Run!' yelled Silver, firing again into the group of Bronzes, forcing them to find cover. She'd bought him time and he mentally chalked it up as one he owed her. He scrambled to his feet and crawled round the flattened milling machine, reaching up to grab the petri dish as he went.

Feeling pretty pleased with himself, he didn't notice the last Jackboy until he almost crawled on top of him.

For a second neither moved until Snowdog launched himself forward, lowering his head and slamming his forehead into the shaven-headed ganger's nose. The Jackboy roared in pain, hands flying to his face.

Snowdog sprang onto the squirming Jackboy and forced the barrel of his gun under his chin. He closed his eyes and pulled the trigger. The Jackboy's head exploded, showering Snowdog with blood and brains, the crack of the gun's discharge lost in a cacophony of shotgun blasts that erupted around him.

Splinters of concrete and glass showered him and he desperately attempted to squeeze himself into as small a target as possible. He could hear Tigerlily and Silver yelling colourful curses and threats at the Bronzes. He tried not to picture the images in his head.

It was clear this situation had gone way too far. Something drastic was required. He checked the clips of each pistol. Each had less than half a mag left. He slowed his breathing, getting ready to go for it. Death or a blaze of glory. Muscles tensed, he was about to move when he caught sight of a dark sheen of metal underneath the Jackboy's bloodstained overalls. He grinned as he reached down and pulled out a leather bandolier with crude, homemade grenades hung along its length.

Some with his name on, he guessed. He was about to unsnap one of the grenades from the bandolier then stopped, smiling to himself.

To hell with it.

He quickly pulled the pins on all the grenades and rose to his feet, swinging the heavy belt round his head. Yelling an obscenity, he lobbed the bandolier towards the sheltering Bronzes.

The boom of a shotgun caused him to duck back behind the crate. But not before he had time to savour the cries of alarm as the Bronzes realised the deadly nature of what he'd thrown them.

The frag grenades simultaneously detonated in the midst of the Arbites troops. Razor-sharp pieces of white hot metal scythed out from the explosion and men died as the shrapnel shredded their bodies. Snowdog covered his ears at the terrific blast as the pressure wave rolled over him, tumbling him from his hiding place. The echoes of the detonation rolled back and forth, mixed with the shrieks of the survivors and the dangerous groaning of tortured metal.

The roof now took on a noticeable downward bulge, water beginning to pour from rapidly developing cracks. With hundreds of tonnes of metal above him, that move with the grenades probably wasn't the best idea he had ever had.

It was time to get greasy and slip away.

He stood and sprinted towards Silver and Tigerlily, sparing a glance at the carnage he'd caused. Three of the Bronzes were dead, a fourth on his knees, clutching his ruined belly, vainly trying to hold in his bloody entrails. The leader he couldn't see. It was too much to hope that Gunderson had been killed; that fragger was way too slippery for that.

Sure enough a black figure rose from behind the wreckage and levelled his shotgun at the running ganger. Silver fired on him, but he didn't flinch. A fragger he may be, but he was a brave one, Snowdog admitted grudgingly. Silver's shot impacted on his armour, but the thick breastplate deflected it. Snowdog ducked as Gunderson fired, feeling lashes of hot fire rake across his back as scatter shot scored through his leather waistcoat, shirt and skin.

His ears were ringing with gunfire, but not before he heard the metal ceiling of the factory give out one last hideous metallic scream of protest, chunks of plascrete and metal crashing to the floor. He saw Silver discard the empty shotgun then, following Tigerlily, dart into the corroded sewer entrance they had earlier tagged as their escape route if things went loco. With a wild yell, he lurched and skidded along the floor, following them into the darkness of the sewer entrance.

SNOWDOG BREATHED DEEPLY, then wished he hadn't. The stench of the Erebus Hive sewer network was overpowering, shot through with the reeking odours of six million people's waste.

He stood knee deep in foetid, rank effluent, sludgy with refuse. Man, he was never gonna get this off his boots! The darkness was absolute; a number of turns in the sewer had cut off the little light that filtered down into the waste pipe. Snowdog reached into his pocket, grunting as pain razored up his back from the trails the scatter shot had blazed, and withdrew his lighter. He flicked off the brass cap and struck the flint.

Weak light flickered, revealing the full extent of their refuge. The steel pipe was perhaps one and a half metres in diameter and stagnant with filth. The murky liquid was unmoving, blocked further up the pipe by piles of trash and rubble.

'You okay?' asked Silver genuinely. 'I was sure that Bronze had you tagged for sure.'

'He almost did. He's a stubborn one, that Bronze. He's been lookin' for me for Spirit only knows how long. Didn't get me yet though,' replied Snowdog.

'I think we might be near the bug nests,' said Tigerlily, the fear in her voice unmistakable. 'We're gonna have to step lightly, less we want to end up sliced and diced.'

Snowdog nodded. Ever since the Space Marines had kicked the tyranids off this world, the local boys of the Imperial Guard and Defence Militia had had their hands full hunting the remaining tyranid creatures that had gone to ground in the underhive. Despite their efforts there were still broods of the smaller beasts nesting in the moist darkness of the lower levels of Erebus Hive. When the 'nids had attacked the hive, Snowdog had fought hand-to-hand in a militia unit as sickle armed beasts burst through every culvert and recyc unit, slaughtering hundreds of the lower hive dwellers. Snowdog had seen enough bugs to last a lifetime and certainly didn't want to see any more.

But the war had been over for three months now and Snowdog had wasted no time in getting back to the serious job of dealing in illegal narcotics and guns. The devotional vids and posters might claim it was every citizen's job to help in the eradication of the tyranids, but for Snowdog it was back to business as usual.

'You get the Kalma drops?' asked Tigerlily, a carefully hidden longing beneath her casually asked question.

'Yeah, I got some. But nobody gets none 'till we're home free. Last thing we need is you smacked out if the bugs come for us,' said Snowdog, stuffing the petri dish into the pocket of his waistcoat.

He grimaced and pointed down into the rank depths of the sewer tunnel. It sloped downwards at a shallow angle, descending into darkness.

Now that he had illumination, he noticed the walls were covered in a glistening ooze, a sticky residue that he didn't like the look of at all.

'Looks like we got a long walk ahead of us,' he said. 'Come on, let's go. I don't wanna be hangin' round here longer'n we got to.'

GUNDERSON THREW HIMSELF forward as tonnes of metal and concrete came crashing down. He yelled as a steel beam smashed into his back, slamming him into the ground and he rolled as blocks of stone and iron thundered around him, the noise drowning out his cries of anger and pain. He saw Enforcer Delano crouching next to him, blood streaming from his temple. He jerked his thumb in the direction of the sewer entrance he'd seen Snowdog go down.

The ceiling continued to groan in protest and Gunderson knew that to stay here was to die. Rubble was sure to keep falling around them and it would only be a matter of time before they were crushed flat. Gunderson and Delano slithered their way towards the tunnel. Snowdog had a head start, but he wouldn't be expecting any pursuit.

Gunderson would make him pay for that lack of vision.

THE INTERIOR OF the sewer tunnel wasn't the worst place Snowdog could remember being in, but it came pretty damn close. The stench was appalling and he didn't want to think what the wriggling movements within the effluent were.

As escape routes went, he'd used better ones.

But any gunfight you walked away from in one piece and with a pocket full of Kalma was a good one, so he guessed he couldn't complain.

At last the tunnel began to brighten slightly before emerging into a high vaulted chamber of dim light and dripping echoes. Tunnels branched off the chamber in all directions and without hesitation Snowdog dropped from the tunnel into the chamber. Picking an opening to his left, he began wading towards it.

They had travelled perhaps ten steps when they found the bodies.

Five Wyldern gangers, their skeletons picked clean of meat. The water around them was still stained with blood, so whatever had done this had reduced them to their bare bones in seconds. The underhive was full of creatures that could kill a man stone dead, but Snowdog didn't know of any that could do this to a person so quickly. At least not ones of this world. The killing of the Wylderns reeked of tyranids and he knew they must be close to a nest. Time to get moving.

The Wyldern nearest to Snowdog still clutched a shotgun in a death grip and he grinned as he quickly bent to pick it up.

'Don't even think about it,' snapped a voice from behind him.

He slid his hand towards his holster until the sharp click of a shotgun slide being racked convinced him that it would be unhealthy to continue. He slowly turned and raised his hands in time to see a pair of blood-streaked Enforcers emerge from the tunnel he and the girls had just come from. Gunderson dropped into the water-filled chamber while the second Enforcer covered them with his shotgun.

'That weapon is Imperial property,' said Gunderson. 'Touch it and I'll blow you away.'

'You'd like that, huh?'

'More than you know.'

'So why haven't you?' asked Snowdog.

'Oh no,' replied Gunderson. 'You don't get off that easy, punk. I'm taking you in Snowdog. I'm going to chain you up like the animal you are and let the world see me drag you in.'

Snowdog looked over at Silver and Tigerlily, but, like him, they knew that reacting now would just get them all killed. The two Enforcers were on the edge. Their blood was singing and it would only take the slightest hint of resistance to start them blasting. He'd have to play this one ice cool.

'Listen man. You see these skeletons?' said Snowdog, nodding towards the bodies. 'These boys got their asses fragged by the 'nids that went to ground after the war and my gut tells me there's a nest nearby. You start firing that cannon of yours, you're gonna bring a whole bunch of 'em down on us, so what you say we all just keep calm, ok?'

'You killed my men!' shouted Gunderson. 'Don't you dare tell me to be calm! I am calm! Delano, get down here with the cuffs.'

A hoarse gurgling was the only reply to Gunderson's order and he risked a glance behind him to see what the hell Delano was playing at.

Enforcer Delano still crouched in the sewer outlet, but a massively long talon now protruded from his body, just above his hip. A look of almost comic surprise twisted his features and he groaned in pain as blood dribbled from the corner of his mouth.

'What the hell–' managed Gunderson as the talon was wrenched from Delano's body and the Enforcer toppled into the water. Behind him, its claws stained bright red, was a lithe, muscled creature with a ridged body and lethal looking talons. The beast hissed, exposing glistening fangs and its pale eyes burned with alien malevolence.

Its powerful hind legs uncoiled like a spring as the creature leapt from the sewer outlet towards them. It exploded in mid-air as the solid shot from Gunderson's shotgun blew it apart, the echoes of the blast ringing from the concrete walls. Hurriedly he chambered another shell and ran to help the struggling Delano to his feet as the sound of scrabbling claws and alien hissing came from all around them.

It seemed to issue from every outlet. And it was growing in volume.

'Damn,' whispered Snowdog as he tried to pinpoint the source of the noises. 'Look what you've gone and done now!'

Another one of the creatures dropped from the roof of the chamber, landing with a splash just behind Snowdog. Its talons lashed out at his neck. He ducked and lowered his head straight into the second beast as it powered from the water, its bony skull smashing into his unprotected face. Blood burst from his nose and he yelled in sudden pain, splashing backwards into the water.

Gunderson's and Delano's shotguns fired again as the outlet pipes erupted with dozens of the horrifying beasts, an alien tide of rippling armour plates, chitinous blades and fangs.

Snowdog hauled himself to his knees as two of the creatures stalked through the foamy water towards him. The creatures were hunched over, the front pair of their limbs ending in long, scythe-like blades.

He recognised them almost immediately as hormagaunts, and he'd fought enough of these beasts during the war to know they were in serious trouble. Their bestial faces were drawn and pale, white, lidless eyes seeming to glow with a killing light.

The lead hormagaunt lifted its head, cocking it to one side, tongue darting in and out of its mouth like a snake's. Snowdog put a bullet between its eyes as the second 'gaunt launched itself at him. He threw himself flat and the creature sailed over him, landing in a thrashing pile of claws. As it picked itself up, Snowdog emptied the last of the clip into the back of its head.

More of the creatures dropped from the roof or rose from the sewage around them. The heavy boom of shotgun blasts echoed deafeningly around the chamber as Gunderson and Delano fell back towards Tigerlily and Silver, firing as they went. Tigerlily drew her daggers and hammered them through a 'gaunt's neck, almost severing its head, as Silver snatched her pistols from her weapons belt. Before she could fire, a pair of 'gaunts leapt from the tunnel behind her and smashed into her back. She cried out and was knocked sprawling, face-first into the water. The beasts' claws tore at her back, their talons raised to strike.

Snowdog slammed a fresh clip into his pistol and fired twice into the soft underbelly of one of the 'gaunts, blasting it from Silver's back. Gunderson slammed the butt of his shotgun into the second creature's head, splitting it apart with a sickening crunch. He kicked the alien away as Tigerlily pulled the spluttering Silver to her feet. Snowdog stood and waded towards the girls. He could see more 'gaunts emerging from the tunnels around them and counted at least a dozen. Suddenly his autopistol seemed scant protection.

Gunderson glared at Snowdog, his rage an almost physical thing. Snowdog grinned, knowing that the Enforcer now realised that he would need Snowdog's help if he was to survive the next few minutes.

Delano propped himself against the concrete wall, his groin and legs awash with blood and his face ashen. A circle of hormagaunts surrounded them, at least twenty now. Snowdog hoped they had enough ammo left to deal with this number of aliens.

He dodged as a hormagaunt leapt at him, its talons slashing. He blasted its chest open and dodged as another pounced. He pulled the trigger and the hammer dropped on an empty chamber. He quickly snatched his knife from his belt.

The bug attacked wildly. Snowdog dodged, spun inside its guard and drove the blade deep into its neck, wrenching it upwards. They splashed into the water, the 'gaunt spasming weakly as its lifeblood pulsed from the ruin of its throat.

Snowdog sprang upright, knife at the ready and slashed out at the 'gaunts next to him. Silver tossed him a fresh clip for his pistol and he slid it home. Gunderson fired into the mass of creatures, each blast blowing a 'gaunt into bloody shreds.

'We got to get out of here!' shouted Snowdog.

'You think?' Gunderson snapped

'Head for the tunnel behind us, it's the only one these things ain't come from!'

Gunderson nodded and began falling back. The 'gaunts surrounded them in a rough semi-circle, fangs bared and talons raised. The noose slowly closed, but the aliens held back, seemingly content just to watch their prey.

'Why aren't they attacking?' whispered Silver.

'Who cares?' said Tigerlily. 'Let's get the hell out of here!'

'Sounds good to me,' agreed Snowdog, backing in the direction of the tunnel. The 'gaunts closed in, moving in time with their beleaguered group. Why weren't they attacking, he wondered? Almost as soon as he formed the thought, his question was answered as a terrifying screech echoed from the tunnel behind the circle of 'gaunts and a monster from the darkest of nightmares pushed its alien bulk into the chamber.

Snowdog had seen some hellish monsters in his time fighting the tyranids and had paid close attention when the commissars had shown them the instructional vids detailing the various identified types of alien creatures and their horrifying abilities.

But he was still shocked by the hideous appearance of this creature.

Standing taller than a man, its spine was curved and ridged, with overlapping plates of chitinous, red armour. Its head was distended and burnt looking, with white orbs for eyes and a vast jaw filled with row upon row of needle-like fangs. Its rear legs were muscled like the 'gaunts' and, like them, its forelimbs ended in gigantic scythe-like talons. The limbs on its thorax bore clawed hands and the muscles there bunched and relaxed, the fingers flexing rhythmically in time with its foetid breath.

The beast's chest was a wetly glistening mass of rippling tissue, pink and raw looking. Barbed hooks clicked on the exposed bone of its exoskeleton, almost as though they had a life of their own. Perhaps it had once been a 'gaunt like the others and the isolation from the hive fleet had driven its internal evolution into overdrive, producing this terrifying pack leader. However it had happened, Snowdog realised, it was bad news for them.

'Emperor save us...' whispered Gunderson. Silver hurriedly scrambled into the outlet behind them and reached back to pull Tigerlily up.

'Come on!' said Silver, extending her hand towards Snowdog. He gripped her wrist and hauled himself into the sewer tunnel as the monstrous beast took a thundering step into the water. Snowdog looked back as Gunderson and Delano faced the huge beast.

'Well shoot the damn thing!' he yelled.

Delano needed no further prompting and squeezed the trigger of his shotgun. At such close range he couldn't miss and Snowdog watched as a blaze of purple energy flared around the beast simultaneously with the shotgun's blast. As the searing afterimage of the flash dissipated, Snowdog saw that the creature was unharmed and knew that it was protected by a kind of naturally generated energy field. He'd seen some of the larger tyranid beasts protected by something similar during the war.

The creature's chest suddenly spasmed, the pink folds of skin rippling and undulating with a grotesque peristaltic motion. Thick cords of tough muscle fibre whipped out towards Delano. The barbed hooks punched through the Enforcer's carapace armour and snagged his ribcage, digging into the meat of his body. The flesh hooks retracted on powerful muscles and hauled the screaming Delano off his feet. Gunderson made to grab him, but wasn't quick enough to prevent the beast from dragging him into its deadly embrace.

Delano slammed into the creature, his screams cut off abruptly as its upper talons stabbed repeatedly into his body. Soon the Enforcer's body was reduced to a pulped mess of torn and bloody flesh, barely recognisable as human. While the beast destroyed Delano, Gunderson leapt for the sewer outlet as the beast dropped the mangled corpse into the water. Snowdog helped him up and they sprinted deeper into the sewers, the high pitched ululating screeches of the 'gaunts telling them that the tyranid creatures weren't far behind them.

Gunderson led the way as they moved further into the tunnels, a torch on his shotgun providing some illumination. Snowdog brought up the rear of their small group, casting nervous glances behind him as the screeching increased in volume.

'Come on, come on,' he hissed. 'Let's pick up the pace here people!'

His breath came in short gasps, and he could almost feel the creatures' hot breath upon him. He threw a glance over his shoulder as he ran and swore as he saw the outline of the giant beast behind him. Too close, too close by half!

The tunnel turned and widened into a large inspection chamber, one with a corroded iron ladder at its centre leading up into darkness. The others were past the ladder, still running, but he knew that to keep going deeper into the tunnels wasn't an option. The beast was too fast and there were more of the smaller ones than they had bullets left.

'Woah!' he yelled, skidding to a halt. 'Up here!'

Snowdog scrambled up the ladder, fear lending his limbs extra speed. He climbed into a wider concrete tube, finally emerging into another tunnel, larger than the one they had just left, but with a sliver of light casting a weak glow from one end. Silver crawled from the hole and rolled to one side as Gunderson's head emerged behind her. No sooner had he clambered out when Tigerlily hooked her arms around the manhole's edge and began hauling herself free.

She screamed suddenly and Snowdog grabbed her wrists and pulled as powerful alien limbs began dragging her back down. Tigerlily continued to scream horribly as Silver and Gunderson leant their strength to holding her.

A horrifying ripping noise sounded, and at first Snowdog thought her clothes were tearing. Then, a scarlet gout of blood flooded from the girl's mouth and the three fell backwards, still clutching the upper half of Tigerlily's torso. The glimmer of life was still in her eyes and Snowdog watched in horror as the girl's agonised shrieks trailed into a hideous gurgling.

With a deafening cry, the tyranid creature hauled its bulk through the floor of the tunnel and Snowdog howled his rage at the beast. He rolled to his knees and drew his pistol in one motion, aiming towards its head. He squeezed off several shots, but none were able to penetrate the creature's energy field.

It lashed out with a taloned arm and sent him flying, slashed from hip to shoulder. Gunderson fired his last few shells at the creature as Silver snatched up one of Tigerlily's fallen knives.

The beast towered over Snowdog and he knew that this was it, this was how he was going to check out of this world. Not exactly how he'd planned it.

Its powerful clawed hands, the ones it had used to tear Tigerlily in two, reached down and picked him up, raising him to its fanged maw. Snowdog heard Silver scream his name as he fired the last bullets from his pistol at point blank range into the beast's face. It screeched in agony as one bullet somehow managed to defeat its protective field and blow out its left eye. Its grip convulsed, the claws digging further into Snowdog's body, and he screamed in agony, blood streaming down his sides.

He scrabbled for another weapon, almost insensible from the pain as the claws dug further into his flesh. His hand closed over something in his pocket and he rammed it deep into the creature's throat. He kicked backwards, powering free of the creature's grip, its talons scoring bloody grooves in his body. He felt a bone-jarring impact as his face connected with the concrete and tasted blood as his teeth snapped.

He heard another boom of a shotgun discharge followed by the snap of a hammer slamming down empty. The beast lashed out again at Gunderson's chest, its talon smashing through his armour and laying him open to the bone. The Enforcer tumbled back, unconscious, and dropped his shotgun.

It was all over now, Snowdog realised, and he waited for the fatal blow to land. But for long seconds nothing happened. Then he heard a tortured groaning and an alien hiss of incomprehension.

Snowdog felt a crashing thump beside him and closed his eyes. Eventually, he forced them to open and looked around. The tunnel was eerily quiet, only the sound of ragged breathing and the gentle lap of distant water disturbed the silence. Then Silver laughed, a high pitched laugh of terrified relief and released tension. Snowdog pushed himself painfully to a sitting position and leaned back against the tunnel wall and stared, disbelieving, at the sight before him.

Flanks heaving slowly with its laboured breathing, the vast tyranid creature lay unmoving on the tunnel's floor. Its fanged head was close enough for him to touch, thick saliva drooling from its jaws. He closed his eyes and replayed the last few moments in his head: Tigerlily's death, the gunshots and him ramming something down the alien's throat. It obviously hadn't been a grenade as he'd hoped, but what had it been? Then he noticed a few red capsules trailing from between the creature's jaws and suddenly knew exactly what he'd done.

Six hundred Kalma drops in one go!

As he watched, the alien's chest hiked one last time and its heart finally gave out under the sedating effects of the drug. Its long, rattling death cough faded to a low hiss and Snowdog could feel hysterical laughter building inside him. The beast had overdosed on Kalma. Not really surprising, considering it had taken all six hundred doses of the powerful narcotic in one hit. Silver helped him to his feet and together they stared at the beast that had almost killed them all.

'Some day, huh?' remarked Silver.

'Some day,' agreed Snowdog.

Silver nodded towards the unconscious Gunderson and said, 'What you wanna do about him? You want me to finish him off?'

Snowdog shook his head. 'No, I don't think so.'

'Why not? He'd kill you.'

'Probably,' conceded Snowdog, 'but just think how much it's going to eat at him, knowing we could've killed him, but didn't.'

Silver shrugged and said, 'Have it your way.'

Snowdog winced in pain as they limped towards the light at the end of the tunnel, dizzy from blood loss. But any battle with an alien monstrosity you walked away from in one piece was a good one, so he guessed he couldn't complain.

Yeah, thought Snowdog, it was business as usual alright.

ONLY IN DEATH DOES DUTY END

SALVATION

Johnathan Green

THE ROAR OF their storm bolters drowning out their battle-cries, the veterans of Ultramar's First Company vented their righteous fury against the abomination that was the tyranid race. Shrieking, the hideous elongated head of a hormagaunt appeared in front of Brother Rius, its fanged mouth dripping with strings of saliva. Responding instinctively, Rius turned his weapon on the creature. He watched with grim satisfaction through his visor as the creature's grotesque visage disintegrated. As his storm bolter kicked in his hand, the back of the creature's skull exploded outwards in a splattering burst of purple blood and bone fragments.

As another in a long line of vanquished foes fell before him, Rius found himself looking across the entirety of the vast battlefield. The rocky plain was covered with a seething mass of flesh and armoured warriors, accompanied by a host of support weapons and vehicles. To both left and right the barren plain rose up to meet steep cliff faces, above which the land bristled with a profusion of plants clustered in primeval jungles. The yellow sun shone down on the prehistoric steppes from a cloudless sky. At any other time the conditions could have been described as almost pleasant.

Reacting automatically, Rius turned his storm bolter on an advancing brood of red-skinned termagants, pumping several rounds of armour-piercing shells into the pack before they had even mounted the outcrop. Despite the repulsing fire of the squad several of the cunning creatures managed to infiltrate the Terminators' position.

With an electro-chemical surge, a fleshborer propelled its cargo of living ammunition towards its target. The veteran Space Marine was standing his ground before the milling termagants as they closed on the Ultramarine lines. The borer beetles impacted on the warrior's Terminator armour, many splattering harmlessly against the ceramite plates. A few survived, expending their remaining life energy in gnawing through the armour with their viciously gnashing teeth, but none of the voracious insects made it through to the warrior within the plasteel shell. The Marine's response was to swing his free right hand, enclosed by its power fist, into the termagant's body. The creature's ribcage shattered under the blow, the fist's disruption field liquefying its internal organs.

With a convulsive spasm, a spike rifle in the grip of another of the hive-mind's assault troops launched a harpoon-like projectile. The barbed spike cut through the air with a hiss before embedding itself deep in the power armour of another of Rius's battle-brothers. The Terminator Marine replied with a burst of fire from his assault cannon. The termagant was torn apart by a hail of shells, its ruined carcass knocked back into the genocidal horde.

Despite the Terminators' valiant resistance, Rius judged that soon they would be overwhelmed. As each of the murderous aliens fell it seemed that there were two more all too willing to take its place. Unaffected by grief for the death of their fellows or remorse for their actions, the inscrutable members of the hive-mind were an awesome enemy indeed.

When the *Gauntlet of Macragge* had come out of the warp, the mighty starship's sensors had picked up the tell-tale signals of a massive alien presence. Scanners quickly confirmed the presence of a hive fleet in orbit around the fourth planet in the Dakor star system. Initial long-range scans of the world had revealed it to be in a state of evolution much like that of Old Earth millions of years before the rise of Man. Warm, tropical equatorial seas separated three massive continents which abounded in different environments: great burning deserts, coastal jungles and steaming swamps, forested uplands, globe-spanning mountain ranges.

A search of the *Gauntlet of Macragge's* library banks had revealed that this was the lost world of Jaroth. According to Imperial records, the planet had been settled millennia ago by isolationists and had subsequently become cut off from the rest of the galaxy by particularly violent warp storms which had only abated in the last hundred years. So it was that in a routine patrol of the wild eastern fringe of the Ultima Segmentum, the flagship of the Ultramarine fleet had rediscovered Jaroth. The Chapter's commanders' first thoughts had been that no doubt if any of the human populace remained their society would have reverted to one of superstitious primitivism. The secrets of the Imperium's Techno-Magi would be lost to them. Jaroth would now be a feral world inhabited by a feral people.

The presence of the tyranid fleet decided the matter. Whatever the state of its population, Jaroth was just the sort of world that the Great

Devourer would relish in plundering of all life, human or otherwise. The galaxy-spanning entity that was the tyranid race was voracious in its appetite. Dozens of Imperial worlds had already been totally scoured of all life to provide the alien horror with raw material from which to perpetuate itself. Who knew how many hundred others had been infested by the insidious cults of genestealers, the blasphemous alien monsters working in collaboration with their corrupted human brood-brethren? The Ultramarines Chapter could not let another planet fall to the Great Devourer. It was their sacred duty to uphold the Emperor's laws, to defend the Imperium against the myriad menaces that threatened to engulf it from all sides. The feeding frenzy of the hive-mind's children was as effective at wiping all life from the surface of a planet as the world-scouring process of the Exterminatus, as a score of worlds would testify.

Squad Bellator fought atop a rocky escarpment in the centre of the bleak valley alongside the veteran Squad Orpheus. Here and there granite formations thrust up from a dried-up river-bed. Every outcrop was the scene of some conflict or other, with the bravest warriors of the Imperium fighting desperately to repel the invading alien horde.

Rius, himself a veteran of Ichar IV, was no stranger to the horrors of the hive-mind. But no matter how many times he witnessed the foul abominations, nothing would ever inure him to them. He could only face each battle with the resolve and courage of the Ultramarines, as laid down in the ordinances of the Codex Astartes by the primarch of the Ultramarines, Roboute Guilliman himself, centuries before.

A unit of tyranid warriors emerged from the slavering ripper swarms to confront the Ultramarines. As Rius watched, a bonesword sliced down through the ceramite shoulder pad of one Space Marine's power armour, severing the skin and sinews underneath. As soon as the serrated edge connected with flesh, the nerve tendrils within the bonesword delivered a potent psychic jolt to the warrior's body. The stun would only be momentary but it was long enough for the tyranid, howling in triumph, to remove the man's head from his shoulders with its second blade.

Striding behind the charging tyranid warriors, lording it over his swarm, the hive queen's consort came into view. The hive tyrant was a truly terrifying figure to behold. The monster stood over two metres tall and its presence exuded a malign intelligence that filled the Ultramarines with dread.

Rapid bursts of laser energy struck the hive tyrant, but to no effect: the monstrosity's toughened carapace absorbed the lethal blasts. With unintelligible roars, and no doubt telepathic signals as well, the master of the swarm directed the broods to seek out the humans and destroy them, consuming all available bio-mass in the process as well. The tyrant had to die!

* * *

KILOMETRES OVERHEAD, THRUSTERS fired, desperately turning the vast
spacecraft on its axis, but it was too late, and the *Gauntlet of Macragge*
collided violently with the asteroid-sized pod launched from the hive
ship. The massive spore mine detonated with the power of a thermo-
nuclear explosion, the resultant shockwave shaking the spaceship.

Chunks of bone-like shell as thick as a fortress wall bombarded the
craft. Some shards disintegrated as they struck the vessel's force-field but
the shields had been damaged by the initial explosion and provided
only intermittent protection. Other fragments struck the vast ship like
meteors, wrecking communications antennae and tearing holes in its
hull through which the accompanying shower of acids, algae and virus-
bearing particles could gain access to the craft's interior.

The Imperial Navigators reacted swiftly, bringing the six kilometre-
long vessel under control. Fission-boosters firing, the *Gauntlet of
Macragge* moved off in pursuit of the bio-ship.

The prehistoric world resting six hundred kilometres below appeared
as a welcoming blue-green paradise, its atmosphere streaked with wisps
of white cloud, a total contrast to the smog-polluted planets that were
so often the refuges of humanity. Jaroth's airless moon, no more than a
planetoid that had become trapped by the larger astral body's gravitational pull, rose over the glowing nimbus of the planet. Then the
stricken bio-ship came into view.

From the bridge of the Ultramarines' flagship, Commander Darius
watched through the view screen wall as the *Gauntlet of Macragge* closed
in on the tyranid craft. The gigantic curled body of the organic vessel
was tilted at a strange angle and appeared to be drifting. However, as the
mighty gothic cruiser closed the distance between itself and the tyranid
craft, Darius could see yet more spore mines and other sleek, finned
creatures being disgorged from the bio-ship's gaping hangar-wide
mouth.

'On my mark, hit that abomination with everything we've got!' the
commander ordered the soldiers at their control consoles. Returning to
his throne of command Darius sat down, never once taking his stern
gaze from the monstrosity displayed before him on the view screen. His
brow furrowed. 'Fire!'

A hundred turbo lasers blazed into life, great beams of intensely
focused light energy striking the already weakened tyranid mother ship.
In a blaze of coruscating fire, the nautilus shell of the massive space-
travelling organism splintered, mountainous shards flying from the
creature and its soft internal organs rupturing as its body depressurised.
Its hundred kilometre-long innards spilling into space, the great creature dropped away from the cruiser as it was caught in Jaroth's
gravitational field. The bio-ship plunged towards the planet's surface
through the atmosphere, its shattered shell glowing red hot. As Darius

watched, the organism began to burn, its pink flesh cooking as it hurtled planetward.

THE TERMINATOR SQUAD moved cautiously through the undergrowth with grizzled Sergeant Bellator at its head. The Space Marines covered the jungle in front of them and to either side with sweeps of their guns, monitoring their motion sensors for signs of potentially hostile life. The surrounding trees were alive with sound. Unknown bugs clicked and hummed while mosquito-like insects as long as a man's hand buzzed around the armoured warriors.

With the defeat of their hive tyrant, the tyranid hordes had been thrown into disarray. Pressing home their advantage, the elite warriors of the Imperium had routed the foul alien army. The less determined termagants and hormagaunts had fled immediately but the rampaging, bestial carnifexes continued to hammer the Space Marine ranks.

Even when its fellows lay dead around it, one of the screamer killers relentlessly charged a razorback. Smashing into the tank, the alien horror scythed through the plasteel armour, its razor-edged killing arms flailing. A living engine of destruction, the carnifex had gutted the vehicle and slaughtered its crew before it was felled by a bombardment of missiles from an Ultramarines Whirlwind.

There was a screeching cry from deep within the trees to the right of the Terminators' path. Sergeant Bellator fired off several rounds from his storm bolter into the foliage. All was quiet again.

'Precautionary fire,' Bellator's growling voice came over the Terminators' comm-units. 'It could have been a tyranid.'

Had it been a tyranid? Rius wondered. It could just have been one of Jaroth's indigenous life forms. There was no way of knowing. With the main tyranid force wiped out, the Terminators had been sent into the jungle to carry out a clean-up operation. With the hive tyrant gone, many of the tyranid troops had gone rogue, randomly attacking Space Marines that far outnumbered them or fled into the primeval jungles where it was harder for the Ultramarines to follow.

Although the tyranids had been defeated, the veteran squad was still tense with anticipation. The Ultramarines' lines were miles away and out here in the depths of the jungle they were as much the aliens as the tyranids.

'There's something up ahead,' Brother Julius said, breaking the communication silence. The others checked their motion sensors. Several red blips had appeared at the outer limit of the small displays.

'Be ready, brothers,' the squad sergeant hissed.

The fronds gave way to a clearing. On the far side of the glade was the crumpled fuselage of an Ultramarines Thunderhawk gunship.

It was instantly obvious to the veterans what had happened. A broad hole gaped in the side of an engine housing. Its edges were corroded with an acidic slime and splinters of bone were lodged in the plasteel hull around it. The living cannon of a biovore had fulfilled its deadly purpose. Having been fatally hit by the spore mine, its crew no longer able to control it, the aircraft had come down on the forested plateau.

A scorched path through the jungle showed where the Thunderhawk, its engines burning, had seared through the trees. It had flattened everything in its wake until it ploughed into the clearing, the soft soil thrown up around it putting out the fires.

But what had happened to the crew?

'Spread out!' Bellator instructed and the Terminators immediately began to take up appropriate positions around the crashed craft.

The blips were still present on their motion sensors. From the readings Rius could see that almost all the organisms were actually inside the downed gunship. As yet, however, the Terminators had not made visual contact with them. Were they the injured crew, tyranids or denizens native to the planet? Were they hostile or totally harmless?

As if in answer, Rius heard his sergeant's voice again over his comm-unit: 'Expect the worst.'

Cautiously the squad strode across the glade, the servo-assists in their cumbersome suits whirring, closing in on the Thunderhawk with every step. When the craft had gone down it had probably been assumed that the crew had perished. However, it was just as likely that the crash would have gone unnoticed to the Ultramarines commanders as wave after wave of mycetic spores hurtled down onto the teeming battlefield. Whatever the case, a rescue attempt had not been ordered.

From Rius's motion sensor, it appeared that the creatures inside the Thunderhawk had stopped moving. Were they aware of the Terminators approaching them? There were too many blips for it to be any surviving crew members, the Marine convinced himself – but were they tyranids?

Brother Hastus was the first to reach the crumpled fuselage. He edged his way towards the open cargo bay hatchway as the others covered him. Several seconds dragged by as Hastus checked the interior of the cargo bay. A wave of his power fist and the rest of the squad moved in.

Rius followed Brother Sericus into the shadowy interior of the crashed Thunderhawk, the optical sensors in his helmet adjusting from the glare of the clearing to the gloom instantly. Lightning claws raised, Sericus advanced slowly through the gunship, brushing aside dangling pipes that dripped oily fluid into the chamber.

Rius glanced down at his motion sensor and then immediately looked up at the ceiling in alarm. A six-limbed, insectoid nightmare dropped out of the darkness. His reflexes working far faster than conscious thought, the Ultramarine automatically raised his power fist to protect himself. The creature hit its crackling distortion field and screamed as its carapace shattered; it fell squirming onto the floor behind Rius. Julius stepped over it, thrusting a whirring chainfist into its face. Then another of the purple-skinned monstrosities was on his back.

Genestealers! His worst fears had been confirmed. Before he could train his weapon on the tyranid construct and blow its vile carcass apart, the monster plunged a taloned claw through the back of Julius's armour. It yanked it out again, dragging with it the man's spine, slick with blood.

A hail of armour-piercing shells from Rius's bolter punched through the genestealer's exo-skeleton and the alien's corpse joined that of Brother Julius on the floor of the cargo bay.

Something heavy slammed into Rius, sending his heavily-armoured body sprawling on the metal floor with a resounding clang. Gripping his left arm between its vice-like jaws, another hissing genestealer was trying to bite through the ceramite shell to get to the flesh within. The creature was swiftly dispatched with a bullet to the temple but even in death the genestealer's jaws refused to release their grip. Several more shots shattered the creature's skull allowing Rius to extract his arm.

To his left, Brother Sericus was grappling with two of the tyranid creatures, one gripped in each fist. A jet of orange flame illuminated the cargo bay as Brother Hastus kept yet more of the creatures from approaching his overwhelmed fellows.

Rius clambered to his feet, shaking the genestealer's blood from his suit. Brother Bellator stood in the open hatchway, assailed on all sides by the rest of the genestealer brood, defending himself as best he could at such close quarters with his power sword. The savagery and ferocity of the genestealers was terrifying. His storm bolter blasting, Rius rushed to the sergeant's aid.

Another flare from Brother Hastus's flamer struck the frenzied press of purple bodies surrounding Bellator and the reek of burning alien flesh filled the chamber. With a sizzling flash an oily puddle ignited, the flames rushing back through the cargo bay following the trail of black liquid to where it cascaded from a broken fuel pipe. Sericus's horrified gaze followed the progress of the fire, his chainfist still embedded in the metal wall through the skull of a twitching genestealer.

Rius reached the edge of the hatchway and the overwhelmed sergeant as the Thunderhawk's fuel tanks erupted in a conflagration of molten metal and oily smoke. The force of the explosion threw the Ultramarine out of the cargo bay, flinging him right across the clearing. Rius's body slammed into a thick tree trunk. The unconscious Terminator slumped to the ground, the weight of his heavy armour embedding his body in the soft ground. Flames engulfed the wreckage of the gunship.

RIUS OPENED HIS eyes slowly, his vision taking a few seconds to focus. Above him were wooden beams and the underside of a thatched roof. Cautiously he tilted his head to one side.

'Hello,' said a small voice. Sitting only a few feet from him was a human child. Her keen blue eyes regarded him with intense fascination. She wore a simple smock and her waist-length auburn hair hung in a plait over one shoulder.

'H– hello,' Rius mumbled in reply. His tongue felt thick and there was the taste of stale saliva in his mouth.

'My name's Melina,' the girl-child said. 'What's yours?'

Still only half-conscious, Rius tried to focus on the girl's question so that he could provide an answer, but he couldn't. A nebulous fog obscured that part of his memory from him.

'I don't know,' he muttered, bewildered. 'Where am I?'

'You're at home, in our house. Why don't you know your name?'

Ignoring the girl's question, Rius scanned the room from where he lay. It was small and spartan. The only other furniture in it apart from the bed was a chair and a small table on which rested a wash basin. Lying on his back in a rough wooden bed, he could feel the straw mattress beneath him.

'You do have a name, don't you?' the girl persisted.

'Come away now, Melina. Let our visitor rest.'

Rius swivelled to find the source of this second voice. A man had entered the room. He also wore plain peasant clothes and although only in his thirties, Rius judged, he had already begun to lose his hair.

'You must be tired,' the man added, addressing Rius himself now. 'We will leave you in peace.'

'No!' Rius found himself demanding, something of the old authority in his voice returning. 'What happened to me?'

'You do not know?' the man asked, incredulously. 'Are you not a warrior of the Emperor himself, fallen from the stars?'

Rius stared at the man with incomprehension. 'Am I? How did I get here?'

'We saw the stars falling to the earth and knew that it was an omen. The menfolk set off into the untamed lands as our elders instructed. We found you in the forest. You were unconscious and badly injured,' the man explained patiently. 'We brought you back to my farm and did what we could for you. At first we were not sure if you would survive but your holy armour had helped to keep you alive. You have been asleep for almost a week.'

Desperately, Rius tried to clear the fog from his mind and piece together his shattered memories. He could remember nothing clearly from before the moment when he had awoken. There were only trace images of terrible, unreal monsters and the distant sounds of battle, like the last lingering fragments of a nightmare that are forgotten with the coming of dawn.

'Who am I? What am I?' Rius's voice was no longer aggressive and demanding, more like that of a pitiful child.

The man and his daughter looked at him sadly. 'I am sorry,' the man spoke wistfully. 'We can heal your body, as best we can, but we cannot minister to your mind. We cannot help you to remember. That is something that you will have to do yourself, given time.'

A sorrowful silence descended over the room for several minutes. Nobody moved. 'You saved me,' Rius finally said, humbly. The man smiled. 'Then I know what I must do,' Rius continued. 'I owe you my life so now I must repay the debt. I pledge myself to your service. I will do whatever you wish.'

Rius tried to sit up and immediately white-hot daggers of pain shot through his body. His face a mask of agony, he collapsed back onto the bed.

'You must rest,' the man chided, gently. 'Tomorrow is a another day. Then we will see.'

EVERY DAY JEREN the farmer and his family tended to Rius's needs, bringing him his meals and seeing to his injuries. The little girl, Melina, was a constant companion. The time Rius spent with the child, hearing of her youthful adventures or helping her with her letters, filled him with joy and gave him new strength to face the long haul to recovery ahead.

But it was not to be a long recovery. Within days his wounds had healed as if they had never been. He was able to leave his bed and walk again. He began helping out around the farmhouse where he could. Jeren and his family, along with the other villagers, were in awe of Rius's restorative powers. The injuries he had suffered would have taken a mortal man months to recover from, if he did at all.

'Truly he is a warrior from the stars,' the people said and heaped blessings upon the Emperor for sending them a saviour. Yet each day Rius still came no closer to resolving his own internal struggles, no nearer to remembering who he was or where he came from.

Only a fortnight after his arrival at the farm, Rius was able to set to work in the fields. Jeren and his family were the owners of a few tidy acres at the edge of a village which consisted of nothing more than a collection of farms, a mill and the local tavern. During the following months he learnt much about the people of the village and their customs. They spent most of their days toiling in the fields in order to raise crops from the unforgiving land. It appeared that the humans fought a constant battle with the surrounding jungle, the 'untamed lands', as the farmers called them. Wherever trees were cleared to provide more land for growing cereal crops or to graze animals, the primeval forest reclaimed an acre left fallow on the farm's boundary. Weeds seemed to grow more readily than wheat and much of the villagers' time was spent clearing them from their fields. It seemed like the forest didn't want the humans there and was trying to evict its unwelcome tenants.

Rius joined Jeren and his family in their own battle with the jungle. He would be the first up at dawn, taking a mighty axe to the twisted trunks, and the last to return to the farmhouse at dusk. The other villagers marvelled at the star-man, as they called him, for his strength was many times that of the other humans. Soon he was also helping the other farmers, single-handedly repairing broken wagons and erecting barns for the grain harvest. There was not one person among the villagers who did not welcome Rius's assistance.

But for all he learnt about the resilient, magnanimous people who had taken him in, he was still no wiser as to his own origins. Perhaps, he began to think, the villagers were right, that he had been sent from the stars in order to help these kind people in their plight. This growing conviction was strengthened by news that came to Jeren's farm one chill morning.

A small party of farmers arrived at Jeren's door, out of breath and in a state of agitation. Jeren and the farmers spent a few minutes in anxious conference before turning to Rius.

'What is it?' Rius asked, concerned.

'Last night Old Man Hosk's place was attacked by something that came out of the forest. Hosk died trying to defend his home but his wife and children escaped.' Jeren paused, as if he hardly believed what he was about to reveal himself. 'They say it was a monster as big as a house and with the strength of a giant. And then there were the terrible, unearthly screams heard outside Kilm's farm during the night. This morning, Kilm found his entire herd slaughtered in the fields and his grain store razed to the ground. Everyone in the village is too terrified to go after the beast. They want you to hunt the monster down for them and kill it.'

'You're the only one that can kill the Screamer, star-man,' one of the petitioners added. 'You will help us, won't you?'

The Screamer… the name troubled Rius. He was certain that he had heard it before – and that it spelled danger. Despite his unease, however, now was his chance to repay these people for their kindness and fulfil his purpose. 'Of course I will.'

Taking up his axe, Rius left the farm with Jeren and the other villagers, and headed for what remained of the Hosk homestead. At the head of the valley in which the ruined farm lay, he saw that the farmers' descriptions of the devastation had not been exaggerated. Most of the buildings had been demolished as if something huge had ploughed straight through the wattle walls.

Suddenly the uneasy quiet of the morning was broken by a blood-curdling, high-pitched bestial scream that cut through Rius like a knife. 'What was that?' he demanded, turning to the crowd of farmers huddled behind him.

'That was the Screamer,' one of them replied, nervously.

The howling beast emerged from the line of trees on the far side of the valley. Although still over a couple of kilometres away, thanks to his enhanced eyesight, Rius was able to make out the monster quite clearly. He saw the bleached, bone-like dome of its head; the great curved arms; the crushing hooves; the tough, chitinous hide.

Instantly Rius's mind was awash with terrifying images and recalled sensations: slavering jaws, burning acid death, stinging tentacles, blood-drenched talons, fetid decay-ridden breath, a nightmare of purple and crimson. It was as if someone had opened the floodgates that had been holding back his memory. Temporarily stunned as forgotten experiences came crashing back into his mind, all Rius could do was stand stock-still, staring at the beast that had banished his amnesia.

'What is it, star-man?' Jeren asked.

'No, not that. Rius. I am Rius,' the Space Marine mumbled, shaking his head as if coming out of a troubled dream. 'I know who I am, what I am.' His thoughts and words became more focused and determined: 'I know where my destiny and duty lie. Where is my armour? Where are my weapons?'

Hefting aside the bales of straw, Jeren uncovered the trapdoor set into the floor of the barn. 'I always thought that one day you would ask for it back. When we found you it was encrusted with dried blood and in a condition not befitting a warrior of the Emperor. I cleaned and polished it, then laid it here, together with your mighty weapons, for safe-keeping.' The farmer raised the trapdoor to reveal the gleaming blue armour that lay there.

The Space Marine held up the helmet, a shaft of sunlight catching its whiteness in a dust-shot beam. Reverently, Rius removed each piece of the centuries-old Terminator armour from its resting place. As he did so, his gaze lingered on the badges of honour won through decades of conflict on a hundred worlds. Pride welled up within him as he took in every crack and inscribed line of the great stone icon fixed to the left shoulder pad. Only the most honoured of the Emperor's veterans wore the Crux Terminatus.

The winged skull carved into the chest plate of the armour attested to another righteous victory against the enemies of humanity. The Purity Seal granted him by the Chapter's chaplains was still intact too. Its blessing had certainly not proved wanting for Rius: it had kept him alive while the rest of his squad had been condemned to death as a result of the accursed tyranids' intervention at the Thunderhawk. Pride turned to sadness as he mourned his departed battle-brothers. He would never fight at their side again. The coming challenge he was to face would be as much for them as for the Emperor and the people of this unforgiving planet.

'I would like to be alone now,' the Space Marine said, turning to Jeren. 'I must prepare for battle.'

As Rius strode out of the barn he looked nothing like the man that had entered. His mortal frame was encased within the metal body of a Terminator and mighty he looked indeed. He had donned the armour of his ancestors and chanted the litanies of war. Now he was ready to confront his foe. He addressed the overawed farmers gathered outside the barn. 'This day I go to face my destiny.'

'Will you return?' Jeren asked.

Rius turned his helmeted head towards the horizon. These people had shown him such compassion, hospitality and friendship. Now he could finally repay his debt to them. 'If the Emperor wills it. If not, my death will serve the greater good.'

'What is your name, warrior?'

'I am Brother Rius of the First Company of the Ultramarines Chapter of the Imperium, may it never fail.'

'Then farewell, Brother Rius. May the Emperor's spirit go with you, as do our blessings.'

Rius saluted the man who had done so much for him and then paused before departing. 'Jeren, will you do something for me?'

'Of course, my friend. Name it.'

'Remember me.'

With that the Ultramarine turned his back on humanity and strode off down the track away from the farm, towards the primeval jungle to meet his destiny.

BROTHER RIUS FROZE. There it was again, a rustling in the undergrowth ahead of him. He checked his motion sensor. There was definitely something there, but was it his quarry or yet another tree-fox? He had hunted the beast for three solid days without resting, having followed its tracks from the ravaged farmstead that now lay many miles behind him.

With a bellowing scream the carnifex broke through the tangle of fronds before him, all four of its razor-edged killing arms scything wildly at the vegetation as it ran. Instinctively, Rius hurled his heavily-armoured body to one side, out of the way, himself crashing through the undergrowth. As he hit the ground, his storm bolter was already spitting round after round of devastating fire in the direction of the rampaging tyranid.

Still screaming, the carnifex ground to a halt and turned, ready to charge Rius a second time. The screamer killer well deserved both its name and the reputation that went with it. The piercing cry of the carnifex was enough to discourage the most resolute of men, while its diamond-hard, sickle-shaped arms could tear apart Rius's ceramite armour as easily as it could his flesh. Its chitinous hide was virtually impenetrable to normal weapons and the great mass of its rounded body made it unstoppable as it stampeded across any battlefield.

This must be the last of its foul kind on the planet, Rius decided – left behind, as he himself had been, after the defeat of the hive-mind's forces.

As the Space Marine struggled to get to his feet, almost cursing the bulky suit in which he was encased, the monster charged again. The carnifex hit the Terminator with the force of a mortar shell, forcing the air out of his lungs and throwing him bodily through the air. Rius crashed to the ground, splintering the branches of a tree on the way down, landing at the top of a steep, densely-forested slope. The impetus of the charge and the subsequent momentum of his own body sent Rius rolling over the edge, tumbling down through the undergrowth.

He came to rest at the bottom of the slope, stunned and crying out in agony. It was like trying to wrestle a tank! Doing his best to suppress the pain mentally, Rius got to his feet. The fall had knocked out a servo-assist in the left leg of his suit so that he now walked with an acute limp. It would also slow him down.

He was standing in a clearing at the edge of a great plateau and, looking out beyond the cliff edge, he saw the prehistoric terrain shrouded by the smoke of distant grumbling volcanoes. Down in the broad valley, partially buried under a layer of ash, were the indistinct outlines of alien skeletons and twisted metal hulks. This was where the battle for Jaroth had been won – and where the final conflict in the war would take place.

A high-pitched screech accompanied the sound of a huge shape ploughing through the jungle towards the Space Marine. The carnifex burst through the trees – and stopped. A disgusting purple fluid oozed from several small holes in its chest where the extremely tough bone and cartilage had been punctured. He had managed to wound the beast, the Emperor be praised! However, his excitement almost instantly turned to disappointment. The flow of alien blood stopped and before his very eyes the wounds began to heal themselves. The carnifex was regenerating!

The great creature's shoulders heaved as if the tyranid was breathing heavily. The deafening scream continued as the carnifex pawed the ground with its crushing horned hooves. A crackling field of bio-electrical energy flickered around the scissoring arms. As Rius watched transfixed, the creature convulsed violently and a glowing green ball of plasma emerged from its fang-lined mouth. Trapped in the energy field of the beast's claws, the carnifex was able to determine the direction in which it would fire the incandescent missile.

Rius ducked as the scorching ball of plasma hurtled towards him. The blazing gout splashed against the Terminator's back, bathing the armour in licking green flames. At once the ceramite began to sizzle and dissolve. Still safe as yet inside his suit, Rius raised his bolter, took careful aim and fired. As many shells rebounded off the reinforced carapace as penetrated it, and those that did wound the creature seemed to make no difference as the tyranid's supernatural vitality and single-minded desire for slaughter drove it onwards. A new pain shot through the Ultramarine's nervous system as the bio-plasma reached his skin, having eaten through the armour. Rius realised that there was only one thing to do. He braced himself. As the rampaging monster ran at him he prepared to meet its charge, not flinching as the distance between the pair rapidly decreased.

As the monster hit him head on, Rius grabbed the creature around its waist. At the same moment he could not contain his agony and screamed. A jagged, curving arm sliced through his armour and deep into his side. The Ultramarine was now face to face with the tyranid. Surprised by its enemy's retaliation, the creature lost control of its charge and stumbled, its momentum carrying the two of them rolling towards the precipitous edge of the plateau.

The hulking monster towered over him. Rius gagged at the stench of the carnifex's reeking breath, its grotesque face mere inches from his visor. The Marine could feel his life-blood seeping away. It was now or never.

With the last of his failing strength he lifted his gun and rammed its muzzle between the monster's jaws. Depressing the trigger he emptied the rest of the cartridge into the carnifex's mouth. Shells blasted through the back of the creature's malformed head; others ricocheted around inside its toughened skull, liquefying its tiny brain.

Rius knew he was dead, but it no longer mattered. He had reclaimed his honour and identity and repaid his debt to the people who had saved him from ignominy. Thanks to them he could die the death of an Ultramarine. Trapped within the carnifex's grasp he could not stop the great bulk of the beast dragging him with it as it toppled over the edge of the plateau. Locked in the inescapable embrace of death, Brother Rius and the tyranid fell into oblivion. The Battle for Jaroth was finally over.

HELL IN A BOTTLE

Simon Jowett

'LET CHAOSSS REIGN!'

Kargon's battle-cry carried over the sounds of carnage and burned itself into the minds of killers and victims alike. Continents away, bloodletters paused to raise a shrill answering cry, before returning to their appointed task: the complete desecration of another of the Imperium's shining homeworlds. The towers of Ilium were falling.

Detonations filled the air as a squadron of Marauder ground attack craft punched through the pall of smoke that hung over the capital city. Chaos hammer air-to-ground missiles kicked free of their wing-mounted cradles and screamed earthwards. The jewel-like spires of the Administratum complex shattered and fell, dark plumes of debris blossoming miles into the air. The Imperial garrison's concern for civilian casualties had been abandoned. Only one strategy remained: destruction of the invaders, whatever the cost.

At an unspoken signal from Kargon, several of the nearest bloodletters turned their attention to the attacking aircraft, each raising its weapon skyward. Sword, axe or spear, these weapons were primarily conduits for the unearthly power of Chaos which, focused by their wielders' rudimentary wills, leapt skywards, towards the attacking Imperial craft.

Organic matter first: the flesh of every human pilot slid, gathered itself, then reformed. Tumours burst on skin and writhed with void-born life. Every bone hummed with imminent destruction as Chaos invaded its blood-dark marrow. In seconds, every pilot's sling-seat was occupied by a grotesque malformation of cells vibrating to an ever-higher pitch.

As the dull reports of exploding flesh painted the cockpits red and black, the Marauders' power plants overloaded, the smooth mathematics of their operation unbalanced by the Chaotic assault. The aircraft spun crazily out of control, some spiralling across the sky, others ploughing into the planetary crust, all finally engulfed in fireballs of pyrotechnic annihilation.

As the bloodletters returned to the task of dismantling the capital city brick by brick, soul by soul, Kargon surveyed the madness and saw that it was good. Dubbed 'The Seed-Bearer' by those who sought to invoke his presence, Kargon had feasted on the entrails of a thousand worlds. Drawn to breaches in the membrane between warp space and the material universe like a shark to fresh blood, Kargon knew only one purpose: strike, violate, move on. Soon Ilium would lay behind him, forgotten, like so many worlds before.

'ILIUM ISS OURSSS?'

The assembled horde – a hideous confederation of lesser daemons, mutant spawn, bloodletters, Chaos warriors and hybrids of every lifeform that had been infected by the contagion of Corruption – bowed their heads in affirmation. The question was unnecessary. The sounds of conflict had been replaced by an absolute silence that spoke of only one thing: victory. The tang of burning flesh hung heavily in the air, as it did over every city on Ilium. The pyre before which Kargon and his cadre stood reached as high as the tallest of the once-proud towers and painted the sky with its slick, black smoke. The pestilence of humanity had been wiped from the planet. Kargon and his followers had drunk deeply of their souls. There remained only one more act to perform: the Ritual of Seeding.

'Let it begin!' Kargon commanded. With a shuffling of feet and a creaking of armour, four mighty Chaos daemons stepped forward from the assembly to stand in the clear space before Kargon and the pyre. Creatures of unstoppable violence, they stood, wings folded, their raging blood-lust quelled by the dark charisma of their leader. An awed hush descended over their fellows. There was no room in the semi-sentient minds of the Chaos-spawn for the subtleties of religious feeling, but they knew when they were in the presence of one of the High Mysteries of Chaos.

With a sibilant hiss and crack, the brazen breastplate of the first of the selected daemons peeled back along hidden seams, exposing pallid, grey-white flesh. Thick, dark veins pulsed beneath its semi-translucent surface. The pulses grew quicker, stronger as the veins began to swell, pushing out against the restraining flesh. A low, bubbling moan issued from the creature's throat, accompanied by the sounds of three more breastplates opening.

A low animal murmur drifted through the watching crowd as all four sacrificial candidates began to tremble, their exposed flesh quaking and distending, caught in the grip of a dark, palsied ecstasy.

The chest of the first daemon, now bulging far beyond the limits of its armour, split explosively, expelling the tightly-wound veins across metres of ground. The earth was soaked by purple-black ichor as the veins continued to pulse and flex of their own volition. With a sigh of almost post-coital satisfaction, the daemon fell first to its knees, then face-forward into the dirt.

One by one the other three fell, all signs of life exhausted but for the mass of pulsating veins that continued to coil and uncoil on the ground before them, growing fatter with every pulse, rubbing slickly against each other as they approached their own apotheosis.

The veins, now as thick around as the barrel chests of the daemons from which they sprang, burst in a cannonade of viscous fluid. The assembled horde drew back, but Kargon stepped forward, his breastplate now open, revealing a wet maw, from which pale tentacles flashed to taste the raining droplets.

From the depths of Kargon's chest uncoiled a single, thicker tentacle. Ignoring the dark rain that spattered his ornate armour, it drove itself into the pool of ichor at his feet, into the ground beneath as if searching for the core of the planet itself. Kargon stood rigidly as the tentacle pulsed once, twice, then withdrew, coiling back on itself, settling once again deep within the Seed-Bearer's chest. The smaller tentacles that ringed Kargon's maw licked hungrily along its length, cleaning away all traces of the ichor.

'The ceremony iss complete. The sseed of Chaoss growsss here!' Kargon announced, his armour sealed, his voice soft with satisfaction. Scoured clean of human life, Ilium was now the cradle for Chaos' seed. In time, new life would grow: twisted, hideous, pliant to the will of Kargon's masters – an infection waiting to spread.

'OUR TASSSK HERE isss complete!'

Kargon's words rang out across the glassy plain on which his entire force stood. They had travelled from every continent, every shattered city, every ruined sector of Ilium to gather on this patch of desert that had once been the control centre of the Imperial garrison. The sand beneath their feet had been scorched, melted and fused by a final, futile act of suicidal defiance: the detonation of the garrison's remaining nuclear stockpile. Here and there, fragments of the garrison buildings protruded from the cracked surface like ancient standing stones, their original purpose erased by the blight of Chaos and already forgotten by the victorious invaders.

'But there are other worldsss that long to bear the harshhh fruit of Chaosss! We shall journey to thessse worldsss, harrow their souls and make them fit to receive the sssseed of Chaos!'

Kargon gestured towards the Chaos Gate that had been erected on the plain. Though quiescent, its design would dizzy any human onlooker. The sigils etched on its surface glowed with a menacing, lambent radiance, awaiting Kargon's command.

'The command isss given!' As he spoke, Kargon noticed the unusually restive atmosphere that permeated his troops. After such a complete victory, they would normally exhibit a stolid complacence. Having fed on a planet's worth of souls, they would be satisfied, ready to move on. Instead Kargon sensed something that would normally accompany their arrival on a new world, one that promised a rich harvest of pain: hunger.

'The command isss given!' Kargon repeated. The gate should have already spun into life, the component parts of its multiple lattice structure turning in ways that violated every law of motion as it tore a new hole in material space. But the lattice remained stubbornly immobile, the tides of warp space beyond Kargon's reach.

A puzzled shuffling rippled through the ranks of daemons. They, too, sensed that something was not as it should be. Kargon ignored them. Within his ancient helmet, supra-dimensional lenses realigned themselves over his multi-faceted eyes, focusing both inward, to the fluid shard of Chaos that burned at his heart, and out, beyond Ilium, where he found...

Nothing. A barrier beyond which he could not reach, beyond which there appeared to be nothing for his inhuman senses to grasp, no clue to the reason for this confounding turn of events.

'There musst be a reassson!' Kargon muttered, while an unaccustomed sensation gnawed at the edges of his awareness.

Hunger.

THE REASON SAT, blinking sweat from eyes that felt as if they had been seared by gazing into the very fires of Hell. Before him a periscopic sight hung from an articulated cradle. Each twist of its operating handles provided a new angle on Kargon and his troops or offered mind-numbing views of the planet-wide devastation. Along one wall of the small annex in which he sat, a bank of printers chattered out statistical assessments of the speed and efficiency of Kargon's victory. His name was Tydaeus, instructor-sergeant of the Iron Hearts Space Marine Chapter, designated supervisor of the Mimesis Engine and, for the last hour, he had struggled to comprehend what he had seen.

Wrenching his gaze from the viewfinder's binocular eyepieces, Tydaeus tore a strip of parchment from the nearest spool. The arcane sigils of the Adeptus Mechanicus gave the same answer to the question he had asked for the seventh time in as many minutes: Ilium was secure, isolated from every other system in the outpost. The only way to make it more so was to begin stripping gears and rods from the very guts of the Engine itself.

However, Tydaeus was a technician, not a tech-priest; this would have to do.

Tydaeus sat back in his chair, closed his eyes and tried to calm the hurricane of images that roared within the confines of his skull. Images of invasion, of merciless assault, death and desecration, of a vile act of planetary humiliation that no human had ever seen before and lived to report. None of which could be said to have truly happened at all.

Ilium was a fiction, one training ground of many that could be generated by a bizarre machine set deep in the bowels of a training outpost that was all but ignored, even by the Chapter to which it belonged. Ancient technology, old before the Emperor first ascended the throne, had been unearthed and used to create an addition to the training of Space Marine initiates: worlds on which initiates could fight, die and fight again, learning from their mistakes without paying the usual price for a failed strategy – their own death and the deaths of their fellow Marines.

Lexmechanics, artisans and logises had spent decades constructing the Mimesis Engine. Not only Ilium, but simulations of a thousand unreal worlds were created, amalgams of every planet on which Space Marines had fought and died. Doubts were raised about the sanctity of such an enterprise, the purity of any technology that set out to re-make the universe. Many were reminded of the foul desire of Chaos-cultists and the dark gods they worshipped to do exactly the same thing.

In the end, ecumenical concerns had little to do with the side-lining of the Mimesis Engine. No Space Marine worth his salt would waste more than a sneer on it. 'A Space Marine prays for only one chance – the chance to die serving the Emperor!' opined Primarch Rubinek, on hearing of the project's completion. In the face of this opposition, the project's supporters proposed that the Mimesis Engine be assigned to the Iron Hearts, to be used in the earliest stages of their initiates' training. Lexmechanics would monitor the combat performance of these initiates and thus evaluate the Engine's usefulness.

During the decades that followed, initiates had come and gone, climbing into the rod- and wire-strung battlesuits that enabled them to interact with the worlds generated by the Engine. Each exercise was preceded by ritual invocations of the Emperor's protection from any possible taint of Chaos that might arise from contact with the Engine and would end with a Service of Absolution in the Iron Hearts' Chapel of Martyrs. Over time, interest in its use dwindled, fewer initiates were sent to do battle with the generated simulacra of daemons, genestealers, orks and eldar and the maintenance team was reduced until only Tydaeus and a servitor named Barek remained.

'They're just waiting for it to break down,' Tydaeus had complained to Barek on more than one occasion. 'Then they'll simply forget to repair it.' Barek would nod or grunt, then go on about his business of climbing around and between the Engine's cogs and gears to apply lubricating unguents to the fast-spinning components. Throughout the long hours they spent in each other's company, Tydaeus was the only one who spoke. Hour after interminable hour, he would watch the Engine grind through one of its default settings after another, sink deeper into his chair and dream of the glory that should have been his.

This day had started as every other. Argos, Belladonna, Celadon – the unending cycle of worlds ran its course while Tydaeus, paying scant attention to the scenes being played out across the eye-sockets of the viewfinder, brooded over the opportunities for real combat on behalf of the Emperor which had been denied him by the very Imperium he longed so desperately to serve.

Evangelion. Fortelius. Galatea. Hyperious.

Ilium.

THE INVASION HAD already begun. Tydaeus stared in bewilderment at the figures on a tape scrolling from one of the tutorial calculators: a rout was in progress on a world primarily used to instruct initiates in the basic elements of planetary defence. Ilium's default setting was one of the most boring of the entire catalogue. Jerking upright in his seat he pressed his eyes to the viewfinder, and manipulated its array of handles and dials. Unbelieving, he watched as a tide of daemons rampaged across the imaginary homeworld, putting its artfully-rendered citizens to the sword, axe and claw.

'Maybe this is the breakdown they've been waiting for,' Tydaeus muttered as he tore off the most recent diagnostic print-out.

SIMULATION RUNNING: ILIUM
SIMULATION STATUS: STANDARD
OPERATING STATUS: NOMINAL

'Your days are numbered,' Tydaeus informed the Mimesis Engine. He felt a certain satisfaction at the prospect of it being junked and of his being re-assigned... but re-assigned to what? Weapons maintenance? Sub-technician in the map room? Every possibility held nothing but further humiliation for a Space Marine who had been deemed unworthy so many years before.

THE AMBUSH HAD been well set. Tydaeus's team detected no trace of their quarry's proximity until the jaws of the trap closed around them.

'Stand and fight, Marines!' the company's leader cried, before a double hit from the merciless crossfire took him out of the fight.

'For the Emperor!' Tydaeus cried in an attempt to rally the company, which was already down to less than half-strength. He pumped shell after shell into the surrounding jungle foliage. Shadows moved among the thick-boled trees.

'Tydaeus! Down!' A shout from behind, followed by a bone-jarring impact.

A charge detonated overhead, in the space he had occupied moments before. Half-rolling, half-sliding in the mud into which he had been pitched, he struggled round to face his saviour.

'Seems I owe you, Christus!' Tydaeus acknowledged. His fellow team-member flashed his familiar, gap-toothed grin. 'Still got your bolter?'

'Always, by the Emperor!' Christus replied, patting the weapon.

'Good,' said Tydaeus, as he gathered his legs under him. Lewd sucking noises burst from the mud as he freed himself from its embrace. 'Because there's only one way out of this!'

Tydaeus sprang forward, his bolter dancing in his grip as he fired charge after charge into the foliage ahead. There was the dull thud of an impact, most likely on a breastplate. A body crashed into the undergrowth. A second thud – another body fell.

'Right behind you, brother!' Christus bellowed, sprinting after Tydaeus, his own bolter dancing in his hands.

Crashing through the cover behind which their attackers had lain in wait, Tydaeus paused. Two bolt rifles lay, abandoned, in the mud. With a crash and shout, Christus joined him.

'These trees are thick enough for a battalion to hide behind!' Christus commented as they scanned the immediate area. What light filtered down from the dense forest canopy served only to throw impenetrable shadows across the spaces between the immense trunks.

'There!' Tydaeus jabbed a gloved finger towards a gap between two trees. 'Movement!'

Christus loosed off a volley. Tydaeus was about to join him in pounding the shadows themselves into submission, when a sudden nagging at the back of his head prompted him to turn.

The figure charged from behind a tree to Tydaeus's right. Fast. Saw-toothed blade already descending. Too close to bring his bolter to bear.

A short step to the left and a twist of his body took Tydaeus out of the blade's path. Another short step, this time towards the oncoming attack, and an abrupt, stiff-armed jab caught the attacker full in the face.

Tydaeus was well-braced for the impact, his attacker was not. Boots sliding in the mud, he sprawled backwards. The attacker's helmet, jarred loose by the power and angle of Tydaeus's punch, spun away into the shadows.

'By the Golden Throne, that hurt!' Initiate Caius declared, shaking his head, then prodding gingerly at his temple, over which a bruise was already beginning to form. 'I was out of ammunition, so hand-to-hand was my only option. Should have known better when I saw it was you!'

Tydaeus stood over the fallen Initiate. Lifting his bolter, he casually drew a bead on Caius's rueful expression.

'Boom,' Tydaeus said, as the siren indicating the end of the exercise stilled the sounds of combat in the clearing behind them. 'You're dead!'

TYDAEUS'S HAND HOVERED over the intercom, images of long-distant triumphs drifting through his mind. Caius, always too easy-going, never sufficiently focused on a task, had fallen during his first mission with the Scouts. Christus, the born warrior, was currently leading a company on the latest of a string of successful search-and-destroy expeditions. Every one of the initiates with whom he had trained had earned the right to receive the Space Marine gene-seed and had gone on to serve the Emperor in the front line of the crusade against the forces of Chaos. Many had perished, earning themselves a place in the Iron Hearts' Chapel Book of Martyrs. The others continued to win glory for themselves and for the Chapter.

And what of Tydaeus? Tydaeus, Initiate of Honour. Tydaeus, of whom many had spoken as a potential company commander, perhaps even Chapter Master, given time.

Ah, yes. Tydaeus. What became of him?

'YOUR BODY HAS rejected the gene-seed.'

Chapter Medic Hippocratus was blunt. Years spent in the field, dealing with the most appalling battlefield injuries and carving the invaluable progenoid glands from the bodies of fallen Space Marines, had blasted away any pretence of a bedside manner. Tydaeus sat across from him, stiff-backed, braced for the news but still unable to quiet the rage of his emotions or the flu-like palsy that had gripped him since the third and most recent attempt to introduce the gene-seed into his system.

'As far as we can tell, there's some problem with your DNA's assimilation of the seed. Your body reacts to it as if to an invading organism. There's nothing more we can do. Any further attempts to introduce the seed would run the risk of producing intolerable mutations. Report to the Chapter adjutant for re-assignment. That is all.'

With those words and a wave of his gnarled right hand, the grey-haired apothecary brought Tydaeus's life to an end.

'RE-ASSIGNMENT...' THE WORD surprised Tydaeus even as it passed his lips. His hand still hovered over the intercom. He should contact Tech-Priest Borus, inform him of the Mimesis Engine's aberrant behaviour and accept the inevitable: the Engine's shut-down and his re-assignment. Ahead of him stretched a future spent watching initiates prepare for their own moment of glory: their assimilation of the gene-seed and their acceptance into the Brotherhood of the Marines.

Not yet. Eyes still pressed to the viewfinder, Tydaeus re-focused his gaze on Ilium. There was something about the invaders, about the way they moved as they piled one atrocity after another upon the surface of the unreal planet. The Mimesis Engine was able to generate the apparent form and behaviour of a vast array of life-forms, but, over years spent squinting through the viewfinder, Tydaeus had come to recognise small, apparently insignificant deficiencies in its creations.

Just as a portrait of a man might capture his appearance, hint at the manner of his movements, but fail to record the particularities of his personality, so the Mimesis Engine could not, to Tydaeus's eyes, produce entirely convincing simulacra. Every ork, genestealer or bloodletter an initiate met on one of the generated worlds was just an approximation of the truth, inevitably – perhaps fatally – incomplete.

As he continued to watch the Chaotic hordes slash their way across the monitors, Tydaeus saw the very inconsistencies of manner and action that he would not expect to see in the artificial enemies of one of the prescribed exercises. A certainty – an impossibility! – began to grow in his mind that these invaders were real.

The outrageousness of the notion warred with his understanding of the relationship between warp space and the material universe. The Mimesis Engine was a part of the material universe and so, too, were the worlds that it generated. Was it so unreasonable to suppose that a confluence of currents in the warp tides could allow a cadre of daemons access to one of those worlds? The longer he pondered the question, the longer he watched Ilium drown in the blood of its unreal inhabitants, the more certain Tydaeus became of the answer.

Ilium had been subjected to countless imaginary assaults by aliens and demons, but this time the daemons were real.

For a moment, a figure appeared, then vanished as Tydaeus panned across yet another scene of utter carnage. Not a bloodletter. Taller, broader, wearing a more individual suit of encrusted armour. Tydaeus's worked the viewfinder's controls, panned back across the scene, until...

There! Half as tall again as the tallest Space Marine, encased in a suit of cracked obsidian from which hung the trophies of a campaign of unspeakable horrors. From its gestures, it appeared to be directing the actions of the other daemons. From the crown of its helmet's shallow dome spewed a sheaf of living tentacles. In one claw-gloved hand it held an axe whose shaft would stand higher than any Marine.

Taking his hands from the viewfinder's controls, Tydaeus stabbed sigil-etched buttons, yanked at toggle switches. A low rumbling shook the floor of the annex as whole systems of gears were thrown into reverse, connecting rods withdrawn and re-aligned. It verged on the blasphemous but, if he could trap the daemons within the Ilium simulation, he could...

He could what? The answer was already there, in the shadows cast by long years of frustration, but he couldn't bring himself to acknowledge it. Not yet.

A printer spool chattered. Ilium had been isolated. Tydaeus ordered another print-out, then another. In the time it took the printer to deliver each new screed of parchment, whole continents went black, overrun by the invading daemons.

Tydaeus returned his gaze to the horde's foul commander, drawn to the inhuman efficiency of his progress across Ilium, apparently still oblivious to the world's unreality, of the trap that had already shut around him.

As he watched the horde assemble on the desert plain, a new certainty grew in Tydaeus. Here was a province of Hell, trapped within a machine-turned cage of unreality. Here was his chance for glory.

All thoughts of glory were blasted from his mind by the spectacle of the Ritual of Seeding. Had every world that fell before this creature been sub-jected to this last act of violation? To defeat him would be to exact holy vengeance on behalf of every such planet. A righteous fire blossomed in Tydaeus's chest that could only be quenched by the annihilation of this daemonic abomination.

The black-clad figure gestured towards the Chaos gate. The flame of Tydaeus's outrage was doused by a rush of fear. If the daemons should escape…

The printer delivered its final report: Ilium was secure. Confined within the new alignment of the Mimesis Engine's operating parameters, the Chaos gate remained immobile. Tydaeus noticed a change in the attitude of the assembled horde. Was it apprehension? Were creatures spawned on the far side of the Eye of Terror capable of feeling fear?

'Time to find out,' Tydaeus muttered, sitting back from the viewfinder and swinging the chair, which was suspended above the floor on its own hinged and jointed armature, towards a row of control panels set against the wall opposite the bank of printers. Via more rune-encrusted switches and levers, he urged into life a section of the Engine which had lain dor-mant since the last group of initiates had completed their training exercise on another of the device's worlds. Another low rumbling rippled through the annex. Before he could re-consider what he was about to do, he stepped down from the chair and walked through the door that had swung open as the last switch had been thrown.

'LORD OF THE Golden Throne, stand with me in my hour of danger. Make me proof against the taint of Chaos, against which I pledge my life in your service…'

As he climbed into one of the battlesuits that hung in ranks in the large chamber adjoining the annex, Tydaeus chanted the Liturgy Before Battle that he had learned as an Initiate. His long familiarity with the suit's design enabled him to close it about his body and hook up the last of the motion-sensing wires without the assistance most initiates required.

The battlesuit looked absurd – a smooth carapace hanging limply from wires and harness – but Tydaeus knew that, once connected to the Mimesis Engine, he would be encased in an exact copy of a Terminator battle-suit. His heart hammered in his chest and a small voice whispered in the back of his mind, informing him of the insanity of what he was about to do. Ignoring them both, he swung a blank-visored helmet from its cradle above the suit and lowered it over his head.

Blind within the helmet, Tydaeus breathed deeply to calm his heart and silence the whispering voice. All that mattered now was what he could achieve. He knew that, in the annex, the dials were counting down the remaining seconds of the time he had allowed himself to step into the inner chamber, don the suit and settle the helmet in place. He had selected a full array of weaponry. He had seen the enemy. He knew what he had to do.

Did time stretch this way for every Space Marine? Did the last seconds before battle seem to stretch to infinity? Were their palms sweaty, did their double hearts pound and their breath come in shallow gasps? Tydaeus already felt closer to the brotherhood that had been denied him.

Still blind. Still waiting. The temptation to remove the helmet and return to the annex had become unbearable when Tydaeus was blinded by the sudden return of his sight. Blinking rapidly, he looked across the glassy plain.

Daemons – hundreds of them! Tydaeus stood a few metres to the rear of the assembly. He had seen their kind thousands of times before, running missions for initiates. He had watched this cadre since their arrival on Ilium, but nothing could have prepared him for this. The kaleidoscopic variety of sizes and body-types assaulted his mind's sense of what a living thing should be. Some he recognised as having once been human: Chaos Space Marines, once-proud brothers who had sold their souls to the Dark Gods. The individual horror of each daemon was magnified to a greater power by their number. The wave of unreasoning, destructive hatred that emanated from them was palpable.

Tydaeus struggled to remind himself that, for all their power, they were unwittingly trapped here on a world that could barely be said to exist at all. Even now, Tydaeus could simply pull the plug and they would be consigned to oblivion, unable to comprehend the manner of their defeat.

But that was not why Tydaeus was here. He was here to fight, to bring their leader to his knees and so prove his fitness for a Space Marine's assignment, a Space Marine's respect!

Thus resolved, he fired a volley into the hulking throng, determined to make the most of the element of surprise. Alerted by the explosive demise of their fellows and baying their surprise, the closely-packed bloodletters and other atrocities against Nature struggled to turn to face their attacker. Tydaeus strode forward to meet them.

Ducking a wild slash from a serrated blade,. Tydaeus answered with one of his own. His chainsword bit into daemon flesh, carved a gaping furrow and left the bloodletter thrashing out its life on the cracked ground. His first kill! Tydaeus's mind sang as he blasted two more onrushing void-spawn with bolts from his pistol. Another blade rang against his armour, the battlesuit deflecting the strike and allowing its wearer to claim a fourth daemon-kill.

'For the Emperor!' Tydaeus cried as a warped ork-daemon hybrid dissolved before his attack. How long since he had last sent up that cry? Kicking free of the despairing grasp of an eviscerated Chaos Marine that stubbornly clutched at his boot, he waded on into the throng.

'I have arrived, daemons!' Tydaeus bellowed. 'I am Tydaeus of the Iron Hearts – and I am your doom!'

STANDING BY THE inactive Chaos gateway, Kargon felt the wave of surprise that swept through his followers' ranks before the images reached him because of the low, animalistic link that they shared. Through their eyes he saw Tydaeus, first as a bobbing figure, glimpsed between the shoulders of other daemons, the view obscured as they struggled to turn in the confused press, then as an armoured image of death, his chainsword descending, his bolter spitting explosive annihilation.

'Thisss cannot be!' Kargon hissed. The human population of Ilium had been wiped out but, even so, no single Space Marine should be able to cut such a swathe through his troops. For the first time in his long existence, The Seed-Bearer knew the numb confusion of the defender faced by an overwhelming foe.

TYDAEUS STRODE ON, conscious thought now a distant memory, moving through the ingrained patterns of combat taught him during his years as an initiate. Devoid of strategy, the daemons rushed towards him, their close-packed numbers working against them, causing their weapons to clash, providing Tydaeus with the largest possible target for bolter and chainsword.

Turning to avoid the thrust of a wickedly hooked spear, Tydaeus was surprised to see the bloodletter that held it knocked aside by another of its kind. The second bloodletter casually stomped its fellow's head into the ground as it pursued an attack of its own. A black chain, encrusted with the dried gore of a thousand kills, snaked toward Tydaeus, wrapping itself around the arm he raised in defence. He let himself be jerked forward, his breastplate thudding against the carmine scales that covered the bloodletter's chest, before firing his pistol point-blank into the daemon's face. The bloodletter fell back, its head a smoking ruin. Tydaeus strode on, noting with surprise that similar internecine skirmishes had broken out around him.

KARGON UNDERSTOOD. SURPRISE had been supplanted in the minds of his legions by another emotion: a desire to satisfy the hunger that had gnawed at them since Ilium's fall, a hunger that Kargon shared. The souls on which they had fed had proved insufficient; their limbs felt heavy, weighed down with the fatigue of the starving, as if the souls of Ilium's inhabitants had been mere illusions. The sudden appearance of another human offered further nourishment – nourishment that every Chaos-born creature was willing to trample over its fellows to reach.

Illusion: Kargon understood that, also. Altering the alignment of his sensory organs, the Seed-Bearer probed the landscape on which he stood, on which his troops were being cut down like so many stalks of grain. Going beyond mere appearance, he sought some trace of an organising principle. Planes of colour were stripped away by his gaze. A matrix of turned metal revealed itself; cogs, differentials, gears and rods meshed and turned with expertly-machined smoothness to create a pattern that was complex, yet regular. Real, yet unreal...

'A conssssstruction!' Kargon breathed. Now he truly understood. Illusion, so often the means by which the forces of Chaos had fogged the minds of men, was the foundation of the world that he had conquered, of the souls on which he and his troops had fed. Intent on conquest, they had been unwittingly starving since their arrival. Now this new threat, an interloper from the world outside the illusion, had come to take advantage of their weakened state, had come to claim the Seed-Bearer's soul as his prize.

'That ssshall not be!' Kargon rasped. He stepped towards the nearest rank of bloodletters, who had by now joined the hungry press. A phalanx of lesser daemons took to the air and arrowed towards the still-distant attacker. Several bloodletters turned, distracted from their blood-lust by the presence of their leader. Kargon's axe, designated Soul-Cleaver by the Imperial archivists, was already descending.

Dull surprise registered in the bloodletter's mind as Kargon's axe buried itself in its chest. A thin pseudopod extruded itself from between two plates of Kargon's armoured glove, slid across its surface and wormed its way into a similar crevice in the axe's handle. The bloodletter's life ebbed away, drawn along the axe and the slick, gelatinous connection of the pseudopod to swell the first of Kargon's shrunken, famished cells.

Not enough. This, Kargon's first taste of real nourishment since his arrival on Ilium, served only to awaken his hunger to a sharper, more exquisite degree. Levering free his axe, Kargon struck again. A second bloodletter fell, Soul-Cleaver's blade lodged at the junction between shoulder and neck. The daemon's body jerked spasmodically as its own depleted vitality was sucked away to replenish the strength of the dark god whom it served.

Not enough. Kargon struck again and again, wading through his troops, cutting them down without a thought, feeding, driven by the knowledge that the nameless Space Marine was working his way towards him in similar fashion. When the last wave of his troops fell and he faced his nemesis, the Seed-Bearer would be ready.

TYDAEUS'S MIND WAS alight with righteous fury. The plain behind him was piled with the bodies of his victims. If all daemons were such easy prey, he wondered why it was that they had not already been wiped from the cosmos? If one man could send so many of their number screaming back into the void that spawned them, why had so many planets fallen, so many warriors not returned home during the long centuries of conflict?

Could it be that the Emperor, or those who enacted his will among humanity, were wrong? Could it be that the gene-seed of the Space Marines was not the means by which the invading forces of Chaos would be repelled, but by the inner strength of men such as himself? This would be the lesson he would teach the Imperium: that true warriors were born, not bred like dumb livestock. He would cast the head of the black-armoured desecrator of planets before the high altar of the Iron Hearts and they would have to listen to him! The old men of the Adeptus Terra might cry blasphemy, but they would be unable to ignore the truth of what he had done.

He had long since exhausted his bolter blowing foul flying daemons from the sky. Chainsword in hand, its self-cleaning mechanism whining in protest, Tydaeus continued to carve a path through the bloodletters, severing limbs, bursting chests with cut after cut. Instead of rushing to their doom, the daemons now pulled back from his advance, parting like a curtain before the hurricane of his approach, until the daemon that he sought stood before him. The leader of this dark army, their commander and their god.

'Abomination!' he breathed, aware for the first time that his breath was coming in ragged gasps, that his chest burned from the superhuman effort he had expended in fighting his way to this point. But, behind his visor, his eyes were bright with holy fire. Fatigue was nothing. He stood on the threshold of immortality.

KARGON'S AXE SLICED through the air and met Tydaeus's sword with stunning impact. Tydaeus staggered back from the blow, boots sliding in the viscera of a recent kill. Dropping to one knee to avoid the daemon's savage back-swing, he slashed at Kargon's legs. His whining blade bit, held for a moment, before sliding free. The Seed-Bearer's armour held. Kargon stepped forward, forcing Tydaeus to retreat and parry blow after blow.

How long had they danced thus across the plain, hemmed in by the surrounding bloodletters and their brethren? How long had the daemons' cries echoed around his head? Time had lost all meaning to Tydaeus, almost from the moment that he'd charged at the monolithic black figure, determined to end the fight with one stroke. The daemon Lord fought with none of the imperious disdain with which he had directed the invasion of Ilium, but his power was still appalling. The cold rage with which he hurled blow after blow against Tydaeus threatened to rob the would-be Space Marine of his will to fight.

'For the Emperor!' In the heat of this last battle, Tydaeus's entire existence had been boiled down to this one cry. Driving himself forward, he feinted, then spun and struck at the hand that held the axe.

A cry like the cracking of the earth issued from the domed helmet of the Seed-Bearer. A fissure had appeared in the obsidian gauntlet. Veined ichor spurted from the wound, spattering Tydaeus's helmet and breastplate. Hope welled up within him and he drove forward once more.

Now it was Kargon's turn to retreat. Tydaeus rained blow after blow against him, anxious to breach the armour that covered the daemon's vital centre – that ravening maw, that slavering organ of desecration. Kargon's defence seemed to have degenerated into an uncoordinated flailing with axe and free hand. Tydaeus stepped closer. The end, he was sure, was near.

A vice closed around Tydaeus's sword-hand, another gripped his shoulder. His boots kicked at the air as Kargon lifted him from his feet. Too close! In his desire to finish things, he had stepped within the daemon's reach. Despite his injuries, Kargon's sheer physical strength was incalculable. Soul-Cleaver hung forgotten from Kargon's wrist as he drew Tydaeus closer still.

Straining to twist free from Kargon's grasp, Tydaeus still had time to notice that the cracks in the Seed-Bearer's armour were more than mere scars of combat. They pulsed with life, as if the stone-like carapace was organically connected to the body within. As he watched, the pulses quickened.

With almost geological slowness, Kargon's breastplate cracked and yawned lazily open.

'No!' Tydaeus seemed to hang over a bottomless pit, a fissure that led down into his own heart, to the depths of his own ambition – to his doom, and that of the training outpost in which his terror-stricken body still stood.

Deep within that pit, something stirred and began to snake towards the light.

TYDAEUS BARELY FELT the impact as the tentacle punched through his breastplate, fastened on something deep within him and began to feed.

He could accept death as the price for his own failure – that, after all, was the warrior's code. It was the knowledge that flooded his mind, even as Kargon emptied him of his soul, that caused him to cry out in anguish. The Seed-Bearer was not interested in his soul, nourishing though it might be after the unsatisfying fare of Ilium's unreal inhabitants and the meagre souls that motivated his followers. Kargon wanted from Tydaeus the one thing he alone was able to provide: a gateway to the material universe, the truth behind the illusion of Ilium.

'Emperor forgive me!' The words, Tydaeus's last human thought, emerged into the silence of the inner chamber before, with a wet explosion, Kargon peeled back the barrier between illusion and reality. Tydaeus's body hung in the air, a twisted blasphemy of blood and bone, as the gash in the fabric of material space grew wider, setting off incursion alarms throughout the outpost.

Kargon stepped towards the connecting door, beyond which lay the annex and, after that, the outpost whose inhabitants were already scrambling in response to the alarms. Behind him, his remaining followers erupted through the gateway, their hunger thickening the air.

'Sssouls!' hissed Kargon, Daemon Lord of Chaos. 'Ssspace Marine sssoulsss!' His fingers flexed around the haft of his axe, the fissure with which he had enticed Tydaeus into his grasp now sealed.

'It isss time to feed!'

TENEBRAE
Mark Brendan

CHINKS OF REDDISH, grey glow filtering between eddies in the layer of atmospheric debris announced the break of dawn over Tenebrae's capital. The city known as Wormwood had stood for the past fifty years of the seven hundredth century of the forty-first millennium. Now Wormwood was dying. The screams of men mingled with the gibbering of daemons and the thunder of weapons. Upset by the warping influence of Chaos gates opening to provide access to creatures who had no rightful place in the material world, the burgeoning clouds over the city periodically rained blood, sometimes toads, upon the death-strewn streets.

The old man strode with uncharacteristic haste through the looming, vaulted halls and thoroughfares of the Adeptus Arbites' fortress of Wormwood's war-torn central plaza. Governor Dane Cortez reflected that the pandemonium within the building was almost as distressing as the chaos without. An ageing man, he nevertheless carried his tall, thin frame with authority. His hawk-like features, coupled with the resplendent robes of his office which billowed in his wake, lent him an air of power and mystique. This was but a well-practised front, providing a facade of strength to a man inwardly broken and in turmoil.

All around Cortez, the subjects of his planet, his charges, panicked and fled before the unholy invaders. Even now, within this very building, the Arbites struggled to order the evacuation of civilians to a heavily-defended landing pad on the roof of the great edifice. This final chapter in his personal catastrophe was almost too much for Cortez's ageing heart to bear, but he knew he must appear strong in the face of adversity if there was to be any hope for the survivors.

Striding through the hall of his inauguration, the milling citizens of Tenebrae parted to allow Governor Cortez passage.

Amazing, he thought. Even in the hour of my greatest failure, they continue to show me deference.

At his heels, a constant two steps behind, trotted his vulpine advisor, Frane. The snivelling wretch burbled a continuous stream of sycophancy and unctuous nonsense which the governor had long since learned to politely ignore. As they passed underneath yet another cyclopean archway on their way to the fortified command chamber express elevator, a commotion caught Cortez's attention in the ornate hallway. A young man had somehow wrestled the bolt pistol from the holster of one of the grim-faced Arbites. Before the security men could stop him, he sprayed his wife and their infant son, cutting them down where they stood, white-faced and terrified. As the lawmen descended on the wretch with their power mauls, he used the space cleared around him to turn the weapon on himself. The man's chest erupted into a fine red mist as he pumped the deadly explosive bolts into his own torso.

Cortez closed the lift doors on this scene of carnage, and felt his inner spark wither a little more inside him. The ancient elevator shuddered into life and began its rapid ascent.

'One more heretic bloodline severed. Praise the Emperor,' Frane remarked in what he obviously considered his most superior fashion.

The two heavily-armed guards in the lift maintained their statuesque stoicism. Cortez regarded Frane with open disgust, earnestly hoping that the insidious man did not mistake his own expression as contempt for those poor people who now lay dead. Dead because of their superiors' complacency.

Because of my own complacency, Cortez mentally corrected himself.

ARRIVING AT THE relative safety of the command chamber, Cortez ordered Frane and his guards to evacuate with the rest. He would remain to put his affairs in order. Frane protested – just enough to escape possible future recrimination, Cortez noted – but was summarily ignored. He, too, eagerly joined the evacuation of the rest of Wormwood's cowed administration, finally leaving the Governor to his own council.

The command chamber was spacious, and Cortez noted abstractedly that for now, at least, the generators still worked. Bright strip lighting threw a sterile, artificial glare from the polished white surfaces of the fittings. Dane Cortez moved slowly towards the broad window to watch the horror unfold. Chaos and heresy engulfed his home before his stricken eyes. Cortez realised that he must present a forlorn figure gazing wistfully from his eyrie, and he desperately attempted to maintain his tall and dignified bearing, despite the terrible events which had overtaken him.

Cortez had served his time in the military, reaching the exalted rank of commander, fighting on a hundred planets in a dozen systems. But with time he had sickened of war, and in the final years of his military career he had begun to realise that he needed a measure of peace to discover himself. By then his influence had not been entirely insubstantial, so strings had been pulled and the name of Tenebrae had been mentioned.

Tenebrae! The planet had seemed ideal at the time, and Cortez had thought that securing the governorship would solve all of his problems. Standing at the impressive window, Cortez laughed ironically to himself. There was, after all, no one else to hear him.

In the street below, the horrible hissing and popping of plasma-cooked bodies mingled with the screams of the wounded to teach the old man above the meaning of fear. Far above the streets, a cold and unhealthy train of thoughts flooded the mind of Tenebrae's ruler with uncomfortable clarity.

Perhaps there is no escape, he mused, plucking absently at the ornate brocade of his cuffs. Life itself is fear, the universe is fear, and vitality itself naught but a morbid energy, fed by the joyous relief that it is the next man who is dead and not oneself. Tears flowed down the pain-wracked cheeks of an old and broken man. Is fear of death the only joy of life?

Shocked by his own thoughts, Cortez felt strangely ashamed by this obscure revelation, for he was yet a man with a military background, and still found it difficult to surrender to fear. 'Now I truly am a man alone, and yes, I am afraid!' he muttered, and terror fluttered within his heart.

As explosions wracked the palace, and the screams of the dead and dying reached even through the reinforced windows of his chamber, their leader stood immobile. Cortez's eyes looked on, but his anguished mind was lost in distant thought as he tried to wrest some solace from the comfort of memory.

Cortez's mind groped back through the years to the first days of his affair with Tenebrae. 'A harsh mistress indeed, and given to treachery at the last,' he whispered, his mind drifting ever on. He recalled those first impressive documents, records he studied earnestly in preparation for his posting as governor and overlord. Even now, he could recite the text. It had become a shallow litany to him, bereft of all meaning other than the comfort brought by the repetition of familiar words.

Tenebrae – forty-five light years from Fenris, the ancient bulwark of the Space Wolves.

Tenebrae – in the Prometheus star system.

Tenebrae – the planet of eternal darkness.

Cortez gripped the guard rail at the window as terror washed giddily over him. In truth, he knew that Tenebrae was nothing more than a world which should never have borne life at all. Perhaps in the very act of settling this world, the Imperium had transgressed into areas best left untouched. Unbidden, the words flowed like a prayer in sibilant mutterings from his thin lips.

Tenebrae – a world a mere 180 million miles from Prometheus, a Class-A super-giant which burns 10,000 times more brilliantly than Sol, the sun that brought life to Terra itself.

Tenebrae – at some point in its aeon-shrouded past, a miracle befell the scorched rock of the planet. A meteor struck, throwing a thick pall of ash and vapour into Tenebrae's thin atmosphere.

Tenebrae – protected by a tender blanket of thick ash clouds from the worst of Prometheus's destructive radiations.

Tenebrae – the stage was set for oceans to form and the theatre of life to perform its first acts.

Cortez wiped an unsteady hand across his pale and sweating forehead. The words brought no comfort. None at all. 'Maybe it was always a trap, the hand of Chaos guiding even that fateful meteorite.'

The old governor stumbled from his vantage point, his mind in turmoil. Instinctively he sought solace at his great desk, hands automatically sorting through the jumble of papers in his desk drawers, even as his mind whirled through uncontrollable planes. He smiled wanly at the mass of agricultural data before him. Ten years of research. Utterly irrelevant now. Just memories of better times.

Cortez shuffled through the records of colonising scientists, reading as if for the first time about the eyeless, slug-like worms which crawled in the anaerobic filth of Tenebrae's shorelines, creatures which were the planet's best evolutionary effort in the absence of sunlight.

While plasma licked hungrily at the walls of his bastion, Cortez absently scanned through lengthy reports about the sulphurous algae-trees glowing in tide pools in their own leprous light.

The planetary overlord toyed with his ornate letter opener. He considered that in truth, for such an apparently drab and lacklustre world, Mistress Tenebrae had proved that she harboured terrible dangers for the unwary. He considered, not for the first time, whether her proximity to the Eye of Terror, abominable gateway to the heart of Chaos, had sealed her fate. Was it this which had whispered the many temptations and terrors into his dreams – and were those nightmares long established in the hearts of the dispirited inhabitants of the planet of eternal darkness by the time his governorship had commenced?

An explosion rocked the palace and a once-valuable glass ornament tumbled from its marble plinth to shatter into countless fragments. Cortez barely shrugged as the spray of razor shards brought scarlet droplets to his forehead.

'Yes,' he muttered. 'She sold her soul long before my time.'

A COLOSSAL RHYTHMIC pounding started outside. The governor's attention tore away from his reminiscences and he scurried back to the window to see what new horror transpired in the streets below. Lumbering past the window of Cortez's shelter, with strides which easily cleared the smaller buildings, Tenebrae's Emperor-class Titan pounded through the city.

'Prosperitus Lux!' Cortez snorted ironically. It was typical to name such a war machine on a recently colonised world thus, the hopes and delusions of the people it served to defend reflected in its title. Prosperitus Lux had not been scrambled quickly enough to be effective against the invasion, and had consequently failed in its protective capacity. Now it must surely fall along with the rest of the world.

'As with everything else in this sorry situation,' Cortez moaned, 'it is me, my own indecision which is to blame!'

While the problem had still been a civil matter, of heretics and malcontents rioting upon the streets of Wormwood, Cortez had been unwilling to send in the Guard. He preferred instead to leave such matters for the Arbites to resolve.

'Idiot! Blind, stupid idiot!' Repeatedly cursing himself for a fool, Cortez came to the bitterest conclusion. The conclusion that his ineffective governorship was the primary cause of their defeat.

He gazed in wide-eyed desperation as the hulking form receded from view, trying to deny the evidence of his eyes. The Titan was listing badly, flames gouting from its hull. Greenish clouds of plasma periodically vented from the carapace, and Cortez well knew that this indicated a catastrophic reactor breach. From his fortified window, the governor could see the tiny faces of the proud crew flash past, mouthing Os of fear and anguish. He knew the machine was doomed along with all the souls on board.

'Doomed as my planet!' he groaned aloud. At last he acknowledged that this situation was down to him, the great Governor Dane Cortez, and in the end the responsibility had proven too much.

EVEN NOW, FACING utter defeat at the hands of warped creatures from the very abyss, Cortez could not stop the flood of hateful memories which assaulted his mind. Amidst the papers strewing his desk, Cortez's leaden eyes fell on the long-ignored Adeptus Arbites reports of cult activity. The unbelievable reports of Chaos worship which had so swiftly burgeoned from a couple of isolated incidents in the wastelands into a full-scale heretical rebellion stared back at him, undeniable evidence of his inaction.

'The signs were all here, all here!' he wailed, scattering the reports from his desk with a wild sweep of his hand. In the secret place of his heart, Cortez long knew that Tenebrae bred a certain dissolution of the senses. He had felt the lassitude of the spirit which left such sophisticated lifeforms as humans craving sensation. Perhaps, Cortez supposed, such a biologically primitive environment resulted in a correspondingly underdeveloped spiritual climate.

Whatever the reasons, the passing of his years of governorship on Tenebrae had seen worship of the Emperor slide further and further into meaningless abstraction, and the whispers from the Eye of Terror grow ever more strident. Now the end was upon him, Cortez could see clearly why it had happened. He derived small comfort from the knowledge that there wasn't a thing he could have done about it, but that did not excuse him of his responsibilities.

Cortez was certain that in the eyes of mankind, he would be held culpable, perhaps even complicit, in the disaster which had befallen his planet.

'They will make their own excuses,' Cortez groaned, aware that elsewhere in the galaxy the powers of the Imperium would doubtless create their own, unfavourable subtexts for why he had not undertaken the obvious and lawful course of action. That is to say, why he had not called upon the Inquisition.

'Heretic Cortez!' he wailed. 'Cortez, thrall of Chaos!' Cortez tortured himself with such thoughts of how history would perceive him, for he was yet merely human, and subject to human pride. Losing Tenebrae was one thing, losing his life another, but losing his name and dignity too?

SLUMPING WEARILY INTO his great, padded chair of office, Cortez remembered the day when vast, baroque battle barges, covered in the hateful iconography of the Chaos Gods, had appeared from the warp to hang silently over Tenebrae's atmosphere. They had rained fleets of jagged landing craft towards the planet's surface. Now the payload of those death carriers stalked the streets of Wormwood: twisted, malevolent machines and beings who left tragedy, ruin and terror in their wake.

'Why? Tell me? Why?' Cortez implored to empty air. 'This backwater planet may not mean much… but it is my home!' Despair overcame him and anguished, gulping sobs wracked his aged frame. 'Why did I ever come here? Why?'

When he had been offered the governorship of this world so many years ago, he had taken it gladly. A small backwater world, of little importance. A place to be happy and untroubled. A place to put his memories of military service and the horrors he had seen behind him. It had become a place of fear and death.

'Why?'

Picking a leaf at random from the pile of reports on his desk, Cortez selected one of the many fateful reports on Tenebrae's heretical activity. Yet another report which he had personally ensured the Inquisition had never received.

The Inquisition? Cortez thought resentfully. If he had requested their assistance, and in truth he knew that they represented the only force in the galaxy capable of preventing events of such enormity, then he also knew he would be standing in despair at this very window again.

The cure? Every bit as lethal as the disease! The irony caused his tear-stained lips to form a rictus grin, and Cortez shook his head. 'The only difference lies in the fate of the victim's souls!' he shouted aloud, as if addressing a rally of doubtful subjects. 'If I called the Inquisition,' he shrieked, 'we would now be watching the grim troops of the Imperium ranging through our beloved thoroughfares supplying "absolution".'

He had left the military after becoming involved in such cleansing operations, for he had come to call them by another name. Murder. Genocide.

'Oh, what's the use in any of it?' he sobbed, crushing the hateful reports between his balled fists. Ripping and shredding, Cortez systematically began the destruction of all the useless paperwork which had bound him to his desk when he should have been leading his people.

His ravings were abruptly interrupted again, this time by an urgent rapping at the door of his office.

'Who's there?' Cortez demanded irritably.

'Jezrael, Captain Jezrael, sir!'

A good man. One of the best. Loyal. Sanity tugged at Cortez insistently. He stopped scrabbling at the remaining papers and readjusted his robes. 'You may enter.'

The captain of the Arbites curtly entered the office and stood to attention. He was a tall, solid man, dressed for battle and brandishing a bolter.

'Sir! We're evacuating the last of the civilians now, sir! You must leave now, sir, if we are to have any chance of survival, sir!'

Cortez smiled weakly at the soldier, then indicated the doors with a slender, wasted finger. 'You go, Jezrael. You have served Tenebrae well. See to it that her people continue to prosper elsewhere,' he said in a tired but kindly voice.

'Sir?' queried the captain, confusion creasing his uncomprehending face.

'I will remain here. It is my duty.'

The governor forced himself to stand and faced the soldier with steely eyes. 'Now go, captain. That is an order!' he barked, some fire returning to his voice.

With that, Jezrael struck his breastplate in salute, turned curtly on his heel and was away. The doors swung behind him and shut with a quiet click.

WANDERING OVER TO his window once more, Cortez felt as if he was in the grip of some strange dream. His attention was once more captured by the ruined streets of Wormwood. Thirty floors below, swaggering gangs of Chaos-warped Marines strolled amongst the wreckage. Their booted feet crunched on the shattered stained glass that once illuminated Wormwood's proud buildings. Any pockets of survivors they chanced upon were swept away in a vague wash of bolt gun shells, swatted like gnats.

Following in the wake of the Traitor Marine cordon, Cortez glimpsed a procession, of all things, approaching the plaza. A victory train of incongruous gaiety and celebration attended by ragged heretics and capering daemons, to the governor it looked almost medieval. Here a plague bearer, foul daemonic servant of Nurgle, dipped an infected finger into the wounds of a dying man; there a heretic carved designs into his own flesh in the vile name of Slaanesh.

At the centre of the march, an honour guard of traitors from the Word Bearer legion of Chaos Marines, four in all, reverently bore a large, upright metal cylinder approximately twelve feet in height and six in diameter. Cortez's uncomprehending eyes took in its rich decoration, bas reliefs of foul, warp-spawned creatures carved from an oily green rock which filigreed the shining silver surface. Wisps of ephemeral vapour emanated from vents atop the singular device.

Perplexed, Cortez watched the procession draw up outside the Adeptus Administratum building, seat of his governorship and the centre of the civil service on Tenebrae. The traitors came to a halt and the square began to fill with the adulants of Chaos. The Word Bearers carried their load up the long, broad steps to the forecourt of the building. Between the majestic pillars of the entryway, now defaced with graffiti and riddled with holes and abrasions from small arms fire, the large casket was set down.

Cortez viewed the events unfolding beneath him with mingled intrigue and disquiet. Something was afoot here which he did not understand, a puzzle that called to him, enticing. The creed of the God-Emperor had always taught unquestioning servitude, and that had sufficed for Cortez. But here, the shadow of his own mortality looming longer and longer, he wanted to at least fathom something of the nature of this forbidden enemy. His destroyer. His doom.

He saw the crowd in the square stirring, becoming agitated. The governor knew instinctively that this had something to do with the contents of that dread casket.

'What is that?' Cortez was only dimly aware of the dread rising like a behemoth to join his curiosity.

Far below, the roiling Chaos throng waited impatiently for the coming of the thing which Cortez could not see. 'Vog! Vog! Vog! Vog! Chastise! Chastise! Chastise!'

Cortez was at once afraid and awfully fascinated by what could be lurking behind the seals.

'Vog, Vog?' he mumbled, transfixed by the growing sense of rhythm. Vacillating, nervous, he was unsure if he even wanted to know the truth at all. Perhaps it was fitting that a plunge into the unknown would draw closed the final curtain on his life. He drew a breath. He watched. He felt ready.

A door cracked opened on the graven cylinder, and a billowing carpet of vapour escaped, to roll down the steps in heavy fetid waves. Cortez quickly reached for his field glasses to better view the spectacle.

'Terminator!' he gasped, and his blood ran cold. An armoured figure stepped over the threshold of the cylinder with a heavy, deliberate tread. The governor could see that this creature's eyes were closed, as if in a trance.

'Stasis slumber,' he whispered, hoping for a logical and less than sinister explanation.

Then recognition struck him as if with a physical blow, and he reeled back from the hated window. In a sudden flurry of revelation Cortez knew what transpired below.

'Vog!' he whispered, barely able to form the name. Cortez now remembered where he had heard the name before. This was Lord Vog, the Chastiser of Worlds. Also known as the Apostate of Charybdis, Vog was a notorious creature of Chaos from beyond the Eye of Terror. Vog was a Word Bearer priest, a twisted parody of the chaplains of the Imperial Space Marines. He was also rumoured to be mutant, a being whose voice could loosen the veil betwixt reality and the warp.

'Bringer of demons!' Cortez gasped, horrified that such an entity sought out Tenebrae for its ministrations.

With terror came a strange dulling of his senses, and Cortez was surprised to find that now he was more curious than ever, for he knew beyond doubt that Vog's presence could only signify one thing: the absolute defeat of Tenebrae. The Chastiser was here to perform a victory mass for Chaos.

The governor shuddered involuntarily, watching Vog as though hypnotised. Slithering over the collar of his Terminator armour came a glistening, slender tentacle. Vog's head tilted back and he inhaled sharply. The whites of his eyes showed through slits as the slimy, pink limb writhed and whipped with its own, unwholesome volition.

An aperture on the side of the Terminator's thick neck dilated and oozed a glutinous clear fluid. The point of the tentacle dug into the hole and began to feed its length into the Apostate's neck. The skin on his throat bulged obscenely, its moisture catching glints of the weak light. Vog came fully awake when the organ was in place, embedded in his larynx.

Lord Vog stepped out into the twilight of Tenebrae. All eyes were upon him and Cortez almost joined the chorus of his demented acolytes as a great cheer rose up from the adoring crowd. Vog scanned his congregation imperiously, his chin held high. Lord Vog radiated arrogance and pride and, it seemed to Cortez, a strange nobility every bit as impressive as the great Space Marine leaders he had encountered during that distant military service.

As Vog started his address to seal the victory of Chaos, the governor marvelled at the way the Apostate's voice carried throughout the broad plaza.
His words were at once perfectly clear to Cortez, yet somehow buried within
a sonic murk which was truly inhuman. The cacophony from the Apostate's
mouth covered a broad spectrum of sound and was counterpointed by an
eerie chanting. This sound, which might have emanated from the very pit of
hell itself, redolent with the torment of a million damned souls, all came
from the lips of a single man. For such was the Eulogy of Pandemonium,
the corrupt chorus of the Word Bearer chaplains.

'Those gullible fools who daily endure the worship of that rotting monolith, the Emperor, would do well to heed the word of Lorgar.' Vog's voice
clutched mockingly at Cortez's heart. 'We offer our worship to true gods
who govern the affairs of mortals. Not a mortal whose affairs are governed
by the delusion that he is a deity.'

The discord of his address and the dreadful import of his words wracked
the Governor's soul with its vile, atonal reverberations. Cortez doubled over,
gasping, and attempted to block the unholy sound by clasping white, trembling hands over his ears. Kneeling on the sterile floor of his office, high
above the ruin of his world, Dane Cortez convulsed with long, shuddering
sobs of denial. It was over and there would be no atonement for him.

THE TONE OF the address had changed. Lulled by the droning, white noise of
the Word Bearer's pontifications, Cortez was drawn, almost hypnotically,
back to the window.

His attention was drawn and held by the sight of a corpse far below him.
It was huddled in a corner of the forecourt where Vog was giving his speech.
Yet another mute testimony to a tired, frightened old man's failure. The
body was that of an Imperial trooper who had fallen trying to defend the
Administratum building.

'Rigel Kremer.' The name swept into his memory, but there was no space
in Cortez to mourn one friend in the midst of such atrocity. The name
seemed... inconsequential. As his consciousness swam to the chant, Cortez
found that he could find room to marvel at the play of light on the wet lips
of Rigel's wounds.

'Beauty or horror?' The old man abruptly cackled, seeing that the warm,
red defilement of flesh almost looked beautiful when viewed in a certain
way.

'Rigel?' Cortez asked querulously, as if expecting some answer from the
corpse below. 'Rigel, how soon will your carmine beauty give way to the
lurid hues of putrefaction? Your attractive red liquid fester into rank, black
necrotic fluids?'

Cortez's wet eyes glazed over, drained of vitality and volition as bizarre,
alien thoughts flayed at the layers of his consciousness, sinking keen
talons into his essential being.

'Then what, Rigel? Answer me! I am your lord, damn you!' Cortez's fingers scrabbled in futility at the window as the Chastiser's voice droned ever on. 'After decay has taken hòld of the sack of meat that was once you, Rigel, what then?' He wagged an admonishing finger at the distant body. 'Let me tell, you young Kremer, let me tell you!' Spittle flew unheeded from snarling lips and smeared the window. 'Your thrice-damned carcass will generate new life. Oh yes, Rigel, maggots will burst from the eggs laid around your eyes and mouth, and bacteria and mould will break you down into nutrients for the humblest of plants to thrive on'.

Abruptly, Cortez leapt back from the window and screamed in anguish, terror and horror. He was appalled at the heretical train his thoughts had taken, realising that somehow the droning voice of the false priest below had slid into his stream of consciousness, tempting him. And he had succumbed so easily.

Tears of shame and loss burned on seamed, leathery cheeks.

'All for nothing?' He shouted, anger beginning to blaze within his core. 'All this to no end save Chaos?' Anguished, he was assaulted by a rush of memories. They overwhelmed him as if eager to escape his corrupted mind.

The long and fraught journey through life. The disappointments, and the fresh hopes. But most cruel of all was the opening of his eyes to the excesses of tyranny during military service. He had left the Imperial armies to become a planetary governor and use his new found understanding to make a better life for people.

'A better life! All I wanted was a better life!' He sobbed, chest heaving with barely controlled misery.

'And this is how the mighty Imperium repays me?'

This dead end. This inevitability.

Cortez howled aloud. In a frenzy of violence, the old man heaved his desk over, scattering precious artefacts and ornaments to be trampled unheeded.

'Oh Emperor, where are you now? Have you forsaken me?'

Regret, disappointment, terror and misery were gone in a blinding explosion of all consuming, inarticulate rage at this most subtle of temptations, and at just how badly he had been betrayed by uncaring fate. Bellowing like a maddened beast, Cortez pounded on the window with liver-spotted fists.

'Where is my Emperor?' he howled in self mockery.

And what succour could the Emperor offer this poor, tormented soul now? he thought bitterly, face reddened in helpless anger. Striding to his neatly ordered shelves, he cleared them in one swoop of his arms. The medals of the various campaigns in which he had served and the sundry paraphernalia of his office he hurled across the chamber with an inarticulate howl.

'As the traitor claimed, so you are!' he shrieked, pointing accusingly toward the skies 'A… a… a deluded rotting monolith!'

The last medals clattered from his fingers with a finality that told him he no longer had any allegiances.

'Only myself now!'

In that moment of deepest betrayal, of deepest loneliness, of deepest despair, Dane Cortez hated with the purity and intensity that could change worlds.

'Why have you forsaken me?' he cried challengingly. 'Why?'

Red, shifting haze started to appear within the room. Cortez stared aghast yet transfixed as the fabric of space and time dislocated. Charnel smells assaulted his nostrils as shifting, nebulous figures coalesced within the gathering miasma.

'No!' he shrieked, his shrill voice an entreaty to the uncaring gods of both Chaos and men.

An awful eerie, mocking laughter ballooned within his skull. His only answer.

A warp gate was opening.

Too late Cortez realised what he had done. By the very act of resisting the temptation he had been subjected to, the violence of his maddened thoughts had opened the way for the crazed servants of Khorne, the lord of blood and war. The one faction missing from the assault on Tenebrae had come in full glory.

Crimson light glowed eerily as the gate widened, allowing sleek, red-skinned humanoid figures access to this dimension. Heavily muscled and fearful in aspect, they stepped into the chamber, uncertainly at first, as though unfamiliar with the sounds and textures of this realm.

Cortez backed away, mouth agape, choked with stark terror.

Cruel mouths were filled with rows of carnivorous, glistening fangs. Nostrils flared wickedly as they smelt his mortality. Blazing daemonic eyes fixed him with a predatory glare. There was to be no escape from that malign intelligence or the bloodlust so driven by it. The bloodletters wielded serrated black swords which were enchanted with the power of death, fit to reap a harvest of souls for their lord.

The old man scrabbled at his belt for the laspistol as the snarling fiends shook themselves free of the fading warp gate. Grinning in terrible anticipation, they loped towards the heavy wooden desk, long tongues flicking down to the bases of their chins in expectation of the soul-kill.

Cortez knew without a flicker of doubt that he was about to die.

'And for what?' he lamented, gibbering in near mindless terror.

Death stalked ever closer, and he was overcome by a sulphurous blast, the infernal reek of Hades.

To die for the Imperium – unwieldy and uncaring behemoth which would have as soon put him to the sword had he approached them for help?

'No!' he cried, and the bloodletters hissed appreciatively. A tang of terror was such a sweet morsel.

Then for the foul abominations released by his very own weakness?

'No! Never that!' Cortez shrieked, backed hard against the far wall of his chamber.

As the daemons approached, bearing his doom on their wicked blades, a solution began to form in Cortez's anguished mind. Against all odds, the governor found a new strength of resolve within him.

He determined it would be neither. Not the Imperium nor Chaos. The answer was obvious. So obvious that he smiled even as he unlatched his holster flap.

So obvious.

The daemons paused momentarily, confused by the unexpected change of emotion. Fear they knew. Terror they relished. Confidence they despised.

The delay was enough.

'For me,' he whispered.

Before the daemons could strike, Dane thrust the muzzle of his ornate laspistol into his mouth and depressed the trigger.

Against all the odds, he had escaped. Finally he was at peace.

DAEMONBLOOD

Ben Counter

THE SPACE MARINE and the Battle Sister gazed across at the sight before them. It was an ocean of corruption. It was a continent of evil.

The morass undulated gently, lit by the phosphorescence of vast colonies of bacteria and fungi. It spread so far through the subterranean darkness that it formed the horizon, and far away island-sized buboes spurted like volcanoes. Rivers of ichor oozed across the slabs of fat and tattered, stretched skin, bursting with the sheer immensity of the creature it contained. Here and there huge spires of splintered bone jutted up from the vile sea, picked clean of flesh by the layer of flies that hung as thick and vast as a city's smog and obscured the cavern's ceiling. This sea of flesh was dead, yet alive. It was the diseased green-black of decay, and yet it pulsed with the life of the pestilences that had made this rank, boiling ocean of filth their home.

Sister Aescarion of the Ebon Chalice tore her eyes away from the sight, bile and vomit rising in her throat. What she saw was a manifestation of everything she had been taught to fear, and then to hate, throughout all of her life. Yet there was little room for fear here, or even hatred. It was a blank revulsion that overwhelmed her.

She was lying on her side, still wearing the fluted angel-wing jump pack, for she had landed badly on the thin promontory of rock which arced over the sea. Instinctively she checked her auto-senses. The respirator in her power armour was working hard to filter out the toxins in the air, and warning runes flashed all over her retinal display.

Hurriedly she tried to remember where she was, and the image of the heretic city flitted back into her mind. Far above them, on the planet's surface, the city of Saafir raged as the heretics and their daemonic allies fought her brothers and sisters. And here was surely the heart of Saafir's evil, encapsulated in an unimaginable sea of writhing corruption.

Beside her stood Sergeant Castus, the deep blue armour of the Ultramarines glinting strangely in the half-light. He had removed his helmet, and held his bolter by his side. His centuries-old armour sported several fresh dents and bullet scars, a testament to the ferocious battle which he and the Sister had fought to get here. Like all Space Marines he was tall, and his dark hair was cropped close. His face was as strong and forbidding as a cliff of rock, his eyes fixed grimly on the sight before him.

Aescarion grasped her simulacrum, rolling the ivory beads in the black gauntlet of her power armour. In spite of its comforting presence she knew the sea was alive, and that it could tell they were there. She knew that it would not make do with merely killing them.

'Brother Marine,' she called to Sergeant Castus, her voice small and quiet when usually it was strong and inspiring. 'Close your mind to it. Look away!' Castus did not seem to notice her.

I have my faith, she told herself. I am alive where no human should have a right to survive. The Emperor is with me always. I have my faith. But I fear for the Space Marine. Why do I fear so?

A ripple of movement shivered through the air. Aescarion reached out and grasped the haft of her power axe where it had landed next to her. Its head, like a giant chiselled shoulder blade, thrummed angrily with the power field around it. She could not hope to hurt the creature in front of her, but she was not ready to die on her knees, and death in battle with such a thing would be a glorious end in itself.

Am I really going to die here, asked that voice of faith deep inside her? *A spirit true to the Imperium never dies. And the Marine? He would have great strength of mind, as he had been trained – but strong enough?*

A kilometre or so across the corpse-ocean, a chasm many leagues long sluiced apart, revealing layers of fat and necrotic muscle beneath, bloated and useless organs. Further away, two orbs the size of cathedrals rose up from the mire with a great, vile sound like a hundred bodies being pulled from a swamp. They shed their filthy membranes to reveal a gleaming black surface. Castus took a few steps away from the rock's edge, but he did not take his eyes off the monstrosity.

It was a face. A mouth and two eyes. When it spoke, it was with a voice felt rather than heard, deep and slow, and Aescarion could feel the waves of malice that swept across the promontory along with the thing's noisome breath.

'What curiously small creatures you are to present such a thorn in my side.' The words roared and rumbled through the air, thick with dark amusement. 'What little bundles of ignorant flesh. I am Parmenides, called the Vile, chosen Prince of Nurgle. I am the virus which the Plague God sends to infect your mortal worlds. I am the festering in your wounded empire. Do creatures as insignificant as yourselves have names too, I wonder?'

'Sergeant Castus of the Ultramarines, Second Company,' the Marine replied in a defiant voice, as if he were trying to impress the daemon prince.

The horrific gaze turned to Aescarion, questioning.

'I would not give you my name, though it cost my soul,' the Battle Sister snarled, and she gripped her axe tighter.

'Such a shame,' Parmenides replied. 'But the girl I can understand. Her mind is most infertile. What has she ever questioned? They teach her and she believes.' The corners of the chasm turned upwards. The thing was smiling. 'But you, my man. You are different, are you not? You can travel across the stars – but you do not know what lies between them. I could show you, my boy. I could show you why your omnipotent Emperor chooses to let his Imperium of toy soldiers be eroded by Chaos.'

Parmenides's immense face rose up in a vast static tidal wave that surrounded them like an amphitheatre of flesh. He gazed down on them from above, drowning them in his blank gaze. Sister Aescarion took an involuntary step back, then held firm. Sergeant Castus continued merely to gaze upon the corrupt being, his eyes steely, jaw set in righteous defiance.

'Now ask yourself, who is in the ascendancy? Every year more and more worlds are lost to you. No matter how you lie to yourself that the warp is held at bay, you know deep in that untaught part of yourself that humanity will fall. The girl cannot see the inevitable. But you can. And do you really want to be dragged down by the Imperium as it sinks? You will die knowing your efforts were futile. You will die knowing that you know *nothing!*'

Castus shook his head slightly, but whether he was refuting the monster or agreeing with it Aescarion could not tell.

'I can give you flesh that will not wither, only change and become home to a civilisation of pestilence. Do not follow the Imperium when it falls. With my help you can crush it beneath your heel, and become an Imperium yourself, my boy! I can show you what secrets this dark little universe contains. I can show you what it really means to exist in a world your Imperium is blind to.'

Castus's face was set but uncertainty flickered in his eyes like lightning. Aescarion could sense the insidious psychic worming that would even now be burrowing for his soul, but the Ultramarine was fighting it, trusting in the Emperor, refusing to bow before Parmenides's strength.

Castus tried to hold his hands up to his face and block out the sights and sounds that were trying to change him, but he was pinned by great chains of psychic energy, to the rock where he stood, utterly immobile, held wide open and totally vulnerable to the mental ambush. He tried to remember the years of training and conditioning in the temple of his fortress-monastery. He felt himself getting more and more desperate as he tried to recall all those words of steel that had been spoken to him by the Chaplains ever since he had first set foot in the Chapter's aedificium. But they were all slipping away, as his mind was dissolved by Parmenides's will.

'Nnnoo… nnnnn…' the Space Marine grimaced as he tried to form the words of defiance spinning in his mind.

It was a new type of fear he felt now. He had known what it was like to feel the air shredded by bolter shells and laser fire, to anticipate, every second, the hot bloom of pain. And he had become used to it over the years, until it was not a real fear, but an understanding of the constant danger that accompanied a sacred duty to defend the Imperium.

This was so different. Here, his body was not at stake. His mind was the prize, his spirit, his very soul. A Space Marine should never feel fear. But Castus felt it now, a fear of change to the part of him that had always remained the same, a part of him that was as sacred to him, in its own way, as the Imperium itself.

'Domina, salve nos…' he hissed through his teeth, grimacing, a thin trickle of blood running from one nostril.

With a mental shrug, Parmenides cast a dark psychic mantle around Castus's soul – a vast, terrifying emptiness, crushing, draining his spirit.

Castus knew that if he had ever been strong enough to earn the armour of a Marine, he would have to be stronger now. 'Imperator, in perpetuum, in omnipotens, in umbrae…'

Aescarion tried to drag herself towards him but the very air was drenched with power and she, too, could barely move – she felt as if she were entombed in rock. Her ears buzzed with a low, savage laughter, and the abhorrent image before her was shot through with red flecks as her head pounded. 'Never break!' she yelled at the top of her voice, unsure if Castus could hear her. 'Never break!'

From between Parmenides's eyes a shimmering psychic lance leapt out and transfixed Castus, laying him open, white arcs of energy leaping off his armour to the rock, lighting him up like a beacon in the darkness. Every fiendish trick the prince could muster was poured into Castus's disintegrating soul.

The crushing power smashed Castus to his knees with an involuntary scream of panic. Deep in his mind he scrabbled madly, grasping for the memories that were stripped from him and were incinerated by the force of Parmenides's malice. Endless hours of battle blistered and died. The liturgies of the Ultramarines were blasted from his memory. And below even that, a past, a childhood, all were flayed away and burned. The threads of personality that had held him together melted in the psychic fire until all that was left were the most base instincts. The flame left him seared clean of all that had made him a Space Marine of the Emperor. Castus was reduced to an animal with no morals, no duty, no memory of the almighty Imperium that had borne him.

And no faith.

A tide of cold horror rose in Aescarion's heart. Castus was limp, swaying where he knelt, his skin pale, blood running from his nose and ears. All his mental defences had been peeled away and the shrill scream that she could hear in her soul was the sound of Parmenides's foul mind savaging the Marine's spirit like a predator tearing apart its prey. Castus had been strong – but this foul Chaos filth had been stronger.

'Do you join me? Do you belong, fleshy little ignorant man?' the daemon prince's voice rose amidst a screeching psychic crescendo. 'Answer! Answer! Do you embrace knowledge, and the plague, and the true path of humanity? Do you transcend your sad little species? Will you watch them fall beneath you, while you walk the stars?

'Do you join me?'

In a heartbeat the mental chains shattered, and Aescarion could move again. But she knew that this was the worst sign, because it meant that Castus had succumbed.

'Yes!' Castus yelled in a monstrous, throaty voice that was not his, throwing his arms wide apart as if offering himself to sacrifice. 'Oh yes!'

Parmenides laughed, and great walls of flesh pounded against the walls of the promontory, sending debris crashing around them. Aescarion was not going to die here. She was not going to join the Emperor, not just yet. The moment Castus gave himself to Chaos, he had given her something to avenge.

She swung her power axe above her head and rushed at Castus, smashing the blade down amidst its howling blue power field. Castus blocked it with his forearm and his hand was severed in a waterfall of sparks. He looked back at her, not with the eyes of a man, but with the same black, filmy, liquid eyes of the Daemon prince, and smiled at her with Parmenides's malevolent grin. His skin was scarred and pockmarked by the heat generated by the daemon prince's invasion, his teeth were cracked and shattered. His body had been wracked and broken enough – but that was nothing compared to the mutilation of his soul.

He did not bother to draw his combat knife or raise his gun. He simply drove the heel of his remaining hand into Aescarion's breastbone and sent her sprawling across the rock with a strength not even a Space Marine should have.

The Sororitas clung to the rock and saw the waves of filth rising towards her. She drew her stiletto combat knife from its sheath, but instead of rushing at her new nemesis and dying a good death, she drove it into the casing of her own jump pack. In two strokes the fuel inhibitor was sliced out, clear fuel spurting onto the stone.

'Damnation tuum,' she growled through clenched teeth. A heartbeat passed and her jump pack erupted into life. She rocketed into the air on a plume of flame as all the fuel was ignited at once. Her ears were filled with the roar of superheated air. The savage heat slammed against her and knocked her half-unconscious. The pack fused solid. The armour on her back began to melt and her hair caught fire.

As she soared upwards and prayed that she would be immolated before falling back into the cavern, far below her the enfolding waves of Parmenides's corrupt flesh covered Castus. In the darkness below Saafir, a new champion of Chaos was born.

As they withdrew from the burning ruins of the city of Saafir, the Imperial forces found Sister Aescarion, broken and shattered. Her fellow Sororitas had taken her from the rubble and transported her to the Order Hospitaller in the Ecclesiarchal Palace on Terra. In the dark majesty of that most ancient of worlds, the priests and apothecaries grafted new skin on to her back and furnished her with a new suit of black power armour and white dalmatic from her Order's vaults. They gave her back her hair, so her red-brown ponytail hung between her shoulder blades as if it had never been seared away. But she still had her scars, tiny scorches around her hairline, like hundreds of toothmarks.

When she gained consciousness in one of the wards of the Order of the Cleansing Water, they told her a story she already knew. They told her how the Ultramarines and the Sisters of the Ebon Chalice had been selected to support the Imperial Guard in assaulting and recovering the heretic city of Saafir. About how the cultists they found there were cut down in hails of bolter fire until suddenly a tide of foulness had bubbled up from below the streets, carrying daemons of the Plague God with it: grinning, one-eyed abominations carrying swords of venomous black metal, tank-sized beasts that killed with a touch of their bestial tentacles, and millions of tiny, pestilent abominations, which giggled insanities as they swarmed into armoured vehicles and even between the joints of power armour. Aescarion was familiar with the way the Marines and Sisters had been forced back, selling every inch of ground for a few drops of daemons' blood, but were finally forced to abandon the city to its fate as the forces of Nurgle grew overwhelming in number and ferocity.

Aescarion answered with a tale of her own, telling how her Seraphim squad had been cut down in mid-air by the poisoned blades of the Plaguebearers and vast thunderheads of fat, purple flies. How she and Castus had found themselves alone in the carnage, facing an assault that oozed straight up from hell. And finally, how the streets had given way beneath them and delivered them into the underground chamber containing the vilest creature imaginable.

She told them of Castus's fall from the Emperor's light, and they hung their heads in shame.

AT ONCE THE Ultramarine armour had been fused to his muscular frame. The blue surface and white Chapter symbol blistered off and the plasteel plates transformed into a living metal which thickened and split, drawing itself into biological curves which oozed dark fluid at the joints. Sometimes he could catch scenes reflected in the dull surface – a darkness descending from the skies, the tear that splits reality in two, Nurgle himself emerging laughing from the shattered remains of the galaxy.

The Plaguebearers that attended to him brought him a morningstar. The haft was cut from the leg bone of some monstrous beast, and the head had been hacked from a stone so black it drank hungrily at the light, and a dark halo played about it constantly. To hold it, he had a new hand made of overlapping plates of dark purple crystal, which flexed and gripped with a cold, alien strength.

On his other arm was a shield as tall as he was, bound in layers of human skin. The varying shades had been wrought into the triple-orbed symbol of Nurgle, and it was drenched in such sorcerous elixirs that it could turn the blows of gods.

The helm they placed on his head had a single eye-slit through which he seemed to see better than with any auto-senses. This was just as well because his implants had soon fled him, wriggling out of his new flesh like metallic maggots.

The Plaguebearers looked upon him with approval in their single glowing eyes, their ever-grinning mouths stretching wider. Castus held his new arms high above him and screamed a never-ending scream, so that even Nurgle on his throne of decay would hear him in the warp and perhaps smile a little at the dedication of his new servant.

THE CULTISTS HAD no time to react as the circle of angels dropped around them from the ceiling of the space hulk's dormant engine room, stitching vermilion threads through their bodies with twin bolt pistols. The cultists were naked to the waist, their bodies and faces daubed with crude symbols in woad of strange colours, their skin white and tarnished by the touch of decay, their eyes black and empty. But armour would have helped them little here, as the concentrated fire cut them down before they could hope to fight back.

The graceful black Sororitas armour flashed in the light of Sister Johannes's hand flamer as it spat a gout of blue-hot flame into the centre of the circle, carving a charred canyon through the torso of one and setting two others alight. The cultists howled, spinning like madmen as the blazing chemical adhering to their skin tore its way into their muscles and organs, until their unholy life was burned from them. They slumped to the ground, skeletons of smouldering ash.

Aescarion's axe-head sliced down into one cultist's shoulder, severing the left side of his body to leave him staggering, almost comically lopsided as his organs spilled out onto the floor. Canoness Tasmander had wanted to present Aescarion with an ancient power sword, in recognition of her famous strength of faith beneath Saafir. But she had refused it: it was too elegant a weapon with which to despatch heretics – they should be slaughtered like animals and pounded into the very earth. That had been a long time ago now – now she was in command of a new Seraphim squad who had become her sisters – but the axe remained beside her just the same. And it was that axe which descended upon the hulk's ill-prepared defenders, lopping off limbs and splitting carcasses like a butcher's cleaver.

A spattering of lasgun fire broke against the walls; one impacted on Aescarion's greave. 'By sections!' she yelled and the Seraphim broke their killing circle, their jump packs hauling them into the air from where they swooped down onto the remaining cultists. The last heretics died so quickly they didn't even have time to scream.

The hulk seemed to have been built by giants. In itself it was the size of a hive city, and everything inside it was immense. In the engine room, ornate turbines as big as city blocks loomed above, too high for their crenellated tops to be visible, and immense pistons bridged the shadows. Everywhere had been daubed with the primitive slogans and symbols of the Plague God, and a reek of death and despair hung in the fetid air. This was a dark, terrible place. But for Aescarion, that was good – because it meant she must be close.

The majority of the hulk had been deserted, and they had spent days picking off the few lifeforms on the scanner. This squad was now as familiar to her, after years of missions, as the Sisters she had lost on Saafir, and they were good, even for the chosen Seraphim.

She was good, too, she knew, for she had learned a great deal of warfare since Saafir. There was a new purpose to her, beyond the service of the Ecclesiarchy. It had driven her to pursue Castus across the stars for almost longer than she could recall, and now her nerves were on fire, because she had found him.

'How far now, Ismene?' she asked.

'Not far, my sister,' Ismene said, the ancient scanning device's pale green glow lighting her face. It showed that she was no longer a young maiden, fresh from the Schola Progenium – they had been hunting darkness for a long time now together. Strong, but not young.

'Then follow.' Aescarion strode through the darkness towards the corridor leading to the ship's control centres.

Sister Johannes looked up from examining the smoking corpses she had created. While Aescarion's scars were unobtrusive, Johannes's formed a web of chewed-up skin spread across her face. They were a relic of a past mission to a hive city and an altercation with a chainsword, and made her look like a savage. 'Forgive me, Sister Superior, but how can you be sure it is him?'

'I do not know him well,' Aescarion replied, fixing her Seraphim with a cool gaze, 'but I know him well enough. Follow.'

The rest of the squad checked their ammunition and marched into the corridor. The walls were streaked with foulness, blood and viscera. Scraps of skin clung to the edges of the metal. The passage grew narrower and narrower, until finally they came to a bulkhead that blocked their way. The symbol of Nurgle was smeared on it, in blood both human and otherwise.

'Grenades,' Aescarion commanded, and hacked the door off its hinges.

The Sisters threw their krak grenades into the space beyond. Aescarion's auto-senses snapped her pupils shut in front of the sudden light.

She was not afraid. She just wanted to see if he really was here, at last.

The flare died down and the captain's suite was revealed in tatters, its elaborate hangings and fine furnishings first defiled by the presence of corruption, then scoured clean by the armour-piercing shrapnel. The intricate murals on the ceiling could just be made out under the filth and scorching, and at the far end a huge, ornate window looked out into space, a black velvet tapestry studded with a billion points of light.

The quartet of blasts had not killed him. Aescarion had not expected them to.

He stood in the flickering wreckage, a standing stone of a warrior, his bright armour twisted beyond recognition and corroded gunmetal grey. One hand was composed of dark amethyst cut into a thousand facets, catching the starlight in sinister forms. The eye-slit of his helmet pulsed with a sickly yellow glow, and his hands bore a full bodyshield and a monstrous ball and chain. He swung the morningstar slowly above his head, thrumming in the air and leaving an eldritch trail of reeking black fire behind it.

Aescarion felt a cold shadow of the horror she had felt many years ago. But that was not all. There was some pride, sinner that she was, that she had managed to track him down even though he had been sowing decay across the galaxy since he had first been turned. And most of all she felt that most wonderful thing: the blank hate of the Sisters of Battle, the refusal to accept that such an enemy could exist, the absolute certainty that to kill him would be right. Aescarion unholstered her bolt pistol and levelled it at Castus's face.

'Damnatio tuum,' she cried, and the Sisters fired in unison.

Castus took most of the shots on his shield, the rest going wide or ricocheting from his armour. Two penetrated and raised sprays of blood, but he stood firm. The champion of Nurgle swung his morningstar once and

drove it downwards, shattering the face of the nearest Seraphim in a
shower of bone. The next he drove to the ground with his shield. Instinctively she flipped her jump pack switch and hurtled away from him,
hitting the far wall and tearing like a fly against glass.

Aescarion yelled with rage and dropped the pistol, taking her axe in
both hands and rushing at her nemesis. Castus turned to catch her on his
great shield, flipping her over with her own momentum. She hit the
ground hard and felt something break.

A cataract of flame caught the champion off balance. Johannes's mutilated face was twisted into a grimace – she made ready to sell her life
dearly, drawing the hulking warrior away from her Sister Superior. Castus
covered his face from the heat and swung the morningstar into her
midriff, flinging her across the room, still trailing flames. A staccato burst
of pistol fire from Ismene lasted only as long as it took Castus to behead
her with a swipe of his shield.

Aescarion, bruised and broken but still alive, struggled to her feet. Castus had changed, too – he was faster and stronger than any Marine. But
she had her faith, which was something Castus could not claim. She had
her faith – and that had been enough once before.

The two circled slowly through the debris. Aescarion's auto-senses told
her that the armour was pumping painkillers through her battered frame
at an alarming rate. The pain was stemmed but she could clearly feel that
the whole left side of her body had been badly damaged.

She looked to where Castus's eyes should be, to see if there was any
semblance of humanity left there. Past the menacing glow, she thought
she could just make out the shadows of a face, a pair of eyes that had once
belonged to a human being.

This might be my only chance, she thought. This may be the last time
I will ever be able to ask him.

It was a question that she had meditated upon for many years, something she simply could not understand. It was something that would keep
her awake at night, and now that she had the opportunity, she had to ask.

'Why did you turn?' she asked calmly. 'Why did you surrender and
desert your Emperor?'

In what was left of Castus's mind something flickered and a memory
sparked. He had seen the woman before, long ago, rising on a column of
flame. This was something Parmenides had not told him about. Could it
be that he had not always been a servant of blessed Nurgle? Was there
something else, a life that also happened to be his?

But that spark of recognition was drowned out in an instant. There was
nothing else. Nothing else but an eternity of beautiful decay, for that was
the inevitable path of everything that lived: to rot, to collapse, to die.

'Why?' Castus's voice was thick and dark. 'Why not? He is no Emperor
of mine. His Imperium is dying beneath him.'

Aescarion tried to hold his gaze, but it was gone, taken over by something inhuman. She slowly swung the comforting weight of the power axe, ready to strike, knowing that he would not hesitate to kill her as quickly as he had done her Sisters. 'It is dying because of weak souls like yours. You defile the spirit of humanity. Eventually you will not even care if you see defeat or victory – all that will matter will be the blood which is shed around you. Your damnation will make a shell of you in the end.'

There was a sound that might have been laughter from inside Castus's helmet. He held the morningstar high, ready to bring it down in a brutal arc.

'My beloved master Parmenides was right,' he sneered, recalling words that he was sure he had never heard before. 'You have no imagination.'

'Really?' Aescarion took a teleport homer from her belt and flicked it to Transmit. 'I would beg to disagree.'

A score of punctures opened up in space-time as the teleport beams locked onto the signal and sent their cargo. Three squads of Battle Sisters materialised with a thunderclap.

In the time it took them to pull the triggers of their bolters, Castus had realised that the woman had used his savouring of the victory to her advantage. Raising both arms above his head and yelling a vile Chaotic curse, he drove the shield and the morningstar into the floor with such force that it shattered and he fell, through the maze of decks and into the darkness below.

The Battle Sisters poured volley after volley into the hole, but as the tongues of fire leapt from the boltgun muzzles a great column of flies twisted upwards from the lower decks. So vast in number were they that the swarm of tiny bodies absorbed every bullet. The insects fell dead to the floor in drifts, many ablaze, but by the time those still living had dissipated, there was no sign of the abomination which had summoned them.

Johannes, still alive, hauled herself over to the edge of the hole and peered down. She spat a gobbet of blood-flecked phlegm into the darkness. 'This isn't getting any prettier.'

Aescarion kneeled behind her, exhausted. 'His master has pulled his puppet strings and dragged him back through the warp to Saafir.' She turned to the Sister Superior of the first squad. 'Search the ship. Kill everything.'

As the Sororitas rushed to do her bidding, Aescarion pondered. She had lost him now. But she had found him once and she could find him again. A link between them had been forged. And if Castus had a weakness, that link would be it.

ON TERRA, THEY said, the very air tasted different, it had the tang of age and of honour. It was heavy with the smell of power, they said. And they were right.

The Ecclesiarchal palace dominated a continent, as if the ground itself had sprouted a great gothic mountain range, fluted and pinnacled, shot through with uncountable temples and monasteries, all the myriad departments of the Adeptus Ministorum.

Deep within this vast creation were the quarters of the Ebon Chalice, the Convent Sanctorum. And within this, the chambers of Canoness Tasmander. Aescarion was not young but Tasmander was definitely old, a white-haired bull of a woman with a heavy face and deep, imposing voice. Her campaigning days were over now, and she administered to the practical and spiritual needs of her younger Sororitas. Once she had been a warrior of rare skill and ferocity, so strong and brutal in the pursuit of her duty that she gained respect even from the squabbling bureaucrats of the Administratum and the immensely proud Space Marines.

She sat in her quarters, at a desk carved from black marble. The room was of similar black stone, an elaborate mosaic of the Order's symbol covering the floor, and all around hung ancient standards and litanies held in power fields to prevent their ageing. In many ways, the canoness herself was a holy relic, old and revered – and still powerful.

Canoness Tasmander had seen many faces come and go on Earth. She had learned to recognise how they changed. Aescarion's had changed more than most.

Standing in the centre of the room, stripped of her armour and dressed only in her simple Sororitas robes, Aescarion lost half of her bulk. She was slender but wiry, with a strange pent-up energy that marked her out as a fine leader. She had been called before the canoness few times before, and then it had been only for praise. But this was different, she knew it.

'Sister Aescarion,' the canoness began, 'you know that I value you as a stalwart of this order. There is not one in the Ministorum who would not have cause to praise your faith. Let that not be doubted – you are one of the foundations upon which the Ebon Chalice is built.'

'Thank you, my canoness.' Aescarion knew that Tasmander would not approve of her pursuit of Castus. She had undertaken it as a personal task, an act of vengeance, while at all times, the Canoness had stipulated, the Order must act as one. But surely, Aescarion told herself, the destruction of such foes as Castus was the reason the Orders Militant existed?

The canoness leaned forward, her voice turning cold. 'There are paths down which our faith may take us which are false. I have seen it many times and it is one of the saddest aspects of my post, may He forgive me. For a servant of the Emperor to pursue harmful goals through nothing worse than devotion is a tragedy.

'I have long approved of your determination and purity of hatred towards the Darkness which threatens us all. But if you look within yourself, you will find that it is personal wrath that drives you to actively hunt Castus, not the good of the Imperium or my orders. A Sister's duties are to the Emperor and the Imperial cult, to the Adepta Sororitas – but not to her own lust for revenge. Your rage takes you away from this order and you are too valuable an asset for us to lose.

'You will no longer be party to any military operation that may bring you into a confrontation with Castus. Are my orders clear?'

Aescarion turned her eyes to the floor. She knew that she had not done anything wrong. Her faith was strong. She could not do anything to harm her blessed Order, she knew that. But now she was barred from acting upon that faith.

Which is the greater, she thought? The orders of my canoness, which have been the word of law since I was not much more than a child? Or my faith, which has driven my soul through this savage universe and never once failed me?

'I understand and obey. But if I may presume, this is a matter which affects me greatly. Castus's turning by Parmenides was the greatest act of abomination I have ever witnessed.'

Tasmander nodded. 'And you could not let that go unavenged. I am not attributing any wrongdoing to you, Aescarion. But the Ebon Chalice is an Order Militant. I can accept absolutely nothing other than total obedience. This order is a legion of Sisters acting as one. I cannot let you fracture that allegiance. Now will you heed the word of the Ministorum and cease this dangerous pursuit?'

Aescarion raised her head and looked the formidable canoness in the eye. The war inside her was over. The decision was made.

'Of course,' she lied.

THE NEXT TIME he stopped to think about what he had become, Castus did not recognise a human being. He had died, and not noticed. Where once his blood flowed there was stagnant, brackish sludge. Where once organs had throbbed with life, there were desiccated twists of petrified flesh. He was not truly alive, but knitted together and animated by the millions of diseases which Nurgle's unholy touch had introduced.

The shield's covering of skin had developed senses – when it fended off blows, he felt pain. The morningstar had become a part of him, the crystalline fist fused around the haft of bone. The helmet had slowly melted and reformed until it and his skull were one. Through its slit he saw only mottled shades of green and purple, the more diseased the brighter. He was something he no longer recognised.

But what did that matter? He had transcended mere humanity. He was the greatest of men. He would see the Imperium fall and live to triumph in its ruins. He should accept these petty changes and rejoice. Shouldn't he?

The warrior gazed down from the promontory. The cavern had not changed after all these decades. Above, the city of Saafir was a mass of festering rot, seeping through the ground, making the whole planet unclean. In the night sky, the nearest and brightest points of light were planets which had fallen to his daemonic hordes. But down below it all, the cavern was the same, with its long, narrow isthmus of stone on which Castus now stood.

And Parmenides, of course. The daemon prince was still there. Castus had long given up wondering if Parmenides was really a majestic demigod who would deliver all he had promised, or a malevolent beast who was laughing at him. He had grown to realise that there were more important things. To serve Parmenides was to serve the greater powers which linked this world to the next with chains of their will. Castus told himself this every second of his waking.

But behind his thoughts, wasn't there something else? Wasn't he a little more than the champion of the Plague God? Hadn't there been a Castus before, a different man but the same? There was only one thing he could say for certain. He had not always been like this.

Below him, the immense waves of decaying flesh rolled and split, and Parmenides's vast face appeared once more, with its malignant grin and dead black eyes.

'My boy,' the daemon prince said, 'you have done much for me. Led my armies. Carved out an empire. Nurgle is much pleased. But now your talents must be turned to another task.'

Castus kneeled on the rock, laying his shield in front of him, ready to receive his holy orders.

'I must confess,' Parmenides continued, 'I cannot see how these little fleshy creatures can be such a nuisance. But now they prepare to strike back at us. A ship is coming, my boy. It is heading for this very planet, such is their insolence, so it is you, my treasured champion, who will demonstrate to them the insanity of their actions. Lead my fleet and be sure to show them the true way of all flesh before you break them. They must not breach Nurgle's sacred boundaries.'

Castus bowed his head. A cancerous shock rippled through the air. The warfleet's ancient teleporters took hold of the warrior's altered frame and hefted him up into orbit to make ready for the foe's arrival.

THE HALL IN the centre of the Convent Sanctorum had been sealed for many days. Although a questioning nature was not encouraged in the Adepta Sororitas, Battle Sister Aescarion could not help but wonder what political machinations could be going on in there, carried out by men who arrived in secret, dressed in shadows. When she was summoned there, she realised the truth almost at once. It had been a long time since the canoness had sought to separate her loyalty from her faith. While Aescarion had done everything she had been told, on all her campaigns skirting the furthest reaches of the Imperium, throughout the savagery of her many battles, she never forgot her thirst for the blood of Castus.

The hall had been a chapel thousands of years ago, rebuilt and absorbed as the Ecclesiarchal palace spread itself across the continent. The grey stonework had been carved with stern gothic fluting, the ceiling was high and vaulted and the air was cold. In the middle of the hall was a large table around which sat the delegates, perhaps a score of them. All but one of them were mere presences. The lights set high in the chapel's ceiling hid their hooded faces.

In the centre of them all sat the only visible being, the inquisitor. He was still dressed in his ceremonial Terminator armour, elaborately inlaid with precious stones, with the massive scarlet Inquisitorial seal on the ring of the power-glove. He had an intense face, drawn and lined, not with age, but with the terrors his calling had forced him to endure, and it looked incongruous amongst the great shifting plasteel plates that gave him the bulk of a walking tank. He indicated Aescarion's designated seat with a wave of the power-glove. It was at the head of the table, and her invisible judges sat in an intimidating crescent before her.

'Sister Aescarion… I am aware of the differences the Ministorum has had with the Inquisition in the past,' the Inquisitor began. His voice echoed grandly around the old stone. 'But I am sure you have seen enough in your service to realise that, while we may go about things differently, we both have similar goals at heart.'

Aescarion had always been suspicious of the Inquisition. With their obsession with secrecy, they seemed to her not far removed from the heretics they monitored. She had herself refused any part in dealing with them in the past. But now, she knew, there might be a chance to realise the wish that she had harboured for most of her career in the Ebon Chalice.

The inquisitor raised his unarmoured hand and a servitor somewhere in the back of the room caused a stellar map to be projected into the air above the centre of the table. A network of fine lines and icons appeared, marking out the western edge of the Segmentum Pacificus. One planet was highlighted.

'The activities of Chaotic forces have always been our primary concern,' the Inquisitor continued. 'The planet indicated is Saafir, which we have been monitoring very carefully for over twenty years. Now, we understand that there is an official position held by your canoness regarding Castus and yourself. Is that correct?'

'That is so.' Aescarion felt a ripple of excitement in her blood. It had been a long time since anyone had dared to even mention that name around her.

The inquisitor nodded gravely. 'A point has been reached where it is no longer feasible, we believe, for this to stand.' He gestured again and several planets lit up around the marked one. 'These are the planets which Parmenides and his foul hordes have secured so far. They are mostly barren worlds in which we have little interest. However, Saafir itself is of considerable material value, with incalculably important mineral resources.'

'I know,' Aescarion replied. 'I was in the force sent to recover it in the first place.'

The inquisitor allowed himself a smile. 'Quite. For these reasons we have been content merely to contain this threat.' A dozen more planets lit up on the map. 'These worlds are under attack now. If Parmenides secures them they will give him a considerable sphere of influence. His empire is, in effect, a Chaotic centre of operations within Imperium-controlled space. This is a state of affairs that cannot be tolerated.'

Aescarion glanced from the inquisitor's face to the shadowy figures on either side. She could feel they were studying her intently, trying to gauge her reaction. What could have brought them here, officials of the Imperium so important their identities had to be kept from her? Then she knew.

'The Exterminatum,' Aescarion breathed.

The inquisitor raised his eyebrows. 'You are perceptive, sister.'

'With respect, inquisitor, though you will know I am not disinterested in the fate of Parmenides, I fail to see why I have been called here. I have pressing duties elsewhere on Terra.' She knew full well why they needed her. But she wanted, she needed to hear them say it.

'Sister Aescarion, Parmenides's area of influence has recently become off-limits to all Imperial craft. Any warfleet we send will be intercepted.' His voice dropped – he was saying this with reluctance, Aescarion realised, because he was so unused to telling such important information to a member of the Ecclesiarchy. 'We know that the forces sent to attack any Exterminatus mission will be led by Castus. Now, in truth, all of our intelligence concerning Castus and most of that concerning Parmenides has come to us indirectly from you. Records from his days in the Ultramarines are next to useless – only you know his mind now.'

Aescarion looked at the inquisitor slyly, 'You need me?'

The inquisitor looked at one of his companions, and the silhouette nodded to him. 'Yes, sister,' he replied. 'We need you.'

'Because only I know how Castus might think.'

'That is not the only reason you are here.' The inquisitor shifted uneasily in his seat, the servos of his armour whirring. This was not something he wanted to say. 'One of the forces which governs this galaxy, and the Imperium within it, is Fate. It is a strange force which cannot be manipulated, only accepted and worked around.

'Part of the reason the Imperium has endured is because we take Fate into account.' Above the table, the map winked off, leaving only the inquisitor lit. 'Lesser leaders ignore it, which is why they all eventually fall. In this matter, it is Fate that connects you to Castus. You are a thread running through his life. Without you, he is completely in the thrall of Chaos. But so long as you are alive, there is a link between him and the Imperium that he cannot escape.

'You were there at the start of this. Fate may well decide that you should be there at the end. This situation may require you to die alongside Castus. I am led to understand that you will accept this.'

Aescarion could feel shadow-hidden eyes examining her. In her mind, she could still see that foul stain of Chaos spreading across the map.

'I could serve my Emperor in no greater fashion,' she said quietly, 'than by scouring Saafir utterly of the filth which infests it.'

ONCE AGAIN, CASTUS had changed. Standing there on the bridge of the Chaos vessel, *Defixio*, Aescarion could see the armour around his barrel chest breathing as he did. Where it had been scored it bled a green, brackish ichor. There were no longer eyes behind the helmet, just a single slash of malevolence. He moved, not like a man clad in armour, but like something wholly biological, primeval and strange.

Castus, for his part, knew that he should recognise her. He had seen her before, more than once, but he could not name her. The face had been younger, certainly, with fewer lines; the eyes brighter, the hair a deeper colour. He recalled dimly that age did these things to humans. But it was definitely the same person, the same black-armoured woman, the same symbol of the flaming chalice embroidered on her white robes. But her name... what was her name? Where had he seen her?

Aescarion had seen this moment a million times in her imagination. All around her lay the shattered wreckage of the *Defixio*'s bridge. The ancient computation banks were torn apart, spilling brass rods and gears onto the floor. The floor and walls were scarred with gunfire. The bodies of the ship's crew lay all around, alongside the mangled corpses of Castus's daemons. Great swathes of daemons' blood spattered across the walls and pooled around the bases of the control consoles, still smoking and bubbling. None had given any quarter, and all had died for their devotion, either to the god of the Plague or to the purity of the Imperium.

Through the great observation port which served for a ceiling, the stars outside marked the fringes of Parmenides's corrupt domain. The warfleet had barely entered the disputed space when the metal fangs of something alive had burrowed into the *Defixio*'s hull and disgorged a horde of Nurgle's finest. One by one the ships protecting the *Defixio* had fallen to the same fate, their huge empty hulks drifting lazily through space like bodies in the water. Only the defenders aboard the *Defixio* had been able to stem the tide, and then only at the expense of their own lives. The two forces had ground each other down in the corridors and engine rooms of the ship, until only two stood.

Aescarion, whose axe blade still smouldered from the blood of a dozen daemons. And Castus, whose morningstar was heavy with gore and whose shield was blistered and slashed. So, as Fate and the Emperor's divine will had decreed, they faced each other once again.

Wearily they began to circle once more, weighing their weapons in their hands. Aescarion knew her chances were slight. She was Castus's match in skill but not strength, and she had none of his toughness. She had faced him twice before, and each time her broken body had needed the attentions of the Orders Hospitaller to heal. And Castus would be a greater warrior than he had ever been. He was wholly Chaotic in form, and lacked the weaknesses of humanity.

But, of course, he had not fought this duel out in full, in every waking second of his life, as Aescarion had done. She had mapped out the tides of the struggle, every move, every outcome. She had seen how he fought. She knew even before she had moved how he would react. Aescarion brought her axe down towards him. Castus thrust his shield in front of him but she knew he would. She drove the blade into the top edge of the shield and split it clean in two. Blood fountained from the torn panels, the warrior letting out a bestial roar of pain. His morningstar swept in a wide black path but the Seraphim ducked it, slicing upwards into his armoured torso.

The axe's blade slashed again and again, a lightning bolt that struck in a dozen places at once, the energy field lashing against the armour so it split and buckled. The wounds were shallow but they were many, for Aescarion knew she could not fell him with one blow. He had to be ground down, whittled away until he could not resist, with blows his supernatural reflexes could not avoid.

My faith has taken me this far, Aescarion prayed as she sliced and circled the warrior. *Now my hatred will take me through.*

Castus was forced back under her onslaught. For the first time he felt panic welling up through long-dead avenues of his mind. He fell to his knees, the blows battering his head now. The blade of bone lashed into his body, the flesh exposed, the armour falling away in chunks. He fell onto his back, his altered blood spurting all around, his blackened, dead flesh drying and contracting as it was exposed to the air. He waited for the final blow that would break him.

This was a feeling he had felt before, so many years before. This helplessness, being laid open before an enemy. This was what it had been like when his mind was flayed away. His faith blasted from him. His soul laid bare for Parmenides to corrupt. The heart-rending memories of that day bubbled up into his mind from the dark corner of his soul where they had festered, just as he had festered for all of these years. He had not always been as he was now. He had been changed. This woman! She had been there when it happened – and now she had come back.

Aescarion looked down at Castus. He was at her mercy at last. Now came the part that could so easily become undone. The speech she had rehearsed all these years.

'It makes no difference if I kill you now,' she spat. 'You are bound to the Plague God. If you die, your soul will join a billion others in damnation. If I let you live, you might wait a thousand years more, and by then you will have no mind left to care what happens to my species. Parmenides offered you knowledge. Now you have it, from me. You have seen both sides of reality – you have served both the Imperium and Chaos. But there is one thing you don't know, one fragment of experience you have not claimed. You do not know how it would feel to become righteous again.'

Castus looked up at her. He knew that he would not live for long, not with his stagnant blood running so freely onto the floor. He stared up at her lined face, and the strands of grey in the hair that he had once seen burning above him.

'You are old,' he whispered through his time-ravaged throat. 'I did not realise it had been so long.'

Aescarion switched off her axe's energy field. The air fell still. 'You have all the knowledge you ever will. You are stronger than any man alive, than any Space Marine I have ever known of. But is it enough? It cannot get any better, Castus. It will only get worse. It might take thousands of years, but it will get so much worse.'

Castus felt his life draining away. He knew well, by now, the ways of death. He had minutes, not years. The words of this woman would not leave his mind. He had thrown everything he had believed in away to be one with the blessed Plague God. Surely he could not return?

Aescarion was virtually unarmed now, but she knew Castus was harmless. Even if he wasn't dying, his thoughts were keeping him docile. There was a war going on in his mind of a kind she knew so well. 'You may think that you cannot be forgiven, that you can never be a part of humanity again. But there is more than one path to redemption.'

More than one path. There is always another way. Castus had walked two paths in his life. He had abandoned one. Could he do it again, with the time he had left?

'Look what the years have done to us both,' Aescarion continued. 'They turned you into an animal. They forced my faith away from the commands of my Order. But all that time has let me come to see that whatever happens here, you will never have the chance to change the galaxy again.

'You have an imagination. Use it. Change your path once more before you draw your last breath.'

THE SICKENING FLASH brought him back into the cavern, returning him to the very place where his new life had begun, so long ago. The Chaos champion struggled, but struggled in victory. His steps were laboured as he dragged his bleeding bulk along the promontory once more to his position above the roiling face of the daemon prince.

'Castus, my boy!' Parmenides had been waiting for his servant's return. 'I see it has been a taxing task I set you. But are you victorious?'

Castus nodded slowly, his last reservoir of energy draining dry.

'The Exterminatus? Is it averted?'

'Better... better than that,' Castus croaked. 'It is... unnecessary.'

The face reared up in its slow tidal wave, a kilometre-wide frown furrowing the cascade of reeking flesh. 'Meaning what, my servant?'

Castus pulled himself up to his full height. With the force of sheer will he unclenched his altered hands. The fingers reluctantly peeled away, the crystal splitting, the morningstar falling from his grip and spiralling down into the corrupt sea.

He spread those fingers and, with what little strength he had left, plunged them into his breastplate. The metal split along the lines which Aescarion's axe had scored, laying open the diseased torso which had been enclosed since he first set foot on Saafir.

The dead organs had been hollowed out and the rotting loops of viscera were gone. Now in his distended ribcage there hung a slim metal cylinder, harmless in appearance – until the daemon prince's psychic sight perceived the gothic letters inscribed upon it:

IN EXTERMINATUS EXTREMIS.

DOMINA, SALVE NOS.

Sergeant Castus of the Ultramarines looked Parmenides the Vile in the eye, and tasted joyfully the fear he saw there.

'Damnatio tuum,' he whispered, and the white light of purity blasted him clean for all eternity.

KNOW THINE ENEMY
Gav Thorpe

THE MASSIVE, SLAB-sided fuselage of the Thunderhawk gunship shook and rattled as it plunged through the upper atmosphere of the planet Slato. The roaring of its massive jets and the rumbling of the air against the armoured hull filled the interior with a deafening cacophony. The air glowed around the falling gunship as the armoured beak of its cockpit and the leading edge of its stubby wings glowed white-hot with the friction of its entry from orbit.

Brother Ramesis, chaplain of the 4th Company of the Salamanders Space Marine Chapter, felt the craft hit an area of low pressure and drop several hundred feet in a couple of seconds, pushing him up into the harness which secured him to the inner side of the gunship's fuselage. As the Thunderhawk plummeted deeper into the thick cloud of Slato's skies the passage became smoother, and half a minute later the pilot activated the standby lights. The padded restraints arched up into the wall above Ramesis's head with a hiss of hydraulics and he stretched his arms, the servos within his powered armour whirring quietly as they matched the movement. He felt pressure on his back as the Thunderhawk's machinery implanted his backpack into the socket along his armour's spine, then dropped the ablative shoulder pads down on either side of his head. Now fully armoured, Ramesis stood up and walked steadily along the decking of the Thunderhawk, passing his gaze over the twenty-six assembled Space Marines. Each was conducting his own pre-battle rituals: checking weapons, comms or armour one last time, wishing each other the Emperor's benevolence or just praying quietly.

Ramesis activated a rune set into a bulkhead and the door to the small chapel-room slid out of sight. Stepping inside, the chaplain lit an ornate brazier in the middle of the altar and then knelt on one knee before it, bringing his clenched fists to his forehead in a sign of worship. Standing, he took his rosarius, the Shield of the Emperor, from the reliquary to the left of the altar. Kneeling again, he cupped the great arcane device in both hands, running his fingers around its circular edge, seeing his face mirrored in the twelve gems set in concentric circles on its black enamelled surface.

'Beneficent Emperor, who rules the stars and guideth mankind,' Ramesis chanted as his thumbs gently pressed the jewels on the rosarius in the ritual pattern, 'Cast thy divine protection over me, your eternal servant. Though I gladly shed my blood in your honour, keep me from ignoble death so that I might continue to serve thy greatness. I live that I might serve thee. As I serve thee in life, may I serve thee in death.'

As he completed his ritual, the rosarius hummed into life. Ramesis could feel the Emperor's protective aura pulsing from its depths and it gladdened his soul. Hanging the rosarius's heavy chain around his neck, Ramesis stood and turned to the reliquary to the right. From within the intricately carved wooden box, fashioned by his own hand during his time as a Chaplain Novitiate, Ramesis took out his crozius arcanum, grasping its two-foot haft tightly in both gauntleted hands. Again Ramesis knelt before the altar clutching the crozius to his chest, its eagle-shaped head resting against the similar eagle blazon embossed on the armoured plastron across his chest.

'Beneficent Emperor, who ruleth the stars and guideth mankind. Guideth my hand that I might smite thine enemies. Invest this weapon with thine anger. Let mine arm be the instrument of thy divine wrath. As you keep me in life, let me bring death to thine enemies.'

With the invocation complete, Ramesis slid the firing stud in the haft of the crozius into its forward, active position. With a simple press of his finger, the eagle of the crozius would be surrounded by a shimmering disruption field, capable of smashing bone and shattering the thickest armour. Truly, the ways of the Machine God are miraculous, Ramesis thought.

As the final part of the Consecration to Battle, Ramesis hung his crozius from his belt and took his golden, skull-faced helm from its position in front of the flickering brazier.

'Beneficent Emperor, who rules the stars and guideth mankind. Let mine eyes look upon your magnificence. Let mine eyes see truly all things fair and foul. Let mine eyes tell friend from foe that I might know thine enemy.' Ramesis placed the helm over his head, twisting it slightly so that the vacuum seals clamped into place. He turned a dial on his left wrist and the helmet pressurised with the rest of the power armoured suit.

'Tactical display,' the chaplain commanded his armour, and his vision was filled with an enhanced image of the outside: details of temperature, atmospheric pressure, light density and other factors were superimposed over his sight. As he rolled his head left and right to check the suit's calibration, Ramesis swiftly completed the other pre-battle procedures, double-checking the suit's power and exhaust assembly, the internal environment monitors, targeting crosshairs and myriad other systems that would keep him alive in the midst of battle, even in the depths of space.

The comm-speaker inside Ramesis's helmet chimed and the pilot informed him they were soon to land.

Ramesis strode out into the main chamber, where the other Space Marines of his force waited for him, their quietly sincere conversations showing they were eager for battle too. At his approach, though, they fell silent.

'Today we are joined by Brother Xavier, who has proved himself worthy enough to move on from his initiation.' The Space Marines raised their fists in praise of the newcomer, who bowed his head in thanks.

'Brother Xavier has served in Tenth Company for twenty-five years, and many are his battle honours,' Ramesis informed them. 'I am pleased to welcome him to our company and this, his first conflict as a full battle-brother, is indeed an honourable and auspicious one. We have come to this world to fulfil our duty as the protectors of mankind., There is no mission more sacred or righteous in its cause.

'Several weeks ago an expedition from the newly founded colony on this world discovered something ancient and terrible. Their explorers found an alien device, a thing of great evil – for it has been placed here by the eldar.'

The Salamanders hissed and snarled in anger, for their Chapter had a long history of fighting eldar pirates. Their home planet of Nocturne had been plagued by the alien corsairs for millennia before the Emperor had arrived to bring them salvation. Ramesis himself had fought against the eldar on numerous occasions and was unreserved in his loathing of the capricious aliens.

'We have been told by the worshippers of the Machine God that this device is a gateway, a portal to the Immaterium,' the chaplain continued solemnly. 'Soldiers from the colony's garrison were despatched to guard this portal while it is investigated, to ensure that the eldar did not attempt to use this gateway to attack Slato. However, they are few and our divine claim to this world, as well as the lives of two hundred thousand colonists, requires that we aid them. We have learned in the last few hours that the eldar have indeed attacked Slato. Even as we descend, their warriors are assaulting the Emperor's servants at the portal. Our augurs and surveyors tell us that they are relatively few in number at present, but if they gain access to their gateway then they will be able to bring on untold numbers of reinforcements. If that happens, our fight to protect this world will be all that much harder.'

Ramesis allowed a moment for his battle-brothers to digest this news. He was glad to be facing the eldar again, for the deaths of many of his ancestors stained their hands and he looked forward to every opportunity to repay the blood-debt.

'Let us pray!' Ramesis commanded the assembled Space Marines. They turned to face him and bowed their heads in acquiescence. As Ramesis spoke he walked along the two lines of warriors, touching each on the chest with the palm of his hand, passing on the blessing of the Emperor and their primarch.

'May the Emperor look kindly on our endeavours today,' he chanted. 'May his eternal spirit steer us ever on the path of light. May revered Vulkan, primarch of our Chapter, watch over us. May we have the strength and wisdom that we will not fail them in honour and duty. Praise the Emperor!'

'Praise the Emperor!' the Space Marines replied in a deep chorus. At that moment a siren sounded twice and the pilot's voice sounded over the comm-net.

'Alien interceptors on an attack approach,' the pilot said hastily. 'Assume battle positions.'

The Space Marines each stepped back into the small alcove which served as their resting place during transportation, grabbing hold of the brass grip rails to steady themselves. Hurriedly Ramesis ducked back into the chapel to extinguish the sacred brazier before taking his own position. The Thunderhawk banked sharply to starboard for a moment, the artificial muscles within Ramesis's armour easily compensating for the movement. The gunship continued to zigzag sluggishly to evade the eldar fighters, before a sudden screech rent the air and a bolt of energy smashed against the armoured fuselage. The blast was mirrored inside the hull in a spray of violet energy, and Brother Lysonis was hurled to the decking. Ramesis took a step forward to aid the veteran-sergeant, but his comrade held up a hand to indicate he was well, before slowly standing up. Sparks of energy crackled around a gash in his abdominal armour, but there was no blood. The blast had just inflicted a glancing hit on the Space Marine. As Lysonis reclaimed his place in one of the unoccupied alcoves, the gunship's reeling interior echoed with the sound of more energy bolts hitting the hull. Another fusillade was followed by the thump of a detonation, sending the gunship falling to one side.

'We've lost two engines,' the pilot informed them in a calm voice. 'Prepare for emergency landing!'

Ramesis felt his weight lightening as the Thunderhawk pushed forward into a steep dive, rushing down towards Slato's surface. For perhaps half a minute the rapid descent continued until the pilot fired the retro-jets, all but stopping the gunship dead in mid-air. The sudden increase in g-forces would have crushed a normal man, but Ramesis hardly even noticed, protected by the strength of his genetically modified physique and further enhanced by his ancient suit of power armour. With a skidding impact the Thunderhawk hit the ground a moment later, sliding to the right for several seconds before coming to a halt. Within a heartbeat the assault ramp had been lowered and Ramesis was charging out, the rest of his force pounding down the ramp behind him.

'THIS IS BROTHER-CAPTAIN Nubean. We have made landfall in the high ground, at position secundus-deca as intended. Ramesis, lead your force to point secundus-octus; I will converge on your position from the other side.' Even carried across several miles by the comm-net, Nubean's voice was as clear to Ramesis as if he were next to him. The chaplain signalled an affirmative and then switched frequencies to address the Space Marines under his own command.

'Advance by squads, pattern Enflamus. Squads Delphus and Lysonis will lead; squad Malesti will form rearguard,' Ramesis ordered in a clipped, precise tone. The three sergeants signalled confirmation and the two lead squads set off at a trot, the long strides of their power armoured legs covering the ground quickly. Ramesis fell in with Veteran Sergeant Malesti, whom he had known since he was first inducted into the Chapter. They had fought together as scouts in the Tenth Company and though Ramesis had advanced more rapidly in the Chapter's hierarchy, they still shared a special friendship. As they ran along, Ramesis modified the comm-net controller on his wrist so that he could talk with Malesti alone.

'Eldar again, my brother. We will have to be vigilant.' Though Ramesis's words seemed grim, he was in a light mood. It had been several weeks since he had been in battle and he had looked forward with anticipation to fighting once more against the Emperor's enemies.

'We have defeated the eldar before,' Malesti replied. 'We know their guile. Their arcane trickeries and sorceries will not avail them against us this time.'

'I share your confidence, brother,' Ramesis said. 'Captain Nubean is a strong commander. The honour of the Fourth Company prospers under his guidance.'

'And yours!' Malesti added with a chuckle. 'In the years you have been our chaplain, our battle-brothers' faith has been sure and steady. They conduct themselves with honour and respect, and do all that we ask of them and more. They do not fail in their duties as warriors of the Adeptus Astartes and they shall not fail us this day either.'

'They'll fight like steppe-lions, of that I'm sure!' Ramesis remarked.

They continued in silence for a while, jogging easily through the waist-high grasses of the plain, turned into a blaze of gold by Slato's setting star.

A few miles to the north ahead of them, the plains rose quickly into the foothills that eventually became a sharp mountain range. In every other direction stretched leagues of cereal plants, heavy with grain. The majority of Slato's landmass was given over to farming. Food grown here would feed the workers on mining worlds and industrial hive planets. Without such agri-worlds, the Imperium's labour forces would starve and the eternal manufacturing of arms and armour would cease, spelling the end for mankind's presence in the sector. It was paramount that Slato did not fall into the hands of the eldar.

IN THE LAST rays of the alien sun, Ramesis's force was continuing its forced march, making their way swiftly along one of the mountain valleys. But for the last few minutes, the sound of cannonfire had been echoing off the valley's steep sides.

'It appears the eldar are engaged in another attack,' Malesti was speculating. 'Landing behind the accursed aliens' position may prove to be an advantage: we can catch them between our guns and those of the Guardsmen at the portal. The Emperor has blessed us.'

'Beware of over-confidence, my brother,' Ramesis warned. 'The eldar are as slippery as a lava serpent and twice as venomous. They may have left a rearguard to protect them from such an attack.'

'True,' Malesti said. 'That is why we have come with two separate forces, so that if one is delayed the other may still fight through. With the Emperor's blessing...' Malesti's voice trailed away. His attention had become fixed on something ahead. Ramesis followed his gaze and saw that the two squads leading the march had halted. He was about to signal Sergeant Lysonis when the comm-net chimed in his ear.

'Chaplain Ramesis, this is Sergeant Lysonis. The valley ahead is filled with woodland, a possible ambush site. Request orders.'

'I'll be at your position shortly. Stay alert,' Ramesis commanded.

A minute had passed before Ramesis and Squad Malesti reached the other Space Marines where they were half-hidden in the long grass and rocks of the valley floor. The woodland ahead nestled firmly in the base of the valley which they had been following, stretching up the mountain slopes to either side. It was impossible to tell how far along the valley the woods continued, but Ramesis did not even consider the option of circumnavigating it. To do so would cost valuable time and still offered no surety that they would reach the site of the gateway unhindered. Ramesis peered at the small forest, trying to discern any activity in the shadowy depths between the thin, tightly clustered boles of the trees.

'Sergeant Lysonis, activate your auspex. See if you can detect anything within those woods.' Ramesis's order was quiet but authoritative.

'We risk the eldar detecting the signal, chaplain. They may not know we are here yet.' Lysonis cautioned.

'Rest assured, sergeant,' Ramesis informed him. 'The eldar are very aware of our presence. Even if their machines did not locate us, their mind-magic will undoubtedly have detected our presence by now.'

The sergeant's head was bowed as he unhooked the auspex from his utility belt and adjusted the dials. As he held it in one hand, passing it left and right in the direction of the woods, its screen threw a flickering green glow onto the black paint of his armour, harshly lighting the helmet from underneath, so that he almost looked like some daemon from the pits of Chaos. Lysonis adjusted one of the many brass dials set next to the display, then tapped a switch into a different position.

'There are definitely human-sized life signals within the woods, chaplain, possibly a dozen or more,' Lysonis reported, replacing the arcane device on his belt and pulling his power sword from its scabbard.

Ramesis looked at the trees once more, seeking any sign of movement or life. There were none. After glancing at the chronometer reading on his visual display, the chaplain made a decision.

'We do not have time to circumnavigate the woods. Prepare for attack. May the Emperor guide our weapons.' As he spoke, Ramesis strode to the front of the gathered Space Marines.

'For the Emperor and Vulkan!' Ramesis cried as he sprinted forward, the actuators of his armour turning every step into a bounding leap across the plain. Around him the Salamanders charged forward too, echoing his battle cry. The air was filled by a soft whistling noise and Ramesis noticed tiny slivers of crystal starting to patter off the armour of the Space Marines around him. Looking into the woods once again, half-seen shadows of movement caught Ramesis's attention as another volley of fire swept into the Space Marines. Behind him Ramesis heard a startled cry. He looked back over his shoulder to see what had happened. One of the Space Marines of Squad Delphus, Brother Lastus, was clutching at his helmet with one hand. Another member of the squad turned on his heel to grab Lastus's arm and haul him forwards. As the chaplain looked on, the toxins contained within the crystal sliver were already seeping into Lastus's bloodstream. The Space Marine gave a choked cry and his body began to shudder. The power armour amplified the shivering Space Marine's movements into flailing paroxysms as Lastus dropped his boltgun and fell to one knee.

'Sniper's needle hit Brother Lastus in the eye-plate,' Sergeant Delphus reported over the comm-link.

'Bring him with us!' Ramesis ordered as he turned his attention back to the woods. The first of the Space Marines were fifty paces from the trees now. Squad Lysonis stopped their advance and as one they raised their bolters and let loose a salvo of fire. Explosive bolts tore through the woodland, smashing swathes of shredded leaf and bark into the air, shattering branches and punching gaping holes into the boles of the trees.

Ramesis heard a high-pitched cry and a figure staggered forward from the shadows, a hand raised to its shoulder where bright red blood was spilling down the ever-shifting camouflage colours of its cape. It was tall and swathed in a long coat that shifted colour to match the shades of the trees and grass. Ramesis aimed his pistol, the crosshair imposed over his vision fixing on the eldar's hooded face. He could see its thin, pointed nose, the delicate features of its high cheeks and brow, and a pair of large eyes glittering with alien intelligence. The chaplain squeezed softly on the trigger and a moment later the eldar's skull exploded, the headless body flung forward several metres by the bolt's detonation.

As he reached the treeline, Ramesis found three more alien bodies. The first had two massive holes blown in its chest, another's leg was ripped off at the hip while the third had been turned into an almost unidentifiable crimson mess by several simultaneous bolter hits. Looking back across the grasslands, Ramesis saw Lastus being carried between two of his battle-brothers who were firing their bolters with their free hands. The wounded Marine was still twitching as his system tried to clear away the alien poisons. The armour of another Space Marine lay close by, sprawled in the grass like a casually discarded doll. The chaplain could see a neat hole in the flexible armour of the warrior's left hip joint where the needle shot had entered. The shot must have hit a major artery for it to have killed the bio-enhanced Space Marine so quickly.

'May thy soul be forever in the light of the Emperor. By His grace he has taken you into his embrace. Serve Him as well in death as your sacrifice served Him in life,' intoned Ramesis, whilst inwardly cursing his force's lack of an apothecary. He could not afford for one of his warriors to carry the dead Space Marine's body and by the time the apothecary from Captain Nubean's formation could arrive, the fallen fighter's gene-seed would be useless. Every gene-seed not recovered was lost forever, weakening the Chapter.

Glancing around, Ramesis saw that all of the remaining men had reached the shelter of the trees. Of the eldar there was no sign. For the next few minutes the dim light was occasionally broken by the orange glow cast by the jets of fire from Squad Delphus's flamer as the Space Marines methodically swept through the trees for any surviving eldar. Ramesis sent Squad Malesti ahead to ascertain whether the route to the rendezvous with Captain Nubean was clear, then sought out Brother Lastus.

The chaplain found him crouched with his back against the trunk of a tree, thumbing bolts from a pouch at his belt into a boltgun magazine. Beside him was his helmet, with the left eyepiece cracked. Blood was dried across the left side of Lastus's face, a reddish stain against his dark skin, and his left eye had been stitched shut. The rest of his face was marked by the scars of the Salamanders' ritual branding. Three dragon-heads were scorched into his forehead, each representing a commendation from the company captain, whilst several lines were scarred along his nose and chin, each scar burnt forever as recognition for a particularly noteworthy kill. As Ramesis approached, Lastus looked up.

'I'd swear that devil-spawned eldar had been aiming for Brother Nitrus next to me. No accuracy, these aliens!' the Space Marine joked.

'How are you faring, brother?' Ramesis asked, crouching next to Lastus and removing his own helmet.

'I can fight on,' Lastus declared with a wide grin that curled the lines of his scars into ragged swirls. 'The toxin is still affecting my hearing and smell, but my vision is almost clear. Well, through this one, anyway.' He stuck a thumb towards his good eye.

'And how is your aim, Brother Lastus?' Ramesis asked. He needed to know how much he could rely upon his battle-brother in a firefight.

'Still true, lord,' Lastus assured him. The Space Marine gestured towards his helmet. 'That's an old Mark VI Regis pattern. It can compensate for the loss of one eye by boosting another signal through the remaining optical link. I won't even realise I'm handicapped. It fits a bit tightly – I almost asked for a different helmet when the armour was given to me – but praise the Emperor I persevered with it.'

Ramesis stood up and told Lastus to report back to Sergeant Delphus. With a salute the battle-brother fixed his helmet back on and strode off towards the other Space Marines.

Sergeant Malesti strode up to Ramesis and reported that the firesweep was complete; no other eldar had been discovered.

'Understood,' Ramesis replied, rubbing a hand through the short curls of his hair before donning his own helmet once more. 'Lead the force to the ridge. The eldar definitely know now from which direction we approach, and Captain Nubean will not want to tarry long waiting for us.'

RAMESIS AND HIS force arrived at the rendezvous point first. As the sun dipped below the horizon, Ramesis's vision was augmented by the aura-intensifier of his helmet, bathing his view of the landscape in a red sheen. From the crest of a ridge the chaplain could see the repeated glow of the Imperial Guard guns, further up into the mountains. It was another hour before Captain Nubean and his Space Marines marched into view. With the aid of the artificial eyes of his armour, the chaplain could see the shimmering heat surrounding the advancing force, plumes of pure white jetting from the exhaust vents cut into their armoured backpacks. Their guns glowed a dim red, which Ramesis knew could only mean they had been involved in a protracted battle. As they came closer, Ramesis did a quick head count: there were twenty-one of them, seven less than had set out. Several more appeared to be wounded and as Captain Nubean approached with his command squad, Ramesis could see that Apothecary

Suda's reductor was covered in the dark red of Space Marine blood; he had been busy extracting the progenoid glands from the missing warriors. The gene-seed he had recovered would allow the Chapter to create more Space Marines to replace those that had fallen.

'We were ambushed shortly after insertion,' Nubean explained as he stopped in front of Ramesis. 'They came in fast, carried inside two fast, skimming transports, our weapons unable to penetrate the force shields protecting the vehicles. There was another anti-grav tank there too, gliding out around us, trying to pick us off with rapid volleys from a pulse laser. Brother Kolenn managed to take it down with his lascannon, but not before Squad Mauria lost three warriors. We were mostly facing regular line troops, which did not present much of a challenge. Their shuriken catapults were unable to penetrate our armour, while our bolters punched them off their feet with every shot! It was the specialists, the ones they call Striking Scorpions, that caused me the most consternation – we've fought them before, Ramesis…'

'I remember. It was on Corronis IV. Close combat experts, with those infernal laser dischargers in their helmets,' Ramesis said, gesturing with a finger either side of his jaw to imitate the aliens' strange mandible-like weaponry.

'That's them,' Nubean agreed. 'Their armour was as good as ours; our bolters were virtually useless. They had managed to slip behind us, elusive scum. It was Squad Goria that they attacked first. Their leader had some kind of power glove that punched through Sergeant Goria's chest with ease. We managed to stave off the others by getting a crossfire on the alien wretches, and once that distraction had been disposed of we could concentrate our fire on the close combat fighters. We left none of them alive,' Nubean finished with a grim smile.

The captain pointed to a Space Marine whose left arm ended at the elbow in a blackened stump; with his other arm the wounded warrior was gesturing expansively to Sergeant Lysonis, not at all disconcerted by his injury.

'Brother Kahli's plasma gun detonated, but he brought two of the enemy down first,' Nubean explained. 'That's the fourth time in the last seven missions I have had a plasma weapon failure, though this is the first time it has been so catastrophic. I will have words with the Master of the Forges when we return. It matters not that our plasma weapons are ancient artefacts, I need them to be better maintained.'

The captain turned his gaze towards the distant flashes of fire coming from the distant Imperial Guard encampment. 'We must press on. I want to reach the Imperial Guardsmen before dawn,' he said, turning his attention back to Ramesis. 'It was well we did not try to mount an airborne landing at the battle sector itself. We came across a pair of the enemy's anti-aircraft vehicles about four miles back. They have gigantic crystalline lasers; they would have shot the Thunderhawks out of the sky with ease.' With a thin smile, the captain directed Ramesis's attention to two thin columns of smoke to the south. 'Still, they won't be causing us any more worries.'

The captain's face grew serious again. 'I only wish we had more time for proper reconnaissance, but the Imperial Guard cannot be expected to hold their defence while scouts locate the main eldar positions.'

'I've never known the eldar to form a static camp, captain,' Ramesis commented.

'That is true,' the captain agreed, his helmet moving slightly as he nodded his head. 'If we had waited to find them we may have wasted what precious time we have. As you once taught us, Ramesis, we must always temper action with wisdom. Though we live for battle, a war is fought with wits as well as weapons.'

'I'm afraid I cannot take the credit for that, brother,' Ramesis confessed with a wry smile. 'I took it from the sermons of Chaplain Gorbiam, my tutor during my time as a Novitiate.'

The captain removed his helmet and took a deep breath. His forehead was pierced by eight service studs, each representing ten years of loyal duty to the Emperor. A pink scar cut from his right cheek to his chin, standing out against the supple sheen of his dark skin. Like the other Salamanders, his face and throat were covered with burns, each medal of honour intricately etched into his flesh. His dark eyes gazed solemnly out into the darkness, the weight of several hundred years of battle hung in that look. With a nod to himself, the captain replaced his helmet.

'Enough talk. Move our battle-brothers out.'

THE SPACE MARINES advanced more cautiously, sending out regular patrols to search for eldar ambush sites. Ramesis was with Brother-Captain Nubean and Brother-Epistolary Zambias of the Chapter's librarium. They had been marching for half an hour when Zambias held up a hand and Nubean signalled a halt. Without a word the librarian took off his helm and stared up into the sky where the stars of the galactic rim were scattered across the cloudless night like a fine dust. The librarian's face was gaunt, his bald head glistened with waxy sweat. His eyes were milky white with no pupils, as though he were blind, yet he gazed up into the heavens with a furrowed brow, as if searching for something. Ramesis saw a pale eldritch light playing around the psyker's eyes as he used his powers to scan the surroundings for other minds.

With a slow blink and a long exhalation, Zambias closed his mind once more. 'The eldar have broken off their attack. They are moving further north,' he told Nubean and Ramesis.

'Then we advance quickly while they regroup!' Nubean barked, waving a hand forward to signal the surrounding squads to start moving again.

'Have you no clues as to the eldar's intent?' Ramesis asked Zambias as they broke into a run.

'Their witchery is strong, as you know, brother-chaplain. I cannot penetrate their minds, I can only sense their presence. It leaves a foul stain upon the air, a corruption on the aura of this world. These lands belong to the Emperor, they abhor the presence of these vile aliens,' the librarian explained, his clenched fist showing his anger at the aliens' desecration of Slato.

'I have pondered upon this myself, brothers,' Nubean said. 'I have been in contact with the lieutenant in charge of the Imperial Garrison and there are a number of factors which puzzle me. I would welcome your guidance in these matters.'

'With our weapons we bring the Emperor's judgement; with our minds we bring his wisdom,' Zambias replied, putting his helmet back on.

'Three times the eldar have launched a full frontal assault on the Imperial positions,' Nubean said. 'That is unusual. The eldar are as fast as lightning on the plains, striking then disappearing as quickly. They know they are no match for massed guns, yet three times they have hurled themselves onto the tanks and squads of the Imperial Guardsmen.'

'I believe they are acting in haste,' Zambias answered after a moment's consideration. 'The force they left to waylay Ramesis was small, composed entirely of their so-called "Rangers", experts in infiltration, disruption and delaying tactics. Even the host they sent against us was not a large proportion of their warriors, if the auguries assessed their strength correctly. It seems they are concentrating everything they can spare on the portal and the humans defending it. Their usual strategy of hit and run would bleed us dry if we did not take the offensive, ensuring them a good chance of victory. Yet here they are, throwing their warriors into the teeth of the Imperial army. They are desperate to break through, of that much I am certain.'

'What matter is it whether they are desperate or nonchalant? They will die under our bolters either way!' Ramesis spat, taking his bolt pistol from its holster and brandishing it fiercely at the horizon. 'If they choose to make themselves easier targets then we should be grateful. I have little stomach for fighting the eldar. They slink and crawl and slither like serpents, never standing and fighting like honourable warriors. Their witchcraft is potent, their machines of war fast and manoeuvrable; it will be better for us that they forego such tactics to stand and fight for once.'

'That is true,' Nubean agreed with a nod. 'We fight for a just cause, for the eldar cannot be allowed access to their infernal portal. If they reach their device they'll bring more of their kind to this world and slaughter the colonists, and it will be lost to the Emperor. We must ensure that does not happen.'

'Why do we not destroy the portal and end this matter immediately?' asked Ramesis.

'There is an agent of the Machine God in the Imperial Guard force,' replied Zambias. 'I believe he wishes it preserved for study.'

'Ach! The Machine God. Politics.' Ramesis's simple statement conveyed his contempt. 'I do not pretend to understand why we waste time with such matters. We fight, we kill, we are victorious. That is what it means to be a Salamander.'

'And what would we be without our armour and our weapons, Ramesis?' Nubean gently chided the chaplain. 'You above all others know that we exist only to protect the Emperor's domains and his servants. If the Mechanicus wish to examine this thing, as foolish as it seems to us, it is our duty to protect them whilst they do so.'

As he pondered this, Ramesis cast a look at the mountains around him. The light of Slato's twin moons had not reached into the valley yet and everything was swathed in shadow. They were jogging easily through the long wild grass, their passage only broken by the odd clump of withered mountain trees or cluster of tumbled boulders.

'That is another curious matter here, brothers,' Nubean said, picking up on Ramesis's earlier words. 'The eldar excel at the sneak attack, the hidden blow, but they forewarned the garrison of their approach. They sent them an ultimatum – allow access to their portal or be destroyed. Why would they give up the element of surprise, when perhaps they could have swept away the defences with a single conclusive assault?'

'Perhaps they wished to terrorise the Guardsmen, in the hope that they would not have to fight at all?' Ramesis offered, not trying to hide his lack of faith in the courage of the Imperial Guard.

'Equally, an attack with total surprise might have swept aside all resistance and given them access to the reinforcements they desire,' Nubean countered, adjusting his right shoulder pad as he jogged along, so that it sat better on its actuators.

'Ramesis is correct,' Zambias said, pulling his force sword from its scabbard. Psychic energy flowed through the blade, causing faint blue flames to play along its length. 'It matters not what their devious scheme is. They will fall before the blade of the Emperor's anger all the same.'

THE SPACE MARINES reached the pickets of the Imperial Guard force without encountering any more eldar, though twice Zambias informed them that an enemy psyker had tried to break through the Epistolary's psychic shield. The Imperial Guard were in poor shape. The charred hulls of both of their tanks sat smoking in the darkness. The bodies of the dead were lined up, their faces covered by helmets, in a line that stretched for thirty paces. Ramesis could see the thirty metres of killing ground which the Guardsmen had cleared in front of their line. It was scorched, pockmarked with craters and shell holes, yet there was no sign of any eldar dead. Ramesis presumed that the enemy had taken them back when they had been forced to withdraw from the sheer weight of the Guard's short-range volleys of las-fire.

The few surviving Imperial Guard squads sat around campfires, their long greatcoats and peaked helmets ragged and stained from battle. Their lieutenant hurried through the darkness to greet the newcomers. His eyes were ringed with fatigue and stress and his dark blue tunic was unbuttoned. A bandage was wrapped around the thigh of his left leg, blood seeping from beneath it in a red stain across his white breeches. He saluted to Captain Nubean in the manner of his regiment, one finger to the peak of his cap.

'Lieutenant Raskil of the Fourth Levillian, seconded to the Adeptus Mechanicus on garrison duty,' he said. 'Praise the Immortal Emperor that you are here to save us.'

Nubean looked down at the officer, the tip of whose head only reached to the Space Marine's chest eagle.

'You are mistaken, lieutenant,' he told Raskil. 'We are not here to save you. We are here to protect the portal from the foul eldar. Your survival is only important with regard to that mission.'

The lieutenant stepped back as if slapped, mouth gaping wide. Before he could say anything more, the hulking form of Brother Zambias was towering over him.

'Where is this alien artefact, lieutenant? I wish to examine it,' the librarian asked. The Imperial Guardsman was still taken aback by Nubean's reprimand.

'I'll, er... I'll take you there myself. Do you wish to rest and eat a little before we see it?' Raskil offered.

Ramesis felt his anger rising. This impudent human was suggesting their physical needs took priority over their mission objectives. He stomped towards the lieutenant, but Nubean interposed himself, holding up a hand to halt Ramesis's approach.

'We do not require any sustenance yet, lieutenant,' the captain interjected swiftly. 'However, we must attend to the defence of this position before any other matters. Please detail your sergeants to work with my brothers. Your men can rest for the remainder of the night, my squads will stand watch until daybreak.'

'You realise that night here lasts for eighteen hours?' Raskil asked.

'We are aware of Slato's rotational cycle, lieutenant,' Nubean said, his voice betraying his confusion at the officer's inquiry.

'And your men are going to stand watch until daybreak, some ten hours away?' Raskil continued incredulously. 'I can detail some men for watch duty, it isn't a problem.'

That was too much for Ramesis. He stepped around Captain Nubean and stared down at Raskil.

'Your men require food and sleep. We do not!' Ramesis felt like he was stating the obvious. 'If your men do not receive these things, their combat performance is adversely affected. We have no such weakness. We can fight for a month on the proteins contained within our armour recycling systems alone. You also suffer from stress-related physical and mental disorders over protracted periods of conflict, which is why I will ignore these insults. Our brothers will stand watch. Please do not question the captain's wisdom again.'

Lieutenant Raskil gave a worried glance at the three giant Space Marines standing around him. Looking across the camp he saw the other Space Marines moving into positions from which they could keep watch to the north and south, along the valley. He wasn't surprised to notice his own men giving the massive warriors a wide berth, moving out of their way when they approached.

'Follow me then. Magos Simeniz has been analysing the… the objective for several days,' he said finally, setting off to the rear of the encampment.

RASKIL LED RAMESIS and the other Marines into an even, bowl-shaped depression which was surrounded on three sides by steep cliffs, just behind the eastern side of the ridge where the Guardsmen had set up their defence. The artefact at its centre was instantly recognisable as eldar in design. The obelisk stood roughly twice the height of a man and was constructed from a deep purple stone. eldar runes were painted in gold leaf along its length. Delicate strands of silver wire hung from rods in the ground around the portal, tracing out a hexagram. The air was filled with a hissing sound, which was emitting from a square box, two foot across and covered in dials and valves, which was sat nearby and linked up to the wires by coils of cables. The whole area was lit by the flickering flames of three braziers placed in a triangle around the dell. As they strode towards the alien creation, a stooping robed figure shuffled into sight from behind the machinery.

'Ah, Raskil, there you–' the figure started, then halted as he noticed the Space Marines for the first time. As he turned to regard them, the flames illuminated the face beneath the heavy cowl of his robe. Parchment-like skin hung in fleshless folds from his cheeks and his back seemed permanently hunched. From his right eye socket protruded a strange optical device with several different sized lenses which slid back and forth as he adjusted his focus. His nose was also absent, an air hose coiling from the middle of his misshapen face to a small cylinder at his belt.

'Come, see this!' Simeniz offered, beckoning to them with his right hand, from which protruded a number of small antennae. He led them to the far side of the analysis machine and pointed to one of the numerous screens showing a succession of sine waves and curving graphs. The Adeptus Mechanicus agent pulled a small plug from a receptacle implanted into the side of his forehead and plugged it into a matching socket in the machine, the wire linking him to the plug glistening with a thin sheen of blood. The screen which he had indicated began to change as the tech-priest chanted a low, almost sub-vocal, invocation. The outline of the artefact appeared in solid green lines and as the adept chanted faster, swirling orange dots began to form into concentric ovals that span in a seemingly arhythmic pattern around the centre of the monolith.

'You see?' Simeniz demanded, stabbing a finger at the screen with obvious excitement.

'We do not understand the workings of this machine,' Nubean said, looking blankly at the ever-moving image.

The tech-priest gave a snort of derision and flicked a switch which locked the moving shapes in place, before pulling the mind-plug from its socket.

'That is a definite warp-coil energy wave,' the tech-priest said slowly, as a patient adult would address a child. 'Our suspicions were correct: this edifice is capable of opening a warp gate, enabling objects to pass through. Rather large objects if my calculations are correct. However, there have been some anomalies. The wave signature is not consistent with any point of warp-interface we are aware of. It is as if it led to somewhere that is part of the warp, yet is separate from it.

'Also, it has been increasing in magnitude since my arrival. I am certain that someone is trying to activate it remotely.'

'Can you prevent that happening?' Ramesis asked, looking up at the great obelisk. The construction seemed to absorb the light from the braziers rather than reflecting it, staying in constant shadow. Being near to such an alien thing, with the scent of otherworldly evil hanging in the air, made Ramesis's spine tingle with some preternatural sensation of foreboding.

'I could potentially destabilise the warp field, but that could prove catastrophic if I am incorrect,' the tech-priest suggested, with a shrug of his slight shoulders.

'Be prepared to do so if I give the order,' Nubean said. 'We will endeavour to preserve this portal intact for your study, but our orders are to prevent the eldar from fully activating it. We will destroy it if necessary, for the lives of two hundred thousand colonists could be in danger.'

'Colonists?' Simeniz asked with a sneer. 'There are always more colonists – but we might not find another specimen of this quality for another five centuries.'

'If the eldar reach this portal, then it will be lost to us anyway,' Zambias said. The librarian held out his hands to either side and walked slowly towards the portal stone, gradually bringing his hands together in front of him as he did so.

'I can feel evil in this place. Ancient, alien evil,' he said, turning back to the group.

'We will be ready for it,' Ramesis answered confidently.

* * *

IT WAS STILL several hours before daybreak when the eldar attacked again. Ramesis had been with Zambias and Nubean for the whole night, positioning their warriors and the Imperial Guard for the best defence. The bulk of the force was stationed watching the northern approaches, where the eldar had attacked from before. However, Nubean had ordered Ramesis and a small contingent to guard the south, in case the eldar used their swift skimmer vehicles to launch their attack from the other direction. There were forty-four other Space Marines, as well as some sixty Imperial Guardsmen, and Ramesis was feeling confident that they could hold out. He was with Squad Lysonis when the first firing erupted to the north, on the right flank of the defenders.

The Imperial Guardsmen sent a steady stream of volleys into the darkness, the harsh white flare of their lasguns burning brightly against the dark. Sleek beams of blue energy struck back from the shadows, followed by a succession of flickering plasma bolts which impacted into the ground with blinding explosions. Ramesis's suit had automatically imposed a filter over his visor to stop his vision being impaired by the glaring light of the attacks, but he knew that the Guardsmen would have difficulty seeing anything in the darkness. As he watched, a fist-sized star of energy shot from the gloom and impacted into the chest of a Guardsman, flinging his ragged corpse a dozen metres across the ground. Ramesis could hear the bellowed orders of the Imperial Guard sergeants, and in the occasional seconds of near-silence his ears picked up the shrill whine of eldar shuriken catapults tearing through the night air.

'We hold here. That may simply be a diversionary attack,' he told Lysonis, turning his attention away from the firefight that was raging a hundred paces to his right. Checking to his left, Ramesis saw the heat auras of several eldar craft skimming forward slowly, silently stalking towards the Imperial position.

'Magnify,' he told his suit, and his field of vision suddenly zoomed in on the faint shimmering lines of three eldar war machines. They flitted a couple of metres above the ground, dodging between the scattered rocks and trees. They were long and sleek, with a curved armoured canopy at the front and an exposed gun cradle to the back. Ramesis recognised them instantly as the craft he had been told the eldar called Serpents or Vypers, something like that; swift two-man attack vehicles armed with a lethal heavy weapon. As they came closer, the sleek, menacing lines of the craft could be seen more clearly, gliding steadily towards the Imperial defenders.

There was no need for him to warn his brothers; he could see they were tracking the eldar's progress as well. Taking a deep breath to steady himself he pulled his bolt pistol and crozius from his belt and waited patiently for the aliens to get within range. A sudden glow from the slender weapon of the closest craft indicated a heat build-up, and a moment later a blue bolt of energy sliced out of the night, punching cleanly through the armour of Brother Kammia where he stood on the hillside fifty metres to Ramesis's right. The Space Marine stood there for a second as if nothing had happened, faint wisps of vapour steaming from the gaping hole through his torso. Then the warrior's legs folded under him and he fell to the ground, his armour clattering noisily as if suddenly empty.

The Space Marines reacted immediately, a lion's roar tearing the sky apart as they opened fire with their bolters in a mass volley of fire. Each bolt traced into the shadows on a tiny tail of flame, to explode a second later with a distinctive cracking noise. Ramesis watched the tiny eruptions spatter across the hull of the lead craft, shrapnel sent flying in all directions. As Ramesis switched his optics to normal view again, the Space Marine beside him, Brother Arthetis, braced his legs and brought his missile launcher to his shoulders. The Vypers were swinging past, the gunners swivelling their elegant weapons to direct their fire against the Space Marines. Arthetis swung at the waist to point the tubular missile launcher at the closest, before pulling back heavily on the trigger. A blossom of orange fire erupted from the back of the missile launcher. For a second it appeared that the missile had not seen its targets; its course would take it straight past the last Vyper. Then the spirit within the missile became aware of the aliens swooping past and with a small flicker of a guidance jet it altered course. A moment later the krak warhead exploded, turning the rearmost of the three craft into a rapidly expanding ball of flame which tumbled into the ground with another explosion.

The Space Marines tracked the surviving Vypers, continuing to fire their bolters. Ramesis saw one bolt impact into a control plane before detonating, shearing the fin off completely. Its stability lost, the craft dived towards the ground and the chaplain saw the gunner lift his arms to shield his face a moment before the nose ploughed into the dirt. The skimmer's momentum sent the craft cartwheeling down the hillside, shards of curved armour flung in all directions. The last surviving Vyper flitted back into the shadows of the crags and disappeared from view.

THE BATTLE HAD raged for a couple of hours, the eldar preferring to dart in and inflict some casualties before withdrawing back into the darkness, rather than mounting a full-scale assault. Such tactics made it almost impossible to judge the eldar's numbers, but the shattered wrecks of two of their grav-tanks littered the ridgeline, and Lysonis had reported over fifty of their dead found in the surrounding area. During the last assault Ramesis had been caught in a hail of fire from a shuriken catapult, an alien creation that could send a storm of razor-sharp discs slicing through their target. The chaplain's ancient armour had held firm, though, and a row of the monomolecular-edged discs spread in a neat line from just below his left shoulder to his right hip. When the battle was won he would have Techmarine Orlinia carefully remove them so that Ramesis could keep them as a memento of the battle. He would repaint the armour himself, however, and thank it for the protection it had given him.

It had been over an hour since the last attack and Captain Nubean, convinced by the lapse of time that this was not some kind of feint, had led his command squad and Squad Delphus after them, determined to harass them and stop them regrouping. He had been gone for perhaps a quarter of an Imperial hour, having left Ramesis in charge of the remaining Imperial forces.

Those forces were much depleted. The eldar attacks had been highly efficient; only twenty nine of the Guardsmen and twenty-seven Space Marines were fit for fighting. Ramesis knew that many of his fallen battle-brothers would fight on if asked, but it was imperative that they allowed their enhanced bodies every opportunity to heal themselves so that they might fight at full effectiveness later when they were really needed. Most of the troopers who had fallen were dead, shredded by shuriken, blown apart by starcannon plasma bolts or torn in half by high-powered laser weapons. Ramesis was looking at one corpse in particular, that of a young corporal whose face looked so serene and at peace. Strange, Ramesis thought in a detached fashion, considering his legs and half his spine have been vaporised. Then Ramesis's comm-link chimed and the body was instantly forgotten.

'I'm returning with some of the eldar,' he heard Nubean report.

The connection was cut before he had a chance to reply, but Ramesis was delighted that the captain had captured some of the filthy aliens so that they could be interrogated as to their plans and the strength of their army. It was not long before Ramesis caught sight of the returning Space Marines. Nubean was striding purposefully up the hill, accompanied by Zambias. His bodyguard was behind him, and between their massive torsos Ramesis caught occasional glimpses of the alien captives.

All three wore long flowing robes and tall, jewel-encrusted helms. Their slight forms seemed emaciated next to the immense physiques of the Space Marines, but the aliens were slightly taller. Intricately shaped eldar runes hung from their garments on fine threads, swaying gently as they walked forward. The one in the centre was the most ornamented and Ramesis realised with a start that this must be one of the legendary farseers, the powerful psykers said to command the eldar. The other two were warlocks; he had encountered them before, powerful battle-witches who were obviously serving as some kind of honour guard for the farseer. All three moved with an effortless grace, easily keeping pace with the Space Marines despite the long strides of the captain and librarian. Nubean and Zambias were about ten metres away now, and Ramesis could clearly make out the three aliens following them. Something was nagging at the back of his mind, but before he could work out what was amiss Nubean was standing directly in front of him.

'Come, brother! We have matters to discuss, and urgently,' Nubean said without formality, already striding past Ramesis in the direction of the portal.

It was then that Ramesis realised that the eldar were not bound in any way at all, and with a shock he noticed they still carried their weapons: shuriken pistols in finely-crafted holsters and long swords carried in scabbards hung with many tassels and runes.

'What devilry is this?' the chaplain demanded, sighting his pistol at the farseer. It was obvious that the Space Marines were under some kind of foul influence of the eldar's psychic powers.

'Calm yourself, Ramesis!' Nubean shouted back, putting himself between the chaplain and his target. 'The situation has changed. Put down your weapon.'

'Weak-minded fool!' Ramesis hissed, pointing his bolt pistol at the captain. 'This is some cursed eldar mind-trick!'

Zambias once more stepped between the chaplain and captain, laying his heavily-gauntleted hand on Ramesis's pistol.

'There is no trickery here, brother,' the librarian assured him calmly. 'We are both free from influence.' Zambias's helmet was hung from his belt and Ramesis could see his eyes were normal, betraying no sign of mental powers being used.

Ramesis hesitated for a moment and studied the librarian's face. Seeing nothing but the honourable and honest face he had come to know and respect over the last few years, he took a reluctant step back, lowering his pistol. The three eldar strode past without even glancing at the chaplain, acting as if nothing at all had happened. Their alien haughtiness infuriated Ramesis but he managed to keep his anger in check – for the meantime.

THE PORTAL WAS being guarded by Brothers Amadeus, Xavier and Joachim, and they eyed the group of eldar accompanying Nubean very suspiciously. Raskil's men and the other Space Marines were left watching the valley, in case this was a subtle ploy to lure the Emperor's servants into some false sense of confidence and security. As the group entered the natural bowl containing the eldar artefact, Magos Simeniz looked up from where he was adjusting the wire hexagram around the portal, his jaw dropping almost comically when he noticed the nature of his visitors.

'What are they doing here?' he demanded, stepping protectively in front of his analytical engine. The farseer took a pace forward and raised his hand in some kind of alien gesture, his fingers splaying open and then closing into a half-fist. When he spoke, the eldar's voice was musical, every syllable and sound perfectly formed and intoned, spoken without hesitation.

'I am here to deactivate the opening-ward, the device of power you call a portal,' the farseer waved an arm hung with several thick golden bracelets in a fluid gesture towards the obelisk.

'This is trickery! You will open the gateway to your fiendish home and bring more of your warriors,' Ramesis claimed, striding to stand next to Simeniz.

'Interference would not please us,' the farseer said gently, with an inclination of his head. 'The voices of our home and forefathers have sent us here, the runes guiding my dancing path to your presence. There is one who comes here, born in nightmare and feeding on fear. He is Kha-rehk, leader of the Fanged Maw. He comes and slaughters you all, sating his thirst with your peoples' essence.'

Ramesis stared at the eldar leader, fixing his gaze on the two green, gem-like ovals he assumed served as eyepieces in the helmet. It was impossible to tell what the farseer was feeling or thinking; the alien's bowed head could be a demand or acquiescence. Captain Nubean removed his helmet as he joined the chaplain, Magos Simeniz scurrying close behind. The captain's eyes were troubled and Ramesis could see that the responsibility he held was weighing heavily on his shoulders.

'Everything has been explained. Well, I think I understand,' Nubean told the others. 'A band of eldar renegades are trying to use this portal to attack the colonists. This farseer has arrived to close the portal completely, so that it can never be used again. We must act quickly to sever this bridge between realms.'

'No!' Simeniz cried suddenly, a crazed look in his natural eye. 'They're trying to keep it a secret from us! They want to hide their wonderful technology from the Machine God!' With a hiss the tech-priest launched himself at the farseer, his fingers spread like claws. Ramesis reached out to grab the deranged adept but the farseer acted more swiftly. The eldar psyker made a short gesture with the fingers of his raised hand and Simeniz's head was surrounded by a faint rippling nimbus of yellow light, stopping him in his tracks. Zambias had taken a step forward, his hand on the hilt of his force sword, but no sooner had he moved then one of the warlocks was barring his path, a glowing witchblade brandished in its hands.

'Release him!' Nubean demanded and the farseer flicked its fingers again with an almost bored shrug. Simeniz fainted to the ground. As Ramesis stooped to one knee to check he was alive, the tech-priest opened his eye and groaned sleepily.

'It told me things,' Simeniz whispered. 'Showed me a glimpse of the portal. It was wonderful.' The tech-priest struggled to his feet and gazed wide-eyed at the farseer, who had turned its attention to the portal itself.

'What do you care about our colonists?' Ramesis demanded of the eldar.

'Nothing,' the psyker admitted with a dismissive wave of a long-fingered hand. 'More of your warriors discover the butchery and seek answers. You stumble across our Craftworld as she drifts peacefully through the stars. You do not understand what has happened and the guilt for the spilling of blood is laid upon us. Your warships gather and attack us. We destroy all of them, but many of my kin die doing so. We wish to avoid this outcome. We did not wish to fight against you. If the Dark Kin break free from the webway we will need the strength of both our forces to turn them back.'

'How do you know this?' Ramesis asked, still convinced that the eldar were trying to trick them somehow.

'How do you know that you are awake? Or even alive?' the farseer said.

'Speak plainly!' Ramesis demanded.

'We waste time!' the eldar leader snapped back. 'I will gladly leave you all to die in the most agonising manners, if you would kindly leave assurances that my kin are not responsible for your deaths or the eradication of your intrusive little dunghill of a town. I must close the webway arch and I must be doing it now!'

The farseer raised its hand and pointed at the portal, chanting softly in its own strange, melodic language. As Ramesis watched, the analytical engine gave a shriek. Simeniz leapt to man the status displays, his fingers working furiously at a series of switches and dials.

'The... the portal's beginning to open,' he said in an awed whisper. All eyes turned towards the stone. A dark corona of energy was forming around the obelisk, tendrils of white power crawling along its surface. A dull hum filled the air and as they watched the silver wire of Simeniz's analysis matrix began to melt.

'Treachery!' Ramesis bellowed, bringing up his bolt pistol and firing at the farseer. There was a flare of psychic energy and the bolt dropped to the ground, unexploded. Behind the farseer, Ramesis saw Zambias exchanging sword blows with the warlock in front of him. Amadeus, Xavier and Joachim fired their bolters at the other warlock, but the eldar side-stepped neatly past the volley and struck out, its witchblade slicing across Amadeus's chest with sparks of psychic power.

Ramesis pressed his thumb to the power stud of his crozius and turned back to the farseer. Suddenly, the chaplain's mind exploded. He felt quicksilver shards of mental energy piercing his soul. It seemed as if the universe itself was shrieking in his ears and light as bright as the sun blinded him. Gritting his teeth, Ramesis forced his eyes to focus on the farseer, who was still standing calmly in the middle of the hollow, his attention fixed on the portal, one hand still outstretched towards it.

'Vulkan give me strength!' Ramesis cried, throwing off the farseer's mental attack with a sudden surge of willpower. Ramesis was two strides from the eldar when it snapped its head towards him like a mantis spying its prey. The farseer opened its right hand and its witchblade leapt from the sheath across its back and settled into his grip. Ramesis brought his crozius around in a vicious back-handed strike, smashing the power weapon into the alien's head. Gems scattered across the ground as the farseer reeled. Ramesis brought his arm back for another attack, but the eldar reacted quickly, spinning on its heel to deliver a double-handed blow with its witchblade. Ramesis thought the eldar had missed for a moment until he brought his arm forward to strike again with the crozius. In a moment of disbelief, Ramesis noticed that his right arm stopped just above the wrist. Glancing down in a detached fashion, the chaplain saw his crozius lying on the ground, his gloved hand still gripping its haft.

The witchblade slashed out again and Ramesis dived to one side, the alien weapon smashing across his left shoulder pad. Sparks fountained into the air from the severed auto-actuators as Ramesis rolled and regained his feet. The farseer seemed to glide towards the chaplain, advancing without walking, the Witchblade blazing with power. The eldar took a wide-stepped stance, its robes billowing in a psychic gale of power, and brought the blade in a slow circle around its head. Ramesis noticed that one of the eye-jewels had been shattered and he could see part of the farseer's face. An almond shaped-eye stared back at him with contempt in its gaze. As the farseer advanced, the eye's yellow iris began to glow, filling up with tiny sparks of energy until it was a small star of white light.

With a thunderous explosion of energy, the farseer was knocked down onto one knee. Behind the sprawling eldar stood Xavier, Ramesis's crozius gripped in both hands. The Space Marine struck down again and again, battering the farseer's head and back until the alien stopped moving, its blood seeping into the dirt. Looking around, Ramesis saw that both warlocks were dead too. Brother Amadeus was on his back, Zambias helping him hold in the organs that were trying to spill from the massive slash through his chest bone. Simeniz was cowering on the ground, sobbing gently, covering his eyes. Nubean strode over and grabbed the back of the tech-priest's robes in one hand and lifted him off the ground.

'Stop the portal opening!' he demanded, hurling Simeniz towards the logic machine.

The portal-stone was glowing white-hot with energy. A cold wind seemed to emanate from its surface causing the braziers to flicker madly. The tech-priest set to work, while Ramesis strode to where Xavier was standing over the farseer, alien blood dripping from the crozius arcanum in his hands.

'This is a good omen, brother!' Ramesis grinned, pointing towards the crozius. 'The Emperor has obviously marked you as special. When we return to Nocturne I will enter your name into the Novitiate of the Promethean Cult. You will make a fine chaplain one day.

'Thank you, brother. I pray to live up to your expectations,' Xavier replied, the honour shining in his eyes.

Ramesis clapped his left hand on the young Space Marine's shoulder pad and looked at the stump of his other arm. Already his genetically-modified blood had clotted and stopped the bleeding, his power armour releasing pain-numbing elixirs into the nerves around the injury. When they returned to the fortress-monastery, the Master of the Forges would fit him with an artificial hand. Such prosthetics were common amongst the Salamanders. There would be no shame in it.

'I think I'm too late,' Ramesis heard Simeniz mutter.

All eyes turned to the tech-priest where he stood hunched over the analyser.

'What did you say?' Nubean demanded, his dark eyes narrowed.

'I'm too late...' Simeniz repeated, pointing at the portal. The white energy had formed into a swirling ring of power many paces across, a purplish shadow staining its centre. The air was filled with a piercing whining noise, somehow loud but also just at the edge of hearing. Without any order being given, the Space Marines began to back away from the alien artefact, taking up a position on the crest of the rise. Captain Nubean was shouting over the comm-net, demanding all squads to assemble on the hill.

With a crack louder than thunder the portal yawned open, creating a massive oval of pure blackness that stretched three dozen metres across the whole width of the depression. Within the blackness of the void there blinked cold, distant stars. Nothing happened for several heartbeats, then suddenly the renegades burst from the ellipse of energy. Gunfire flashed out of nowhere and more eldar leapt into view, each of their rifles spewing a hail of deadly crystal splinters. More eldar riding midnight-black jet bikes covered in scything blades flashed into existence, their screaming engines sending them racing past the startled humans. The Space Marines and Imperial Guardsmen opened fire as more and more evil creatures slid into existence. The skin of these eldar was pale to the point of being white, contrasting harshly with the black of their armour, which was made of flexible plates festooned with glittering blades. Hooks and barbs hung from chains around their wrists, loins and necks, and many of them wore extravagantly coloured crests on their high-fluted helmets.

Watching as the dark portal spat forth a sleek anti-grav vehicle packed full of howling warriors, Ramesis knew at the last that the alien farseer had been right. Their force could not hold against the alien host on its own. The war engine glided slowly forward, menacing in its calmness. The creatures aboard it brandished cruel curved and serrated blades, and fired pistols indiscriminately into the mass of Imperial servants before them. The exotic cannon mounted on the prow of the renegades' craft spat a ball of dark energy at the Space Marines, slicing easily through the armour of Brother Lastus. More and more warriors leapt through into the world, accompanied by packs of alien beasts which had no skin, their flesh and muscles clearly visible in the light of the constant gun fire. With ear-splitting howls the hunting pack bounded up the slope, their fanged jaws and clawed feet tearing a bloody path through the Imperial Guardsmen. More skimmers were sliding into view, bearing a seemingly endless stream of depraved and vicious warriors.

Firing his bolt pistol at the charging aliens, Ramesis knew a fear like he had never experienced before. If their forces had been combined with the original eldar force, without being weakened by days of fighting each other, they would have been able to stem the tide of renegades pouring through the breach in reality. Now the servants of the Emperor stood alone. Ramesis knew that they were doomed; their only hope of victory had been shattered by his own hatred and inflexibility.

Determined that he would not die alone, Ramesis snatched the power-sword clenched in the hand of Malesti, who lay dead in the dust. The hollow was full of the aliens' corpses, yet more and more seemed to spill forth into the battle. Screaming with rage, the chaplain charged into the centre of the throng. Ramesis was surrounded by their warriors as he hacked blindly left and right, felling an enemy with each blow. The whining of anti-grav engines was deafening and the chaplain was knocked to one knee by the downblast of something large sweeping overhead. The noise of guns and blade-on-blade swirled around him, accompanied by a cacophony of screams which were suddenly drowned out by a deafening bellow of inhuman rage. He was hemmed in on all sides by shadowy warriors, his armour rent and torn from the blows of his enemies, his real enemies. As the darkness closed in on him the last sight he had was of their thin faces laughing with cruel glee.

INNOCENCE PROVES NOTHING

NIGHTMARE

Gav Thorpe

JOSHUA WAS DREAMING. He knew he was dreaming, because he could distinctly remember laying down to sleep, wrapped in a thin, ragged blanket, out in the desert that he now called home. Inside his dream he found himself standing in a dank grotto of trees, the light dim and the air tinged with the thick, musty smell of rotting vegetation. The trees' leaves hung limp and almost lifeless, pale and sickly on thin, twisted branches. Overhead the watery light of an unfamiliar moon broke through fitfully as a desultory breeze sighed through the foliage around him.

Looking around, Joshua could see that the grotto was surrounded by steep-sided cliffs, broken only by a single cave entrance. It was carved in the shape of a giant mouth, jagged stalactites hanging down just inside the opening like a row of fangs. The dark pits of a pair of hollows just like skull eyes glared at the young man from above the cave entrance.

Greetings, young friend.

The Voice was inside Joshua's head, felt rather than heard. He knew the Voice well, for it had spoken to him many times over the last few years. At first the young man had been afraid of the Voice, but over time he had felt less and less threatened, despite the strange things it sometimes said. This was the first time that the Voice had been in one of his dreams, though, and it was stronger, somehow louder than normal.

'What is happening?' Joshua asked, his words also thought rather than spoken aloud.

You are dreaming, that is all. There is nothing here that can hurt you. There is no need to be afraid, the Voice replied.

'How are you here too? You have never spoken to me while I slept before. Why have you never spoken to me in my dreams until now?' Joshua was not afraid. The Voice was soothing, calming him.

You would not let me into your dreams before. You did not trust me until tonight. Now you know that I am your friend, I can speak to you anywhere. It was you who let me into your dream, Joshua.

'Where is this place? Is it real, or is it a dream-land?' Joshua asked, though he was unsure why, for he knew that he was dreaming. There was no place on the whole of arid Sha'ul where plants could grow in such abundance, except perhaps the gardens of Imperial Commander Ree.

It is not a real place, I helped you create it. We are going to have an adventure together. Do you remember when you were just a child, you used to have adventures in your mind. You would slay the Emperor's foes, those daemons and monsters, with a bright sword.

'I remember my daydreams, yes. But that was when I was little. I am fifteen now, too old to have childish adventures,' Joshua argued.

You are never too old to have adventures, Joshua. In this land you are a hero. People will welcome you, adore you even. Not like in the world of the waking, where you are shunned, where you were driven from your village by your own friends and family. Here, no one will hate and despise you for what you are.

The Voice was very persuasive. It knew everything about Joshua; his childhood, his thoughts, his emotions. In the lonely times since Joshua had fled from the mob who had once been his friends and relations, it had been his companion, soothing his troubled thoughts with its presence. The Voice always knew the exact right things to say to make him forget the loneliness. It had taught him so many things about the gifts he had been given, the gifts the ignorant peasants of his village had called witchery.

The Voice had explained everything. It had taught Joshua how others were jealous of his talents and how, out of jealousy, they became angry. It had shown him the way to practice his skills, so that he could control them, rather than letting them take him over. Sometimes it had asked him to do things, unpleasant things, but Joshua had always refused, and the Voice had never been angry, never shouted or complained. It had been like a father to Joshua, ever since his real father had reported him to the Preacher and Joshua had been forced to flee or be burnt at the stake.

Come, Joshua, in this world where you are a hero. Your adventure awaits you.

As JOSHUA STEPPED towards the sinister cave mouth, two strange figures appeared, as if out of nowhere, and barred his path. The creatures were hunched and deformed. Pale, lidless eyes glowered at him from sunken sockets. One opened its mouth to speak, revealing a circle of razor-sharp teeth lining its mouth, but all that issued forth was an incomprehensible burbling and hissing.

'They will not let me pass,' Joshua told the Voice without speaking.

Then you will have to make them, Joshua.

'How can I fight them? I have no weapons, no armour,' Joshua replied. His heart felt heavy with a sense of inevitability, as if he knew what the Voice would say next.

Here in the dream you can create weapons. Your mind is your weapon, use it!

Joshua stared at his hands, picturing them holding a long-bladed sword. As if at his command, a hefty metal falchion appeared in his grasp, its semi-transparent blade shimmering with an unearthly blue light.

See! the Voice crowed. *Here in this world you have real power, Joshua. Here you are the master. Now – strike them down!*

Joshua hesitated for a moment. The daemons were backing off from the holy fire of his sword, panicked gurgling sounds spewing from their lips.

They are foul, Joshua thought to himself. I am the master here. Taking a deep breath, he stepped forward decisively. One of the daemons lunged for him and he reacted without thought. The blade screamed as it swung through the air. Without pausing in its sweep, the sword sliced through the outstretched arm of the attacking daemon, which howled in pain. Another stroke clove the daemon from shoulder to groin. The other creature turned to run, hobbling away on its twisted legs, but Joshua was faster, striding effortlessly after the fleeing beast. A single backhanded stroke separated the daemon's neck from its head, and Joshua watched with distaste as its dark blood spread across the ground, soaking into the dead leaves, making them hiss with wisps of acrid vapour.

Good, good, the Voice congratulated Joshua. *You have vanquished your foes. Now, enter the cave, pursue your quest.*

Casting one last look back at the fetid woodland, Joshua stepped beneath the tooth-like stalactites and plunged into the darkness of the cave.

INSIDE, THE CAVE had turned into a twisting, downward-sloping tunnel, with smaller paths branching off in different directions. As he progressed through this maze, the Voice was unerringly guiding Joshua as he sped through the depths. Joshua didn't feel like he was walking, the sensation was more like floating, moving speedily through the network of passages. As he reached another fork in the tunnels, more daemons ran into view, each as twisted and ghastly as the first he had encountered. They held wands and staffs that began firing bolts of white lightning at Joshua. As they exploded against the walls all around him, the young man ducked back into a side passage. Joshua used his mind to weave a shield around himself. Glorious power flowed through his limbs, creating a shifting miasma of miniature stars which whirled around his body. Stepping out into the main tunnel once more, Joshua advanced towards the daemons. Their energy bolts flared harmlessly off Joshua's mental shield, but more and more were arriving.

Eradicate them. They must not stop you!

Joshua held up his hands and concentrated. Each fist burst into eye-searing purple flames and he hurled the balls of magical fire at his foes. The sorcerous flames exploded around the tunnel, engulfing a handful of daemons, burning them in an instant and scattering their ashes through the air. Joshua hurled more fireballs, incinerating the daemons as they charged towards him, the storm of their lightning blasts dissipating harmlessly around him. Joshua was filled with elation – he was unstoppable. More and more daemons fell to his attack. Soon the daemons were dead and none rushed forward to replace them. The air was heavy with the stench of charred flesh. Seeing the scattered lumps of burnt carcass, Joshua was suddenly struck by a deep sorrow. He stopped dead.

'They stood no chance, did they?' he asked the Voice.

Of course not. Spare them no pity! Inferior creatures exist only to serve. If they fight against that purpose, they are utterly worthless. Destroying them was a mercy, for they had wandered from the path of service. They are nothing.

Joshua found the Voice's words disturbing. It had not been the first time the Voice had spoken of destroying inferior beings. Often it was callous and heartless, it seemed to him.

The Voice seemed to have sensed his thoughts.

Did not your own people try to destroy you? Did they pause to listen to your pleas for mercy? Did they try to understand you, to comprehend your innocence? No, they did not. They wanted to kill you for what you represent to them, driven by their misguided fear and loathing. It was they who forced you into the wilderness, condemned you to a life of loneliness and misery. Were it not for me, you would have died out there, young, weak and vulnerable as you were. But I protected you, nurtured you. They are below your consideration, they deserved to die!

'But these were daemons, not people, weren't they?' Joshua demanded, worried by the Voice's tirade.

Of course, of course. This is all a dream, Joshua. None of this is real.

Joshua paused for a moment, considering the Voice's words. It had spoken hurriedly, as if trying to cover up a mistake, angry with itself for letting something slip. There was a glimmer of a thought forming at the back of the young man's mind. But before Joshua could work things out, the Voice was telling him to move on, insistent and urgent. Joshua gave up trying to figure out the Voice's purpose and let himself be guided further into the winding labyrinth of caves.

* * *

IT WAS NOT long before Joshua was forced to stop once more. Ahead of him, the narrow, sloping passage was barred by a great iron portcullis. He sidled up to it and looked miserably at its bars, each as thick as his arm.

'You've led me the wrong way!' Joshua complained unhappily to the Voice.

I have not! You must trust me. This is no real obstacle. Merely break the bars and continue.

'But how can I bend these?' Joshua demanded. 'Even the strongest man could not move this portcullis, and I am weak and feeble.'

You hear me, but you do not listen, Joshua! Others have said you are weak, but you know that you are strong. You are stronger than any full grown man. Listen to me, not the doubts placed in your head by fools who do not understand you. Who would you believe? Peasants who grub in the dust and dirt all day, or me, who has already shown you so much, brought you so much?

I guess you're right, Joshua thought, though he was still unsure. He grabbed two of the bars in his hands and strained with all of his meagre muscles. They did not move an inch. Panting, with sweat dripping down his cheeks, Joshua stood back.

'I told you! I'm not strong enough,' he complained.

Stop whining, Joshua, you sound like one of those pathetic preachers who sermonise about the follies of the universe without ever having left their shrines! Bend the bars with your mind, not your body. There you are strong, there you have power.

Joshua took several deep breaths and stepped up to the portcullis once more. Closing his eyes, he grasped the bars again. The metal felt hard and cold in his hands, but he began to pull at them, this time imagining them to be as flimsy as reeds. When he opened his eyes the bars of the portcullis were rent from the frame, leaving a twisted gap wide enough for him to slip through.

As he stepped through the hole, Joshua felt the tunnel constricting around him, suddenly becoming very narrow.

'It is too small,' he told the Voice.

Why is everything an obstacle to you, Joshua? You complain endlessly.

'I'm sorry,' Joshua apologised. Almost contritely, he focused his mind, making his body supple and lithe, almost boneless. With this achieved, he found he could pass through the narrow crevasse with ease.

Well done. You see, nothing is impossible to one such as you.

Joshua grinned to himself, basking in the Voice's delighted praise, and continued to move through the winding fissure.

FOR WHAT STARTED to seem like an eternity, Joshua eased himself through the small tunnel, around turns and corners, always heading gently downwards. Suddenly, though, the tunnel stopped and Joshua felt himself fall for a moment. He landed with a thick splash and, as his eyes grew accustomed to the dull light, he saw he was standing knee-deep in filthy swamp water, at the bottom of a deep pit. The smell was truly nauseating and Joshua felt bile rise in his throat as he gagged at the stench.

Joshua waded a couple of steps through the murk, looking around him. To his right, a massive, formless thing rose from the mud, filthy water cascading off its slimy hide. Tiny eyes peered at him across the shadows, and its true shape was hidden by gigantic folds of blubbery flesh. It reached towards him with a spindly tentacle, uttering a high-pitched mewling noise. Disgusted, Joshua slapped the tentacle away.

'I don't like this adventure any more,' Joshua told the Voice, feeling sickened and tired.

This is the object of your quest, Joshua. Kill it and you can return home.

'Why do you always ask me to destroy something?' Joshua demanded. 'You've always nagged me to go back to the village to kill them, always told me that I have to destroy others if I want to survive. Why?'

It is just the way things should be. For us to rise to the power which is rightfully ours, we must dispose of those who would oppose us. People will always willingly follow a master, but you must first remove their existing master before they will follow you.

'But I don't want to be anybody's master.' Joshua hung his head sullenly. Beside him, the marsh-thing was huddled against the wall, murmuring with a low, gurgling noise.

Then kill this creature and we will go home. I will never communicate with you again. You can be all alone in the wastelands – friendless, homeless, a vagrant who will never be welcome. Is that what you wish?

'I could get used to the loneliness,' Joshua argued, staring down at the marshy ground as gas escaped in a flurry of bubbles beside him.

You could get used to the loneliness? How often did you weep, that first year in the wilderness? How often did you stand atop the high cliff at Korou and think of leaping off? How often have you longed to return to your family, dreamt that they will welcome you back with smiles on their faces and open arms? This will not happen, Joshua. You will always be alone if you do not let me help you. Never again to know friendship. Never will you meet a pretty girl and wander in the marketplace buying gifts for each other. Never will you meet the woman of your dreams and marry her, to the jubilation of those around you. You are loathed, hated, cast out. You are a vagrant, a menace, a mutant. You are in league with daemons! You have betrayed the Emperor! You will ultimately destroy those who you once loved and who once loved you!

'That's not true! It's not!' Joshua screamed aloud, his voice echoing off the damp pit walls.

It is what they thought of you, loathsome wretch that you are. You were a weakling, a failure. They had no choice but to want to kill you! Now you have no choice but to kill them!

With a howl, Joshua turned on the bloated fiend of the pit, his hands reaching through the folds of flesh to grab its throat.

'They never understood!' he screamed. 'It wasn't my fault! I never did anything wrong! I never chose to be like this! They should have listened to me! I tried to tell them! I tried! Damn them all to hell! I never did anything wrong! I would never hurt anyone!' Joshua's screaming became primal and incoherent, a high-pitched wailing which carried a lifetime of suppressed anger and bitterness. The desperation that only an abandoned child could know reverberated around the chamber in a rending banshee screech that seemed to last forever.

As he howled, Joshua's hands closed tighter and tighter on the monster's throat, slowly choking the life from it. Its feeble limbs thrashed wildly in the mud, throwing up sprays of foul liquid. Joshua felt all of his anger and hate pouring into his arms, imbuing his grip with a vice-like strength. With a final effort he snapped the creature's neck, its tentacles falling limply into the murky water, a foul dribble of slime trickling from its fat lips.

Suddenly Joshua released his grip and he stood back, horrified, watching the foul corpse slip silently back into the filth.

'I'm going now,' he told the Voice with his mind, panting, his whole body trembling with emotion. 'I don't like your adventures. I don't like what you say to me, what you've made me do. I never want to hear you again. I will learn to cope with my life, without your venomous whispers in my ear. I never again want to feel as ashamed as I do now. Return me home and then leave me.'

As you wish, Joshua. You have already done all that I need of you. Simply think of yourself back in the woods and you will leave this place. You will not hear my voice again. But I will be near, of that you can be certain.

JOSHUA WOKE UP with a start, his eyes snapping open. For a moment he did not know where he was. All around him grew lush plants, and he found he was resting against the thick trunk of a tree, whose branches spread high into the air above him. Looking around, he saw a high wall encircling the area, broken only by an ornate gate, wrought in the shape of a grinning mask.

With a shock, Joshua realised that these must be the gardens of Imperial Commander Ree's palace. To be caught here would mean imprisonment for him, despite his young age. He stood quickly, putting the tree between himself and the gate.

How had he come to be here? He had been dreaming, but he couldn't remember of what; the dream had slipped away like morning mist. And why had the guards not found him sleeping and oblivious to everything, right here in their midst?

Trying to calm himself, Joshua relaxed his mind, letting it flow from the restricting confines of his body, just as the Voice had taught him to do. He found a group of guards not far away, could feel their agitated thoughts. Gently, he slipped his mind next to theirs, one by one, touching them only briefly so that they would not know he was there.

Lasguns had no effect on them...

Just burnt them, Emperor's mercy. Bodies everywhere...

A rat would've had problems getting down all the way to the Imperial Commander's bedchambers...

Sentries on the gate cut down...

Strangled and his neck broken. What kind of person would do this...

Nobody could have removed that ventilation duct without heavy machinery...

No sign of them since, either of them. Just disappeared without trace...

Somebody had killed the Imperial Commander? Joshua was desperately confused. It would go ill for him if they found him here after the Imperial Commander had been murdered. They might think he had something to do with it.

As he looked around desperately for a way to escape, Joshua had a sudden flash of recollection. The dank woods from his dream were a twisted version of the gardens that now surrounded him. Had it really been him? Was this where it had started?

He closed his eyes and hung his head in his hands. The preachers had always warned that the daemons of the warp could possess a person, drive him to do things like this. Joshua's mind reeled.

They had said that... that the ancient, formless denizens of the Empyrean were formed from the sins of the impure and craved after the material universe like a starving man hungers for bread. They could not normally enter the realm of the living, but instead guided unwitting mortals, and sometimes willing servants, to help them break through the boundaries separating the spaces between the stars.

They sought to dominate other creatures, to make them subservient to their immortal and alien whims and needs. It was why they sought out witches and warlocks, because they were the best tools for such monstrosities. It was why the Inquisition and Ecclesiarchy were always hunting down those of magical prowess.

But the Voice had always told Joshua this wasn't true! It was a lie propagated by the Imperial authorities because they feared the power of the blessed ones. Joshua's thoughts were lurching, but through the muddled haze of his mind he caught a strange smell, the metallic reek of blood.

Opening his eyes, he looked about him, but could not see anything. Then he looked at his hands for the first time. Both were stained red, smeared with dried blood.

The Voice, his only friend when all else had deserted him so cruelly, had lied to him, had lied from the very first moment. It had used him, manipulated him. And now it had made him do the most terrible thing ever, and then deserted him, just as his own family had deserted him before. Joshua's howl of fear and desperation echoed off the stone walls.

And in the warp, something laughed.

ANCIENT HISTORY

Andy Chambers

Cross the stars and fight for glory
But 'ware the heaven's wrath.
Take yer salt and hear a shipman's story.
Listen to tales of the gulf,
Of stars that sing and worlds what lie
Beyond the ghosts of the rim.
But remember, lads, there ain't no words
For every void-born thing.

– Shipmen's labour-chant,
Gothic Sector, Segmentum Obscurus

NATHAN RAN DOWN the stinking alley, panting and sweating. He could hear shouts and a scuffle behind him as they pounced on Kendrikson. His mind raced faster than his feet across the cracked slabs. *Poor old Kendrikson. Still – better him than me.* He leapt over a prostrate body almost invisible in the darkness as the irony of the situation struck home. *At least that's the last time he'll try to get me killed.*

At the corner he risked a glance back. A lone streetlume cast a pool of yellow light over a scene that looked suspiciously like one from some Ministorum morality play. Four burly, shaven headed men in dun-coloured coveralls were hauling Kendrikson to his feet. He seemed unduly surprised, nay stunned, to be cast in the starring role of the eponymous incautious reveller laid low by local ruffians, cultists or worse – surely a punishment from the God-Emperor for his carelessness and self-indulgence.

327

The image was shattered when the officer stepped out from the shadows to congratulate the men on their catch. Nathan had never seen an Imperial Naval officer before but he had no doubt that he was looking at one now. Tall, poised, immaculately dressed in a tailored uniform coat and a pair of glossy black boots which had probably never trodden the dust of a planet for more than a few hours. He would surely be a junior officer to be in charge of a gang like that, trawling through the back alleys of Juniptown to fill out some labour team aboard his ship. Junior or not, he radiated the absolute assuredness that only generations of breeding and a lifetime of training engenders.

Nathan started to back away as his mind raced on. There were rumours that Imperial ships would come from Port Maw to Lethe, but everyone said that sort of thing when there was a war among the stars. Half the people hoped the fleet would come and save them from Sanctus-knows-what, while the other half were afraid that the fleet would bring the war to their doorstep. Nobody had ever thought that the Navy would come to steal a tithe of men and take them away on ships. Men who, if only half the stories were true, would never be seen again.

Kendrikson was off for a cruise and there was nothing Nathan could do about it. He certainly didn't intend take on a pressgang single-handed.

'Well, well,' said a finely cultured voice from behind him. 'It looks like young Rae missed one – get him lads!'

A blow struck his head, bright stars flashed before his eyes and he fell into waiting arms which bore him off even as his consciousness slipped away.

NATHAN WOKE TO the sound of a voice speaking. It sounded deep, resonant and faintly amused. He was amongst a crowd, being propped up by a stranger. The voice rolled on through his confused awakening like martial music: proud and insistent.

'…I could take this ship twice around the galaxy and wander the void for a hundred years if the Emperor wished it. One thing would bring me back to the hallowed worlds of humanity before we'd been out for more than a year! Crew! You lucky fellows have won the chance to serve aboard one of the sector's finest ships, the *Retribution*. Remember that name with pride and affection and all else should come naturally.'

Nathan must have looked confused because the stranger, a thin, dark man with tired eyes, whispered to him: 'It's the captain. 'Ere to welcome us aboard – sez it'll likely be the first and last time we see's 'im.'

Nathan blinked and gazed about him.

A vast, curving wall disappeared out of sight above them. It was pierced by arches showing a night sky speckled with stars. Halfway up it a buttressed gallery swelled outwards and it was from there that the captain spoke. His voice must have been amplified somehow, because a normal man's voice would have been drowned by a distant rumble which seemed to radiate from the worn stone floor they stood upon. A jolt of panic shot through Nathan as he realised they must be aboard some ship. No, an Imperial warship, he corrected himself. Even as he watched the stars in the windows were sliding across it almost imperceptibly. They were already underway.

NATHAN WAS INDUCTED into a gun crew: number six gun of the port deck, known to its crew as Balthasar. Him, Kendrikson, the tired-eyed man – who introduced himself as Fetchin – and five others were beaten, stripped, shaved, deloused, tattooed with their serial numbers and issued with dun-coloured coveralls, apparently tailored so that their one size would fit no one. The gun officer for Balthasar, a Lieutenant Gabriel, seemed decent enough and didn't revel in their humiliation. He and his enforcers, his armsmen, simply crushed their individuality and made it clear that they were to obey orders and cause no trouble. He was even good enough to explain to them that men were a commodity on a warship, like food or fuel or ammunition. When the ship ran out, it came to a world to resupply. Simple as that. Even before the lieutenant had finished his little speech, Nathan had hardened his resolve to escape at the first opportunity.

They were set to work in a gunroom, a cavernous, hangar-like space which reeked of grease and ozone. It was part-filled by cranes and gantries but dominated by the breech of Balthasar, apparently some sort of gigantic cannon as big as a house and nested at the centre of an insane web of power coils, chains, coolant pipes, wiring, hydraulic rams and less easily identified attachments. By the unspoken rule which applies to all new recruits, the old hands set them to work on the most mundane, laborious and unwelcome tasks in the gunroom. In this case that meant long, hard work-shifts scraping off corrosion – which an old hand named Kron helpfully pointed out bloomed like a weed in the moist, oxygen-rich air inside the ship – or chipping away frozen coolant from the branches of piping. They ate on the gundeck too, their food arriving on square metal trays through an aperture in the wall.

Food breaks were accompanied by the arrival of the crewmen the old hands referred to as armsmen. They came through one of the two heavy pressure doors that led into the gunroom, from the direction which Nathan had nominated as 'south'. The armsmen wore leather harnesses over their coveralls and carried long clubs and stubby pistols or shotguns. They kept a respectful distance while the guncrew ate, but their attitude spoke of a readiness to do harm if necessary. Once the food was consumed and the trays returned to their slot, the armsmen left through the north door, presumably to perform the same, apparently pointless function in the next gunroom.

Again, it was Kron who explained the purpose of the armsmen's vigil to the new recruits. 'They're here to make sure everyone gets their own share, lads.' Kron told them. 'An' that nobody takes what isn't theirs.'

Fetchin seemed shocked. 'So yer can't even keep a crumb for later? Or swap some wi' yer mate.'

Kron's answering grin was an ugly sight, particularly because he, like many of the old hands, had been patched with steel over old injuries. In Kron's case the tech-priests had left him with a half-skull of polished metal and set with a red-glowing eye. 'Not unless you want a few extra lumps to nurse, no,' he chortled.

Seeing disbelief still written on their faces he added more quietly: 'Was a time, years ago, when we had a… bad captain. He didn't keep a watch, boys. Was alright at first, the bully boys didn't take too much and no one starved. But then we were caught in a storm 'tween Esperance and the K-star for months, the ether was torn apart by cross-chasers and remnants so much that it was all the Navigators could do to keep us from being lost. Pretty soon men's hunger made 'em desperate, an' desperate men'll do terrible things.'

Kron closed his real eye, blocking out bad memories.

Nathan had seen plenty of desperate men around Juniptown in wet season, when work was scarce or non-existent.

'I've seen floors swimming with blood after fights over a husk of bread. The captain's right to keep a watch,' he said.

Kron looked at him curiously for a moment and then nodded. 'That's right, lad. Better to be harsh now than deadly later.'

Food was palmed and traded and fought over anyway, but in a quiet, cautious fashion which Nathan suspected the armsmen chose to over-look. Several times he tried to speak with Kendrikson but each time his old rival ignored him or, if Nathan pressed him harder, fled away from him. The old hands brooked no fighting so Nathan took it no further. He judged that the old hands were right: punishments for fighting were liable to be swift and brutal.

At the end of each workshift the crew slept in a low bunkroom beneath the gundeck. armsmen arrived to drive them below, although they needed little persuasion to drop their tools and find their way down into the gloomy, red-lit chamber. There were no exits from the bunkroom saving the hatch which led back up to the gunroom. cleansing and purging was undertaken in ridiculously small metal cubicles off the bunkroom. Nathan watched and waited but opportunities for escape never presented themselves. Soon work-shifts and sleep-shifts rolled relentlessly past until all sense of time was lost, until there was only toil and rest from toil, and then toil renewed.

* * *

IT WAS ONLY after the ship had left the Lethe system and passed into warp space that Nathan began to understand why men were a commodity. The warp made everything different somehow. Even the cavernous gundeck felt claustrophobic and oppressive, as if immense pressures existed just beyond the hull. Then the dreams had started, nightmares which left the mind dark and full of half-formed images upon waking. Some men screamed and wept in their sleep without knowing why, and others just grew more and more introverted and silent. Fetchin was one of these and Nathan had seen a weird light coming into his eyes long before it happened.

It was the end of the work-shift. The crew was straggling down the hatch to the bunkroom, more reluctant now that the dreams had come. Fetchin was last of all, listlessly scouring at a corrosion spot long after the others had moved away. The armsmen stepped forward with hard faces and Fetchin backed away with a stooped, almost scuttling gait. Almost at the top of the ladder, Nathan stopped and turned, his mind fumbling for some encouraging words which might persuade Fetchin to go below.

Before he could speak Fetchin backed into another of the guncrew. The man cursed and roughly thrust Fetchin away. From there it seemed as if Fetchin was possessed by devils. He pounced on the man with a snarl and bore him down. A horribly throttled gurgle escaped the thrashing pair and Fetchin rolled away, his lips and chin bloody with the ruin of the man's throat. Two men tried to pin the devil-Fetchin's arms but he slipped through their grasp like an eel, raking clawed fingers across their eyes with a hysterical, wordless scream.

The armsmen came pelting up and the first to reach the scene swung at Fetchin's shoulder with his long club, probably aiming to break his collarbone. The blow never connected. Fetchin grasped the downrushing arm with preternatural speed and swung the armsman away with a horrible cracking, popping sound which spoke of dislocated joints and snapping bones. The madman turned suddenly and bounded towards the bunkroom hatch. Men scattered as his last manic leap sent him hurtling straight at Nathan.

Nathan saw the animal fire in Fetchin's eyes in the age-long instant as he leapt and felt his guts turn icy. There was not a scrap, not a hint of the mild, world-weary colleague he had come to know. All reason was lost in that glare, and Nathan was frozen in it.

Suddenly Kron was between them, so quick that Nathan didn't even see him step in the way. Kron swept the flailing arms aside and punched two stiffened fingers into Fetchin's windpipe before his feet had touched the ground. Fetchin was knocked sprawling by the impact and let out a low growl as he skidded across the deckplates. Nathan felt shocked; Kron's deadly accurate blow should have left Fetchin dead or unconscious, he felt sure.

Click-clack BOOM.

The sound of the shot echoed around the gunroom. A frozen tableau was left in its wake. An armsman stood with shotgun levelled, smoke curling from the muzzle. Fetchin slid down the bulkhead leaving a bloody smear, a fist-sized wedge of raw flesh and entrails blasted from his midriff. Nathan, splattered with still-warm blood, not able to understand how Kron had moved so fast.

The armsmen drove them below with kicks and blows before another word was said. Kron was surprisingly kind and turfed out the old hand who bunked below him so that Nathan did not have to sleep beneath Fetchin's empty berth. When they were brought up for the next work-shift a scoured spot on the bulkhead was all that was left of Fetchin.

NATHAN WOKE TO the sound of screaming. He lurched up with a half-strangled yelp, almost braining himself on the bottom of Kron's bunk. He stared wildly about him, gulping for breath. The oppressive red light of the bunkroom still surrounded him, the cloying odour of sour sweat and grease still fought the sharp tang of coolant in the air down here. The room was quiet save for the drip of the condensers and the assurance of night noises made by forty sleeping men.

Nathan wiped a shaky hand across his eyes and peered over towards Kendrikson. If anyone had screamed it would have been Kendrikson; he had nightmares nearly every sleep-shift. They all did, but Kendrikson just couldn't take it. Perhaps he had a guilty conscience, or perhaps he was just some dumb thief who was completely terrified by being shut up in one of the Emperor's warships. But Kendrikson's bunk was empty; he must have gone to relieve himself.

The scream came again, but it was tinny and distant, carried along by the conduits from another bunkroom. Pity the poor devils in there, thought Nathan, every one of them wide awake and praying the screamer didn't go berserk and start clawing and biting at them. That he didn't turn into a wild beast like Fetchin had.

Nathan lay back in the narrow bunk and tried to recapture sleep. He tried to imagine all the other shipmen doing the same. Start with this gundeck. Kron had told him there were forty guns with forty crews each, that's sixteen hundred, another gundeck on the other side for three thousand two hundred. Then there were the lance turrets, port and starboard, nobody seemed to know just how big the crews for those beasts were, call it another sixteen hundred a piece. This was working well, his eyelids were drooping. That was six and a half thousand souls (give or take). The torps probably had a crew much bigger than a single gun but less than a whole deck – maybe a thousand. That made seven and a half... engines must be at least two or three thousand more...

A rasping cough snapped him back to full wakefulness. A bittersweet cloud of smoke was drifting down from the bunk above. Nathan sighed. Kron, it was always Kron. 'Ain't sleeping too good?'

'Nah. Bad dreams,' Nathan replied. Kron was the oldest hand on the gundeck. Even Lieutenant Gabriel listened to him, sometimes, so it often paid to listen too.

'Really? Not like Fetchin, I hope,' Kron wheezed. It was a statement – or a cruel joke – not a question.

Nathan decided to take it as a joke and chuckled quietly. 'No, not like Fetchin,' he said. 'Just more dreams of the ship.'

Kron harrumphed quietly and another cloud of smoke wafted downwards, the feeble breath of the recyclers apparently insufficient to even pull it up and away. 'It's lucky to dream of the ship,' Kron said, his voice sounded a little wistful to Nathan, as though Kron were talking to himself. 'I used to dream of it a lot when I was young.'

Nathan wouldn't like to have to guess Kron's years. Apparent age varied so much from one world to another that it was a long shot at best. Take into account all the warp-time Kron must have had and Nathan would be naming a figure somewhere between sixty and three hundred. In the time it took him to think that, a slithering sound came from above and suddenly Kron was there, pipe in hand, right beside Nathan's bunk. The red light turned his polished skull, with its sharp nose and glowing eye into a gargoyle's head. His living eye twinkled.

'Come walk with me, young Nathan. Let's go up on deck.'

Nathan sat up and warily eased himself out of the bunk. 'What about the armsmen?' Nathan asked. Kron just snorted and started to pick his way, soft as a cat, to the hatch.

The gunroom was dark, its spars and columns rearing up with cathedral-like splendour into a gloom broken only by the jewel-like gleam of ready-lights and power indicators. They edged around to the far side of Balthasar over snaking cables, Kron sure-footed and Nathan trailing behind. As they rounded one of the pillars Nathan froze as he heard a squeak of oiled leather. Kron stepped on and virtually walked into an armsman.

The armsman brought up a torch and snapped it on, a little too quickly and awkwardly to have been lying in wait for them. Nathan slipped back round the pillar and out of sight so he didn't hear what was said, but after a few muttered words the armsmen swung away, whistling a little ditty and heading for the far end of the gunroom.

'Yeh can come out, lad,' Kron called. 'Ole Leopold won't bother us.'

Nathan came forward. 'I'd thought they would never stoop to fraternising with gunners, the armsmen I mean,' he said.

'Not while others're about, but come sleepshift they'll talk and trade like anyone else – they're crew just like us, just trusted enough to bear arms all th' time.' Kron seated himself on a stanchion and gestured expansively to another. Nathan took a last glance round before warily sitting also.

Kron gazed at him steadily while he got out his pipe again. 'So what's your story, young Nathan?' he asked.

'I don't have a story,' Nathan replied carefully. 'If this is about Kendrikson, my business is with him alone and I'll thank you not to intrude.' That earned an arched eyebrow and Nathan suddenly felt he was mistaken, Kron hadn't brought him up here to find out what was going on between him and Kendrikson.

'No,' Kron said, 'I mean, tell a story. That's how it's done among shipmen. When we want to really talk we tells a story, that way we can tell our secrets without saying them right out so others might hear.'

When Kron said that, he looked meaningfully at the outer hull plates, which Nathan could see from here were covered with writings, layered one over the other, marching lines of faded Gothic script which continued up and out of sight towards the ceiling.

A sudden chill crept down Nathan's spine. He was sure he heard a vague creak of metal up at the north end of the gunroom. 'What do you mean? What "others"?' he hissed.

Kron raised a hand to stop him 'That's jest what I mean. Let me tell you a story about how mankind got among the stars: a tale of ancient times.'

Kron began to speak clearly and surely, without the customary drawls and breaks in his speech. It was almost as if he were reading from a book, or reciting a tale told many, many times before.

'Once, long ago, Man lived on just one island. The broad oceans surrounded him and he believed himself alone. In time, Man's stature grew and he caught sight of other isles far off across the deep ocean. Since he had seen everything on his island, climbed every peak and looked under every stone, he became curious about the other islands and tried to reach them. He soon found the oceans too deep and cold for him to get far, not nearly a hundredth of the way to the next island. So Man returned and put his hand to other things for an age.

'But in time food and water and air ran short on Man's island and he looked to the far islands again. Because he could not bear the cold of the ocean deeps, he fashioned Men of Stone to go in his place, and the Stone Men fashioned Men of Steel to become their hands and eyes. And the Stone Men went forth with their servants and swam in the deep oceans. They found many strange things on the far islands, but none as strange or as wicked as the things that swam in the depths between them; ancient, hungry things older than Man himself.

'But these beasts of the deep hungered for the true life of Man, not the half-life of Stone, so the Stone Men swam unmolested. At first all was well and the Men of Stone planted Man's Seed on many islands, and in time Man learned to travel the oceans himself, hiding in Stone ships to keep out the cold and the hunger of the beasts. All was well and Men spread to many islands far across the ocean, such that some even forgot how they came to be there and that they ever came from just one island at all.'

Kron's tale wound on, telling of how the stone men became estranged from humanity by their journeys through the void. This led to a time of strife when the Men of Steel turned against their stone masters and mankind was riven asunder by wars. A thousand worlds were scoured by the ancient, terrible weapons of those days before the Men of Stone were overthrown, and a million more burned as flesh fought against steel. Worst of all, the beasts arose and were worshipped as gods by the survivors. Once proud and mighty, Man was reduced to a rabble of grovelling slaves. Finally one came who freed man from his shackles and showed him a new way to reach for the stars. This path was forged from neither stone nor steel but simple faith. Faith guarded Man from the beasts of the void as steel or stone could never do.

NATHAN CAME TO himself with a start. Kron's sonorous voice had lulled him into a strange, half-dreaming state. He looked back at the wall and its inscrutable scripture. Faith. Faith kept the beasts at bay. Beasts that turned men into creatures like Fetchin. Each line of script covering the wall was a prayer to the God-Emperor for protection. Centuries of devotion layered like stratified rock to keep whatever was out there... out there. He could feel Kron's expectant gaze upon him, the red eye burning like a ruddy star in the gloom. Nathan uncomfortably tried to ignore the scratching noises he thought he heard coming from the gloom. Just nerves, he told himself, or rats, of course. Still, no harm in watching the shadows.

'I don't know many tales,' Nathan hedged, trying to recall one about the Emperor or the Great Crusade. He felt Kron's tale must be a parable of ancient times, set before the Crusades. They were spoken of only through the preachings of the Ecclesiarchy. In the Lethe system, a legendary time of righteousness and purity recalled in the Ministorum's most reverential sermons, usually as a comparison to the immorality and irreverence of modern times.

'Tell us about you and yon Kendrikson then,' Kron prompted.

Inwardly Nathan cringed, but he sensed that Kron could be a big help to his chances of survival, let alone escape, and he had told a tale first. Warily, Nathan began.

'Me and Kendrikson don't go back far, but in the short time I've known him I've decided that I need to kill him. My youthful prospects were not exceptionally good, truthfully they were much given over to petty crime and associating with undesirables. However, thanks to Kendrikson I'm now an unwilling recruit in the Emperor's Navy. That appears to mean lifetime incarceration in a steel cube twenty paces across until death by insane shipmate, starvation, disease or enemy action intercedes. This wasn't my first choice in life.'

Nathan stood suddenly. There was no doubt about it now, someone or something was creeping towards them as stealthily as it – or they – could manage. He gently lifted a steel hookbar from the deck and held it ready. Kron, seeing his look and actions, similarly armed himself with a long spanner. All the while Nathan kept talking, so as not to alert their stalkers. He told Kron about how he and Kendrikson had both served on the *Pandora*, an ageing lugger hauling ore and oxygen between the outer mines of Lethe. He even told him about how they had both actually been in the pay of a businessman dedicated to transporting goods of a rare, valuable and illegal nature with no questions asked.

Nathan had just got to their last voyage on the *Pandora*, and how Kendrikson had sold him out to the pirates when their skulking stalkers attacked. They came out of the shadows in a rush, three pale shapes and one dun coloured one. Nathan made a two-handed swing at the first to reach him. The steel hookbar caught it on the side of the head with a meaty crack and it dropped as if poleaxed.

It was a man. Pale, near naked, with a matted beard and bloodied shock of hair. A second leapt forward, jagged blade swinging, while Nathan was still recovering from his initial blow. He managed an awkward parry with the hookbar and the man pulled his blade back for another hack. Nathan followed through with his block and crashed the end of the hookbar into the wildman's elbow, making him yell and drop his blade. The third dove in between them and drove Nathan back with a flurry of blows.

He blocked a few strikes with the ungainly bar, but gave ground and almost stumbled on a trailing pipe. In desperation he ducked under a cable conduit as his assailant made an overhead cut. The blade sliced into the shoc-lines with a shower of fat sparks. The man convulsed and his face clamped into a rictus grin of agony as current flowed remorselessly between blade and deck through him. As Nathan dashed past him he was starting to smoulder, the blade glowing orange in his deathgrip.

The second man had retrieved his blade and made as if to strike as Nathan ran up, but the superior reach of the hookbar finally paid off. Nathan slammed it bodily into his ribs. The momentum of his charge skewered the man on its cruel head, splintering ribs and ripping open a gouting wound. Nathan abandoned the wedged bar and plucked the blade out of the man's fingers, giving thanks that his enemies seemed disorientated and slow, as if they were half-starved or dim-witted.

Nathan sprang forward towards the last foe, a figure in shipman's coveralls bending over the prone body of Kron. Nathan's nape hairs prickled as the figure lurched up. Blue wych-fires writhed about his limbs like angry snakes and sparks poured from its fingertips. By some reflex Nathan ducked away from a hissing bolt of energy which lashed out from an out-stretched hand. It still caught him across the left shoulder and sent fiery needles of agony lancing into his very bones.

If he could have shouted in agony he would have, but his lips only parted in a soundless gasp as a wave of numbness washed through him. Nathan fell to his knees on the deck and fought his unresponsive body as it dragged him down, down. The figure stepped closer. Through blur-ring eyes Nathan could see the complex weaving of tattoos beneath his skin, glowing through it with lightning-brightness. Even the coveralls were rendered translucent by that glare, and bones stood out coal-black as he raised a spectral hand in a gesture full of menace.

With his final ounces of strength he struck back at his foe the only way he could, hurling the blade stiff-armed as he slid to the deck. Before he blacked out he felt a thunderclap of pressure and a wave of heat before blackness closed over him.

NATHAN'S EYES FLICKERED open. He pulled himself up to a sitting position and retched. Only moments had passed. Smoke was still rising from the corpse beside him and the sweet stench of cooked flesh hung in the air. The thrown blade protruded from the corpse's larynx, and Nathan knew he should never gamble again after fluking that shot. But, despite the blade, the massive burns across the body looked like they had been just as fatal. Vagrant flickers of static still trailed along rigor-stretched limbs. Nathan mustered his courage and stared into the blackened face. It was Kendrikson, patently no mere smuggler after all. He stepped well clear of the corpse as he staggered groggily to where Kron lay.

Faint breath sighed from Kron's lips and the burns on his body didn't look fatal. Nathan paused at this, his head throbbing and mouth dry with fear, and considered how he might be able to judge such a thing given his lack of experience. Regardless, he could not simply leave Kron lying insensible so he decided to follow his instincts and attempt to revive him somehow. By shaking him and calling Kron's name, Nathan was soon rewarded with a moaning and stirring. Seconds later Kron's real eye flick-ered open; his redgem-eye remained dim.

'Wh-wh-what? Wh-where am I?' he whispered with trembling lips.

'On the gundeck,' Nathan replied. 'There was a fight…'

He broke off. Kron had raised his hands and was touching his metal half skull and dim jewel-eye. 'It's still on me!' he suddenly yelped. 'Get it off before it can crash-start!'

Nathan stood in shock. Kron's voice was different and he was starting to thrash around in a most un-Kron-like fashion. Nathan snatched for his wrists in fear that he might injure himself and the strange voice grew shrill with panic. 'No! Don't let it take me... don't let it...' Kron's new voice trailed away and his body slackened in Nathan's grip. As Nathan lowered him gently to the deck he noticed Kron's jewel-eye was flickering back to life.

'Ai, Nathan,' Kron said, his voice normal. 'Lost my way there for a sec. Ye were about to tell me how ye escaped from the pirates?'

Nathan stared at him. Kron seemed to have no recollection of the fight or his bizarre behaviour. Nathan squatted down, watching Kron carefully as he slowly looked about, taking in the carnage around him.

'There was a fight,' Nathan explained again. 'Kendrikson and some new friends tried to kill us, well, perhaps just kill me and capture you.'

Kron stood with no apparent signs of pain or weakness, and walked over to Kendrikson's corpse, where he bent down and retrieved a half-melted spanner. 'I struck him with this,' he told Nathan. 'I didn't realise he was a Luminen.' Kron fell silent, staring down at Nathan with that red, cyclopean eye for a long, long minute.

Nathan had a greasy feeling of fear in his stomach as he gazed back. Kron was obviously not entirely whole or sane. He had called Kendrikson a Luminen, a word which stirred disturbing memories in Nathan's mind. It might be best not to remind Kron of his equally disturbing words and actions. Better now to find out about the Luminen Kendrikson and his allies. Kron was holding Kendrikson's scorched head in his hands now.

'Why do ye think they were out to catch poor Kron?' the old man asked. Kron turned away to hide the act, but his hands still made an ugly cracking noise as they crushed Kendrikson's skull.

'I have absolutely no idea who they were,' Nathan snapped, 'let alone what they wanted with you! Kendrikson was... was... I don't know, possessed? What is a Luminen?'

Kron clicked his tongue a few times, a curiously mechanical sound like that of the *Pandora*'s clattering old logic engine. Before he could reply there was a flicker of lights at the south end of the gunroom; echoing shouts followed. Kron turned and scurried towards the north end without a word. After a second's indecision, Nathan followed, struggling to keep sight of Kron's disappearing back while not tripping on a cable or cracking his head on a stanchion.

He caught up with Kron as he bent over a thick pipe in a shadowed corner beside the script-marked outer wall. The pipe was made of many rings of metal half the height of a man. Kron pulled apart two of the rings and slipped inside, turning to hold the rings apart and jerking his head for Nathan to follow. He ducked within, realising as the rings creaked back into place that he had heard the same noise before Kendrikson and his allies had attacked.

They belly-crawled along the pipe in silence, the way lit only by Kron's cyclopean eye. Bundles of wires ran along the bottom of the pipe, most filthy and blackened but some more recent, their bright colours encarmined by Kron's unflinching gaze. Dozens of dog-eared labels clung precariously to the different bundles. Many were torn off or unreadable, others bore legends such as Lwr diff, aaz/3180 or Ar.ctrl 126.13kw in careful gothic script.

The pipe gave out in to a black crack, chasm-deep with cabling spilling off into its depths like a frozen waterfall. Kron led Nathan on to a short bridge of pipes that crossed to the other wall which was splotched with bright blobs of enormous silver like soldering marks. At the far side Nathan stopped, unnerved by Kron's continuing silence and the cold, lightless spaces he was being led into. Time for some answers.

'Kron,' he whispered, 'where are we? And where do you think you're taking me?'

Kron turned to face him before replying. 'She's an old ship, lad. She fought and sailed the void for nigh eighteen centuries in the Emperor's fleet, an' before that she slept in a hulk for another twenty. That's where I–' Kron clamped his mouth shut and his eye blazed. He gazed round warily before speaking again. 'We're between the hull plates here. Yon weld marks are from when she took a salvo in the flank during the assault on Tricentia.'

'And where are we going?'

'Somewhere that's safe, where we can hide 'til the armsmen finish their search; hide an' talk in peace.'

'Won't the armsmen follow us down here?'

'Nay lad, wi'out a fully armed servitor crew an' a tech-priest they couldn'a use their guns for fear of cracking somethin',' Kron said.

'And where is this sanctuary of yours?'

'Not ten strides yonder.' Kron pointed.

Nathan took a long, hard look at the narrow ledge of rotting cables that ran along the wall from the end of the pipe bridge. His burnt and aching body already throbbed from the efforts he had forced it through after the fight. Now, as the flush of adrenaline left him and the icy chill in the air replaced it, he doubted his arms and legs could carry him on such a precarious path. He hesitated and swayed involuntarily on the bridge, which suddenly seemed rather precarious in itself now he came to think about it.

'Kron, I don't think...'

Too late, the old man was swinging off along the ledge with the agility of a monkey. With him, the wan red light that served as the only illumination was vanishing fast.

Nathan hesitated only a moment before a hot flush of anger drove him forward onto the ledge. He'd be damned if he would let this walking enigma disguised as an old man abandon him to the dark and potentially more of Kendrikson's feral allies. He grasped a shoulder-high seam of wiring and pulled himself firmly over to get a foot on the cabling, trusting his weight to it as he pulled his other foot into place. Bloody-minded determination hauled him along three paces of the ledge. He made two more with his heart in his mouth and fingers fumbling blindly for purchase on the wires before his foot slipped off the cables.

His body swung out alarmingly, and only his recently gained handholds on the wiring-seam stopped him pitching off the treacherous ledge. He desperately scrabbled to get his foot back on it. His hands were as weak as water and his heart was thumping so hard his arms quivered. After a few seconds of naked terror he got his foot back on and hugged himself to the wall, teetering as his legs shook. He couldn't let go of the wiring now, his legs were too weak to trust and his hands couldn't hold his weight for much longer. He couldn't go forward, he couldn't go back. Every iota of his strength was necessary just to hold him where he was, with the blackness below sucking at his remaining scraps of vigour.

Nathan clutched closer still to the wall and plucked up his courage, carefully shuffling one foot along the cabling. He shifted some weight to it and shakily drew the other foot closer. With a supreme effort of will he unhooked one hand from the wires and reached out to grasp them further along. Then he rested and sweated before shuffling his foot forward again. So he went for the remaining five paces: slide, grip, shuffle, rest; slide, grip, shuffle, rest; slide, grip…

NATHAN ALMOST FELL into the opening when he came to it. The horrible sensation that he might fall off just as he pulled himself to safety was almost overwhelming. Once inside the opening he sat trembling for only a moment, before summoning the energy to crawl further away from the edge.

The interior of the narrow space looked like the choir stall of some Ministorum chapel. Narrow seats crammed along either wall beneath gothic arches of tubular metal. At the far end a porthole of stained glass was lit fitfully from behind by swirling colours. Kron stood silhouetted against the glass. He turned to face Nathan and pressure doors rolled shut behind him, shutting the dank breath of the crevasse outside. 'Well done, lad. I was thinking ye weren't goin' to make it.' His voice sounded as smooth and calming as the raspy little goblin could make it.

'What the hell did you leave me alone out there for?' Nathan demanded.

'To see if you're as tough as I'm thinking ye are.'

'Oh really, and do I pass muster?'

'I'll be needing to hear the end of your story to know that.'

'That's got nothing to do with this!'

'Come, lad, I can tell by the look in yer eyes that you don't think that's true. "Coincidence" is just a name that fools use for events they don't understand.'

Nathan blinked at Kron and gave a mental shrug. What harm could it do to finish the story if it gave Kron one less thing to be evasive about? 'All right, but then you better give me some answers or I'll crawl right back out of here and tell it to the armsmen.

'As I said, I opened the inner hatch to the cargo bay. Once it was open I overrode the outer hatch controls and hung on tight. I knew the drums in the bay were badly secured because me and Kendrikson had been too busy watching each other to make a decent job of it. The outer hatch blowing was enough to break them free and dump them into the void between the *Pandora* and the pirates. I was almost crushed by the stampede of metal cylinders but by the Emperor's grace and a strong grip I was able to keep a hold and stayed on the ship instead of being flung out among the cartwheeling drums outside.

'A few seconds later the first drum connected with the docking thrusters of the pirate ship. I'd been playing for time, just hoping to upset their approach, but the drums were filled with liquid oxygen. The touch of the thrusters was enough to make them explode like bombs. Dozens of the cylinders exploded in slow, slow motion, the tendrils of fire reaching back further into the cloud and detonating the rest. The escalation scared me badly and I hauled myself within the inner hatch and closed it an instant before the expanding bubble of flames washed across the *Pandora*. The deck bucked and the handful of drums which had not escaped with their fellows rolled around and clashed angrily.

'In a second the shock wave had passed and I looked out of the hatch to see the pirate ship spiralling off, fires clinging to it and debris leaking from it like a blood-trail. I went forward and up to the bridge where that slob Captain Lage was defecating in his britches. Lage claimed that Kendrikson had held him at gunpoint and forced him to cut the engines and wait for the other ship. Minutes before the explosion Kendrikson had taken a raft and left the ship. Naturally he had taken all of the archaeotech we had been smuggling with him.

'I was surprised when I heard Kendrikson had been seen in Juniptown on Lethe. I'd thought he was dead or long gone. I knew I could pick up a bounty for his head so I went hunting for him in the back alleys, which is home turf for me. But both me and Kendrikson were seized by men from the *Retribution*. And that is how I began my new career in the Imperial Navy...'

'Ye never actually knew Kendrikson?' Kron asked softly.

'No, I knew of him, worked with him, but he avoided me and most people from what I heard, he was a guy so weird he didn't even have a nickname. He was just "Kendrikson", and that said it all. Alright, I've told you my tale now it's time for you to give me some answers. No stories, just tell me the truth. 'Who were those men with Kendrikson?' Nathan glared at Kron, daring him not to answer, to push him over the edge into screaming fury.

'Them's muties, shipmen that's spent too long sailin' the void an' lost their faith. The beast song's in their heart now and they live like lice on the innards o' the ship; sometimes they'll even grab compartments and feast on the poor shipboys if they can. Once in a century the captain'll put the ship into port and flush her guts with poison to clear 'em out but 'tween times there's always muties in the crossways and trunks. Seein' as we're in a big war right now there's more than ever, and they'll be lookin' to call the beasts aboard all the time, invite 'em in as it were. Out there's whole squadrons who've succumbed to the beasts in men's hearts in past times, ones I reckon we'll be fightin' soon enough. Kendrikson probably pretended he were possessed to scare 'em into obeying him. The pirates' ship ye saw, did it have a mark on it? A rune or sigil?'

'Yes it did, most do. I don't see–'

'Did ye see it well enough to know it again?'

'Yes, but I'm asking the questions now.' Nathan had recovered enough energy to stand and hauled himself up to face Kron. 'What's a Luminen? I asked you before and you didn't answer but now you're going to tell me. What made Kendrikson a Luminen and how did that give him lightning in his veins and the power to melt steel like wax?' Nathan took a step closer, looming over Kron in the narrow space. 'Tell me!'

Kron grinned up at him before turning and pointing at the stained glass. 'I bet the pirates' symbol looked like that.'

Nathan gaped. The intricate, geometric designs of the window centred around a central icon. A halo of gold with rays so short and square that they looked like crenellations on a castle wall. In the centre was a grinning skull, picked out in loving detail with strands of platinum wire and swirls of crushed diamond. He snapped his gaze back to Kron. 'What does it mean?'

'It answers both your questions, lad. Kendrikson and yon pirates came from the same place. They made him a Luminen, took him an' made crystal stacks of his bones an' electro grafts of his brain, gave 'im skinplants and electros so's he could summon lightning an' channel it an' much more. He was a war-child of the Machine God, what the uninitiated call an electro-priest, though not one in a hundred can hide his power an' look like a normal man like he did.'

'The Machine God – you mean the tech-priests of Mars, don't you, the Adeptus Mechanicus?'

Kron nodded solemnly and Nathan suffered a painful insight into the awesome power that organisation wielded within the all-powerful Imperium. Tech-priests ministered to machines and engines on every civilised world, every interstellar ship. The Navy might man its ships but the tech-priests ran them. Their prayers and runes brought life to cold, dead metal and their forge worlds produced weapons in their billions for the Emperor's eternal war against aliens, heretics and traitors. In theory at least killing Kendrikson made him one of the latter. A sobering thought indeed.

'All right then, what's this place. Those look like shuttle controls. Am I right in presuming that it's an escape pod of some sort?'

'Aye lad, a cutter. Good for a planetary hop if ye don't mind the waiting as she's a mite slow.'

'Given what I've just heard I'd jump ship now if we weren't in the warp.'

'Death by fulguration if they catch ye,' Kron muttered with an honest-looking shudder.

'Well, we can't go back. If they find out who Kendrikson was and who killed him I'd wager they'll come up with something even more unpleasant.'

'Nay, lad, if anyone knew who Kendrikson was he wouldnae have been in the gunrooms. Tech-priests only come to repair battle damage and such.'

'So Kendrikson was originally out to get back the archaeotech for the tech-priests and got pressganged accidentally, but why didn't he tell the Navy who he was? They would have let him go for sure.'

'Many times servants o' the Emperor bury their real selves behind false memgrams and such, makes 'em hard to ferret out even wi' soul-seers. Their real purposes run in the background, watching the puppet show through the eyes and ears until they're in position to accomplish their mission. Then they become a whole different person. The Luminen part was just standing by for orders, but it must have decided that you needed killin' to keep its past buried.' Kron let that sink in for a few seconds before passing judgement on the matter.

'No one'll know we did for 'im if we get back before roll call, 'cept Leopold mebbe and he ain't going to say for fear o' bein' called derelict.'

Nathan was safe as long as Kron didn't rat on him, but he had a feeling that Kron was happy to keep their secret for the time being. They were partners in crime. 'I'm willing to bet that there's another way back into the crew quarters without crossing the gunroom.'

Kron grinned.

'HAJJ.

'ISIAH.

'KENDRIKSON.'

The sergeant-at-arms leant over and whispered something to Lieutenant Gabriel, who paused over the great ledger he had open before him. Nathan swallowed hard. This was where Kron's theory came to the crunch. Getting back from the cutter had been easier than he had hoped. A narrow culvert led back from the crevasse into the cubicles by the bunkroom. Nathan had carefully memorised every twist of the trunking and was determined to go back and familiarise himself further with it in the very next sleep shift. But for now he must see whether the Angel of Retribution was at Kendrikson's side or not.

Lieutenant Gabriel gazed at the assembled company, eyes blinking as if he were struggling to recall Kendrikson's face. He turned and murmured a question to the sergeant, who shook his head curtly in response. Gabriel made a small mark in the ledger and continued.

'Krait.

'Komoth.'

Roll call held an additional pleasant surprise: when Lieutenant Gabriel assigned the duty roster Nathan found himself placed on the Opticon crew. His momentary puzzlement was soon answered when it became clear that he was to be Kron's apprentice. He stole a look at the old man, who looked blandly innocent of course, and made a mental note of the apparent influence he could wield. Nathan wondered what the role of apprentice entailed, and for that matter what the Opticon was. A dim memory floated forward that the Opticon was involved in observation outside the ship. He certainly knew that the Opticon crew usually worked high up on the main gantries above Balthasar's breech on what amounted to an extra half-deck a good twelve metres up spiral steps of skeletal iron-work.

Whatever the duties, they could scarcely be as onerous and repetitive as the labours he was tasked with at present. As he ascended he could see other members of the guncrew moving to repair the damage he and Kron had caused in their desperate fight. The bodies were gone but charred cabling and slashed conduits were visible. Nathan wondered grimly how often they had repaired such damage without knowing its cause. The adage that 'ignorance is bliss' seemed to dominate shipboard life, but with good cause if what Kron had said about the muties was true. The grim pressures of warp travel became all the more nightmarish with the thought that there were malevolent entities clustered beyond the hull. Beasts that thirsted for human lives and souls, whose subconscious calls drove men mad. Nathan suddenly stopped climbing the steps as the thought struck him that he was going to help Kron observe those beasts and the Empyrean, the alternate dimension that they swam in.

The curses of the men behind made him move on, accompanied by a perverse desire to see the sinister beasts. He had mixed feelings when he reached the raised deck and saw a row of five shuttered arches lining the hull wall. There were ten in the Opticon crew and the burly rating named Isiah placed two men at each shutter. At first Nathan and Kron busied themselves greasing the shutter runners and cogs at its head and foot. After a quarter watch or so Isiah received a message from the comm-box he carried and relayed an order to raise the shutters. Kron smartly threw a lever and the shutter rose smoothly up to reveal an expanse of black glass which rose higher than his head and as wide as his outstretched arms. As Nathan glanced around at the other crews he noted a sense of nervous anticipation behind their actions, as if raising the shutters was an act of hidden significance.

Nathan was still gazing expectantly at the black glass when the scream of a siren shocked him rigid. The titanic blast of noise seemed to make the very deck plates tremble and was followed by a booming voice which rang like the word of the God-Emperor: 'ALERT STATUS ALL STATIONS!'

Kron turned and ran for a set of lockers at the side of the Opticon chamber, hotly pursued by the rest of the crew. The men started pulling on pressure suits which Kron dragged from the lockers. The significance of the situation was becoming readily apparent to Nathan by now. They were going into battle, very soon. Those ridiculously cumbersome-looking, heavy, rubberised pressure suits and thick-bowled helmets could be all that stood between them and the void.

To his surprise, Nathan managed to finish clamping himself into a suit before anyone else.

The helmet locked down onto a broad ring across the shoulders of the suit but had a visor made up of different layers, the last of which was little more than a slit in the armour plate. He slid back all the layers and saw Kron had done the same. Nathan felt relieved that he wouldn't have to breathe the stale, sweaty air inside the suit just yet. 'How long does this oxygen last?' he asked Kron, tapping the dented brass cylinder plumbed into the side of the suit's chest.

'A watch or so for somun' as big as ye.'

'Just eight hours? They don't want us to get any ideas about wandering off, do they?'

'Ye can always get more air on the ship and if ye… part company wi' the ship an' ye're not picked up they wouldnae be able to find ye anyway. Ye'd be drifted too far into the void.'

'Alright, what do–'

The deck lurched beneath their feet and there was a sickening sensation of falling for a second. Isiah shouted at them to get to their stations. Nathan noted that the rating now bore a pistol and what looked suspiciously like a shock-maul and sprang to his post as best as the suit's heavy boots would allow.

The monolithic siren blasted twice. A commanding voice spoke: 'BATTLE STATIONS. BRACE FOR IMPACT!'

The deck shuddered and dropped again. This time the falling was longer. Nathan slid the visor down, grabbed a stanchion and braced his legs. He felt sick and hollow. The suit was stifling. He fought an urge to tear the helmet off and scream his lungs out. An insistent, intellectual part of his brain kept telling him to be calm and that the ship was simply preparing itself and surging majestically into battle. But the animal instincts of his body felt every jar and shake as an infernal choir of death screams.

The ship lurched and fell again. This time Nathan actually felt his feet leave the floor. He felt as though part of him was being torn away, all the roiling emotion in his body began coalescing into a tearing sense of dislocation. A tangible shock rang along the length of the ship and Nathan realised they had left warp space.

The black glass of the Opticon flashed white and then cleared to show a scene of awesome beauty. A night-sky bisected by titanic thunderheads of cloud reared above a fiery sunset. Static lightning cobwebbed the depths and climbed up to blush the clouds with purple. Stars stood out sharp and clear, their own fires made to seem cold by their distance.

'The void never looked so beautiful or terrible before,' Nathan whispered, his fear drained away by the majesty of it all. Kron's voice crackled in his ear-pieces.

'That's right lad, 'cause through this glass ye see as the ship does; heat, light, magnetism, radiants and etherics are all clear to her.' Kron slid out a large circular lens which was attached to the window frame by a system of brass rods and runners. The thick frame of the lens held two number counters and two raised icons. Kron expertly tracked it across the surface of the window. The numbered wheels of the counters span in response, one horizontal, one vertical.

The ship shuddered again, and Nathan swayed against the window, his helmet ringing off the unyielding surface alarmingly. The sensation of almost being pitched out into the void was enough to make his palms sweat inside the cursedly thick gloves. As he straightened up, Isiah was barking orders to the crews to search different co-ordinates. Kron slid the lens across until the metriculators showed 238.00 by 141.00, their search area. At that spot the lens resolved a dark area which had shown occasional vagrant twinklings into an asteroid field, rolling mountains of stone lit by the star's fiery light.

'What are we looking for, Kron, just rocks?' Nathan asked with shaky levity. The old man was tracking the lens back and forth across the field with deft, economical movements. Each time he reached its periphery he depressed one of the runes, and the tumbling stones shown in the lens were outlined in red with strings of numbers showing speed and distance which remained in the glass after the lens slid away.

'Anythin' that might show us where the foe's a'lurkin; a glint here, or a bloom o' heat there.' Kron never took his eye from the lens as he spoke, Nathan slid back his topmost, armoured visor so that he could see better.

'You mean engine heat trails like those?' he stated, pointing to a set of needle-thin arcs which shimmered near the edge of the field.

'CONTACT! MARK-TWO-FOUR-ZERO BY ONE-THREE-SEVEN!' Kron roared, Isiah shouting it back, word for word, over the crackling comm.

The lens now showed broad, vaporous trails of red which curved back around the furthest asteroids. There looked to be four to Nathan, although they were already merging and dissipating.

'They're closing in, lad, I can smell it.'

Kron tracked the lens along the trails and cursed as they disappeared behind a glowing streamer of dust. Moments later an incandescent spearhead of heat blossomed out of the cloud, dust and lightning rolled off it in plumes as the lens starkly announced it as Enemy vessel [class: Unknown]. 51,000l. Closing.

A burst of activity on the deck below drew Nathan's attention. Through the grilled floor he could see Balthasar's breech had been swung open and the gunners were hauling flat plates covered in short spikes into the open maw. Even through his thick suit he could hear the gunners' cheers as they slammed the sub-munitions home. On the lens light and shadow now etched out the enemy, showed the silhouette of crenallated battlements and barbed buttresses as the spearhead rolled abeam on the white-hot stabs of myriad thrusters. Grand cruiser, the display read, Repulsive class.

A ripple of serried flames geysered from the Repulsive's flank as she completed the turn, and a storm of black specks arrowed towards them. Nathan gasped in horror as a heartbeat later the specks started to explode in gouts of flame. At first they looked distant, small puffs of colour against the void, but the projectiles kept coming, surging forward through the fiery chains to detonate in turn. In moments their view of the enemy was obscured by a firestorm which was rippling ever closer. The flames filled every window in the Opticon by the time Nathan slammed his visor fully shut.

The Repulsive's salvo crashed down on the ship itself with hurricane force. Nathan staggered as the deck rolled beneath him and a mighty, rushing wind roared beyond the hull. A lash of dazzling purple light blazed through the glass, cutting the incendiary cloud like elemental lightning. It was gone in an instant before it returned in a retina-burning sweep which slammed into the ship with a bone-jarring impact. Nathan's spine crawled with the sensation of unseen energies straining and crackling before a rush of scorching heat washed over him.

At last he was glad of the suit's cumbersome protection, though even with it he felt as though he had been suddenly cast into a great oven. The heat was a palpable thing, pushing down on him like a great hand and burning his throat as he tried to breathe. Nathan saw several of the Opticon crew collapse into pathetic heaps, one with flames licking about him. After what seemed like hours but could only have been seconds of heart-stopping fear the burning suddenly stopped, leaving a horrible tang of smouldering rubber inside his helmet. Sirens blasted and an almighty voice boomed over the chaos: 'PORT WEAPONS PREPARE TO LOCK-ON. TARGET MARK-TWO-SIX-NINE BY ONE-SIX-ZERO.'

Iron discipline drove the shipmen to their tasks, that and the grim instinct that to live they must fight and win. The ship had been wounded but it could still fight back. Fires were doused, the dead and injured dragged away. The firestorm was lessening and a moment later the decks ceased to rattle as the ship finally burst clear of the enemies' salvo pattern. Kron's breath rasped in Nathan's earpiece as they slid the lens back over the grand cruiser contact. The Retribution was coming across the enemy's bow, and the metriculator's count showed the enemy as closing.

'LOCK ON.'

Kron activated the second rune on the lens frame. A stylised cog superimposed by the Imperial eagle sprang into existence within the lens but the runners seemed to be jammed and Nathan had to help him drag the device over the target contact. The lens showed the ornate spearhead foreshortening into a shark-finned ziggurat of bronze as they pulled across the front of her. Where the icon rested the hull of the grand cruiser was illuminated as if by a ghostly radiance which played over shimmering walls of force.

'FIRE MAIN Batteries!'

The lights dimmed for a moment as capacitors charged and then the ship resounded with the clamour of the guns. Nathan felt the pressure of unseen forces hit him like a slap as forty guns hurled their payloads across the void. A moment later he saw the spreading cloud of projectiles cleaving towards the enemy. No spreading storms of fire this time, the munitions detonated right beneath the enemy's prow. Invisible walls fell beneath the onslaught and a rain of destruction crashed across the battlements of the ziggurat-fortress. Debris haloes puffed from it like smoke rings.

'FIRE MAIN LANCE ARRAYS.'

Ravening white spears of pure power stabbed at the foe, tearing redglowing gouges across its hull, globs of molten metal spun away and flames leapt from the wounds. The grand cruiser lurched visibly under the impacts, and began to twist away from the salvo. Even as it did so, two heat trails appeared from behind the grand cruiser, coming up fast to slash at its rear with a spiralling net of laser bolts. Nathan felt a flush of relief. The other two ships must be allies, and now their mutual enemy was caught between two fires. Below, the gunners were rushing to reload Balthasar for another shot, while a small team struggled to pin a whipping power line which sparked furiously. He looked back at the lens in time to see a swarm of bright flares pulling away from the enemy cruiser's prow. Ominously the tiny heat trails curved to alter course towards them and it soon became apparent that although these new weapons were not as fast as the projectiles fired before, they were considerably bigger. Sirens blared.

'ALL STATIONS PREPARE TO REPEL BOARDERS.'

The relief Nathan had felt rapidly evaporated. The enemy must have launched boarding torpedoes, simple attack craft packed with the troops, bombs, incendiaries, corrosives, nerve agents and other hellish weapons necessary to wreak havoc if they got aboard. It was bad enough to be caught up in the titanic duel between warships but now the enemy was coming to strike at them face to face, all the time with the prospect of being crushed like an insect by the pulverising contest going on outside. Isiah rapidly passed out weapons from an arms-locker: blades, shock mauls, stubby autopistols and chunky shotguns. Nathan found himself equipped with a worn-looking pump gun and a clip of shells. He risked a glance at the windows as he was fumbling to slot the shot-filled cylinders into the breech of the gun. They now showed finger-long missiles with beaked prows powering, as it seemed, straight for him on harsh coronas of light. The sirens blared a repeating four-tone alarm.

'PORT TURRET STATIONS: OPEN FIRE!'

Nathan cursed as he dropped a shell onto the grating; his fingers felt like sausages in the thick suit gloves. Outside lasers sketched livid traceries across the void as the short-range turrets laid down their barrage, shells and missiles exploded in gouts of orange incandescence as the Retribution's barbettes joined in. The first rank of the beaked projectiles were consumed or broken open and tiny, struggling figures spilled into the void as they spiralled away. But still more torpedoes surged through the barrage and angled in, cutting their flaring drives on a final approach.

Nathan slammed the last shell into place and carefully pumped the action to chamber a round. At the last instant before impact the torpedoes appeared to swell enormously, becoming as big as shuttles before they disappeared from view. A ringing impact threw Nathan to the quivering deck and an endless cacophony of screaming, tearing metal followed. It was so loud it made him quail at the bone-crushing violence of it, of the sheer force that was ripping through the metres of armour plate to breach the hull.

Finally the tearing slowed and stopped until only the screams of injured gunners and the hiss of escaping air penetrated Nathan's helmet. The Opticon deck had twisted and now part of it sagged away towards the lower deck. Nathan crawled to the edge and saw there was terrible carnage below. A great crocodile-snout of steel and brass projected through the hull plates near Balthasar's breech. Deckplates were twisted back; stanchions and pipes had been bent into an insane ironwork jungle with flowers of steam and spraying fluids. The surviving gunners were taking up defensive positions, aiming their assortment of shotguns and pistols at the invader.

As they did so, cannons coughed into life around the crocodile's snout. Gunflashes strobed as the autoweapons hammered explosive rounds across the interior of the gunroom. Men were blasted asunder where the rounds struck and hot shrapnel whickered around the metal walls injuring others. The snout was grinding open now and a horde of nightmarish figures spilled out of it to add their fire to the fight. At first they appeared like men in the flickering light, but their insane glee marked them apart. They capered as the gunners' pitifully few weapons tore into them, filling that crocodile maw with twitching bodies. They roared with mad laughter as they blazed back with their own guns and threw devilish bombs which burst into pools of hungry, incandescent flame wherever they landed.

Nathan sighted on a twisted figure as it pulled back its arm to throw. The pump gun crashed and the figure fell into a burning pool of its own making. The flames spread, engulfed the crocodile snout and the next two who tried to rush through it were eaten alive by the incendiary. Even so a group of the attackers were out in the gunroom now, dashing through the wreckage to hurl themselves on the gunners. Vicious hand-to-hand combats broke out all across the deck, the foes' hooks and crooked blades clashing against the gunner's pry bars and line gaffes.

The pump gun was useless now the melee had reduced all ordered fighting to a shambles.

'We've got to help them!' Nathan shouted to Kron.

Kron's helm nodded ponderously back and they both slid themselves down the twisted Opticon deck to drop down onto the gundeck. Isiah and two other survivors of the opticon crew followed and they waded into the brawl in a loose knot. Nathan used his gun as a club, smashing the skull of a black-clad figure who was about to gut a fallen gunner. He winced as the gun crunched into its misshapen head, fearing the ageing weapon would fall apart in his hands.

He pumped the action to chamber a round to reassure himself it still could, just as two figures leapt at him out of the smoke. Their mad eyes glared from behind leather hoods, looking so like Fetchin's that Nathan almost hesitated before he blasted one in the midriff with the shotgun. He pumped the slide to chamber another round but it jammed halfway. Cursing, he swung the gun up to block a saw-bladed knife as the other foe slashed at him but he was borne back as his attacker leapt bodily onto him, pinning the useless gun between their bodies. Panic stole Nathan's strength as he struggled against its maniacal attack. Drool spilled across his face as the creature tore away his helmet with its free hand and pushed him to the deck.

Nathan dropped his gun and scrabbled to keep a grip on the knife-hand as his foe leaned his weight against it, pushing it inexorably towards his exposed neck. For a long second Nathan saw every detail of the thing astride him with horrible clarity. Flames billowed behind a head made jagged by the short horns thrusting out through its leather mask. Cartilage-textured tubes twisted in and out of its flesh like parasitic worms. It was either naked or covered in human hides marked with brands and stigmata. It stank like a week-old corpse and it muttered mad, excited prayers as it bent to the task of murdering him. If what he had been told was true this thing must have been human once. Every shred of its humanity was gone now, eaten up by insane gods that had reduced it to living offal that worshipped its own butcher.

Sickness lent Nathan an awful strength, a burning desire to wipe out these horrors that had been unleashed on them. With a supreme effort born of revulsion Nathan shoved the creature back. Suddenly it convulsed, then slumped and its dead weight bore him back down again.

Nathan rolled free to see Kron pulling an axe from the abomination's neck. Isiah and the others had disappeared into smoke. Only corpses surrounded Nathan and Kron. Nathan's helmet visor had been smashed, rendering it useless. Without it he realised how thin the air was becoming. The flames all around were turning ghostly as they hungrily ate at what remained. Even the screams and sounds of combat were becoming subtly muffled.

'We have to stop more of them getting aboard!' Kron shouted to him through his own damnably intact helmet.

Nathan nodded his understanding. Grabbing up some firebombs from the corpse and found a short halberd from among the fallen before heading for the heart of the inferno. He felt filled with a kind of righteous fury at the turn of events, like things couldn't get any worse and it was time for some payback. Somebody had to pay for him landing up in a situation as dire as this, and with Kendrikson already dead it was going to have to be their insane, murderous enemy.

The snout stood open as before. The flames were dying away in its maw and Nathan could see more twisted figures gathering to rush through. He fumbled to find an activation stud on the rune-etched bomb before giving up and simply lobbing it as the figures started to run forward. Then another, and a third from Kron, turning the entryway into a sea of corrosive fire as the bombs burst on impact. Nathan turned to shout to Kron an instant before an armoured giant burst through the conflagration with a brazen roar.

Before Nathan could react the heavy pistol in its fist barked twice and Kron was thrown back with a flash and shower of blood. Nathan felt an icy bolt of fear trying to force his feet to run but it was already too late. The figure charged forward with nightmarish speed, an ironclad monster of myth, skull-helmed and laden with death, a screeching chainsword in its other fist slashing down at him in an unstoppable arc.

Nathan hurled himself aside and brought up the halberd to block the slash. It was a mistake. The power of the blow threw him back, jolting his arms as the shrieking teeth of the saw tore chunks from the halberd's steel haft in a shower of sparks. The giant wielded its huge blade with ease, and in the blink of an eye its shrieking blade circled and swept down at him again. Nathan leapt back but the sweep of the chainsword tore the head from the halberd and slid along the arm of his suit, chewing through it and tearing at his flesh. A cold flush of painlessness told Nathan that the injury was severe; his body was already trying to shut out the agony.

In desperation Nathan thrust the jagged end of the halberd haft into the thing's barrel chest. It rang off an armoured plate and buried itself deep in a nest of cables beneath where its ribs should have been. The giant warrior didn't even flinch as it sent him sprawling with a blow from its heavy pistol.

Death was close. One of his eyes was blind and Nathan felt an abnormal calm as he accepted that these were his last seconds of life. The world seemed to slow to an insect crawl as the armoured warrior stepped towards him, raising its keening sword for a killing blow. Nathan felt only a pang of disappointment that he would never know more of Kron's strange wisdom; so much must have died with him. The pounding of Nathan's last heartbeats sounded like a distantly thumping drum.

Thump. One armoured boot crunched down. Flecks of blood span away from the motion-captured teeth of the chainsword as it soared upward. Nathan looked down at his right arm and saw it was crimson from shoulder to wrist. Everything wavered as he started to black out.

Thump. The other boot crashed down. The blade was raised almost to the top of its arc. Nathan was aware of movement where Kron had fallen, and a tiny spark of hope flared that he might still be alive, might save Nathan somehow if only he were quick and could defeat this unstoppable colossus. Logic sneered at his paltry hopes from the dark recesses of his brain.

Thump. The blade began to sweep down, gathering momentum. Nathan's world was shrinking, the vision from his remaining eye darkening until he could barely see. Paltry hopes and all conscious thought were corroded away by the sea of agony raging through his arm.

Thump. Nathan saw the blade had entered his dimmed world and part of him welcomed it, teeth flashing bright as a shark's hungry smile in the gloom. The pain would be over soon, that could only be good. A spectral hand seemed to reaching over him to touch the blade, as if the God-Emperor himself were placing a benediction on his slaughter. The hand was crawling with blue fires and sparks cascaded from its fingertips.

Thump. A flash of light leapt from hand to blade, and with it the chainsword exploded and was hurled away from the giant's fist. The hulking warrior staggered and started to raise his pistol. Kron stepped forward into Nathan's circle of vision and raised a hand.

Thump. A ravening bolt of brilliance crackled from Kron's hand onto the warrior's chest plate and rent it asunder in a thunderclap. The mighty figure was thrown off its feet, its pistol sending explosive rounds flashing off wildly from its owner's convulsing death-spasm.

Thump. The chainsword, molten and twisted rang down on the deck-plates. Nathan clasped his left arm to his right shoulder and instantly felt warmth flood through his blood slick wounds. The armoured warrior crashed to the deck beside its smoking sword. Nathan tried to breathe more deeply to clear his head but found he couldn't. The orange flames all around were shrinking into bluish flickers. The air was nearly gone.

Kron squatted down beside him as the ship shook, as if from some internal explosion. Nathan could see the chest of Kron's suit was shredded and bloody, a death-shot surely. Wreckage dislodged by the shockwave crashed down nearby with horrible clangour. Kron didn't even flinch as he calmly removed his helmet. As the helmet came away, Kron's eye blazed as never before. It was glowing with the fierce light of furnace. Nathan tried to blot out the horrible intensity of that glare in his dimmed world but couldn't. It bored into him, so that it seemed like Kron the man was shrunk to nothing more than a wraith, that the crimson brilliance trailed behind it like smoke.

Kron's lips moved, but Nathan had to strain to hear their faint whisper through the rarefied air.

'Don't you worry, shipmate, Kron'll see to ye.'

'L-Luminen!' Nathan gasped.

'No,' Kron whispered.

Nathan's body was trembling uncontrollably as shock set in. His vision had almost dimmed completely, apart from a harsh, red light floating nearby.

'Not that at all.'

A helmet clamped down over Nathan's head, dimming the light and bringing a welcome darkness.

NATHAN AWOKE ON the floor of the hidden cutter. His arm was in a sling and a bandage covered one of his eyes but he otherwise felt rested and healthy. Kron was sitting in one of the narrow pews, watching him.

'How de ye feel?' he inquired with genuine concern.

'Good,' Nathan grunted as he sat up. 'How long was I out?'

'Five hours. I took time to fix ye up, an' me too, and rest some 'fore we go back up to the gunroom.'

Nathan felt a sense of relief. He had feared Kron would ask him if he wanted to jump ship. The aftermath of a battle offered the best chance Nathan would likely get for an escape to go unnoticed. But somehow the prospect seemed a lot less appealing now he had seen what was out there waiting for mutineers and faithless men to fall into its clutches. In fact Nathan was feeling an unfamiliar amount of regard for the God-Emperor after his experiences, a craving for the protection the Ecclesiarchs promised could be gained from the blessings of the Holy Master of Mankind.

But that left him in here with Kron, not-a-Luminen Kron who could defeat a champion of the mad gods with his own lightning. No ordinary gunner, for sure. A servant of the Emperor? Somehow Nathan didn't think so. If anything he really did look like a gargoyle in this setting, a red-eyed piece of malevolence that had detached itself from the stonework and come down to blaspheme among it. Perhaps someone hiding out then, disguised among a faceless mass yet always moving from one world to another. It would be a superb cover. Unremarkable, beneath attention and yet guarded by the awesome might of an Imperial warship. Ultimately, whatever other misgivings Nathan might have, Kron had saved his life and that put him firmly in Kron's debt. He began to say so but Kron waved his thanks away.

'Don't be too thankful, lad. I had to fix your eye with what was to hand down here. I'm 'fraid I might have made a terrible job out of it. Take the bandage off. Tell me if ye can see.'

Nathan knew what was coming even before his fingers brushed cold steel around his eye. The lens of it was hard and slightly curved to the touch. He bore the metal-sealed scars of his first engagement as part of the Emperor's Navy, but his vision was perfect. Nathan shuddered as he recalled Kron's unnerving personality shift after the fight with Kendrikson, when he had seemed like a slave desperate to escape his inactive bionic eye.

'Kron?' Nathan began tentatively. 'Who are you really?'

Kron chortled. 'A princeling who was stolen by gypsies.'

'Don't start that again.'

'Very well, I'll put it this way, lad… Cross the stars and fight for glory…'

THE TOWER
CS Goto

THE NARROW, DARK corridor that led out of the ciphers' bloc was filthy. Little piles of dust were pushed up against the walls, congealed into paste as they mixed with whatever liquid seeped down the damp stone. In front of each doorway along the length of the passage, Lexio could see wedges of floor swept clean by the outward-opening doors themselves, and orderly footprints left in the dust as the other ciphers had hurried off to their duties. The marks were in the same place every day, and Lexio had memorised them all – memory was his special skill, after all. Just from the marks on the floor, Lexio could tell whether anyone was sick, missing, or merely running late. Not that they ever were.

The menials in this quadrant of the tower always started their day in the corridors immediately adjacent to the Hall of Historical Correction. It was the mysterious centre of their world – for they could never enter it – around which revolved an entire unexplored universe of passageways and chambers that they would never see. They would fuss and shuffle in their own special, inexplicable manner, working their way out from the great hall in concentric rings of meek bustle, never looking up from the dusty flagstones at their feet. By the end of their working day, they would have passed through the realms of the ordinates and prefects, and would have reached the habitation area of the ciphers, buried deep in the subterranean realms of the tower's foundations, tucked under the rather decrepit western wing of the immense edifice. The menials themselves lived another two storeys down, in a sector of the tower that never got cleaned. The professional sanitisers of the legendary Tower of Idols lived in the dustiest, most squalid conditions imaginable.

The cleaning timetable had been designed to ensure that the most important parts of the tower got sanitised first. It would not do for the Historicus to arrive at the great hall in the morning only to find it covered in the layers of dust and industrial grime that quickly accumulated during the day and night in the sleepless tower. To permit such a thing would be tantamount to the most unimaginable heresy. In fact, in an effort to avoid insulting the greater agents of the Emperor, a junior ordinate had struck upon the idea of making the menials' working day slightly longer than a calendar day. This had the advantage of making the menials think that they were always behind schedule, forcing them to work in relay teams so that one was always cleaning the corridors outside the Hall of Historical Correction before another had reached the ciphers' bloc. The relay teams shared a single salary between them, and none would dare complain because of the tremendous honour accorded to them; menials were recruited from the population outside the tower and were the only non-hereditary members of the Administratum to be granted the title of adept. The ordinate responsible for this stroke of genius was destined for the ranks of the prefectus.

As he did every morning, Lexio shook his head and ran his delicate fingers through the cobwebs that had collected around the doorway to his hab-unit overnight. For some reason, despite the intricate genius of the cleaning routine, his doorway was perpetually filthy. He resented having to walk through the grime – he was a hereditary cipher, not some scurrying menial. But, like an obsessive compulsive, he ran his well-scrubbed fingers through the dirt every morning, collecting gloopy sediment under his nails, and cursed under his breath at the incompetence of the lowly, salaried workers: adepts, indeed.

Lifting his feet carefully into neat little steps, avoiding the cracks between the flagstones and deliberately treading into as many of the existing footprints as possible, Lexio made his way through the half-light of the corridor. He had done this so often that an onlooker would no longer think that he looked unnatural as he shortened and lengthened his stride to fall in with the patterns on the floor. Indeed, he didn't even have to look down at his feet – he knew where all the markings were and could make this precise journey in pitch darkness if he had to; a four-dimensional map of the route between the ciphers' bloc and the Hall of Historical Correction was etched indelibly into his memory. He knew exactly where to place his feet at any given time, in any given location along the way, depending on the esoteric vagaries of the menials' routines and the movements of the other officials in the quadrant.

Of course, Lexio didn't know that he knew the route in such intricate, perfect detail. He had simply repeated the journey so often that he no longer had to think about it. It had seeped into his muscle-memory, bypassing his cognitive faculties altogether. Indeed, on a traumatic occasion a number of years before, Lexio's walk to work had been dramatically interrupted by the exhausted collapse of a menial in the passage way in front of him. The man had fallen off a ladder and broken his neck as he thudded into the stone floor before Lexio's feet. Suddenly jolted out of his routine and unsure about which way to turn next, it had taken the cipher nearly half an hour to retrace his steps back to his hab-unit in order to start the journey again. He lived in mortal dread of this happening again.

It was one of the ironies of his vocation, reflected Lexio as he lapsed into reverie once more, letting his feet take him up the first flight of steps towards the cleaner air of the ordinates' sector of the western wing itself, that he was fated to remember everything and yet have no conscious access to his memories. It was a unique skill, and one that was highly prized by the Administratum. The ciphers of the Tower of Idols were carefully selected from specific bloodlines, which were interbred under rigorously controlled conditions, and the special verbatimem talent was meticulously cultivated in dedicated academies. Tests were conducted each year. The traditional families would prepare their children for the tests for years before; fathers and grandfathers passed on the secret arts of self-hypnosis which enabled the child to memorise dictation without showing any knowledge of the message that they were carrying. Some families had been in service since the time of the Emperor himself, and they were exceedingly proud of their honourable lineage as Imperial adepts.

Lexio stopped abruptly and took one step back. He was not feeling very relaxed this morning, and he had already made a mistake – overshooting this leg of his journey by a full stride. Somewhere in the depths of his consciousness, a whispering voice started to chant his family's memory mantra, calming his mind so that he would make no more mistakes of this nature in the day to come.

As he stepped back automatically and a heavy vehicle rumbled past his face without stopping, obliterating the footprints that he had erroneously left in the dust in front of him. As it did every morning, the vehicle carried the prefectus secondus on his way to the Hall of Historical Correction. Without giving the matter any thought at all, Lexio turned sharply and walked along the wide corridor in the wake of the prefectus, keeping his feet neatly in the track-marks of the vehicle.

This wide, low corridor connected the ordinates' wing to the more elaborate sector inhabited by the prefects. It was wide enough for fifty ordinates to walk side by side in the busiest times of the day, but its ceiling was so low that any one of them could reach up and touch it if they cared to. Above the passageway was another, exactly the same. And above that was another. If he listened very hard, Lexio could hear the footfalls of the officials on other levels bustling through the wide corridors on

their way to their stations. The sound formed part of the familiar background noise of the tower, and it reassured everyone that they had a
special place in a huge, magnificent machine. Lexio, of course, hardly
noticed it at all anymore. He simply knew what tone he should hear and
what volume it should be at different times of the day. Today, it sounded
perfect, which was a relief.

As the passageway ran through the prefects' sector, getting closer and
closer to the Hall of Historical Correction, it grew steadily more impressive. The ceiling started to withdraw into the heavens and pillars began to
rise out of the ground to support the suggestion of vaulted details. By the
time the corridor left the prefects' realm and reached the edge of the Historicus's district, it was more like a cathedral, with a great vaulted ceiling
soaring into the invisible heights. But Lexio never looked up. Instead, he
recognised this location by the increased traffic and by the sudden clean-
liness of the floor – it was as though this end of the corridor was cleaned
and polished constantly. Without thinking about it, Lexio could feel the
tension drop out of his shoulders as his muscle-memory realised that he
no longer had to be so careful about where he put his feet – there were
no dusty footprints for him to follow here, only cracks to be avoided.

After two hundred and seventy-four steps, Lexio turned sharply to his
right and ducked into a low, dark passage that sloped upwards towards the
next level. This little tunnel was clearly never cleaned at all – presumably
the Historicus never had cause to stoop into these service tunnels and thus
the menials had no incentive to clean them – and the angled ground
squelched and slid slightly as Lexio's feet compressed the accumulated
grime. It was too dark for him to see where the cracks or other footprints
were, and he had never been able to see the ground to learn their position,
so he shuffled nervously and rapidly through the confined space, emerging into a gloriously lit hallway on the other side, after twenty-eight
slippery steps. Pale morning sunlight streamed into the ornate, gothic
space through giant circular windows that ran the entire length of the hallway, casting long shadows across the shiny white floor. Each window
depicted a scene from the glorious history of the Imperium, beginning
even before the Horus Heresy and reaching up to the present day with the
last stained-glass image. Visitors to the Historical Correction Unit would
walk along the resplendent timeline, over immaculately polished white
marble, before reaching the great doors at the end of the hallway. The picture was certainly one of a heroic and sanitary Imperium.

Lexio's walk changed slightly as he made his way down this impressive
historical line. It was not that he was intimidated by the weight of history
itself, since he never looked up at the icons emblazoned on the windows,
nor even by the responsibilities that awaited him when he reached the
great doors. Rather, he was conscious that his feet were dirty and that he
would leave grimy footprints on the pristine marble. He lifted his feet

high and only touched the balls of his feet to the ground with each step, keeping away from the cracks between the huge slabs of stone. According to his four-dimensional mental map, Lexio should have timed his arrival perfectly to coincide with the start of the next cleaning relay, so his footprints would be eradicated within fifteen minutes.

Today, something was different about this grand hallway, and the trauma of difference shivered its way into Lexio's consciousness like a maggot into an overripe fruit. As his higher functions wrested control from his muscle-memory, he looked around and found himself in the middle of the Procession of History. It took a moment for him to calm his nerves, as he realised that he could actually see the great doors ahead of him – there would be no need to return to his hab-unit and make the journey all over again. Thus calmed, Lexio cast his eyes back down onto the shimmering white marble at his feet and he struggled to work out what was different. What had disturbed him so much that it had broken his automatic, daily routine? There were no menials with broken necks lying across his path this time.

After a few minutes of focussed concentration, the picture began to resolve itself in Lexio's mind. He studied the pristine floor and watched the gradually shifting forms of the shadows creeping across the marble. One of those dark smudges on the ground was slightly different from the previous day... from all previous days. It was just a tiny difference, just the hint of a protrusion where there should have been smooth uniformity.

Lexio gingerly raised his eyes from the ground and looked up at the glorious image on the window, blazing in reds and golds in the sunlight. The picture showed a giant red Space Marine with the wings of an angel, flourishing a great sword but contorted in agony. This was the first time that Lexio had ever seen the visage of the Adeptus Astartes, and a pang of guilt plucked at his soul, as though the powerful images were supposed to be reserved for those greater and better than him. But he mustered his courage and narrowed his eyes, concentrating on the pillar that rose at the edge of the great window. The intricate stonework sported an array of icons and the swirling form of High Gothic script. Right up near the arch that folded back over the top of the glorious window, Lexio could see a small gargoyle with a sneering face and two long horns. He traced the line of light from the hideous sculpture to the ground, and realised that the erroneous shadow was being cast from that ugly face. Squinting against the light and straining his eyes, he saw a tiny fleck of black between the gargoyle's horns. It was almost nothing – almost not there at all – but its tiny shadow betrayed it to the perfect memory of Lexio.

Now what am I supposed to do, thought Lexio, wringing his hands anxiously and looking around at the bustle of other officials in the Procession of History, hoping that one of them might notice the flaw in the morning routine.

* * *

THE FEET MADE him stop moving. They were directly in his path, blocking the route of his broom and apparently unwilling to move aside. Gingerly, Cregg prodded at them with the harsh bristles of his brush, half hoping that they were not connected to anything, so that he could simply sweep them up and continue with his rounds. He was running a little late already this morning, and he really wanted to make up some time in the gleaming Procession of History – it was always so sparkling clean that he was sure he could get away with a cursory sanitization just this once.

The feet didn't budge. Instead, a whispering cough sounded down from above them, as though somebody was trying to attract Cregg's attention. For a moment, he wondered whether this was some kind of test. He had been warned about such things by the veteran menials: prefects lying in wait for an unsuspecting menial and then tricking him into looking into their eyes. The results of an errant glance depended upon who was telling the story. In the depths under the western wing, huddled around a sputtering, oily fire during the short, cold off-hours, Cregg had heard about how the gaze of a prefectus could turn a menial to stone, or wipe his memory so that he forgot who he was. He had even heard of menials being dragged out of the tower altogether and thrown back amongst the non-adepts outside, for daring to look into the eyes of a superior, hereditary official. Whatever the truth of it, Cregg had never once looked up from the floor outside the dungeon-like confines of the menials' sector, and he didn't mean to break that practice now.

After a couple of experimental prods, Cregg manoeuvred the broom around the feet and attempted to continue on his route. But the feet moved, stepping carefully over the crack between the marble slabs and coming to rest again directly in front of Cregg's sanitizer. It seemed that the feet were determined to prevent Cregg from successfully performing his Emperor-given duties. In a flash of anger, Cregg's mind boiled with sudden resentment at the heresy being performed, and his knuckles whitened as his hands tensed around the handle of his broom. He pushed the brush forcefully against the feet, without looking up.

'Excuse me, my lord,' he whispered, barely audible. 'I must press on… for the Emperor,' he added, hoping that the hallowed name might budge the feet through sheer resonance.

There was another vague cough from above the feet, and then a thin, stuttering voice. 'Um, look, erm, t… there's a b… bit of a p… problem h… here.'

Cregg stopped jamming his sanitizer against the feet, hardly able to hear the weak voice above the sounds of its bristles against the stone. That really didn't sound like the voice of an adept who could turn him to stone or wipe his memory with a single word. He looked again at the feet. They were wrapped in simple, unadorned, dark grey cloth, soled in thick rubber. Coating the heels, Cregg could distinctly see the unpleasant, granulated sheen of grime. Then, looking back to where the feet had been only seconds before, Cregg winced as he saw the sticky suggestion of a pair of footprints polluting the marble.

Where in the world could a hereditary official have so sullied their feet, wondered Cregg? Unless, Brother Greck had completely failed with his cycle of cleaning before him, Cregg could see no way that these could be the feet of a prefectus.

Slowly, and with great trepidation, Cregg lifted his eyes slightly. The grey feet were connected to grey leggings, which were buried beneath the long folds of a plain, featureless grey smock. Squinting his eyes and feeling faintly nauseous with tension, Cregg lifted his glance the last few centimetres and saw the face of a hereditary official for the first time since he was selected for service in the tower, five years earlier.

The face was pale to the point of whiteness, with a thin sprinkling of grey stubble over its jaw and scalp. Etched into the sickly, sunless skin were a series of complicated lexiographs, written in neat, black vertical lines down the side of the face and neck, disappearing under the featureless material of the smock. But, after all of his fear about the petrifying gaze, Cregg could not see the man's eyes, since they were averted – they seemed to be staring up towards something on the huge window at the side of the Procession of History. Indeed, the man was pointing in that direction with his hand and muttering something inaudible under his breath, as though talking to himself.

THE SENTRIES STOOD in silence, half hidden in the deep shadows of the ornate, arched doorway. There were no windows in the corridor that led into the Great Hall of Vindicare, and no lights shone out of the cavernous space beyond. The entire temple was cloaked in darkness, as though shimmering on the edge of existence. The endless, labyrinthine corridors twisted and snaked in tortuously indirect patterns, turning back on themselves and suddenly stopping in abrupt dead-ends. Some of the flagstones were wired with explosives, and others did not really exist at all, hiding pits of excruciating pain beneath their silent charade. In places, there simply was no floor, and the unwary risked falling into the unspeakable abyss below the ancient temple, where forgotten horrors lay waiting to feast on the careless and the stupid.

Even if an assailant were stupid enough to attempt unauthorised access into the Vindicare temple, it would be a rare individual indeed who could make it through the maze of tunnels, around the myriad traps, and live to confront the sentries who seemed to haze into translucence at the entrance to the Great Hall. And these were no ordinary sentries – they were amongst the most honoured and exalted of the Vindicare brethren, standing a tireless vigil before the most sacred site of their faith. They were enwrapped in the ritual synskin of their creed, which seemed to absorb the faint light and render them almost invisible, and were armed with an incredible array of exotic blades, many of which had never seen the light of the sun outside the temple's confines.

On this particular morning, a svelte and graceful figure flicked through the darkness of the Vindicare temple, sweeping through the web of passageways with practiced ease, stepping around the false flag-stones and vaulting the moments of yawning abyss without giving them a second thought. She seemed to know where they were before she reached them, springing up to swing from a well-placed handrail or to walk the thinnest of ledges set into the black stone walls. All the time, her simple black robes fluttered and billowed behind her; thanks to the unique way in which the fabric had been folded, the flowing material made no noise as it rushed in her wake.

Without hesitation, the mysterious figure vaulted into the air as she emerged into the darkness of the corridor that led to the Great Hall. Reaching up with her slim arms, she grasped hold of the tails of a hanging, black banner and hoisted herself up behind it, climbing it with arachnoid ease. She could feel the attention of the sentries focused along the long, narrow corridor below her, but she didn't stop moving.

Reaching the top of the banner, she pulled herself up onto the thin horizontal pole from which it was suspended, and stood motionless for a moment, hidden in the vaults of the ceiling. With a sudden spring, she threw herself forward into space, catching the detail of a delicate carving in one hand just as her momentum failed and she started to fall. Pivoting around her arm, her fall was transformed into a flowing arc that flung her across the ceiling.

Landing softly above the arch of the doorway that led into the hall, she could see the tops of the heads of the two sentries only four metres below her. Bending down to touch her hands to her toes, she gripped hold of the ledge at the apex of the arch and let herself fall forward, swooping through the doorway like a pendulum and up into the Great Hall on the other side, coming to rest on the equivalent ledge on that side, facing the wall.

Scanning the dark expanse of the hall, she could see nothing at all. The walls had been constructed out of vividium – a stone amalgam that actually soaked up light, rendering any space that it enclosed into complete blackness.

Having expected no less, the figure was unsurprised. She climbed silently up the wall, digging her fingernails into the tiny cracks between the great blocks of stone and pulling herself towards the invisible ceiling. After a few moments, she reached a thick ledge which supported a row of black gargoyles. Melting into the space behind one of them, she settled in to wait, unseen and utterly alone.

'Ah, Nyjia, I have been waiting for you. There is something that you must do,' came an even voice from the darkness beside her.

THE SCRIPT IN the book had been etched in an obscure and ancient language, and it made Thucydia's head spin when she looked at it. It was almost as though it had been designed to be difficult, even painful to read. In the dim light around her desk in vault 47589.c3 of the Historicus Librarium, Thucydia rubbed her forehead and rocked back into her chair. She looked along the aisle on either side of her at the hundreds of other desks receding off into vanishing points in both directions, each at the head of a perpendicular aisle of book stacks, and she shook her head in awe at the scholarship going on around her. Each of the curators at those desks was descended from one of the finest scholar-families in the segmentum. Some of them could trace their lineages all the way back into the very pages that they were studying.

Pushing her palms into her eyes and rubbing them dryly, Thucydia leaned back over the manuscript in front of her and forced herself to focus once again. The language was an archaic form of Vindracum, itself a perverted form of an early version of the Imperium's Gothic script, dating from the time of the Wars of Vindication. Thucydia was probably one of only a handful of people in the galaxy who could still read this text, with all of its spidery contortions and unvoiced ideographs. It was an unusual written language, since it had no sound at all, as though the agents of the ancient Vindicare temple who employed it had no use for noise.

Like her father before her, Thucydia was chasing a loophole in the history of the Imperium, struggling to find one of the thousands of missing pieces from the immense, sprawling jigsaw that was the story of man's conquest of the stars. She had inherited her position in the Tower of Idols from her father, just as he had passed on his rare linguistic sense together with mountains of notes about the aftermath of the Wars of Vindication. Thucydia herself had managed to narrow the scope of her research to the machinations of the early Vindicare Masters. It seemed to her that their sinister and stealthy hands lurked behind many of the catalytic events of that time, but she could find no record of them at all. It was almost as though they had done nothing for millennia. Even the most cursory glance along the great windows in the Procession of History would reveal the profound absence of the entire Officio Assassinorum. It had an invisible history, which was both incredible and unbelievable – two of the most intriguing characteristics of a historical puzzle.

THREE MENIALS WERE fussing around the base of the ladder, one holding onto each side and the third standing on the bottom step, acting as a dead weight. The highly polished marble floor was not the best surface on which to erect such a crude climbing device, but it was the first thing available at hand, and the most sophisticated technology available to adepts at the level of menial. The feet of the ladder slipped and skidded on the cold stone as the three menials struggled to keep it in place, stumbling and tripping over each other as they did so. Part of the problem was their refusal to look up from the ground, so none of them really knew what was going on above them or around them.

Meanwhile, nearing the top of the ladder was the excited and trembling form of Cregg, his hands uncertain on each new rung and his feet shaking under his own weight. He was studiously looking down towards the ground, but realising with increasing excitement that looking down from such a height widened his horizons significantly. He could see, for example, the image of the winged warrior emblazoned on the window itself, and, standing anxiously on the ground next to the bottom of the ladder, he could see the cipher wringing his hands and muttering to himself, looking nervously up and down the Procession of History.

Taking a few more steps, Cregg reached up his hand to grasp the next rung only to find that there wasn't one. With his gaze still trained diligently on the ground, he moved his hand from side to side experimentally, as though believing that the next step on the ladder might have moved slightly. With the creeping dread of realisation, Cregg slowly raised his eyes from the ground – he had reached the top.

As his eye-line finally drew level with his head, Cregg found himself staring into the face of a muted grey, granite gargoyle. He flinched as he saw it – never having been so close to such a thing before. The three menials at the base of the ladder groaned with the effort of keeping the fidgeting Cregg upright, but he quickly regained his composure in the face of the inanimate stone horror.

For a few moments, Cregg stared at the ugly sculpture in front of him, wondering why anyone would want to decorate a glorious, clean procession with such polluted forms. Then he wondered how long it must have been since anyone had cleaned it. Automatically, he pulled the sleeve of his smock over his hand and spat onto the cloth, before proceeding to buff the hideous face into a faint gleam.

'Ah, y… yesss,' came the uneven voice of the cipher from the ground. 'P… perhaps you m… might fet… bring down the t… tube?'

Cregg shook his head, jolted out of his sanitization reflexes by the stuttering anxiety of the grey cipher below him. Then he nodded with determination and reached out his hand to feel behind the head of the gargoyle. There did certainly seem to be something lodged in the thin gap at the back. His fingers quested around the metallic tube, scraping at its almost frictionless surface with little effect. He needed more purchase on it.

Leaning forward still further, Cregg levered himself a little higher by wrapping his left arm over the top of the gargoyle and reaching round behind it with his right. His fingers poked at the cold, slick tube on the other side, and he could feel it starting to work free of the stonework.

Lexio saw it all happen at once, as a yelp of desperation sounded from one of the menials holding the ladder. The ladder slipped out of the menials' grasps and its base skidded out towards the centre of the hallway, knocking a number of officials over and sending others scurrying out of their regular routines. Meanwhile, Cregg was left hanging by one arm from the gargoyle's neck, whimpering and crying in fear. Most importantly, however, the little tube slipped out of the masonry and fell end over end towards the ground, clinking and clattering as it struck the marble.

'Um, you should h… help him, please,' said Lexio to the other menials as he hopped from one marble slab to the next, heading towards the fallen tube – the aberration that had caused so much trouble already. When he reached it, he pulled his sleeves down over his hands so that he wouldn't have to touch the offending article with his skin, and picked it up. Peering inside, he saw a small roll of paper, covered in strange spidery squiggles that he could not recognise.

BACK IN THE familiar darkness of her chambers in one of the outer towers of the temple precinct, Nyjia unfastened the clasp that held her cloak secured around her shoulders and let the layered material slip to the ground into a pile around her ankles. Those luxurious robes were only suitable for the deference required within the Temple of Vindicare itself, and she would have no need for such false humility once she arrived in the Tower of Idols to perform her duty. The Vindicare Master in the Great Hall had been very clear about the importance of secrecy, and she was not about to take any chances with a direct order from the grand master of her temple.

Her small, circular room was lit only by the tiny javelins of light that shot through the cracks in the windowless walls of the spire. In fact, there were no windows at all in the Vindicare temple, giving the interior the atmosphere of perpetual night. Every year, some of the new initiates – all of them orphans of Imperial officials fostered in the Schola Progenium – would go insane because of the lack of daylight. They were the lucky ones, since they would be removed from the temple before the serious conditioning began and the others started dying. A class of twenty pre-selected, would-be assassins might be reduced to two before the end of the third year of training. One of those would inevitably die in the final initiation ceremony nine years later, when the two would confront each other in their last trial – as much a test of their will to kill as of their technical ability to do so. Given that there were only one or two classes started in each year, this meant that the temple produced only one or two fully developed assassins each year – something that placed a huge responsibility onto the shoulders of each, and something which made them extraordinarily valuable to those rich or powerful enough to employ their services. In the long, shrouded history of the Vindicare temple, these patrons had not always been agents of the Emperor. This was not something that they cared to advertise.

The tiny threads of light from the walls flicked at her pale, scarred skin as she pulled back the curtain that surrounded the synth-shower that occupied nearly a quarter of the room. It was a complicated device, used in some form by each of the temples under the auspices of the Officio Assassinorum, although each used a unique chemical mix of its own.

Nyjia adjusted the valve-array that set the mixture for the spray, checking each dial carefully to ensure that there were no errors. It was a matter of life and death, since an incorrect setting could lead to asphyxiation as the synskin was applied or simply to death afterwards if the armoured properties of the membrane were inadequate.

Selecting three exotic blades from the rack beside the shower, Nyjia pulled a series of levers and then flicked a switch as she stepped up onto the pedestal at the focus of the various nozzles and jets, tugging the curtain closed behind her. Closing her eyes, she could feel the delicate spray accumulating in layers over her body, clinging to her limbs like coats of rubberised paint. The pattern of the rain was specifically programmed for her body, focusing around the major muscle groups to augment their strength, and around her vital organs to provide maximum protection. Thin layers sealed the bladed weapons into place on her thighs and calf. The Vindicare synskin also contained reservoirs of oxygen and metabolic suppressor chemicals, in case the assassin had to stay in hiding for long periods of time.

Sliding the shower curtain back with a snap, Nyjia stood glistening in the speckled light of her dark room, her body shimmering in the slick, membranous armour that hugged her figure like a second skin. She paused for a moment as the synskin dried, letting the fingers of light dance over her perfect form, before vaulting down from the pedestal and snatching her long-barrelled rifle from its fittings on the wall. She spun it once in her hands, checking its balance, and then flipped it over her shoulder into the harness moulded into her back. Without a moment's hesitation, she stalked out of the chamber and slipped invisibly out of the temple precincts.

'YOU'RE ELEVEN MINUTES late, cipher,' hissed Kayle, looking Lexio up and down and trying to work out what was different about him this morning. All these ciphers look the same, he thought agitatedly.

Lexio shuffled from one foot to the other, twisting his hands anxiously around the metallic tube that he had found in the Procession of History outside the hall. He was looking down at his feet, keeping his eyes fixed on the join between the two flagstones and concentrating on keeping his feet away from it. He knew better than to look up at the face of a prefectus, especially a secundus who was in the process of reprimanding him.

'Stop fidgeting!' snapped Kayle, unable to abide the pathological peregrinations any further. 'Report to your station and wait to be summoned. The Historicus himself will be here shortly, and I am sure that he will have use for you.'

'B… but sir…' began Lexio, still staring at the ground.

'What!' clipped the prefectus, his impatience with this underling reaching breaking point.

Lexio found himself simply unable to speak. He had often reflected that it was strange that he could never find any words of his own when confronted with a senior official, but that he could recite long, intricate messages for hours without fumbling even a single syllable. Today of all days, with such dramatic events to report, he had no words at all. Instead, he just stared at the ground and pushed his hands forward with the little black tube balanced in his up-turned palms.

'What! What? What's this?' bleated Kayle, snatching the object from Lexio's shaking hands. Without ceremony or appreciation for the significance of this item in Lexio's traumatic day, Kayle tugged the roll of paper out of the tube and cast the metal aside. He casually cast his eyes over the spider ideographs etched into the paper and then nodded, as though it all suddenly made sense.

'I see,' he said, handing the paper back to Lexio without looking at him. 'I presume that this is a document from the Archeotechium? A new find?' he continued, without waiting for confirmation from the cipher.

Lexio shuffled and spluttered slightly, unable to articulate himself, but Kayle pressed on, ignoring him. 'You should take it down to vault 47589.c3, curator 14.259. Wait there for the translation and then bring it back to me – your memory key will be my face. Do you understand?'

Lexio nodded uncertainly, his mouth working soundlessly. 'N… not… ar… arch… not from there…' he managed, finally.

Kayle's eyes snapped round to inspect the gibbering cipher. 'What? Not from where? What are you talking about? Just go and get it translated and bring the translation back to me,' he said sharply, shaking his head at the very concept of an orally-challenged cipher.

A commotion erupted outside the hall as a number of menials crashed about carrying a ladder. 'What's going on this morning – it's a disaster,' muttered Kayle as he realised that he was the ranking prefectus in the vicinity. He turned and strode towards the Procession of History, leaving Lexio wringing his hands in the middle of the great hall.

THE BRIGHT LIGHT streamed through the stained glass windows, casting long shadows and sending hazy colours kaleidoscoping across the white marble floor. Nyjia lay back against the ceiling with her legs and arms spread out by her side, the fabric of her suit finding purchase in the intricately worked stone. She watched the commotion in the Procession of History below her die down, as an important-looking official strode out of the huge doorway at the end of the hall and barked some commands at the scurrying menials. Three of them ran off with a ladder, and one shuffled over to the official, muttering something that Nyjia could not make out – she couldn't even read his lips because his face was turned towards the ground. He was gesticulating nervously and pointing up towards the little statues around the top of one of the great windows. The official's face was contorted and twisted in disgust as he listened to the menial speak, as though repulsed by his very presence. Then he nodded abruptly and dismissed the lowly adept, a look of relief washing over his face as the scruffy man shuffled away down the hallway.

Nyjia didn't even breathe as she held her motionless position against the ceiling, watching the people passing backwards and forwards along the Procession. She was obscured in the deep shadow of one of the wide vaulted domes that ran the length of the hallway, and she knew that nobody would be able to see her from the ground even if they looked up from their own feet, which they never seemed to do.

After a few hours, she could see a pattern emerging in the traffic below her, as menials, ciphers and ordinates bustled through the Procession in the course of executing their duties. She watched the ebb and flow of the life blood of the Tower of Idols and realised how perfectly predictable everything was, as the officials pulsed through the corridors of the Administratum, utterly oblivious to her unexpected presence.

She waited for the lull in traffic that occurred every twenty-three minutes, and then she dropped down from her vantage point on the ceiling, catching hold of one of the elaborate chandeliers that hung in the Procession, swinging underneath it and turning a neat somersault before landing lightly on the ledge above one of the stained glass windows. She edged silently along the thin protrusion of rock until she reached the gargoyle's head – the traditional drop point of the Vindicare agents inside the tower. Reaching her hand down behind the sculpture, Nyjia realised that the Vindicare Master had been right – somebody in the tower had discovered too much. The small, metallic message tube was gone.

Climbing back up into the shadows on the ceiling, Nyjia crept, crawled and leapt her way over towards the great doors at the end of the hallway. The second part of her mission now initiated.

THUCYDIA LOOKED UP irritably from her desk and squinted through the lamplight. A grey-robed cipher stood uneasily next to her table, looking up and down the aisle as though worried that somebody might see him. He had a small roll of paper in his clasped hands, and he was rocking agitatedly from one foot to the other.

'Yes?' said Thucydia simply.

'Please translate this. I'll wait,' said Lexio, clearly chanting the words he had said to innumerable curators on numberless occasions in the past.

The curator snatched the little scroll from Lexio's grasp and flipped it back and forth, quickly scanning both sides of the paper before pressing it flat against the surface of her desk. There were only a couple of lines of text scribbled onto it, but the dialect was quite unusual, and Thucydia scrunched up her face as her brain raced to recall the correct words. The Archeotechium was always uncovering new documents, but most of them were useless – worthy merely of being filed.

When the content of the message finally seeped through into her consciousness, Thucydia could hardly contain her excitement. She leapt up from her chair and paced backwards and forwards, muttering under her breath as she tried to work out its precise significance for her inquiries into the machinations of the Vindicare Masters. It seemed to fit exactly into the historical hole – it was a ready-made explanation for how the Vindicare temple had kept itself out of the official histories.

She rushed off down one of the aisles of bookshelves, searching for the most closely associated documents in the collection, leaving Lexio standing alone by her desk. He had no idea why the curator was so excited, and he didn't really care. His own excitement about the events of the morning had already been squashed by the prefectus secondus's matter-of-fact, routine response to his discovery, so he would simply wait for the curator to dictate the translation, just as he did every day.

Suddenly Thucydia yelped and tugged down a giant box of documents. Struggling under its weight, she hurried back to her desk and thumped it down on the table, already starting to rifle through the thousands of pieces of paper within. As though remembering something incidental, she abruptly stopped and looked up at Lexio. For a moment, she wondered why anyone else would be interested in the translation of this document – as far as she knew, Vindracum was a dead language, and the note could be of only historical interest. But it was not her place to ask such questions, and a cipher would certainly not know the answers – he was a virtual automaton. She gave a level three memory key, so that the cipher would not have access to the content of the message, and then dictated the translation.

Lexio blinked a couple of times, always slightly disorientated by the process of initialising his verbatimem. His consciousness literally switched off for the duration of the dictation, and the message went straight into the lower, subconscious reaches of his mind. When he came back to normal consciousness, it took him a while to realise how much time had passed. In this case, just a few seconds, it seemed. Already, however, the curator had her head stuck in the box of papers and she was quite clearly finished with him.

Lowering his eyes back to the flagstones on the ground, Lexio walked slowly down the main aisle of vault 47589.c3, heading for the huge, spiralling stone staircase that would take him back up into the Great Hall, after forty-seven floors of historical vaults. For a moment he wondered about the content of the message lurking in his mind, but then he resigned himself to the long, routine trudge up the stairs. Perhaps today wasn't so exciting after all.

PANTING AND DRIPPING with sweat, Lexio carefully lifted his foot over the last stair and placed it deliberately into the very centre of the first level flagstone. Drawing himself up after his advanced foot, he straightened his smock, smoothing out the creases and breathing heavily.

The Hall of Historical Correction opened out before him, riddled with reading desks and kilometres of document stacks. The huge domed ceiling was nearly three hundred metres away – it was actually the roof of the great tower itself – and the frescoes painted onto it over the centuries were barely visible – just vague blurs of colour in amongst the dancing shadows. For a moment, Lexio paused and cast his gaze up into the heavens, watching the distant forms swim in reflection of the bustling commotion on the ground. He wondered whether it was quiet up there. Sometimes, in moments of heretical weakness, he even wondered what lay beyond that huge dome.

The vast hall was circular in shape, since it stretched all the way to the external walls of the great spire in each direction. The single, circular wall was covered in tapestries, banners, and icons dedicated to the great scholars of the Imperium. Their harsh, disapproving eyes stared down at the officials of the Historical Correction Unit, suffering no indolence.

On the far side of the hall, opposite the magnificent winding staircase that provided access to the research vaults below, were the twin doors that led out into the Procession of History. And in the very centre of the hall was the glorious throne of the Historicus himself, sparkling with gold and hoisted fifty metres into the air. It was supported on a complex matrix of platforms, each fashioned into the shape of one of the great classic tomes of the Imperium. The elaborate pedestal had been designed so that envoys and messengers from the other parts of the tower would all have designated platforms on which to await the attentions of the Historicus. For Lexio, this meant twenty-seven paces short of the bottom platform on the left-hand side. After all, he was not awaiting the Historicus himself, but his prefectus secondus.

As he shuffled across the flagstones towards the throne, lifting his feet carefully over the cracks and skipping occasionally to avoid stepping onto a pile of papers, Lexio realised that the Historicus had already arrived for the day. He was enthroned and dispensing directions to the most senior prefects. Looking up, Lexio saw that the prefectus secondus was standing at the left shoulder of the Historicus, looking very pleased with himself. He seemed to see Lexio approaching the designated interview point, but his face snarled in displeasure at the thought of having to descend from his pedestal to interact with the snivelling cipher. Quite used to this response, Lexio came to a halt exactly twenty-seven paces short of the base of the pedestal, and resigned himself to wait patiently for the prefectus to acknowledge him. After his long journey and his troublesome morning, he was glad of the rest.

NYJIA SPRANG FROM the head of one gargoyle, just catching hold of another with one hand, letting the momentum swing her into a vertical arc. She flipped soundlessly through the air, landing softly and precisely on one foot, balanced perfectly on the tiny rock protrusion of an engraving in the wall. After a quick glance around and down, she dove headlong from the wall, plummeting ten metres before catching hold of a banner-pole and spinning herself across to the other side of the huge dome. She landed neatly at the base of a near-vertical flagpole, and wrapped herself around it, tugging her long rifle free of its harness on her back as she did so.

This was the perfect angle, she thought, as she brought the reticule into focus on the head of the fat official, sitting in the gaudy, golden throne far below her. He was surrounded by petty administrators, and only a near-vertical shot like this would make a clean kill.

Holding her breath, Nyjia brought her metabolism almost to a standstill, letting the chemicals in her synskin bleed into her system to keep her alive while all of her muscles locked into position, giving her perfect stability. The fat man in her sights rocked and laughed, stuffing his face with food and spitting it at his assistants as he bellowed and cackled orders at them.

Nyjia thought about the trigger and visualised the man's head exploding in the reticule. And then it happened.

THIS IS IT, thought Thucydia, pulling out a bunch of yellowing, old documents from the bottom of the pile. It all suddenly made sense, as she read the accounts of how various Historicuses had met untimely deaths throughout the history of the Tower of Idols. They had all been engaged in research into the Vindicare temple, which just happened to be located on the same planet, but they had all died without leaving any significant documentation on the affairs of the mysterious assassins.

She turned the little scroll in her hands, reading the message over again, as though unable to believe that the text was so simple and straightforward. It explained everything.

Shaking her head and chuckling slightly at the wonderful simplicity of historical conundrums, she clipped the message scroll to the front of the pile of documents and stuffed them all back into their box. Then she picked the box up and walked off down the long aisle in front of her desk in vault 47589.c3. Finding the correct shelf amongst the kilometres of stacks, she pushed the box back into place and shuffled off back to her desk.

Looking along the endless line of curators at their desks in the 589th reading room of level 47, she smiled to herself with the knowledge of a job well done. Her father would be proud of her, as the history of the Imperium took one small step closer to completion. Case closed.

PANDEMONIUM WAS LOOSED in the great hall, as the Historicus's head exploded into a rain of bony shards and splattered mush. Lexio looked hesitantly up from his position twenty-seven paces shy of the throne, fearful that one of the senior officials would see him stealing a glimpse at the Historicus. Instead, he saw the face of the prefectus secondus stretched into a scream and covered in ichor as he scrambled down off the matrix of platforms towards the ground.

The face of the prefectus was exactly what Lexio had been waiting for, and he closed his eyes as the memory trigger activated his verbatimem. His conscious mind receded and he chanted the translation of the message scroll without any awareness of what he was saying. The message made Kayle skid to a halt next to the cipher and stare at him in disbelief.

'You must kill the Historicus today – they know too much.'

LOYALTY'S REWARD

Simon Jowett

THE VOX-ENHANCED BELLS of the nearby Ecclesiarchy chapel were sounding vespers when Kleist spotted them. They had only just stepped into the bar. There were three of them – well-dressed, but not ostentatiously so. They wouldn't have looked out of place among the crowds in one of the uptown bars or restaurants, but here, close to the landing fields, they stood out among the off-duty loaders and packers who made up the regular clientele at the Split Pig.

Several heads turned as the newcomers made their way slowly towards the bar – then turned quickly back to stare into drinks or strike up conversations with companions. The strangers' expensive suits couldn't hide the heavy muscles beneath their fabric or the air of suppressed violence that hung around them like a dark cloud. Even Ernst, the bar's permanently-stewed mascot, didn't try to tap the newcomers for a free drink.

The walls shook and a dull roar filled the bar as a heavy cargo shuttle passed overhead, drowning out the sound of the call to worship as it made its way from the landing fields to the Merchants' Guild transport barge that waited for it in low orbit. The fields were busy day and night; Equus III was the most ore-rich world on this edge of the segmentum and Praxis its most prosperous city. The Split Pig was not a place to go if you wanted peace and quiet.

From his booth at the rear of the room, Leon Kleist scanned the bar's dimly-lit interior, hoping to spot a group of Imperial Guard troopers on shore leave from their orbiting transport. The Split Pig was a favourite among Guardsmen in transit with only a few hours of furlough before their next journey through the warp. No luck.

373

Kleist looked back towards the bar and saw one of the newcomers beckon to the bartender. The young man stopped stacking glasses and sauntered towards the stranger, wiping his hands on his apron, ready to take his order. Kleist knew that the stranger didn't want a drink; he and his companions wanted information.

While he talked to the bartender, the stranger's companions surveyed the room. Kleist slid as far back into his booth as possible, while still keeping the three of them just in view. He felt the beginnings of panic swirl in his gut. What had he been thinking? He should have kept his mouth shut! His eyes darted nervously towards the rest room door. All he needed was a chance to...

The ascending shuttle's sonic boom rattled the glasses on their shelves. None of the regulars took any notice. The bartender continued talking; Kleist saw him point towards his booth. But all three strangers glanced upwards, surprised by the aerial concussion. One of them slid a hand inside his jacket, unconsciously reaching for a concealed weapon.

Kleist ran for the door.

From behind him came the sound of chairs being overturned, shouts and the sound of glasses breaking. He slammed through the door and raced down the short, poorly-lit passageway towards the rest room. The door swung shut behind him, cutting off the noise.

Before it reached the latrines, the passageway branched right. Kleist took the turn and sprinted towards the door that led to the alley behind the bar. He knew that it would be a matter of seconds before the three strangers were on his tail – there wasn't enough of a crowd in the bar to slow them down for very long – but, once he was outside, he stood a better chance of losing them.

Kleist cursed himself as he ran. If he hadn't stayed for that last drink. If the drunken conversation hadn't turned to old man Gaudi's death.

And if he hadn't started shooting his mouth off.

He straight-armed the door at the end of the passage and found himself in the garbage-strewn alley. From here he could go left, across the main street and head home – though only the Emperor knew what he would tell his wife – or right and take the back way towards the landing fields. There was a local Arbites sub-station at the field gates, but Kleist couldn't risk the planetary representatives of Imperial law probing too deeply into his business dealings. Right now the idea of being on some distant world felt very appealing. Unfortunately, he was not alone.

'Hey, Leon, I've been looking all over for you.'

The man was tall, well-dressed in the same unobtrusive style as the strangers in the bar and carried himself with the confidence of someone who knew that, in this case, a one-on-one confrontation meant the odds were already stacked in his favour. A thin scar ran the length of the right side of his face, from the hairline of his slicked-back, sandy-coloured hair, almost to the point of his narrow chin. He was not a stranger.

'Mister... Mister Kravi...' Kleist managed to stammer. And then his world exploded.

HE DIDN'T REMEMBER landing in the filth at the foot of the wall. He rolled painfully onto his front and pushed himself up onto all fours. His mouth was full – it felt as if he had swallowed as much of the muck as now covered his clothes. He spat. A large gobbet of blood hit the back of his left hand. As he stared at it, blinking away the tears that had inexplicably appeared, fogging his vision, another joined it, this time falling from his nose. He raised an unsteady hand to the centre of his face, pressed gently and felt the grinding of cartilage against bone. Fresh tears welled up in his eyes.

'That hurt, Leon?' Someone was standing over him. A pair of expensive-looking shoes stood in the muck a short way from him. Kleist craned his neck to look up at the man who spoke.

The fist slammed into the side of his face. Stars exploded behind his eyes and his supporting arm gave way. Gasping with pain and surprise, he inhaled a mouthful of filth.

A hand reached for his shoulder, turning him onto his back. Coughing, fighting down the urge to vomit, he stared up at Mikhail Kravi, right arm of Aldo Graumann, the Protektor, or local boss, for the Haus Gaudi, which had run this part of the hive for as long as anyone could remember.

'I... I'm sorry!' Kleist stuttered. Feet sliding in the slime that coated the alley's flagstones, he began to push himself away from Kravi, towards the rear wall of the bar, expecting every heartbeat to be his last.

'Sorry for what, Leon? Sorry for shooting your mouth off to your buddies in the Transport Confederation, or sorry for making me come down here and bruise my knuckles on your face?'

Kravi seemed amused to watch him slide along the ground, then push himself up into a half-seated position against the wall. Only now did Kleist dare to shift his gaze from Kravi's face.

He noticed that the three strangers from the bar now stood a short way behind their leader, hands clasped, mute witnesses to his humiliation.

Kravi dropped to his haunches in front of Kleist, and locked eyes with him.

'You see, Leon, word reached Mister Graumann that you'd been telling your pals that now Graf Gaudi was dead, Emperor bless his departed soul, you didn't see why you should keep on paying tribute to... what did you call him... "his whore-hopping whelp"? Was that it?'

Kleist started shaking his head in a feeble, pointless attempt at denial. Kravi reached out, caught his chin in one large hand and held his head still.

'That's the Graf's grandson you were calling a whelp, Leon. The new Graf. You think that, just because he's young and likes to have a good time, that he's not going to be interested in taking care of business?'

'N–no,' Kleist spluttered. A mixture of blood and alley-filth dribbled down his chin. He wanted to say something, anything that would prevent Kravi from hitting him again. 'It... it was the drink.'

'You know, that's what I thought, when Mister Graumann told me what he'd heard. You meet up with some friends and colleagues, you eat, drink a little too much wine, it goes to your head and you say some crazy things.' Kravi's voice was soft, reasonable. 'I knew you wouldn't have forgotten all the help the old Graf had given you, all the contracts he put your way, the competitors he persuaded not to bid for runs along your routes. He gave you the route from the refineries to the landing fields and I knew you respected him for that.'

Kleist tried to nod, but Kravi's hand was like an iron glove clamped around his jaw.

'I knew, once you'd had time to think about it, you'd respect the new Graf in just the same way. More, even. I guess that's why you came to this toilet, instead of one of the nicer places near your home: to think things through. Am I right?' He released his grip on Kleist's jaw and the older, fatter man nodded like a chastened child.

'That's good.' Kravi stood, smoothed back some strands of hair that had fallen about his face. 'Now there's going to be a gathering in honour of the new Graf's accession. Everyone's going to be there, paying tribute. And I know whose tribute is going to be the biggest of all, don't I, Leon?'

Kleist nodded again. He had noticed a clammy sensation between his legs and realised that, at some point, he had wet himself like a newborn. Hot tears – not of pain, but of humiliation – rolled down his cheeks.

'I'm glad we had this little talk.' Kravi beckoned to his men and they moved forward, passing Kravi as he stepped away from Kleist. 'My associates here are going to tidy you up and get you home safely to your lovely wife and that very pretty daughter of yours. The gathering is the day after tomorrow at the compound. That gives you time to organise your tribute in the proper manner. If you look out of your window before then and happen to see one of my men outside your home, don't worry. He'll be there to make sure nothing interferes with your preparations.

'After all,' Kravi added as two of his men hauled Kleist to his feet, 'you know we only have your best interests at heart.'

THE LAYOUT OF the Haus Gaudi compound had changed little since its construction at the end of the First Age of Vendetta, the blood-soaked decades that followed the founding of Equus III's first industrial colonies. This was a rich world; the opportunities for profit – legitimate or otherwise – were boundless. The houses that would one day control the black

economy of Equus III grew out of loose-knit gangs of street thugs, entre-
preneurs who had failed to prosper in legitimate trade, crewmen who had
grown tired of life aboard the Merchant Guild's ships, and discharged
members of the Imperial Guard regiments which had accompanied the
first settlers.

The First Age of Vendetta saw allegiances harden into blood loyalty as
the gangs jockeyed for position and power. The weaker houses were
absorbed by the more powerful, the better organised, or else they were
eliminated. An observer who looked only at the spires and towers of
Equus III's rapidly expanding cities, or at the vast wealth generated by the
burgeoning trade in refined ores, would be unaware of the war being
fought in the shadows.

Franz Gaudi, the first Graf, had seen his house come close to extinction
during this time. He was determined that it should not happen again. The
compound, set on the banks of a lake on the outskirts of Praxis, beyond
the curtain wall that marked the boundary of the hive proper, most of it
constructed below ground level and surrounded by a high, hexagonal
wall, was the result.

The Second Age of Vendetta was a quieter, less blood-soaked affair,
marked by assassinations and the occasional skirmish over territory. Like
the players of some abstruse intellectual game, the Grafs of the remaining
houses directed their street-soldiers against their rivals, gaining control of
the illegal interests in one territory, only to lose control of another. Where
the First Age had lasted decades, the Second lasted centuries.

Bruno Gaudi had been young and ambitious when he became Graf.
Over time, he saw both his sons die – one by an assassin's blade, the other
gunned down on a street corner – and came to the conclusion that, during the whole of the Second Age of Vendetta, there had been only one real
casualty: profit.

From its unpromising position at the end of the First Age of Vendetta,
Haus Gaudi had grown to become one of the most influential criminal
entities in Praxis. When its Graf spoke, people listened. For Bruno, the
only real surprise was how readily the other Grafs agreed with him. Endless vendettas had got in the way of doing business, had depleted the
houses' funds and wasted their manpower. Peace, they agreed, was the
only answer. Ritual and respect should replace the blade and the gun.
Each house could then concentrate on exacting tribute from those who
operated within their agreed territories; violence would be directed only
against those who refused to pay. After lengthy negotiations, the Second
Age of Vendetta came to an end around the long table in the subterranean
sanctum of the Gaudi compound.

'GRAF GAUDI, IN honour of your grandfather's memory – may the
Emperor bless his soul – and of your accession, I offer this in tribute.'

With a trembling hand, Leon Kleist placed the dataslate on the polished surface of the long table. Viktor Gaudi, pale-skinned and
sharp-featured, clad in a high-collared suit of crimson velvet, reached forward, picked up the slate in one slim, elegantly-manicured hand and
thumbed its screen into life.

The room was panelled with dark wood and discreetly lit; the back-lit
screen cast a pale green glow over his face. Gaudi raised an eyebrow as he
read the display, then passed it back to the slightly older man who stood
at his left shoulder – Filip Brek, formerly a minor member of the dead
Graf's inner circle and Viktor's companion on his visits to the fleshpots of
Praxis, now elevated to the major role of Grafsberator, the Graf's most valued advisor.

'You have been most generous,' Gaudi said quietly. 'Exceptionally so. In
memory of my beloved grandfather, I thank you.'

'The honour is mine,' Kleist replied, more loudly than was necessary, in
an attempt to disguise his nerves. Kravi and his boss, Graumann, stood
behind him, flanking the door, overseeing the tributes from their part of
the hive. Kleist was the last; he could feel their gaze burning into his back.
Before ushering Kleist and the others down the long corridor to the sanctum, Kravi had checked the slate, then shown it to Graumann.

The older man had whistled appreciatively – and so he should. Kleist
had liquidated over a third of his assets to ensure that this tribute was sufficiently extravagant for him to escape another beating.

'The Haus Gaudi does not forget its friends.' Gaudi nodded towards the
door, ending the interview. 'Aldo, stay a while,' he added as Kleist took an
unsteady step backwards, then turned. Ahead of him, Kravi stepped forward to open the door. As Kleist passed, Kravi nodded and smiled a
self-satisfied, predator's smile before following him into the corridor and
closing the door behind them.

'You did well in there, Leon,' Kravi said as they walked along the corridor. Panelled with the same warm, dark wood as the sanctum, it was
lined with niches, in which busts of long-dead Grafs stood atop stone
plinths. Kravi kept pace with Kleist, one or two steps behind him, a menacing voice at his shoulder. 'There's just one more thing I wanted to ask
you.

'Your daughter – what does she like to do?'

'THE GRAF'S PLEASED with you, boy,' Graumann blinked as his eyes adjusted
to the afternoon sunlight. The second of Equus III's twin suns was dipping
towards the tops of the trees that ringed the lake. He had found Kravi
standing at the battlements atop the hexagonal wall that surrounded the
compound. In all the years since its construction, no one had ever tried to
breach the wall, but its rock-and-plasteel bulk, metres thick, looked capable of withstanding any assault short of orbital bombardment.

'Yeah?' Kravi might sound relaxed, unconcerned, but Graumann knew that was an act. He remembered the hot-tempered young street hustler who had been caught boosting liquor from a vehicle owned by a trader under Haus Gaudi protection. He had already been given a working-over by Graumann's men, but he still stared defiantly out at Graumann from a swollen, bruised face. Normally, his men wouldn't bother their boss with such an incident, but Kravi was the son of another trader under Gaudi protection. Apparently, the kid had seen Graumann's men, their expensive clothes and cars, and decided that their line of business was more appealing. Graumann had found himself admiring the boy's guts and decided to give him a chance to learn the business from the inside.

'You won't regret it,' Kravi had slurred through split lips. Graumann had laughed out loud at that – even then, when most people would simply be grateful to still be alive, this kid was trying to hustle him! But Kravi had made good on his promise; Graumann did not regret taking him on.

'The Graf asked about Kleist's tribute,' Graumann said. Taking a silk kerchief from his pocket, he dabbed at the sweat that beaded his forehead after the climb to the battlements. He was getting old, older than he liked to admit, even to himself. 'I told him that you'd prevailed upon Leon's better nature. He liked that. He's got something in mind, I can tell. Now the old Graf's gone – Emperor bless him – he's looking to stir things up.'

'Stir things up how?' This time, there was no mistaking the interest in Kravi's voice.

'He didn't say, but, as I was leaving, someone came into the sanctum through another door. Not a Haus man. Seemed pretty friendly with Brek.' He patted the broad expanse of jacket that covered his midriff.

'Something in here tells me things are going to get interesting.'

THERE WAS NO recoil when he triggered the alien weapon. For a moment, Kravi feared that the firing mechanism had malfunctioned. If this was so, and if all of the weapons the Graf had delivered to the Graumann crew were defective, then he and his men would die here, in a storage depot under the protection of Haus Reisiger.

And then his target – a heavily-built Reisiger enforcer – dropped suddenly to his knees, his features pulped, the top third of his skull sheared off. The laspistol he had been in the process of drawing from a shoulder holster concealed inside his jacket clattered to the floor from nerveless fingers, then the corpse pitched forward and lay still.

The corpse's companions – four of them, foot-soldiers making their regular circuit of Reisiger turf, collecting tribute from the businesses under their Haus's control – reacted with shouts of anger and surprise as they reached for their own concealed weapons.

Kravi and the three men who flanked him cut them down with short, silent bursts from the elegantly-crafted rifles they each held. Their smooth curving lines and long tapering barrels made them look more like pieces of sculpture than weapons; their pistol grips, set behind curved magazines that jutted forward like the teeth of some huge sea-beast, had been designed for slimmer hands, possessed of longer, more delicate fingers. This, combined with their weight – much less than an autogun or bolter – gave Kravi the impression that he might be holding a child's toy, rather than a firearm, but the bloody chunks that now lay scattered across the depot floor bore mute witness to their deadly capabilities.

Kravi poked the air with a finger, directing his men to take up positions on either side of the open doorway, then ran forward, weapon held at hip-height. As he had expected, two of the Reisiger crew had remained outside the covered warehouse section of the depot, guarding their vehicle. The first appeared in the doorway, pistol drawn, coming to investigate the cries from within. Kravi fired and the thug fell back, his chest a ruin. The second, seeing his comrade fall, ducked to one side, away from the doorway.

'The wall – there!' Kravi pointed to the metal wall to one side of the door. His men stared at him for a moment, puzzled. 'Shoot the damn wall!' he repeated. According to Graumann, Brek claimed these fragile-looking things could punch through light armour plate.

Kravi's men each fired a sustained burst at the wall. By the time they released their triggers, the metal hung in shreds and the man behind it lay in pieces. Two of Kravi's men – Gregor and Rudy – stared down at their rifles, wearing comical expressions of almost religious awe.

The squeal of protesting vulcanite came from outside the warehouse. Kravi ran through the door in time to see the Reisiger crew's vehicle tearing away from them, on a swerving, barely-controlled course towards the depot gates. Depot workers in the auto's path scattered to avoid being run down. Those in the clear had turned from the wagons and tractors they were working on to stare at the carnage.

Gregor had followed Kravi through the door. He raised his rifle, sighting after the speeding vehicle. Kravi put out a hand, pressing the barrel down.

'Let him go,' Kravi said. 'He'll be our messenger. He's seen what we can do with these.' Kravi hefted his rifle. In the sunlight, an iridescent sheen swirled just beneath the surface of the weapon's carapace. The metal of which it was composed – if indeed it was metal – had not been mined on Equus III, or any other world in the Imperium. Looking down at the shifting pattern, Kravi felt a thrill run through him – a mixture of fear and elation.

'He'll tell his Protektor and his Protektor will tell Reisiger: Haus Gaudi is taking over.'

* * *

IN THE SANCTUM beneath the family compound, Viktor Gaudi listened to the reports. Haus Volpone was losing its hold on the docks as Protektor Seynitz's men moved in. Graf Malenko's men had taken a beating in the smelting districts – it remained to be seen whether they would attempt a reprisal on Gaudi territory. Viktor doubted it – word would already have reached them of the death of Graf Reisiger, gunned down while presiding over a council-of-war in his favourite restaurant. According to that report, there was barely enough left of Reisiger, his closest advisors and their bodyguards to make one of the stews the old Graf loved so much. Since then, large numbers of Reisiger men, protektors as well as foot-soldiers, had been defecting to Haus Gaudi.

An audacious move, the assassination had been planned and led by Graumann's protege, Mikhail Kravi. Kravi's hand-picked crew hijacked a pantechnicon on its way to make a delivery to the restaurant and, disguised in the coveralls of the delivery firm, had strode unopposed through the kitchens and into Reisiger's private dining room. By the time the Graf's bodyguards realised anything was amiss, the air was thick with high-velocity mono-molecular disks. At a stroke, Graumann's young lieutenant had torn the heart from Haus Reisiger. Grown soft during the years of the truce, none of Reisiger's remaining heirs had the experience or the will to rally their house against Haus Gaudi's annexation of their territory. Viktor had already sent word that Kravi was to be acknowledged as a Protektor in his own right and given control of the depot district that had formerly been under Haus Reisiger protection.

'I take it that our merchandise has met with your approval, Graf.' The merchant stood before the long table, looking down at Viktor with dark, heavy-lidded eyes. He wore the same bland, neutral expression as he had when Filip had introduced him to Viktor in the salon of the Leather Venus, one of the more salubrious establishments in Praxis's pleasure district. Using the most polite, convoluted form of High Gothic, he had requested an audience. Viktor, tired from the night's exertions and more than a little drunk, had agreed and left Filip to make the arrangements. He had arrived on the day of the gathering, alone, carrying a long, slim case made from what appeared to be some kind of wood, inlaid with ornate icons. It had reminded Viktor of the case in which his grandfather stored his favourite antique hunting rifle. Its contents, however, could not have been more different.

'We'd be happier if we knew where those unholy relics came from,' growled Friedrik Engel, before Viktor had a chance to speak. From his seat on Viktor's left, Brek shot a look along the table at the old man who sat on the Graf's right. He opened his mouth to speak, but Viktor held up a hand to quiet him. His grandfather's Grafsberator, Viktor only kept Engel by his side to appease the old Graf's retainers – and to make it easier to dispose of him when Viktor's position was secure. Engel didn't approve of

Viktor's plans, or the means by which he had set about achieving them, but his sense of loyalty to the family had kept him in line thus far.

'As I explained to your new Graf,' the merchant replied smoothly, as if unaware of the sudden tension in the room, 'I am merely a representative of a larger concern, one that specialises in supplying – shall we say unusual – material to those who might make best use of it.' Though he was addressing Engel, he was still looking at Viktor. His tone was polite, emollient, but the implication was clear: his business was with the new Graf, not an ageing subordinate. Viktor felt the old man bristle and smiled.

'Our ships came upon a drifting hulk. Its exact location is of no concern. Within its hold were certain artefacts. When the news reached us of Graf Gaudi's accession, it occurred to us that others might seek to take advantage of the situation – to move against the family before the new leader had settled into his position – and so we offered our services. From what I have heard, things are going well for Haus Gaudi.'

'They are indeed,' Viktor agreed. 'Though the words of the Divine Emperor rightly teach us to be wary of the work of alien hands, the fact is that a gun is a gun, nothing more. Better that such weapons should be in the hands of our men, rather than those of our rivals.' Viktor directed his words at Engel and now it was Brek's turn to smile. The younger man had just repeated, almost verbatim, the reasoning Brek had used to quell Viktor's misgivings at the sight of the curved, shimmering surface of the shuriken catapult nestling within the merchant's case.

'When you contacted me to request this audience, you said that you had more merchandise that would be of use to us?' Brek addressed the merchant, who nodded.

'Oh yes,' the merchant replied. Viktor thought that, for the first time, the flicker of a smile played across his thin lips. 'There is so much more that we can show you.'

KRAVI HAD BEEN at prayer when he received the summons. Kneeling in the dark, incense-heavy atmosphere of the Ecclesiarchy sub-chapel, he had been giving thanks for his recent elevation to Protektor of the first district he and his crew had wrested from Reisiger control. That it was the Emperor's will that he should have achieved this was beyond doubt. Was it not written in the Holy Books of Terra that the Emperor of Man would help those who helped themselves?

Any doubts he did have centred around the means by which he had achieved so much in so short a time. After Graf Reisiger's death, merely the sight of the shuriken catapults was enough to un-man the Reisiger crews Kravi and his men had faced. He smiled at the memory of the Protektor of a neighbouring district who, upon his first sight of the weapon in Kravi's hands, immediately pledged his stammering allegiance to the Haus Gaudi without a shot being fired.

Be not tempted by the works of the Alien, for they are abominations. Equus III was a loyal world and Praxis its most devout city. Like all of its inhabitants, Kravi knew large sections of the Books of the Emperor by heart. Regular chapel attendance was taken for granted by the members of every Haus on the planet. It was not unusual for a Gaudi, Reisiger or Malenko foot-soldier to kneel in prayer beside a member of a rival family, or a judge from the Arbites. Whatever happened on the streets outside, the sacred ground on which Ecclesiarchy buildings stood was neutral territory.

There was no denying that the weapon he had used to carve Graf Reisiger into bloody slivers had been created by alien minds to be used by alien hands, perhaps against the loyal human servants of the Imperium. As he knelt in the chapel, Kravi had taken a breath before offering thanks for their delivery into the hands of Haus Gaudi. Then he waited, head bowed and heart hammering, for judgement, for some sign that he was damned.

Instead, he had felt a hand on his shoulder, followed by a familiar voice, whispering. 'You're wanted at the compound.'

As they walked briskly down the chapel steps in the fading evening light, Gregor had told him that every Protektor had been summoned to attend upon the Graf immediately. Gregor had driven to the chapel in Kravi's personal vehicle – a sleek, powerful two-seater which Kravi had accepted in lieu of tribute from a trader whose depots fell within his newly-acquired territory – so that he might drive out to the compound directly. Before slipping behind the wheel, Kravi had instructed his lieutenant to let Maria Kleist know that he would be late for tonight's assignation.

As he drove towards the compound, the canyons of the city's streets giving way to fields and woodland, he laughed at his earlier doubts. There had been no bolt from the chapel's rafters, sent by the Emperor in retribution for his daring to use the alien weapons. None of the chapel's priests had denounced him from the high altar as marked by abomination. For all their gleaming strangeness, these 'works of the Alien' were no different to a laspistol or a bolter.

Equus III's second sun was setting as he approached the compound, casting a crimson glow across the high wall. Sentries stood atop the battlements; the curving metal stocks and thin, tapering barrels of their weapons glittered in the fading light.

The compound beyond the wall resembled a vehicle bay at the landing fields. Kravi was one of the last of the Gaudi Protektors to arrive. Graumann was already below ground, a sentry informed him as he hurried towards the low, bunker-like structure that was the only part of the sanctum to protrude above ground. As he stepped between the bunker's heavy doors, Kravi felt – as he had in the frozen heartbeat that preceded the assassination of Reisiger – that he was taking another decisive step towards his destiny.

THE HIGH-PITCHED squealing threatened to burst his skull as he crashed into the bathroom. The side of his head connected with the door-frame and stars shot across his already-blurred vision as he groped his way towards the sink.

He made it just in time. His cramping guts contracted in a spasm that almost dropped him to his knees and shot a column of vomit into the metal bowl. Elbows locked, he supported himself against the sink and gagged for air. He managed a brief glimpse of his reflection in the ornately-engraved mirror set above the sink – long enough to take in blood-shot eyes set in a puffy, blotched face framed by hair that was dishevelled and lank with sweat – before his stomach clenched again and another yellow and green stream splashed into the bowl.

This time he was able to draw enough breath to let out a low, animal moan. The squealing had subsided, but his knees were trembling almost as violently as his guts. If he threw up for a third time, he feared that his arms would give way and he'd end up lying on the bathroom floor in a pool of his own waste.

He retched, then coughed and spat out a last gobbet of bile. Nothing else left, it seemed. Kravi closed his eyes and took a deep, shuddering breath.

That must have been some party, he told himself. Wish I could remember some of it.

There was a shape in the star-flecked darkness behind his eyelids. A darker shape against the darkness. Its outline was regular, many-sided. There was something written across its surface...

Kravi's knees felt strong enough to support him, so he eased himself upright and lifted an experimental hand to the side of his head that had collided with the door-frame. A bruise was already rising, but the skin hadn't been broken. He took another deep breath and opened his eyes.

The light was like slivers of glass pressed against his eyeballs. Kravi gasped, blinked rapidly and raised a hand to shade them before focusing, with some difficulty, on the image in the mirror.

It was no prettier than before. He looked like someone who had just risen from his bed after a week-long fever. As he struggled to recollect the events of the previous night, he peered more closely at his reflection. He noticed what looked like an elongated teardrop, rust-brown in colour, at the corner of one eye. He prodded at it with a finger and it flaked away at his touch. Blood?

There was blood caked around his nostrils too, he noticed. Alarmed, he turned his head to one side. There, running in a thin line from his ear to the corner of his jaw, was more. He turned his head in the opposite direction. His ear-lobe was caked in what looked like an enormous brown scab.

What, in the Emperor's Name, had happened at the compound last night? Had there been some kind of drunken brawl? Kravi remembered the squealing, the pressure inside his skull, as if something was trying to force its way inside his head.

There had been something in the room. Not the sanctum, but one of its annexes. The furniture had been cleared to make way for it. A solid shape, carved from a single block of black stone: a polyhedron. There had been markings on its surface – shapes, sigils of some kind – but they had been almost impossible to make out because the stone, though highly polished, reflected hardly any of the light cast by the candles that had been set around the room's perimeter. All of the other Protektors had been there; Graumann had nodded a greeting from the far side of the room. The Graf had been there, too, and Brek, but he didn't remember seeing Engel, the old Grafsberator. There had been someone else standing beside Gaudi, a face Kravi hadn't recognised, with hooded eyes and thin lips curled in an unpleasant smile.

Kravi groaned as another cramp rippled through him. Despite their violent evacuation, his guts felt heavy, bloated. It occurred to him that a drink might calm them down – and immediately discounted the idea as they clenched and rolled again.

Looking down into the sink, he saw that the yellow and green vomit was draining slowly and glutinously away. He thumbed the faucet and splashed his face with cold water, cupping his hands over his eyes to ease their aching.

Hangover or not, you've got work to do, he told himself. As the new Protektor he had to show his face, prove to his men, and to those who owed him tribute, that he was in control.

He didn't feel as if he was in control. He didn't feel as if he had a hangover. His bowels rolled over yet again. It felt as if they were moving of their own accord, settling into a more comfortable position. He looked down at his flat, muscled abdomen and realised for the first time that he was naked. He didn't remember getting home last night; he didn't remember undressing. He had jolted awake to find himself sprawled on the couch in his new apartment's living room, wood-panelled and softly-lit in imitation of the Gaudi sanctum.

As he looked down at himself, he half-expected to see evidence that something was moving beneath his skin.

'Like it or not, I need a drink,' he muttered. The first mouthful of liquor came back up almost as quickly as he swallowed it. His guts cramped and twisted, but he persisted. The second mouthful burnt its way down his bruised throat, but didn't return. By the time he took his fifth and sixth pulls on the bottle, a pleasant numbness had spread through him and he felt ready to face the day. He showered, dressed, then called Gregor to pick him up.

When Gregor arrived, Kravi took the half-empty bottle with him.

'SORRY, MIKHAIL, BUT the old man ain't takin' any calls.' Grisha Volk's voice came from the vox-unit's handset. 'He's cancelled all his tribute meetings, too. Didn't say why. He ain't looking too good, though.'

Sitting in the back of the armoured limousine he had 'inherited' from Graf Reisiger, Kravi knew what Volk – his replacement as Graumann's chief lieutenant, a stolid, loyal soldier – was talking about. He had seen Gregor's look of surprise when he had opened his apartment's front door.

'He really tied one on last night – we all did,' Kravi replied – the same answer he gave to Gregor's unspoken question.

'That's what I figured,' Volk said with a chuckle.

'Tell him I'll be in touch tomorrow,' Kravi said, then cut the line and sat in silence for a while, looking out at the city streets – his streets – that flowed past the vehicle's darkened windows. Something was nagging at his memory: the Graf's words from the previous evening, about how the shining alien weapons were just the beginning, and that he was going to show the assembled Protektors the means by which Haus Gaudi's hold over the city would be made secure for years to come.

Then what? There had been chanting, first in High Gothic, then in a language Kravi couldn't properly recall. Not so much words as noises: clicks and squeals...

With the memory of the squealing came that of the pressure, building inside his head. With suddenly unsteady hands, he unstopped the bottle and lifted it to his lips.

'Where to, Mikhail?' Gregor asked via the inter-vox from the driver's cab, separated from the passenger compartment by another sheet of black glass. Kravi swallowed twice, draining the bottle, before he replied.

'Home.'

GRAUMANN WASN'T TAKING calls the following day, or the next. Neither were any of the other Protektors. Several had not emerged from their homes since the evening at the compound. For those whose territories had been in Gaudi hands for generations, that was not a problem. For Kravi, however, it was vital that he showed his face – however blotchy and blood-shot it might still be – to those traders, shopkeepers and bar and restaurant owners who until recently paid tribute to the Reisigers.

The drink helped. It steadied his hands and eased the cramps that still woke him early each morning. Not that his sleep was undisturbed, either. The memories of ghoulish, lurid dreams hung about him when he woke, too indistinct to remember clearly, though fragments would suddenly jump into unnaturally-sharp focus at odd times during the day: the Gaudi sanctum, the assembled faces of the other Protektors, subtly but monstrously changed, voices chanting in deep, immeasurably ancient voices, offering power in exchange for obedience. At such moments, Kravi would reach for the bottle again.

The liquor had another benefit: by clouding his mind, it allowed him to ignore the questions that nagged at him when sober. How did the alien weapons reach Equus III? Where did the black stone polyhedron come from and what did the sigils etched into its surface mean? These were questions that Kravi feared to face, because he already knew the answers.

Guns were one thing. The Dark Gods were another.

On the day he received the summons, he waited until dark before travelling alone to the Palace of the Ecclesiarchy.

As he stood at the foot of the broad marble steps, looking up at the vast double doors, decorated with an intricate bas-relief carving of the Emperor's triumph over the heretic Horus, he surprised himself by thinking of his father. Woyzek Kravi was a devout man, who raised his sons to trust in the Emperor's all-knowing wisdom and who never bothered to hide from them his distaste for the men who came to collect tribute in the name of Haus Gaudi.

To their faces, however, he was always unfailingly courteous and respectful and this, Mikhail, his eldest son, saw as proof that they and the people they served had power over his father.

That power fascinated him, grew into a desire to become one of them. He kept his early adventures into petty crime a secret from his father but, when Graumann accepted him into his crew, Mikhail could not resist visiting his father's office, dressed in a fine new suit and the newly-adopted arrogance of a Gaudi foot-soldier.

He had expected rage, but all he saw in his father's eyes was disappointment. Whenever they met during the years that followed, always as a result of Gaudi business, neither father nor son acknowledged their blood-tie. Only once did Mikhail ask after Emile, his younger brother, who had harboured ambitions to join the ranks of the Ecclesiarchy. Woyzek Kravi fixed his son with a steady gaze and informed him that Emile had been accepted as a student in the seminarium attached to the palace.

Two brass censers, each taller than two men, stood inside the main doors. Kravi walked between them, wisps of their pungent incense clinging to him as he passed. Ranks of pews spread out to either side as he walked down the nave's long central aisle. Supplicants sat or knelt in prayer, just as many hundreds of thousands of others knelt in the subordinate chapels located throughout the city. A low, almost sub-sonic hum filled the air. It came from the choir stalls at the far end of the aisle, ranged before the high altar: invocations of the Emperor's goodness and might, chanted and repeated endlessly by rotating shifts of priests and students. The hymns of praise never ceased, day or night.

Kravi scanned the vast space until he spotted what he was looking for: a priest, stepping through the iron gate set in the grille separating a side-chapel intended for private worship from the rest of the palace. The priest closed the gate, drew a ritual sigil of protection in the air before it, then moved off along a side-aisle. Quickening his pace, Kravi hurried after him.

'Father.' Kravi's voice was little more than a whisper. The priest turned. Kravi half-expected to see his brother's face framed by the hood of the priest's robe. Thankfully, a stranger returned his gaze.

'My name is Mikhail Kravi,' he told the priest, then paused. On Graumann's turf and now on his own, mention of his name usually produced some reaction. This time there was none. The priest remained silent, his gaze steady.

'I am a... a businessman and a loyal follower of the Emperor, blessed be His name,' Kravi continued, now doubting his wisdom in coming here. Fear had driven him to the palace, fear of what might await him at the Gaudi compound, to which he had been summoned in three days' time. That fear had been replaced by a cold, appalling sense of what he was about to do: break the first rule that any foot-soldier was expected to learn, the only rule he would carry in his heart until the day he died. Never speak of Haus business to an outsider.

'That is as it should be,' the priest replied. Kravi thought he saw a flash of impatience cross the other man's features. 'The Emperor watches over us that we may live secure from the works of the unholy, the blasphemous and the alien. If you have come to reaffirm your faith in his righteousness, take a seat. I am required to be elsewhere, but I will send a novitiate to guide you in the Litany of Renewal.'

'No!'

The priest took a surprised step back. Kravi hadn't meant to raise his voice, but he knew that, if he didn't speak now, he would not have the will to speak again. 'My faith is strong. I'd not be here if it wasn't. There's... there's something you must know. The Dark Gods. They're here–' His guts spasmed, cutting him off. He gasped, forced down the urge to retch, then continued, 'They're here. In Praxis. I have seen them.'

THE CEREMONY HAD begun. The confined space of the sanctum annexe was filled with the sound of thirty voices, chanting in unison. Viktor stood at the centre of the candle-lit room, flanked by Brek and the merchant, basking in the palpable sense of power that had already begun to permeate the atmosphere.

All but one of the Protektors had answered the summons. As they arrived, Viktor had detected a nervousness, but also a sense of anticipation. He understood the mixture of feelings – he had felt the same when Brek and the merchant had brought him before the polyhedron that now stood, altar like, at his back. There had been pain, uncertainty, but that had passed. When he gazed upon the stone-set sigils, he saw only his future: more wealth and power than could have been imagined by the Grafs who had come before him and, if the rasping voices that spoke to him from the depths of the black monolith were to be believed, immortality.

Only Kravi, the newest Protektor, had failed to answer the summons. He would have to be removed, replaced. Viktor had decided to send Graumann, the boy's mentor, to do the job. As the chanting grew in volume, now underscored by a deeper, resonating tone that seemed to emanate from a past beyond reckoning, from a dimension beyond that through which mere humans moved, Viktor felt a vague sadness that Kravi would not share in the riches to come.

The sudden rush of ecstasy swept the thought from his mind. His spine popped as he arched backwards, energy racing along the vertebrae, then igniting within his skull. Colours blossomed behind his eyes – a spectrum the human brain was never meant to perceive. With a strangled half-moan of blasphemous pleasure, he dropped first to his knees, then forward onto all-fours. The thing inside him thrashed against his ribs, coiling about itself in a voluptuous frenzy.

His head snapped up as another jolt ran through him and he saw that he was not alone. Most of the Protektors were also on their knees; several lay on the polished wood floor, writhing and groaning.

He caught sight of Graumann, trembling like some palsied beast. As he watched, the older man's face began to melt, the skin running like tallow, remoulding itself into a series of new countenances, each more impossible than the last, as the power of the Lord of Change coursed through him.

At first, Viktor thought the series of dull, muffled concussions came from within him, another manifestation of the power that was being channelled into the room through the monolith. Only when he heard the merchant's curse did he suspect that something was wrong. Fighting against the fog of delirium that clouded his mind, he looked around the room. Several of the others had noticed it as well. The walls and floor vibrated as impact followed impact – the sounds of an attack, transmitted through the earth from the compound above.

THE THUNDERHAWK DROPPED vertically out of the night sky above the Gaudi compound, its bay doors already open. Its armour-clad cargo launched themselves into space, flares of exhaust from their jump packs slowing their vertiginous descent. Bolt pistols coughing throatily, they fired as they fell, clearing most of the guards from the compound wall before their ceramite-booted feet touched earth.

The more quick-witted of those left guarding the vehicles parked in the compound managed to loose off volleys of shuriken fire at their attackers. Most of the shots went wide, but one, at least, found its target, cutting through a jump pack's fuel line. Suddenly engulfed in a ball of flame, the armoured figure plummeted to earth, ploughing through the roof of a limousine. A number of the foot-soldiers let out a small cheer of triumph, which was quickly extinguished as the still-blazing figure tore its way out of the vehicle, pumping round after round across the courtyard as the fuel that covered its power-assisted carapace burned harmlessly away.

The Gaudi foot-soldiers knew the battle was already lost, but trapped within the walls which were intended to keep them safe, they now had no choice but to fight back against the killers who had fallen into their midst. They were huge, half as tall again as any normal man and almost twice as broad, clad as they were in dull grey armour, emblazoned with the Imperial seal. Shuriken fire spattered against their breastplates like summer rain as they moved across the compound with deadly, implacable purpose. Those who threw down their alien weapons fared no better than those who died fighting. The Grey Knights of the Ordo Malleus had their orders: none who had dared lay hands on the works of the alien were to live.

By the time the gate exploded inwards in a shower of fire and debris, the compound was quiet. The Rhino transport that nosed through the ragged gap had been set down by the Thunderhawk far enough away to avoid detection and had sped towards the compound while the dropship delivered the rest of its cargo. Grinding to a halt in the centre of the courtyard, its tracks smeared with the pulped remains of fallen Gaudi foot-soldiers, the vehicle's side and rear hatches swung open and ten more grey-armoured figures emerged and immediately moved to set up a secure perimeter.

The Rhino's last passenger was far less physically imposing than his travelling companions. In contrast to the ceramite and plasteel wargear of the figures who now moved about the compound, gathering up the alien weapons and stowing them within the Rhino, the suit he wore would not have looked out of place on the streets of Praxis's business district. A tall man, he still only reached the shoulder of the Grey Knight who greeted him.

'The compound is secure. We await your orders,' the Space Marine's voice emerged, electronically-filtered, from his helmet grille. Although he no longer wore his jump pack and his armour bore a patina of sooty scorch marks, the insignia on his armour's shoulder plates marked him out as a sergeant of the 4th Company, the Pax Mortuus. His name was Alexos, the leader of the airborne assault team.

'So I see.' Inquisitor Belael gestured towards the low, bunker-like structure that was the only visible sign that the compound comprised more than the shattered courtyard in which they stood. 'The informer provided us with a detailed description of the chambers that lie below ground. Take your men. Clear every room. Inform me when you have located the abomination.'

'In the Emperor's name.' The Grey Knight nodded and turned away. As he marched across the compound, his assault team formed up behind him. Some had exchanged their bolt pistols for bolters, others for meltas. A krak grenade took care of the single door set into one face of the bunker and they filed cautiously inside.

Almost immediately, the sound of gunfire burst from the open doorway. The Grey Knights who had remained above ground turned, weapons held ready. As was suspected at least some of the compound's defenders had waited in hiding, while their fellows died. Judging by the way the sounds of combat grew fainter, they were able to offer little resistance to the downward progress of the sergeant's team.

Standing by the Rhino, Belael yawned. He had slept very little over the three days since the Palace of the Ecclesiarchy here on Equus III had alerted the Inquisition to the presence of a newly-formed cabal of Chaos worshippers in Praxis. He never slept well when travelling and, immediately upon his arrival in the city, had conducted his own interrogation of the informer. The company of Grey Knights, in transit after the successful completion of another operation against the followers of Chaos, had arrived while he was interviewing Kravi.

He had found Kravi to be a dullard, barely able to comprehend the forces in which he had unwittingly become enmeshed. But even the most slow-witted may do his duty in the war that was raging across the Imperium and beyond. Belael smiled as he remembered the look of almost childlike gratitude that spread across the informer's face when he told him that his loyalty to the Emperor and to mankind would be rewarded.

Oh, yes, Belael had assured him, he would see that he was appropriately rewarded.

THE ANNEXE WAS a scorched ruin. The stench of cooked flesh hung thickly in the air as Belael stared at the sigils etched into the surface of the black stone monolith: blasphemous names, among which one stood out – Tzeentch, the Lord of Change. The polyhedron had operated as a channel for his unholy energies, but that channel was now closed. One of the crisped bodies that lay about the floor of the room would have been its human attendant. He must have warned his masters soon after the attack began. To all intents and purposes, the monolith was nothing more than an inert lump of rock. Soon it would not even be that.

'Set the charges,' Belael instructed Alexos. 'Then mine the entire compound. I have summoned the Thunderhawk. I will perform the Rite of Exorcism from the air.'

'In the Emperor's name,' the Grey Knight replied.

'Indeed,' Belael nodded. 'Once this place is little more than an unholy memory, I shall have one more job to do. In the Emperor's name.'

SITTING ALONE ON the low, hard cot in the bare cell, Mikhail had lost track of time and of how many times he had repeated his story – first to the priest in the vast nave of the palace, then to the priest's superiors, in a series of smaller chambers set high in one of the palace's spires, and then, in the cell in which he now sat, to the inquisitor. With each telling, the reality of the events he described seemed to become more distant, less real. Had he misunderstood the events at the compound? Had he broken his vow of silence for nothing? If this were the case, he could expect swift and deadly retribution from Haus Gaudi. If he wanted to avoid that, he would need protection – the kind of protection even the Haus would recognise.

'Your loyalty to the Emperor and his works shall be remembered – and rewarded,' the inquisitor had told him.

Mikhail now knew what kind of reward he most desired: induction into the priesthood. No Haus in Praxis, or any of the other cities on Equus III, would harm a member of the Ecclesiarchy. That his brother was already a priest would surely stand his request in good stead. Of course, it would mean starting over, back at the bottom of the heap, but he had done that with Graumann's crew and the Ecclesiarchy was just another organisation, like the Haus. He was smart, he would learn how to get things done, catch the eyes of his superiors and rise through the ranks. Perhaps he would be sent off-world, where the opportunities for advancement would be limitless.

'Preacher Kravi' – the title had a nice ring to it.

The thud of heavy footsteps sounded on the other side of the cell door. His guts cramped and spasmed. Just nerves, he told himself as he pressed a hand against his abdomen. Just nerves.

The door swung inwards and the inquisitor stepped into the room, followed by a towering figure: a living statue, cast from a dull grey metal that seemed to absorb the light from the cell's single ceiling light. The Imperial eagle spread its wings across the figure's chest and a human head sat atop its shoulders, whose eyes regarded Mikhail with a coldness he imagined to exist only in the gulfs between the stars.

'Did you find them?' Mikhail managed to tear his eyes from the grey apparition and turned to the inquisitor. 'Was I right? I have been waiting...'

He paused, searching for the right words to begin his petition for acceptance into the Ecclesiarchy. If an Imperial inquisitor was to lend his approval to Mikhail's request, surely none would argue.

'I have been praying that you found the blasphemers before their power grew stronger,' he continued, the words coming out in a rush. 'I... I know that I've not lived a conventional life. I have done things others would consider wrong, but... but I have always loved the Emperor. I have always been loyal. My one hope is that I may make amends for my past, prove my loyalty even further...'

Belael smiled, and raised a hand to halt Mikhail's flow.

'We found them. As you suspected, they had assembled to perform another of their unholy rites. We brought it to a premature end and wiped their stain from this world. Had the stain been allowed to spread, it would have been necessary to sacrifice this city, perhaps this world in the process of their annihilation.'

'Emperor be praised!' Mikhail, anxious to prove his piety, blurted out. 'I sought only to be of service to the Golden Throne. My greatest wish is to be of yet more service. Perhaps if...' He faltered as he saw the smile drop from the inquisitor's face.

'There is indeed one more service you can render to the Emperor.' In his eyes, Mikhail now saw something of the coldness he had noticed in the eyes of the grey-clad hulk that stood behind him. 'There remains one last fragment of the unholy seed your former employers sought to sow on Equus III. It must be eradicated.'

'Of course!' Mikhail gushed. 'If you need a guide, someone who knows his way around Praxis, I–' Then the meaning behind the inquisitor's words slammed home, cutting off his words.

'No!' he gasped, wincing as something inside him began to twist and thrash, claws scraping against the cage of his ribs. Belael only nodded. Taking this as a signal, the Grey Knight stepped forward, raising one massive gloved hand. Seeing that hand held a bolt pistol, emblazoned with the Imperial seal and sigils of power, Mikhail tried to say something, anything that would delay the inevitable. All that emerged from his throat was a low, guttural snarl, as if the thrashing thing within him had seized control of his voice.

'I call upon the cleansing fire of the Emperor's gaze to purify this tainted vessel.' For the second time that day, Belael began to intone the Rite of Exorcism. Ignoring his words, Mikhail scrambled backwards across the narrow cot until his back pressed against the wall of the cell.

'As the Emperor sacrificed Himself into the eternal embrace of the Golden Throne, so it is right and proper that all those tainted by the unholy and the blasphemous should submit themselves to his judgement.' Belael's words bored into Mikhail's mind. Legs still kicking in a futile attempt to get further away from the mouth of the bolt pistol and the steady, cold gaze of the figure who held it, he raised his hands in a final pleading gesture. Absurdly, he found himself thinking of Leon Kleist, grovelling in the filth outside the Split Pig.

'By fire and shell shall they become clean. Through sacrifice shall they receive their reward.'

The bolt pistol coughed once and Mikhail Kravi, loyal servant of the Emperor, received his reward.

RAPTOR DOWN

Gav Thorpe

THE FLIGHT DECK was a hive of activity. The murmuring of tech-priests resounded off the high gantries amongst the chatter of rivet guns and the clank of ordnance loaders. Welding torches sparked bright blue-white in the yellow glow of the standby alert lighting and figures hurried to and fro. The Marauders of Raptor and Devil squadrons were arrayed herringbone-fashion along the length of the maintenance bay as tech-adepts and servitors crawled across them, repairing battle damage and loading new ordnance. Flight Commander Jaeger stood and watched it all with a faint sense of satisfaction. Everyone was performing well today – the pilots, their gunners and bombardiers, and the bay crews were all operating like a well-oiled machine. He cupped his hands to his mouth to shout across the din.

'Ferix, how are the repairs going?' he bellowed across the decking to the robe-swathed tech-adept monitoring the maintenance on Jaeger's own Marauder, Raptor One. Ferix hurried over with short, quick steps and nodded curtly. Over the adept's shoulder, Jaeger could read the insignia that he himself had painted onto the nose of Raptor One after their last mission. It was the Raptors' motto – Swift Justice, Sure Death – in bright white against the dark blue paint of the Navy colours. Underneath in gold was the squadron emblem, an eagle rampant in shining gold. It was reassuring to Jaeger, the familiarity he now shared with Raptor One after their bloody baptism together a year and a half ago.

'All craft are battle-worthy, Flight Commander Jaeger,' Ferix told him, his hands concealed within the voluminous sleeves of his robes. 'Raptor Three should be de-commissioned for several more hours preferably, but is operational within tolerable limits.'

'Good. Let me know as soon as weapons load and check is complete. I'll be on the bridge,' Jaeger dismissed Ferix with a wave of his hand and turned away. As he walked across the flight deck, he cast his gaze around him, looking at the bulky shapes of the Marauder bombers in the gloom and the smaller Thunderbolt interceptors in the launching alcoves on the far side of the massive chamber.

All this is my domain now, he thought, not for the first time. It had been eighteen months since Raf's death had left Jaeger in charge, a year and a half of responsibility to command and lead nearly a hundred pilots and flight crewmen, to mould them into a fighting team worthy of the Imperial Navy.

He could see the men of his own squadron, the Raptors, taking a well-earned meal break at the battlestation mess tables on the starboard side of the flight deck. He saw the veterans – strong, disciplined men like Marte, Arick, Phrao and Berhandt. But there were too many new faces for the flight commander's liking, men untested in the heat of battle until today. For a year the cruiser *Divine Justice* had continued her patrol, unable to replace the losses she had suffered at the hands of the orks. Only three months ago she had returned to dock and new crews were drafted in from the flight schools. Unlike the ratings, flight crews needed to be trained professionals; you couldn't just send a press gang onto some Imperial world and see what you dredged up. For a year the *Divine Justice* had been home to only half the aircraft her holds could carry and launch. Jaeger was glad that they had seen no serious action during the rest of the patrol – a few skirmishes with outclassed pirates, the odd smuggler, but nothing like the baptism of fire and death that had been the duel with the ork hulk.

Jaeger realised he was at the lifter now, and stepped into the small chamber. He cranked the dial to 'Bridge deck' and slammed the grating shut. A moment later he was swiftly ascending amongst the clatter of chains and gears, the floor of the lifter shaking gently beneath his booted feet.

Untried boys! he cursed to himself. But for all his worries, the operation was proceeding with little difficulty. Having barely had time to refit and re-crew at Saltius, the *Divine Justice* and her three frigate escorts, the *Glorious,* the *Apollo* and the *Excellent,* had been despatched with orders to support the Imperial Guard invasion of the Mearopyis system. Even now, they were in orbit over the third world of the system, running escort to the dropships and making ground attacks against enemy supply bases and communications centres.

They were here to fight the noctal – spindly, insectoid aliens who had conquered Mearopyis and enslaved its human population several thousand years ago. Finally, the Imperium had arrived to take it back and once more bring the light of the Emperor to the people of the subjugated world. Casualties had been light so far. Admiral Veniston's rites of engagement had been very specific. The noctal fighters were incapable of orbital flight, unlike the Thunderbolts and Marauders of the *Divine Justice*. The squadrons were hitting hard and fast, dropping from orbit, bombing and strafing their targets before powering back up to the ships waiting above, safe from harm. The enemy fighters were swift and agile, but they couldn't be everywhere at once and only a single Marauder had been lost, and no Thunderbolts had yet been taken down. Jaeger had heard that the squadrons from the other ships of the fleet were having similar successes.

Perhaps this is not such a bad time to test out the new hands, Jaeger considered. No massed air battles, strict orders and a safe haven would allow his men to settle, with enough risk to keep them on their toes, but also safe enough that they'd survive to learn from the experience. Survival was the key, in Jaeger's mind. No flight commander wanted a continuous draft of newcomers flying his craft; he wanted experienced, dedicated crews who would return time and again, their mission complete.

With a thunk, the lifter reached the top of its shaft, eighteen decks up from the flight bays. Jaeger pulled back the door and stepped out, swapping a salute with a gunnery lieutenant who stepped past him. He marched up to the double doors leading to the bridge and nodded to the shotgun-wielding armsman standing guard. The armsman turned and activated the comm-set on the wall behind him, announcing Jaeger's presence. There was an affirmative and several seconds later the bridge doors swung back with a hiss of hidden pistons. Stepping through, Jaeger saw the bridge was in its normal state of organised confusion. Tech-adepts scurried to and fro, augur and surveyor servitors announced target dispositions in monotonous drones, officers snapped orders over the comm-net and flunkies and menials of every description hurried here and there taking notes, making reports or simply repeating messages from one officer to the next.

In the middle of it all stood Captain Kaurl, like a rock amidst the swirl of a rising tide.

The stocky, bearded officer had his hands clasped behind his back, his feet spread as if braced on a buffeted dropship rather than a stately cruiser. He nodded as a lieutenant passed on some piece of data and then looked at the main viewing screen. It dominated the centre of the bridge, five metres high, and twice as long.

The main picture showed a duel between three Imperial cruisers and two noctal superdestroyers. Cannon-fire and missiles streaked from the Emperor's vessels, flaring into bright green flashes as they impacted on the energy shields of the alien ship.

Bright white las-fire erupted from one of the superdestroyers, a flickering coruscation of energy bolts that impacted on the void shields of one of the cruisers, their energy dissipating harmlessly.

Various sub-images charted fleet positions, dropship manoeuvres and sundry other details. In the bottom left, a tracker field flickered on and off in one of the *Divine Justice's* docking bays, drawing a supply shuttle down onto the armoured deck, heat wash from its engines causing the image to waver on the screen. To the top right, a spread of torpedoes rocketed across the void. As they neared a noctal vessel the front of each peeled open, ejecting a storm of plasma and fusion warheads which rippled across its silver-grey hull in a riot of orange and red. Along the bottom of the screen, wings of Starhawk bombers manoeuvred between the las-fire of a superdestroyer's defence turrets, the armoured surface of the alien ship splintering into a shower of shrapnel as their bombs punched deep inside before exploding.

Jaeger turned his attention back to the main image and watched as retro thrusters flared into life along the length of one of the Imperial cruisers. Slowed in its course, it began to sweep to starboard, turning slowly at first but gathering pace as its forward momentum slowed. Another jet of engines halted the turn and the main engines increased to full. Its broadside opened fire again and this time the noctal shields failed, missiles and plasma blasts raking into its engine decks.

Fires blossomed and spread, burning white hot as air rushed out of the punctured hull of the enemy superdestroyer in explosive bursts.

'Jacques!' Kaurl called out, snapping Jaeger's attention from the ongoing space battle.

'Sir!' he replied crisply, saluting formally. The captain responded with an equally formal nod.

'How are things going?' Kaurl asked, taking Jaeger by the arm and leading him into his personal cabin off the main bridge. It was fitted out in wooden panelling, a deep red grain that leant an air of calm. He sat beside the captain on a long sofa whose plush covers matched the rich décor of the room.

'I have made post-mission reports, sir,' Jaeger replied with a frown. 'Everything is in there.'

'Not everything, Jaeger,' smiled Kaurl. 'Numbers, yes, but nothing else. They don't tell me how you feel the invasion is progressing.'

'Everything seems to be going smoothly, exactly to plan I would say,' Jaeger told the captain after a moment's thought. 'Better than planned.'

'And that worries you?' Kaurl seemed to read Jaeger's thoughts.

'Every plan is perfect until it makes contact with the enemy,' Jaeger recited the line from the Navy battle dogma. 'Then it usually falls apart; it doesn't exceed expectation.'

'Emperor's blood, man!' cursed Kaurl, standing up and glowering at his flight commander. 'Are you never happy?'

'No, sir, I'm not,' Jaeger replied solemnly, looking back up at Kaurl, his face impassive.

That was slightly untrue, he thought; I'm happy when I'm flying. That's the only time. A thought occurred to him then. There was someone he hadn't seen over the past twelve hours since the attack had begun. 'Where is Admiral Veniston, sir?'

'Admiral Kright has been recalled to sector command. Veniston has taken command of the fleet and transferred his flag to the battleship *Holy Dignity*,' Kaurl answered. 'I've got my own ship back, thank the Emperor,' he added with a conspiratorial grin.

'Not meaning to be rude, sir, but the Raptors will be ready to launch any minute,' Jaeger fidgeted with the collar of his flight suit and glanced at the chronometer that sat on the desk behind Kaurl.

'Of course, Jacques, you get out there and bomb them to hell and back,' Kaurl nodded towards the door. Jaeger nodded thankfully and hurried out on long strides.

'I almost feel sorry for the noctal,' Kaurl muttered to himself as the door closed behind the eager flight commander. 'Almost.'

'TARGETS ALL STORED, weapons ready to go,' Berhandt announced gruffly. Jaeger glanced to his right across the cockpit towards his bombardier. He opened the comm channel to the rest of the Marauders. Both the Raptors and the Devils were in on this one, escorted by the interceptors of Arrow and Storm Squadrons.

'Everyone has their orders, let's make sure this one goes smoothly,' he told them.

++They won't know what's hit them!++ crowed Phrao's tinny voice in Jaeger's ear.

++We gonna make a fireball so big they'll see it back on board!++ chipped in Logan, squadron leader of the Devils.

'Let's cut the gossiping. Prepare for atmospheric entry. Let's not lose our heads,' Jaeger chided them. In the last twelve hours they had flown five missions with nine-tenths of their targets utterly destroyed. He wasn't about to lose a craft because some hothead forgot their procedures.

++Raptor Leader, this is Arrow Leader, moving ahead to intercept positions++ Squadron Leader Dextra's voice was quiet and distant over the comm-link.

++Raptor Leader, this is Storm Leader, taking position on your rear quarter++ Losark added as Jaeger watched the bright spark of the Arrow's engines forging ahead towards the world below.

It nearly filled the cockpit: a yellowish globe swirled with orange and red dust clouds. Down there, three-quarters of a million Imperial Guardsmen were forging their way across the plains, in a massive strike determined to seize the noctal's capital within a day. The Imperial strategy relied upon a single swift hammerblow that destroyed the noctal's command before their reserves could react and bring superior numbers to bear on the Emperor's soldiers. And so far it seemed to be working – resistance was scattered, the noctal seemed to have had no warning that the Imperium had arrived. The first the aliens had known of the attack, Imperial dropships had already touched down.

The Marauder began to shudder as it entered the upper atmosphere of Mearopyis. The control stick in Jaeger's hand started to judder as the air resistance strengthened. Thermals and turbulence began to make the massive aircraft dip and weave as it streaked down towards the clouds. Ahead Jaeger watched the shapes of the Thunderbolts commanded by Dextra disappear into the cloud cover, slipping silently from view. As air pressure built, Jaeger disengaged the attitude jets along the Marauder's wings; it would fly like a conventional aircraft now. As the first few wisps of cloud began to coalesce across the cockpit windows, Jaeger turned the comm-link dial to talk to the *Divine Justice*.

'This is Raptor Leader. Entering cloud cover now. What's the latest on enemy craft?' he reported.

There was a pause, and Jaeger could imagine the bustle on the bridge as a lieutenant sought out the information and relayed it to the comms officer.

++Raptor Leader, this is the *Divine Justice*. Small enemy interceptor patrol last reported one hundred and fifty kilometres to local west. Larger concentration, approximately fifteen craft seen over target area at 0844 ship chronology.++

Jaeger absorbed this news without comment. As the air campaign had continued, the enemy had responded and now there were fewer targets left, it was inevitable that they would receive better air cover. Jaeger had argued hotly that the noctal airbases were the target of the first strikes, but Kaurl had informed him that priority had been given to targets that stood in the path of the advancing Imperial army.

'Time to target?' he asked Berhandt. The bombardier glanced at a screen to his right.

'About twenty minutes, depending on headwind,' Berhandt replied with a shrug.

Jaeger thought this over in silence. The last report had been thirty minutes old, plus another twenty minutes until they arrived. Would the enemy aircraft still be there? Would there be more of them or less?

'*Divine Justice*, this is Raptor Leader. Please inform me as soon as new data available on target's air cover.'

As he made the request, Jaeger forced himself to relax. Adaptability was one of his greatest strengths, and he felt confident he could react to whatever situation developed.

But can the others, he asked himself sourly? This invasion was the first time many of them had been under fire. So far their orders had been simple to execute and had gone by the book. How well would they react under real stress, with Jaeger barking orders out over the comm-net; orders that might save them from being shot down if followed quickly and accurately? He had drilled them long and hard in the simulators and on training flights, mercilessly pushing them each time, berating them loudly for the smallest errors. They thought he probably didn't know, but he'd heard they called him the Iron Tyrant for his strict, disciplined approach. He didn't care; they could call him all the names in the Imperium if it meant they listened to him and learnt from his experience.

He had served under three flight commanders over nearly ten years as an Imperial Navy pilot. All three had impressed upon him the importance of duty and discipline, and it was a message he was determined to impart to his own men. He felt a responsibility to each of them, to give them the training and leadership they needed to excel, to become what the Emperor expected of them. It was why he was so hard on them, why he was the Iron Tyrant, because each small failure reflected on him in his own conscience.

'Arrow leader, move ahead and see what's waiting for us at the target,' Jaeger ordered into the comm. 'Storm Leader, remain in position ready to engage enemy from the west.'

He hated fighting blind; the memory of the attack on the space hulk was still burnt into his mind. Twenty-one men had died that day because no one had told them what they were up against.

Veniston had called it 'acceptable losses', but there was no such phrase in Jaeger's head. No loss could be tolerated and already he felt guilty for the crew of Devil Five which had been shot down by groundfire on the first mission over Mearopyis.

This time is different, he told himself, trying to build up some conviction. This time our orders are simple. We have rules of engagement written specifically to protect my men. In, attack and then out again. They were the rules and he was bound by his duty to the Navy and his men to follow them.

++Raptor Leader, this is Storm Leader. We have enemy incoming from the west. Permission to engage?++

'Go ahead, Losark,' Jaeger replied, staring out of the cockpit window towards the west for some hint of the enemy aircraft, but nothing was to be seen yet.

++Okay Storm squadron, let's chalk up some more kills++ confirmed Losark, making Jaeger smile inside his facemask. The Storm squadron leader was the best dogfighter on the *Divine Justice*, but Dextra was his senior by two years and was always just a few kills ahead in his tally. Jaeger had wagered extra drinks rations to the whole of Raptor squadron that Losark would surpass his rival's total by the end of the campaign.

He watched as the Thunderbolts, eight of them, screamed overhead and banked to starboard. The squadron split into two wings of four craft each, one accelerating up towards the cloudbase, the other dipping towards the ground. Jaeger saw a sparkle in the distance – the Mearopyis star glinting off metal as the enemy fighters closed in.

'Maintain course to target,' the flight commander ordered the Marauders. 'Gunners prepare for interlocking fire, pattern omega.'

As he finished, he heard the whine of electric motors as Marte swung the fuselage gun cradle into position. Through the reinforced screen, Jaeger watched as missile trails ghosted away from Storm squadron arrowing their way across the skies towards the Noctal plains. A moment later and a bright explosion lit up the sky, an expanding star of blue created by a missile's impact. As the blast dissipated, a haze of white smoke was left drifting on the gentle wind.

'One less alien,' Berhandt muttered contentedly to himself from beside Jaeger.

The dogfight approached as the speedier noctal fighters burst between the two Thunderbolt formations, intent on the bombers. Jaeger saw vapour trails arcing across the sky as the Imperial interceptors banked round to follow the alien craft, but he knew they were too slow to catch them and the Marauders would have to look to their own guns for protection.

'Power up the lascannon,' Jaeger ordered Berhandt, who gave a satisfied grunt and swivelled his seat to grip hold of the nose-gun's controls. Jaeger switched the comm-link to address all of the Marauders.

'Hold your fire, wait for my order,' he steadied them, knowing that if one trigger-happy soul started firing, the rest would join in and probably waste their limited ammunition.

He could make out the noctal planes more clearly as they streaked towards him at the front of the double arrowhead of Marauders. They were racing in fast, keeping a tight formation. That was good; the closer the aliens stayed together, the more chance the firing from the turrets would hit something. Another ten seconds trickled past as Jaeger watched the bright specks turn into distinct shapes.

A bolt of green energy erupted towards the bombers as the lead craft fired its laser, the flash passing comfortably overhead.

'All crews, open fire!' Jaeger bellowed into the comm-mic. An instant later Raptor One shook with the thunder of autocannons and heavy bolters firing and a stream of tracer rounds soared across the shrinking gap between the two squadrons. More las-bolts blasted past, one so close it left a streak of after-image seared across Jaeger's eyes for a few seconds.

'Come on, up a bit... up a bit, you alien scum!' muttered Berhandt, his face pressed down into the targeting visor of the lascannon. The noctal had dipped, trying to take the Marauders from below. But there was to be no refuge there either, as the guns of the lower squadron, the Devils, opened fire and the three sleek aircraft were surrounded by a storm of tracers.

'Got yer!' cackled Berhandt, pressing the firing stud. The lascannon burst into life, a beam of white energy lancing out to pass straight through the nearest foe. The enemy craft disintegrated, its triangular wings spiralling groundward until they were out of sight, the main fuselage utterly vaporised. As the noctal planes screamed past, Jaeger got a good look at their shape. They were like blunt darts, their stubby delta wings stretching from in front of the cockpit to the rear of the plane. Four tail fins surrounded bright blue jets as Jaeger tracked its course through the side screen, looking over his shoulder as it zoomed away.

Fire from Raptor Four, Phrao's Marauder, caught one wing of the noctal fighter, shredding it into hundreds of shrapnel fragments that scattered in its wake. Control lost, the plane went into a wild rolling spin, tumbling headlong through the rest of squadron, whose gunners easily tracked it and sent a fusillade of fire into it until finally it broke in half before exploding.

++I'll get the last one++ Losark assured him over the comm.

'How many kills behind now?' asked Jaeger, laughing softly.

++Three to go, Raptor Leader++ came the squadron leader's reply, his eagerness conveyed even across the crackling comm-net.

The Thunderbolts soared past just metres away, afterburners on full, the wash of their passing juddering the control column in Jaeger's right hand.

'Continue course to target, estimated time to attack is…' Jaeger glanced up at the chrono-display in the top left corner of the cockpit window. 'Thirteen minutes.'

'Five minutes until target in sight,' Berhandt's rough voice reported. Jaeger glanced over towards the muscled bombardier who was intent on his bomb targeter. The glowing green display underlit his face as he stared into the aiming reticule, making final adjustments to the optics with a series of switches and dials on his control panel. He never took his eyes from the reticule. Instead his fingers danced over the controls as if powered by a will of their own – in fact they were driven by a familiarity only years of experience could develop.

If they survive, all of the crews will be as good as him, thought Jaeger as he watched the bombardier at work. *It's up to me to ensure that they do.*

Jaeger knew that at times he was guilty of pride, but he had a dream that one day Raptor squadron and the *Divine Justice* would be recognised as the best across the whole segmentum. He wanted the admirals at Bakka to know he was there, to hear of his great work. It was a good ambition, he told himself.

The flight commander turned his attention back outside the canopy as the Marauders' altitude dropped. They were to make a low-level attack first, dropping their massive payload of incendiary explosives on an enemy bunker complex. After circling around they would make a second attack run with missiles and lascannons, picking off anything smoked out by the firebombs. It was straight out of the tactics manual, performed in drills and simulated battles a dozen times by the pilots and bombardiers.

A subtle movement to Jaeger's right caught his attention. Something was stirring in the yellow haze to the south-west. It looked to Jaeger like a dust cloud, quite a large one, several dozen kilometres away. Checking the gauges above his head, Jaeger noted a strong headwind, which would probably blow the dust storm in their direction. Concerned, he opened up the long-range comm channel.

'*Divine Justice*, this is Raptor Leader. Any reports of storm activity on our approach?' he asked, still looking intently at the swirling cloud of ochre sand and dust.

++That is negative, Raptor Leader. Strong winds, low cloud, no storm activity++ came the reply after several seconds.

'Okay, *Divine Justice*. Please monitor this channel, I may have found something,' Jaeger told the officer in orbit, an uneasy feeling growing in the pit of his stomach.

Turning in his seat, Jaeger punched a few runes on the screen display and, after a swirl of static, a chart of the local geography was superimposed over the front canopy window. He focused the map onto his current recorded location and, glancing up again to check the direction towards the storm, placed its position. It seemed to be issuing from a long canyon complex that ran for hundreds of kilometres perpendicular to the axis of the Imperial attack, some twelve kilometres behind the forward Guard positions.

'They would have checked it out,' he muttered to himself. Berhandt looked up at him quizzically.

'Somethin' wrong?' the bombardier asked, looking out of the cockpit to follow Jaeger's gaze.

'Ferix!' Jaeger snapped, glancing over his shoulder down the length of the Marauder. The tech-adept emerged from his maintenance alcove, trailing a twist of cabling. 'Talk to one of the missile auspexes, find out if it can see anything in that dust cloud.'

Ferix nodded, and ducked through a low hatchway into the maintenance crawl space that led to the starboard wing. His voice arrived in Jaeger's ear direct through the Marauder's internal comm system.

'Initiating activation sequence, aktiva cons sequentia,' the tech-adept intoned, reciting the rites out loud. His voice took on a different timbre as his brain merged with the mechanical workings of the missile, feeling its spirit moving inside him, divorcing him from the world of the flesh. 'Librius machina auroris dei. Contact established with machine spirit of "Flail" missile, designate 14-56. Praise the Machine God. Ignis optika carta mond. Invoking surveyor sweep over target area. Calculating... Calculating... Calculating... Targets present, multiple, unknown designation.'

'Emperor's claws,' cursed Jaeger hotly. Something was inside that canyon, hiding from orbital surveillance. 'Can you be more specific, how many is "multiple"?'

'Unknown, target acquisition beyond recall capacity,' Ferix replied. His voice lost its distant edge. 'Flight commander, this missile type has a half-kilobrain of memory, capable of storing information on seventy-five separate targets.'

'So there's more than seventy-five possible targets down there?' Jaeger demanded, the clenching sensation in his stomach moving up to his throat. 'More than seventy-five armoured vehicles?'

'That is correct,' came Ferix's dispassionate reply. 'Smaller objects are disregarded.'

'In all that's holy–' came Berhandt's response, who had been listening in, eyes locked to Jaeger's.

'That's enough to cut their supplies... We have to warn the Guard!'

'You HAVE VERY specific orders, flight commander,' Kaurl's stern voice told Jaeger over the comms network. ++Proceed with the attack as planned.++

Jaeger glanced at the small display screen just to the left of the control stick. Ferix had re-mapped the wiring of Raptor One so that the artificial eyes of its missiles were directed towards that display. There were one hundred and twenty-three separate signals there now and still rising as they approached the canyon. Jaeger eyed the small blobs of green light with hatred. His two squadrons were enough to seriously dent the enemy force, but it would be risky. Added to that, the captain had specifically ordered him to ignore them.

If the counter-attack was allowed to continue, though, who could tell what damage it would do to the whole war effort? Speed was the basis of the assault, and if it was slowed down by an incursion into its supply lines, the whole invasion might falter. If it faltered, all would be lost as the noctal used the time to gather their armies from across the planet. Who could tell if they had more ships in the vicinity, each now warned and powering its way to raise the orbital siege of the alien-held world? And what of the humans below?

The noctal had been so shocked there had been no time for them to bargain or use them as hostages, but millions of lives could end in torment and death if the noctal regained the upper hand.

Jaeger felt torn in several directions at once. He had his orders, they were very specific and Captain Kaurl had said as much. If he attacked the enemy column – whatever else happened – he would have to face a court of inquiry for disobeying those orders. Also, this noctal army was bound to have defences against air attack; after all they had been suffering badly from airstrikes for the last twelve hours. If this counter-attack was as important as Jaeger thought it was, it would have every available protection. And that meant a lot of added risk. Risk to himself, his planes and their crews. Risks Jaeger was loath to take. Had he not, minutes before, been ruing the day he led Raptor squadron on that deadly attack against the ork hulk? And now here he was, contemplating disobeying a direct order to lead his men down a canyon full of the enemy, into Emperor-knew-what kind of trouble and bloodshed. Jaeger swallowed hard and made his decision.

'Raptors, Devils, change of plan,' he announced to his command through gritted teeth. His duty was ultimately to the campaign as a whole, and through that to the Emperor. He had no other course of action open to him. 'Follow me to the enemy, free attack once you are in range.'

++Let's do some huntin'!++ came Gesper's reply from Devil Two.

++Behind you all the way, sir++ agreed Phrao.

'Come in low and fast, hit them with everything you've got, then make for the *Divine Justice*,' Jaeger was talking quickly now, feeling adrenaline surge through him as he banked the squadrons towards the canyon and nosed Raptor One towards the ground. 'No waiting around!'

++Raptor One, this is Storm. We are on intercept course to enemy fighters over new target.++

++Storm One, this is Arrow One, you'll have to get there before me!++

Even as the message ended, Dextra's Thunderbolt screamed across Jaeger's field of vision, its jets at full burn leaving a brief after-image in the flight commander's eyes. It was swiftly followed by the shapes of the other four Thunderbolts, spreading out in readiness for the coming battle. As Jaeger continued to bank, Storm squadron roared overhead, just seconds behind the Arrows.

'We'll be at the canyon in twenty-five seconds,' Berhandt reported.

Jaeger nodded and levelled the Marauder, pushing up the engines to maximum as Raptor One powered towards the enemy a mere two hundred metres above the softly undulating dunes of Mearopyis.

'Fifteen seconds to canyon,' Berhandt informed him, bent once more over the aiming reticule.

Above him, Jaeger could see the fighters duelling in and out of the rising dust cloud. A moment later and the sand and grit was swirling around the Marauder, skittering off the windshield and obscuring everything past a couple of metres.

'I hope those engine filters hold, Ferix,' Jaeger glanced over his shoulder to the tech-adept in the maintenance bay.

'I fitted them myself, flight commander,' Ferix assured him coldly, bringing a smile to Jaeger's lips beneath his air mask.

'Ten seconds to target,' came Berhandt's countdown. 'Nine… Eight… Seven… Six… Five… Four… Three… Two… One… Target acquired!'

Jaeger felt rather than saw the ground drop away beneath him and banked the Marauder to port, heading north, and down into the canyon. Flickers of green las-fire illuminated the dust cloud ahead and to either side, but none was close yet. A hum started in Jaeger's ear as Berhandt locked-on one of the flail missiles, its warning tone rising to a screech as it became aware of its target's location.

'Fly sweet vengeance!' Berhandt spat, pressing down on the firing stud. A half-second later the missile streaked downwards and then levelled, disappearing into the dust on a trail of white fire. Jaeger felt his heart beat once, then again, then there was a bright patch in the storm and a moment later a muffled boom shook the canopy.

'Fuel carrier, I think,' Berhandt commented, not looking up from the sighting array.

The dust began to thin rapidly and soon Jaeger could see the bottom of the canyon, still half a kilometre below. *No wonder the orbital augurs didn't notice this, it's as deep as the pits of hell,* he thought. Another missile flared off towards the enemy, its vapour trail joined by eight more as the other Marauders opened fire. They jinked and wove as strong eddies in the wind, caused by the funnelling effect of the deep canyon, forced them to adjust their flight path towards their prey.

A couple of seconds later nine explosions blossomed in rapid succession in a cluster across the canyon floor, but Jaeger still couldn't make out what they were firing at. Now more ground-fire was lancing its way along the natural trench towards them. Pulses of tracer fire combined with the green las-blasts he'd seen earlier, but the enemy were aiming too high.

Looking away at the target-screen for a moment, he saw a grouping of several dozen stationary vehicles ahead.

'See that cluster?' he asked Berhandt as a shell whistled past a few metres to his left. The bombardier nodded and adjusted a couple of dials on his visor.

'Squadrons, assume formation Bravus for main payload drop,' Jaeger ordered the two squadrons into position to maximise damage from the bombing run. Without warning, he heard a detonation close behind, and twisting in his pilot's seat he looked out of the side window. A Marauder was banking off, flames engulfing its tail and rear fuselage. Its uncontrolled descent took it into the canyon wall a second later, its fuel tanks and plasma chamber exploding in a shower of flames and debris.

'Who was that? Who did we lose?' Jaeger demanded over the comm.

++Devil Three, Scairn's plane++ came the reply from Cal Logan, the Devil squadron leader.

++Dammit! We've lost two engines!++ L'stin cursed, before Jaeger could answer.

'Raptor Three, get back to orbit!' snapped Jaeger, noticing that las-bolts were streaking down towards them as well as from the ground.

'Arrow, Storm! Strafe enemy positions on the canyon walls!' Jaeger's voice was clipped, harsh, as he focused his mind on what to do next. 'Raptor squadron continue with bombing runs. Devil Squadron use missiles and lascannons to provide covering fire.'

A series of affirmatives sounded in the flight commander's ear. Jaeger levelled out the Marauder's course to prepare for the bombing run. He couldn't afford to evade the incoming fire, it would make aiming almost impossible for Berhandt. A splintering crack appeared in the canopy between him and the bombardier as a las-bolt ricocheted off. Jaeger heard other impacts rattling along the length of the fuselage as green flashes of laser energy and yellow tracers converged on him, the lead plane.

He knew Ferix was now working at full stretch, monitoring any malfunctions, coaxing Raptor One's own systems into repairing themselves, welding, cutting and binding where that wasn't possible. He could hear the tech-adept chanting liturgies of maintenance and repair behind him. A red warning light flashed on the panel to Jaeger's right – one of the engines was leaking plasma. Without thought, the flight commander shut down power to the damaged jet and boosted up the others, stabilising the Marauder's flight path with small movements on the control stick.

++Raptor Four is down, Raptor Three is down++ reported Phrao heavily. ++Storm and Arrow have broken off, they're out of fuel.++

'Emperor damn it all to hell!' snarled Jaeger, looking back and up over his shoulder for a sign that any enemy fighters had survived the air duel. A sudden blood-curdling shriek over the inter-squadron frequency deafened him, forcing Jaeger to shut down the comm and switch off the pitiful cry. He adjusted one of the secondary view screens on his panel to display the rear camera shot. Another Marauder was tumbling groundwards, wreathed in smoke and flames, its wings spinning away on separate trajectories, trailing burning fuel. His chest tight with apprehension, he opened up the comm-link again.

'Who was that?' he demanded.

'Bombs away!' Berhandt called out, sitting up from where he'd been crouched over the bombsight. Jaeger's head whirled as so many things clamoured for his attention.

++It was Devil One, sir++ came Phrao's delayed reply.

Jaeger closed his eyes for a moment and took a deep breath, steadying himself. Opening them again, he looked at the rear view to see massive red flames bursting over the dark shapes of the enemy attack column. The fireballs continued to expand, the special incendiaries igniting the air itself with their heat, filling the canyon from wall to wall with crackling, hungry flame.

Another massive detonation followed, and then another as the other Marauders dropped their devastating payloads. Jaeger saw secondary explosions along the ground as fuel tanks expanded and burst and ammunition was set on fire. Another blossom of brighter fire, in the air this time, showed where a tailing noctal fighter had flown straight into the inferno as it had attempted to close from below.

Berhandt was firing off the remaining missiles, as were the other Marauders. In front and behind, the canyon was a blaze of destruction. Burning wrecks littered the valley floor, while the firebomb damage continued to creep along the walls and into the air, slowing now, billowing black smoke now rising thousands of metres into the clouds.

'That should give the ships in orbit something to aim at, if nothing else,' Berhandt commented gruffly, switching his attention to the lascannon controls.

Jaeger spied a group of vehicles along the east wall and banked the Marauder smoothly towards them. More ground fire sprung up to meet them, sporadic at first but building in intensity until once more Raptor One was banging and clattering with impacts, and the air became iridescent with multiple las-blasts impacting into her thick armour.

'Just another couple of seconds,' Berhandt told him, and Jaeger could hear the grind and whirr of motors as the multi-barrelled anti-tank gun swivelled in its nose mount. A movement to Jaeger's right attracted the flight commander's attention and he look across, flicking his gaze between this distraction and the approaching canyon wall. It was a bright spark of blue, growing bigger very quickly. With a start, Jaeger realised it was an incoming missile.

'Oh s–' Jaeger's curse was cut off by an explosion just to his right and behind him. He heard Marte bellow in pain and Raptor One dipped suddenly to starboard, smashing Berhandt's head against his sighting array.

'We've lost the whole wing!' screamed one of his crew, the panicked wail making their voice unrecognisable.

'Into the saviour pod!' shouted Jaeger, punching free of his harness, and releasing the dazed Berhandt as the Marauder's erratic lurch tumbled him across the bombardier's chair. He could feel Raptor One plummeting down nose first and had to almost crawl his way up the fuselage. Ferix was there, ushering the others into the armoured compartment, and he saw Marte being bundled in by Arick, the old veteran's flight suit ripped to shreds, blood pumping from half a dozen shrapnel wounds in his chest.

Pushing Ferix and Berhandt in first, Jaeger grabbed the door. As he swung it shut he saw the ground screaming up towards him through the canopy. A las-bolt shattered the front screen and the wind howled in, almost wrenching the door from his grasp.

With a wordless, bestial snarl he grasped the handle with both hands and slammed it shut.

'Strap in, sir!' Arick pointed towards the empty seat.

'No time,' Jaeger replied, punching his fist into the release button. Explosive bolts ignited around the base of the pod, hurling it outwards from the doomed wreck of Raptor One. As it tumbled in flight, Jaeger was thrown onto the wall then the ceiling, before the pod steadied on its retro jets and he fell to the floor, dazed, his leg twisted, sending flares of pain up his spine.

'Are you–' Arick began to ask, but red filled Jaeger's vision and he heard rather than felt his head thump against the floor. The sound of his blood rushing through his ears filled his mind before unconsciousness swept through him.

JAEGER OPENED HIS eyes and winced as sunlight blinded him. He was sitting with his back to the saviour pod, out in the Mearopyis desert somewhere. Ferix was changing the bandages wrapped around Marte's chest, while Jaeger's own numb right leg was splinted, so he guessed it was broken. Arick noticed he was awake, and the young man crouched down in front of him, face solemn.

'Raptor One, there's nothing left of her.' The youthful gunner was almost in tears.

Jaeger gulped and gathered his thoughts. He pushed himself to his feet, wincing at the pain in his leg, and looked around. Just on the horizon was a massive plume of dust.

'Don't worry, it's the Guard advancing on the capital,' Arick reassured him.

'Other… other losses?' Jaeger asked quietly, keeping his eyes on Arick's.

'Two thirds of the Marauders are destroyed,' Arick's reply was hoarse, and this time there really was a glint of moisture in his eyes. 'Half the Thunderbolts. Seven pilots dead. Losark won't be getting any more kills, I'm afraid. Thirty-three other crew members dead. Fourteen wounded, including Marte who has shrapnel lodged in his spine, and you.'

'So, almost the entirety of the *Divine Justice's* flight complement destroyed,' sighed Jaeger bitterly. 'Was it worth it, Arick?'

'I think so, sir. You saved thousands of lives, by my reckoning,' Arick replied with a fleeting grin.

'I doubt the Imperial Navy will see it that way,' Jaeger answered with a heavy heart, already picturing his court martial. He sat down again and rested his chin against his chest for a moment, eyes closed against the harsh light. With another sigh he looked up at Arick, into his fresh, grey eyes. 'They'll hang me for this disaster.'

He gazed out at the distant army, rumbling towards the enemy capital, intent on recapturing this world. Was it worth it, Jaeger asked himself? He honestly didn't know.

FOR THE EMPEROR!

DEFIXIO
Ben Counter

'ORKS!' SCREAMED SOMEONE over the radio, and the concussions of the first crude shells rang through the ground into the reeking, cramped interior of the *Defixio*. Samiel shouldered the massive weight of the sponson's heavy bolter and squinted through the vision slit. He could see nothing of the ambush, just wisps of smoke drifting in from the front of the convoy, but he could already hear the confusion of noise building up – broken voices over the comms, dull thuds from up ahead, and the Exterminator crew around him getting to battle posts.

He was bad luck, they said. Samiel was beginning to think they were right.

'Crew, load up!' came Commander Karra-Vrass's voice over the rumble of the tracks and the ringing of explosions. Samiel glanced round to see Graek heaving the autocannon rounds into their chambers, gang tattoos rippling across his back. Above him, the skinny form of Damrid crammed itself into the turret gunner's chair.

'*Defixio* requesting target locations,' barked Karra-Vrass into the comms, but all he got was static shot through with screams. He turned back and shouted over the noise of the *Defixio's* engines. 'Crew, I want targets, now! Light armour and infantry priority!'

There was a vast, terrible, crunching explosion and Samiel's vision was filled with an orange-white sheet of flame billowing towards him.

He darted back from the sponson as a tongue of fire licked through the vision slit, his gas mask's intake suddenly choked with smoke and fumes. There was a hideous wrenching sound as Dniep gunned the engine and the *Defixio* ploughed through the wreckage of the shattered tank ahead of them.

'What the bloody hell was that?' bawled Karra-Vrass.

'Hellhound!' shouted back Samiel. 'They got Lucullo's Hellhound!'

Burning bodies tumbled across the dark earth outside, and Samiel was thankful he couldn't hear them scream.

'Targets!' The voice was Damrid's, up in the turret, bringing the *Defixio's* autocannons to bear.

Kallin, on the opposite sponson, opened up and suddenly the *Defixio's* interior was full of the staccato battering of the heavy bolter's reports, hot shell casings everywhere. 'Come get some, ya groxlickin' sons a' bitches!'

Karra-Vrass swung open the front hatch and put his head out to see what was happening.

When he came back down the side of his face was dark with soot. 'Get the halftrack!'

Samiel didn't hear over the din, but he knew that Damrid would be muttering a word to the Emperor, like he always did, just before the twin thunderclap of the autocannon blanked out the world for a split second.

All of *Defixio's* firepower was brought to bear on the orks apart from Samiel's sponson. He couldn't see the orks, and now thick smoke was sweeping across the valley from what must be half the convoy burning up ahead. It was choking the interior, too, but the crew barely noticed. Every breath a Chem-Dog took was drawn through a respirator or jerry-built gasmask, and most of them were used to breathing stuff that would kill most people.

Graek yanked the glowing-hot shells out of the breech and slammed another two home, and Kallin continued to fill the air with bursts of heavy bolter fire.

'Samiel, get me targets!' shouted Karra-Vrass. Unlike the rest of the crew his voice was unimpaired by ugly implants or a gas mask – Savlar aristos didn't have such things because back home they breathed clean, imported air.

'Nothing, sir!' replied Samiel, and even as he said it a monstrously crude jet intake sucked the smoke away and he was looking at the underside of the ugliest, squattest aircraft he had ever seen. It flew so low it must have clipped the vox aerial, sounding like a nuclear wind and followed by a score of rickety buggies, half-tracks and bikes crewed by insane greenskins, teeth bared and guns roaring. They barrelled down the side of the valley at astonishing speed and one of them slammed into the *Defixio's* side, so the tank slewed wildly and Samiel was thrown onto his back. Gunfire rattled along the *Defixio's* armour and Damrid swung the turret towards the horde.

Then, the roar of the dog-nosed fighter again as it spiralled down for another pass. This time cannon shells lanced down from above, ripped chunks out of the ground, and burst through Samiel's side of the *Defixio* like a hammer through glass. Samiel heard no noise, because the din had built up into a wall of white noise that filled his ears. Through the yawning hole in the tank's side he saw a swarming mass of greenskin maniacs sweeping down into the valley.

Samiel realised he had been blown clear across the tank's interior, and that Kallin's gun was still firing wildly even as the wall of white noise toppled over and everything went blank.

WHEN HE WOKE, all he saw was the grim grey sky of Jaegersweld. There was only one planet Samiel had seen uglier than this one, and that was Savlar itself. The Guard was supposed to be a way of getting off Savlar and the Dead Moons, with their chem-pits and convict-cities. All the Guard had done for him was drag him from planet to misbegotten planet, kill his friends, make him a jinx. Because he had been a sole survivor, he had used up more than his fair share of luck already and whoever had to serve with him next would have that little bit less luck to go round. Sole survivors were as unlucky as it got.

Still, he wasn't dead yet.

He sat up and felt the ache running down his limbs, and the sharp shots of pain where his skin had been hit by shrapnel. He took a breath of Jaegersweld's damp, unhealthy air, and heard the metallic sigh as it was forced through the implants inside his ribcage. Samiel's implants were more sophisticated than most, because those willing and able to work as administrators were worth keeping alive for longer than the average Chem-Dog. But the Guardsmen of the Savlar regiment, of course, had little respect for such skills.

They were towards the top of the valley slope. The *Defixio* stood nearby. The profile of the Exterminator-class battle tank was broken by all manner of salvaged and stolen bits Dniep had bolted on – armour plates, trophies, stowage. Kallin had tied a string of ork hands around his sponson mount, the freshest still glinting with moistness, the oldest shrivelled and rotted. The Savlar regimental markings were stencilled onto one side of the turret – on the other, splattered on in Dniep's loose hand, were the bold white letters that read *DEFIXIO*.

The tank had been sprayed in the drab brown-grey camouflage scheme common to everything on Jaegersweld, but the various shades of the bits and pieces bolted and tied on made it something very different from what must have rolled out of the factory on some far-flung forge world. Samiel was coming to realise that it was their tank now, their home and their protection as well as the weapon they were ordered to use. And because it was theirs, the crew made sure that in the process of repairing and maintaining it, they left it looking like it had been through its fair share of battles and firefights – they said almost everything had been replaced on the hulking vehicle, until it was almost entirely composed of what they had installed or repaired. The tank belonged to the crew far more than it belonged to the Imperial Guard, and that was just how the crew wanted it. Dniep himself was kneeling at the *Defixio*'s other side and welding a huge sheet of salvaged metal over the hole in the side armour, which would become one more battle wound carried proudly like a badge of honour.

'Looks like all yer luck's used up after all.' Samiel looked up to see Kallin standing over him. Kallin was a big guy, tall and broad-shouldered, with skin so appallingly pitted and eroded by the constant rain of chemicals he had lived through that Samiel had seen healthier-looking corpses. The unsophisticated respirator implants under his jaw confirmed he had grown up in the chem-mines of the Dead Moons, which was a feat in itself. 'Miracle we made it this far, with a jinx.'

'Save it for the greenskins, Kallin.'

Kallin stooped down and pushed his ravaged face close. The ork bones hanging round his neck jangled like wind chimes. 'You're a jinx, boy. One of them things sent down to plague us, like the greenskins ain't bad enough. Don't you start thinkin' we'll look out for you or miss you when you're dead. Graek's dead and we're on our way out, and it'll all be because we went and took in a jinx.'

'Graek's dead?'

Kallin indicated the loader's body, laid out in the shade of a rock, one side of his torso dark red and swollen under the tattoos. 'Dead as they come. Busted all his ribs, turned his guts to groxfood. Like I said, miracle if any of us make it now. Jinx and a Guild boy, Emperor's teeth.' He saw Samiel's confused frown, and smiled with a mouthful of teeth stunted from inhaling acidic air. 'You didn't know about Karra-Vrass? You know that damn stick he carries?'

Samiel nodded. Karra-Vrass always carried a silver swagger stick, but Samiel had assumed it was just a gimmick, like other officers insisted on wearing full dress medals or parade swords.

'It's a badge of office. Made of titanium. He's not just any aristo, he's from the Guild. When he's not playing soldier with a tank full of us plebs, the bastard sits in orbit and sells the filth we churn out of the Dead Moons. People like him worked everyone I know near to death. Most of us aren't even cons, we're second generation or more, but they don't care. Long as they keep the trade going, we're just machines to make them creds. Used up Graek like he used up half the men on the Dead Moons.'

When Karra-Vrass approached with Damrid, Samiel couldn't help noticing the shining swagger-stick the officer still held in his hand. In the other was a salvaged visor-scope, just one of the pieces of 'non-standard' equipment that tended to turn up in any Chem-Dogs vehicle.

'We're not rejoining the convoy,' said Karra-Vrass.

'Why not?' asked Dniep, looking up from his hurried weld job.

'Because it's not there. We lost about three-quarters strength in that ambush, and the tail-end must have retreated. We can't hook up with them because our comms are out and the orks have us cut off.'

'Then what do we do?' said Kallin, quick to anger. 'Wait for a greenskin patrol to skin us alive?'

'The nearest regimental HQ is the Cadian 24th, fifteen hundred kilometres west.'

'Three days across ork-held land?'

'Exactly, Kallin. I wouldn't like to think you were questioning this course of action.'

Kallin muttered something under his breath that Samiel was glad he didn't quite catch.

'Now, crew,' continued Karra-Vrass, 'since Samiel is back with us I think this is an appropriate time for a reading. Damrid?'

'Sir.' Damrid stepped forward, fishing a small prayer book from his ill-fitting fatigues. He began to speak of hope and duty, of how they were all sinners who wanted only to survive that they might redeem themselves in the Emperor's service. The words were familiar to Samiel, who had heard such things so often before in the chapels of the administrative colony where he had once lived. But he knew they were not meaningless, even if he had trouble believing them – devotion was the only thing keeping many Guardsmen sane. And even he, sometimes, found himself calling to the Emperor for help – especially when he fought his way out of a flaming wreck and felt the flames on his back as he leapt from the white-hot explosion behind him…

He was a sole survivor. Perhaps the Emperor had already heard him once, and wasn't ready to grant a miracle a second time. Maybe that was why he was supposed to be so unlucky.

Samiel and Damrid buried Graek's body quickly – orks were little more than animals, and they could home in on a spoiled corpse like any other beast. Samiel didn't object when Damrid rifled through his dead comrade's fatigues and pocketed the few trinkets and ammo rounds he found – he'd done the same himself, to friend and foe.

'Is it wrong…?' asked Damrid falteringly. 'Is it wrong to lose a fellow man and think we're better off without him?'

'I don't know,' replied Samiel. 'I didn't know him long.'

The last handful of damp earth was thrown over the dead man's face. 'You didn't want to. He was bad. The worst.'

'What did he do?' It wasn't a question that was generally asked of a Chem-Dog, for a man's crime was his own damn business. But Graek was dead, and he wasn't about to complain.

'A slaver. He ran with the… the uncleans. Some Arbites tracked him down, but he found them first, and when he finished with them they say you couldn't tell they had ever been human.

'And he never changed, that was the worst. He never saw the light. He never stopped hurting people. When we evacuated the civilians out of the south, he went missing for days, and after he came back we'd hear stories about families burned in bunkers and children hunted down for sport. They blamed it on the orks, but Graek had some… some things he kept. I think he was the worst sort of person.'

Samiel was grateful for an unhealthy shudder from the *Defixio*'s engines as they kicked protesting into life. 'Dunno if they'll hold together,' Dniep was saying. 'Fuel's not a problem, you can run a Leman Russ on boot leather and bad language. But she took a big hit back there and the track drives are looking shaky.'

'Will it last?' Karra-Vrass's voice was dispassionate – he must have known that his life depended on the *Defixio* not breaking down, but he didn't sound like it.

Dniep stood up, wiping the oil off his hands onto his stained fatigues. 'Three days? Be surprised, sir. But then again, sometimes even I get surprised by how much punishment these things can take.'

'Good.' The officer raised his voice. 'Burial detail, are you finished?'

Damrid raised a hand. He had rolled up the sleeves of his fatigues and for the first time Samiel noticed something – a tattoo, a skull surrounded by barbed wire, with a barcode underneath, at the top of the boy's arm. It was one of the many symbols branded on the fresh convicts brought in to keep up the population of the Dead Moons, which meant that Damrid wasn't second generation like Samiel had assumed. He was a con. What had he done, this boy? You heard tales of kids slung into the chemmines for stealing loaves of bread or failing to cheer when the planetary governor waved to the crowds. Poor lad. Life could be bad enough without being sentenced to a slow death when you were hardly old enough to know what right and wrong really were.

'And weaponry?'

'Loaded and ready,' came Kallin's voice from within the hull.

'Very well. The orks will have patrols out looking for survivors and we must not give them the chance to find us. We roll immediately.'

They clambered into the *Defixio*, Damrid into the turret to take the first lookout, with Karra-Vrass alongside Dniep at the front. Kallin and Samiel, meanwhile, slumped against the sponson mounts to catch some of the noisy, cramped downtime that passed for sleep on the move.

You CAN'T DREAM when you're not asleep, but it still felt like a nightmare. It wasn't that long ago it had happened, but he knew it would be burned across his mind's eye until he breathed his last. It was the reason he was on the *Defixio* at all, and the reason they all thought what only Kallin spoke – that Samiel was a jinx who had used up too much of his luck. His previous tank, an Executioner, had found itself surrounded and outnumbered by the light vehicles and bikes the greenskins rode like madmen.

He saw the billowing black-red of the fire and felt the heat across his face. He felt the cold earth against his back heating up as fuel spilled over the ground and rippled towards him, on fire.

He could see, as if they were in front of him right then, the silhouettes of his old crewmates, fire at their backs and orks at their front, blasting away with sidearms at their assailants. When the magazines had gone up from a lucky warbike shot the rear of the tank's hull had been torn off and Samiel had tumbled out while the burning wreck slid to a halt, and there his crewmates had made their stand.

Living on a planet like Savlar meant you valued every scrap of pride you scrounged, and the men who crewed the shattered tank weren't going to let themselves be taken prisoner by anyone or anything. Samiel watched as one was cut down by explosive shellfire, another ground beneath the wheels of a warbike that slewed insanely close.

And then the plasma coils went critical. An expanding globe of white-hot energised plasma, like a new star, incinerated the crewmen and burned a hole in the ork attack.

When the smoke cleared and the bodies were recovered, Samiel was the only one alive. His injuries were minor, and the orks hadn't even noticed him in the confusion. He heard them all say he was the luckiest Guardsman on the planet.

But they weren't smiling when they said it.

'No use, sir. Goes as far as I can see.' Samiel snapped out of his half-sleep, and once more he was back inside the stale hull of the *Defixio*. He knew something was wrong because the tank was only moving slowly now, and Karra-Vrass was replacing Damrid at the turret hatch.

Damrid dropped down onto the floor.

'What's happening?' asked Kallin, also jolted out of his own half-dreams.

'Minefield,' came the reply, and Samiel realised it was probably the worst possible answer. Orks made no attempt to conceal their mine-fields, but they laid a hell of a lot and didn't care if they lost a couple of their own to them, meaning the fields were always big with no way through. They also had a habit of packing them with so much explosive they left craters the size of command bunkers – current Guard wisdom was that the orks laid mines more because they liked the noise than for any strategic advantage.

Karra-Vrass came back down and pulled a folded-up map from inside his greatcoat. He laid it out on the floor – it showed the northern part of the continent across which the *Defixio* was trying to travel. Samiel saw just how far they had to go, and how much of the ground they had to cover was covered in the green markers of known ork camps and out-posts.

Karra-Vrass stabbed at the map with the end of his swagger stick. 'Dniep, is this our position?'

'Near enough.'

Between the *Defixio* and the Cadian HQ lay a plain bounded by con-tours – in the world outside, those contours were ragged, torn ranges of loose earth and landslides. No kind of country for a tank.

'The minefield will have no safe channels, and the high ground is not an option. However, the field is not particularly deep. Defusing is possi-ble.'

Everyone looked at Dniep. He had a knack with anything technical – Samiel had heard tell of the miracles he had worked with the stubborn Leman Russ engines, and no doubt he could have taught the Tech-Guard Engineers a thing or two about clearing mines. 'I could do it,' he said, with an uncharacteristic bravery that made Samiel realise just how desperate a situation they were in.

'What about patrols?' asked Kallin. 'We'd be waiting here for hours, the bloody greenskins could pick us off for fun.'

'Dniep could stay.' It was Damrid who spoke – by now all the crew were crowded around the map. 'If someone marked the mines first, he'd defuse them in half the time. We'd have a driver in case we got jumped. He'd have to go out and clear a path afterwards, but not for as long. We'd still be targets, but we'd have a better chance.'

'And we'd leave a man behind if we had to run for it,' added Kallin grimly.

Karra-Vrass began folding up the map. 'We're not leaving anyone. But we may find ourselves in a firefight a man short. We're already down a loader.'

'So, who do we need the least?' asked Dniep.

And this time, they looked at Samiel.

IT WAS DARK by then. Jaegersweld had two moons, one large and bright, but its light was filtered through many layers of ever-present cloud and a sickly, grey glow fell over the landscape. The minefield was obvious enough – some explosive-packed devices stuck above the ground, more of a challenge than a trap. But while they might have been animals, orks were a very cunning type of beast. They would have some buried so you couldn't see them, and those were the ones Samiel would have to spend a long time marking so Dniep's foray would be as short as possible.

Samiel told himself it could be done – it wasn't far across. And it cer-tainly had to be done, for the loose, muddy hills on either side would be near-impossible for the *Defixio* to clamber across, even with Dniep at the controls.

Hopping down from the front hatch, Samiel was acutely aware of just how exposed he was. Outside the tank, he felt soft and vulnerable.

Inside the tank he was on home ground, a tiny bubble of the Imperium around him. Now he was behind ork lines, and alone. He checked his gear – flare gun, bayonet (another of Dniep's 'finds'), a bag of spent shell casings to mark the mines.

It wasn't slow work, but there were a lot of mines, densely packed to make the huge chain explosions the orks liked so much. He looked up every now and again to check for glints of approaching machinery against the grey-black horizon, and listened for the juddering drone of an ork engine. Once or twice he heard the chatter of gunfire far off, but that might mean anything in an ork warzone – they could be launching a major assault or just taking pot shots at one another for fun.

That they were so difficult to predict was the worst thing, because you couldn't just herd them into killing zones or cripple their economic base or any of the other things that worked with good old-fashioned humans. The only thing that worked was hatred. There was no sympathy, no honour. You had to exterminate them, all of them, because they were seemingly designed to spring up again at the slightest chance. Samiel knew that war against the orks would never end – even if they were wiped off the surface of Jaegersweld, the Guard would just be packed off to the next planet that became infested, and it would begin all over again. For Samiel, it had become a case of getting out alive and hoping that some distant commander would grant him a plot on a conquered planet as reward for a lifetime of fighting, so he could let someone else do all the hating. But if he really had used up all his luck already, as the others suspected, then he didn't fancy his odds.

The sound that alerted him was the squeal of metal on metal as the *Defixio*'s turret turned to face something he couldn't see. Samiel looked around him – he was more than halfway across the minefield, a long trail of shell casings marking the hidden mines. The *Defixio* was too far away – if he ran for it now it would probably move before he got there and he'd be left standing in full view of whatever was attacking. He obeyed the first rule of the Imperial Guard, and kept his damn head down.

The autocannon fired and an explosion bloomed some way off. A group of vehicles was illuminated for the briefest moment – bikes, huge clunking things like battering rams on wheels with speeds limited only by the insanity of their riders.

Orks. They had been found, and now the greenskins were moving in for the kill. They were crazy, these bikers, but they were as dangerous as it got for a tank – they carried the crudest of explosives which could crack open a Leman Russ with ease. Samiel had seen it done. And now it was going to be done to the *Defixio*.

The red-hot exhausts and muzzle flashes were visible now as the bikers careered down the valley at tremendous speed, and the *Defixio* was moving.

It was heading the only way it could – towards the nearest ridge of surely impassable ground. Karra-Vrass was gambling on the tiny chance that the *Defixio* might make it, because the other chances were the minefield and the approaching orks, and those odds were worse still.

It wouldn't make it. No way. Kallin's sponson chattered away at long range at the bikes, and after a worryingly long wait (Damrid must be having to load it himself, thought Samiel, remembering Graek's shattered ribs) the autocannon fired again. Two bikes tumbled flaming to a standstill, but the others sheared through their wreckage and stayed on course.

The *Defixio* was at the foot of the ridge and began to climb, the loose earth already slipping under its tracks. The tank wouldn't have outrun the bikes at the best of times and now it was slower still, hauling itself painfully up the crumbling slope as the bikes roared around it, sweeping towards its near side. Samiels's sponson fired and the closest bike's front wheel was shredded, flipping the bike over and sending the ork rider somersaulting into the *Defixio*'s side. Samiel realised that Karra-Vrass himself must be manning the gun.

The officer's aim was good but there were only so many rounds he could squeeze off, and the lead biker threw a grenade, fuse sparkling, at the tracks as he slewed past. The explosion was loud even from where Samiel was lying and he saw links of track flying. Three more followed as the bikers passed, Karra-Vrass's gun still firing but blindly through smoke and shrapnel.

Samiel knew they didn't think much of him – in fact, they would probably have preferred one less gunner than a sole survivor and the misfortune he brought. But they were still his comrades, and they were still soldiers of the Imperium up against aliens. He couldn't just let them die.

He stood up, pulling one of the flares out of his bag, and lit it. When his eyes adjusted to the sudden glare he saw the lead biker had spotted the flash in the darkness and was wheeling in Samiel's direction, the others following.

Samiel considered dropping the flare and running – but ork mines were unstable and the weight of a man would set even the tankbusters off. His heart, already racing, quickened further when he realised that the safest thing he could do was stand his ground and face the bikers' charge.

'Come on, you green bastards! Come and get some!' he yelled over the roar of the bikes' engines.

It was probably the bravest thing he had ever done. Probably the last, too. Would anyone survive to tell the story of how he died? Could the crew in the *Defixio* even see what was happening? Samiel couldn't think of an answer because his mind was full of the bikes screaming towards him. He could see the lead bikers' bared teeth in the light from the flare, see the pinpricks of white in its tiny piggy eyes and the blur of the front wheel…

It was some way into the minefield when it careened straight into an anti-vehicle mine so scrappily made it stuck out of the ground half the height of a man. The noise was so vast Samiel was totally deafened, and a column of earth burst out of the ground. An instant later a huge chain explosion erupted with such force Samiel felt himself picked off his feet as the concussion hammered over him. He slammed onto the ground, breath knocked out of him, mind reeling, the whole world a swirling madness of white noise and explosions.

When the noise subsided and he opened his eyes, he saw the air thick with smoke coiling from a rip in the ground longer than the skid from a dropship crash. The wan moonlight made strange shifting shapes in the smoke, and the smell of burnt fuel was dizzying. A bike wheel, licked with flame, rolled slowly along the ground.

By the Emperor, thought Samiel, I'm alive.

I can't believe it. I'm alive.

Through his near-deafness he caught the ragged sound of an engine gunning and the smoke parted to reveal the last biker, blackened and battered with blood-flecked teeth bared, clinging to his bike as it tore towards Samiel through the blast zone. Samiel acted on reflex – he lashed out his gun and fired. It was then that he realised he was armed only with the flare gun.

The sparkling white flare spiralled towards the bike and shattered against the handlebars like a firework, leaving an incandescent comet trail as the bike hurtled forward. Samiel could see the ork's manic grin and the wicked squinting eyes behind its goggles, and knew he was going to die.

There was a massive wash of heat as the bike took off at the last second in a ball of flame, somersaulting over him and cartwheeling across the plain. The rider was thrown off, on fire, further into the minefield – Samiel covered his head just in time to protect himself from the inevitable shower of debris from another detonating mine.

Samiel watched as the flames guttered out. For the second time in half a minute he was quite astonished to be alive. He lay back on the ground, suddenly exhausted, and got his first real sleep for months.

'You ARE ONE lucky bitch, Chem-Dog.' The voice was Dniep's. It was morning, and the sun was flooding the dank valleys of Jaegersweld with drab grey light. Samiel felt he was propped up against the slope. He was aching again, but mostly unhurt.

'Them greenskin bastards cleared us a path,' continued Dniep. 'And that last one, you must've caught his fuel tank. Went up like a flare shell, saw it from here. Even Kallin was impressed.'

Samiel looked across to the minefield – there was indeed a scar running right across it, plenty wide enough for the *Defixio*.

Dniep scratched at the acned skin around his throat implants – he had escaped the worst ravages of the chem-mines because he had been too useful fixing the machines to risk at the workface, but he was still damned ugly. 'So you solved us one problem, Samiel, but now we got us another.' He indicated the hulk of the *Defixio*, smoke still coiling off it. The tracks on the near side had been unpinned and lay limp on the ground. 'We found enough links, but a coupla pins got sheared. Scavved one soon enough, but we can't find another. Not for the life of us. And it'll be our lives, too, 'cause we're stuck out here in the open with a tank that won't move and a bunch of greenskins wondering why their mates haven't come back.'

'You should have woken me, I could have helped–'

'Karra-Vrass said to let you sleep. And didn't none of us argue with him, neither. Besides, we're not going to find it. We need something thin enough to fit but strong enough to take the strain. Miracle we found one.'

But Samiel went out and looked anyway. It wasn't that he dared have any real hope – he just couldn't lie there and wait. The orks would come, he knew, because they had a knack for being everywhere on a planet at once, and many Guardsmen swore greenskins could hunt a man down by scent alone. He kept low and always checked the horizon for approaching orks, once or twice spotting something dark and moving and hitting the ground until he was sure it was gone. And, as he expected, there was nothing that might serve as a track pin half-buried in Jaegersweld's heavy earth, just metal fit only for scrap. There was no hope, but he didn't allow himself be consumed with the knowledge that he would die. Many a time he had heard better Guardsmen than him discover how slight their chances were, then shrug their shoulders and reply that hell, a man's gotta die somehow.

Nevertheless his steps were heavy and his head low as he clambered back over the ridge. And the sound he heard was engines.

He hurried down the loose slope to see the *Defixio* warmed up and ready to roll, smoke pumping from inefficient exhausts, trinkets and grisly trophies shaking with the unhealthy vibrations of the cylinders.

The front hatch went up and Kallin looked out. There were a few more scavenged trinkets around his neck and hanging from his various ammo belts and pouches – a Chem-Dog out foraging always came back with some new toys. 'Samiel, ya grox-lover! Get in!'

Samiel sprinted the last few metres and climbed in – the rest of the crew had been waiting for him. With a nod from Karra-Vrass, Dniep gingerly backed the Defixo off the slope. Then, it turned and headed across the wide channel across the minefield, towards the other side of the plain and the Cadian HQ beyond.

Samiel didn't ask what had been used as a track pin. Probably the axle off an abandoned ork vehicle, or even a direct replacement from

another wrecked Leman Russ tank, of which there must be some lying
around.

And then he realised that Karra-Vrass was no longer carrying his titanium swagger stick.

SAMIEL'S TURN AT the lookout came. The last day had been nervous but
hopeful – they had hidden under an overhang when a flight of smoking
ork flyers swooped overhead, and often lurked behind ridges and rock
formations as ork patrols passed close by. Karra-Vrass had told them they
were being hunted by orks eager to remove such an impertinent threat as
a tank that dared run their gauntlet, and the hunters were closing in. But
they had not been spotted, and time was on their side, because they were
nearing their destination.

'Maybe you're not as unlucky as you look, Samiel,' Kallin had said,
which were probably the most charitable words he had uttered in his life.

They now had to cross one last hill before the Cadian HQ was in sight.
There would be some explaining to do – where had they come from? Why
were they alone? Where was the rest of the column? The Cadians would
certainly make a point of packing away anything small and valuable
whenever the Chem-Dogs approached. But they would be able to eat,
maybe sleep, pull a few days light duties before someone figured out how
to get them back to the Savlar regiment.

Samiel didn't fancy the *Defixio* to make it, with a half-busted track and
a hole in the side, especially since a constant supply of Leman Russ spares
was always required. The Cadians would probably break the old Exterminator up and use the bits to patch up their own vehicles in the motor
pool. But even Dniep thought it was a better end than a smouldering
wreck in the middle of a planet no one really cared about.

And now they were at the crest of the hill, the flats beyond rolling out
before Samiel's eyes, the Cadian HQ finally coming into view…

A grinning, lopsided horned skull totem, cut from sheets of metal and
bolted together, stood on the roof of the command bunker. Burned-out
Leman Russ and Chimeras littered the compound. A Hydra flak cannon
stood idle at one corner, pointing down and inwards, barrels still blackened from the fire it had poured into the attackers streaming through the
breaches.

Bodies of men and orks lay in piles around the centres of the heaviest
fighting – the breach, the gateway, the mess and barracks complex where
the men had made their stand. Where the fuel dump had been was a
charred crater ringed with corpses. Buildings and bunkers had been
turned inside-out by demo charges, their contents – furniture, equipment, occupants – strewn across the ground. Those structures still
standing bore scars around windows and doors that had been used as fire
points. Bodies in Cadian fatigues were displayed entwined in the razor

wire that topped the rings of barricades and fences. Everywhere were bullet scars, discarded weapons, and the dead. Especially the dead.

But the worst was outside. All around the HQ was a teeming city of tents and huts, brimming with greenskins. They fought, argued, divided the spoils and feasted on the supplies they had hauled out of the HQ's stores.

The mad bikers that had so taken to Jaegersweld's landscape were buzzing like flies around the camp, eagerly burning captured fuel in pursuit of the blind speed they lived for. Camp fires smouldered, and the breeze brought the reek of burning and filth.

'Can you see it?' called out Damrid from below.

'Stop,' said Samiel.

The *Defixio* ground to a halt. Damrid was the first out, scrambling over the turret seat and pushing his head out of the hatch.

'Imperator...' he whispered, one hand held to the pocket in which he carried his prayer book. 'Xenos malefica... what about forgiveness? Hasn't it been enough?'

Damrid slithered back into the *Defixio*'s hull. Dniep replaced him, eager to see what had caused such shock in his crewmate.

'Those bastards,' he said when he saw. 'Alien bastards. We shoulda known.'

Samiel didn't know what to say. What can you say, when even what little hope a Guardsman allows himself is torn away?

'So that's what broke the lad,' continued Dniep, more to himself than to Samiel. 'He thought he was forgiven, he really did. That's why he never called you bad luck, like the rest of us. The Emperor was watching, he thought, because he had been forgiven.'

'For what?'

Dniep looked at him incredulously. 'No one told you? Damrid's the worst! I mean, I did fixin' for some pretty rough types, and a few people got hurt, and but I never–' Dniep shook his head. 'The lad was on a frontier world, raising hell since he was born. When they sent a mission to tame the place, Damrid and his boys took exception. You know his prayer book? Used to belong to a Sister there. They say that as Damrid was hacking the poor bitch to pieces all she could say was: "He will forgive you. He will forgive you..." over and over. Threw her to the cudbears when they'd finished with her. He started reading the damn book on the prison ship, and by the time he got to the Dead Moons he got it into his head he was forgiven.'

Damrid? It didn't make any sense... but then, sometimes there was a desperation about the way he believed, as if his faith was his only chance and he had to hold onto it no matter what... 'He doesn't look like he went through the Dead Moons.'

'They kept him safe. A chaplain who believes, that's the rarest thing in the system. Worth keeping alive. And when the Guard said they were raising up another Chem-Dog regiment, he was first in line, ready to fight the Emperor's fight and smite the foes of Humanity.' Dniep shook his head and whistled at the sight of the orks running wild across the Cadian HQ, making belts of skin and necklaces of hands. 'And now this. He should've made it. Really should've. Kid like him, just getting through it all without breaking up, that's like winning the war on your own.'

When they had all looked upon the remains of the Cadian HQ and its slaughtered garrison, they slumped down inside the *Defixio* and were silent.

Suddenly Kallin slammed a fist into the side of the hull. 'For this we fight? We drag this lump of metal across a whole damned bitch of a planet and this is what we get?'

They all looked at him, and Samiel wished he would stay quiet, but like the rest of them Kallin had felt hope building up during the journey's last leg and he couldn't cope with having it torn away from him. His voice was rising to a screech. 'Why now? Why couldn't they take the place a month earlier, or a month later, or any time but now? They can't... what happened? Can't these damn Cadians even look after their own HQ?'

Kallin slumped, suddenly exhausted. Dniep spoke weakly, his voice cracking. 'The Jurn regiment is supposed to be south, past the gulf. If we can get down there, and cross it–'

'No.' Karra-Vrass's voice was strong. That was why he was an officer, thought Samiel grimly. He was as broken as the rest of them, but he could conceal it. 'We would be passing through the ork drop sites. When we are found here we will be executed quickly, for we are on the frontier and prisoners would use up too many supplies. If we break for the south we will be imprisoned, enslaved, probably used as playthings, and then we will die anyway. The gulf cannot be crossed, there have been enough prisoners that have tried.'

'So what then?' Kallin's voice was like a child's. Samiel was almost sure he was weeping. 'We die?'

Karra-Vrass looked at him. 'We die.'

'Everybody dies.' Samiel realised that he was the one speaking.

'The truest of things,' replied Karra-Vrass. 'All lives end.'

'So it is willed,' said Damrid. His face was pale as a dead man's and he had a faraway expression. It was said a man could gain a place at the Emperor's side by his conduct when all seemed lost, for even in the moments of the most terrible desperation, He was watching, He was judging.

This was Damrid's last chance. If he died well, maybe that would mean he'd be forgiven, after all.

'But how many know when their time comes?' continued Karra-Vrass. 'How many can see the end coming, and be prepared? Not many. Of all those of our brothers-in-arms who died, only we can ready ourselves. It is in death, more than anything, that a man can be measured. Isn't that right, Damrid?'

'So it is willed,' said the boy again.

'Their patrols will catch up with us within the hour. Their camp sentries will be onto us long before that. We don't have much time, but it will be enough. We have been given the greatest gift that any man could ask, for now we have a purpose. We will spend the rest of our lives battling the alien foe, not because we are ordered or because we must, but because we choose to do so, to make our deaths mean something. It could be otherwise – we could die in flight, or cowering, or under the slaver's whip. But we will not.'

Samiel looked up. It shouldn't mean anything, for still they were all dead men. But somehow, it did. They could butcher his friends, strip away his hopes, wage a war that forced him to spend his life in exhaustion or fear cooped up in a tank on a planet he hated. They could turn him into no better than a bad seed. But by the Emperor himself, those greenskin bastards couldn't make him die for nothing.

He was on his feet, shivering with excitement and pride. Karra-Vrass stood, too, and smoothed out the creases in his greatcoat.

'Crew, load up,' he said.

Every Savlar vehicle was equipped with hermetic seals around the hatches and doors – these they sealed, so that even breathing the same air as the Chem-Dog crew would be a privilege the orks would have to fight for. Karra-Vrass took off his officer's greatcoat, rolled up the black sleeves of his uniform, and slammed two autocannon shells home into the breech. Damrid calmly recited those hymns that meant the most to him – the ones about never despairing, because every good man has his place in His plan, even if that man in his humility knows it not.

Karra-Vrass checked his sidearm, a duelling pistol that somehow he had managed to keep hold of even though its ivory handle and fine workmanship would have caught the eye of the most honest Chem-Dog. The others did the same with weapons they had as trophies or charms – Kallin's ugly snub-nosed gun looted from a dead ork, a shotgun Dniep hid under the driver's seat, a rusted sergeant's sword Damrid had kept. A rummage through the *Defixio*'s gear produced an old but working laspistol, which Samiel took.

This is the last gift I will ever receive, he thought. It felt like the first.

They did not have long to wait. As darkness approached once again, a greenskin foot patrol approached from the camp. Perhaps fifty strong, they stalked low in the gathering gloom, led by one a head or two taller than the rest, one arm hacked off and replaced with a brutal three-fingered claw that spat sparks from a power field. They had axes, guns, clubs.

Kallin whispered sharply to Karra-Vrass – from his vision slit, he could see one of the bike patrols that had been hunting them approaching fast from the opposite direction. They were trapped.

Good, thought Samiel. If you've got to go, then this is the way to do it.

Karra-Vrass glanced up at Damrid. The lad nodded back.

'Fire,' said Karra-Vrass.

The twin explosions burst in the midst of the orks, blasting two or three to flailing limbs. Some tried to scatter but the leader grabbed a couple by the scruffs of their necks, flung them forward, pointed with his monstrous claw and bellowed a command that could only be the charge.

They ran forward brandishing their weapons. Samiel heard Karra-Vrass roll the smoking casings out of the breech and haul another two shells in, as strongly and smoothly as Graek had done.

'Range?' called the officer, voice strained with the effort of forcing the breech cover home.

'Close!' shouted back Damrid.

'Fire!'

The two blasts merged into one as a hole was torn out of the advancing patrol. Some were thrown forward to collide with their fellows in the front, and two of them were thrown into the air in bits. Samiel took the opportunity – slowed down and in disarray, the leader cracking two heads together to stop his troops from fleeing, the patrol was a fine target. He opened up with his heavy bolter, seeing orks stitched through with explosive shells, illuminated in the muzzle flare. Two or three more went down, and the charge was halted. Now Dniep crunched the gears and the *Defixio* turned towards the orks.

Samiel kept firing, keeping ork heads down, and he could hear the wet crunch of greenskins going under the *Defixio*'s tracks.

Kallin was already firing on his side, meaning the bikers were almost upon them. The foot patrol blazed away with every chance they were given, and shells were impacting fiercely on the *Defixio*'s hull. The noise was appalling, for the orks liked their weapons loud – but Samiel didn't care. They could make all the noise they wanted, they weren't taking down these Dead Moon scummers without the hardest fight of their lives. His heavy bolter roared with the defiance he felt boiling inside him, and another ork was run through on a lance of hot steel.

There was a sound like a thundercrack as a crude ork grenade went off, buckling the metal patching the hull at Samiel's side. Shells ricocheted off the edge of Samiel's vision slit, but he didn't flinch. His ammo belt was running out and Karra-Vrass rammed another one into the heavy bolter's breech. Samiel glanced at him in gratitude, saw the officer understood, and went back to firing. He could barely see the targets now, his vision was full of a heaving press of green flesh as the orks tried to swamp the *Defixio*.

Another grenade went off and Kallin swore, his heavy bolter torn off its mounting by the explosion. Without pausing he grabbed his ork gun and opened fire at the talons clawing at the breached hull. Samiel could hear the bikes now, even above the rest of the din, as the riders dismounted and added their weight to the assault.

There was a shriek of metal and suddenly the *Defixio* was open to the sky – the lead ork was standing over them, power claw holding the turret he had just ripped clean off the tank. Damrid tumbled back down into the hull, grabbed the sword and began to hack at the green arms and heads that appeared over the edge of ragged metal. Kallin's side gave way seconds later and he was fighting back the encroaching greenskins with his bare hands, ammo expended.

One of the greenskins got Dniep, an axe swinging down and burying itself in his back. Karra-Vrass opened fire with his duelling pistol, each shot hitting home, and Samiel followed suit, laspistol bolts burning into green skin. He heard Kallin yelling obscenities as he was dragged through the hole in the hull by a dozen clawed hands, and Samiel felt sure Kallin would have wanted to go out swearing.

The massive ork reached down and grabbed Damrid in its claw, hoisting him clean out of the tank, shearing through the boy's skinny body, tossing him aside, roaring its rage and showing its huge fangs. Karra-Vrass grabbed an autocannon shell and rammed it into the monster's mouth with the strength of a man who knows he has run out of time. The ork swiped at him with the power claw, batting him aside, and shots from the swarming orks tore into the officer's torso.

Samiel snatched up Dniep's discarded shotgun. He could feel the greenskins all around him, teeth biting into his legs, claws sinking into his shoulders. But there was no pain, not at the end, not while he still had his mark to make.

He fired a single round from the shotgun, aimed right into the face of the immense ork leader. With a roar like the end of the world the auto-cannon shell lodged in its jaw detonated, blowing the beast's head clean off, tearing a huge chunk out of its monstrous body. It swayed, as if it hadn't realised it was dead – then it fell.

Knowing that he had died giving as good as he had got, his heart pumping sheer glory through his veins, Samiel fell under the heaving mass of greenskins and felt no more.

'You're a lucky swine,' said the voice. It wasn't Savlar – the accent was different. 'Well enough to talk?'

'Just.' Samiel was surprised to hear his own voice replying. He opened his eyes – Jaegersweld's sunlight was never very bright, but he still squinted after so long…

Asleep? Unconscious? Dead?

The shadow in front of him became the shape of a man. A lined face and grey hair, dressed in Cadian fatigues. A colonel, Samiel saw from the chevrons on his shoulder.

'You mind telling me what happened here, son?'

'Ran into some orks, sir.' Samiel could hardly believe he was speaking. He had thought he must be dead before, twice… but this time he had been certain. He had been there waiting for it, and when it came he faced it and refused to let it take him without a fight.

He struggled into a sitting position. Behind the colonel was the smoking shell of the *Defixio*. He wouldn't have recognised it as a tank at all had he not spent the last, greatest moments of its life inside it. Skeletons surrounded it, just as charred.

The massive jawbones and beetling craniums of orks were everywhere, with a couple of human skulls that had once belonged to his comrades.

'Took a lot of them with you. Must've thought you were dead, eh?'

'I was sort of counting on it, sir.'

'Like I said, one lucky swine. Fuel tanks went up and threw you clear. Week or two with the Sisters in the field hospital and you'll be back in action.' The colonel looked over Samiel's tattered fatigues, and the gas mask that hung round his neck. 'You from Savlar?'

'Yes, sir.'

'Steal anything and we'll hang you.'

'Yes, sir.'

Samiel could sit up but he couldn't walk – one leg was busted so bad he couldn't feel it. As he was loaded onto a stretcher he could see the rest of the Cadians clearing up the debris of the ork camp they had overrun in recapturing their HQ. The ork totem was being taken down from the roof of the command bunker, and the bodies lined up in mass graves.

Nothing Karra-Vrass had said was true. His friends (they were his friends in those final hours, without a doubt) had died no better deaths than the hundreds of Cadians days earlier, or the poor souls killed when the convoy was hit. They hadn't achieved anything, not really – the war on Jaegersweld would carry on without them. The Imperium was exactly the same as it would have been had none of them ever lived.

But that wasn't the point. They felt they were achieving something in death. Even Karra-Vrass believed his own words, of that Samiel was sure. They believed they were dying for a cause, they had been allowed to confront their deaths head-on and not have it finding them without warning as they cowered alone. How many Guardsmen on Jaergersweld could say that?

It was a terrible place, this galaxy, that ate up the lives of men. But sometimes, there was hope. Sometimes, there was something you could salvage from it, some dignity and pride, even if it was right at the end. It was more than most men got in the Guard, or on the Dead Moons, or anywhere else. Samiel couldn't properly understand it himself. But the crew of the *Defixio* had won a fine and noble victory of their own.

Now, of course, Samiel was a sole survivor twice over, and it would be a miracle if anyone would ever so much as look at him without muttering something dark under their breaths about how that man had used up enough luck for a hundred men. But there were worse things. In fact, he had something to be proud of – he had died a total of three times now, and two of those were pretty good send-offs. That wasn't a bad strike rate.

The Cadians began to carry him back to the HQ compound, through the wreckage of the ork camp. One of the stretcher-bearers glanced round at him, and must have wondered why, when he had a shattered leg and every one of his friends was dead, all this crazy Savlar kid could do was smile to himself.

ANCIENT LANCES

Alex Hammond

A DRY HEAT slid over the barren wastes with the rising of the sun. As light pushed at the edges of the darkness, the shadows fell away to reveal the dead in their many hundreds. Dakat City was nothing but rubble and corpses. Broken steel and concrete lay spread out on the baking sand. Only carrion insects moved about the devastation, nibbling on flesh, darting across dead eyes.

Al'Kahan looked out across the sea of carnage. His eye did not blink. Heavy artillery must have pounded the city for hours. The bunkers were torn open. The network of hives beneath the city would be running with blood. It would pool in the lower places. The smell of it would remain there forever.

His mare stirred beneath him. She had a heart of iron but liked the slaughter of innocents no more than he. Al'Kahan turned to face his men. Veteran tribesmen all, they were the best sons his home world had to offer. Each should know his steed as well as his steel. The philosophy of his people. The horse was their kin, their companion. Without it they could never prevail.

The battalion looked across at Al'Kahan, their dark eyes and rough hearts moved by the scene before them. They wore the marks of their clans upon their cloaks, carved from bone and stitched onto the hides of great bison. Beads of honour hung from their beards, holding the complex plaits in place. Al'Kahan spoke, his voice breaking the stillness of the spent battlefield.

'This is our first and last day. Last, for we shall no longer be sworn to the sword of the Imperium. First, for we shall die or succeed. To die is to pass on to the plains of our ancestors, to join them in the great hunt. To succeed is to be given a world to make our own.'

Al'Kahan stood upon the back of his horse, so that he could see the entire body of men. Lifting his eye patch he spoke. 'We own each battle. It has cost us one and all, brother man and brother horse. We are the Sons of Atilla. Our destiny stands before us.'

Al'Kahan dropped into his saddle and pulled hard on his reigns. His mare stood high on her hind legs and kicked at the air. In a second, the silence was broken for the last time on that day. Two hundred hooves struck the ground in unison, sending carrion beetles scrabbling and used shells flying. Al'Kahan's Atillan Rough Riders were on the move again.

They swept over the broken lands, skirting between battlefields. As they rode, they found only the dead, but the tracks of their enemies were all too clear. Heavy tanks and many infantry: this was an enemy unconcerned with subterfuge, an army of fire and iron.

'Honourable Al'Kahan?' A giant tribesman, Tulk, rode beside him, livid face scars denoting many kills.

'Speak, brother.'

'Those who lead the Prakash XIIth have made contact. They're being surrounded. Cut off on the salt flats. They will make their stand there.' Tulk grunted in disdain.

'They will fall if surrounded.'

'If the spirit of the hawk is with us, we may have speed enough to aid them,' the large tribesman said, looking to the sky.

'Indeed, if we fight with our ancestors by our side we could break the enemy's line. Create a weak point, from which they may make their push. Use the communicator: let them know that the sons of Atilla will save their hideless backs once again.'

CRESTING AN EMBANKMENT, the riders looked out over the Great Lake. Its life blood dried up, it shimmered in the haze of a high sun. A dark column snaked like a viper across the salt flats, heading inexorably for a much smaller, ragged mass. Al'Kahan paused briefly, his men arriving close beside him as he looked through binoculars at the forces ahead. He turned and called out.

'The enemy artillery is their key. Like a fist from heaven it has smashed every settlement we have passed. We must outflank it and destroy it. Our ancestors are with us today, this I know for a wind has travelled with us across this barren land. Feel it at your heels when you strike for their heart.' Al'Kahan raised his lance and readied it in the harness of his saddle. 'Save your lances for their artillery. Do not engage their main force. Ride like the wind, my brothers.'

Al'Kahan let out a deep, wordless cry, his voice holding strong. The riders followed suit, their voices rising high above the thick heat. Al'Kahan felt a shiver pass through his bones, electric like the thrill of a kill. His lance felt good in his hand, like it had always been there. He was first to break the war cry and set his steed to battle. The pounding of the hooves rang about the great expanse. Tulk screamed their position down the communicator array on his back. A flare from the Prakash XIIth rose high into the air. A reply signal, they were prepared.

Al'Kahan's heart felt as though it was keeping pace with the rushing horses. The closer the enemy, the tighter he gripped his reins. His cloak spun and twisted in the air about him. His eyes wept with the sting of the rising salt from the flats and the wind in his eyes.

A shell landed close by. It sent a horse and rider spiralling through the air, the mare whinnying as it slammed to the ground. It died on impact. Its rider fell beneath a hundred hooves. Honed in battle craft the men spread wide. Another shell fell amidst them, its shrapnel slicing flesh and fur. But artillery fire could not compete with the riders' speed.

They were closing on their greatest threat. Ahead, foul Chaos Marines, their ancient armour warped and corrupt, skirted like giant cockroaches behind their machines. Here they nested, chittering, calling and screaming in a language that bore into Al'Kahan's skull, as though it was trying to devour him. All around them, screaming hordes of cultists howled insane hymns to their warped masters.

Al'Kahan's warrior's heart shuddered to look upon them all. He gripped his studded reigns tighter, letting the iron studs tug at his flesh. The pain helped distract him from the abominations ahead. Airborne jet bikes tore the sky apart as they ripped forward from within the enemy's column. Lasfire and bolter shells began to rain down upon the riders. Men were thrown from their horses, the beasts remaining riderless within the charge. Al'Kahan leapt the body of a dead horse, its skull ruptured, a rider trapped beneath it.

The first of the riders had reached the enemy's line. They did well, their steeds ploughing through the line of cultists. Some were cut down, spurts of blood slicing through the air like jets of steam.

Tulk led a second wave. His men had stowed their lances in favour of lasguns. Every shot rang true, but few penetrated. In answer, hot metal shells ploughed into his unit. Horses fell, colliding with one another on their way to the ground. A few riders were able to leap free, but most were cut down or crushed beneath their mounts, their bodies dropping like building blocks smashed aside by a child. Their momentum had been stopped. Men had to take cover behind the dead and dying. The Chaos hordes cared only for the spilling of blood, and rained fire upon dead and living alike.

Al'Kahan wheeled around and drove his unit hard towards his fallen comrades. To remain stationary in battle was to offer victory to the enemy. Vaulting the piled dead, Al'Kahan rode along the Chaos line. He swung his lance like a staff, keeping its explosive tip from striking. The fallen raiders took his cue and charged at the enemy. Atillans rushed the armoured Chaos Marines, their furs soaked in blood. Many were thrown high by the sheer force of the enemy's powered armour, but a few blows found their mark.

'We're slowing!' Al'Kahan cried, circling the fray and rounding up those riders who remained mounted. The ground shook, and for all but a moment, cultist and rough rider alike paused. Barbed tanks, bristling with weapons and equipped with savage scythes and ploughs, began to advance upon the Imperial Guard.

'Pull out! Move, damn you!' Al'Kahan called, leaning down from his saddle to snatch at the grasping hand of a fallen raider.

'Thank you, brother.'

Tulk, Al'Kahan's lieutenant grinned back at him, his sharpened teeth streaked with his own blood. It welled up from a gash on his tattooed face, a fresh memento of this battle and one that Tulk would certainly cherish.

'They're not too tough once you've cracked them open!' he grinned.

The enemy tanks were almost upon them. Men were still trying to scramble free of the fray onto stray horses and the backs of their colleagues.

Al'Kahan swore. 'We need time.'

'It would be an honour, Al'Kahan,' Tulk said.

Al'Kahan kicked hard into the flanks of his horse and rode high over the mounting dead. He charged straight towards the first of the tanks. Flanks dripping with sweat and blood, Al'Kahan's mare struggled forward, irregular hoof falls alerting him to her waning strength.

'One more charge, daughter of Atilla,' he called to her.

Tulk stood upon the horse's back, arms steadying himself against Al'Kahan. He snatched a bulging satchel from the saddle and crouched. Al'Kahan rode alongside the approaching tank, its cruel blades spinning but an arm's distance away. Tulk paused for a moment only, then the giant tribesman flung himself forwards onto the grinding vehicle. Al'Kahan kicked at his mount and they burst forwards, throwing salt high into the air as they galloped around the rear of the machine. Tulk scrabbled up the top of the tank and threw himself back as a hatch burst open. Al'Kahan snatched a throwing disc from his belt. He threw the blade with abandon, not caring whether he cut down the Marine or gave Tulk a painless death. It ricocheted off the hull and up into the cultist's face. The man fell, gun pumping, back into the tank's innards. Amid screams, the vehicle spun wide and bucketed right. Tulk pulled a grenade from the satchel and popped its pin. He threw it deep into the machine and looked about, wild frenzy in his eyes.

Al'Kahan spurred his mount on. Tulk threw himself down a little ahead of his comrade. An explosion ripped the tank open, throwing Tulk into

Al'Kahan's horse's flank. All three collapsed to the ground. Two more tanks pressed onwards. Dazed, Al'Kahan turned, trying to catch sight of his men. A dull pain at the base of his spine drew his attention to his legs, trapped beneath the horse.

'Tulk?' The tribesman did not stir. The tanks rumbled on towards the Atillan commander. Al'Kahan scrabbled desperately at the satchel at Tulk's side but could not reach it. He reached back and caught hold of his lance. Using it, the Atillan prodded gently at the satchel, praying the explosive tip would not trigger, setting the grenades off. The surface of the salt flats came away in large plates as the satchel dragged slowly towards him. The noise of the tank filled his entire body. Al'Kahan slowly drew the satchel close enough to open.

The shadow of the tank fell across him. Scythes and blades cut up the corpse of Tulk, harvesting flesh. Al'Kahan drove his hand deep into the satchel and pulled a pin. At the same moment, he braced the lance hard against the carved insignia on his armoured breastplate. Al'Kahan threw the satchel beneath the lead tank and let the vehicle's plough catch the tip of his lance. Flame and sulphur engulfed him for an instant as the lance tip detonated, throwing him backwards and away from the exploding tanks.

Al'Kahan floundered, tumbling backwards across the salt flats, unable to slow his momentum. He prepared for the sharp, crushing pain of hooves. Instead he found himself wrapped in something soft. The smell of home... fried bison and corn bread. Was this the hereafter?

Al'Kahan opened his eyes. Wrapped about him was a thick fur cloak. He had been scooped from the ground, two young riders supporting him between horses.

'We have you, honourable commander,' a young rider with tangled braids said.

'A steed! I need a fast mare. We must destroy their artillery,' Al'Kahan wheezed.

'Great commander–'

'I know I'm wounded. My chest is pierced, my life blood falls to the soil. If we do not fight we will lose this battle and my name will be dishonoured. Better to die than to live dishonoured.'

Ten more riders arrived to regroup, some carrying additional men.

'Gather the lances! And get me a horse!' Al'Kahan screamed.

An Atillan dismounted while others circled, sweeping down from their saddles to snatch up the unused lances of fallen riders. They lay, scattered like kindling, across the battlefield, daring the foolish to tread upon their explosive tips.

Al'Kahan propped himself up in a saddle. The sucking wound in his chest was like a blow hole, gouting forth blood and pain.

'Son of Atilla,' Al'Kahan called to the dismounted rider. 'Get behind me. Take your clan tassels and hold them hard to my wound.'

The rider held Al'Kahan tight, his grip stemming the flow. 'You hold my old life in your hands. Quite literally.' Al'Kahan coughed, feeling his life's blood wearing thin.

No cry was given. In this moment, actions spoke louder than any horn. Al'Kahan spurred the new steed forwards, the young warrior on his back bracing his wound and bearing several lances. The remaining riders followed suit, their steeds catching up with the old commander. They spread out with an unspoken synchronicity, pulling alongside one another. A line of riders, thirty strong, churned the earth as they flung themselves hard at the enemy.

'Ready lances!' Al'Kahan commanded. The artillery loomed closer. It was larger than he had expected. Giant cannons pointed skywards, seeming to stroke the bellies of the clouds. Mortars with gates as dark as the mouth of the warp grinned like daemons. Tracked platforms churned up the ground beneath them, ripping huge trenches into the ground. These machines were eager to belch their deadly shells upon the good men of the Emperor.

As they rode, the Atillans passed the lances from hand to hand with spider-grace. All were equipped twice over. The Chaos Marines and their cultist forces caught sight of the rough riders. They scrambled low across the ground, throwing themselves hard behind the rare pieces of cover that jutted, like blast craters, from the ground.

'Steady!' Al'Kahan called, air escaping both from his mouth and the wound. His head spun, oxygen depleted.

A barrage of laser and lead whipped across the riders. Explosions from mortars and grenades rent the ground.

'Now!' Al'Kahan cried. On this mark, every man slid effortlessly to the right side of his horse, bodies pressed flat against his steed's flanks. Some horses were hit, some fell, but more rode on.

'For Atilla!' one warrior cried as the cavalry swept high and hard over the enemy lines. Ignoring their assailants, the riders doubled their speed. The pounding of hooves echoed deep into the earth. Sweat and blood were swept from horse and man, leaving thin red wakes in the shimmering heat. The riders lowered their lances. Artillery crews, still scrambling to load their cannons, scrambled for hand weapons. The Atillans let forth a single war cry, twenty sounding as though they were a hundred.

The explosive-tipped lances found their marks. Thick iron plates were torn from machines, hulls dripping with wires, gutted. Explosion after explosion, like a string of firecrackers, burst out across the battlefield. Rounds of ammunition, like rain from the heavens, filled the air. Al'Kahan threw grenade after grenade at stockpiles of munitions. The rear of the Chaos army was engulfed in cleansing flame. Burning tracks and fragments of metal still fell as the Atillans moved on to cut down the fleeing.

AL'KAHAN RAN HIS hands across his chest. It had healed well. The scar was impressive, the largest on his battle-worn torso. The soft sounds of the battlecruiser filled the room. Transparent plasteel windows, like the hollow eyes of the dead, looked out across the stars. Al'Kahan stared at a sharp blue nebula, crackling with lightning and flame. The lulling hum of the starship's engines and the glorious scene before him made Al'Kahan almost long to remain in deep space, almost.

He looked down a the large Imperial Eagle that hung from his chest from chains of gold. He could feel its weight through the layers of fur and hessian he wore. His cloak bore further trophies and medals, their shining metal like strange ticks amongst the pelts. Al'Kahan considered his reflection in the window. Broad plainsman's hat, trimmed with fur, single wild warrior's eye, long braided hair. He could hardly distinguish between his dark black locks and the snow leopard's mane he wore about the top of his cloak. Both were worn with age and dark from a thousand blood stains.

'Commander!' A voice from behind.

Al'Kahan turned about slowly. A commissar; dark leather coat, black peaked cap, trimmed and adorned with silver skulls; eyes like flint.

'Commander. I trust you have healed.'

'Indeed, Commissar Streck.'

'Your Imperial Seal fits you well.' The commissar turned towards the window.

'It feels good about my neck.'

'As well it should. You have served the Emperor well.' The commissar worked a crank, shielding the window and throwing the room into neon bright.

'A hundred battles.'

'Time for you to take your place as lord of your own province on Dagnar II.'

'I look forward to such an honour.'

'Really?'

'I could be no less certain.'

'Interesting. I thought your people longed for their homeworld more than any other. The Ice Warriors of Valhalla long for the sun, the Alderian Shock Fighters hate their deathworld, the Gorchak Fire Sentinels thirst. But the Atillans never tire of hunting bison, warring amongst their clans... or at least that's what the Adeptus Ministorum have always held.'

'I'm sure they have their reasons.'

'Most assuredly.' Commissar Streck turned and made to leave the room, then paused. 'However... you have an irregular choice. In three days we will

dock with your home world. A unique opportunity. We need to take on
new steeds and other supplies for your founding, then head off to Dagnar
II, and from there on to Olstar Prime. If you were to stay you would not be
dishonoured. You could return to your hunting grounds.'

'Why?'

'Let me simply say that I have long maintained that with time a warrior
of the Emperor comes to know only battle. I look forward to being able to
prove this in a report to the Ministorum. A... test case, if you will.'

'I see.' Al'Kahan looked down at the seal on his chest.

'The ship will dock for a week only,' Streck said. 'You have your Emperor's
blessing.'

'ONE WEEK, COMMANDER,' Commissar Streck called from across one of the
many loading bays of the massive space vessel. Al'Kahan did not turn to
acknowledge the man. Rather he waded through the air, thick with fuel,
towards the towering bay doors. He longed to feel the soft soil of his homeworld beneath his feet, not lifeless steel.

Al'Kahan's furs, bundled upon his back, weighed heavily on his shoulders. Filled with gifts and trophies from the Emperor, they were foreign
objects on Atillan soil. A twisting path of conduits and gantries crowded
and cluttered Al'Kahan's progress. The Emperor's ship, even now, with its
foul vapours and grinding noises, tried to hold him back from his homeland. The land to which his soul would be forever joined.

Al'Kahan reached the bay's vast external doors. Two men from the
Prakash XIIth – boys only – stood at their stations by a smaller, man-sized
doorway. One stepped before him. Al'Kahan pulled his papers from his
coat and pushed them hard into the young Guard's forehead. The man
stumbled backwards. Al'Kahan swept his feet from beneath him with a
solid throw from his leg and spun about letting his heavy furs catch the
other in the neck. The second fell to the ground just seconds after his companion. The papers, heavy with seals, fluttered down to land on the ground
between the men. Al'Kahan stepped through and was struck by the winds
of home. He held his breath and strode out onto the sloping walkway, then
leapt down into the knee high grasses of the open plains of Atilla.

The massive space vessel towered from the grasslands. It would block out
much of the sun as it rose, its shadows turning around the countryside like
a giant sundial. The long grasses surged and crested in the warm evening
breeze. They washed around Al'Kahan, slapping against his thighs as he
strode on. The ship had put down next to a small Imperial outpost, which
huddled in a wide, blasted-earth clearing. More a collection of scattered
administrative buildings than an organised base, the buildings looked like
squat dung heaps.

Worse still, like buzzing flies, Atillans were gathered in groups about
the buildings. Approaching them, Al'Kahan saw that there were more

than he'd initially thought. Many lay huddled together drunkenly amidst pools of bile and filth. Some shivered around small fires. As Al'Kahan drew near, he saw that they did not cook desert hen or bison side, but something else, something more akin to a rodent.

Mongrels and beggars scuttled out of Al'Kahan's way as he strode on. The deeper into the quagmire of scorched earth and hastily erected bunkers he went, the more Al'Kahan worried he would never escape it. It was as though he were entering the heart of the dark plains, that dire place to which the dishonoured dead passed on. Smaller spacecraft, not bearing the glorious eagle of the Imperium, had landed here too. Rogue traders? Mercenaries? Pirates? Al'Kahan cold not be certain. All that he could tell was that these men were making a living off his people. From out of the side of one of these ships a pledge trader was at work. Beggars and wounded queued in a soulless line outside the small craft. A dark, heavy-set man was passing out food in battered tin bowls.

'Sister, what are you doing?' Al'Kahan leant in to talk to a woman in the queue.

'I am hungry, brother.'

'Where is your clan, your husband?'

'He left to fight for the Sky Emperor. I came here to find peace.'

'I see no peace.'

'Can I help you?' A trader type in long, mesh-armour robes strode forward to stand face to face with Al'Kahan.

'You have made beggars of my people,' Al'Kahan sneered.

'We offer them food in return for performing small tasks on our ship up in orbit,' the trader said pulling aside his coat. 'Join the queue or leave.' He revealed the handle of a laspistol underneath his garments.

'I know what this is,' Al'Kahan said to the assembled tribespeople. 'This is a ploy. These men are slavers, they will take you up to their ship to imprison the strongest of you and slay the others!'

'What? That is simply untrue!' The trader turned to face the crowd, his hands held open in a gesture of platitude.

Al'Kahan grabbed the trader by the back of the neck and thrust him forward to the ground. Throwing back the man's coat, Al'Kahan revealed a set of manacles at his belt.

'Look!' he called to the crowd. 'What merchant has need of these?'

Al'Kahan drove the slaver's face further into the ground. Others drew near. Al'Kahan snatched the man's laspistol from beneath his coat. 'Back off!' Al'Kahan growled holding it to the back of the floored slaver's head. 'Return to your tribes!' he screamed at the beggars, 'This is no way for Atillans to live!'

Al'Kahan spat to the ground and strode into the night. The blank faces watched him go in silence. No one moved, no one left.

The eyes of his ancestors were beginning to appear in the heavens above him. He still recalled each pattern, each constellation, from that time many years ago when, with a boy's foolish notions of the glory of war, he had set forth into those stars to fight for the Emperor God. His ancestors would guide him, guide his own eyes to the hunting grounds of his people. Al'Kahan imagined what they would be doing – perhaps feasting after a great hunt, gathered around the fires. He would walk from the light of each hearth to meet with old friends and new warriors. Young men keen to gain their first scars on the field of battle. It would be so good to be back.

THE NIGHTS HAD passed slowly. Al'Kahan slept alongside the tired old mare he'd bought from a trader back at the outpost. The animal was as scarred and wrinkled as Al'Kahan himself. Its breath was shallow when it slept, a constant reminder of his own mortality. He found he had somehow lost the knack of lighting a fire, and had had to use Imperial Guard-issue flame flares to keep himself warm.

There were few signs of his clan on the plains – the marks made by the herds were old, and there were no fresh horses prints either. On the third night, though, he came across an old camp, tents bunt to the ground, and clan banners buried in the dirt. There were no bodies. Amidst the charred remains, Al'Kahan found a lasgun, its charge burnt out. It bore no markings. Had his people taken to using the weapons of the Imperium?

On the fourth night, Al'Kahan wound his way along Kapak Canyon's massive ridges. It was a wide gulf, as though the finger of some god had stripped back the earth revealing its inner workings. In the valley there were channels like arteries, boulders and outcrops like cancers and ancient caves like hollow sockets. If his clan had been attacked this would be their place of refuge. It had been that way for hundreds of years. Only the Hawk's Shadow clan knew of the tunnels and the ridges and could hide here for many days. In a hidden valley, through the disguised arch of a rocky outcrop, he saw at last the familiar tents of his clan. They were smaller than he recalled, more ramshackle. A few mongrels fought over a bone in the moonlight. He could see no guards.

Al'Kahan gritted his teeth and dismounted. He strode on, his arms wrapped tight around the fur bundle he had brought from the ship. The dogs ran away barking into the night as he approached. A young Atillan, facial scars still fresh, stepped from the shadows, his sabre drawn.

'Back off,' Al'Kahan mumbled.

'You are in the territory of the Hawk's Shadow Clan.' The boy stepped closer, bringing his sabre to bear. 'You will back off.'

'I am Al'Kahan. I am one of the Hawk's Shadow.'

'There is no one by that name amongst our clan.'

'You are too young to know any better.' Al'Kahan proceeded to continue past the boy.

'Drop what you hold or my sword will drink of your blood,' the boy snarled.

'No. I am Al'Kahan!'

The boy lunged at him. The old warrior stepped aside, grabbed hold of the boy's arm and smartly lifted upwards. The boy let out a high scream, dropping his sabre, and clutched at his shoulder joint.

'It'll snap back in,' Al'Kahan sneered.

Taking up the fallen sword, Al'Kahan strode towards the nearest hut. Tribespeople had run out at the screaming of the boy. The warrior slashed back the curtain across the entrance to the tent.

'Alyshfa!' Al'Kahan called for his wife.

A battered tribesman stood up, casting aside his furs. His face and body were scarred and wan.

Al'Kahan slit open another tent. She was not here either. A woman sat surrounded by many children her face worn, her eyes red from crying. The babes were thin, they began to cry and scream.

Al'Kahan entered more tents. With each slice of the sabre, the tragedy of his tribe was revealed to him. Outsiders slept with tribesmen. Stinking carcasses, some many days old, were being used for food. Horses were lame.

'Alyshfa!' Al'Kahan called, slashing open another one of the wretched hovels. A man sat bolt upright from beneath a mound of furs, a terrified look in his eyes. There was a familiar woman's form at his side.

'Alyshfa! Your husband has returned!' Al'Kahan yelled as the man leapt up and snatched at a hunting lance resting high against the roof.

Al'Kahan brought his sabre down on the tribesman's outstretched hand. It fell to the floor. The tribesman let out a howl. Al'Kahan grabbed him by his braids and threw his naked frame out of the door.

'Al'Kahan!' a sombre-eyed woman, her hair greying, shouted back at him. Her skin read like life's map, a map Al'Kahan could hardly read. He half-recognised her as she snatched hold of his hand.

Al'Kahan spun hastily to face the tribesmen entering his door and shoved Alyshfa back onto the bed. One of the advancing tribesmen swung hard towards Al'Kahan's head. He ducked and wrenched a fur rug from the ground, tripping the tribesman who crashed through a large water vase. The floor flooded. Another man rushed Al'Kahan. He stepped into the warrior's path and smashed the hilt of his sabre into his face.

'Come on, you whelps!' Al'Kahan barked out of the hut. 'Let's see how many it takes until you show me your respect!'

Suddenly he felt a sharp pain across the back of his skull. Staggering around he saw Alyshfa above him, a heavy iron pot held tightly in her hand, a streak of his blood on its hard base.

AL'KAHAN OPENED HIS eyes. Above him he saw blankets hanging from the support beams of the leather tent. His head was throbbing. He lay on the ground in the damp furs. Alyshfa sat on the ground beside him, holding a sabre to his neck – the sabre he had given her on the day he left.

She had aged more than he. Her eyes were as though they had seen the horrors of the warp, her hair streaked grey and knotted. She still had a noble bearing, but it seemed as though she was struggling to maintain it, to save face before him.

'You hit me.' Al'Kahan reached to feel the crown of his head.

'You were destroying my tent.'

'You are my wife,' Al'Kahan mumbled. He could taste the blood from his cut lip.

'Was! I was your wife.' Alyshfa placed the sword at her side. 'When a wife's husband departs on a sky ship, she becomes widowed. She may choose a new husband after the time of mourning.'

'You are no longer widowed. I have returned.'

'I mourned your passing. A fool, you took to the stars. You fought for the Sky Emperor. You left. What more is there to say?'

'I have returned to my people. I see that they need me.' Al'Kahan sat up slowly. It dawned on him that he was arguing with her as though he had only departed yesterday. She had her temper still, as he had his. Some things on Atilla had not changed.

'We are fine without you, Al'Kahan. Your place is no longer amongst us.'

'All the traditions have been forgotten. I was attacked by a boy, too stupid to know the rules of hospitality. Who is headman now?'

'Po'Thar is dead. Like I said, a lifetime has passed since your leaving. Our tribe is no longer glorious. We starve, our tribesmen are but boys. Traditions are our last concern.'

'That saddens me.' Al'Kahan stood gingerly. 'It is a pity. Our traditions are what make us Atillans.'

'There are new traditions. Things are changing.' Alyshfa handed Al'Kahan a damp rag. He placed it on his head.

'They have changed all too much. Where are all the men?'

'They rode against the warlord, Talthar. Our herd was stolen and they sought to bring it back.'

Al'Kahan paced around the perimeters of the tent, trying to clear his muddled head. He peered outside the flap. A crowd had gathered outside, they stood back from the tent as they caught sight of Al'Kahan. There were very few able warriors, ten at the most.

'Our warriors were defeated?' he asked Alyshfa, turning back to the room.

'Survivors told of a fortress, of weapons bought from sky traders. They rode against it and tried to attack, but could not assail its walls or defeat their guns.'

'Where is your… husband?'

'With the wisewoman. She is mending his wound.'

'I can pay for a new hand.'

'He is proud. He will neither take your money nor let a machine replace his flesh.'

Al'Kahan regarded the woman he had only known as a girl. She wore the sorrow of his tribe like a veil, but beneath it he could still see some inkling of pride.

He strode out of the tent. The crowd staggered backwards, some men reaching for sabres. Al'Kahan held up his hands. They stared intently at the figure who had arrived a frenzied madman.

'Come dawn,' Al'Kahan said, 'come dawn we will make plans to renew our tribe.'

'WELCOME, THE ONCE-proud tribes of Kapak Valley.' Al'Kahan stood upon the back of a horse, looking out over a rabble of wounded men, boys and women who had turned against the traditions. 'I am Al'Kahan. I have served the Sky Emperor and have returned to rejoin my people. Here I have found nothing but sorrow and tears. This warlord refuses the ways of our people by plundering and stealing bison and setting rock and stone to earth to make a fortress. These plains belong to all. Our ancestors divided them equally, so that we could all be free to ride the lands and eat of their harvests. This Talthar is an enemy to us all, an enemy to our traditions, to our ancestors.'

The few warriors present stirred in their saddles. Many spat into the earth, their sharpened teeth glinting in the stark light.

'I came home seeking the traditions I had long held in highest honour in my heart. On other worlds Atillans fight, united by their love for their homeland, their brother horse and the freedom to which we aspire. I say that this warlord, Talthar, is little more than a brigand. I say we ride against him. I say we string him from the gates of his own damned fortress and let the carrion feast on his innards. Through battle we will know the truth. In battle we will find victory. By battle we will save Atilla's soul and restore the tribes to their glory!'

Faces turned away and heads dropped. The ground was stirred by soulless hooves, dragging against the earth.

'Do not turn away! You must trust in the ways of the ancestors. We will overcome this man. He is no daemon. His fortress is but earth. Our steeds tear up the earth as they ride; his fortress is nothing!'

'It is no use, Al'Kahan.' Alyshfa's husband, Ke'Than, turned to him from his saddle. His dark braids and scarless face betrayed his youth. His eyes were keen and tough, like black pearls. Ke'Than jabbed his stump in the departing crowd's direction. 'Their spirits are broken.'

'They no longer have the hearts of true Atillans.'

'Things have changed.'

'Changed for the worst, Ke'Than.'

'Perhaps, but then nothing lasts forever.'

Al'Kahan jumped to the ground. He reached down and grabbed a handful of rich, black soil. 'I have travelled to many worlds and one thing never changes. There is always war.' Al'Kahan stood casting the dirt aside. 'If change is what Atilla wants then change is what she will get. Go and talk to them. Tell them I know how to crack open this fortress.'

FEWER HAD COME than before. Al'Kahan looked out into a crowd of faces, grim and unimpressed. He looked to the low ridge above him. There Ke'Than sat, awaiting his instructions.

Al'Kahan turned to the crowd. 'Not even stone is impenetrable.'

He waved his sabre in the air and Ke'Than kicked his steed into life. The beast thundered across the ridge, throwing up earth all about it. Ke'Than gripped hard to the reigns and lowered his hunting lance in the crook of his injured arm towards a broad boulder before him. The warrior braced himself as a great explosion ripped through the stone. Shards of rock, like leaves from a tree, fell down around the assembled riders.

The crowd gasped.

Al'Kahan held up his own hunting lance. 'I have twenty of these explosive heads. Your lance shafts are not as strong as those of steel, so they will have to be reinforced. But with them we can break open that fortress. We can defeat this warlord.'

THE CHILL WIND of dawn passed through Al'Kahan's hair. It moved the long grasses that grew on the highest parts of each hill. Below him, a morning mist was starting to rise. Around Al'Kahan were gathered fifty riders from the broken clans of Kapak Valley. Riders of varying ages sat atop a mixed rabble of mares and geldings, their faces filled with grim determination. They were few. The boys amongst them had never seen battle, nor ever killed a man.

Al'Kahan turned to face them. His stallion shifted beneath him. His eye passed along the row of riders before them.

'I will not lie. Today, we ride outnumbered. Today, we fight against a superior force, behind walls of stone. Today, we may lose our lives.' Al'Kahan reached around to the furs he'd brought from the starship.

'But these are things you all know.' He started to unwrap the large bundle. 'I promise you this: whilst this day may not be fought in the traditional way, you will not dishonour your ancestors. They will look upon you with great joy – for you fight to free their sons, the founder's children – our brothers who lie in the bowels of that fortress.

'Let me promise you this also.' Al'Kahan produced a plasma rifle and several grenades from the furs, their Imperial Guard insignia plainly visible, 'With these weapons we will conquer! We will ride with the force of a thousand and crack open the walls of their fortress like lightning from the heavens. We will split their heads and bring the full fury of the clans upon them!'

The riders cheered. Al'Kahan swivelled his horse and plunged down into the mist towards the plains in which the fortress sat. White tendrils quickly enveloped him as he dived, near blind, down the steep incline leading to Talthar's fortress. The riders followed into the miasma, the sound of their steeds and beating hearts the only sign that they did not ride alone.

After what seemed like many hours, the ground levelled out and the mists thinned. The fortress, the size of a small star cruiser, loomed ahead of them. It was jagged and sinister, and pieces of scrap metal soldered to iron stakes rose in vicious angles from the ground before it. These would slow down the cavalry. Its walls looked climbable, for the stone was roughly hewn – but peppered with murder holes and lookout towers as it was, this would be nigh-on impossible. Al'Kahan's men slowed; struck dumb with apprehension, some began to falter. Strong actions were needed.

Al'Kahan, plasma rifle in hand, unleashed a volley of burning power that ripped though the iron stakes and lit up the entire valley in white light. The tense air was filled with static. His men rallied and rode like the crazed, relying on the experienced warrior's skill with the rifle to destroy the pikes that threatened their charge. Al'Kahan desperately tried to destroy each barricade before his men collided with them, but some riders struck the barbs. But he kept on firing; if the charge was slowed, they would become bottled up and be shot to ribbons.

The riders rode on, the remnants of the deadly barricades now just ash. Men appeared at the fortress walls. Shotguns and rifles added dull staccatos to the high-pitched cry of Al'Kahan's plasma rifle.

'Face away!' Al'Kahan cried as they neared the fortress. Imperial Guard-issue flash grenades rose high into the air, detonating at spaced intervals like fireworks. The men behind the barricade screamed, blinded by the flash. The riders resumed their charge.

'Lances!' Al'Kahan cried out over the sound of his weapon.

The riders obliged, lowering the explosive tipped weapons to face the stone walls. 'Level up!' The riders pulled alongside one another, creating a convincing line. The hooves, like thunder to the lightning of Al'Kahan's weapon. A storm of retribution was in full sway.

Too late, the doors to the fortress opened to release the warlord's own riders. Al'Kahan's men braced themselves as their lances struck the wall. The tips exploded, ripping great holes in the stone. Sharp rubble ripped at their faces and tore at their furs. One rider fell beneath a hail of debris; his mare kept running. The warlord's riders swept around to follow Al'Kahan's men.

'Hawk's Shadow and Desert Thorn take the compound! The other clans with me!' Al'Kahan cried above the havoc. The riders separated. Al'Kahan's force turned and prepared a charge.

The enemy riders had the better speed. 'Keep going!' Al'Kahan called, pulling four grenade pins. He threw low and hard at the oncoming riders. Startled faces broke into screams of fear as the grenades hit the ground and went off, tearing earth and flesh. The enemy charge fell short. Now his riders had the momentum. Horse met horse, rider set upon rider and a desperate battle broke out.

Al'Kahan wielded the plasma rifle as a club, knocking a rider to the ground to be trampled under the churning hooves. Sabres flashed as Al'Kahan's men jostled with the warlord's. The slow press of horse's bodies was like a giant python, gradually constricting around the battlefield. Men desperately clung to their steeds; to fall was to die under this crush. One of the warlord's men made a rush for Al'Kahan, sprinting across the backs of several close-pressed horses. Al'Kahan turned and released a volley from the plasma rifle. It went wide, barely slowing his attacker.

The rider leapt upon Al'Kahan and they both slid towards the ground. His attacker stabbed again and again with a short knife. Al'Kahan felt the blade penetrate his side. Without thinking, he smashed his forehead into the attacker's face. Al'Kahan rolled to one side and let the screaming man fall beneath the stamping hooves of his enraged mount.

After regaining his saddle, Al'Kahan saw that his men had gained the advantage and had all but finished what remained of the warlord's cavalry. Al'Kahan pulled at the dagger in his side.

THE MEN OF Hawk's Shadow and Desert Thorn hurdled through the holes in the shattered wall and passed into the warlord's compound, Ke'Than at their head. The place was filled with the booty of war; strange machines traded from merchant pirate's lay sprawled about the fort, while coal-black pipes, like spilled entrails, made riding hard. Women and children ran for the mud huts and stone houses that lined the walls. A mass of warriors armed with pistols and sabres rushed from their barricades. They looked shell-shocked and desperate.

Ke'Than snatched his sabre from his saddle and swung it high above his head. With a clean stroke he beheaded an oncoming warrior before the man had a chance to react. Another drew a shotgun on him. The weapon cracked out across the air. It clipped Ke'Than in the shoulder. Barely noticing, Ke'Than brought down his sabre hard. The warrior brought his shotgun up to parry the blow. From the back of the horse the blow was savage. The warrior's wrist snapped, the shotgun singing free from his hands. Both warrior and weapon fell to the ground, the gun misfiring as they collided together. Soft tissue sprayed across Ke'Than's face and he turned away. Around him, his clan had the advantage over the remaining warriors. In the distance, a dark shape appeared on the far side of the melee.

'Who is it?' Al'Kahan arrived at Ke'Than's side.

'Talthar, the warlord,' the other sneered.

Covered in dark furs, criss-crossed with black straps and leather harnesses, Talthar charged forward on the back of a giant black stallion, a whirling chainsword in one hand. Al'Kahan groaned out as the foreign weapon sliced through sabres and limbs alike. The warlord's face had a crazed look, his scars and toothless grin slick with the blood of Al'Kahan's men. With tearing precision, he cut down five men in but a few seconds.

'Here!' Al'Kahan screamed and drew the warlord's attention. The warlord commenced a charge. Al'Kahan spurred his horse towards him. They crossed the short distance neither slowing, their eyes wild.

Al'Kahan leant and whispered to his mount: 'Brother horse, I thank you for your spirit and blood.'

The warlord was upon him, the chainsword spitting gore. Al'Kahan pulled hard against his mount's reins. The inexperienced creature buckled and fell to the ground, the momentum from its charge causing it to slide hard into Talthar's own steed. The black stallion stumbled over the sliding Al'Kahan. In this instant, Al'Kahan jammed the butt of his plasma rifle against his shoulder and fired. The white blue light, mercury bright, cut up through horse and rider. Talthar screamed as his leg was engulfed in searing agony. His monstrous steed crashed to the ground on top of Al'Kahan.

The old warrior felt a biting pain scream through his leg. Something had torn and his foot was bent at a weird angle. Close by, Talthar howled. He was still alive, covered in the gore of his steed, his chainsword cutting a path through the smouldering flesh about him. Al'Kahan rolled to one side as the savage weapon tore through his cloak. He dragged himself across the ground, his tired arm muscles straining to move his substantial bulk.

'I will... have... your head!' Talthar wailed, dragging himself after Al'Kahan.

'You have offended our ancestors! You will die!' Al'Kahan shouted back, looking for a weapon.

'You are no different to me,' the warlord shrieked, swinging the chainsword wildly. 'You offend our ancestors with your alien weapons.'

'Never!' Al'Kahan cried, reaching his plasma rifle and snatching it up.

The warlord swung, the whirling blades of the chainsword spinning furiously towards Al'Kahan. Al'Kahan fumbled with the rifle. It had not charged fully. He brought the gun up to meet the chainsword, waiting for the biting pain of its serrated teeth. The sword dug deep into the rifle's fuel cell. A flash of white-blue flame leapt up the sword and through the warlord's body. He screamed briefly and collapsed, a charred husk.

Shaking the noise from his head, Al'Kahan looked up through the gore and saw a group of riders assembled above him.

Ke'Than grinned down. 'We are victorious, mighty Al'Kahan. You have restored us to glory!'

A LARGE FIRE burnt high that night. The thick scent of bison meat filled the air for miles around. The broken tribes were united, joined to sing of blood and glory. None would pass to sleep without the aid of ale. One soul was not present: the greatest of the Hawk's Shadow, Al'Kahan. Once the wisewoman had done her work, the old war commander passed from the camp quietly, early in the festivities, his leg braced. Al'Kahan left his old hut and disappeared into the darkness of the Atillan night.

At dusk on the next day, Al'Kahan found himself at the starship, the air fouled with its noxious fumes. By one of the entry gates, a lone figure stood. Al'Kahan dismounted and approached.

'I thought as much,' Commissar Streck said. 'I could see it in your eyes the day that you left.'

'I owe as much. Without the Emperor's weapons, we would not have won.'

'Ah yes. You defeated the tyrant. Good for you.' Streck shifted slightly; his black coat creaked. 'Why not stay and be their leader?'

'I no longer know this place.'

'You are one of us, then?'

'No.' Al'Kahan strode past Streck towards the towering starship. 'I am an Atillan.'

ORK HUNTER

Dan Abnett

KEYSER, WHO THEY call the sergeant but who wears no rank pins I can see, calls a halt. He gets up on the limed trunk of a massive fallen cypress and stands, sniffing the air.

We wait, thigh deep in the stinking soup below.

The wet air seems to fill my lungs with steam, and I want to cough, but the Skinner nearest me, a lean brute with charcoal-blackened eye-sockets and piercings down his ears, fixes me with a savage glare as if he can tell what I'm thinking. Keyser waves three scouts ahead, and that leaves thirty of us, twenty-two Skinners and eight Jopall Indentured. I'm halfway down the file, the swamp water bubbling and oozing around my legs, dust flies swirling round me.

The silent halt seems to last an eternity. There are spiders in my hair. I can feel them.

Captain Lorit, looking as out of place as the rest of us Jopall in his white-flecked, jade green fatigues and white peaked cap, wades forward. 'What are we–' he begins.

The Skinner they call Pig, standing to the captain's left, surges forward and takes my commander in a choke hold, clamping one greasy paw across his mouth. The captain struggles, wild-eyed, and Pig tightens his grip. The reason for Pig's nickname is self-evident – slabby and fat, with vastly developed muscle groups stretching his tattered tunic, he has a face ruined by scars and a ragged snout of flesh where his nose was bitten off.

Pig's muscles tighten further and the captain begins to turn blue. We Jopall look on in silent disbelief.

Keyser drops his hand and the Skinners un-freeze and move again. Pig releases the captain and throws him, gagging, face down into the water.

Keyser's jumped down off the cypress by then, and drags the captain up with one hand.

'He assaulted me! That man assaulted me! Put him on a charge!' The captain spits out weed and slime, indignant. Keyser doesn't put Pig on a charge. He punches the captain in the throat and silences him. The Skinners laugh, an ugly sound. Pig snorts, a far, far uglier noise.

'I thought we covered this in basic back at Cerbera. When I signal silence out here in the Green, I mean silence.' Keyser's voice is as sharp and taut as a wire. He says this to the captain, who is too busy grovelling and vomiting in the liquid mud to listen attentively.

HE TURNS TO the rest of us. 'We've got a scent of the 'skins. Close by, no more than a kilometre. Arm, load and follow. No noise. Especially you skinbait.'

That's what we are to them. Not Imperial Guard, not fellow troopers, not noble soldiers from the Jopall Indentured Squadrons. No matter most of us are from good, up-hive stock, no matter our comrades are even now defending the walls of Tartarus Hive against the Invasion.

We are skinbait. Nothing. Lower than scum.

For these Skinners set the value of scum. There are juve-gangs from the Tartarus underhive I'd have more respect for.

It is my considerable misfortune, mine and the other members of my squad, to have been sent to Cerbera Base to undergo jungle warfare training with the ork hunters just as the war for beloved Armageddon began. There is no hope of rejoining our company or hive. We are stuck for the duration, seconded to one of the most notorious units of 'skull-takers', the so-called Keyser's Skinners.

Once in a while, from very far away, we hear the thump of artillery or the scream of ram-jets. Open war is being waged in the lands beyond the jungle, far away. It may as well be on another world. Word is Yarrick himself had returned. Oh to be part of that!

Oh to not be part of this... I believe the Skull-takers have been fighting the feral greenskins for so long, they have begun to mirror what they fight. The least of them are painted and pierced, the worst have implanted tusks jutting from their jawlines. All have ork finger-bones, teeth and ears dangling from them as grisly trophies. They have no official chain of command. They respect no rank or authority other than their own. I have been told they elect their leaders. Think of that!

We edge forward now, slopping through the pools of mire; thick, sticky fluid like mucus. Dragonflies, with stained-glass wings as wide as a man's arm span, cross the glades, beating the air louder than the blade-fans of the air-cars in Tartarus's elite district. Skaters as big as my hand skitter across the sheened water.

Pig tells us we're wading through sap, sap drooled out of the fleshy cycads and root-ferns all around. He snorts again. It's hard to catch my breath, the air is so humid. The Skinners though... they move so silently. They disturb nothing. They make no ripples, leave no trace. Their damn boots never get stuck in the mud-pools. Their sleeves never catch on thorns. Fronds never whip back as they pass. Bark doesn't snap as they climb over it. Even cobwebs remain miraculously intact, as if the Skinners were never there.

For coarse brutes, they move with unimaginable care and enviable skill. We Jopall blunder like fools amongst them. I spent four weeks last summer on a covert training course at the Hades Hive Guard Academy. I did well. I thought I was good. How... how in the name of the Emperor who watches us all do you not make a ripple when you wade through water?

We stop once more, and I lean against the bole of a giant ginkgo. Something has laid a clutch of wet, yellow eggs in the fabric of my jacket cuff. The size of rice grains, they glisten. I shudder and make to wipe them off.

A dirty hand grabs mine and stops me. It is the Skinner with the blackened eye sockets.

'Don't touch them. Rot-wasp eggs. Be thankful they chose your fancy jacket to lay in and not your ear, or your genitals, or your tear-ducts.'

He scrapes the eggs off me with the blade of a rusty shearknife.

I look at him, bewildered.

'You wanna wake up with larvae munching out of your nose? Eating out your brain?'

I shake my head. Who would?

He chuckles.

'What's your name?' I ask.

'Deadhead.'

'No... your real name.'

'Er... Rickles,' he replies, as if he has to think about it. Then he turns away.

'Don't you want to know my name?' I call after him.

He turns back with a shrug. 'No point remembering the name of a skin-bait who'll be dead by tonight. I'll never use your name anyway.'

Anger puffs up inside me, dry and fire-hot despite my sweat. 'I'm Corporal Ondy Scalber of the Jopall Indentured, you scum-sucker! Remember it! Emperor help you that you do ever have to use it!'

He grins, as if my forthright attitude has impressed him.

But he punches me in the mouth anyway.

We press on, the ever-quiet Skinners silently punishing every clumsy stumble of us Jopall. We reach a glade where the vast upper canopy is broken and sunlight streams down bright as lasers. There are flowers here, floating on the frothy, weed-choked water, huge flowers with shocking pink heads. Vast insects too, slow and drowsy, buzzing the air like chainswords and dripping nectar from each hideously limp proboscis. A pallid white serpent with vestigial limbs slides through the murk between my legs. My friend, Trooper Rokar, starts to whimper. He has just discovered that something unseen and submerged has gnawed off the cap of his boot... along with two of his smaller toes.

I was in a scholam with Rokar. I pity him. His injury. His weakness.

The scouts come back, two of them. We never see the third again. They confer with Keyser for a while. Then he tells us, low and mean, there's a nest nearby and we must fan out.

Rokar is whimpering even more now, and begins to climb up into a tree. The captain tries to call him down. Rokar shakes his head, refusing, terrified.

Keyser gets him out of the tree. He throws a stab-knife and impales my old friend through the sternum. Rokar drops and hits the ooze with a wet slap. His body sinks.

'He was no use to us anyway. A liability. Worse than a liability,' Keyser tells the captain.

The captain is speechless with rage and horror. We all are. I don't know what to think or feel any more.

I am sent on the right hand side of the fan advance, with Deadhead and Pig, and another Skinner called Toaster who hefts a heavy flamer unit. Trooper Flinder of the Jopall is with us.

Pig stops us under the shade of a horsetail and smears foul smelling grease over our skin from a dirty pot. Now we smell as bad as the Skinners, and I notice for the first time that they are caked in the stuff. It isn't just dirt. It's deliberate.

'It's skin tallow,' Toaster sneers as he explains while checking the hoses of his sooty flamer. 'Now you won't smell of soap and humans.'

Pig has just daubed us with ork grease, blubber fat from their pestilent bodies. My stomach turns over.

We edge onwards. Flinder and I try to be as silent as the Skinners. Our efforts seem laughable. Then Deadhead stops me again, and points down at the gossamer skein my shin was about to break. He traces it back to a clump of flowering moss and gently exhumes a clutch of stikk-bombs, wired to the cord.

Keyser appears.

'Good work, Deadhead. Good eye.'

'Wasn't me who found it, sir. It was Ondy there.'

I look round, delighted to hear my name used.

'His shin, anyway,' Deadhead adds, and he and the Skinner boss laugh out loud. Curse their filthy hides.

WE CROUCH IN sap-water for half an hour, not daring to breathe. Bird calls and insect chirrups wing through the air. Some of them are natural, some are disguised signals. I can't tell them apart.

Deadhead waves us on.

As we cross a deep culvert of mud and slime, I see movement in the far tree-line. I've always had a good eye. It's the one skill I'm still proud of. I make something pustular and green amid the Green.

So I don't hesitate. I raise my lasrifle, and fire a stuttered burst.

Something big and green and tusked and monstrous slumps out of the foliage, its chest cavity exploded, and drops into the mere.

Then hell breaks loose. There are 'skins all around us, throwing themselves up out of the ooze, spitting out the hollow reeds they were breathing through. They are lean, malnourished, pale things, with jutting teeth like anthracite and deep-set eyes like diamonds. They howl and whoop. They stink. They wield heavy cleavers, cudgels and crude sidearms.

We're all firing. Gunfire explodes from the other elements of our formation. The wet air becomes cinder dry with ozone from the laser discharge. Las-rounds pepper through the leaf cover and fill the air with sap-vapour.

Toaster triggers his flamer and wastes the curtain of foliage before us. Swine-shrieks issue from the raging fire, piercingly harsh.

I fire, on full auto now, dropping 'skins around him. A rusty cleaver takes Flinder's head off his shoulders in a welter of blood and frayed tissue. I see Captain Lorit lifted right up out of the water on a primitive spear that transfixes his gut. He screams, piteously, flailing his limbs.

I had fixed my bayonet hours before, as per the Skinners' briefing. Now, with las-rounds expended and no time to change the clip, I stab and gut and slash.

Deadhead is nearby. He has wrested an ork lance from some dead grip, and is splitting skulls and whooping like a 'skin. Toaster fires again, his belch of flamer vaporising a tide of charging 'skins so that nothing but their fused skeletons slump in the steaming water, dribbling molten fat.

I impale a charging 'skin on my rifle-blade. It howls and pulls towards me, dragging the weapon out of my grasp. There is a plate-metal hatchet in its massive paw already wet with human brain tissue.

I pull my autopistol and blow its face apart.

'Throw! Throw!' yells Deadhead, tossing me a clutch of stikk-bombs.

We hurl them together into the densest part of the 'skin press. In the flash-wash, slivers of shrapnel flutter back, stippling the water with a million separate impacts.

The orks turn and melt away, as if they were never there.

We regroup. Five Skinners are dead. I am one of only three Jopall left alive. I slump, hollowed by shock, against a lichen-covered rock with the others of my hive as the Skinners lock down the perimeter and take the spoils.

'What do you want?' Pig asks, and I turn.

He is sawing the head off an ork corpse with a serrated knife.

'What?'

'An ear? A tooth? You earned it.'

My gut tosses in revulsion. 'Skin ichor is leaking from the sawed incision he is working and forms a stinking slick on the water's surface.

'Don't make a mistake now, Ondy Scalber.' It is Deadhead. His voice is low. 'A mistake?'

'Pig's offering you a trophy. Can't remember the last time Pig did that for skinbait. It's an honour. Don't refuse it.'

'A tooth then,' says I, turning back to see the butchery.

'Yeah,' agrees Deadhead. 'He had a good eye back there. Saw them first.'

Pig nods, snorts, and digs his blade in.

'A good eye? Then that's what he'll get. A good eye for Good Eye!' Pig and Deadhead laugh.

Pig hands me the trophy. It dangles like a pendant on its long rope of blood-black optic nerve.

I can't refuse. I take it, tie it to my dog-tags. It thumps against my chest like a rubber ball at every move I make. As soon as Pig is gone, I'll lose it.

The Skinners build what they call warning shrines. Ork skulls and limbs spiked on posts or nailed to trunks. The idea is the 'skins will now shun this area because it stinks of murder and defeat. But the Skinners wire up the remnants to grenades anyway, in case the 'skins decide to recover their dead.

It's what Keyser calls a win-win situation.

Keyser. I see him across the clearing as the Skinners raise the ork heads on display all around us. He is bent over the eviscerated body of Captain Lorit, who is cruelly still alive. Toaster says Keyser is giving the captain last rites. I see the sudden twist of Keyser's hand. That wasn't last rites as we know it.

The nest is close. We move in, forming small groups. I find myself with Pig, Toaster, and two other Skinners called Slipknot and Buck.

In the glade ahead, swathed in vapour, rises a great, ghostly tree. I sense it is not one tree but several that have become wrapped around each other over time. Hundreds of metres tall and thousands of years old, the great, entwined trunks are lifted clear of the water by a vast raft of winding roots. Birds flitter in the upper canopy. Beetles crawl and gnaw on the exposed roots.

We enter the root system, finding a tunnel half-filled with rank water. The roots coil and interlock above our stooped heads, reminding me of the interlocking arch vaults of the glorious Ecclesiarchy chapel back home on Jopall.

Toaster leads the way. We can smell the leaking promethium of his blackened flamer.

Buck shows me how to take a strip of field dressing and soak it in the swamp water to make a breath mask. Already, the pungent smoke of fires deliberately lit by the scouts on the far side of the nest is creeping back to us.

I breathe through wet gauze.

They're on us a moment later. Toaster scours the tunnel with his flamer, but they're pouring out of side turnings we didn't even see. I'm killing them even as I realise these are youngsters, small ork spawn no taller than my waist, weeping and shrieking as they run from the smoke.

Children. That's what we'd call them.

I don't care any more. Slipknot and I push down a side-vent, clawing our way through the tangles of black roots, and engage fierce 'skin youths, who jab at us with short spears and broken blades.

No match for las-fire.

'This way, Good Eye!' I hear Slipknot shout.

Then I'm into a larger root cavity, with Buck and Slipknot on my heels. We can still hear the rasp of Toaster's flamer nearby, and smell the burning promethium.

Feral orks are all around us now, many full-grown and massive. Some have guns. Slipknot is blown apart by a bolt round. His left hand slaps against my shoulder as it is blown clear of his carcass.

I kill the ork with the bolter. Then Buck and I pepper the cavity with random automatic fire. Green blood splats and sprays in the close air.

An ork is right on top of me, howling, raising a blade in a meaty paw bigger then my head. My gun is out. I fumble. It sees the eye bouncing across my chest and it seems to make it pause. I need no further urging. I slam the bayonet up into its jutting chin so the blade-end punches out through the back of its skull. Its huge jaws, spasming shut as it dies, bite the end off my lasgun.

I take up its blade in my right hand, holding my autopistol in my left. With the blade I dash out 'skin brains. With the pistol I wound and cripple and kill. I am plastered with 'skin blood now, as feral as the things I slay, murderous, wanton, out of my mind.

Jopall seems a long, long way away. Further than ever before.

And I know now I can't go back there.

Not now.

Not after this.

Toaster comes in behind us and yells for us to drop. Buck does, and I pull my head down as the flamer wash gusts like a sun's heat over our heads, incinerating the rest of the chamber.

We're all laughing as we clamber out of the nest. Golder and Spaff, the remaining Indentured Squadrons, look as me as if I have run mad. I know how I must look to them, singed and filthy and covered in 'skin blood that is baked like treacle. I don't care. I don't care what they think. I don't care for anything any more.

KEYSER IS FIGHTING the boss. Driven out by the smoke and carrying a ragged stomach wound, the massive 'skin has found himself cornered in a sap-pool east of the nest. Keyser confronts him. We all group around to watch. No one interferes. We just watch and whoop and chant.

Like orks.

The 'skin boss is one hundred kilos heavier than Keyser, and massively muscled, with molars like daggers and tusks like bayonets. It wears a turtle-shell breast plate, and carries a hooked bill on one paw and a gutting knife in the other. Its torn belly oozes foul-smelling ichor, making the thing crouch.

Keyser, lank and lean in tattered camo-fatigues and webbing, his skin white with paint, has only a shear-knife. They circle and jab. We stand around the clearing, clapping and cheering, chanting 'Key-ser! Key-ser!' like animals. The boss circles in, sidestepping Keyser's blade and taking a decent cut of meat from Keyser's left thigh with its bill. In return, Keyser swings and kicks the monster square in its wounded abdomen, throwing it back into the water in a spray of slime.

The boss rises to its feet awkwardly. Keyser is now limping from the ragged slice in the meat of his thigh, a slice that has flapped the skin open to show pink meat and gleaming white bone.

Another swing with the bill, an evasive deflection from Keyser's knife. How can he go on with a wound that bad, I wonder?

But he does. Keyser splashes through the churning, foamy water and rips his blade along the boss's forearm, causing it to drop its bill.

Then Keyser swings in counter-clockwise and buries his blade up to the hilt in the boss's throat.

Gurgling and aspirating mists of blood, the boss falls on its back, surging water across the clearing under its vast bulk. And dies.

We chant Keyser's name so loud that leaves shake lose and drop from the canopy.

ONDY SCALBER IS dead. He died somewhere and somewhen in the glades of Armegeddon's vicious jungles.

I only barely remember him now. He was a good sort, I suppose.

What I am become now, only time will tell. I hate it, yet I love it too. It is a way of life and of death that appeals to me in its simplicity. To hunt, to kill, to be a better hunter and better killer than the brutes we stalk. To be Good Eye.

One day, perhaps, I'll remember Jopall and the life I had there. Perhaps. I may wake screaming in the night, dreaming of it. I may not.

The Green waits for me. There I will do my work, in the Emperor's name. There I will find my glory.

THE RAVEN'S CLAW

Jonathan Curran

'MY LORD GOVERNOR, I see shadows ahead. I see ravens wheeling, but beyond the shadows there is only darkness.' The man was nervous, wary.

'Are we in danger then, Rosarius? Are all our schemes to come to naught? Look again. Look again!' his master insisted.

'My lord, I– I cannot tell... Wait, there is something, the darkness is clearing... I see fire. No... a star, it is falling in the night... falling from the sky. What does it mean? No, no, wait... it is gone, I can see no more.'

'Then try harder. We must not fail. Too much is at stake here. You've got to protect me until all this is over. This place is full of treachery and I trust no one. If anyone so much as thinks ill of me I want to know about it. We're taking a massive gamble here, and I want to know that it's going to pay off. Don't worry, when it does, I will remember who my loyal servants are. Keep looking – I must know when victory is close.'

Governor Torlin turned on his heels, and stalked over to the windows. He was a short man, but his gait was commanding, almost a swagger. He stood with both hands resting lightly on the sill, looking out over his capital. Far in the distance he could see flashes of light as the defence troops struggled to hold the city's perimeter. The triple-insulated glass dampened the sounds, but even from this distance, he could see distortions in his vision as the steady crump-crump of artillery caused the plexi-glass to vibrate. He couldn't tell whether the explosions were coming closer, but he knew it couldn't be long before the walls were overrun and the city brought to its knees. He started to stroke the lines of medals on the chest of his gaudy dress uniform, as he always did when he was lost in thought.

Rosarius, a thin, sallow man dressed in dark robes, stared at his back. His milk white eyes, blind since his days at the Adeptus Astra Telepathica, gazed unseeing into the void. He could hear the governor's breathing, sense his faint odour of tension and fear, feel the intense electrical activity of his brain. He could almost tell what he looked like, so well did he know his aura, but he ignored these false clues to reality, and concentrated instead on the images he could see with his inner eye. Far beyond the window, he could feel the desperation of the Guardsmen holding the walls, feel the determination of the attackers, their mad lust for battle as they threw themselves against the defenders. He sent out fingers of thought, searching for pathways to the future, like tendrils, snaking their way into possibility. He searched for clues to potential outcomes, the easiest way to victory, the conclusion of their plans. He shook his head in frustration – whichever way he looked, all he could see was darkness, and stars falling from the sky.

In the distance, high in the sky, a flash of light amidst the orange and red bursts of plasma and high explosive caught the governor's attention. Sunlight on metal, moving fast. He followed the object downwards, until it disappeared from view, leaving a thin trail of scorched air behind it from its white hot entry shield.

THE DROPSHIP fell out of the sky like a burning comet. Inside the hold, a hundred men struggled to stay upright, holding tightly onto the steel cords that held them fast against the wall. The ship rocked as anti-aircraft fire exploded like deadly orange flowers around it and servo motors struggled to keep the ship upright against the buffeting gale of explosions and shock waves.

Altitude ten thousand feet and counting. The voice was metallic and harsh.

Vero stood still, his feet apart, bracing himself against the wall, willing his mind to slow, to calm down. Around him men groaned as the rapid descent caused their ears to bleed and their senses to spin. His head felt groggy and painful from the changes in pressure caused by their fall. It was dark, the only light a dirty red glow from the power room. The heat was almost tropical and the air was thick with sulphurous fumes from the badly regulated engines.

Altitude five thousand and counting.

An explosion thumped the outer shell of the ship with a giant's fist and span it around violently like a cork in a whirlpool. Vero could hear bones snapping as bodies jerked against the cables holding them to the walls. The dim red lighting flickered twice, then seemed to stabilise itself.

Altitude two thousand and...

The ship hit the broken ground with a jolt that forced the pneumatic shock absorbers to groan and wheeze like an asthmatic old man. Vero felt as if his spine was being pushed up through the top of his skull. His muscles automatically reacted to the sudden feeling of heaviness as the planet's gravity took over abruptly from the weightlessness of freefall.

He moved his arm and the bindings that bound him fast to the wall automatically increased resistance around his wrist, limiting his movements. His wrists were chafed raw where the tight steel bonds had cut into his flesh, and his body ached from sitting motionless, thrown around by the violently descending craft.

It had seemed like hours since he had woken, an eternity in the dark, hearing the engines rumble. Time in his own head had lost meaning and focus, he felt confused and disorientated. His head felt heavy, full of strange images that came unbidden in the near-darkness. His memory was restless. He couldn't remember being captured, and he couldn't think of any reason why he should be bound up in this manner. He struggled to remember how he had come to be here, chained up in a plummeting ship heading only Emperor knew where.

The first thing he remembered was waking up confused, unable to even remember his own name, but he had seen a single glistening word tattooed on his forearm – Vero – and assumed that that was his name. Looking around now at the similarly tattooed men around him, he felt that his guess was correct. Some of the men seemed to know each other and as they woke up, greeted each other with rueful smiles and shaking heads. A low buzz of conversation started up in parts of the hold, others were silent. He'd questioned a couple of them, but they hadn't known who he was. He didn't recognise his clothes, nondescript khaki fatigues, and even his own body looked strangely unfamiliar. His thick-set hands were scarred across the knuckles, but his legs looked strong and sturdy through the rough cloth. But he did not know them as his own.

THE FAR WALL cracked open, harsh white light spilling across the men. A shadow fell in front of the door, and a figure appeared. The newcomer was hefty and grizzled. His dull brown Imperial Guard uniform was torn and a dirty bandage covered most of his head. He pressed a button on his belt unit and the steel bonds holding the prisoners against the wall relaxed. The cuffs opened, allowing them to rub life back into their limbs. The man moved into the hold and aimed his electro-prod at the nearest captive, lying recumbent on the floor. The man's body jerked as the electrode touched his torso, but he didn't get up. Whatever fate awaited them on this planet, some, at least, had been mercifully spared.

'Come on, you pigs, move it! Out, out, out!' the burly man shouted at them, his accent harsh. Other guards appeared, brandishing weapons at the men. Slowly, a ragged line started to form. Vero, struggling to get up through the burning cramp in his legs, found himself beside a huge bear of a man, stripped to the waist, fluorescent tattoos glistening on his thickly muscled neck and arms. Vero stumbled as he approached the ship's ramp, and the man caught his arm, preventing him from falling. He grinned at Vero, though much of his mouth was hidden behind a shaggy, ginger-brown beard. Almost concealed beneath the thick hairs on his arms, Vero could read the word 'Whelan', and he nodded his thanks.

'It's the sedatives they give you for the journey,' Whelan muttered to him quickly. His voice was deep, almost a growl. 'They make you a bit unsteady on your feet, and that's also probably why you don't remember anything. Trust me, I've seen it before. You can't remember anything now, but it'll come back.'

Vero didn't have time to ask where Whelan had seen it before. The big man seemed to know a lot more about what was going on than Vero himself did.

The faint light became much brighter, causing Vero to shield his eyes from the glare. He realised that it was only weak sunlight, but it seemed strong to him after so much time locked in the darkness of the hull. The sky was a watery grey, and a light drizzle was falling, quickly wetting Vero's dark hair through. For a moment it was quiet. A soft breeze blew, and it felt like the breath of heaven. Vero stretched, flexing his muscles where the cruel bindings had cut into his flesh. He winced as the raw weals opened again, the fresh wounds livid on his olive skin. Despite the inactivity of the trip, he still felt strong and fit. Behind him, the dropship sat on the pitted ground like a large black beetle, towering over the people standing underneath, sheltering from the rain beneath its black armoured carapace.

Then the shelling started again.

The men all ran from the cover of the dropship, the crashing of shells drowning out the sounds of their feet. Vero felt as if he was running in a vacuum. He could not feel his legs, cramped as they were from the journey, his ears deafened by the pounding of the incoming shells. The guards were herding them towards a low building built from crude concrete. Vero and Whelan stopped in front of it, with the rest of the prisoners, shifting their feet to try and restore circulation.

'Whelan,' Vero began, looking around him at the motley assortment of soldiers, 'where in hell are we? And what am I doing here? Do you know me?'

The larger man looked pointedly at the tattoo on Vero's arm.

'Vero, is it? Well, I don't know you, but you've answered your own question.' He looked grim. 'We are in hell. It doesn't matter a damn what planet we're on. All you need to know is that you're part of the Fourteenth Esine penal battalion. The "Holy Fourteenth", they call us, but the Emperor alone knows why. Are you telling me that you really don't remember anything at all? You don't even remember how you came to be on the penal ship in the first place?'

Vero shook his head. A couple of other men strode over to where they were talking. Whelan smiled, the gap-toothed grin splitting his shaggy beard in two.

'Well, look who we have here! Which sorry rock did you two crawl out from under? I didn't see you on the ship when I was cruelly shaken out of my beauty sleep.' Whelan greeted the newcomers by knocking his knuckles against theirs.

'Vero,' Whelan continued, still smiling. 'Let me introduce you to a couple of the dumbest dirtbags around. This here is Oban. In his time he's been done for assaulting a senior officer, second-grade treason, heresy... Oh,' he added at a scowl from Oban, 'make that reformed heresy – this guy's now one straight up, down the line catechismic fellow.'

'That's right,' Oban affirmed, nodding his head vigorously. He was a sharp-featured man, with a broken nose that seemed almost too big for his face. Oban held out his clenched fist chest high to Vero, and after a second, Vero knocked his own knuckles against it. Oban smiled. He looked like he was about to say something, but Whelan interrupted him.

'Me and Oban are old hands here. How many tours we done now, Oban? Six all told I think, including this one.'

Oban sucked in his breath. 'Let's call it five, Whelan. We'll make it six when we're off this dustbowl in one piece. Emperor willing.'

'And this here is Creid.' Whelan pointed at the second man, a tall, rangy figure in battered fatigues, who grinned at Vero from behind a pair of blast goggles. 'I don't even know where to start with this guy. You name it, he'd done it. Law of averages says he should be dead, the amount of tours this guy's had to do. But some people are just born lucky, I guess. Eh, Creid?'

'You said it, brother.' Creid pulled his goggles up onto his forehead to peer at Vero. Creid's right eye had gone, and a crude bio-implant glittered coldly in the socket. Creid noticed Vero's somewhat startled look, but did not seem to take offence. 'Some crazy smuggler took my first eye during the battle for Sonitan VII – stray blaster shot,' Creid volunteered. 'The docs said I was lucky it wasn't my whole head that got blown away, but they patched me up good and proper. Said it was my due reward for bravery.' He shook his head at the memory.

'Silence!'

A path suddenly appeared through the throng for the man who spoke. He swaggered through the crowd of men, a bulky plasma pistol banging against his lean thigh as he moved. A hush fell on the group as he turned to face them.

'I am Commander Bartok, and I am senior officer here. I will be commanding you for this little fracas.'

The officer was young, probably less than twenty – this was most likely his first command. Despite his strong words and careful swaggering walk, he looked inexperienced and nervous. He was tall and slim, boyish even. Neat sandy hair was brushed down smartly over a broad forehead.

Whelan muttered something about 'Damned rookies!' under his breath, and Vero knew just what he was thinking.

'OK, you lot, this is the end of your journey,' Bartok continued in a voice plainly unused to being raised. 'Where you are doesn't matter, but I'll tell you why you're here. This Imperial outpost is under attack, and we're still waiting for reinforcements. In the meantime, the Imperium has seen fit to send you lot to help us, and empty its prison ships at the same time.' He stroked his officer's insignia as he spoke, as if to reassure himself of his authority amongst so many men. 'I'll be blunt. I don't like penal battalions – you're all scum as far as I'm concerned – but I don't have any choice in the matter. You're here and you're going to fight.'

Vero looked around. There were more men than he could easily count. Many of them were prisoners such as himself, but still more were Imperial Guardsmen, dressed in standard grey uniforms, with the symbol of a purple glove on their armbands. A purple glove... it meant nothing to Vero; he had no idea which planet he was on, let alone which unit he was meant to be fighting with. The officer continued.

'Listen up! Our job is to defend the perimeter. And don't think of trying to escape – there's nowhere to go. If the enemy catches you, they'll kill you – and if I catch you, you'll wish they had killed you. The governor's psyker himself has foreseen victory for us, and he's the best telepath in this system – nothing gets past him, so we have got nothing to worry about.'

Men passed through the group, distributing lasguns and combat knives. Vero took the weapons he was given, turning the unfamiliar shapes over in his hands. The lasgun's metal and plastic felt strange, but as he turned the butt and grasped the handle, his hands slid into position, seemingly of their own volition, and his finger caressed the trigger. It just felt right somehow. Vero shifted his weight around, rocking gently on the balls of his feet until he felt totally comfortable toting the weapon. He checked what he somehow knew was the power gauge, and flicked the safety catch on and off, noting everything. Whelan glanced at him curiously.

'Used one of these before?' he asked.

'I don't know... I don't think so.'

'You seem to know what to do,' the other man said with a shrug.

Vero looked down at his hands. He felt his muscles heave, and as he looked at his fist, he saw the tendons stretch and become hard. His knuckles, when he touched them, were like steel. He felt a surge of adrenaline pump through him and strength flood through his body. Strange thoughts filled his head. Marble corridors, skies bright with stars, the low hum of machinery. He stood stock still, trying to latch onto the thoughts, but they fluttered away from him, dark as ravens' wings.

'Right, you sorry lot, lock and load, and let's go and get ourselves some action!' Bartok was yelling. 'You four,' he finished, pointing at Whelan's little group, 'you're with me. You,' he said to Oban, 'you're comms. Let's move out!' One of the Imperial Guardsmen handed Oban a comms-unit, and he hefted it onto his back without complaint.

Whelan scratched his beard thoughtfully, and looked at Vero. 'Come on, we'd better shift our butts, or else we're gonna get a bolt in the back of the neck for lack of zeal. I reckon that kid commander's dying to take a pop at somebody, and if we're in the way we're as likely to get it as anyone else. These sort of people are famous for fragging their own side as often as the enemy's. Stick with us. As I said, this is my sixth penal tour of duty. I've survived so far, even been commended for valour once. Stay close and you'll get through alright.'

Vero didn't seem so sure, but the feel of the weapon in his hands, at least, was reassuring. They set off behind Bartok, jogging alongside the other prisoners from the dropship, heading for where the sounds of battle were loudest.

'ROSARIUS, YOU FOOL, are you a telepath or are you not? Have you served me so faithfully for so long, only to have your powers fade at the moment when I need them most? What is the use of shadowy images, when what I need are facts!' Torlin's voice could not disguise his furious rage. He swept a pile of papers off his enormous desk, sending them fluttering around the chamber.

'My lord, for a second I saw something, but then it was gone. This darkness troubles me more than I can say. For a moment, I saw the raven again, then stars, marble halls. And now nothing. I am as blind now in the ether as I am in your world.'

'You fool, Rosarius, there is nothing there for my victory is certain. I don't need for you to start getting the jitters now. You're an old man; maybe you should leave the predictions of war to me. We go on.'

'My lord, I beg you...'

VERO'S UNIT ARRIVED at the perimeter defences to find themselves in the midst of a ferocious firefight. Hundreds of men were crammed into makeshift concrete battlements and the roofs of bunkers, and beyond these positions, Vero saw a sea of rubble where weeks of artillery bombardment had shattered the outer edges of the city. The air buzzed with laser fire and the roar of heavy weapons. The sounds of battle raged in his ears. He felt strong.

For the first time he could see the enemy up close. As far as he could tell, they were human like him, and from the number of casualties on this side of the wall, well armed. As they moved into position, a man he didn't know, standing right next to Oban, was hit by enemy auto-cannon fire.

One moment he was firing into the distance, the next there was a roar and tatters of the man's flesh covered them. Vero wiped the mess from his face, tasting the metallic tang of blood on his tongue. He followed Whelan's example and ducked down behind the crenellated walls. The pair of them began firing out across the ruins.

Across this nightmare landscape, Vero could see hundreds of bodies, scattered and broken, limbs cut from bodies by powerful laser fire or ripped apart by the relentless artillery. The ground shook every time another shell landed, and it seemed as if the corpses were dancing on the ground, their arms and legs jerking in time to the exploding shells.

The stones before them shook. Looking down, Vero saw gloved fingers clutch the stone of the parapet in front of him, and before he could react, the largest man he had ever seen swung over the wall. Dressed from head to toe in dull grey battle armour, he swung a huge chain-axe at Vero's unprotected head. Vero heard the rasping of the axe's teeth chewing the air as it swung towards him. Acting from pure instinct, he jumped backwards and sideways, putting space between himself and his assailant. The axe missed Vero's head, but the whirring blade shattered the barrel of his lasgun. Splinters of hot metal flew in all directions. One hit Vero's forehead, and blood welled into his eye, making him blink. Vero dropped his useless weapon, and pulled his combat knife from its boot sheath. He dropped into a crouch, balancing his weight on the balls of his feet. Somewhere deep inside his own mind, Vero found he was watching himself with a mixture of admiration and alarm.

Trying to concentrate, he ducked under the next swing and threw himself at the enemy, inside the arc of the chain-axe. He could smell stale sweat and blood, but as his opponent staggered back, Vero forced the steel point of his knife in towards the man's chest and pushed hard, shattering ribs and severing muscle.

As he plunged the ice-tempered blade deep into his opponent's chest, Vero felt something take him over. Some savage spirit possessed him and he twisted the blade, feeling it bite into soft tissue, then brought his knee up to push himself away from the falling body, pulling the knife with him. The man gasped and died in front of him on the broken ground, his madly staring eyes clouding over as blood gouted from the wound in his shattered ribcage.

Vero staggered back as sensations flooded through him. He didn't remember ever having learnt to use a combat knife, yet at the precise moment the crazed man had leapt at him, he had felt something take him over, some instinct, some training, that had enabled him to pull the knife from his boot, twist it in his hand and plunge it fatally into the chest of his opponent.

He opened his mouth and yelled, a guttural howl of triumph – and he felt a sudden flash of memory illuminate his mind. He struggled to hold on to it, but it slipped away like a sump-eel, slithering away from his conscious will, leaving him none the wiser. But for a second, he had seen in his mind's eye the image of stars burning behind a huge glass window, heard the sound of feet rustling on polished stone, and a smell like… like something he couldn't put his finger on. Then it was gone and the moment passed.

He sensed movement to his left and wheeled around, snatching up his dead assailant's chain-axe. A soldier had vaulted the parapet, a knife gripped between broken teeth as he used one hand to pull himself up and over the concrete wall. In the other he waved a battered bolt pistol. The man was covered in scars, and his hair stuck up in tufts all over his head. They looked at each other for less than a heartbeat… then Vero clenched the lever on the weapon's handle, and the chain-axe snarled into life. He lunged, and there was a deafening scream as his opponent fell gasping into the mud, arm severed at the shoulder.

Suddenly, as if at a signal, the walls before them were being scaled by tens of warriors, swarming over the parapet. Shocked, Vero jumped back, and looked around for his companions. He saw Whelan laying down a withering blanket of las fire, as Creid and Oban lobbed frag grenades that Commander Bartok was tossing over to them from the bottom of the wall, forming a human chain of destruction.

And then Vero was fighting for his life, swamped by attackers, carried along by the press of enemy bodies. He lost sight of his comrades for a few moments as he swung his stolen chain-axe in a whirling figure of eight before hurling it at the closest foe, cleaving his skull in two. He picked up a laspistol from a fallen Guardsman, quickly checking the power cell, and cleared himself some breathing space. Grabbing Whelan's shoulder, he shouted above the din.

'Where's Bartok?'

'Gone!' came the answer in a growl.

'Dead?'

'No chance. Run off!' Whelan looked pale, obviously sure that his sixth tour was turning into his last.

Vero assessed the situation. 'Fall back!' he shouted at the others. They looked at him suddenly, and he was momentarily confused, unsure where the sudden note of command in his voice had come from. They began to retreat, using the ruined walls as cover. Enemy artillery shells sailed over their heads in the direction of the city, the eerie whistle making the men shudder. Vero grabbed Creid by the shoulder, as he lobbed his final grenades.

'Come on!' he shouted, pulling the man away, 'fall back, follow me.'

They did so, suddenly surrounded by fleeing Guardsmen, making for the cover of the buildings, fiery laser shots stabbing the darkness behind them. Vero lost sight of Creid in the confusion, swept away in the general rout, and he prayed silently that he would escape with his life.

There was a roaring noise next to them and Oban stumbled, his legs seeming to give way under him.

'Whelan, help me!' Vero shouted, slipping on the blood-slick ground. The larger man grabbed Oban's arms and helped Vero drag him towards a ruined building nearby. They may all be dead men, with no one to bury them after this debacle was over, but Oban was a comrade-in-arms; besides, he had the comms-unit, and there was no way any of them were going to get out of this mess alive if they lost all contact with command.

They made it through a burnt doorway that led into some sort of ware-house. Molten plastic fell from the ceiling in droplets of lethal rain. Whelan and Vero put Oban down and leant against the wall, panting from both fear and exhaustion.

Vero ran one hand through his hair as Whelan knelt to examine Oban. When Whelan stood up again there was blood on his hands, and a look of concern on his bearded face.

'What's the score?' Vero asked warily.

'Still hanging in there, but I don't think he's gonna last much longer. Both legs are shattered, and he's losing blood faster than I could hope to stop it. I'm surprised he's got this far.' Whelan looked around, eyes full of panic. 'What the hell are we going to do now?'

Vero shook his head. He hefted up Oban's comm-unit, but the cheaply mass-produced unit was broken, the casing cracked and scored by the explosion. He threw it down in disgust and sat down wearily on a slab of rubble. The sound of shellfire was still in his ears. He rubbed his sore eyes, feeling the sting as acrid smoke was rubbed into them from his face. A water bottle lay half-hidden by rubble, no doubt dropped by a fleeing soldier. Vero sniffed the contents cautiously and then swigged at the brackish water inside. He tried to remember the thought that had entered his head as he killed the enemy soldier, but it was gone for good. He cursed. His memory was clear since coming to this planet, but as for what had gone before – nothing. He closed his eyes and tried to retrace his steps since arriving, searching for some clue as to who he was and what he was doing.

In his mind's eye, he saw movement: a tracked vehicle making its way towards them. Could it be safety, or the enemy? He couldn't tell, the image was unclear. He felt as if something was happening just beyond his reach.

'What is it?' Whelan asked him, looking concerned. 'Can you hear something? What's happening?'

In the corner of the room, Oban moaned, and blood ran in streams from his mouth and nose, but Vero hardly noticed. He could hear the sound of a raven cawing. He saw a face swimming in front of his eyes.

Grizzled grey hair, arrogant, aristocratic eyes, some sort of uniform, medals. He remembered how his strength had returned so quickly after landing on the planet, despite his weakness on the ship. He remembered how he had mastered the weapons, his instinctive fighting when attacked at the wall. He remembered the hardening of the tendons in his hands and his fingers twitched. And then, nothing. His mind went blank, and all he could see was the ruined building they were hiding in, and Whelan kneeling next to Oban.

'Whelan,' he said in a thick, pleading voice. 'Something's happening to me.'

'MY LORD GOVERNOR, the situation is getting too dangerous. For a second I almost saw something, but now I can see no outcome for our strategy except destruction. We must escape, and soon.'

'But the rebels are so close, how can we fail? Everything is proceeding exactly as we planned it. What can go wrong?'

'My lord, even in a psychic darkness, I can usually see something, some glimmer of intent, of the future. Here I can see nothing.' Rosarius's voice was cracked with strain. 'It is true that my powers cannot see danger ahead of us, but that is why I have cause for worry. I have never had my second sight so blinded. There are futures hovering on the edge of my vision, but there is a cloud, like ink in water, confusing, blocking everything. If I could foresee our doom, that at least, would allow me to plot a course away from that outcome. But there is nothing.'

'Then we will leave for the bunker. It will be safer there. Perhaps I was foolish returning to the city, but I wanted to be there to watch as the city fell.'

Rosarius shook his head at his master's egocentricity. Pressing a button on the governor's barren desk, he spoke into the comm-link.

'Sergeant, prepare the governor's personal transport. We'll be there in a few minutes.' As the two of them turned to leave, Rosarius reflected, not for the first time, on the limits of his own psychic powers in not forewarning him of the ill-luck of his appointment as personal advisor to Torlin.

Leaving the ornate double doors standing open, they clattered down the grand staircase, not trusting the lift. Lights flickered as the generator struggled to cope with the demands of the power shields protecting the governor's official residence.

Under the palace, the governor's personal liveried Leman Russ armoured personnel carrier was belching black smoke, causing Rosarius to wheeze. Torlin prayed that the inefficiencies of his governorship hadn't extended as far as his own personal transport, and that the mechanics had added the extra side armour as he had demanded. His bodyguard, thirty hand-picked soldiers of impeccable loyalties, snapped to attention as he appeared. He nodded at them curtly and waved a vague salute. While the governor and Rosarius climbed into the Russ, strapping themselves into the seats, the bodyguard piled into two Rhinos. The driver sealed the hatch behind them. To Rosarius it sounded like the closing of a coffin.

The driver gunned the engine, and they lurched forward, nearly jolting Governor Torlin's head from his shoulders. 'For pity's sake,' he growled at the driver, 'be more careful. I want to get out of here alive.'

The Russ, with its escort of Rhinos, drove slowly through the burning city, slowing often to manoeuvre around ruined buildings and shell-pocked roads. The light outside was made eerie by the many magnesium flares sent up by the spotters, but the sound of small arms fire had faded. The governor didn't know whether this was a good sign or not. Even through the vehicle's filters, he could smell the smoke from the burning buildings, the stench of corrosive chemicals, burning plastic, and, faintly, the odour of charred flesh as the victorious rebels lit their celebration pyres. His city was deserted, its citizens long fled. Torlin listened with half an ear to the sound coming from the comm-link with their escort, and chewed his nails thoughtfully. Rosarius was slumped against his seat, seemingly lost inside his robes.

'Fury One, we have snipers point two zero zero. Over.'

'Fury Two, I see them.'

They could hear the ricochet of shells bouncing around the armoured hide of the APC, and then the returning rattle of bolter fire.

'Snipers neutralised.'

'Fury Base, we are on our way, ETA thirteen minutes and counting. Over.'

'Receiving, we are awaiting your arrival. Keep us updated. Over and out.'

Suddenly, Rosarius sprang bolt upright, his eyes crazy with fear. 'My lord!' he exclaimed. 'I see fire, fire from the sky!'

The comm-link from the lead Rhino screamed: 'Incoming, incom–'

The explosion drowned out the rest of the voice.

THE BLAST ROCKED the ruined building where the two survivors were holed up, dislodging great chunks of plaster and rubble from the ceiling. Vero crept towards the ruined window, keeping his head back for fear of sniper fire. Peering across the wrecked boulevard he saw the smoking ruin of a tracked armoured vehicle, fire raging from its engine. Across from it, another similar vehicle had been completely buried in rubble from a building hit by the missiles. Between the two was a battle tank, lying on its side, the upper track still revolving, the tread shattered. The tank's massive lascannon drooped, useless, its barrel bent beyond repair. Sparks flickered across the undercarriage and oily black liquid leaked from the cracked carapace.

The liquid slowly crept its way towards the sparking underside and Vero knew whoever was inside had only moments before the vehicle went up in flames.

'Cover me,' he found himself shouting at a startled Whelan. Vaulting from the window, Vero ran across the open ground, lasgun fire from snipers in the rooftops in the next block following him, spitting up shards of rock behind his feet, and the returning fire from Whelan flickering around his ears.

He leapt onto the moving track, using its motion to propel himself over the stricken tank and into cover. Bracing his boots against the wet earth, he unsheathed his knife, wedging the point of the blade into the crack between the top of the vehicle and the access hatch. He leaned on the blade, praying it wouldn't break, but the adamantine tip held strong. With a groan of metal, the hatch opened, belching a cloud of hot smoke into the night air. Blinking against the fumes, he peered into the shattered interior.

Slumped against the control was the driver, but he could see immediately that he was beyond help: a supporting strut from the chassis had driven deep into his chest. The gunner was moaning gently, but the blood bubbling from his mouth was arterial red, bright oxygenated blood; he would not last more than a few minutes.

In the darkness beyond he saw a figure, pinned to the floor by a broken stanchion of metal from the armoured walls of the vehicle. He looked closely. Grey hair, aristocratic eyes, the medals on his chest. He'd seen this man before.

Suddenly memory exploded inside his head like the heart of a star collapsing under its own weight.

HE WAS SITTING at the end of a low bier in a hall of highly polished marble. In front of him, a man dressed in dark robes was reading from a large, leather-bound book. Around them both were banks of humming machinery, dim green screens which flickered with images. He could hear the soft whisper of leather slippers on polished stone. Tech-priests moved gently through the aisles between the rows of ancient machines, adjusting, taking readings, reciting prayers.

The humming became louder. Gentle hands were placed upon his shoulders, easing him back so that he was lying flat on a warm, padded bench. Above him was a large monitor, and on it he could see the face of a robed man. His face was aged but unlined. The man spoke and his voice, calm and measured, seemed to bypass his ears and speak directly into his brain.

'Averius, Callidus assassin, relax. Be still and relax.'

The procedure was carefully explained to him. 'It's quite simple, I assure you. A man's mind is made up of two parts. The first part includes memory, your personality, thoughts that are unique to you. Then there is the part which controls your day to day functions, your knowledge of weapons, infiltration, poisons, everything that enables you to function as an assassin, as well as your animal instincts, the fight or flight, your powerful instinct for survival. All we are going to do is to temporarily erase the first part, allowing you to get past the normal psychic screening with which the ever-paranoid Governor Torlin surrounds himself. You will have no recollection of who you are, or what your mission is, so his sanctioned psyker will have no forewarning of you until it's too late. You are Averius, and so this mission has the code-name Vero.'

A helmet, humming with power, moved down over his head, covering his eyes. He saw faces, scenes of battle, carnage, the rage of guns, and then a face framed by grey hair, eyes full of ambition and a palpable thirst for power. His quarry: Governor Torlin. Images from his own life, past terminations, death throes, passed before his eyes, spooling backwards, and then there was only darkness.

THE VERY NEXT thing he knew he was in a metal comet, falling to earth, his arms bound tightly behind him. Now everything was clear. He was Averius, Callidus assassin – and he had found his quarry.

Next to the governor, a terrified-looking elderly man dressed in dark robes looked at him. He muttered softly to himself. Averius leaned over to hear him better.

'You... you are the raven?' the psyker croaked. 'Why did I not see you? Why could I not read your mind? Why could I not predict your coming?'

Blood trickled from his nose, his breath coming in gasps. The assassin raised his fist.

'Be silent, psyker,' he spat, and his hands cut off the old man's questions.

Averius pulled roughly at Torlin, ignoring the man's moans as the broken metal pinning him to the Russ tore through his flesh. He pulled him out of the vehicle, and dragged him to the building. He felt a wave of heat, as the leaking fuel flooded one of the sparking circuits, and the tank exploded in a ball of molten metal and plastic.

Whelan was waiting for him back in the ruined building, covering his return from the shelter of the shattered window.

'Vero, who is it?' he asked as the assassin stalked back into their crude shelter and flung his prize roughly onto the ground. When there was no answer, Whelan grabbed his upper arm and swung Averius round to face him.

'Vero, what is it?' he asked, but the assassin looked at him blankly. All previous thoughts of comradeship were erased from the assassin's mind by the full knowledge of his mission.

'You are in my way,' he stated simply. He swung his hand out almost lazily and Whelan was sent flying, knocked unconscious by the force of the blow. The assassin gazed dispassionately at the prone body of his comrade, a look of surprise etched onto the man's unconscious face.

The assassin's fingers began to twitch and shake painfully. He looked down in alarm at the fingertips. He was suddenly wracked with pain, his whole body seeming to lift up and shake itself from deep inside. Averius could feel the polymorphine flowing through his system, and his body contorted as if it was trying to throw off its skin. He felt himself grow taller, broadening out, and from his fingertips he felt a pricking as finely honed steel needles slid out from under his fingernails, razor-sharp and slick with toxic fluids. At last he was complete: the tools of his trade, his raven's claw, hidden to prevent discovery of his mission until he had found his prey.

The governor croaked from behind him as he came to. The assassin picked up the water bottle from where it had been lying amidst the rubble on the floor, holding the man's head up to allow him to take a sip of water. Averius wanted his quarry to be able to answer his accuser.

'My lord,' the assassin began, as he always did. 'I come at the express order of the Officio Assassinorum.'

The governor started into full awareness: his eyes focused, then opened wide with panic. 'The raven,' he croaked. His voice was wild, delirious.

Averius slapped him, lightly, on one ash-grey cheek.

'Wake up. Concentrate. I come to give you the Emperor's absolution.'

'What do you mean? I have done nothing, I have no need of absolution,' Torlin blustered.

The assassin ignored him. 'I have come to bring justice to this planet. You have been watched. Do you think your lapdog telepath could protect you from justice. He knew your thoughts, and his knowledge shone like a beacon to the Adeptus Astra Telepathica. Did you think treachery like yours could be hidden away?'

The governor was beginning to lose himself to utter panic. The assassin could see sweat starting to bead on the man's ashen forehead. He knew he was a dead man. But confession could at least bring a clean death. Absolution would be swift. The assassin pressed his fingers to the governor's temples and concentrated his thoughts.

'You thought that you could encourage these rebels, make it possible for them to destroy the Emperor's forces stationed here on your little world.' Averius could barely keep the scorn from his voice. 'Then when they were victorious, you thought you would take your place at their head. Your ambition thought to lead an army across the galaxy, carve out your own empire.'

The governor gazed into the assassin's eyes, and he could see the fires of his betrayal burning. His imagination spiralled out into the vast distance of space. Torlin's mind became full of an unshakeable image: his Emperor and erstwhile master seated on the Eternal Throne of Terra. His heart ached as the assassin forced him to confront his betrayal.

'But why should you not be annihilated along with the rest of your rebellion?' Averius pressed on. 'Death is the easy part. Anyone can die – every day countless thousands die on countless thousands of worlds. As a human being, you are less than nothing. We could have launched a strike from space, bombed your palace, destroyed you in an instant. You would have died without ever knowing why. But as a heretic you are never beneath our notice, and every heretic who dies unrepentant is a failure of orthodoxy. I am here to accept your repentance.'

In the assassin's eyes, Torlin saw the Emperor hold out his hand towards him, saw the hand getting bigger and bigger until it threatened to engulf him. As he watched, it withered, became a claw, a raven's claw, and then fell to dust.

'You have sinned most grievously against the Emperor, and I am here as his judge and executioner. You will die, but you must die repenting your faults.'

The governor began to weep, great welling tears.

'I repent, I repent,' he wept over and over. Eventually his voice fell to a whisper. 'Forgive me.'

The assassin flexed his fingers, feeling the sharp needles fill with toxins from the bio-engineered pump inside his hand. He turned to the craven governor.

'Torlin, Imperial Governor of Tadema's World, you have sinned against the Emperor. I accept your repentance and grant you the Emperor's mercy.'

He held the governor's head still with one hand, cradling it as one would a child's, and pressed the fingers of the other against the man's face. The needles slid through the soft flesh of the governor's eyes, piercing nerves and tissue, passing the deadly poison into the man's brain. After a wile, the hand holding him up opened and Governor Torlin fell lifeless to the floor.

Absolved.

The assassin stroked his hand over the penal tattoo on his forearm. The letters morphed gently into arcane runes, and he knew that they would transmit a signal through the ether to the Callidus temple. Far off in space, the Imperial reinforcements, held back until his crucial mission was completed, would swing into action and White Scar Space Marines would start dropping onto the planet. His mission was over, and he could now return for debriefing.

Pressing his thumb against the governor's forehead, he activated a bio-implant buried deep within his hand. He felt a brief flare of heat, as if he was passing his hand over a lit candle. When he removed the thumb, a mark was burned into the cold skin of the man's head. The stylised mark of a bird.

A raven.

EMPEROR'S GRACE

Alex Hammond

THE BURNING FLAMES leapt high, throwing long shadows about the vault. The cold floor beneath his feet refused him comfort. Light robes adorned his body, clinging to him, providing little warmth. Streck stared into the dark, eyes straining to pierce the gloom. Above and all around him, a thick silence suffocated anything that dared to make an impact on the stillness.

A noise. Streck turned, his sleep-clogged eyes still trying to get their bearings amidst the flickering shadows.

The flames flared into monstrous life. The dark corners shrunk, betraying the shape of the room. High arching supports held aloft a roof of unimaginable height. Shining steel pipes funnelled the flames into the hall, their light revealing a man in black, military medals peppering his coat. A soft buzzing became apparent; it had always been there, echoing through the halls.

The man, dark-eyed and swathed in the coat and sacred insignia of the Cult of the Emperor, approached. The flames grew, casting light upon a huge lexicon, the Imperial seal burnt into its cover. The dark man stepped forward and opened the book, its pages reflecting flickering light onto his face. Streck stared into his own eyes. The halls erupted with flame. The buzzing grew shrill and flung Streck into the howling consciousness of a warzone.

Screeching attack sirens. His narrow stretcher bed. Bolt pistol in his hand. Streck rose, smoothed his commissar's uniform, placed his peaked cap on his head and rushed upstairs to his command post.

* * *

STILL. THE CHIRPING of the large, horned insects had stopped when the bombardment began. Lieutenant Lownes could still see their multi-coloured wings, like stained glass windows, fluttering as the creatures darted desperately between the thick mangrove patches.

'Intelligence of a cat,' Lownes whispered to the young Guardsman next to him.

'Sir?'

'Those insects have the intelligence of a cat, soldier.' A pair of kaleido-scope wings hovered close by the man's head. The Guardsman raised his lasgun.

'Steady, son. It's just taking a look at you.'

Olstar Prime. Recent Imperial colony in unclaimed space; a jungle planet rich in deep ores and petro-ethers. Lieutenant Lownes and his squad had been brought in specially from Catachan. Similar climate, similar terrain – High Command figured they'd be perfect for helping in the defence of the main colony installation. The problem was that 'perfect' needs ground support, covering fire and capable shelling, something the last functioning elements of the Valis Fifth Guardsmen and the local garrison on Olstar Prime were a little hard pressed to supply when the word 'Eldar' crackled over the airwaves.

'The orders are clear. We're here to destroy their commander and weaken their position. The local garrison and colonists will try and keep the bulk of their force at bay,' Lownes whispered to his squad huddled in the ebbing shallows of the mangroves. The heat and mist had covered brawny arms and combat knives in a dewy sheen.

'So the rumours are true?' Sergeant Stern asked, batting an insect from his pack with the back of his huge hand.

'Yes, we face eldar. No one's come in contact with them yet, might have something to do with their technology, but they're definitely out there. The alien devils have the colonists terrified while the local defence forces have no taste for battle – although facing down those sorcerous weapons doesn't appeal to me either.'

'Shuriken catapults, sir.'

'Sorry?' Lownes looked up, scanning his men.

'Sir.' It was the new Guardsman, a young, bullish lad with close-cropped hair. 'Shuriken catapults, they use magnetic impulses, fire spinning discs.'

In mock horror, Lownes made a religious symbol in the air. 'Didn't know we had an eldar expert amongst us. What kind of heretic are you?' He laughed and a cloud of insects rose from the ferns around him. 'Glad to have you along.' Not even a chuckle from his squad. They were apprehensive, and Lownes knew it. 'Make it clean and we'll make it through, Emperor willing. See you all at base camp.'

The Jungle Fighters each gripped their nearest comrade by the forearm, in a brief, silent display of camaraderie.

'Alright.' Lownes released the young soldier's arm. 'Let's move out.'

There is a skill to moving in waist high water and ignoring the strange movements brushing past. The Jungle Fighters of Catachan had got it down to a fine art – that and at least four unarmed fighting styles and extensive weapons training.

The bulbous mangrove trees sat still, the only things with sense enough not to try and move about in the quagmire. Lownes led his squad into cover behind a vine-swathed clump of the trees. Spiny trunks scratched at the exposed flesh of the fighters. A cocktail of combat drugs staved off all but the most extreme of injuries. Many a fighter had lived to see another day thanks to the potency of the Imperial chemists' brews.

A splash in the water to the left of the squad brought their honed reflexes into action. As silent as nightfall, Stern raised his lasgun. Lownes grabbed his infra–red scope and peered through it. An eldar, with a long, fluted pistol-like weapon strapped to its steel-slender body armour. It moved gracefully through the water; the swamp seemed to have little effect on its movement. Soft, discordant sounds, like an unearthly wind, came from the alien's respirator. Two, three… four in total. Outnumbering them and unseen, Lownes had the drop on them. Yet the men shuddered as the beings came into view.

Three sharp gestures from their commander and the squad went into action. Lownes tugged on two grenades and timed them long. They splashed into the water beside the two eldar on point. One moved close to the ripples in the water and stared upwards, assessing where they had come from. A second too late. The frag grenades cracked loud over the swamp. Burning body armour, flesh seared to metal, splashed into the water about Lownes's squad. Waves rushed about the grove. The Jungle Fighters leaped into the thick grenade smoke as the remaining eldar sprayed humming death from their shuriken catapults.

Tree bark and burnt foliage dropped down into the silent world of the swamp as Lownes swam in the shallows towards the unsuspecting eldar. Half his squad followed, respirators bubbling air to the surface the only sign of their passing. Chainsword spinning, Lownes exploded out of the water; the squad followed, lasguns firing controlled bursts into the mass of body-armoured warriors around them. The needle-sharp teeth of Lownes's mechanical sword ripped into an eldar, removing wrist and weapon in one fluid motion.

The aliens fell back in the face of the Jungle Fighters' numerical superiority, standing behind the tallest of their number, dressed differently in flowing robes and a strange elongated helmet. A pair of green eye sockets glowed. The robed figure raised its hand. A spray of low-powered lasfire from the remaining eldar channelled into one massive bolt that swept through the Jungle Fighters. Stern and four other men fell to the beam, identification tags and flesh fusing in one. The remainder of the squad threw themselves away from the gunfire and found precarious cover behind what remained of the mangrove trees.

The battlefield was still.

'Their leader, it's… it's psychic,' the new Guardsman stammered to Lownes.

'I guessed, son.' Grim faced, Lownes struggled to suppress the drugs in his blood that screamed at him to rush into deadly action against the eldar. 'It doesn't matter. They're all the same when they're dead.'

FOR THE PURITY of the Empire, in deed and mind. Let my body be a machine of war. Let courage be my companion and never let it leave my side even in my darkest hour. Blood spilt in the name of the Emperor is glory; fear is the death of courage and the death of me.

Commissar Streck prayed, staring down from the fire base at the jungle below him. Pitch floated on the shallow waters, blazing in the lasfire glare, only to show the deaths of more Imperial Guardsmen. The screams of the dying echoed through the low ridges. Many of the Valis Fifth would die in battle for the Emperor today. The dead were in their own realm now and had their own judges. It was not for Streck to judge the dead, but to monitor the living and see that they showed courage in battle. His commission was brief and to the point: Spiritual guidance necessary. Instil courage and condemn fear. Victory unlikely.

A rocket screamed through the air and collided with the armour of the steel plateau on which Streck stood. The commissar grabbed hold of the railing but it came away, rusted at the joints. Streck rolled backwards towards the edge of the platform. Below him he could see the vile eldar closing in. The line of bases that acted as the first defence, out in the tangled jungle, were falling. Streck's sinewy arms strained, muscles shuddering as he hoisted himself back onto the platform.

The commissar stumbled through the smoking wreckage of the lower levels of the base checking bodies, and administering the Emperor's Grace to those who could not be saved. He made for the remaining soldiers huddled beneath the main supports of the fire base. Pip-pupilled terror screamed in their eyes; shaking hands drooped lasguns at the floor. Because of the smoke they had not seen him yet.

One of the Guardsmen stood and staggered out of the bunker. Streck prayed that he'd turn back. For fear is the enemy of man. It stays his weapon in anger and dilutes his potency.

'State your name and rank, soldier.' The Guardsman staggered round as Commissar Streck stepped out from the smoking wreckage.

'I, uh, I need a medic.' The Guardsman blinked, blurry-eyed, as the black overcoat and cap of the Imperial commissar swam before his eyes.

'Name and rank?'

'Retner Ganch, Guardsman, Valis Fifth, sir.' The words dribbled from the slump-shouldered shape.

'Are you aware of the punishment for desertion?'

'Can't fight... lost gun, lost fingers.' Ganch wriggled the nubs of a bloodied stump.

'And for each who has turned their back on battle there will be death. For they are dead already as weapons for the Emperor and lost to his halls of glory.' As Streck spoke the sentence, the Guardsman dropped to his knees, tears streaming down from his bloodshot eyes. 'Even worse are those who show fear in the face of judgement, for in death they have neither pride nor glory.'

Commissar Streck raised his pistol to the Guardsman's head, distancing himself so that the deserter's blood would not stain his clothes.

'If we must die, then we will die with courage,' Streck turned and bellowed at the remaining men. Another rocket struck the base, tearing through both plascrete and armour plating, but he did not flinch. 'The Emperor rewards those who show courage. They will join him at his halls and be recorded for ever in the annals of our heroes.'

Streck looked across the faces of the men before him. Youths, none more than two decades old, stared back at him. Mass-produced helmets rested loosely on their heads; the fit was almost always imperfect and required firm straps to provide any protection. Giddy-eyed and silent, the Guardsmen sat ineffectually in the mud. Streck was sick with rage. These men had not even caught sight of the aliens that assailed them, yet they were terrified.

'Do you not fear the death of a coward? There is no place for them. They will be spurned and hated by their fellow men, for they did not fight to better humanity. They lie slack-kneed and stupefied as the daemon weapons of the eldar come closer, every second making the last moments of their life those of a coward!'

Streck fired his pistol into one of the trembling Guardsmen. A brief shriek was all he relinquished. The dead man slumped forward, helmet tumbling into the blood-slick mud.

Shaking hands now readied weapons and began to release rapid volleys of lasfire through the fire-slits in the remaining parts of the bunker. Streck, pleased, set himself against a supporting beam and began to fire into the undergrowth, praying that his shots would ring true. He knew they were being surrounded. He could sense the unholy beings gathered in the swamp about them. Dusk was coming and they would renew their assault in the night, their alien eyes penetrating the darkness.

LOWNES, KNEE HIGH in swamp water, fingered his last grenade.

'They can't give us any support. The Basilisks are tied up shelling their main strike force,' the new Guardsman said, closing the console of a communicator.

'I need cover, all of you. And make it clean.' Lownes stripped off his pack and readied his lasgun. 'On my mark.'

'One.' Lownes twisted the grenade's pin. 'Two.' The squad raised their rifles. 'Three.' Thrashing through the water like a charging beast, Lownes ran for an embankment close to the eldar. The squad fired in unison, lasers slicing jungle vines and igniting small gas pockets. The fury of their renewed assault scythed through the eldar. They shot down all but the robed eldar, the dead aliens' body armour cracking open to reveal pale skins glistening like shelled oysters.

An immense geyser of swamp water reared into the sky. Lownes had almost stood on his own grenade. In the second that the water spouted, Lownes tumbled out from behind cover and started firing at the robed eldar. Lasfire crackled about it. Lownes threw himself at the eldar psyker, chainsword sending rapid pulses up his arm. The eldritch being brought up its thin staff to parry the blow. Sparks danced around crackles of energy. Lownes reeled within the electrical maelstrom. Death only a heartbeat away, the seasoned Jungle Fighter threw down his lasgun and snatched at his combat knife. On his knees, Lownes plunged the simple blade into the eldar's side. The field dissipated. The chainsword shattered jewels and mesh armour. Like a burst of air rushing forth from a vacuum seal, the psyker expired.

THE SWAMP HOWLED with the sounds of the night creatures, their shrill, staccato voices beating at the air like tiny hammers upon a discordant chime. Streck found some solace in the noise. He had heard that the eldar possessed keen senses, their hearing unmatched. These night calls would make them uncomfortable. As if on cue, a shot rang out in the darkness and the screeching stopped, only to start again a few seconds later. Streck chuckled. He had long since learnt to find pleasure in his enemies' pain.

What remained of his command force lay scattered about the wrecked bunker. Eyes downcast, each man sat contemplating his fate. Some men looked over the personal possessions they kept about them: gang bandannas from their home world, farewell gifts from lovers, trinkets and keepsakes of all descriptions. Others simply stared at the mud, or shivered in the swamp water. Only a few talked. In one instant it occurred to Streck how far these men had been gathered from to defend this jungle planet. How each had come from the far distant world of Valis to die together in defence of the greater cause. The power of the Emperor was vast. He prayed the Great One would smile on them tonight.

Streck had ordered the men to conserve their energy packs. Until such a time as someone got a clean aim at an eldar, no one was to fire. Silent as death's scythe, a spinning disc as fast as light skimmed into the armoured shell and struck the man closest to Streck in the head. His face a bloodied mess, he died before he could scream.

The Guardsmen fired wildly into the darkness. Lasfire lit up the bunker for a few seconds.

'No! Where I'm firing.' Streck screamed. 'Fire on my lead!'

The men still fired in all directions. A wave of enemy fire swept down into the bunker and cut more Guardsmen down. Limbs severed, screams ceased. Their wild firing was serving only to reveal their positions. A flash revealed two eldar rushing forward from the dark cover of the mangroves. Their feet hardly splashing the shallow water, they moved with terrifying grace, long hair running wild from hard armour crafted from sorcerous materials. Chainswords screaming, they fell upon the revealed Guardsmen, slicing through flesh and bone like it was water.

Streck spun and levelled his bolt pistol at the carnage. Men were falling by pairs, dual cries of terror sending others running.

'Hold your ground! For the Emperor!' Streck felled one of the eldar, three shots cutting cleanly through the lurid helm of the alien degenerate. The butchery stopped for a second. The remaining eldar withdrew its spinning blades from the carcass of a dead man and let the glowing green eyes of its helm look the commissar up and down.

'Let the Emperor's might be mine!' Streck spat bloody spittle as explosive shells cracked from his pistol, jarring his hand and throwing him backwards.

The alien leapt high over the commissar's shots. The shells burst against the roof of the bunker, each getting closer to the lightning-fast eldar as it sailed through the air. Streck tumbled through the mud, listless limbs flapping against the ground as the eldar darted after him, twin swords held high above its head like a matador.

Streck kicked a trembling Guardsman into the path of the eldar and it cut him down without slowing. Shots rung off his assailant's carapace. Streck rushed a prayer to the Emperor.

Steaming with sulphurous heat, the eldar dove at Streck. Bracing for the pain, the commissar blinked. It was all the time needed. Opening his eyes again, Streck looked up and traced the jittering death spasm of his assailant. It lay on the end of a large, crude chainsword. Engraved words following the blade read Catachan IV.

Lieutenant Lownes, dour face slick with the heat, looked down at the commissar. 'It would appear you're surrounded.'

IT TOOK SOME moments to cover the dead and regroup under the dripping steel bunker. Half the fortification was ripped open down one side, and Lownes set two Jungle Fighters to block it with whatever rubble they could scavenge and cram into the space without being shot.

'Why did they let you through, lieutenant?' Commissar Streck said, looking down over the Catachan commander.

'False hope. You've held out this far – thought you'd be saved.' Lownes continued bandaging a Guardsman's arm. 'There's only five of us. Not nearly enough to help dig you out of this one.'

'We're doomed? Is that what you think, lieutenant?' Streck stared into the Catachan's eyes.

Lownes stood and gestured at the huddled, forlorn figures. 'No, it's what they think.' He grinned at the commissar. 'I've been in worse situations than this.'

'Really?'

'Well they're not tyranids, that's a start.'

Streck turned his back on the Catachan and looked out through the dark hole that was once a bunker wall. 'I will wait until daybreak before I command the men to attack. We make our stand here. The glory of the Emperor will aid our fight.'

'They won't let us make it through to daybreak. They'll shell this bunker to rubble before they let us see their positions. We need to set a trap, lure some in and get out of here,' Lownes replied. The commissar turned to face him.

'When the Great One was fighting the foul Horus, do you think he set about creating a trap to "lure" him to his death. With will alone he defeated the fiend, not simple tricks. Was he not–'

Lownes shook his head. 'Commissar. Sir. I am not questioning doctrine, rather trying to get my men and yourself out of here alive. Glory can wait for another day.'

'Glory must be the sole aim of each man, each day. His mind a temple, his body a weapon in the service of the Emperor.'

Lownes looked up at the roof, then fixed Streck with a steely glare. 'I hate to say it, sir, but this particular temple should be condemned – and all of the Emperor's weapons are running out of ammunition.'

THE PREPARATIONS TOOK only a few moments. Lownes and his men scampered in and out of the bunker, low to the ground like crabs. Others ran the detonating cable they'd scavenged from the burnt-out fire base along the ground. Commissar Streck looked on, his face a granite scowl. In his head he played through the various positions he could take. From depths he had not penetrated for some years he drew out fragments of doctrine, of teachings and precedents. The rebellion on Ultar III, bloody merciless suppression, the Emperor's Grace for those whose minds were mortally fatigued. Streck formulated, stipulated and prepared his judgement, dark eyes impenetrable to those who would dare look the commissar in the face.

Only one man did. 'Commissar, we are ready, thank the Emperor,' Lownes called from a precarious position atop the bunker.

Streck stood well back. The Catachans had jury-rigged several grenades at weak points about the rubble strewn about the outer walls of the bunker.

'There's double-thick plating up that end,' Lownes said, pointing. 'Everyone up there.'

'What exactly are you suggesting we do, lieutenant?' Streck sneered.

'We've rigged the outside with explosives. This bunker is now one big grenade.' Even Streck shuddered a little at this suggestion. 'All we need to do is lure them in and let the thing rip.'

'How do you propose we do that?'

'Surrender,' Lownes grinned.

'Alien heretics are not known for taking prisoners.'

'Exactly.'

'I DON'T SEE them coming.' The jungle was still in the bright dawn light.

'You won't until they're close enough to make a kill,' Lownes called, keeping his voice low. He continued staring out from the bunker, lasgun sight fixed on the young Guardsman. The small figure shuffled forward towards the edge of the clearing, gazing nervously all around him.

'They're fast, sir.'

'I know, son. That's why I sent you out there. You've got reflexes that would make the Departmento Munitorium consider giving you special training.' Lownes was nervous too. He couldn't make out any movement in the faint light of the waking day.

'Think so, sir?' The Guardsman lowered his white flag for a moment as he looked back over his shoulder.

'Keep your eyes sharp, soldier.'

'Well?' Streck's voice rung the length of the bunker.

'Nothing yet, commissar.' Lownes flicked his head; sweat had saturated his bandanna and was beginning to run into his eyes. 'Tense, isn't it?'

'You make sure your men are ready and I'll take care of mine.' Streck turned his back on him and stalked the length of his retinue.

Lownes motioned with his hand and the three remaining Jungle Fighters crept forward, keeping their heads low. 'We have the surprise,' Lownes whispered to his men. 'We may be outnumbered but we've been through much worse and lived. Get through this and I'll look into getting us into Segmentum Solar, closer to home.'

Streck's voice came ringing down the length of the bunker as he walked along the line of nervous Imperial Guardsmen. 'Fear is the province of the weak and unworthy. There is no glory for those who run from battle or fail to raise their weapon in anger. Others who come after you will remember this day if you fight with valour. We are outnumbered – this planet is destined to be taken. There are too many of the obscene enemies of the Emperor and too few of his servants.' Streck removed a copy of the Imperial Scriptures from his overcoat. 'I am a hard man but I give you my blessing for what it is worth. For each man lost–'

'Lieutenant! They're coming!' the Guardsman screamed from outside, running hell for leather for the bunker.

'Keep that flag waving!' Lownes yelled as he motioned his men into action. A tall, slender shape, moving fast amongst the trees, took aim on the young Guardsman. Lownes reached out and grabbed the sprinting soldier by the lapels, swinging him into safety. A dozen shuriken ripped the white flag out of the Guardsman's hand, shredding it against the thick concrete wall.

Honed reflexes snapping into action, one of the other Jungle Fighters raised his lasgun and cut the alien down with a single shot. Its seared body armour glowed faintly in the dawn light as it dropped like cut bamboo into the swamp. The Catachans fell back from the bunker opening, firing neat bursts at the charging eldar as they crossed the clearing.

'Everyone back… and pray this works.' Lownes snatched up a small control panel, twenty lines patched into it. The first inhuman figure was silhouetted in the bunker's doorway.

'Everybody down!'

'Emperor protect us!' Streck cried as Lownes slammed his hand down on the panel.

A rush of air, like a deep space air lock blowing, dragged at the Imperial Guard huddled in the bunker. Men cried and blood burst from ear drums as the explosion raged through the confined space. Flame rushed about the soldiers, setting some alight. Lownes grabbed the brave young Guardsman and threw his flaming body to the ground, holding him down to smother the flames. Commissar Streck screamed prayers to the Emperor as the flames rose higher.

Then silence.

STRECK WAS THE first to open his eyes. Gashes in the bunker roof bled shafts of light into the dust-choked darkness. The pages of his book of scripture lay scattered and burning around his collapsed body.

The commissar struggled to his feet and staggered out of a ripped hole into the warm dawn air. It was filled with the smell of burning steel, harsh and metallic, lapping at the edges of his nostrils. A dozen eldar lay on the ground; some moved, others lay still. Streck stumbled towards one of the aliens, its leg pinned to the ground by a steel girder. The eldar flapped uselessly at the beam, the blood running freely onto the ground marking the minutes it had left to live. Streck dropped to his knees and grappled with the creature's helm, ripping it from side to side, rocking loose the bonds that fastened it. The eldar slapped at Streck, making limp, childlike attempts to knock him to the ground. Streck stumbled backwards as the helm came loose, revealing the pale white skin of the alien.

'Heretic scum,' Streck panted. 'Look upon the face of man!' Streck raised his bolt pistol and held it to the eldar's forehead. The alien closed its eyes and sat still. Streck holstered his weapon and pulled himself to his feet using the girder that impaled the eldar. The creature screamed, a hollow, soulless noise. 'No mercy for you, degenerate.'

'Commissar, get down!' Lieutenant Lownes burst from the bunker, a lasgun under each arm. Streck snapped his head around and saw several more eldar rushing from the shadows of the jungle, fluted weapons pointed in his direction.

Streck fell backwards and pulled an eldar's body over him just as a barrage of spinning discs collided where he had been standing. Lownes unleashed a volley of burning hot laser fire from each of his weapons. They seared eldar armour, sinking deep into the soft flesh beneath. A humming shuriken clipped Lownes's arm. Reacting to the stinging pain, the seasoned warrior dropped to his stomach to give himself cover.

'For the Emperor!' Lownes called from his prone position, waving his hand high in the air.

The remaining Imperial Guardsmen opened fire, using the precarious cover of the destroyed bunker. Their shots flashed through the superheated air, slamming into both eldar and muddy swamp. From the edges of the vegetation, Lownes's Jungle Fighters unleashed everything they had. Streck had not seen them move through the mangroves to cut off the eldar. Grenades threw wads of swamp filth up into the air, toppling the eldar.

Lownes lunged forward, holstering one lasgun to unstrap his chainsword. A wounded eldar lurched forward at Lownes from the swamp. Its chainsword whirled close to Lownes's head, metal teeth spitting mud across his face. Lownes brought his own sword up against the eldar's. The creature slammed a quick succession of blows against the Catachan, Lownes catching each with a narrow parry. He held the last of the eldar's blows on his chainsword, drove his lasgun into the alien warrior's chest and fired. The force from the gun threw the eldar back into the muddy water, its chainsword still spinning as it jerked in a death spasm.

Lownes caught sight of the commissar's muddy uniform amidst the dead eldar.

'You still alive, commissar?' Lownes asked, dragging an eldar body off Streck.

'I will not run. Help me to my feet and let me fight for my glory.'

'You've got shellshock. It might only be temporary.'

'Let me fight,' Streck spluttered, blood trickling out of his ears and mouth.

'You're hardly able to stand. You'd better serve the Emperor by getting out of this alive, sir. We must retreat.'

Lownes hoisted the commissar onto his shoulder and begun to stagger through the swamp, away from the battle. Streck fired his pistol uselessly in the direction of the remaining eldar forces.

'Fall back to the main installation!' Lownes shouted over the noise of the battle.

'No!' Streck cried. 'We hold our ground and fight to the last!'

The ragged band moved in increments from the bunker, some supporting others on their shoulders. Every few steps, men would have to take cover and return fire on the advancing eldar. Lownes kept pace with the men, hacking aside any vines or large fronds that slowed their progress. After an hour's forced march, guns levelled every step of the way in fear of more eldar, the Guardsman reached the central installation, the key Imperial defence position in this sector of Olstar Prime. Lownes staggered forward, the commissar struggling on his back, until he passed under the heavy gates to the compound and fell to his knees.

'How dare you challenge a commissar!' Streck screamed at Lownes as the lieutenant knelt, panting on the ground, his face crimson. The commissar flailed himself to his feet, tottered for a moment and then stood erect. 'How long have we been out of the battle?'

'It's over, Streck.'

'Over?'

'The surviving elements of the Fifth are returning; my men are guiding them through the jungle as we speak.'

'They know the way back!' Streck snapped.

'They're taking an alternate route.'

'Creeping back like dogs on their bellies!'

'The same way we got back alive.'

'You have threatened my immortality today, Lownes. I have fought gloriously in every battle I have joined. I have never turned my back on the enemy. I have suffered countless wounds and remained alive, to fight again for the sanctity of man and the honour of the Emperor!'

'Save your preaching,' the Catachan said, shaking his head. 'I serve the Emperor just like you, but I would rather fight than die a lone fool striking out against a hundred enemies. If I can find a way to make a difference I will, but I will not die in some forsaken swamp for no reason other than glory.'

'Glory is found through death.'

'Glory is what I make of it.'

Commissar Streck stared at the Jungle Fighter. Both men stood still, Lownes's eyes cast to the ground.

'I'm going to find my men.' Lownes turned his back and left the compound.

HE STOOD TALL amongst the returning Imperial Guardsmen. The battle over, few walked upright, their energy spent. Even those unwounded walked like men with a death sentence, their eyes towards the ground, bodies near paralysed with dread resolve. Amidst scant cheers, the Catachan Jungle

Fighters arrived, leading the Guardsmen through the massive barricade gate. Catachan, a planet of fringe dwellers, souls sworn to the Emperor despite lives spent in obscene pursuits. For Streck these troops were worse than barbarian outriders. They fought in no formation, wore no real uniform, misused weapons and showed no honour in battle. They did not stand and fight but nipped at the enemy's heels like dogs.

Lownes stood at the head of the returning men, his face dour, despite his heroics on the battlefield. No cheer passed his lips, no smile broke his face. Dead and living travelled through the gates. Bodies upon stretchers covered by shrouds soon separated from the file of men; like driftwood cast out of the sea by waves, they were directed towards the morgue and crematorium. Above everything hung a persistent roaring, as merchant ships – not bound by illusory notions of duty and honour – heaved into orbit from the refugee-choked landing pads, every space filled with those who could afford today's asking price.

Streck followed the Jungle Fighters through the complex. People scurried about frantically like ants, laden down with bundles of equipment and rations. Many of the civilian buildings had been stripped, Guardsmen protecting the military installations. Streck was unsurprised by the Catachan's destination when they finally pushed open the crude metal doors of the last open saloon. In the dim light, a woman divesting herself of clothing betrayed their motives.

So soon after the glory of battle! Streck was sick with the thought of what these men were truly like. No sooner had their bodies done the glorious work of the Emperor than their weak spirits drove them into the clutches of flesh and alcohol.

Without really thinking what he was doing, the commissar entered through the back of the saloon, clenching his book of scripture tightly in his hand. The bar owner's pockmarked face twisted white as the agent of the Emperor's law entered. Streck sat amidst the din and smoke and watched. He had never entered the saloon before; military business had never given him reason to.

The woman moved listlessly. Streck assumed she was shutting out the desperate, doomed faces of those about her, the reminders of her own fate. The Catachan were more sullen than earlier. They drank and watched the woman dance with loveless eyes. Streck looked across their faces. Scarred, brows furrowed, they stared dark-eyed into their glasses. Their lips moved in crude motions, mouthing words with such effort that Streck could read their lips through the filth laden air.

Glasses. Streck hadn't realised until now. Every soldier drank, bar one. Lieutenant Lownes just stared into the table, into darkness. Streck considered the man. He had disgraced so many by leading them in a retreat from the battle. Perhaps he had realised the truth of his actions, felt the guilt of a coward. Streck considered the value of a court martial again. It would set a precedent, of course, but men bearing ranks as high as Lownes's were not exempt from execution.

Lownes stood, bade farewell to his men and left the saloon. Drifting after him, Streck wove through the crowded room, all eyes turned away uncomfortably moments before he passed. Streck knew this behaviour as shame, for those who serve the Emperor well know their actions are true and will only receive praise.

A TROPICAL HEAT washed over Olstar Prime, sucking fluid from every pore. Streck stalked Lownes through the compound: Lownes striding forward, a giant powerhouse riding the waves of combat drugs that still tingled along his limbs; Streck lean, tall, keeping pace. Lownes returned to the steady flow of the dead through the colony gates. He walked amongst them, pulling back each sheet.

Streck hung back and watched, trying to pierce the motivations of this man. His reports described him as a loose cannon, but honoured him numerous times with no less than thirty successful engagements to his name. He himself had seen how the Jungle Fighter had led his men and those thrown in with him by fate. He spoke the words of the faithful and did not show any signs of heresy – but he had challenged a superior officer and refused the command of a commissar. Offences punishable by death, yet Streck remained undecided.

Lownes walked along the 'Road of the Dead', as the colonists called it, for it led to the installation's mortuarium. A house that might contain his body one day, and if not this one, definitely some other mortuary in another dark place of the galaxy. Streck had noticed long before that Imperial Guard drop pods often contained morgues, as though death was just another element of battle that needed to be taken care of. Lownes entered and approached the line of bodies gradually being pushed towards the furnace.

Streck watched as Lownes continued his dismal search. The end result: five shrouded figures, red bandannas draped across them. Lownes stood over them in the damp chill of the vault. Drawing out his combat knife, Lownes held out his left forearm; steely muscles twitched as he scored five long gashes across it. Placing each body bag into the crematorium, Lownes ignited them. Once they were consumed he rubbed some of the combined ashes produced by the furnace into the wounds. Ritual scarification. Crude but not without honour, Streck mused.

A steel stretcher-bed in the barrack block was Lownes's next port of call. The Catachan end of the barracks was covered in an array of war trophies and coloured banners. It was far short of the Spartan neatness that Streck called for in his own thorough examinations of the Imperial Guard quarters. Streck's aversion to the Catachan Fighters had never led him past this part of the barrack compound. Now he peered in through a window like a thief.

In the still of nightfall, Lownes produced his lasgun and began stripping it down with rapid, staccato movements. each hand operating on its own task. Streck watched Lownes go through this ritual again and again, mesmerised by the symphony of assembly and disassembly. The soldier's wounds still wept, yet he ignored the pain.

Streck considered for long moments. He knew that a mould must be flexible enough to create versatility in what it cast. In those days of judgement, the Emperor cast and recast his actions, each one different, each one enough to hold back the traitors and heretics that threatened the purity of mankind. Had he not done so, the pattern of his thinking would have been revealed, he considered, and his battle strategies useless. Skills Streck still believed he must hone. Maybe he should teach himself a little more flexibility in both strategy and judgement. Let Lownes be the man he must, Streck thought; let him be cast from the mould a little rough around the edges. Perhaps it was a test set by the Emperor, a test of his ability to reason with the faith to have the courage to engage fully with the scriptures, not just the Lore of Punishment and Retribution alone. After all, had not Lownes served the Emperor well? Maybe the Catachan should not be condemned so harshly for his actions.

Streck had learnt long ago never to let down his guard. Two years ago, three Imperial Guardsmen had attempted a mutiny whilst he was engaged in combat with a renegade Space Marine. Their escape was forever burnt upon his mind.

The rustle in the bushes beside the barracks was entirely noticeable. Streck caught sight of a figure darting into the barracks. A surprise attack? Bolt pistol at the ready, he peered into the room again. In the darkness he saw two figures – Lownes and a second, a woman. Streck peered harder but could only make out silhouettes. A flare of light from within and for an instant Streck saw all. Lownes's torso, exposed, deep cuts and wounds wet with blood. The deep orange flashes emanated from a cauterising device the woman was applying.

When his wounds were treated, Lownes leaned to pull a pack from beneath his bed. He had carried it with him throughout the battle. Streck had paid it no heed, figuring it for rations or repair equipment – he knew the tales of the Catachan's self-sufficiency.

The Jungle Fighter opened the bag and held it open for the woman. Streck could see her properly now as she looked appraisingly over the contents of the bag. She was striking, hair cut short in the style of a native Catachan, a long scar running down one cheek to the point of her sharp chin. Her jump-suit and flak jacket showed she was not a soldier; a merchant guild badge hanging from her chest was all that identified her.

The woman reached into the bag and began to examine its contents, Lownes's solid form obscuring them from Streck's view. The commissar hurried quietly around to the half-open door and found he could see completely into the room.

'You will help me get my men off this place?' Lownes was asking.

'Lownes, how long have you known me for?' the merchant replied, sifting through the bag.

'A long time… since we were young. But I know this will just be business. This will make up the final payment?'

'Given that I don't have enough time to barter you down, I'll agree – but that's only because I know you, Lownes.'

'And that's passage for all of them.'

'We've got just enough room.' The merchant turned.

At last Streck saw what Lownes was trading: eldar weapons!

'Lieutenant!' the commissar burst into the room, bolt pistol drawn.

'Streck!' The half-assembled lasgun lay on the bed beside Lownes. He reached for it but its parts clattered onto the steel floor, lost amongst the mesh grating.

'Lieutenant Lownes, you are charged with attempted desertion and possession of heretical weapons!'

'What?'

'This subterfuge, these plans to flee are not warrior's work. You have defamed your body as a machine of the Emperor. The Emperor gives you life and you, in turn, give him yours. This is a warzone and you have sullied yourself with this illicit transaction.' Streck spat the words out in a frenzied babble. 'As a champion of the Emperor you betray us all.'

Lownes put himself between Streck and the merchant. 'I am doing what is best for my men, as always.'

'Your men are servants of the Emperor. You are a servant of the Emperor. To possess such weapons is heresy and punishable by death – but to seek to flee a righteous war is to have all honour stripped from your name after death. Your spirit is marred. You can not be remade. Trust in the Emperor, not the embraces of a woman!' Streck raised his pistol.

'Save it, Streck,' Lownes said, somehow calmer now. 'It's not loaded. I removed the clip earlier, when you were unconscious.'

Streck pulled the trigger anyway. Nothing happened.

The two men jumped as one. Streck ejected the empty clip from his pistol onto the ground, grabbing a fresh one from his belt and slamming it into the gun. Simultaneously, Lownes flung the contents of the bag out onto the bed and grabbed an eldar pistol, pointing it at the commissar.

'This is lunacy!' the merchant cried, struggling to push herself between the pair, Lownes's arm holding her at bay. 'Look, commissar, I can fit you on board, no charge. I'll get you out of here before the whole place goes down. It's the deal of a lifetime.'

'Let my men leave, Streck. You'll never hear from us again,' Lownes pleaded.

'You will be sentenced to death,' Streck said through gritted teeth.

'My finger is on the trigger. I will fire as soon as you do.'

'My aim is good.' The commissar steadied his gun.

'So is mine. Look, this is madness. We can both live.'

'And for each who has turned their back on battle there will be death. For they are dead already–'

'Incoming!' screamed a voice from outside. Metal plating ripped and the ground cracked open as a massive explosion rocked the compound. In the barrack room, however, neither man moved despite the shaking ground.

'Eldar! Here they come!' cried a different voice from out by the gate.

Streck paused for a moment. Lownes stared him straight in the eyes, the merchant woman looking on in terror.

Suddenly one of Lownes's men was at the door. 'Sir, it's the big one. They've breached the– Lieutenant?'

Other Jungle Fighters arrived behind him, weaponless and bloodied. Neither Streck nor Lownes moved.

'For they are dead already–' Streck began.

'We have enough time to escape. We're not going to win, commissar!' Lownes insisted. 'This planet is lost, but we can live – criminals, perhaps, but alive! Come on!'

Streck paused in his litany and regarded Lownes with eyes of steel. 'Oh yes. We could run,' he snarled. 'Then another planet will fall, overrun by alien degenerates intent upon the destruction of humanity. Creatures driven by such a desperate vengeance that they will fight on until every last one of us is destroyed. Unless we remain defiant, fighting on despite this madness. Face the task in hand and make the difference. For each enemy dead in this last stand, it will be one less enemy to be fought in the future. Each man can make a difference: "As weapons for the Emperor and lost to his halls of glory!"' Streck finished, his voice level with unshakeable faith.

Lownes stared at the commissar's set expression, his mind racing in confusion.

There was a deafening roar and a pressure wave slammed against the barracks, sending men and fittings flying. Plaster and bricks blew into the room, leaving several holes in the wall.

'They're inside the–' someone screamed, their voice cut off as a line of shells sliced through the room like a scythe. The merchant woman was thrown backwards into a corner. Picking himself up off the floor, Lownes started to move towards her, but he knew already that she was dead.

He looked at Streck, who had somehow remained standing throughout the bombardment, then down at the eldar weapon in his hands. He dropped it as if it was diseased, then looked back at the commissar, face set. 'Very well. Let's do it. Let's make a difference. Give me a lasgun.'

'Thank you, Lieutenant Lownes,' Streck said calmly, handing over a weapon. 'For the Emperor!'

'For the Emperor!'

Moments later, the ragged, lit-up doorway to the barracks was filled with the contrasting silhouettes of the Catachan lieutenant and the commissar. Then the pair of them dove, guns blazing, into the metal-filled air of the white hot night.

ACCEPTABLE LOSSES

Gav Thorpe

'CAPTAIN ON THE flight deck!'

The assembled aircraft crews of the Imperial cruiser *Divine Justice* moved as one. Captain Kaurl strolled into the vast hangar to the resounding clang of one hundred boots stamping in near-perfect unison on the steel-mesh decking. Walking two strides behind the stocky flag captain, Flight Commander Jaeger looked over his new comrades.

Most were dressed in regulation fatigues, standing smartly where they had been working or lounging before their commander's arrival. Jaeger's eye was drawn towards a particular crowd off to one side, towards the rear of the aircraft bay. There was something surly about their bearing: their uniforms were not quite so smart, their posture not so rigid as the other flight crews; their attention not totally focused on the newly arrived captain. Instinctively, Jaeger knew that they were Raptor Squadron, his new command.

That explained a couple of things, at least: Kaurl's slightly amused look when he had greeted Jaeger earlier, and the glances from the other flight commanders during his initial introduction. So, the Raptors were in need of some discipline? Well, Jaeger would soon knock them into shape.

Jaeger realised that Captain Kaurl was addressing the flight crews and tuned his wandering mind into what his new commander was saying.

'...and I expect every one of you to accord Flight Commander Jaeger the same amount of respect and co-operation you gave to his predecessor, Commander Glade. Proceed with your duties; we break from dock at 0500 hours.'

With a nod, the captain sent the gathered men back to work and turned to Jaeger.

'I see from your look that you've already spotted Raptor Squadron,' he said plainly.

Jaeger nodded slightly, keeping his expression as neutral as possible.

'They're not as bad as they might seem at first,' Kaurl continued. 'There are some damn fine pilots there, and with the right man in charge they'll make a fine showing. I think you're that man, Jaeger, and I'll be watching your progress with interest.'

'Thank you, sir,' Jaeger replied, pleased the captain had confidence in him. 'I don't think you'll have anything to worry about from Raptor Squadron.'

'Go and meet your men then, I'll see you later. Give them a chance and they'll prove themselves worthy of the Emperor's Navy.'

The two officers exchanged respectful bows before Kaurl turned on his heel and strode from the flight deck. Jaeger took in all the sights, sounds and smells of his new home. Although most flight decks had similarities, each always had a unique odour, a different edge on the lighting, variations in layout and a hundred other small details that made it special. The flight deck of the *Divine Justice* had space to carry, prepare and launch ten of the massive Marauder bombers, along with a complement of ten Thunderbolt fighters. All of the aircraft were currently in their docking bays, each nestling in its own arched alcove along the sides of the flight deck. Above the flight commander's head, a labyrinthine criss-cross of gantries and steps hung in the distant shadows, centred around a pair of enormous cranes capable of picking up and transferring the planes to the launching bays. The chatter of the flight crews filled the cavernous chamber with a constant murmuring, and the fragrances of the tech-priests' unguents and incense hung heavy in the air, mixed with the more mundane smell of oiled metal and human sweat. Taking a deep breath, Jaeger started towards his new flight crews.

As he strode across the flight deck, Jaeger quickly inspected his new men more closely. Despite Kaurl's parting words, he was not impressed with what he saw. They slouched amidst a scattering of crates, idly passing the time arguing heatedly, playing with dice or just sprawling around relaxing. All but a few wore loose-fitting, light grey fatigues, presenting a drab, uninspiring sight. Some of them turned to look at the flight commander as he strode briskly over, and a couple managed to get to their feet. One of them, a gunner from Jaeger's own plane judging by his insignia, pulled himself upright and snapped off a sharp salute.

'Fine day!' proclaimed the gaunt-looking gunner. 'May I welcome you to the auspicious role that is flight commander of Raptor Squadron.'

One of the others, a burly-looking bombardier, shot a murderous glance at the man.

'Shut it, Saile. The new commander don't want to hear your creeping!' the bombardier warned, his sweat-beaded brow knitted in a glowering scowl.

'That's enough from both of you!' Jaeger snapped, irritated by their indiscipline. 'Let's get something straight right from the start: I don't like you, any of you.' Jaeger made a point of looking them over slowly. 'From what I've already seen, you are a bunch of shoddy, undisciplined, no-hope slackers. Well, not any more!

'You will address me as Commander Jaeger. Unless directly addressed by me, in non-combat situations you will only talk to me by first receiving permission, in the manner of "Permission to speak, Commander Jaeger?". Are those two simple facts absolutely clear?'

The men looked at Jaeger in stunned disbelief.

'I believe the words you are looking for are, "Yes, Commander Jaeger",' he prompted, eyebrows raised.

Their reply was quiet and faltering, but it was a start.

'Ahm, permission to speak, Commander Jaeger?' came a quiet voice from one of the men around them.

Jaeger looked at the flyer who was stepping lightly between the others to stand in front of him. He was swathed in the voluminous robes that marked him out as one of the tech-adepts, responsible for the mechanical and spiritual wellbeing of the planes, as well as the 0 itself. The man's neck was criss-crossed with wires and scar tissue, and an interface plug dangled from the back of his right hand. In battle, the tech-adept would literally wire himself into the Marauder bomber, monitoring any damage and prompting the plane's repair mechanisms into action.

'Granted,' Jaeger said with a nod.

'As I am principally a member of the Adeptus Mechanicus, and only aligned to the efforts of the Imperial Navy by secondary venture, I consider your treatment of myself and the other tech-adepts as subordinates in a very serious light,' the tech-adept said, his chin raised proudly to look the tall flight commander full in the face.

Jaeger grabbed the man's robe, pulling him up until he was on the tips of his toes. The adept's hood fell back, exposing more bio-wiring. The coils of thin cable sprung from his shaven head like metallic hair, attached to his scalp through a hundred scabrous incisions in the skin. Some of the others stepped forward but were stopped in their tracks by a murderous glance from their new commander.

'While you fly my planes, I am your commanding officer!' Jaeger snarled. 'I don't care what rank you have in the worship of the Machine God – on this flight deck and in the air, you answer to me! Make no mistake, I have every intention of turning this squadron into a respectable fighting unit. Cooperate and you may come through it with your lives and your rank. Go against me and I'll chew you up and spit out the pieces.'

Jaeger let go of the adept and stalked off, cursing himself for losing his temper. But if there was one thing that Jaeger hated, it was sloppiness. He had seen too many good men die because of another's carelessness, and he wasn't going to let it happen again.

JAEGER ORDERED THE men to stand down, pleased with their performance during the training session. As they sloped off to their communal sleeping chambers, Jaeger headed back towards the bunkroom he shared with the other three flight commanders. Jaeger wiped the sweat from his face with the palm of his hand, and was glad to be leaving the heat of the flight deck, warmed beyond tolerance by the bombers' engines. As he walked down the corridor towards the officers' quarters, Jaeger heard the clump of boots on the metal deck and turned. Marte, one of his gunners and a veteran of many years service, jogged slowly up, saluting as he approached.

'Permission to speak, Commander Jaeger?' the man asked cautiously.

'What's on your mind, gunner?'

'Excuse my saying, but I don't reckon you're as hard-edged as you make out, sir.' The gunner was sheepishly inspecting the backs of his hands, avoiding Jaeger's stare. 'We – that is, the other lads and me – we were wondering how you ended up as our flight commander. I mean, what did you do wrong?'

'What are you getting at, gunner?' Jaeger rested his hands on his hips. 'And look at me when I speak to you,' he added, annoyed at having to address the top of the gunner's bald head.

Marte looked up reluctantly to meet his gaze. It was obvious that the other crew members had put him up to this. 'Well, getting stuck with Raptors,' the gunner explained quietly. 'I mean, you seem like you know what you're doing, so why did you end up in this dead-end assignment?'

'"Dead-end"? Raptor Squadron may not be spectacular, but you're all competent, dedicated men. Why should this command be so bad?' Jaeger asked, genuinely puzzled.

'So you've not heard the stories, sir?' The gunner's face was a picture of incredulity.

'I don't listen to rumours, I deal with facts and my own experiences,' Jaeger snapped, annoyed that the gunner considered the flight commander the type to listened to scuttlebutt.

'Very wise, sir,' the old gunner said quickly. 'Look, Raptors get the worst deal, it's that simple. If there's some dirty work to be done, we'll get it. You must have seen the records, we've got the highest loss rate for the last three tours. That idiot Glade didn't help either, Emperor rot him.'

To Jaeger, the gunner was making no sense at all. 'What about the other Marauders?' he asked. 'Devil Squadron?'

'The Devils?' The gunner laughed, a short and bitter noise. 'They don't know the meaning of hard work. Flight Commander Raf is Admiral Veniston's nephew, if you take my meaning...'

The veteran gunner was shaking his head, as if his surprise at the flight commander's ignorance had reached a new level. Jaeger had had enough of being treated like a naive youth who had just earned his commission.

'You and all those other scurrilous gossips can rest assured that by the time I'm finished, Devil Squadron will be polishing our boots,' he promised, his voice hard, his eyes boring into the gunner. 'Remember, a crew is only as good as they think they are. Captain Kaurl is behind me on this: all you need is a morale boost and things will fall into place. Now go and get some rest!'

The old gunner hesitated for a moment, giving his commander a doubtful look, before hurrying back down the corridor, leaving Jaeger to his thoughts.

Raptor Squadron wasn't inherently bad, the flight commander mused. They'd just started believing the things that were said about them. If it was true that the admiral's favouritism for his nephew was costing lives, he'd have a few things to say about that. For now, all he could do was watch and wait. And hope that things weren't as bad as they seemed.

'EMPEROR'S BLOOD! THAT'S a sight to set a man's heart trembling!' Admiral Veniston exclaimed. Only eight weeks into her patrol, the *Divine Justice* had run into serious trouble. Magnified on the main display screen of the *Divine Justice's* bridge was a scene of utter destruction, the like of which the ageing officer had not witnessed for many years. The terrible wreckage of a Navy cruiser, what little remained, spun slowly across the stars. In the distance could just be made out the dark shape of an ork hulk, the source of the carnage. One of the command crew looked up from the glowing green read-out in front of him.

'Surveyors identify her as the *Imperial Retribution*, admiral. 80% structural damage – she's taken one hell of a pounding,' the crewman reported.

Veniston nodded. 'Aye, she has. And the question is: how do we avoid a similar fate?'

Captain Kaurl took a step forward, a glint in his eye. 'I suppose dropping back into the warp and forgetting we found her is out of the question?'

As the command crew chuckled, Veniston directed Kaurl into the conference chamber with a flick of his head. Within the small wood-panelled room, the two were able to speak more freely.

It was Veniston who spoke first. 'Seriously, Jacob. How the hell are we going to take out that damned hulk?'

'The tech-priests made a long-range assay.' The captain activated a comm-screen and brought up a rough schematic of the hulk. 'The bulk of the weapon systems are located near the front. If we could come at it from the rear we could probably give her enough of a pounding while limiting the return fire.' As he spoke, Kaurl drew his finger over the screen in a wide circle, to finish pointing at the hulk's main engine block.

The admiral frowned. 'There's only us and the frigates, we can't take her on from more than one direction without being taken apart piecemeal. If she can bring her guns to bear, even the *Divine Justice* won't survive for very long. Just how do you suggest we get the greenskin scum on that hulk to sit still long enough for us to let rip with the torpedoes and batteries, Jacob?'

Kaurl rubbed his short-cropped beard. With the press of a rune, he imposed a series of arrows and notations onto the diagram of the hulk. 'Well, now that you mention it,' he said, 'I have had one idea. The orks won't have a problem hitting something the size of the *Divine Justice*, but that doesn't mean they're invulnerable...'

THE ORDER TO prepare for launch had been issued an hour ago. Now the flight crews were hurrying to finish their last tasks. Jaeger's second-in-command, Phrao, was leading the crew in prayer, kneeling with heads bowed beneath the fuselage of their Marauder, chanting hymnals with admirable concentration. Jaeger looked up to where Arick, one of the dorsal gunners, was clambering around on top of the Marauder's fuselage.

'What's with them?' Jaeger called up.

Arick looked down from where he was polishing the twin barrels of his auto-cannon atop the spine of the Marauder.

'Do it every time. S'posed to bring the Emperor's blessing,' the gunner called down.

'I guessed that, but why beneath the Marauder? Isn't it more practical to do it in the open?'

Arick shrugged, although the movement could hardly be seen inside the thick folds of the vacuum suit he was wearing. 'Meant to bring the Emperor's power through the plane. You know the score, you must've seen other crews doing something like that before every flight, a special ritual. Like Jeryll reading out the Articles of War, and me polishing this damned big gun, though I know the maintenance crews have oiled it plenty since we got our orders. Surprised you don't do something like it yourself.'

'Yes... Yes, you're right, there is something I nearly forgot,' Jaeger replied distractedly.

Standing in front of his massive Marauder, Jaeger called for his crew to gather in front of him, ready for briefing. His gaze turned to the nose of his craft and the gilded Eagle Rampant that shone from it. The design was repeated on the gloves of his dress uniform and printed on all of their helmets. It was the blazon of the Raptor Squadron. A fine name, but was it a fine crew?

As his crew congregated, he looked at each of them in turn. Over the two months that had passed since leaving the dock at Bakka, he had come to know the men better, although only real combat would show him their true mettle. There were the gunners, Arick, Marte and Saile; each had proved his accuracy on the simulation ranges, but word was that Arick lost his cool in the heat of battle, and Saile was basically a coward. Still, trust not in rumour, Jaeger's old captain on the Invincible had taught him.

The tech-adept, Ferix, had been no problem since Jaeger's rough treatment of his fellow Adeptus Mechanicus at that first encounter. Ferix was frowning, however, as he climbed down from the Marauder's engine, obviously annoyed that his attempts to consecrate the Marauder to the Machine God had been interrupted. Jaeger would give him time to finish his rituals before they launched; there were enough variables to worry about without offending the Marauder's spirit with hasty ceremonies and hurried prayers.

The last over was Berhandt, the bullying, muscle-bound bombardier. For all his rough accent and large frame, the flyer had a shrewd mind. He'd have to be watched, however, Jaeger had decided, since much of the pessimism of the squadron seemed to originate from him, one way or another.

Once all five of his crew were present, Jaeger stepped onto an empty munitions crate that the servitors had not yet moved. Clearing his throat, he spoke out strongly and surely, wanting to instil his crew with the confidence that they demanded. If they didn't believe in him now, their hesitation or doubt could get them all killed once they were in battle.

'As you know, many bomber crews have certain customs to ensure the Emperor's grace and no bad luck. Well, this is something of a tradition for me, a little ceremony I go through before my first combat flight with a new squadron, just to make sure nothing bad happens – to any of us. Don't worry, it doesn't take very long,' Jaeger assured them, seeing their distracted gazes. They wanted him to get his little pep-talk over as quickly as possible, and he could empathise with that.

'It's an old tale from my home planet. I come from Extu, in case you hadn't heard already – bit of a backwater by many of your standards, but we've a strong sense of honour and courage, so I'll not be running away from any fights.'

Jaeger saw nods of agreement from Marte and Arick. The others shuffled their feet uneasily, embarrassed by being told a story. Not all cultures were like the one on Extu, Jaeger knew; in some societies tales were seen as childish rather than important teachings for adults and children alike. Though he sometimes cursed others for their ridiculous habits or customs, in his years of service in the Imperial Navy, Jaeger had learnt to accept all manner of viewpoints and outlooks on life.

'Anyway, to my tale, as told to me by Faith-Sayer Gunthe. It tells of the great Emperor Eagle, whose claws are sheathed with fire and whose eyes are all-seeing – and of how he banished the Chaos Serpent from our realm. One day, the Chaos Serpent, the eternal enemy of the Emperor Eagle, steals one of the sacred eggs from the Emperor Eagle's nest whilst he is away hunting. The Chaos Serpent takes the egg back to her lair, and wraps herself about the egg to keep it warm, to make sure it incubates. When the Emperor Eagle returns, great is his dismay to find one of the sacred eggs missing. He searches far and wide, but he cannot see the missing sacred egg.

'Meanwhile, the egg hatches, and the young Eagle is welcomed into this world by the Chaos Serpent. "Greetings," says the Chaos Serpent, "I am your mother, you will learn what I teach you and listen to my every word." And the Eagle learnt the foul, twisted ways of the Chaos Serpent.'

Jaeger looked over his men, pleased to see they were all paying attention now, even Ferix whose own religious beliefs taught him to worship machines over human beings.

'The young Eagle's radiant golden feathers were tarnished with spite.' Jaeger's mouth twisted in disgust as he pictured the fallen Eagle in his mind. 'His glistening eyes were misted with false hope and his claws were blunted by disobedience. All the while, the Emperor Eagle continued his search, seeking ever further for his lost sacred egg. At last, one day, he came across the Eagle, now fully grown, and at first the Emperor Eagle was glad. But as he spoke to the lost Eagle and saw what it had become, the Emperor Eagle became most displeased. He commanded the young Eagle to remain where he was and sought out the Chaos Serpent. He found the treacherous, false creature hiding in the shadows nearby, but the Emperor Eagle's keen eyes still spotted her.'

Jaeger half-closed his eyes, remembering the first time he'd heard the tale when he was a small child. The next part was his favourite and had served to inspire him all the way through his upbringing by the Schola Progenium and through his flight training at Bakka. It was this that had first given him the ambition to be a pilot, and when times had been hard, he'd told himself the story in his mind. Each time it gave him the strength to persevere through his hardships.

As the other flight crews had finished their pre-flight rituals, they had drifted over to listen to the flight commander's speech. Now all twenty-nine of them stood in front of him, gripped by his words. Taking a deep breath, Jaeger continued.

'Swooping down upon his massive pinions, the Emperor Eagle seized the Chaos Serpent in his flame-wreathed talons and swept the Chaos Serpent high into the air. For a long time they flew. "Why do you attack me so?" enquired the Chaos Serpent, in feigned ignorance and innocence.

'"You have taken one of mine own from me," said the Emperor Eagle, "and twisted it with your dark ways so that it is no longer tall and proud and fulfilling its righteous destiny. That is a crime for which there can be no mercy." And the Emperor Eagle dropped the Chaos Serpent into the bottomless dark pit that is the Eye of Terror, condemning the Chaos Serpent to eternal imprisonment, agony and torment for what she had done to the young Eagle.'

Pausing for a moment for dramatic effect, he could see that the tale was having the desired affect on the assembled crewmen. The men were listening with rapt attention now, and for the moment would listen to, and more importantly believe anything he cared to tell them. His own pride was inspiring them, giving them the confidence to follow him wherever he led them.

'The Emperor Eagle returned to his offspring,' Jaeger continued, his intense gaze meeting the stare of each of the men in turn. '"You have been done a great wrong," the Emperor Eagle said, "made that much greater for I cannot correct it, but can only punish the guilty. There are no amends to be made. You are my child and yet I cannot suffer you to live now, twisted and malignant as you are." The young Eagle looked at the Emperor Eagle and the nobility of his birth rose through the filth of the Chaos Serpent's false teachings. "I understand, oh great Emperor Eagle," and the young Eagle bent back his head to show his breast to the Emperor Eagle. With one sweep of his flame-wreathed claws, the Emperor Eagle tore out the young Eagle's heart, burning it to ashes – for none can live that have been touched by the Chaos Serpent, not even the children of the Emperor Eagle.'

The sycophantic gunner, Saile, clapped enthusiastically; a few smiled in grim appreciation while the rest awaited his explanation with dutiful silence.

'For we are the talons of the Emperor!' Jaeger said, his voice deep and full of conviction, his right hand unconsciously making the shape of a grasping claw across his chest. 'Just as this ship is named the *Divine Justice*, so too must we be the instrument of the Emperor's vengeance. No mercy, no forgiveness, just the surety of swift justice and sure death!'

'Swift Justice, Sure Death' was the squadron's motto, and hearing it spoken so confidently, with such emotion, had a startling effect on the crew. Jaeger could see their anticipation, eager for battle like they had never been before. They had pride in themselves, for the first time in years.

'So, what are we?' Jaeger yelled, his hand now raised in a fist.

'Swift Justice, Sure Death!' came the replying cry from twenty-nine throats. It echoed around the flight bay, making the crews of the other squadrons turn in surprise. Jaeger grinned, his heart beating fast.

'Damn right! Let's give the enemy a taste of the Emperor's claws.'

* * *

JAEGER GRINNED AS he gazed out of the cockpit's canopy and saw the rest of the Squadron flying alongside the ship's hull, each pushed forward on quadruple tails of plasma. Beyond them, he saw the firing ports of the Divine Justice's gun decks opening slowly, revealing battery upon battery of massive laser cannons, mass drivers and plasma projectors. Immense firepower, enough to destroy a city.

The comm-link in Jaeger's helmet crackled into life.

++Thunderbolt fighter squadrons Arrow and Storm ready for rendezvous.++ The familiar voice of Flight Commander Dextra, given a metallic grate over the long-range communicator.

Jaeger flicked the brass transmit rune on the comm-link panel to his left. 'Good to hear you, Jaze. Take up a diamond-ten on the aft quarters.'

++Affirm, Raptor Leader.++

As the smaller fighters took up their escorting position around the bomber squadron, Jaeger increased the throttle, taking his plane to the front to form a flying-V formation, with his Marauder as the arrowhead. The craft swept over the prow of the cruiser, looking like tiny flares of light against the backdrop of the immense torpedo tubes.

'Bridge, this is Raptor Leader. Formed up and ready to attack; awaiting target data, by the Emperor,' Jaeger reported.

Berhandt gave a thumbs-up signal as the target information was transmitted from the *Divine Justice*. The bombardier's gruff voice gave Jaeger the details over the internal communicator. 'It's a point at the rear of the 'ulk, in the engines somewhere. Can't tell what it is exactly, this far out.'

'What do you mean?' Jaeger asked.

'Just what I said, sir. It's just some co-ordinates, no details of target type and a notation that says the attack trajectory is at your discretion.'

'Very well. Inform me as soon as we get further details,' Jaeger replied, before addressing the rest of the squadron. 'Listen up, Raptors, this is the real thing. No bickering, no whining and no stalling. I am not going to let you get me and your flight comrades killed. We're here to blow things up in the name of the Emperor, and that's what we're damned well going to do!'

Jaeger smiled as he heard the laughter of the other crew members come over his headset. Sitting back in the pilot's seat, he began to relax. It would be a while before they were anywhere near within range of the hulk's considerable defences, and being tense for two hours was sure to do his reactions no good, not to mention the nerves of his crew. To occupy his mind, Jaeger went through the pre-battle checks once again. He ran his eye over the cockpit's interior to check everything visually. There were no chinks or scratches on the tinted armoured shielding of the Marauder's cockpit. The snaking wrist-thick pipes that twisted from the control panel in all directions seemed to be intact, with no insulation breaks or kinks. The pressure gauges of the engine had their needles pointing comfortably in their green quadrants, and numerous other dials, meters and counters indicated that nothing was amiss. Jaeger tested the flight controls, worried by the stiffness he was feeling in the movement of the control column. A few gentle turns and rolls later and everything seemed fine, easing Jaeger's suspicions.

Berhandt had told him that this Marauder had been almost cut in half by an eldar laser during its last mission. It had been then that his predecessor, Glade, had been sucked out into the void, never to be seen again. Jaeger cursed himself for such morbid thoughts and to calm himself he began to think of his home world. Unfastening a couple of catches, Jaeger pushed his helmet onto the back of his head and closed his eyes. With a thin-lipped smile, he began whistling a hunting chant from back home.

VENISTON PACED BACK and forth across the command deck of the bridge, watching the various screens that gave updates of the progressing battle. As the *Divine Justice* slowly moved in closer to the hulk, the smaller ork ships in its escort were trying to break through the cordon of frigates to attack the cruiser. They were having little success, and the one or two that managed to get within range were soon obliterated by the overwhelming firepower of the *Divine Justice*'s gun decks. The floor shook with regular throbs as the immense plasma drives pushed the ship towards the distant foe, bringing all on board ever closer to death or glory. One of the communications officers was muttering sharply to Captain Kaurl, while he glanced over his subordinate's shoulder at a flickering screen, directing the efforts of the escorts and fighters.

'Is there a problem, Mister Kaurl?' Veniston enquired as he stepped up to the captain, trying to keep the tension from his voice.

'Not really, sir,' Kaurl answered, standing up straight to look the admiral in the eye. Veniston raised an eyebrow in query. 'A wave of ork fighter-bombers has made it through the blockade. They'll be intercepting the Marauders of Raptor Squadron shortly. But the fighter screen should be able to protect our bombers,' Kaurl assured the admiral, rubbing the tiredness from his eyes and running a thick-fingered hand through his dark hair.

'Send the Thunderbolts on an intercept course,' Veniston decided, looking past Kaurl at the display screen. 'If the orks get too close, the bombers will have to slow down, and timing is all-important. If the Raptors don't attack in time, the whole plan will be off course and the hulk will still be fully mobile when we get within range. We can't let that happen, Jacob.' The admiral's eyes narrowed and his jaw clenched tightly for a moment as he considered the prospect of the *Divine Justice* suffering the same fate as the *Imperial Retribution*.

'What if a second wave of fighters comes up? They'll be unprotected...' the captain protested, his voice suddenly hoarse with the prospect.

'If that happens,' Veniston stated coldly, 'then we shall pray that the Emperor is watching over us.'

The admiral turned towards the main display again, indicating that the conversation was ended. Kaurl suppressed a grimace and turned towards the waiting comms officer.

'New orders for Arrow and Storm Squadrons,' the captain began.

THEIR THUNDERBOLT ESCORT had peeled away regretfully a few minutes ago, and now the Marauders were on their own. As Raptor Squadron thundered towards the hulk, more details of the battle ahead could be seen. A swarm of ork attack ships duelled with the frigates escorting the *Divine Justice*. Manoeuvring just outside range of the orks' crude weapons, the Imperium ships were taking a heavy toll; the wreckage of at least five ork vessels was drifting lifelessly across the battlezone. Much closer now, the hulk seemed truly immense. Around it orbited a cluster of defence asteroids, floating bases crewed by the orks and bristling with rockets and gun batteries. Some were simply pieces of the hulk that had broken off but hadn't escaped the pull of the hulk's gravity. Others, Jaeger had been taught in Command Training, were deliberately captured by the orks, who used bizarre field technology to grasp onto asteroids and debris, purposefully creating a swirl of obstacles to protect themselves against attack. Whatever the cause of their orbit, and whether they were just floating chunks of stone and metal, or had been fitted out with rocket pods or gun turrets, throughout the navy they were known simply as Rocks.

As Jaeger considered this glorious example of understatement, there was a sudden hiss of escaping gas and the control stick in his left hand started juddering uncontrollably.

'Ferix!' Jaeger snapped over the internal comm-link. 'These damned controls are playing up. I need stability right now, if you don't mind.'

The small tech-adept crawled into the cockpit and took the toolbelt from his waist. Pulling a glowing, gold-etched device from one pocket, he set about the fastenings on a panel under Jaeger's legs. As Ferix unscrewed the compartment beneath the control column he began a low-voiced chant: 'To see the spirit of the machine, that is to be Mechanicus. To find the malaise of malfunction, that is to be Mechanicus. To administer the Rite of Repair, that is to be Mechanicus.'

Jaeger let the man drift from his attention as he looked through the armoured glass of the cockpit. The frigates had done a good job punching a hole through the ork attack ships, leaving the way clear for the Marauders. However, something wasn't quite right. Jaeger's spine tingled with some inner sense of foreboding. Looking at the approaching hulk, a sinister suspicion began to rise at the back of his mind.

'Berhandt, can you get a fix on that Rock, five o'clock, about twelve by thirty-five?' Jaeger asked the bombardier, his unease rising.

'Got it,' the bombardier replied, a question in his voice.

'Plot a trajectory prediction, impose it over our course.'

'Okay, Commander Jaeger. Metriculator processing right now. Coming through… Damn! You were right to ask, sir. We're heading straight for the damn thing!' Berhandt exclaimed.

'Avoidance course?' Jaeger knew that there wouldn't be one even as he asked.

'No, sir. Not with the time we've been given. Emperor's mercy, we're gonna have to deal with the bloody thing ourselves…' The bombardier's voice was barely a whisper.

Jaeger pressed the long-range communicator. 'Bridge, this is Raptor Leader.' he announced. 'We have a problem.'

THE BOMBER SQUADRON banked round slowly, shaken by the engine blasts of the vast rockets soaring past. Each of the ork missiles roaring from the Rock was larger than a Marauder, designed to blow apart a massive starship but equally capable of wiping out the whole squadron with one unlucky blast. Crude faces had been painted onto the tips of monstrous rockets, leering grins and sharp-teethed devils seeming to leap from the darkness on columns of raging flame.

Jaeger was listening in to the comm-net, his mood grim.

++This is the *Apollo*, we cannot disengage currently.++

++This is the *Glorious*, unable to reach your position in time.++

And so it went on, each of the fleet's frigates too busy or too far away to attack the rapidly approaching Rock. Another flare erupted from the ork defence platform in front of the Marauders, hurling six more rockets at the incoming bombers. Jaeger switched to the inter-squadron communicator.

'Split one-four, on my lead,' he ordered, his voice low and abrupt. 'We've only got time for one pass. Make it count.'

As an icon flashed green on the panel beside him, Jaeger switched frequency to listen to the incoming message.

++This is Tech-Priest Adramaz of the *Excellent*++ a tinny, unfamiliar voice reported. ++We have surveyed your target and established a primary detonation point. Transmitting information now. It appears to be some kind of power source, which may destroy the target if you can hit it. I would make your departure as expeditious as possible though, we are unsure how large the resultant blast will be.++

'Thanks, Adramaz,' Jaeger replied, turning to see if Berhandt had received the information.

The bombardier gave a nod as the targeting data for the Rock's reactor was received and with the turn of a dial and a flicked switch, he transmitted the details to the other Marauders. Berhandt swivelled in his seat to grasp the forked control stick that guided and fired the Marauder's nose-mounted lascannons. One shot from those could punch through a cubit or more of reinforced armour and smash apart rock with equal ease.

'Signature suggests it ain't laser shielded,' the bombardier said, smiling grimly. 'A couple of good hits should do the trick.'

Jaeger broadcast to the rest of the squadron again. 'Lascannons only on this one; save your missiles and bombs for the main target.'

Phrao's voice came back first. ++What do you mean 'main target'? Ain't this what we're here to destroy?++

'This is just incidental!' Jaeger snapped back. 'Our main objective is on the hulk itself.'

++You're joking! Five Marauders are going to have as much effect on that beast as a swampfly biting a grox's backside!++ Drake chipped in.

Jaeger barely suppressed a growl before opening up the comm channel. 'We don't make the orders, we just follow them. If you have a problem with that, we can sort it out back on the flight deck. We've got a job to do, so let's just stay calm. We'll deal with this Rock and then we'll push on to our main objective.'

++If we get that far!++ Phrao's voice, even taking the hiss of the comm-net into account, was rasping and bitter. ++Damned Raptor's luck!++

Jaeger stabbed at the transmit rune. 'Silence, all of you!' he snapped 'Everyone listen to me right now. You all know your jobs, you've all flown combat missions before. So I'll hear no more of this "Raptor's luck". Is that understood?'

A series of affirmatives were broadcast back and Jaeger nodded to himself. Doubt sows the seeds of fear, the abbot of the Extu Schola Progenium had taught him when he was young. Crush it at birth or suffer the growth of heresy.

Flicking his gaze over the control panels, Jaeger saw that all systems were working within acceptable levels. Everything was ready. He took a deep breath, his hand poised over the comm-link. Letting it out slowly, he touched the rune.

'Raptor Squadron, this is Raptor Leader.' Jaeger made his voice deliberately calm, even though inside his heart was racing and he could feel the excitement of combat beginning to surge. 'Break and attack! Break and attack!'

A DOZEN SMALL turrets swivelled into firing position and unleashed a torrent of shells at the Marauders as they screamed in towards the Rock, their engines at full burn. Dodging through the hail of death, now was the time for each pilot to prove his worth. Jerryl took the lead, followed by Jaeger, then the other bombers. From his position, Jaeger had the perfect opportunity to see the magnificent Marauder bomber in action.

They were huge metallic beasts, each weighing more then three battle tanks, with a wide wingspan. Designed for limited range space combat as

well as atmospheric missions, the Marauder manoeuvred with small vec-
toring engines along the fuselage and wings whilst in the ether, and
massive control planes and a quad-ramjet when they dipped into a
planet's atmosphere. Nicknamed 'Big Brutes' by the flight crews, each
Marauder was a flying fortress. Its two dorsal twin-autocannon were capable of unleashing a hail of fire that could punch through the armour of
enemy planes and tear apart crew and engines, while the tail-gunner's
triple heavy bolters could fire a dozen shells a second at enemy interceptors or strafe soft ground targets. On the nose were the lascannons for
precision targeting, and six Flail missiles hung from the wings, each with
a plasma warhead capable of creating a crater over fifty feet in diameter
or cracking the armoured hull of a spaceship. For more wholesale devastation, the Marauder's hull also incorporated a spacious bomb bay which
could deliver a payload of explosives or incendiaries.

As he contemplated the sheer destructive potential of just a single
Marauder, Jaeger found his faith in the Imperium renewed. The Adeptus
Mechanicus had designed this awesome fighting machine. The Schola
Progenium of the Ministorum had given him the fervent faith to serve the
Emperor. The Imperial Navy had taught him how to control this murder-
ous creature of metal. And now he was here, once more about to deliver
fiery judgement upon the heads of the Emperor's enemies. For Jaeger,
there was no finer feeling.

As Raptor Squadron roared closer to the Rock, the enemy response grew
in ferocity. With stomach-churning suddenness, Jaeger pulled up from
the dive towards the Rock, bringing the Marauder's nose level with the
horizon of the small asteroid. Where a second before he had been flying
in open space, now there was ground beneath him. As always, it took a
couple of seconds to fight off the disorientation, and while he took a few
deep breaths, he subconsciously sent the Marauder into a series of short
climbs, dives and banks to throw off the enemy gunners. Glancing hits
ricocheted around the armoured hull, filling the air with sporadic metallic clangs. A close hit set the plane shaking, and warning runes flashed red
across three of the control panels that covered every surface of the
cockpit. Ferix's voice sounded over the comm in alarm.

'Armour breach! Check your vacuum seals and utter the Third Canticle
of Protection, praise His name.'

Jaeger went through the routine of checking the fastenings on his helm,
muttering under his breath: 'Deliver me from the void. Protect me from
the ether. Guard well my soul.'

The bombers were almost within firing range and the fire had slackened
as some of the Rock's gun turrets were blind-sided by the mass of the
asteroid. A surprise burst of fire engulfed Jerryl's plane, stripping away
great shards of metal. Phrao's plane swept low, its lascannon blasting
apart the ork gunnery turret, exacting instant revenge. Jaeger could see a

gaping hole in the starboard wing of Jerryl's Marauder, trailing sparks as severed power cables discharged their energy into the vacuum.

'Raptor Three, what is your condition?' Jaeger enquired urgently.

++Lost starboard controls, handling shaky. I don't think I can hold her, permission to disengage?++

'Okay, Jerryl. Break off and return home,' Jaeger said through gritted teeth.

Suddenly the comm-net icons flashed for a priority message. ++This is Admiral Veniston. Do not disengage, Raptor Three: circle around and reform for attack on primary objective.++

Jerryl's reply came through a hiss of static. ++What the... Damned controls... Order received.++

Jaeger watched as the lead Marauder pulled up, taking it out of the attack run. Easing his control column left and right, Jaeger steered his craft through the shells screaming towards him. Guiding the Marauder over the steep lip of a crater, Jaeger saw the reactor housing for the first time: a crude conglomeration of twisting pipes and power relays. Berhandt gave a grunt as the ork's power generator came within range of his lascannon. Bolts of laser energy flashed towards the Rock, sending up plumes of smoke and dust. Berhandt's lascannon spat forth another volley of fire, tearing through metal and rock.

'Emperor's blood, missed!' cursed Berhandt, punching his fist against the lascannon controls.

Twisting in his seat as he steered the Marauder away, Jaeger watched as Phrao's bomber made its pass. As the craft swept towards its target, leaving a trail of swirling debris in its wake, two bolts of light struck the reactor full on, turning the generator's armour into a molten slurry and punching through to the highly unstable plasma chamber within.

++Spot on!++ Phrao shouted gleefully. ++Pull away!++

Jaeger's left arm ached as he wrenched the column back and right, pulling the Marauder into a spine-bending turning climb. Through the side-screens, Jaeger could see small eruptions breaking out across the Rock as a chain reaction spread from the reactor to the turrets and rocket batteries. Forks of electrical energy began to arc into the air and the reactor went into critical overload. A cloud of gas exploded through the Rock's surface from an underground tank, sending shards of rock spinning dangerously close to the following Marauders, before the gas was eaten up by a shaft of blue flame. Raw plasma spewed from the molten remains of the generator, pushing the Rock off its trajectory, sending it spinning further away from the hulk. With an explosion that momentarily blinded the flight commander, the Rock burst apart, sending fragments of debris hurtling in every direction. The victorious cries of Jaeger's crew and the other pilots rang in his ears.

'Steady, Raptors, that was just the warm up,' Jaeger chided them 'Now for the real target. Form up; Jerryl take the rear.'

++Affirmative.++ Jerryl responded. ++Where for now, sir?++

Jaeger grimaced to himself. 'Not sure,' he answered slowly. 'We haven't received full target information yet.' Damn it, he thought to himself, the whole mission briefing was hazy. This whole thing was beginning to stink, but of what he wasn't yet certain.

++Let's get this straight.++ Phrao's voice was heavy with sarcasm. ++We don't know what we're attacking, we've just got a deadline to meet. That's it? We just fly in there, easy as you like, drop a few bombs, fire a few shots and go home? Somehow I don't think it'll be that easy.++

'Cut the chatter!' Jaeger ordered, his mood grim. He agreed with the other pilots, but he'd be damned if he was going to sow doubt on the command skills of Kaurl and Veniston halfway through a mission.

The Marauders roared onwards, the hulk growing ever larger through their cockpit windows. Its massive bulk blocked out a swathe of stars, looking like some lurking shadow waiting to swallow up the Marauders, luring them to their doom.

CAPTAIN KAURL COUGHED gently to attract the admiral's attention. The senior officer pulled his gaze from the monitoring station and turned round, one eyebrow raised in question.

'We are in position to initiate the second attack wave, Lord Veniston.'

The admiral rubbed one haggard cheek with his hand, gazing at nothing in particular.

'Sir? Shall we proceed?' Kaurl pressed.

Veniston's eyes were flints. 'Very well, Jacob. Launch Devil Squadron. Proceed with the attack on the engines themselves.'

WITH THE DEBRIS of the Rock scattering slowly in their wake, the Marauders headed onwards towards the hulk. Pressing a series of runes above his head, Jaeger turned on a small viewscreen just above the front canopy, and a flickering, fractured image of the view behind the bomber crackled into existence. The flight commander watched as the *Divine Justice* moved in towards the hulk, its awesome plasma drives pushing it forward on great trails of fire. The two surviving frigates formed up in front of the cruiser, ready to defend their capital ship against the few remaining ork attack ships.

Jaeger could picture the commotion on board the massive warships, as gun and torpedo crews scurried to and fro, readying their weapons for action. He imagined the gun decks bathed red in combat lighting, the gunners sweating and cursing as they heaved power cells into place or loaded shells the size of his bomber into the breaches. In the torpedo bays, hundreds of men would be bending their backs to the chains, hauling the massive projectiles, ten times the size of a Marauder, along the loading rails. In the engine room, the men would be sweating heavily, the heat of the thirty plasma reactors permeating even through their thermal shielding and the crew's protective suits. He didn't envy them their task: hard work in very cramped conditions for little recognition or reward. Moreover, pilots were all volunteers, while many of the thousands of men who laboured in the depths of the fighting ships were criminals serving their penance to the Emperor, or simply unfortunate men taken unawares by the press gangs. And yet, he thought, everyone serves the Emperor, each in their own way. They will receive their due honours in time, whether in this life or not.

Something caught Jaeger's attention from the corner of his eye, but before he had a chance to look properly, Arafa was screaming in his ear.

++Incoming! Ork fighter-bombers, moving in on an intercept vector, closing fast. Where's our damned fighter screen?++

Jaeger was transmitting even before Arafa had finished.

'Storm Leader, Arrow Leader!' he rasped, throat dry with sudden fear. 'This is Raptor Leader, we need cover and fast! We have...' Jaeger checked the display in front of him '...eight fighter-bombers incoming!'

++Okay, Jaeger.++ the fighter commander came through immediately. ++We're on our way. Arrow Leader out.++

'Everyone, keep sharp!' Jaeger ordered over the squadron comm-link. 'Gunners mark your targets, watch for the crossfire. Tight formation. Don't let them get in amongst us. Drake, you're uppermost; cover the blindsides.'

Jaeger forced himself to calm down, loosening his white-kuckled grip on the control column. He kept his gaze firmly on the slivers of light that marked the approaching orks. Now was the time to trust in the gunners.

THE ORKS WERE jinking and swerving as they closed in on Raptor Squadron, surrounded by a cloud of tracer shells and pulses of laser light as the Marauders' guns opened fire. Each enemy craft was different, haphazardly constructed from crudely cut and bent metal plates, pushed screaming across the stars by hugely oversized engines that spluttered multi-coloured trails. Each was decorated differently too: some painted in bold stripes of red and black or red and yellow; others embellished with ork glyphs that were indecipherable to Jaeger; others still just a mess of jagged patterns and bold colours. Blazing cannons protruded from the nose of each interceptor and their wings were hung with bombs and missiles.

The Marauders were flying close in to each other, relying upon mass of fire to drive off the attack, rather than trying to evade the much more manoeuvrable ork aircraft. Their gunners covered each other's blind spots, trying to keep up the almost impenetrable wall of fire that was needed to keep the fighters at bay until the *Divine Justice*'s interceptors could arrive.

'Got one!' Arick shouted from behind Jaeger, as an ork fighter exploded into a billowing cloud of shrapnel and rapidly burning fuel. Then the fighters screamed within range, raking along the length of Drake's plane, sending splinters of metal flying. A few stray rounds ricocheted off the shield in front of Jaeger, causing him to flinch, but the armoured glass held out against the impacts. As the enemy swept overhead, the dorsal guns on the Marauders swivelled to track them, spraying salvo after salvo of fire into the ork formation. Through the armoured view panel to his left, Jaeger saw one of the craft caught in a crossfire by Phrao and Drake's gunners. The enemy's cockpit shattered, causing it to tumble out of control towards Jerryl's stricken Marauder. As the bomber laboriously swung out of harm's way, its damaged wing twisted, until it sheared off completely. Lurching out of formation, the Marauder flipped madly out of control, and was suddenly in the centre of a devastating crossfire from the orks. Jaeger averted his gaze, but in his mind's eye he could picture the lifeless bodies of the crew drifting out towards the stars.

With Jerryl's covering fire lost, the ork fighter-bombers closed in on the rear of Raptor Squadron, twisting nimbly between the volleys of fire from the tail gunners. The situation was looking grim: the orks could simply pick them off one by one now that the formation was disrupted. If they just carried on flying straight towards the target they'd be sitting targets and wouldn't last more than a couple of minutes.

'Break formation for dogfight!' Jaeger ordered. 'Drake, Arafa, circle round and get–'

Jaeger's order was interrupted by a message from the *Divine Justice*. ++This is Admiral Veniston. Maintain formation, proceed towards primary target without delay.++

Jaeger gripped the control column, trying to quell his rising fury. Was Veniston deliberately trying to get them killed? He stabbed at the commnet button again. 'This is Jaeger. Repeat: break formation, take out these damned orks, or we can forget about our target!'

As the Marauders pulled away from each other, Jaeger dragged his plane round in a tight circle, the control column juddering in his hands. Berhandt was crouching over the lascannon controls, staring intently through the firing visor for a target. Jaeger spotted a fighter expertly tailing Drake's weaving Marauder. Jaeger brought his own craft down above the ork craft, glancing across to check that Berhandt was ready. The slicing beams of the bombardier's lascannon were joined by Arick's fire from above their heads. It tore through the tail of the ork fighter and sent it listing off uselessly, fountains of sparks spraying from its ruptured fuselage.

A rattle of shells against the hull snapped Jaeger's attention to his left, where another enemy fighter-bomber was roaring towards him, its cannons blazing away. Something punched through the hull just behind the flight commander and he heard a muffled cry over the internal communicator.

'What's happening back there? Saile? Marte?' he demanded.

He was answered by Marte's deep voice. 'Clean head shot, Commander Jaeger. Saile's dead.'

Everything was anarchy. Jaeger watched the Marauders twisting and weaving, trying to shake off the much quicker ork craft. The enemy was everywhere, the fighter-bombers looping around the squadron, unleashing hail after hail of fire from their cannons.

Arick's voice filled the internal link: 'Come on, scum! Yeah, just a little closer... Take that! Damn, just winged him! Oh, you hungry for some as well, filth? Emperor, these scum are slippery...'

Jaeger pushed the Marauder into a steep dive, the mass of the ork hulk sliding across his field of vision through the canopy. He saw Drake's Marauder being tailed by a trio of fighter-bombers and realised the first attack wave had been reinforced by more of the ork craft. Glancing down at the on-board scanner, he realised that the bomber's sensor arrays were damaged and hadn't picked up the new arrivals. The flickering amber and red lights across the whole panel showed that nearly all the plane's systems were in need of serious repair. Glancing over his shoulder, Jaeger could make out Ferix clambering about in the gloom, frantically re-wiring cables and sealing split pipelines, muttering prayers all the while.

Turning his attention back to the outside, he watched helplessly as a volley of fire from the orks shredded the tail of Drake's Marauder. But then, without warning, the fighter-bombers tailing Drake exploded into widening blasts of twisted metal. A moment later, three Imperial Thunderbolts screamed through the cloud of burning gas, their engines at full throttle. The comm crackled into life.

++This is Arrow Leader. We have them now. Break for your target.++

With a howl of relief, Jaeger opened up the engines to full and flicked the transmit rune on the comm panel. 'Just in time, Dextra! Stay lucky and I'll see you back on board.'

The interceptors had punched a hole in the fighter-bomber squadrons, leaving the route clear for the bombers to proceed towards their destination. Jaeger banked his aircraft around to head for the opening, his eyes fixed on the huge ork vessel ahead.

'Raptor Squadron, this is Raptor Leader,' Jaeger announced over the squadron frequency, trying to keep his voice calm, despite his trepidation and pounding heart. 'Follow me in.'

'CHECK MISSILE AND bomb links,' Jaeger ordered the squadron. Behind him, Berhandt touched a pair of runes and frowned as they failed to light up. Snarling, the bombardier brought his fist down sharply on the display and grinned cheerfully as his faced was bathed in green light. He looked towards Jaeger and gave a thumbs up.

'This is Raptor Leader,' Jaeger broadcast to the squadron. 'Prepare for bombardment of primary objective.'

As a series of affirmatives came back across the comm-link, Jaeger gave a quick smile to himself. They'd got through. Not all of them, admittedly, but hopefully they'd get the opportunity to avenge Saile, Jerryl and the others.

++Look at the size of that beast.++ Arafa's awed voice came over the ether.

'Less talk, men, stay sharp,' Jaeger interrupted 'We've come too far to mess up now.'

Despite his stern words, Jaeger could understand the other pilot's feelings. The hulk was truly massive, dwarfing even the majestic size of the *Divine Justice*. As the squadron moved closer and closer to their target, and the hulk grew larger and larger in their sights, Jaeger could make out more details. He could see where three or perhaps four different starships had been compacted together, forming outcrops of twisted metal, jutting at a bizarre angle from where innumerable other craft and asteroids had been compressed together by the tides of warp space to form the central mass of the drifting hulk. It looked like a gigantic wedge of crumpled and torn metal and rock, the size of a city, weighing untold millions of tons. How the orks managed to populate one of these randomly wandering behemoths, the Emperor alone knew. That they could was bad enough, but when the green-skinned savages managed to activate dormant engines or build their own immense drives, that turned an uncontrolled, erratic menace into a dire threat. The bulk of the ork vessel shimmered with the frozen particles that encrusted its hull. Billowing gases vented from unseen ports, creating a wreath of lazily-moving smog around the hulk's huge girth. It had a kind of savage beauty: a wracked sculpture of tortured metal that somehow seemed to be cleaving elegantly across the stars.

Jaeger's thoughts hardened. Inside that bizarre, sprawling shell were thousands, possibly hundreds of thousands of orks waiting to devastate some planet; to spill across continents in a wave of wanton destruction and killing. He remembered what had happened to the *Imperial Retribution* and pictured Saile's corpse in the sealed gunnery chamber behind him. All thoughts of beauty slipped from his mind immediately. The hulk was a threat to the Emperor's domains; a stain upon the galaxy. It was his duty to destroy it.

Checking the targeting data scrolling across a small, dull yellow viewscreen just above his head, Jaeger banked the Marauder in towards the hulk to assume the best attack trajectory.

'Raptor Squadron, this is Raptor Leader,' Jaeger growled, turning over the attack pattern in his head. 'Praise the Emperor, it's time.'

* * *

THE MARAUDERS SPED across the chaotic hull of the ork hulk, diving low to swoop beneath ruined gantries, swerving around twisted columns. With the Marauders this close, the defence turrets had little time to react to their presence, sending up a harmless spray of energy bolts and shells seconds too late.

Jaeger started to chant the mantra that would ease his mind into union with the aircraft he controlled. He would rely solely upon instinct rather than thought, he and the bomber acting and reacting as a single entity. As he felt his mind slipping into the semi-subconscious state he required for total concentration, Jaeger glanced over to see Berhandt hunched over the targeting screen, his fingers subconsciously adjusting the row of dials below it to get the focus and magnitude correct.

Guiding the Marauder across the hulk's surface with one hand, Jaeger activated a series of runes and the canopy in front of him darkened slightly as it interfaced with the Marauder's artificial eyes and ears. A false image of outlines and silhouettes imposed itself over the view through the shield; highlighting particular obstacles, bringing the twisted contours and angles of the hulk's surface into stark contrast for ease of navigation. Patches of static or blankness showed here and there where the Marauder's sensors were damaged or some interfering energy source was fluctuating within the hulk itself.

With Berhandt concentrating on the bombs and missiles, it was Jaeger's task to take control of the lascannon. The flight commander reached overhead and pulled a lever. With a sudden venting of quickly-dissipating steam, the lascannon controls slid forward from the control panel beside Berhandt, four clamps locking the whole control bank into its new position alongside Jaeger. Punching a pair of buttons on the weapon control panel with his right hand, still guiding the Marauder around the obstructions ahead with his left, the flight commander activated the lascannon and the canopy display in front of him was filled with a swirl of static. Quickly adjusting the weapon's sensor array, Jaeger re-tuned the lascannon's false eyes and the cloud of random specks coalesced into moving icons, highlighting possible target points. The blood-red rune of their primary target stood out like a guiding beacon, a procession of angles, estimated armour, trajectories and other information scrolling rapidly alongside it.

'Raptor Squadron, sound off current status,' the flight commander ordered.

++Raptor Two, lascannon's out, missiles and bombs on-line and ready to blow!++

++Raptor Three, all systems acceptable, by the Emperor.++

++Raptor Five, everything's in the green 'cept tail retros. She's handling hard, but we'll be fine.++

'Okay. Assume attack vector Prime, standard diamond,' Jaeger commanded. 'Let's not waste our chance.'

Jaeger slowed his breathing, realising that despite his prayers he was becoming agitated. In a few more moments they would pass over the jagged outcrop of an impacted cargo ship and would have a line to their as-yet unknown target. A hum started in Jaeger's ear through the internal comm, as Berhandt wakened the spirits of the Marauder's self-guiding missiles and they set about seeking their target. As the bomber neared its objective and the missiles' surveyors acquired the targeting point, the hum became ever more high pitched. Tilting the nose of the Marauder forward, Jaeger led the squadron over the wrecked cargo transport. The unidentified target came into full view.

Like a bolt of unholy wrath, a ball of plasma a hundred metres wide swept through the Marauder squadron, engulfing Arafa's aircraft, leaving nothing more than a cloud of gas and globules of molten plasteel.

Drake was on the comm-link instantly ++Emperor's blood! It's a damned gun battery! Why didn't they tell us it was a damned cannon? What the hell were they thinking of? Aren't we attacking the engines?++

Jaeger saw that it was true: a pair of immense guns, each with a barrel wide enough to swallow a Marauder, was pointing directly at the attacking bombers. Jaeger shivered with dread as he saw the scanner's read-out showing the energy build-up for another blast.

'Pull up!' Jaeger cried out over the squadron frequency. 'Break formation! Hit it from the other side!' As he wrenched his own plane into a steep climb, he prayed that the others had reacted in time, as if he could make their aircraft move faster, make them react quicker, through sheer force of will.

As the Marauders dispersed, another volcanic blast of energy hurtled from the cannons, blazing a path through the space where seconds before the Marauders had been. Jaeger thanked the Emperor for his swift guidance, but inwardly he was cursing Veniston and Kaurl with all his might. Why hadn't they told Jaeger that the target was a weapon battery? How the hell did they think he was going to plan an attack properly if he wasn't made aware of all the dangers? Choking back his fury, Jaeger ordered the squadron back into an attack approach, fervently praying under his breath that the huge turret didn't have enough time to traverse and get another shot at them. At this range it could hardly miss.

With agonising slowness, the turret tracked around towards the incoming Marauders. The message 'Deviant Perceived' flashed scarlet across the left window of the canopy and the whine of the missiles became an unbearable shriek.

'Fly, sweet vengeance!' came Berhandt's voice, quoting the words he'd personally inscribed onto each of the missiles as they were loaded.

A salvo of fire from the other bombers joined Berhandt's volley, a rippling wave of death that streaked towards its target on tails of flame, rapidly becoming distant sparks as the missiles sped towards the gun turret. They hit home with a deadly blossom of explosions and the viewscreen showed twisted chunks of metal being thrown in all directions. Escaping gases briefly caught fire in actinic fountains of flaring light.

The red target rune was still active on the canopy screen, shining bright just in front of Jaeger's eyes. He realised with sickening dread that the turret wasn't destroyed. It was still about to open fire once more.

'Lascannons and bombs!' Jaeger ordered, pressing the firing stud of his own plane's weapons with his thumb, spewing forth a salvo of energy bolts. Debris and burning vapours exploded across the hulk's surface as the lasers tracked towards their target, until the gun turret was at the centre of a storm of beams converging from the four Marauders. A warning sigil floated before Jaeger, showing the turret was in position to fire again. In his mind's eye, Jaeger could imagine the huge barrels of the cannons glowing with the suppressed energy inside, waiting to spit forth destruction and damnation.

With a blast that flung Jaeger back in his seat, the turret exploded in a vast, searing cloud of white plasma and billowing clouds of magnesium-bright vapour. Easing the controls back, Jaeger began to pull the Marauder out of its dive towards the hulk's surface.

Suddenly, Drake's voice was hammering in his ear: ++Control's lost, Raptor Leader. I can't pull up.++

Jaeger watched as Drake's Marauder sped below him, dipping towards the hulk's hull, trailing sparks and burning fuel from its damaged tail.

Get out, Jaeger pleaded. Get to the saviour pod. He gave a heartfelt sigh of relief as he saw the midsection of the Marauder being punched upwards by emergency rockets, sending it spinning away from the hulk.

++Lost Barnus and Cord.++ Drake's voice was hoarse with sadness. ++Their link to the pod was blocked.++

++Raptor Squadron, this is Veniston.++ The admiral's smooth voice cut through the comm-chatter. ++Excellent work, boys. You can come home now.++

Jaeger frowned to himself in confusion. How the hell did destroying one gun turret help the *Divine Justice* against this brute? As he raged, the answer appeared on the display screen far across the rear of the hulk. More Marauders were moving in on the behemoth's engines: the Marauders of Devil Squadron.

Phrao hissed bitterly over the comm-link: ++Trust those damned Devils. We do all the bleeding, they get all the glory!++

'Not this time, Phrao.' Jaeger answered. 'Form up on my wing. Let's give the Devils a hand.'

++I hear you, Raptor Leader!++ Phrao replied happily.

As THE BOMBS and missiles of Devil Squadron erupted across one of the hulk's immense engines, the surviving two Marauders of the Raptors swept low, their lascannons picking out weak points in the armour, punching through buckled shields and twisted plates. Soon a dozen fires were blazing, and the engine ruptured with a swirling cloud of super-heated matter. Explosions blossomed across the whole section of the hulk and one by one each of the massive stellar drives lost power and went dim, leaving the hulk drifting without control. As the Marauders sped back towards the *Divine Justice*, the cruiser was sweeping in victoriously for the kill. Wave after wave of torpedoes sped past; Jaeger adjusted the rear viewer to see the plasma warheads punching massive holes in the hulk's armoured skin. Gun batteries exploded across the ork vessel in bright pinpricks of light. Fires began raging across the hulk's midsection, becoming raging infernos as the atmosphere inside the hulk pushed out with ever-increasing pressure.

As he prepared to dock, Jaeger got one last glimpse of the hulk. Unable to manoeuvre without its main engines, and helpless to resist the Imperial cruiser raking it from the rear, the hulk was slowly deteriorating. Salvo after salvo from the *Divine Justice*'s gun decks pounded into the hulk, ripping off huge swathes with every broadside. Ancient reactors in the hulk's depths began to overload, smashing open gaping holes from within. Then the bomber passed into the shadow of the *Divine Justice* and the hulk was lost from view.

CLEANED UP AND in his dress uniform, Jaeger hurried to the briefing chamber. As he entered, Admiral Veniston was debriefing the Devils. Kaurl was there too, standing silently behind the admiral, his face a blank mask. Jaeger listened to Veniston's praise for Devil Squadron's part in the day's victory, and what he heard set his teeth on edge.

'And I can say without doubt that the whole mission was a complete success,' the admiral said, 'and I am glad that it was achieved with acceptable losses.'

That was too much to bear. Jaeger stepped into the centre of the briefing chamber, blazing with fury. He'd already gone through too much, without having to stand around while the admiral praised the Devils' conduct and said that the Raptors' casualties simply didn't matter.

'"Acceptable losses"?' Jaeger demanded, eyes ablaze. 'What the hell do you mean, "acceptable losses"? I lost fifteen good men on that mission while these flyboys were sitting on their carefully polished backsides waiting for their orders! Fifteen men lost while thirty others watched and waited! If you had sent us out together, we could have handled ourselves better. Damn it, you didn't even tell us what our target was, did you?'

Veniston and Kaurl stared at Jaeger in rank disbelief, which only served to fuel his fury. 'Of course,' he spat, his voice dropping to a harsh whisper, 'we're just the Raptors, we don't really count, do we? Well I'm sorry if we're not related, admiral, but my life is worth as much to the Emperor as that of your own kin!'

Kaurl was beside himself. 'What is the meaning of this, flight commander?' the captain stormed, face like thunder. 'How dare you speak to a
senior officer like this! Call for the Officer of the Watch. Have Commander Jaeger taken to the brig immediately!'

Jaeger clamped his mouth shut with a snort, and bristled in impotent
fury. Without a word or look, Veniston walked from the chamber, ignoring the icy glare that Jaeger shot him as the admiral walked past. Jaeger
felt his arm grabbed just below the elbow and he spun round.

Lieutenant Strand was standing there, flanked by two ratings. 'We've
orders to take you down, Mister Jaeger,' he said, face impassive. Jaeger
nodded numbly and followed them out of the briefing room. After a
moment, Captain Kaurl caught up with the group and dismissed the lieutenant and guards with a waved hand.

'You went too far, Jacques,' Kaurl started, his voice soft, his eyes meeting the flight commander's gaze. 'If you don't have respect, then you don't
have anything.'

Kaurl led the flyer into one of the secondary hangars. Inside were the
coffins of the dead, waiting to be ejected into space during the burial ceremony that evening. On each was an inscribed nameplate, even for those
who had left no body behind: Gunner Saile, Raptor Squadron; Gunner
Barnus, Raptor Squadron; Gunner Cord, Raptor Squadron; Commander
Drake, Raptor Squadron; the row went on and on.

There were twenty-one coffins in all. When Jaeger read the nameplate
of the sixteenth, he stumbled back a step in shock. It read Flight Commander Raf, Devil Squadron. He turned to Kaurl, his brow knitted in
confusion.

'I– I don't–' Jaeger stuttered, lost for words. His anger was gone; he felt
empty.

'The Devils' attack wasn't the "easy in, easy out" mission you seemed to
think it was,' the captain said tersely. 'They still had to get through several
ork attack ships and the roaming fighter-bombers. Raf was killed guiding
his plane into the engines of one of the ork attack ships that was blocking the *Divine Justice*'s approach. He knowingly sacrificed himself for the
completion of the task, and you'll do well to remember him with pride.'

Kaurl stepped between Jaeger and the coffin, forcing the flight commander to look at him. 'I devised the plan of attack on the engines, not
the admiral,' the captain went on relentlessly. 'It was me who decided that
two waves were needed: the Raptors in first to silence the engine defence
guns picked up by the Mechanicus's scan, then the Devils to finish off the
whole mission. If you'd gone in together, would you have had any more
chance of success? Would ten Marauders have had a better chance of
destroying that battery. No, don't reply. You know what I say is true.

'There were two separate targets which required two missions. We
couldn't risk the orks fixing the gun turret while the Marauders were

back on board re-arming and refuelling. It had to be done this way. Neither of the two squadrons had it particularly good, let me assure you. And the reason I didn't tell you it was a battery was to make sure you didn't worry. Come, be honest, if you'd known it was a massive gun battery, would you have been so confident?'

Jaeger considered the captain's argument, and he could see the logic. But that didn't alter the fact that they were sent into a situation without knowing the full risks. 'Taking on a massive gun battery isn't as simple as blowing up defenceless engines, sir,' Jaeger protested.

'I knew it would be hard, and that men would die,' the captain told Jaeger, his eyes showing that he understood the flight commander's concerns. As they spoke, Kaurl led Jaeger out of the hanger and they continued down to the brig. 'Don't you think that every time I order an attack, I don't consider the lives of my men? You had the cover from the Thunderbolts for that second fighter attack. Why do you think it took so long for them to arrive? They were supposed to be escorting Devil Squadron. I didn't sign death warrants for your crews, I gave them a chance to prove themselves, to show what Raptor Squadron could really do. Lord Veniston had the chance to over-rule me, knowing that his nephew was going to be having just as much of a hard time as you were. But he did not.'

'Why the hell not?' Jaeger asked with a flick of his hand. 'What the hell does Raptor Squadron mean to him? Raf was in the Devils, so surely his main loyalty lay there.'

'That's not for me to say. That aside, I know that the admiral was as keen as myself to give your squadron its chance for glory. Without your efforts, the Devils would have been obliterated by the ork cannons, and after that the *Divine Justice* would have been facing a fully operational enemy, instead of a sitting target. Everybody realises that – including Lord Veniston.'

As they spoke, Kaurl led Jaeger into the brig, where Lord Veniston was waiting silently. Jaeger looked at the admiral, and for the first time realised the pain and anguish he must be feeling.

'You can leave the prisoner in my care now, captain,' the admiral said, meeting Jaeger's gaze for the first time. Veniston appeared as calm and collected as ever at first glance, with only the occasional twitch of an eyelid or lip betraying any emotion the admiral might be feeling at his nephew's death.

As Kaurl bowed and left, Veniston stepped up to Jaeger and laid a gentle hand on his shoulder. 'While you are in here, think on what has happened today.' The admiral's voice was quiet but strong. He spoke with years of authority, and for the first time since arriving on the *Divine Justice*, Jaeger could hear what the admiral had to say for himself.

'Your enthusiasm, your dedication, are laudable,' his superior was saying. 'But you must expand your perspective, trust in your superiors. Remember always: the cause justifies the sacrifice. No mission I've ever flown or commanded in the Emperor's name was ever a waste, and while I retain my mental faculties things will stay that way.'

Jaeger didn't know what to say. His mind was fuddled with post-battle exhaustion and his thoughts were reeling, trying to make some sense of the unexpected sequence of events that had followed his outburst in the briefing chamber. 'I'll think on that, sir,' he managed to mumble.

'Just see that you do, lad,' the admiral said. With a cursory flick of his head, Veniston directed the two attendant sentries to lead Jaeger into the small, sparse cell.

As the thick steel door closed behind him with an echoing clang, Jaeger's thoughts were troubled. He sat down on the small bunk and hung his head in his hands. What did Veniston mean, 'No mission I've ever flown'?

In his head, he could not shake a small detail, barely glimpsed as the admiral had taken his hand from Jaeger's shoulder. Jaeger looked down at his black gauntlets, part of the flight commander's uniform required by regulations. Veniston had been wearing black gloves too, each with a small insignia. Picked out in delicate gold thread on Veniston's gloves had been an Eagle Rampant, the unmistakable sign of Raptor Squadron.

BURN THE HERETIC, KILL THE MUTANT, PURGE THE UNCLEAN

PESTILENCE

Dan Abnett

The Archenemy infects this universe. If we do not pause to
fight that infection here, within our own selves,
what purpose is there in taking our fight to the stars?

– Apothecary Engane,
from his Treatise on Imperial Medicine

I

IT IS MY belief that memory is the finest faculty we as a species own. Through the function of memory, we are able to gather, hone and transmit all manner of knowledge for the benefit of mankind, and the endless glory of our God-Emperor, may the golden throne endure for ever more!

To forget a mistake is to be defeated a second time, so we are taught in the sermons of Thor. How may a great leader plan his campaign without memory of those battles won and lost before? How may his soldiers absorb his teaching and improve without that gift? How may the Ecclesiarchy disseminate its enervating message to the universal populace without that populace holding the teachings in memory? What are scholars, clerks, historians or chroniclers but agencies of memory?

And what is forgetfulness but the overthrow of memory, the ruination of precious knowledge, and an abhorrence?

I have, in the service of His Exalted Majesty the Emperor of Terra, waged war upon that abhorrence all my life. I strive to locate and recover things forgotten and return them to the custody of memory. I am a scrabbler in dark places, an illuminator of shadows, a turner of long un-turned pages, an asker of questions that have lapsed, forever hunting for answers that would otherwise have remained unvoiced. I am a recollector, prising lost secrets from the taciturn universe and returning them to the safe fold of memory, where they might again improve our lot amongst the out-flung stars.

My particular discipline is that of materia medica, for human medicine was my original calling. Our understanding of our own vital mechanisms is vast and admirable, but we can never know too much about our own biology and how to protect, repair and improve it. It is our burden as a species to exist in a galaxy riven by war, and where war goes, so flourish its hand-servants injury and disease. It may be said that as each war front advances, so medical knowledge advances too. And where armies fall back in defeat or are destroyed, so medical knowledge retreats or is forgotten. Such are the lapses I seek to redress.

Upon that very purpose, I came to Symbal Iota late in my forty-eighth year, looking for Ebhoe. To provide context, let me say that this would be the third year of the Genovingian campaign in the Obscura Segmentum, and about nine sidereal months after the first outbreak of Uhlren's Pox amongst the Guard legions stationed on Genovingia itself. Also known, colloquially, as blood-froth, Uhlren's Pox was named after the first victim it took, a colour-sergeant called Gustaf Uhlren, of the Fifteenth Mordian, if memory serves me. And I pride myself it does.

As a student of Imperial history, and materia medica too, you will have Uhlren's Pox in your memory. A canker of body and vitality, virulently contagious, it corrupts from within, thickening circulatory fluids and wasting marrow, while embellishing the victim's skin with foul cysts and buboes. The cycle between infection and death is at most four days. In the later stages, organs rupture, blood emulsifies and bubbles through the pores of the skin, and the victim becomes violently delusional. Some have even conjectured that by this phase, the soul itself has been corroded away. Death is inescapable in almost every case.

It appeared without warning on Genovingia, and within a month, the Medicae Regimentalis were recording twenty death notices a day. No drug or procedure could be found that began to even slow its effects. No origin for the infection could be located. Worst of all, despite increasingly vigorous programs of quarantine and cleansing, no method could be found to prevent wholesale contagion. No plague carriers, or means of transmission, were identifiable.

As an individual man weakens and sickens, so the Imperial Guard forces as a whole began to fail and falter as their best were taken by the pestilence. Within two months, Warmaster Rhyngold's staff were doubting the continued viability of the entire campaign. By the third month, Uhlren's Pox had also broken out (apparently miraculously and spontaneously, given its unknown process of dispersal) on Genovingia Minor, Lorches and Adamanaxer Delta. Four separate centres of infection, right along the leading edge of the Imperial advance through the sector. At that point, the contagion had spread to the civilian population of Genovingia itself, and the Administratum had issued a Proclamation of Pandemic. It was said the skies above the cities of that mighty world were black with carrion flies and the stench of biological pollution permeated every last acre of the planet.

I had a bureaucratic posting on Lorches at that time, and became part of the emergency body charged with researching a solution. It was weary work. I personally spent over a week in the archive without seeing daylight as I oversaw the systematic interrogation of that vast, dusty body of knowledge.

It was my friend and colleague Administrator Medica Lenid Vammel who first called our attention to Pirody and the Torment. It was an admirable piece of work on his part, a feat of study, cross-reference and memory. Vammel always had a good memory.

Under the instruction of Senior Administrator Medica Junas Malter, we diverted over sixty per cent of our staff to further research into the records of Pirody, and requests were sent out to other Genovingian worlds to look to their own archives. Vammel and I compiled the accumulating data ourselves, increasingly certain we had shone a light into the right shadow and found a useful truth.

Surviving records of the Torment incident on Pirody were painfully thin, though consistent. It was, after all, thirty-four years in the past. Survivors had been few, but we were able to trace one hundred and ninety-one possibles who might yet be alive. They were scattered to the four cosmic winds.

Reviewing our findings, Senior Malter authorised personal recollection, such was the gravity of the situation, and forty of us, all with rank higher administrator or better, were dispatched immediately. Vammel, rest his soul, was sent to Gandian Saturnalia, and was caught up in a local civil war and thereafter killed. I do not know if he ever found the man he was looking for. Memory is unkind there.

And I, I was sent to Symbal Iota.

II

SYMBAL IOTA, WHERE it is not covered in oceans that are the most profound mauve in colour (a consequence, so I understand, of algae growth), is a hot, verdant place. Rainforest islands ring the equatorial region in a wide belt.

I made 'fall at Symbalopolis, a flat-topped volcanic outcrop around whose slopes hive structures cluster like barnacles, and there transferred to a trimaran which conveyed me, over a period of five days, down the length of the local island group to Saint Bastian.

I cursed the slowness of the craft, though in truth it skated across the mauve seas at better than thirty knots, and on several occasions tried to procure an ornithopter or air conveyance. But the Symbali are a nautical breed who place no faith in air travel. It was tortuous and I was impatient.

It had taken ten days to cross the empyrean from Lorches to Symbal Iota aboard a navy frigate. Now it took half that time again to cross a distance infinitesimally smaller.

It was hot, and I spent my time below decks, reading data-slates. The sun and seawind of Symbal burned my skin, used as it was to years of lamp-lit libraries. I took to wearing a wide-brimmed straw hat above my Administratus robes whenever I ventured out on deck, a detail my servitor Kalibane found relentlessly humorous.

On the fifth morning, Saint Bastian rose before us out of the violet waters, a pyramidal tower volcanic flue dressed in jungle greenery. Even as we crossed the inlet from the trimaran to the shore by electric launch, turquoise seabirds mobbing over our heads, I could see no discernible sign of habitation. The thick coat of forestation came right down to the shore itself, revealing only a thin line of white beach at its hem.

The launch pulled into a cove where an ancient stone jetty jutted out from under the trees like an unfinished bridge. Kalibane, his bionic limbs whirring, carried my luggage onto the jetty and then helped me over. I stood there, sweating in my robes, leaning against my staff of office, batting away the beetles that circled in the stifling humidity of the cove.

There was no one there to greet me, though I had voxed word of my approach ahead several times en route. I glanced back at the launch pilot, a dour Symbali, but he seemed not to know anything. Kalibane shambled down to the shore-end of the jetty, and called my attention to a copper bell, verdigrised by time and the oceans, that hung from a hook on the end of the pier.

'Ring it,' I told him, and he did, cautiously, rapping his simian fingers against the metal dome. Then he glanced back at me, nervously, his optical implants clicking under his low brow-ridge as they refocused.

Two sisters of the Ecclesiarchy shortly appeared, their pure white robes as stiff and starched as the bicorn wimples they wore on their heads. They seemed to regard me with some amusement, and wordlessly ushered me to follow them.

I fell in step behind them and Kalibane followed, carrying the luggage.

We took a dirt path up through the jungle which rose sharply and eventually became stepped. Sunlight flickered spears of light through the canopy above and the steaming air was full of exotic bird-song and the fidget of insects.

At a turn in the path, the Hospice of Saint Bastian Apostate suddenly stood before me. A great, stone-built edifice typical of the early Imperial naïve, its ancient flying buttresses and lower walls were clogged with vines and creepers. I could discern a main building of five storeys, an adjacent chapel, which looked the oldest part of the place, as well as outbuildings, kitchens and a walled garden. Above the wrought iron lych-gate stood a weathered statue of our beloved God-Emperor smiting the Archenemy.

Inside the rusty gate, a well-tended path led through a trimmed lawn punctured by tomb-stones and crypts. Stone angels and graven images of the Adeptes Astartes regarded me as I followed the sisters to the main door of the hospice.

I noticed then, fleetingly, that the windows of the two uppermost storeys were rigidly barred with iron grilles.

I left Kalibane outside with my possessions and entered the door behind the sisters. The main atrium of the hospice was a dark and deliciously cool oasis of marble, with limestone pillars that rose up into the dim spaces of the high vault. My eyes lighted on the most marvellous triptych at the altar end, beneath a stained glass oriole window, which I made observance to at once. In breadth, it was wider than a man's spread arms, and showed three aspects of the saint. On the left, he roamed the wilderness, in apostasy, renouncing the daemons of the air and fire; on the right, he performed the miracle of the maimed souls. In the centre panel, his martyred body, draped in blue cloth, the nine bolter wounds clearly countable on his pallid flesh, he lay in the arms of a luminous and suitably mournful Emperor.

I looked up from my devotions to find the sisters gone. I could feel the subliminal chorus of a psychic choir mind-singing nearby. The cool air pulsed.

A figure stood behind me. Tall, sculptural, his starched robes as white as his smooth skin was black, he seemed to regard me with the same amusement that the sisters had shown.

I realised I was still wearing my straw hat. I removed it quickly, dropping it onto a pew, and took out the pict-slate of introduction Senior Malter had given me before I left Lorches.

'I am Baptrice,' he said, his voice low and genial. 'Welcome to the saint's hospice.'

'Higher Administrator Medica Lemual Sark,' I replied. 'My dedicated function is as a recollector, posted lately to Lorches, Genovingia general group 4577 decimal, as part of the campaign auxiliary clerical archive.'

'Welcome, Lemual,' he said. 'A recollector. Indeed. We've not had one of your breed here before.'

I was uncertain quite what he meant, though in hindsight, the detail of his misunderstanding still chills me. I said 'You were expecting me? I voxed messages ahead.'

'We have no vox-caster here at the hospice,' Baptrice replied. 'What is outside does not concern us. Our work is focused on what is inside... inside this building, inside ourselves. But do not be alarmed. You are not intruding. We welcome all who come here. We do not need notice of an arrival.'

I smiled politely at this enigmatic response and tapped my fingers on my staff. I had hoped they would be ready for me, and have everything in place so that I could begin my work immediately. Once again, the leisurely pace of Symbal Iota was weighing me down.

'I must, Brother Baptrice, proceed with all haste. I wish to begin my efforts at once.'

He nodded. 'Of course. Almost all who come to Saint Bastian are eager to begin. Let me take you through and provide you with food and a place to bathe.'

'I would rather just see Ebhoe. As soon as it is possible.'

He paused, as if mystified.

'Ebhoe?'

'Colonel Fege Ebhoe, late of the Twenty-third Lammark Lancers. Please tell me he is still here! That he is still alive!'

'He... is.' Baptrice faltered, and looked over my pict-slate properly for the first time. Some sort of realisation crossed his noble face.

'My apologies, Higher Sark. I misconstrued your purpose. I see now that you are an acting recollector, sent here on official business.'

'Of course!' I snapped. 'What else would I be?'

'A supplicant, coming here to find solace. An inmate. Those that arrive on the jetty and sound the bell are always that. We get no other visitors except those who come to us for help.'

'An... inmate?' I repeated.

'Don't you know where you are?' he asked. 'This is the Hospice of Saint Bastian, a refuge for the insane.'

III

An asylum! Here was an inauspicious start to my mission! I had understood, from my research, that the Hospice of Saint Bastian was home to a holy order who offered sanctuary and comfort for those brave warriors of the Emperor's legions who were too gravely wounded or disabled by war to continue in service. I knew the place took in the damaged and the lost from warzones all across the sector. But I truly had no notion that the damage they specialised in was wounds to the psyche and sanity! It was a hospice for the deranged, individuals who presented themselves at its gates voluntarily in hope of redemption.

Worst of all, Baptrice and the sisters had presumed me to be a supplicant! That damned straw hat had given me just the air of madness they were expecting! I was lucky not to have been unceremoniously strapped into a harness and placed in isolation.

On reflection, I realised I should have known. Bastian, that hallowed saint, was a madman who found sanity in the love of the Emperor, and who later cured, through miracles, the mentally infirm.

Baptrice rang a bell cord, and novitiates appeared. Kalibane was escorted inside with my luggage. We were left alone in the atrium as Baptrice went to make preparations. As we waited, a grizzled man with an old tangle of scar-tissue where his left arm had been crossed the hall. He was naked save for a weathered, empty ammunition belt strung around his torso. He looked at us dimly, his head nodding slightly, then he padded on his way and was lost from view.

Somewhere, distantly, I could hear sobbing, and an urgent voice repeating something over and over again. Hunched down at my side, his knuckles resting on the flagstones, Kalibane glanced up at me anxiously and I put a reassuring hand on his broad, hairy shoulder.

Figures appeared around us: haggard, tonsured men in long black Ecclesiarch vestments, more phantom sisters in their ice-white robes and horned cowls. They grouped in the shadows on either side of the atrium and watched us silently. One of the men rehearsed silently from long ribbons of parchment that a boy-child played out for him from a studded casket. Another scribbled in a little chapbook with his quill. Another swung a brass censer around his feet, filling the air with dry, pungent incense.

Baptrice reappeared. 'Brethren, bid welcome to Higher Administrator Sark, who has come to us on official business. You will show him every courtesy and cooperation.'

'What official business?' asked the old priest with the chapbook, looking up with gimlet eyes. Magnifying half-moon lenses were built into his nasal bone, and rosary beads hung around his dewlapped neck like a floral victory wreath.

'A matter of recollection,' I replied.

'Pertaining to what?' he pressed.

'Brother Jardone is our archivist, Higher Sark. You will forgive his persistence.' I nodded to Baptrice and smiled at the elderly Jardone, though no smile was returned.

'I see we are kindred, Brother Jardone. Both of us devote ourselves to remembrance.'

He half-shrugged.

'I am here to interview one of your... inmates. It may be that he holds within some facts that even now may save the lives of millions in the Genovingian group.'

Jardone closed his book and gazed at me, as if waiting for more. Senior Malter had charged me to say as little as I could of the pandemic, for news of such a calamity may spread unrest. But I felt I had to give them more.

'Warmaster Rhyngold is commanding a major military excursion through the Genovingian group. A sickness, which has been named Uhlren's Pox, is afflicting his garrisons. Study has shown it may bear comparison with a plague known as the Torment, which wasted Pirody some three decades past. One survivor of that epidemic resides here. If he can furnish me with any details of the incident, it may be productive in securing a cure.'

'How bad is it, back on Genovingia?' asked another old priest, the one with the censer.

'It is... contained,' I lied.

Jardone snorted. 'Of course it is contained. That is why a higher administrator has come all this way. You ask the most foolish things, Brother Giraud.'

Another man now spoke. He was older than all, crooked and half-blind, his wrinkled pate dotted with liver spots. A flared ear-trumpet clung to the robes of his left shoulder with delicate mechanical legs. 'I am concerned that questioning and a change to routine may disturb the serenity of the hospice. I do not want our residents upset in any way.'

'Your comment is noted, Brother Niro,' said Baptrice. 'I'm sure Higher Sark will be discreet.'

'Of course,' I assured them.

It was late afternoon when Baptrice finally led me upstairs into the heart of the hospice. Kalibane followed us, lugging a few boxed items from my luggage. Ghostly, bicorned sisters watched us from every arch and shadow.

We proceeded from the stairs into a large chamber on the third floor. The air was close. Dozens of inmates lurked here, though none glanced at us. Some were clad in dingy, loose-fitting overalls, while others still wore ancient fatigues and Imperial Guard dress. All rank pins, insignia and patches had been removed, and no one had belts or bootlaces. Two were intently playing regicide on an old tin board by the window. Another sat on the bare floor planks, rolling dice. Others mumbled to themselves or gazed into the distance blankly. The naked man we had seen in the atrium was crouched in a corner, loading spent shellcases into his ammunition belt. Many of the residents had old war wounds and scars, unsightly and grotesque.

'Are they... safe?' I whispered to Baptrice.

'We allow the most stable freedom to move and use this common area. Of course, their medication is carefully monitored. But all who come here are "safe", as all who come here come voluntarily. Some, of course, come here to escape the episodes that have made regular life impractical.'

None of this reassured me.

On the far side of the chamber, we entered a long corridor flanked by cell rooms. Some doors were shut, bolted from outside. Some had cage-bars locked over them. All had sliding spy-slits. There was a smell of disinfectant and ordure.

Someone, or something, was knocking quietly and repeatedly against one locked door we passed. From another we heard singing.

Some doors were open. I saw two novitiates sponge-bathing an ancient man who was strapped to his metal cot with fabric restraints. The old man was weeping piteously. In another room, where the door was open but the outer cage locked in place, we saw a large, heavily muscled man sitting in a ladderback chair, gazing out through the bars. He was covered in tattoos: regimental emblems, mottoes, kill-scores. His eyes glowed with the most maniacal light. He had the tusks of some feral animal implanted in his lower jaw, so they hooked up over his upper lip.

As we passed, he leaped up and tried to reach through the bars at us. His powerful arm flexed and clenched. He issued a soft growl.

'Behave, Ioq!' Baptrice told him.

The cell next door to Ioq's was our destination. The door was open, and a sister and a novitiate waited for us. The room beyond them was pitch black.

Baptrice spoke for a moment with the novitiate and the sister. He turned to me. 'Ebhoe is reluctant, but the sister has convinced him it is right that he speaks with you. You may not go in. Please sit at the door.'

The novitiate brought up a stool, and I sat in the doorway, throwing out my robes over my knees. Kalibane dutifully opened my boxes and set up the transcribing artificer on its tripod stand.

I gazed into the blackness of the room, trying to make out shapes. I could see nothing.

'Why is it dark in there?'

'Ebhoe's malady, his mental condition, is exacerbated by light. He demands darkness.' Baptrice shrugged.

I nodded glumly and cleared my throat. 'By the grace of the God-Emperor of Terra, I come here on His holy work. I identify myself as Lemual Sark, higher administrator medica, assigned to Lorches Administratum.'

I glanced over at the artificer. It chattered quietly and extruded the start of a parchment transcription tape that I hoped would soon be long and informative. 'I seek Fege Ebhoe, once a colonel with the Twenty-Third Lammark Lancers.'

Silence.

'Colonel Ebhoe?'

A voice, thin as a knife, cold as a corpse, whispered out of the dark room. 'I am he. What is your business?'

I leaned forward. 'I wish to discuss Pirody with you. The Torment you endured.'

'I have nothing to say. I won't remember anything.'

'Come now, colonel. I'm sure you will if you try.'

'You misunderstand. I didn't say I "can't". I said I "won't".'

'Deliberately?'

'Just so. I refuse to.'

I wiped my mouth, and realised I was dry-tongued. 'Why not, colonel?'

'Pirody is why I'm here. Thirty-four years, trying to forget. I don't want to start remembering now.'

Baptrice looked at me with a slight helpless gesture. He seemed to be suggesting that it was done, and I should give up.

'Men are dying on Genovingia from a plague we know as Uhlren's Pox. This pestilence bears all the hallmarks of the Torment. Anything you can tell me may help save lives.'

'I couldn't then. Fifty-nine thousand men died on Pirody. I couldn't save them though I tried with every shred of my being. Why should that be different now?'

I gazed at the invisible source of the cold voice. 'I cannot say for sure. But I believe it is worth trying.'

There was a long pause. The artificer whirred on idle. Kalibane coughed, and the machine recorded the sound with a little chatter of keys.

'How many men?'

'I'm sorry, colonel? What did you ask me?'

'How many men are dying?'

I took a deep breath. 'When I left Lorches, nine hundred were dead and another fifteen hundred infected. On Genovingia Minor, six thousand and twice that number ailing. On Adamanaxer Delta, two hundred, but it had barely begun there. On Genovingia itself... two and a half million.'

I heard Baptrice gasp in shock. I trusted he would keep this to himself.

'Colonel?'

Nothing.

'Colonel, please...'

Cold and cutting, the voice came again, sharper than before. 'Pirody was a wasted place...'

IV

PIRODY WAS A wasted place. We didn't want to go there. But the Archenemy had taken the eastern continent and razed the hives, and the northern cities were imperilled.

Warmaster Getus sent us in. Forty thousand Lammark Lancers, virtually the full strength of the Lammark regiments. Twenty thousand Fancho armour men and their machines, and a full company of Astartes, the Doom Eagles, shining grey and red.

The place we were at was Pirody Polar. It was god knows how old. Cyclopean towers and columns of green marble, hewn in antique times by hands I'm not convinced were human. There was a strangeness to the geometry there, the angles never seemed quite right.

It was as cold as a bastard. We had winter dress, thick white flak coats with fur hoods, but the ice got in the lasguns and dulled their charges and the damned Fancho tanks were forever refusing to start. It was day, too. Day all the time. There was no night, it was the wrong season. We were so far north. The darkest it got was dusk, when one of the two suns set briefly and the sky went flesh pink. Then it would be daylight again.

We'd been fighting on and off for two months. Mainly long range artillery duels, pounding the ice-drifts. No one could sleep because of the perpetual daylight. I know two men, one a Lammarkine, I'm not proud to say, who gouged out his eyes. The other was a Fancho.

Then they came. Black dots on the ice-floes, thousands of them, waving banners so obscene, they...

Whatever. We were in no mood to fight. Driven mad by the light, driven to distraction by the lack of sleep, unnerved by the curious geometry of the place we were defending, we were easy meat. The forces of Chaos slaughtered us, and pushed us back into the city itself. The civilians, about two million strong, were worse than useless. They were pallid, idle things, with no drive or appetite. When doom came upon them, they simply gave up.

We were besieged for five months, despite six attempts by the Doom Eagles to break the deadlock. Faith, but they were terrifying! Giants, clashing their bolters together before each fight, screaming at the foe, killing fifty for every one we picked off.

But it was like fighting the tide, and for all their power, there were only sixty of them.

We called for reinforcements. Getus had promised us, but now he was long gone aboard his warship, drawn back behind the fleet picket in case things got nasty.

The first man I saw fall to the Torment was a captain in my seventh platoon. He just collapsed one day, feverish. We took him to the Pirody Polar infirmium, where Subjunctus Valis, the apothecary of the Doom Eagles company, was running the show. An hour later, the captain was dead. His skin had blistered and bubbled. His eyes had burst. He had tried to kill Valis with a piece of the metal cot he had torn from the wall brace. Then he bled out.

You know what that means? His entire body spewed blood from every orifice, every pore. He was a husk by the time it was over.

In the day after the captain's death, sixty fell victim. Another day, two hundred. Another day, a thousand. Most died within two hours. Others lingered... for days, pustular, agonised.

Men I had known all my life turned into gristly sacks of bone before my eyes. Damn you, Sark, for making me remember this!

On the seventh day it spread to the Fancho as well. On the ninth, it reached the civilian population. Valis ordered all measure of quarantine, but it was no good. He worked all hours of the endless day, trying to find a vaccine, trying to alleviate the relentless infection.

On the tenth day, a Doom Eagle fell victim. In his Torment, blood gouting from his visor grilles, he slew two of his comrades and nineteen of my men. The disease had overcome even the Astartes purity seals.

I went to Valis, craving good news. He had set up a laboratory in the infirmium, where blood samples and tissue-scrapes boiled in alembics and separated in oil flasks. He assured me the Torment would be stopped. He explained how unlikely it was for a pestilence to be transmitted in such a cold clime, where there is no heat to incubate and spread decay. And he also believed it would not flourish in light. So he had every stretch of the city wired with lamps so that there would be no darkness.

No darkness. In a place where none came naturally, even the shadows of closed rooms were banished. Everything was bright. Perhaps you can see now why I abhor the light and cling to darkness.

The stench of blood-filth was appalling. Valis did his work, but still we fell. By the twenty-first day, I'd lost thirty-seven per cent of my force. The Fancho were all but gone. Twelve thousand Pirodian citizens were dead or dying. Nineteen Doom Eagles had succumbed.

Here are your facts if you want them. The plague persisted in a climate that should have killed it. It showed no common process of transmission. It brooked no attempt to contain or control it, despite efforts to enforce quarantine and cleanse infected areas with flamers. It was ferociously contagious. Even Marine purity seals were no protection. Its victims died in agony.

Then one of the Doom Eagles deciphered the obscene script of one of the Chaos banners displayed outside the walls.

It said...

It said one word. One filthy word. One damned, abominable word that I have spent my life trying to forget.

V

I CRANED IN at the dark doorway. 'What word? What word was it, colonel?'

With great reluctance, he spoke it. It wasn't a word at all. It was an obscene gurgle dignified by consonants. The glyph-name of the plague-daemon itself, one of the ninety-seven Blasphemies that May Not Be Written Down.

At its utterance, I fell back off my stool, nausea writhing in my belly and throat. Kalibane shrieked. The sister collapsed in a faint and the novitiate fled.

Baptrice took four steps back from the doorway, turned, and vomited spectacularly.

The temperature in the corridor dropped by fifteen degrees.

Unsteady, I attempted to straighten my overturned stool and pick up the artificer that the novitiate had knocked over. Where it had recorded the word, I saw, the machine's parchment tape had begun to smoulder.

Screaming and wailing echoed down the hall from various cells.

And then, Ioq was out.

Just next door, he had heard it all, his scarred head pressed to the cage bars. Now that cage door splintered off its mount and crashed to the corridor floor. Berserk, the huge ex-Guardsman thrashed out and turned towards us.

He was going to kill me, I'm certain, but I was slumped and my legs wouldn't work. Then Kalibane, bless his brave heart, flew at him. My devoted servitor rose up on his stunted hind limbs, the bionics augmenting his vast forelimbs throwing them up in a warning display. From splayed foot to reaching hand, Kalibane was eleven feet tall. He peeled back his lips and screeched through bared steel canines.

Froth dribbling from his tusked mouth, Ioq smashed Kalibane aside. My servitor made a considerable dent in the wall.

Ioq was on me.

I swept my staff of office around and thumbed the recessed switch below the head.

Electric crackles blasted from the staff's tip. Ioq convulsed and fell. Twitching, he lay on the floorboards, and evacuated involuntarily. Baptrice was on his feet now. Alarms were ringing and novitiates were rushing frantically into the corridor with harness jackets and clench poles.

I rose and looked back at the dark doorway.

'Colonel Ebhoe?'

The door slammed shut.

VI

THERE WOULD BE no further interview that afternoon, Brother Baptrice made plain, despite my protests. Novitiates escorted me to a guest chamber on the second floor. It was white-washed and plain, with a hard, wooden bed and small scriptorium table. A leaded window looked out onto the graveyard and the jungles beyond.

I felt a great perturbation of spirit, and paced the room as Kalibane unpacked my belongings. I had come so close, and had begun to draw the reluctant Ebhoe out. Now to be denied the chance to continue when the truly dark secrets were being revealed!

I paused by the window. The glaring, crimson sun was sinking into the mauve oceans, throwing the thick jungles into black, wild relief. Seabirds reeled over the bay in the dying light. Stars were coming out in the dark blue edges of the sky.

Calmer now, I reflected that whatever my internal uproar, the uproar in the place itself was greater.

From the window, I could hear all manner of screams, wails, shouts, banging doors, thundering footsteps, rattled keys. The word of blasphemy that Ebhoe had spoken had thrown all the fragile minds in this house of insanity into disarray, like red-hot metal plunged into quenching cold water. Great efforts were being made to quieten the inmates.

I sat at the teak scriptorium for a while, reviewing the transcripts while Kalibane dozed on a settle by the door. Ebhoe had made particular mention of Subjunctus Valis, the Doom Eagles' apothecary. I looked over copies of the old Pirody debriefings I had brought with me, but Valis's name only appeared in the muster listings. Had he survived? Only a direct request to the Doom Eagles Chapter house could provide an answer, and that might take months.

The Astartes are notoriously secretive, sometimes downright blatant in their uncooperative relationship with the Administratum. At best, it might involve a series of formal approaches, delaying tactics, bargaining.

Even so, I wanted to alert my brethren on Lorches to the possible lead. I damned Saint Bastian when I remembered the place had no vox-caster! I couldn't even forward a message to the Astropathic enclave at Symbalopolis for transmission off world.

A sister brought me supper on a tray. Just as I was finishing, and Kalibane was lighting the lamps, Niro and Jardone came to my chamber.

'Brothers?'

Jardone got right to it, staring at me through his half-moon lenses. 'The brotherhood of the hospice have met, and they decided that you must leave. Tomorrow. No further audiences will be granted. We have a vessel that will take you to the fishing port at Math island. You can obtain passage to Symbalopolis from there.'

'I am disappointed, Jardone. I do not wish to leave. My recollection is not complete.'

'It is as complete as it's going to be!' he snapped.

'The hospice has never been so troubled,' Niro said quietly. 'There have been brawls. Two novitiates have been injured. Three inmates have attempted suicide. Years of work have been undone in a few moments.'

I nodded. 'I regret the disturbance, but–'

'No buts!' barked Jardone.

'I'm sorry, Higher Sark,' said Niro. 'That is how it is.'

I SLEPT BADLY in the cramped cot. My mind, my memory, played games, going over the details of the interview. There was shock and injury in Ebhoe, that was certain, for the event had been traumatic. But there was something else. A secret beyond anything he had told me, some profound memory. I could taste it.

I would not be deterred. Too many lives depended on it.

Kalibane was slumbering heavily when I crept from the chamber. In the darkness, I felt my way to the stairs, and up to the third floor. There was a restlessness in the close air. I moved past locked cells where men moaned in their sleep or muttered in their insomnia.

At intervals, I hugged the shadows as novitiate wardens with lamps made their patrols. It took perhaps three quarters of an hour to reach the cell block where Ebhoe resided. I stalked nervously past the bolted door of Ioq's room.

The spy-slit opened at my touch. 'Ebhoe? Colonel Ebhoe?' I called softly into the darkness.

'Who?' his cold voice replied.

'It is Sark. We weren't finished.'

'Go away.'

'I will not, until you tell me the rest.'

'Go away.'

I thought desperately, and eagerness made me cruel. 'I have a torch, Ebhoe. A powerful lamp. Do you want me to shine it in through the spy-hole?'

When he spoke again, there was terror in his voice. Emperor forgive me for my manipulation.

'What more is there?' he asked. 'The Torment spread. We died by the thousand. I cannot help with your cause, though I pity those men on Genovingia.'

'You never told me how it ended.'

'Did you not read the reports?'

I glanced up and down the dark cell-block to make sure we were still alone. 'I read them. They were... sparse. They said Warmaster Gatus incinerated the enemy from orbit, and ships were sent to relieve you at Pirody Polar. They expressed horror at the extent of the plague-loss. Fifty-nine thousand men dead. No count was made of the civilian losses. They said that by the time the relief ships arrived, the Torment had been expunged. Four hundred men were evacuated. Of them, only one hundred and ninety-one are still alive according to the records.'

'There's your answer then.'

'No, colonel. That's no answer! How was it expunged?'

'We located the source of infection, cleansed it. That was how.'

'How, Ebhoe? How, in the God-Emperor's name?'

'It was the height of the Torment. Thousands dead...'

VII

IT WAS THE height of the Torment. Thousands dead, corpses everywhere, pus and blood running in those damnably bright halls.

I went to Valis again, begging for news. He was in his infirmium, working still. Another batch of vaccines to try, he told me. The last six had failed, and had even seemed to aggravate the contagion.

The men were fighting themselves by then, killing each other in fear and loathing. I told Valis this, and he was silent, working at a flame burner on the steel workbench. He was huge being, of course... Astartes, a head and a half taller than me, wearing a cowled red robe over his Doom Eagles armour. He lifted specimen bottles from his narthecium, and held them up to the ever-present light.

I was tired, tired like you wouldn't believe. I hadn't slept in days. I put down the flamer I had been using for cleansing work, and sat on a stool.

'Are we all going to perish?' I asked the great apothecary.

'Dear, valiant Ebhoe,' he said with a laugh. 'You poor little man. Of course not. I will not allow it.'

He turned to face me, filling a long syringe from a stoppered bottle. I was in awe of him, even after the time we had spent together.

'You are one of the lucky ones, Ebhoe. Clean so far. I'd hate to see you contract this pestilence. You have been a faithful ally to me through this dark time, helping to distribute my vaccines. I will mention you to your commanders.'

'Thank you, apothecary.'

'Ebhoe,' he said, 'I think it is fair to say we cannot save any who have been infected now. We can only hope to vaccinate the healthy against infection. I have prepared a serum for that purpose, and I will inoculate all healthy men with it. You will help me. And you will be first. So I can be sure not to lose you.'

I hesitated. He came forward with the syringe, and I started to pull up my sleeve.

'Open your jacket and tunic. It must go through the stomach wall.' I reached for my tunic clasps.

And saw it. The tiniest thing. Just a tiny, tiny thing.

A greenish-yellow blister just below Valis's right ear.

VIII

EBHOE FELL SILENT. The air seemed electrically charged. Inmates in neighbouring cells were thrashing restless, and some were crying out. At any moment, the novitiate wardens would come.

'Ebhoe?' I called through the slit.

His voice had fallen to a terrified whisper, the whisper of a man who simply cannot bear to put the things haunting his mind into words.

'Ebhoe?'

Keys clattered nearby. Lamplight flickered under a hall door. Ioq was banging at his cell door and growling. Someone was crying, someone else was wailing in a made-up language. The air was ripe with the smell of faeces, sweat and agitated fear.

'Ebhoe!'

There was no time left. 'Ebhoe, please!'

'Valis had the Torment! He'd had it all along, right from the start!' Ebhoe's voice was strident and anguished. The words came out of the slit as hard and lethal as las-fire. 'He had spread it! He! Through his work, his vaccines, his treatments! He had spread the plague! His mind had been corrupted by it, he didn't know what he was doing! His many, many vaccines had failed because they weren't vaccines! They were new strains of the Torment bred in his infirmium! He was the carrier: a malevolent, hungry pestilence clothed in the form of a noble man, killing thousands upon thousands upon thousands!'

I went cold. Colder than I'd ever been before. The idea was monstrous. The Torment had been more than a waster of lives, it had been sentient, alive, deliberate... planning and moving through the instrument it had corrupted.

The door of Ioq's cell was bulging and shattering. Screams welled all around, panic and fear in equal measure. The entire hospice was shaking with unleashed psychoses.

Lamps flashed at the end of the block. Novitiates yelled out and ran forward as they saw me. They would have reached me had not Ioq broken out again, rabid and slavering, throwing his hideous bulk into them, ripping at them in a frenzy.

'Ebhoe!' I yelled through the slit. 'What did you do?'

He was crying, his voice ragged with gut-heaving sobs. 'I grabbed my flamer! Emperor have mercy, I snatched it up and bathed Valis with flame! I killed him! I killed him! I slew the pride of the Doom Eagles! I burned him apart! I expunged the source of the Torment!'

A novitiate flew past me, his throat ripped out by animal tusks. His colleagues were locked in a desperate struggle with Ioq.

'You burned him.'

'Yes. The flames touched off the chemicals in the infirmium, the sample bottles, the flasks of seething plague water. They exploded. A fireball... Oh gods... brighter than the daylight that had never gone away. Brighter than... fire everywhere... liquid fire... flames around me... all around... oh... oh...'

Bright flashes filled the hall, the loud discharge of a las-weapon.

I stepped back from Ebhoe's cell door, shaking. Ioq lay dead amid the mangled corpses of three novitiates. Several others, wounded, whimpered on the floor.

Brother Jardone, a laspistol in his bony hand, pushed through the orderlies and ecclesiarchs gathering in the hall, and pointed the weapon at me.

'I should kill you for this, Sark. How dare you!'

Baptrice stepped forward and took the gun from Jardone. Niro gazed at me in weary disappointment.

'See to Ebhoe,' Baptrice told the sisters nearby. They unlocked the cell door and went in.

'You will leave tomorrow, Sark,' Baptrice said. 'I will file a complaint to your superiors.'

'Do so,' I said. 'I never wanted this, but I had to reach the truth. It may be, from what Ebhoe has told me, that a way to fight Uhlren's Pox is in our reach.'

'I hope so,' said Baptrice, gazing bitterly at the carnage in the hall. 'It has cost enough.'

The novitiates were escorting me back to my room when the sisters brought Ebhoe out. The ordeal of recollection had killed him. I will never forgive myself for that, no matter how many lives on Genovingia we saved.

And I will never forget the sight of him, revealed at last in the light.

IX

I LEFT THE next day by launch with Kalibane. No one from the hospice saw me off or even spoke to me. From Math Island, I transmitted my report to Symbalopolis, and from there, astropathically, it lanced through the warp to Lorches.

Was Uhlren's Pox expunged? Yes, eventually. My work assisted in that. The blood-froth was like the Torment, engineered by the Archenemy, just as sentient. Fifty-two medical officers, sources just like Valis, were executed and incinerated.

I forget how many we lost altogether in the Genovingia group. I forget a lot, these days. My memory is not what it was, and I am thankful for that, at times.

I never forget Ebhoe. I never forget his corpse, wheeled out by the sisters. He had been caught in the infirmium flames on Pirody Polar. Limbless, wizened like a seed-case, he hung in a suspensor chair, kept alive by intravenous drains and sterile sprays. A ragged, revolting remnant of a man.

He had no eyes. I remember that most clearly of all. The flames had scorched them out.

He had no eyes, and yet he was terrified of the light.

I still believe that memory is the finest faculty we as a species own. But by the Golden Throne, there are things I wish I could never remember again.

BARATHRUM
Jonathan Curren

NIGHT, AND THE site is quiet as a morgue. The only sound is the gentle clink clink of chains rustling from the high ceiling, connected to the crane mechanisms running from gantries the length of the hangar. Machines hum silently, a faint disturbance of the air the only sign that they are active. The occasional light pierces the twilight walkways and balconies, stairways and alcoves. Archaeo-site R347 is the inside of a great hive, its workers and machines the silent insects, termites in the service of the Machine-God.

Tech-Brother Crans stands bent over a workbench, a tray of thick viscous fluid in front of him. Immersed in the ungúents is an array of fine machinery, tiny metal plates and wires meshed together in intricate fractal patterns. Crans murmurs prayers, manipulator gloves caressing the fine wires, divining rods following the paths of energy locked in the device.

He straightens up, stretching his sore back. Removing the manipulators, he lays them down on the workbench and raises the optical enhancers from in front of his eyes. Balancing them on his forehead, he rubs his tired eyes with his fingers. He's worked with mechanical optics all his life, yet has steadfastly refused bio-implants of his own, maintaining that the optics he was born with would see him to the grave.

Something. A noise, almost inaudible.

Crans turns round.

'Hello,' he calls, quietly, almost so as not to disturb the tranquillity of the place.

He appreciates the silence and solitude, it's why he chooses to work at night. He doesn't want to disturb it. 'Is anybody there?'

Nothing.

He turns back to the workbench, flipping the opticals back down in front of his eyes. The component swings back into view, large as a fist. He picks up the manipulators.

A crash, as something falls behind him.

He spins round, and something fills his vision, the opticals fighting to make sense of the image, magnified hundreds of times.

Then his sight fills with red mist as something hard and sharp shatters the opticals, plunges into the flesh around his eyes, driving through bone and filling his head with fiery pain.

The last thing he hears before the darkness of death overwhelms him is the soft shuffle of slippered feet walking quickly towards him.

ECHO TWELVE BEARING *three three zero, range forty clicks and counting. Requesting landing permission, code blue seven zero seven. Over.*

A burst of static. Then.

Echo Twelve, landing permission granted. Proceed to landing bay seven zero seven.

The Imperial shuttle drifted slowly through the cloud cover, its wings jostled by the heavy thick air. Red dust thrown up by the industrial exchange outlets down on the surface swirled into the engines, causing the rotor-blades to shudder. Wind howled around the tiny craft, as if daemons of the air competed to swallow it.

Inquisitor Anselm watched the red crosshairs of the nav-comm playing across the face of the pilot as he struggled to keep the shuttle on its computer-assisted course. The pilot's right hand was jacked into the shuttle's controls and his bio-eye scanned the clouds for the first lights of the landing bay. Technobabble issued from the cabin speakers as the cogitators spoke to the pilot at a rate of several thousand words mixed with binary codes a minute.

Looking into the swirling maelstrom outside the shuttle's forward screens, he was surprised to see his own reflection staring back at him. A craggy face, weathered by long tours of duty in the Emperor's service made him look older than his years. Long-service studs embedded above his eyes glinted in the winking lights from the console. A shock of close-cropped white hair, dark, hooded eyes, an imperious nose added to his imposing figure, made people think carefully before crossing him. He knew full well the advantage it gave him.

Gazing at himself like this made him uncomfortable, and he turned away. He felt impatience grip him, and he forced himself to stay calm. It was a long time since he'd last seen Cantor, many years, and he freely admitted that he was looking forward to seeing his old friend. But that wasn't the only reason he was pleased to have been assigned this investigation. There was something else, the opportunity to investigate a crime at the very limits of Imperial jurisdiction. Only a short hop from unexplored space itself. He'd never travelled this far before, and now he was entering the atmosphere of Barathrum, a planet that despite years of extensive archaeological investigation, was still a mystery to Imperium scholars. Who knew what may happen this far from the centre of Imperial space? Not that this sort of thing meant anything to an Imperial inquisitor, but at the back of his mind, he knew that heading such an investigation could propel him along the road leading to the highest echelons of the Inquisition.

The shuttle docked, and the pilot unplugged himself from the console, pale from the concentration needed for their landing. Anselm unbuckled himself, and felt his seat relax, its shape melting away from his body. The shuttle's hatch opened with a hiss of compressed air, and as he walked down the rampway, his senses were assaulted with the smells of ozone, oil, metal and industrial solvents. His enhanced olfactory system idly recognised a dozen different chemical compounds, but before his brain had time to register them, he heard his name being called.

'Anselm! Anselm! I'm so glad you've made it.'

He looked over to the double doors facing the shuttle hangar. A tall thin man approached, dressed in brown robes with a leather apron from which hung tools, calibrating instruments and various optical measures. His face was flushed, and he was sweating slightly. They gripped each other's forearms in an old comradely gesture. Cantor indicated that they should walk, and they boarded the enclosed monorail pod that he'd just emerged from.

As the monorail slowly accelerated, Anselm was the first to voice what he was thinking.

'Cantor, it's good to see you. It has been a long time. It saddens me that after all these years, we only get the chance to meet on such an ominous occasion.'

'You've read the transcripts? There is something unnatural happening. I'm glad you are here.'

'It's affected you deeply.' It was a statement, not a question. 'You look flushed. Have you not been sleeping? You look uneasy.'

'No, my sleep is fine. You always were an apothecary first and foremost. But that is not why I am uneasy.'

Cantor reached out and stabbed a finger at the panel of buttons by the door. The monorail slowed, and a light started flashing on the console.

Anselm looked at him. 'What is it? Is there something you need to tell me? Remember that I am the Emperor's ear here. Speak freely.'

Cantor lowered his voice. 'There is something you should know. You are not the only member of the Emperor's Inquisition here on Barathrum.'

Anselm felt something clench in his stomach. 'What do you mean?' he demanded.

His friend paused, and at that moment, the pod slowed to a stop, the doors sliding gently open on a waft of pneumatic air.

The inquisitor stepped out into a long room. At one end was a huge window, filling the whole wall. Silhouetted against the setting sun were two figures, one bulky, the other slight. Anselm strode towards the figures, and as he approached, the pair turned round.

Surprise stopped Anselm in his tracks, but he made an effort to steady himself.

'Grogan! What in the Emperor's name are you doing here?'

The tall man smiled a smile that made Anselm's blood boil. His smaller companion looked confused. He recovered himself quickly, and bowed to Anselm in greeting, a half bow of respect to an equal. Anselm returned the gesture, never taking his eyes off Grogan.

Inquisitor Grogan was tall, taller than Anselm and many years older. His eyes were cold, and seemed fixed on the middle distance, as if permanently watching out across the broad expanse of tundra that comprised his home planet had fixed his gaze far away; a long moustache drooped on either side of his lips, giving him a permanently sour expression. He wore rough clothes tied together with an immense belt from which hung a myriad of tools, knives and weapons, along with devices best left unrecognised. It was as if he wanted to make it clear that he would brook no nonsense of the kind that flourished in courts and palaces across the galaxy. He had a reputation for harshness and inflexibility that Anselm could attest to and that reputation had no doubt preceded his arrival on Barathrum. No wonder Cantor was nervous.

'So,' the smaller man started, 'you two know each other?'

Grogan turned to his companion. 'Anselm was a pupil of mine. When he was first elevated to the rank of inquisitor adept, he was entrusted into my care.'

'That was many years ago,' Anselm cut in, and then stopped, angry with himself. It was a long time ago, long enough for him to have worked through the anger that his time under Grogan's tutelage had left him. He continued. 'The inquisitor and I have worked together before. We know each other's methods well. Our differing approaches will no doubt cover all the possibilities in this situation.' He gave Grogan a meaningful look and was relieved to see him back down. The man merely grunted in reply and indicated the man standing at his side. 'Anselm, this is Eremet. He is the master explorator in charge of the work here on Barathrum.'

Eremet bowed, and extended one hand to Anselm. His grip was strong, the skin rough and weathered. The explorator's face was open, friendly. 'The holy Inquisition is most welcome on Barathrum,' he said. 'You've read Cantor's report?'

'I have,' Anselm replied, 'but I would hear it from your mouth. There are many ways to tell the same story.'

'Follow me then. Perhaps when you see, you will understand more than if you simply listen.'

Eremet led them through a set of double doors and down a short flight of stairs. He pushed open a plain door and they entered a clean bright room that smelled of antiseptic. Racks of surgical instruments lined the walls, and an operating table stood under bright theatre lights. Behind a green cloth screen, just visible from the doorway, stood a row of gurneys, each holding a shrouded figure.

The master explorer moved the screen aside and stood beside the first body.

With a flick of his hand, he removed the shroud from the figure. Despite himself, Anselm felt his stomach heave. He was no stranger to battle and the hideous wounds that resulted from close combat, but this was no war-wound. The face had been mutilated almost beyond recognition, great gouging marks like those of a wild beast scoured the face from top to bottom. The jaw had been broken by the violence of the attack, and the mouth hung open, making it look like the corpse had been interrupted in the process of screaming. One eye had been destroyed, the socket torn across, but the other stared out between curtains of ragged flesh.

Eremet's voice was matter of fact. 'We have lost six of our company in the past eight work cycles. The first to go missing, Aleuk, was found in sector four, one of the mid-city areas, then one by one we lost the others, each one deeper and further in towards the heart of the city. And now, Crans, he was working at the furthest point that we have excavated...'

'How big is the city?' asked Anselm. 'All I saw on the flight in was the bunker and the landing bay.'

Eremet laughed. 'That is all you would see. The bunker is in fact the highest part, the spire if you like, for a great city that has sunk beneath the sands of this planet. It once stood proud above the ground, but something in ages past made it sink through the sand, and now all that lies above the earth is this part.'

'How far does the city extend?'

'The city stretches underneath us for over five kilometres. We've only mapped the core. The deeper we get, the more spread out it is – we estimate up to ten kilometres in diameter at the deepest points – and the less we know. The city is incredibly complex in design, but Cantor is the best tech-priest explorer there is. Every time we were halted in our efforts, Cantor advised us where to dig next, and, each time, we made such progress that we were able to carry on.

'As I was saying, Aleuk was in sector four, about three kilometres down. Our servitors had just cut into a new area – a lot of the work here involves cutting or digging through debris to reach a new level – and this level was much older. There was less concrete and steel, much of the building was formed from great blocks of hewn stone.

'The standard of masonry is extraordinarily high, there's hardly a gap between any of the blocks. It's quite astonishing.

'One of our adepts was taking geochron readings, trying to gauge how old the area was. How it happened we haven't been able to discover but one of the blocks from the ceiling must have been loose. It fell, blocking the corridor he was in and cutting the man off from the rest of the team. It was then it happened. He was attacked. The sound of him screaming in pain and fear could be heard from the other side. It was horrible.'

'You were there?' asked Grogan.

'No, I wasn't. I was here in the medi-bay.'

'Alone?'

'Yes.'

What about the other corpses?' asked Grogan.

Silently, Eremet moved from trolley to trolley, pulling back the sheets that covered the forms, until all the corpses lay exposed, side by side in death like a roll-call of the slain. Each of them was terribly torn, the flesh of each flayed back from his musculature and in places bones, cracked and splintered, appeared through the tattered muscles.

'The others disappeared and were found, each one deeper down in the structure of the city. I had to order the complete shutdown of all our operations until you came.'

Anselm cast a critical eye over the display.

'Has the cause of death been established for each?' he asked Eremet.

Grogan snorted. 'I think the cause of death is pretty self-evident. Attack by some sort of wild beast, could be a 'stealer or some other species of 'nid. Something big and dangerous. Look at that one – his arms have been ripped off. Complication of the simple always was one of your…'

He broke off, and turned to Eremet. 'Master explorator, I think this is a clear-cut case of xeno-infestation, type unknown. Unless there's some other evidence to the contrary, I would say this is not a crime-scene. I suggest that, as we're here, we find your missing tech-priest, hunt whatever's running loose here and move on.'

He turned to Anselm. 'Cantor's already explained to me that the missing tech-priest was scheduled to work on some newly discovered archaeotech, in a recently excavated area, sector twenty-eight. I suggest we start looking for him there. Eremet, do you have weapons here?'

'No – this site has been active for years and we've never had any problems with hostiles. It's away from the main trade routes, we have no trouble from pirates or xenomorphs. The Imperial zoologians who surveyed the planet found no indigenous life that posed a threat, and the planet itself has a green security rating.'

'Well, we have,' Grogan countered. 'So soon there won't be any indigenous life forms around to threaten anyone!' Then he added, as if to himself, 'The Inquisition is a tool of cleansing fire. It's time to light the flame.'

He turned and stalked out of the medi-bay.

'Follow me,' Anselm said and moved swiftly after the inquisitor. They caught up with him in the control room, where he was waiting for Cantor to guide them. The tech-priest handed each of them a torch from a rack, then led the way out of the control room and towards a pair of lifts. Stopping only to pull his combat shotgun from his kit bag, Anselm followed him. Once inside, they stood silently while Cantor jabbed at buttons with his finger. The lift doors closed and a gentle humming sound filled the small room. There was a barely perceptible shift as the lift started to descend. There was almost no sensation of falling but Anselm felt his ears popping before the lift came to a gentle halt about a minute later. The doors opened and they moved out into a vast space.

The room was a hall of some kind. It seemed as if it were once some sort of meeting area or place of worship. There had once been fine paintings on the walls, but age and water damage had destroyed them, leaving only mouldering frames. What had once been furniture was now nothing more than splintered timbers and broken masonry, pushed to one side. The dust lay heavy at the edges of the room, but the middle had been worn clean by the countless feet of the archaeotech priests over the years.

They moved down through the hall, Grogan leading, his great strides kicking up dust. Cantor followed, his soft shoes shuffling, and Anselm brought up the rear. They went through a door and found themselves in a broad corridor, almost a road, leading downwards. On either side of them, doors and corridors led off in different directions. Burnt out machinery, some of it looking incredibly old, was scattered haphazardly around the area. Doors, broken and hanging off their hinges, sometimes blocked a doorway. Every now and again, they passed some dark staining on the walls or floors. It looked as if oil or some carbonised matter had been spilt there.

They came to a crossroads of sorts, lit by the harsh lights of the exploratory team who had set up permanent illumination across the dig area. High pillars held up the roof, now hung with webs of what looked like the spinnings of some long gone creatures. He could see balconies, mezzanine levels, bridges spanning the void above them. Anselm shuddered. He suddenly realised that they were moving through the heart of what had been a great city, a city to rival in splendour any that he had seen, but now ruined and desolate. In his mind's eye he could see shops, warehouses, palaces, gardens, roads and walkways, once splendid, now ruined and empty. He noticed marks in the walls from small arms fire, bolter marks and scorches from lasguns. All was quiet and beyond the perimeter of light afforded by the arc-lamps, he could see nothing. He gripped the comforting bulk of his shotgun, holding it ready as he scanned the darkness. The beam from his torch wavered as he settled the gun's stock into his hip.

Great loops of black cabling snaked back the way they had come, no doubt supplying power to those digging deeper in the bowels of the city. Arc lamps threw stark shadows, and as they passed each lamp, Anselm saw the silhouette of Grogan rear up the wall towards him and then sink down again as the inquisitor strode past, his powerful bulk seeming to leap at him.

His skin prickled. Out of the corner of his eye, he thought he saw movement. He turned his head, shining the strong beam of his torch into the blackness, but there was nothing there, only an empty hole where one part of a wall had collapsed. He turned his attention back to the group.

'Do we know anything about the city, its people?' Anselm asked Cantor.

'Nothing at all,' he replied. 'The city itself is very old, but apart from the buildings themselves, which you can see around you, there is very little that it has revealed to us. It is a bit of a mystery – there is nothing in the ancient chronicles about a city or even a civilisation this far away from the galactic core. Whatever was here was either well hidden from the main routes or kept itself to itself. I would have posited some sort of pirate community or frontier world but the size and complexity of this city denies that. There is almost no evidence of how they lived other than the buildings. There is much damage, it looks like a heavy battle was fought here but over what we cannot tell. The centuries hide a lot of evidence – we found bones but they'd almost worn away to nothing, clothes had rotted, even metal had rusted away.'

Anselm shuddered. He couldn't get rid of the feeling that they were being watched but he could see no sign of anything nearby. The dark windows of buildings seemed to gaze at him blankly but every now and then he felt that something was watching him from behind stone buttresses or broken walls. He shook his head, clearing the visions. He wouldn't allow himself to start imagining that he could see back into the city's living past. He looked ahead. They were coming to a narrowing of the way, almost a tunnel.

He concentrated on Cantor's monologue.

'Much of this part of the city was sealed off by rockfall. We had to excavate heavily in order to get past it, as sensors indicated that the city continued for some way beyond it. Took some doing, I can tell you. This rock's hard as adamantium. Wore away hundreds of drillbits, but in the end… Ah, here we are. As you can see, what we found was well worth the effort.'

They had come to the end of the tunnel. In front of them stood a wall, carved from massive blocks of stone, fitted together with such precision that only the thinnest line separated the blocks from one another. At the base of the wall was an opening, barely two metres high, and only half the width. Surrounding the opening was an inscription in a language they could not read.

'The translation has defeated us so far; it was sent to the Ecclesiarchy for translation but we heard nothing back,' Cantor said, rather sheepishly. 'There was a stone blocking the doorway. I'm afraid we had to use compact charges to remove it. The interesting thing, you'll notice, is that none of the other blocks were scarred by the explosion. The door-block was made of a softer stone than the wall. Why, we've no idea, but we sent the fragments back for analysis all the same.'

Anselm had to stoop to get through the doorway, and when he lifted his head on the other side, he felt his breath catch in amazement. Ahead of him, sloping down, illuminated in the soft light of hundreds of glow-globes, the corridor stretched ahead for what seemed like kilometres. The passageway was barely wider than the door they had entered it by, but the roof stretched hundreds of metres above him. On the floor was a soft fine dust that stirred as he stepped through it.

Grogan grunted. 'Impressive,' he conceded, striding forward, his cloak billowing behind him, throwing up miniature dust-storms. 'But we've no time for sightseeing. My work is fighting heretics, not playing historian. This stuff should all be left underground where it belongs. The Imperium is best guarded with the Emperor's word and a hellgun, not with ancient trinkets. In the meantime I want to find your missing priest as quickly as possible. Or the corpse,' he added darkly. 'If there is something alive down here, I want it hunted down and exterminated so that we can get off this rock.'

Cantor huffed. 'Come on,' Anselm said. 'Until we find whatever's out there, it may strike again.' Cantor led the way down the immense corridor. Anselm gazed up in wonder. The roof soared away into darkness above him. About halfway along, there was a dark strip of rock all the way across the floor and reaching high up the walls on either side.

Cantor noticed him looking at it. 'That's hardened basalt,' he commented. 'It cut the corridor in half. Our cogitators have surmised that at one time a wall of molten lava bisected this corridor, held in place by the Emperor knows what. In time it cooled and hardened into a perfect wall of basalt. We had to cut through it with high intensity laser drills. The basalt extends for hundreds of metres in every direction as if the wall stretched far into the rock like a protective barrier. We knew once we passed it that we were reaching the heart of what had been the city – we think it may have acted as some sort of heat sink or repository for their energy needs. What we do know is that there is still much molten magma near this part of the dig, held in check by the great weight of rock.'

They passed the ring of basalt and after some time, the passageway levelled out. Soon afterwards, it opened up into a room, perhaps ten metres wide. Machinery lay on wheeled trolleys, cables and unlit glow-globes were stacked in piles around the room, and there was the noise of humming. Anselm guessed that the machinery was pumping fresh air into the room and taking away spent air. Above them, balconies overlooked the room, and there was the faint sound of chains swinging in an imperceptible breeze.

Cantor said 'This is the heart of Barathrum. It is the deepest our excavations have brought us.' Then he stopped.

The body lay slumped face down against a workbench. There was a pool of blood around his head, and his hair was matted with it. Blood and brain matter were spattered against the walls. Grogan motioned Anselm forwards.

'Anselm,' he said. 'You're the chirugeon, if I remember correctly. What can you tell us?'

Anselm moved forwards, stepping over the outstretched legs of the corpse. He leaned forward and gently pulled the body round. As it slumped over onto its back, he gasped in horror. The man's front had been torn apart, the chest a gaping cavity, arms hanging limply from sleeves of lacerated skin. Dark holes gazed into nothingness where his eyes had been, and blood had oozed from the sockets, drying into black crusted rivulets across his cheeks.

'I can tell little from here,' he said. 'We must take him to the medi-bay. I will examine him there.'

He turned his face away from the shattered corpse and examined the room in which they had found him. The walls were made of small mud bricks stacked one on top of the other and sealed with some sort of rough cement. There was a glow-globe in the corner and he played it over the wall, the flickering light tracing daemonic patterns on the rough brickwork. Apart from the blood spray near the corpse, there were no other marks on the wall.

Except...

'What's this?' Anselm ran his fingers over one part of the wall. The bricks seemed to be rougher here, the finish less clean. His fingertips found a line, near the floor, almost imperceptible, and followed it up until it was about half a metre above his head. Then it turned sharply, at ninety degrees and continued horizontally for about a metre.

'A door,' he breathed. 'Cantor, look at this.' The tech-priest came close and peered at the line.

'You're right,' he said. 'A door. We'd never have seen this if you hadn't noticed it.'

Grogan barked at Eremet. 'Get servitors down here. I want this area sealed off and I want to know what's behind this wall.'

Eremet nodded. 'I will see to it, inquisitor.'

Anselm made a circuit of the room, remembering everything in case a clue came to him later. Then, reluctantly, they lifted the corpse and wrapped it in a length of tarpaulin, before placing it on one of the machinery trolleys that stood to one side. Anselm, his mind already on the work ahead, guided the trolley as its internal suspensors moved it forwards.

As they passed once more through the labyrinthine passages of the dead city, Anselm again felt the hairs on the back of his neck begin to rise. Out of the corner of his eye, in the dark passages and openings that they passed, he could swear he saw eyes glinting at him, hundreds of eyes staring, unblinking. But each time he turned his head, his torch illuminating the darkness, he saw nothing, only the empty blackness of the tunnels. He was sure it was only his imagination, but he thought he could hear laughter; laughter dusty, dry and alien. He shook his head and the sound disappeared.

The tension must be getting to him, the horrific corpse they had found and the knowledge that Grogan was once again watching him. What if this was some sort of test? What if Grogan had been sent to report back on how he was handling this enquiry, whether he was showing sufficient zeal and devotion?

What if... What if, he told himself angrily, you concentrate on the task at hand and leave the worries for another time. He had a post-mortem to carry out and despite the gruesome nature of the task, he was looking forward to it; a chance to pit his keen intelligence against something that would eventually yield up its secrets.

It took some time before they reached the apothecary's bay. They placed the body on the operating table and unwrapped the tarpaulin. Cantor and Eremet stood back against the wall, trying not to watch, and Grogan pulled a high lab stool up close.

Donning a pair of transparent surgical gloves, Anselm began to work, cutting the shredded remains of the man's clothing away from the body.

He muttered to himself as he did so, a habit from the days when he had a med-servitor to record the results of the post-mortem. 'Hmm, number of deep incisions on the torso, mostly vertical... some bruising of the solar plexus... let's see, ribs cracked on left hand side, heavy blow to the shoulder, no bruising. Most interesting...' His voice died away as he reached across to pick up a pair of oculators and a small surgical pick. He leaned across the body and tentatively lifted up a flap of skin on the corpse's chest. 'Most interesting,' he confirmed as he squinted through the oculators.

'What is it?' demanded Grogan.

'Not ready to say... I just need to...' Anselm mumbled half to himself. He transferred his attention to the man's ruined face. Taking a pad of cotton, he soaked it in surgical alcohol and began to wipe the dried blood from the skin. Under the blood, the slashes were livid, purple and swollen. Cantor looked away and made a strangled gargling sound in his throat. Eremet looked pale. Grogan watched stoically, occasionally rubbing the vein at his temple. In the now clean face, the corpse's empty eye sockets glared evilly and despite their lack of occupants, Grogan felt they were watching them.

It was some time before Anselm spoke again: 'Now this is most interesting...'

This time, Grogan lost his patience. He stood up and leaned over the body on the table. 'For Emperor's sake, what are you muttering about?'

Anselm pulled of the oculators and stripped the gloves from his fingers.

'This is not the work of a zoomorph, a beast, at least not in the way we thought. These slash marks are certainly caused by claws of some kind, though the exact identity of the creature that caused them is beyond my knowledge. However, they are not the cause of death, nor the most interesting part of the examination. Look at the man's head, the area around the eyes, and tell me what you see.'

'This is insufferable,' Grogan declared, but bent his head until his nose was almost touching the ripped nasal cavity of the dead man.

'Throne of Earth!' he exclaimed. Cantor and Eremet jumped up as if they had been stung and crowded round.

'What is it?' the explorator demanded.

Grogan jumped in before Anselm could open his mouth. 'Don't you see?' he said. 'Look at the eye sockets. It seems like the eyes have been ripped out, but look more closely. It's not just the eyes that have gone, it's the bone around the eye socket too.'

'And if you look through the oculator,' continued Anselm, 'the eyes weren't torn out. They were removed. Something, or someone, removed those eyes with great precision, using some kind of device that removed them at high speed and with great accuracy. There are hardly any radial injury marks on the rest of the skull round the wound – this was done with something incredibly sharp – whatever else, I would say this man's eyes were intact when they were removed. But what kind of creature takes the eyes and leaves the rest of the body?'

Anselm ran his fingers through his cropped hair and started to pace the room. He suddenly stopped. 'What about the eyes on the other bodies?' he suddenly exclaimed. He strode to the screen behind which the bodies lay on their gurneys. He rapidly pulled back the sheets and then stopped in disappointment. Whatever the extent of their injuries and cause of death, it was clear to see that the eyes of the other bodies were either intact or at least extant.

He turned to face the others. 'I need to be alone,' he said. 'I need to think about this. I will examine the other bodies. There may be some clue as to how they died that may help us.'

Cantor and Eremet bowed towards the inquisitor and left. Grogan remained.

'Inquisitor,' Anselm asserted. 'I must do this alone. I need to deliver these souls into the Emperor's care and ask their spirits to guide me in finding their killer. To do that I must be alone.'

Grogan looked suspiciously at him. 'What is this? Is this some sort of ritual?'

'No, it is merely that I must examine the other bodies, but I need to have my mind clear to accept whatever the results tell me, no matter how strange or confusing they may seem to my brain. I just need quiet.'

Grogan seemed to consider this. 'Very well,' he said, 'but I want a full debrief.'

'Before you speak to the others,' he added, as he turned and strode out of the room.

IT WAS SOME hours later that Grogan heard a knock on the door of the hab-mod that had been assigned to him. He put away the documents he had been reading and opened the door. Anselm stood there, looking tired but alert.

'May I enter?' he asked. Grogan stood aside and Anselm entered, seating himself at the table strewn with transcripts and documents. Grogan swept them up into a pile and sat down opposite him.

'Well, what have you found?' he asked.

'This is a lot darker than you or I suspected,' the inquisitor began.

Grogan's face twitched and Anselm could have sworn he saw the flicker of a smile pass across the older man's craggy features. Nothing gave Grogan more pleasure, Anselm remembered, than having an enemy, preferably a self-confessed heretic, that he could pin all his fiery, destructive, righteous energies on.

'I've examined all the bodies. Apart from Crans, they all seem to have died in a savage and frenzied attack. They were literally torn apart. Whatever it was that killed them, it was hugely strong, fast as a tyranid, but man-sized, bipedal, with only two arms, and legs for locomotion, not attack. The attack was frenzied, as I say, but I would say from the pattern of the lacerations, it was carried out by someone who was not. In other words, this is not the work of a beast, nor of a deranged madman, but a madman who is cold, calculated and very cunning.'

'I don't follow. How can a killer be mad and yet not mad? You're not making sense?'

'There is something strange about the bodies. They are each missing part of their anatomy. This is something that had been missed in all previous examinations but I made the connection after examining Crans. Even in the case of the body that was missing its arms, while the fact of the missing arm was obvious, what was less so was that the arm had been removed, carefully and surgically, after death. It was amputated, not ripped off.'

Grogan had become still, his jaw twitching slightly as Anselm spoke.

'We are missing a heart, brain, eyes, a number of bones and many kilos of muscle tissue from various parts of the body. In one case the face had been torn away, but in such a way that it would have been undamaged by the removal. The question I put to myself was, why?'

'And what did you come up with?'

'I wasn't able to come up with an answer, until I made a final discovery which meant that the answer to the riddle became secondary to the real truth about what's happening here on Barathrum. This mark was burned into the back of the eye socket of Tech-priest Crans.'

Anselm leaned over and thrust a thin dataslate towards Grogan. The older inquisitor took it and thumbed the activation button. The dataslate glowed pale and illuminated the man's face from below as he gazed at it. Anselm watched as an image, upside down from his perspective at the other side of the table, began to coalesce on the slate's screen. It was a symbol, dark and clear-edged, yet hard to see, as if it was being inspected under ultraviolet light, or another wavelength just beyond the limits of human eyesight. He knew that he wouldn't have been able to describe it if asked. The symbol seemed to twist and turn in on itself like a writhing creature, yet Anselm knew that logically it could not move; it was a snapshot captured on the data-slate, yet it was an image with both meaning and power. Despite himself, he shivered.

'So,' Grogan stated, the word slow and ponderous, hanging in the air between them. 'Chaos has come to Barathrum.'

THERE WAS A knock at the door. Grogan thumbed the slate clear and slipped the inert machine into the voluminous sleeve of his robe and called out: 'Enter.' The door opened a crack and the anxious face of Eremet appeared.

'Your eminences,' he began. 'I think you had better come with me.'

'Has there been another death?' Grogan asked, standing up.

'No, but there has been a discovery. Please follow me.'

'Where are we going?' Grogan asked. Out of the corner of his eye, Anselm could see his companion's right hand wandering towards the holster where he kept his hellgun strapped tight to his thigh.

'Inquisitor Anselm's discovery of the door was followed up, as per orders.' The Excavator seemed nervous, as if the whole investigation was starting to take on a life of its own and was running away from his control. Anselm felt for him. The man's job was risky, but the kinds of risks he faced were ones he could normally tackle – here he was, faced with an investigation with not one but two of the Emperor's finest inquisitors, one of whom was evidently getting increasingly trigger-happy.

Eremet led them quickly through the pathways and tunnels towards the area where they had discovered the body of the unfortunate tech-priest.

This time Anselm felt no eyes upon him and he was glad. He felt a rising excitement: they were starting to make some headway. He had done well to put together the clues held in the bodies of the slain. It was a difficult conclusion to have come to but it held up. If things worked out on Barathrum, there would be nothing standing in his way. Barathrum would be simply the beginning. He would be elevated through the ranks of his brothers and he would lead them. Those who stood in his way would be quashed…

He shook his head to clear it and forced his mind back to the present. He was tired. He had not slept since leaving Atrium two days ago. After they saw whatever it was that Eremet was bringing them to, he would rest for a couple of hours. Or at least take some stim to keep him going and risk the attendant headaches.

THE ROOM WHERE they had found the body was unchanged since they removed the corpse. Anselm could still see the spatters of blood and the dark shadow where the body of the tech-priest had lain in a pool of its own blood. Now, however the single glow-globe had been replaced by an array of harsh arc-lamps, casting their stark light on the scene. To his left stood a doorway, in the place where his fingers had traced out the line in the mud bricks. The doorway led into a room that was filled with lambent light that seemed to create, and then chase away, shadows on the walls. Eremet stood at the side of the doorway and extended his arm, almost as if he were inviting them in.

Anselm took a deep breath, almost without knowing why, and stepped through the doorway, Grogan close behind him.

The first thing he noticed was Cantor, locked in conversation with a recorder, the servitor a mass of audio-visual feeds, spectrometers and devices for measuring humidity and air density. Cantor looked up as the inquisitors entered and ushered the servitor away. It bowed briefly and then went back to its work. Cantor's face was aglow with excitement as he faced his old friend.

'I would say congratulations if you had been a member of my team,' he said. 'You seem to have stumbled onto some sort of heart of our enterprise, I would say, no?' He gestured expansively around him.

Anselm gazed around him in wonder. The room was huge, a great pillared hall, the trunks of the pillars like a forest of great trees. The ceiling was high and seemed to glow with an angry red light, almost as if it were some sort of burning sea. It was this ceiling that lit the room and the waves of light washing across it had caused the play of light and shadow that Anselm had noticed when he had entered. Suddenly, he realised what it was – lava, molten rock, swirling above them, held in place by who knew what artifice. They stood under a lake of fire that swirled in the air above them.

Ahead of him there were great double doors, almost twenty metres tall, each door perhaps five or six metres wide. It seemed to be made from what looked like beaten copper, or perhaps bronze – it glowed dully in the reflection of the ceiling. Around the doors were carved great hieroglyphics in a language that was unfamiliar to him. The glyphs were mainly pictoral, with lines and circles making up the remainder. Although he couldn't read them, they didn't look alien and he was relieved.

He noticed other tech-priests in the room, some directing servitors who lugged great chests of instruments, trailing wires, struggling under the immense weight. Others were taking notes on data-slates, still others appeared to be transcribing some of the hieroglyphics. He watched idly as one of them approached the great copper doors and reached out to touch them.

There was a high pitched hum and a beam of intense red light erupted from a point above the doors and focused on the tech-priest. The luminescence washing over the ceiling darkened momentarily as if someone had thrown ink into a bowl of bright liquid. The tech-priest writhed as he was caught in the beam of light, a silent scream forced from his lips. Then the light was gone and the man collapsed, like a puppet Anselm had once seen on Darcia that had had its strings cut. Grogan ran over to the man and prodded him with the toe of his boot. Nothing happened. He knelt down and pressed his finger to the man's neck.

'Dead!' he announced.

He raised his voice so that all could hear him. 'I want no one to touch this door. I want these glyphs read and deciphered and the results delivered to me in my quarters within the hour. Anselm, I want to speak with you. Privately.' He turned to Eremet. 'Get this place sealed off.'

Cantor faced him, apoplectic with rage.

'Inquisitor! This area is under the jurisdiction of the Adeptus Mechanicus. There is so much to learn here, from the inscriptions, from the structures. You cannot make such an order. We must lose no time.'

Grogan refused to be countermanded. 'On pain of death, tech-priest, I order you to stay away from here. And that applies to everyone.' He whirled on his heels and stalked out of the room.

ANSELM FACED GROGAN across the table in the younger man's hab-mod. The senior inquisitor looked as if he was barely containing his anger. Anselm knew that look. It meant that Grogan smelled the stink of corruption and knew exactly how to deal with it. It also meant that he was not prepared to discuss any alternative.

'I'm ordering immediate evacuation of Barathrum and requesting back up from an Astartes kill-team. I want Terminator squads to scour this place and if they find nothing I will be recommending full Exterminatus.

Barathrum is a threat to the Imperium. The Imperium is a city built behind high walls and these frontier systems are the unknown beyond. It is our job to defend those walls and what shelters behind them, whatever the cost. If there is the influence of Chaos at work here, then I will stamp it out. It is unfortunate but necessary – I will be demanding that the explorator mission here be relieved of its duties and subjected to rigorous review.'

Anselm knew full well what that meant. He had been party to Grogan's reviews before, when he was an acolyte. It meant death for those who confessed, and torture for those who did not. Until they did. They all confessed in the end.

'Grogan, we must investigate further. If there is a manifestation of Chaos here, we must get to the bottom of it, certainly, but we should root out its heart, not destroy the body just to get at the tumour. There is something unspeakably evil here but there is also great good in what we can learn from this planet. You heard Cantor – the archaeotech finds are immeasurable, there may be standard template devices that the Adeptus Mechanicus have only dreamed about. You cannot take the decision to destroy all that these men have worked and died for simply because we have only just begun to understand what has been happening here.'

'That is weakness, Anselm. Everything contrary to the rule of the Imperium is heresy and there can be no exceptions. I'm surprised you do not remember that after what happened on Tantalus. That is what happens when you show weakness.'

Anselm looked into the dark eyes of Grogan. His voice shook with anger.

'I did not show weakness, Grogan, as you well know. It is not weakness to show restraint. What you did on Tantalus was unprecedented and unnecessary. To destroy a planet because of an insurrection that was limited to one city was arrogant, and typical of your approach.'

Grogan's eyes remained enigmatic, unreadable. 'I seem to recall, Anselm, that you were in charge of suppressing that insurrection. A charge you expressly failed to carry out. I did what I did only when the rebellion threatened the stability of the whole star system.'

Anselm kept his voice calm. There was no point in getting angry with Grogan. The man's icy manner would never crack, and Anselm knew from bitter experience that if he lost his temper, he would be the loser. He took a deep breath, and when he spoke, his voice was again calm. 'May I remind you, Grogan, that I had only been on Tantalus for four days when your agents had me pulled out. Of course I failed to halt the insurrection; I hardly had time to open my office.'

'Tantalus was under your jurisdiction. The insurrection should have been crushed. Instantly. Diplomacy is only useful after force has driven the other side to the table. Alone, it is a tool for the weak, for effete

Imperial ambassadors. The Inquisition is not a tool, it is a force in itself. As I'm sure you remember.' Grogan breathed in deeply.

Anselm forced a tight smile to his lips. 'I remember only too well, inquisitor; your classes made a great impression on us all. But perhaps we should concentrate less on what happened in the past, and more on the present.'

There was a shuffle of robes as Grogan stood up. He checked his chronometer. 'I have ordered that no one leave their quarters tonight. Barathrum has moved into its night cycle. There is nothing we can do until light, when the planet has turned its face once more towards the core systems and we can send word back to the Ecclesiarchy.'

'Yes.' Anselm's silence swallowed up the end of the word, and dismissed his erstwhile tutor. The old man gathered up his robes and left, closing the door after him, leaving Anselm exhausted. Why was it that every time he spoke to Grogan, he felt himself back in the Scholarium, being tested on Imperial ethics or some obscure matter from a legal codex?

He moved his weapons case from his bunk and set it on the table. He lay back on the sleeping pallet and closed his eyes, allowing his mind to clear, leaving it open to thought.

ANSELM AWOKE AND looked at the glowing chronometer next to his pallet. He had been asleep for only a matter of minutes but something had woken him. There was a strange scratching sound, almost at the edge of his hearing. No, not scratching, more like a shuffling, soft fabric being drawn across polished stone. He shook his head and sat up. The sound wasn't coming from inside his hab-mod, it was coming from outside, in the corridor.

He moved across to the door, silent on bare feet, rubbing his eyes with tiredness. Opening the door a crack, he looked out into the corridor. There was nothing there. The corridor was empty. He closed the door again, but this time he locked it. He lay back on his pallet and closed his eyes.

ANSELM WAS DREAMING. In his dream, he was gliding through the labyrinth below the dig site. Again, he felt eyes on him, many eyes watching him as he moved through the darkness. Although he had no torch with him, he could see as if it were day, and in his dream, the darkness and complexity of the labyrinth held no fear for him. He came at last to the room where they had found the body. It sat slumped against the wall, its front stained with blood and the empty hollow eye sockets seeming to watch him, a dark fire burning within them.

To his left was the doorway cleared by the servitors and he felt himself being drawn towards it. He passed through, but instead of the great hall with its brass doors and pillars, he found himself in a throne room. Warm light streamed over him. Before him stood a dais with a throne on it. The throne was enormous, bigger then a building, and on the throne sat a great figure, haloed in golden light. In his dream, Anselm knew that this was – praise be the holy throne of Terra – the Emperor himself, great father of mankind.

His heart soared and he felt himself sink to his knees. He looked up into the ancient wise face of the saviour of mankind... and saw it swim before his eyes, seem to melt and flow, and there on the throne sat a beast, the face of a hyena, eyes glowing red with immeasurable evil, the muzzle long, creased in a bestial snarl or smile, he couldn't tell which. The creature stood, its rich robes sweeping the floor. It held out one arm and Anselm could see fine rings glittering on dark fingers. The creature gazed at him.

'Anselm!' it said, the voice deep, dark, rich, evil. 'Anselm, my servant, you have come to me. Anselm!' The voice drove into his skull and his heart began hammering as if it would burst from his ribcage. And then the scene faded and the hammering of his heart became the hammering of someone banging on his door and calling 'Anselm, Anselm! Open the door!'

HE LEAPT UP, dazed with sleep, his fingers instinctively reaching for his shotgun.

'Who is it?' he called.

'Eremet,' came the reply. 'A transmission has arrived from the Ecclesiarchy with the translation of the hieroglyphs.'

Anselm opened the door cautiously.

'Come in. What does it say?' Eremet came in, looking behind him before he closed the door. Silently, he handed a dataslate over to Anselm.

'The transmission was coded and bears the highest seal of your Ordo. I cannot read it.'

Anselm thumbed the power rune and the screen lit up. There was a brief moment while the slate read the print of his thumb and verified his identity. He entered his personal code number, then a jumble of hieroglyphics swam across the screen, resolving themselves into neat rows. Slowly, starting at the top, the glyphs began to change into the regular characters of High Gothic text.

He read: 'Inquisitor Anselm, this transcription is for your eyes only. What it contains is reserved for the highest level of the Ordo and the Ecclesiarchy. The information cannot be revealed to any outside our order.

'The hieroglyphs of Barathrum have been translated as follows:

'*Let it be known that we, the Mugati, humans, descendants of the tribes of the Ilatrum, claimed this world for our people in the name of the Holy Emperor. The land was cultivated and great cities we built in his name. We grew strong, our people were brave; many journeyed beyond the stars amongst their brothers in the armies of the Imperium. Our trade stretched beyond this system. We were a proud people. That pride was our downfall. The eye of the Evil One turned its gaze upon us.*

'*When the warp storms came, we were cut off from our brothers who had left to protect other parts of the galaxy. For years, we trembled in fear as foul raiders came out of the Immaterium to attack us. Our cities fell, one by one and we drew back to our capital. Here was the scene of our last battle.*

'*We fought hard and pushed the foe back, but then it called up Szarach'il, foul servant of their gods, and terrible was the destruction he wrought. Our city could not stand against such a foe, and so it was that our world teetered on the brink of oblivion.*

'*The final battle took place deep in the catacombs beneath the city. Our finest warriors fought a desperate battle, until at last Szarach'il himself stood face to face against Amaril, leader of all our people, brother of the Holy Inquisition.*

'*Amaril knew that Szarach'il could not be killed, nor banished by his powers, diminished as they were by the months of battle. Instead, in a final act that destroyed his mortal body, he bound Szarach'il behind great doors of promethium, sealing them with words of great power such that he should never be released.*

'*Our planet is destroyed, our people no more. I, Dramul, last of the Mugati, have caused these words to be carved on the prison walls that any who read them will know.*'

Anselm felt his heart grow cold. What have we uncovered here, he thought?

Then he suddenly realised why he was here. The Ecclesiarchy had already sent one inquisitor to investigate the events on Barathrum. Why send another? Unless his Ordo had known, somehow, what Barathrum meant. Their archives were endless and ancient beyond memory. Did they send him to Barathrum to prevent Grogan, staunch puritan that he was, from destroying all trace of the daemon from existence? And in the process banish to nothingness all that the Mugati had learnt from their battle, the ancient powers that had bound the daemon in its abyssal prison?

'Where is Grogan?' he demanded.

'He is not in his mod, excellency,' replied Eremet.

Anselm turned and opened his weapons case. Inset in red velvet was an ancient sword. The handle was made from fine wood wound with hand-tooled leather. He released it from its cradle, held it up in front of his face, depressing a button on the handle to test the blade. The metal of the blade hummed and the cutting edge shimmered. He released the button and the humming stopped, the blade inert.

'Come on!' he said to the terrified explorator. 'Let's go and find him. I know where he is.'

As ANSELM DREAMED, Grogan paced his room, trying to wear off his impatience at having to wait until he could call down divine retribution on Barathrum.

He stopped, hearing a soft shuffling sound outside his mod. He opened the door a crack and saw Cantor as he faded into the darkness at the end of the corridor.

He called after him, but there was no answer. Where was the fool going? And after he had specifically forbidden anyone from venturing forth tonight. Grogan turned back to grab his hellgun, and snatched up his chainsword at the same time.

By the time he reached the end of the corridor, Cantor had disappeared. But Grogan knew where he would be heading. The damn fool scholar was going to go and investigate the glyphs.

He followed the footprints they had made earlier until he came to the long straight passage. As he approached the room with the door, he heard the sound of soft chanting. Alarmed, he gripped his hellgun tightly in his left hand, the right fingering the release on his chainsword. Silently, it began to whirr, the light from the glow-globes flickering off its spinning serrated surface.

He stood at the side of the doorway and cautiously peered in.

Inside he could see the great pillars reaching up, their surfaces shifting in the light from the ceiling. Shadows pooled around their bases, anchoring each pillar in its own plot of darkness. The light caressed the carven script set into the walls surrounding the door.

It settled on the figure of Cantor, tech-priest and disciple of the Adeptus Mechanicus as he stood in front of the great copper doors, his arms raised in a gesture of welcome, ancient words spilling from his throat.

'El'ach mihar, cun malaas, an ach! Szarach'il cun malaas!'

The words hung in the air like incense in a temple, and the sound of them hurt Grogan's ears. They were unholy words, words of summoning, words of power. Words of evil. The voice of Chaos.

In front of Cantor the glyphs carved into the great beaten copper doors began to glow, tendrils of luminescence flickering over the images and jumping from rune to rune. The lighted ceiling began to darken, storm clouds the colour of bruised flesh forming in the artificial sky. A tremor shook the earth and the dust rose on the floor at Grogan's feet. Cantor's chanting grew louder.

Grogan stepped out from behind the door, his hellgun pointed straight at the tech-priest's back and bellowed: 'In the name of the Emperor, foul hell fiend, cease your chanting or die.'

What happened next was the very last thing he expected. Cantor ceased his chanting and turned round. His eyes were black pits of darkness, the pupils enlarged hugely, filling his sockets. The face was a rictus of concentration, his mouth wide in the midst of a chant. Then Grogan saw his hands. Where his fingers should be, claws that gleamed like metal had burst from his hands. He could see the tips, glistening with blood.

Cantor lowered his arms, and held them out towards Grogan.

'Welcome, inquisitor!' the mouth hissed but the voice was not Cantor's. It was dark, dry, dusty, the voice of one imprisoned for aeons and not used to forming words aloud. 'You are just in time to welcome me at the moment of my release. But there is still the final invocation, and you cannot be allowed to prevent that.'

The creature gestured to one side and Grogan turned to look in that direction.

From the shadow of one of the pillars emerged a monstrosity from the very pit of hell.

It resembled a man only in as much as it had a head, torso and four limbs but that was where the resemblance ended. The thing lurched towards him, arms outstretched, hands ending in claws that looked like metal spikes driven into flesh. Its limbs were red muscle, flayed raw, dripping with plasma and ichor. The creature's face was seemingly stitched to a skull of sorts, hanging oddly so that the features were drooped and rucked into each other, ending in a gash where a jaw had been secured to the upper skull. Bits of metal and what looked like machinery were attached to the thing at odd intervals, making up part of a leg here, part of its sternum there. It limped towards Grogan, a bloodcurdling hiss issuing from its broken mouth.

Grogan leapt back, hearing as he did so the sound of chanting resume. He had no time to think about it before the foul creature was on him. He thumbed the switch on his chainsword, hearing the reassuring whirr as its teeth carved the air.

The beast covered the ground between itself and the inquisitor in two strides. He could smell the putrid stench of rotting flesh as it reached out for him. The metal claws on its hands raked Grogan's chest, the armour there sparking from the force of the attack. The inquisitor lashed out with his boot and connected with the thing's kneecap, knocking it back. It fell onto one knee but then rose again. Grogan could see the white sheen of bone where his boot had broken the thing's knee but it didn't seem to notice, ignoring any pain it may have felt and lurching back towards the fray.

Grogan cut the air with his chainsword, slashing the creature across one shoulder. No blood spurted from the wound, instead the flesh separated and the pink muscle tissue gleamed wetly.

The thing roared with anger and jumped at Grogan. It landed on his chest, the weight of it knocking the wind out of him. He fell on his back, his right arm up against the creature's chest, trying to stop the slavering jaws from ripping his throat out, foul breath choking him. Held away from his face, the creature began to pound against Grogan's belly with its feet. Pain wracked the inquisitor. Slowly, he pressed the muzzle of his hellgun against the belly of the creature and fired.

There was a roar as the creature was hurled up in the air, and then it landed down on Grogan, the stench of suppurating flesh making him gag. He scrambled to his feet.

And froze...

In front of him the great doors stood ajar. Between them, Cantor stood, outlined in shimmering light.

No, not stood, floated. Suspended in a nimbus of light, the old tech-priest hung, like a heretic on a rack, writhing in pain. Tendrils of light wrapped themselves round his body and spun it around.

The dark voice came again, this time appearing inside Grogan's head without Cantor speaking. At the same time, it reverberated around the room, causing the pillars to shake.

Inquisitor! You are most welcome!

The inquisitor raised his weapon. 'Die, hellspawn!' he spat. He pressed the trigger.

The gun recoiled, there was a flash of light and he saw the shell hurtle towards Cantor. Before it could impact, there was a shimmer in the air as if the very fabric of reality had turned to glue. The bullet slowed, stopped, then clattered to the floor, inert. Then the handle of the hellgun jumped in his hand. Then his chainsword too jumped from his grasp and the two weapons clattered to the ground.

'Really, inquisitor, that showed no imagination.' The voice was sooth-ing, paternal, chuckling as if at a disappointing but much loved child. 'I have called to you across time and space and this is how you welcome me.'

'Who... who are you?' Grogan's voice was shaky.

'I am Szarach'il, the Great Destroyer, Devourer of Souls, daemon, world defiler. Endless was the torment I inflicted on the galaxy. Whole systems fell before me. Then my great crusade brought me to this accursed planet. Nothing could stop me, until I came face to face with one man, an inquisitor from the dawning of your order, who rallied his men. He had studied my kind, he knew he could not destroy me. Instead, coward that he was, he wrought a dungeon for me here and incarcerated me. For an eternity I have languished here in this pit, this abyss, until the scratchings of these Mechanicus slaves woke me from my slumber. They had no idea that this whole planet was my prison, buried as I was at its heart.

'When they broke through the city limits into the prison's outer cham-bers I knew that my time was once more drawing nigh. This one, this tech-priest, he burned for knowledge and delved deep into the planet. Weak though I was after my imprisonment, I was able to control him for certain periods. With each hour, the day of my release grew closer, but what then? I was trapped on the planet with old men and half machine creatures. Their spirits were slight. I would perish without souls, without strength to feed me.

'Then I realised how to live, to thrive and to use the very instrument of the Imperium to release me from this planet and be the instrument of my revenge. Through this man, I stalked the city once more, killing his fellows. How I relished the spilling of blood again after all those centuries. How I laughed at their feeble cries as I ripped the still beating heart from one, the very flesh from the bones of another. I felt free again. And under my instruction, this human constructed the creature you have vanquished. It would protect him from any threat until the doors were discovered and the runes imprisoning me read and broken.

'And I knew that he would be horrified at the killings that he had no memory of carrying out, for by day, he was his own man with no recollection of what he had done while I controlled him. I read his mind and saw his old friendship with the inquisitor. He would seek help from his old friend and that man would come. A man strong, resolute, full of power and ambition, and then, I would have the body that would allow me to escape this planet and cut a swathe of revenge through the ranks of the Imperium. A fitting irony, don't you agree?'

Grogan stood, staggered at this revelation. He took a step backwards.

'Not so fast, human. I have been kept talking too long but it has been many ages since I heard my own voice. Now is the time for action.'

Cantor held out a hand. A tendril of light flickered from it and snaked through the air towards Grogan. It reached him and his body writhed in the coruscating light as the daemon took possession. The moment the tendril touched Grogan, the light that had surrounded Cantor disappeared. The techpriest fell from the air, and crashed in a crumpled heap on the floor. He raised his head and looked at Grogan, his eyes normal again, his body his own. 'I'm sorry,' he whispered and his head fell back. His eyes went blank and he was still.

Szarach'il stretched his new arms and Grogan's features twitched in a parody of a smile. He whirled round at a noise and came face to face with Anselm. The daemon could tell from the look on the inquisitor's face that he had seen everything that had taken place in the last few moments. The daemon raised one hand and Grogan's discarded chainsword flew into his hand. He activated it and waved it experimentally at Anselm.

Anselm raised his own sword and sidled into the room, giving himself some space as he activated the blade. Grogan leapt at him, the sword a blur of whirling teeth. Anselm raised his own in a parry and the two blades met in mid air, sparks flying from the discharged energy. Anselm's arm rang with the force of the blow. Even before, Grogan had been far stronger physically and now the daemon within him added the force of his own infernal strength to that of the inquisitor. Anselm's sword slid down the length of his opponent's and as they broke contact, he spun, swinging the blade down low in a sweeping arc. Grogan jumped, easily evading the blade and a bellow of pleasure issued from his mouth.

'You humans are not as puny as I remembered. This one is strong and I see that you too are skilled with a blade. The contest is pleasing to me.' As Anselm looked at his old master, the man's face seemed to change, and for a second Anselm saw the bestial face of the daemon, his hyena smile, the long teeth; then the vision changed and Grogan's face reasserted itself.

Anselm tried not to think of Grogan as a human any longer; he was a creature of darkness, a vessel for infernal power. That was how Grogan would have thought about it if the roles had been reversed. His former tutor would have had no trouble in executing him if it had been he who had succumbed to daemonic power, no matter how unfortunate it may have been.

He lunged at Grogan, feinted, then pulled back. Grogan bellowed again, and thrust forward. Anselm dodged the thrust, putting out his boot and tripping his former tutor. The creature stumbled and rammed his head against the wall. It turned and for a moment, the eyes changed, and Anselm could see the deep wells of darkness clear and Grogan's own eyes gaze out at him.

'Anselm, my pupil,' he croaked. 'Remember that the path of the inquisitor... is one of holy fire. One must... fight fire... with fire.'

The eyes darkened briefly, then lightened. Grogan made a gesture. His hellgun, lying unnoticed against the wall, flew into his hand. He raised it, towards Anselm... then slowly, shakily, upwards until it pointed towards the ceiling.

'Get.... out!' Grogan croaked and pulled the trigger. The shell flew upwards and hit the ceiling. There was a moment of awful silence and then a tremendous roar. The ceiling shattered above the daemon and an instant later, a cascade of molten lava fell, obliterating Grogan in a waterfall of glowing heat. It hissed as it hit the floor and immediately began to harden, the solid rock being covered with more lava that flowed endlessly from the ceiling, a stalactite of solid fire with Grogan at its core.

Anselm jumped back, scrambling to get away from the river of magma that began to flow towards him. He stumbled and his boots smoked as spraying droplets of lava touched them. The flow was relentless and he felt his eyebrows singeing from the intense heat. Gathering his strength, he ran from the room. Looking behind him, he could see the room beginning to fill with the fiery molten stone. At the doorway, he passed Eremet standing in horror watching the scene unfold, and pulled the speechless explorator along with him.

They ran until they reached the long passageway. Behind them, at the mouth of the passage, there was a wall of glowing rock that was slowly, relentlessly moving towards them. Fear lent them strength and, lungs screaming with the effort, they ran. Behind them, the magma, rose, solid-

ifying as it did so, sealing off the body of his former tutor with its daemon intruder forever.

They reached the command module and Eremet gave the evacuation
order. The archaeotech site at Barathrum was no more. There would be no
more digging after eldritch knowledge here. Barathrum's secrets would
remain locked under countless tonnes of stone, sealed forever.

Later, as he sat, strapped into the seat of the Imperial shuttle that carried them from the planet, Anselm looked back at the archaeosite as it
disappeared under the fury of a newly born volcano. He found himself
pondering Grogan's final words, and for the first time since he was
received as a noviciate amongst the ranks of the Inquisition, he found he
could agree with his old tutor and erstwhile foe. In a universe full of
Chaos and darkness sometimes it was necessary to fight fire with fire.

SUFFER NOT
THE UNCLEAN TO LIVE
Gav Thorpe

YAKOV CAUGHT HIMSELF dozing as his chin bowed to his chest, lulled by the soporific effect of the warm sun and the steady clatter of hooves on the cobbled street. Blinking himself awake, he gazed from the open carriage at the buildings going past him. Colonnaded fronts and tiers of balconies stretched above him for several storeys, separated by wide tree-lined streets. Thick-veined marble fascias swept past, followed by dark granite facades whose polished surfaces reflected the mid-afternoon light back at him.

Another kilometre and the first signs of decay began to show. Crumbling mosaics scattered their stones across the narrowing pavements, creeping plants twined around balustrades and cornices. Empty windows, some no longer glazed, stared back at him. With a yell to the horses, the carriage driver brought them to a stop and sat there waiting for the preacher to climb down to the worn cobbles.

'This is as far as I'm allowed,' the driver said without turning around, sounding half apologetic and half thankful.

Yakov walked around to the driver's seat and fished into the pocket of his robe for coins, but the coachman avoided his gaze and set off once more, turning the carriage down a sidestreet and out of sight. Yakov knew better – no honest man on Karis Cephalon would take payment from a member of the clergy – but he still hadn't broken the habit of paying for services and goods. He had tried to insist once on tipping a travel-rail porter, and the man had nearly broken down in tears, his eyes fearful. Yakov had been here four years now, and yet still he was adjusting to the local customs and beliefs.

Hoisting his embroidered canvas pack further onto his shoulder, Yakov continued his journey on foot. His long legs carried him briskly past the ruins of counting houses and ancient stores, apartments that once belonged to the fabulously wealthy and the old Royal treasury, abandoned now for over seven centuries. He had already walked for a kilometre when he topped the gradual rise and looked down upon his parish.

Squat, ugly shacks nestled in the roads and alleys between the once-mighty edifices of the royal quarter. He could smell the effluence of the near-homeless, the stench of unwashed bodies and the strangely exotic melange of cooking which swept to him on the smoke of thousands of fires. The sun was beginning to set as he made his way down the long hill, and soon the main boulevard was dropped into cool shadow, chilling after the earlier warmth.

Huts made from corrugated metal, rough planks, sheets of plasthene and other detritus butted up against the cut stones of the old city blocks. The babble of voices could now be heard, the screeching of children and the yapping and barking of dogs adding to the muted racket. The clatter of pans as meals were readied vied with the cries of babes and the clucking of hens. Few of the inhabitants were in sight. Most of them were indoors getting ready to eat, the rest still working out in the fields, or down the mines in the far hills.

A small girl, perhaps twelve Terran years old, came running out from behind a flapping sheet of coarsely woven hemp. Her laughter was high-pitched, almost a squeal, as a boy, slightly younger perhaps, chased her down and bundled her to the ground. They both seemed to notice Yakov at the same time, and instantly quelled their high spirits. Dusting themselves down they stood up and waited respectfully, heads slightly bowed.

'Katinia, isn't it?' Yakov asked as he stopped in front of the girl.

'Yes, preacher,' she replied meekly, looking up at him with her one good eye. The other was nothing more than a scabbed, red mass which seemed to spill from the socket and across her face, enveloping her left ear and leaving one half of her scalp bald. She smiled prettily at him, and he smiled back.

'Shouldn't you be helping your mother with the cooking?' he suggested, glancing back towards the ramshackle hovel that served as their home.

'Mam's at church,' the girl's younger brother, Pietor, butted in, earning himself a kick on the shin from his sibling. 'She said we was to wait here for her.'

Yakov looked at the boy. His shrivelled right arm and leg gave his otherwise perfectly human body a lopsided look. It was the children that always affected him the most, ever cheerful despite the bleakness of their future, the ghastliness of their surroundings. If all the Emperor's faithful had the same indomitable spirit, He and mankind would have overcome all evil and adversity millennia ago. Their crippled, mutated bodies may be vile, he thought to himself, but their souls were as human as any.

'Too early for church, isn't it?' he asked them both, wondering why anyone would be there at least two hours before mass was due to begin.

'She says she wants to speak to you, with some other people, Preacher Yakov,' Katinia told him, clasping her hands behind her back as she looked up at the tall clergyman.

'Well, get back inside and make sure everything's tidy for when your mother returns, you two,' he told them gently, hoping the sudden worry he felt hadn't shown.

As he hurried on his way, he tried to think what might be happening. He had heard disturbing rumours that in a few of the other shanties a debilitating plague had begun to spread amongst the mutant population. In those unhygienic close confines such diseases spread rapidly, and as slaves from all over the world congregated in the work teams, could leap from ghetto to ghetto with devastating rapidity.

Taking a right turn, Yakov made his way towards the chapel that was also his home. Raised five years ago by the mutants themselves, it was as ramshackle as the rest of the ghetto. The building leaked and was freezing in the winter, baking hot in the summer. Yet the effort put into its construction was admirable, even if the result was deplorable, if not a little insulting. Yakov suspected that Karis Cephalon's cardinal, Prelate Kodaczka, had felt a perverse sense of satisfaction when he had heard who would be sent to tend the mutant parish. Coming from the Armormants, Yakov strongly believed that the edifices raised to the Emperor should be highly ornamented, splendid and glittering works of art in praise of the Holy Father of Mankind. To be given charge of something he would previously have declared unfit for a privy was most demeaning, and even after all this time the thought still rankled. Of course, Kodaczka, like all the native clergy of Karis Cephalon and the surrounding systems, was of the Lucid tendency, preferring poverty and abstinence to ostentation and excessive decoration. It had been a sore point between the two of them during more than one theological discussion, and Yakov's obstinate refusal to accept the prevailing beliefs of his new world did his future prospects within the Ecclesiarchy no favours. Then again, he mused ruefully to himself, his chances of any kind of elevation within the hierarchy had all but died when he had been assigned the shanty as a parish.

As he walked, he saw the rough steeples of the chapel rising over the squat mutie dwellings. Its battered, twisted roofs were slicked with greying mould, despite the aggressive efforts of the voluntary work teams who maintained the shrine. As he picked his way through a labyrinth of drying lines and filth-strewn gutters, Yakov saw a large crowd gathered outside the chapel, as he expected he would. Nearly five hundred of his

574 *Let the Galaxy Burn*

parishioners, each mutated to a greater or lesser degree, were stood waiting, an angry buzz emanating from the throng. As he approached, they noticed him and started flocking in his direction, and he held up his hands to halt them before they swept around him. Pious they might be, but kind on the nose they were not. They all started babbling at once, in everything from high-pitched squeaks down to guttural bass tones, and once more he raised his hands, silencing them.

'You speak, Gloran,' he said, pointing towards the large mining overseer whose muscled bulk was covered in a constantly flaking red skin and open sores.

'The plague, preacher, has come here,' Gloran told him, his voice as cracked as his flesh. 'Mather Horok died of it this morning, and a dozen others are falling ill already.'

Yakov groaned inwardly but kept his craggy, hawk-like face free of expression. So his suspicions were correct, the deadly scourge had arrived in the parish.

'And you are all here because...?' he asked, casting his dark gaze over the misshapen crowd.

'Come here to ask Emperor, in prayers,' replied Gloran, his large eyes looking expectantly at Yakov.

'I will compose a suitable mass for this evening. Return to your homes and eat; starving will not aid you against this plague,' he said firmly. Some of the assembly moved away but most remained. 'Go!' snapped Yakov waving them away with a thin hand, irritated at their reticence. 'I cannot recall suitable prayers with you taking up all my attention, can I?'

After a few more murmurs the crowd began to dissipate and Yakov turned and strode up the rough plank stairs to the chapel entrance, taking the shallow steps two at a time. He pulled aside the sagging roughspun curtain that served as a barrier to the outside world and stepped inside. The interior of the chapel was as dismal as the outside, with only a few narrow gaps in the planking and crudely bent sheets of metal of the walls to let in light. Motes of dust drifted from the rough-cut ceiling, dancing lightly in the narrow shafts of the ruddy sunlight. Without thought he turned and took a candle from the stand next to the entrance. Picking up a match from next to the pile of tallow lights, one of the few indulgences extracted from the miserly Kodaczka, he struck it on the emery stone and lit the candle. Rather than truly illuminating the chapel the flickering light created a circle of puny light around the preacher, emphasising the gloom beyond its wavering light.

As he walked towards the altar at the far end – an upturned crate covered with an altar spread and a few accoutrements he had brought with him – the candle flame flickered in the draughts wheezing through the ill-built walls, making his shadow dance behind him. Carefully placing the candle in its holder to the left of the altar he knelt, his bony knees protesting at the solidity of the cracked roadway that made up the shrine's floor. Cursing Kodaczka once more – he had taken away Yakov's prayer cushion, saying it was a sign of decadence and weakness – Yakov tried to clear his turbulent thoughts, attempting to find that place of calm that allowed him to bring forth his litanies to the Emperor. He was about to close his eyes when he noticed something on the floor in front of the altar. Looking closer, the preacher saw that it was a dead rat. Yakov sighed, it was not the first time. Despite his oratories against it, some of his parishioners still insisted on their old, barbaric ways, making such offerings to the Emperor in supplication or penance. Pushing these thoughts aside, Yakov closed his eyes, trying to settle himself.

As HE STOOD by the entrance to the shrine, nodding reassuringly to his congregation as they filed out, Yakov felt a hand on his arm and he turned to see a girl. She was young, no older than sixteen standard years by her looks, and her pale face was pretty, framed by dark hair. Taking her hand off his robe, she smiled and it was then that Yakov looked into her eyes. Even in the gloom of the chapel they looked dark and after a moment he realised they were actually jet black, not a trace of iris or white could be seen. She blinked rapidly, meeting his gaze.

'Yes, my child?' Yakov asked softly, bowing slightly so that he could hear her without her needing to raise her voice.

'Thank you for your prayers, Yakov,' she replied and her smile faded. 'But it will take more than prayers to heal your faithful.'

'As the Emperor sees fit,' the preacher murmured in reply, keeping his gaze steady.

'You must ask for medical supplies, from the governor,' she said calmly, not asking him, but stating it as a fact.

'And who are you to tell me what I must and must not do, young lady?' Yakov responded smoothly, keeping the irritation from his voice.

'I am Lathesia,' was her short reply causing Yakov's heart to flutter slightly. The girl was a wanted terrorist. The governor's Special Security Agents had been hunting her for months following attacks on slave pens and the homes of the wealthy landowners. She had already been sentenced to death in absentia in a trial several weeks ago. And here she was talking to him!

'Are you threatening me?' he asked, trying to keep his voice level even though a knot of fear had begun to tighten in his stomach. Her blinking rapidly increased for a moment before she gave a short, childish laugh.

'Oh no!' she squealed, stifling another giggle by covering her mouth with a delicate hand, which Yakov noticed had rough skin peeling on each slender knuckle. Taking control of herself, her face became serious. 'You know what you must do for your parish. Your congregation has already started dying, and only treatment can help them. Go to the prelate, go to the governor, ask them for medicine.'

'I can already tell you what their answer will be,' Yakov said heavily, gesturing for her to follow him as he pulled the heavy curtain shut and started up the aisle.

'And what is that?' Lathesia asked, falling into step beside him, walking with quick strides to keep up with his long-legged gait.

'Medicine is in short supply; slaves are not,' he replied matter-of-factly, stopping and facing her. There was no point trying to make it easier. Every one of Karis Cephalon's ruling class could afford to lose a thousand slaves, but medical supplies, bought at great expense from off-world, could cost them half a year's profits.

Lathesia understood this, but had obviously railed against the fate the Emperor had laid down for her.

'You do realise you have put me in a very awkward position, don't you, child?' he added bitterly.

'Why so?' she answered back. 'Because a preacher should not be conversing with a wanted criminal?'

'No, that is easy to deal with,' Yakov replied after a moment's thought. 'Tomorrow when I see the prelate I will inform him that I saw you and he will tell the governor, who will in turn send the SSA to interrogate me. And I will tell them nearly everything.'

'Nearly everything?' she said with a raised eyebrow.

'Nearly,' he replied with a slight smile. 'After all, if I say that it was you who entreated me to ask for medical supplies, there is even less chance that I will be given them.'

'So you will do this for me?' Lathesia asked with a bright smile.

'No,' Yakov replied, making her smile disappear as quickly as it came.

He stooped to pick up a strip of rag littering the flagstones of the floor. 'But I will do it for my parishioners, as you say. I have no hope that the request will be granted, none at all. And my poor standing with the prelate will be worsened even more by the confrontation, but that is not to be helped. I must do as my duty dictates.'

'I understand, and you have my thanks,' Lathesia said softly before walking away, disappearing through the curtained doorway without a backward glance. Sighing, Yakov crumpled up the rag in his hand and moved to the altar to finish clearing up.

THE PLEXIGLASS WINDOW of the mono-conveyor was scratched and scuffed, but beyond it Yakov could see the capital, Karis, stretched out beneath him. Under the spring sun the whitewashed buildings were stark against the fertile plains surrounding the city. Palaces, counting houses, SSA courthouses and governmental office towers reared from the streets towards him as the conveyor rumbled noisily over its single rail. He could see other conveyor carriages on different tracks, gliding like smoke-belching beetles over the city, their plexiglass-sided cabs reflecting the sun in brief dazzles as it moved in and out from the clouds overhead.

Turning his gaze ahead, he looked at the Amethyst Palace, seat of the governor and cathedral of Karis Cephalon. Its high walls surrounded the hilltop on which it was built, studded with towers from which fluttered massive pennants showing the symbol of the revolutionary council. Once each tower would have hung the standard of one of the old aristocratic families, but they had been burnt, along with those families, in the bloody coup that had overturned their rule seven hundred and thirty years ago.

The keep, punctured at its centre by the mysterious kilometre-high black Needle of Sennamis, rose above the walls, a conglomeration of millennia of additional wings, buttresses and towers obscuring its original architecture like successive layers of patina.

Under his feet, the conveyor's gears began to grind and whirr more loudly as the carriage pulled into the palace docking station. Yakov navigated his way through the terminus without thought, his mind directed towards the coming meeting with Prelate Kodaczka. He barely acknowledged the salutes of the guards at the entrance to the cardinal's chambers, only subconsciously registering that they carried heavy-looking autorifles in addition to their ceremonial spears.

'Ah, Constantine,' Kodaczka murmured as the doors swung closed behind the preacher, looking up at Yakov from behind his high desk. A single laserquill and autotablet adorned its dull black surface, reflecting the sparsity of the rest of the chamber. The walls were plainly whitewashed, like most of the Amethyst palace's interior, with a single Imperial eagle stencilled in black on the wall behind the cardinal. He was a handsome man in his middle ages, maturing with dignity and poise. Dressed in a plain black cassock, his only badge of office the small steel circlet holding back his lustrous blond hair, the cardinal was an elegant, if severe, figure. He wouldn't have looked out of place as a leading actor on the stage at the Revolutionary Theatre; with his active, bright blue eyes, chiselled cheekbones and strong chin he would have enthralled the ladies had he not had another calling.

'Good of you to see me, cardinal,' replied Yakov. At a gestured invitation from Kodaczka the preacher sat in one of the high-backed chairs that were arranged in a semi-circle in front of the desk.

'I must admit to a small amount of surprise at receiving your missive this morning,' Prelate Kodaczka told him, leaning back in his own chair.

'You understand why I felt it necessary to talk to you?' inquired Yakov, waiting for the customary verbal thrust and parry that accompanied all of his conversations with Kodaczka.

'Your parish and the plague? Of course I understand,' Kodaczka nodded as he spoke. He was about to continue when a knock at the door interrupted him. At Kodaczka's call they opened and a servant in the plain livery of an Ecclesiarchal servant entered with a carafe and glass on a small wooden tray.

'I suspect you are thirsty after journeying all this way,' Kodaczka indicated the drink with an open palm. Yakov nodded his thanks, pouring himself a glass of the crisp water and sipping it carefully. The servant left the tray on the desk and retired wordlessly.

'Where was I? Oh yes, the plague. It has struck many of the slave communities badly. Why have you waited until now before requesting aid?' Kodaczka's question was voiced lightly but Yakov suspected he was, as always, being tested somehow. He considered his reply for a moment, sipping more water as an excuse for not answering.

'The other slaves are not my parishioners. They are not my concern,' he said, setting the empty glass back on the tray and raising his eyes to return the gaze of the cardinal.

'Ah, your parish, of course,' agreed Kodaczka with a smile. 'Your duty to your parishioners. And why do you think I can entreat the governor and the committee to act now, when they have let so many others die already?'

'I am simply performing my duty, as you say,' replied Yakov smoothly, keeping his expression neutral. 'I have made no promises other than to raise this with yourself, and I do not expect any particular success on your part. As you say, there has been an abundance of time to act before now. But still, I must ask. Will you ask the governor and the committee to send medical aid and staff to my parish to help defend the faithful against infection by this epidemic?'

'I will not,' Kodaczka answered curtly. 'They have already made it clear to me that not only is the expense of such resources unjustified, but the lifting of the ban on full citizens entering slave areas may prove a difficult legal wrangle.'

'My congregation is dying!' barked Yakov, though in his heart he felt less vehement. 'Can you not do something to help them?'

'I will offer up prayers for them,' the cardinal responded, showing no sign of being perturbed by Yakov's outburst. Yakov caught himself before he said anything. This was one of Kodaczka's traps. The cardinal was desperate to find some reason to discredit Yakov, to disband his unique parish and send him on his way.

'As I already have,' Yakov said eventually. There was an uncomfortable silence for several seconds, both preacher and cardinal gazing at each other over the desk, weighing up the opposition. It was Kodaczka who broke the quiet.

'It irks you to preach to these slaves?' the cardinal asked suddenly.

'Slaves are entitled to spiritual guidance even by the laws of Karis Cephalon,' the preacher replied.

'That is not an answer,' Kodaczka told him gravely.

'I find the… situation on this world difficult to align with the teachings of my faith,' Yakov admitted finally.

'You find slavery against your religion?'

'Of course not!' Yakov snorted. 'It is these mutants, these creatures that I preach to. This world is built upon the exploitation of something unholy and abhorrent and I believe it denigrates everyone involved in it.'

'Ah, your Armormant upbringing,' the prelate's voice dripped with scorn. 'So harsh and pure in intent, and yet so soft and decadent in execution.'

'We are an accepted and recognised sect within the Ministorum,' Yakov said defensively.

'Accepted? Recognised, I agree, but acceptance… That is another matter entirely,' Kodaczka said bluntly. 'Your founder, Gracius of Armorm, was charged with heresy!'

'And found innocent…' countered Yakov. He couldn't stop himself from adding, 'After a fair trial in front of his peers.'

'Yes,' agreed Kodaczka slowly, his sly smile returning once more.

YAKOV'S AUDIENCE WITH the cardinal had lasted most of the afternoon and once again the sun was beginning to set as he made his way back to the shanty town. As on the previous night there were many of the mutants gathered around the shrine. Rumour of his visit to the cardinal had spread and he was met by a crowd of eager faces. One look at his own expression quelled their anticipation and an angry murmur sprang up. It was Menevon who stepped forward, a troublemaker by nature in Yakov's opinion. He looked down at Menevon's bestial features and not for the first time wondered if he had been sired by unholy union with a dog or bear. Tufts of coarse hair sprung in patches all across his body, and his jaw was elongated and studded with tusk-like teeth stained yellow. Menevon looked back at him with small, beady eyes.

'He does nothing,' the mutant stated. 'We die and they all do nothing!'

'The Emperor's Will be done,' replied Yakov sternly, automatically echoed by some of the gathered mutants.

'The Emperor I trust and adore,' Menevon declared hotly, 'but the governor I wouldn't spit on if he were burning.'

'That is seditious talk, Menevon, and you would do well to curb your tongue,' warned Yakov, stooping to talk quietly to the rabble-rouser.

'I say we make him help us!' shouted Menevon, ignoring Yakov and turning towards the crowd. 'It's time we made ourselves heard!'

There were discontented growls of agreement from the others; some shouted out their approval.

'Too long have they lorded over us, too long we've been ignored!' continued Menevon. 'Enough is enough! No more!'

'No more!' repeated the crowd with a guttural roar.

'Silence!' bellowed Yakov, holding his arms up to silence them. The crowd fell quiet instantly at his commanding tone. 'This discord will serve for nothing. If the governor will not listen to me, your preacher, he will not listen to you. Your masters will not tolerate this outburst lightly. Go back to your homes and pray! Look not to the governor, but to yourselves and the master of us all, the Holy Emperor. Go now!'

Menevon shot the preacher a murderous look as the crowd heeded his words, dispersing with backward glances and muttered curses.

'Go back to your family, Menevon. You can do them no good dead on a scaffold,' Yakov told him quietly. The defiance in the mutant's eyes disappeared and he nodded sadly. He cast a long, despairing glance at the preacher and then he too turned away.

THE TOUCH OF something cold woke Yakov and when he opened his eyes his gaze fell first upon the glittering knife blade held in front of his face. Tearing his eyes away from the sharpened steel, he followed the arm to the knife's wielder and his look was met by the whitened orbs of the mutant he knew to be called Byzanthus. Like Lathesia, he was a renegade, and hunted by the Special Security Agents. His face was solemn, his eyes intent upon the preacher. The ridged and wrinkled grey skin that covered his body was dull in the silvery light which occasionally broke through the curtain swaying in the glassless window of the small chamber.

'I had your promise,' Yakov heard Lathesia speak from the shadows. A moment later she stepped forwards, her hair catching the moonlight as she passed in front of the window.

'I asked. They said no,' Yakov replied, pushing Byzanthus's arm away and sitting up, the thin blanket falling to his waist to reveal the taut muscles of his stomach and chest.

'You keep in good shape,' she commented, noticing his lean physique.

'The daily walk to the capital keeps me fit,' Yakov replied, feeling no discomfort as her penetrating gaze swept over his body. 'I must stay physically as well as spiritually fit to serve the Emperor well.'

A flickering yellow light drew the preacher's attention to the window and he rose from the thin mattress to pace over and look. Lathesia smiled at his nakedness but he ignored her; fleshly matters such as his own nudity were beneath him. Pulling aside the ragged curtain, Yakov saw the light came from dozens of blazing torches and when he listened carefully he could hear voices raised in argument. One of them sounded like Menevon's, and as his eyes adjusted he could see the hairy mutant in the torchlight, gesticulating towards the city.

'Emperor damn him,' cursed Yakov, pushing past Lathesia to grab his robes from a chair behind her. Pulling on his vestments, he rounded on the mutant girl.

'You put him up to this?' he demanded.

'Menevon has been an associate of mine for quite some time,' she admitted, not meeting his gaze.

'Why?' Yakov asked simply. 'The governor will not stand for this discontent.'

'Too long we have allowed this tyranny to continue,' she said with feeling. 'Just as in the revolution, the slaves have tired of the lash. It is time to strike back.'

'The revolutionary council was backed by two-thirds of the old king's army,' spat Yakov, fumbling in the darkness for his boots. 'You will all die.'

'Menevon's brother is dead,' Byzanthus growled from behind Yakov. 'Murdered.'

Yakov rounded on the grey-skinned man. 'You know this? For sure?'

'Unless he slit his own throat, yes!' replied Lathesia. 'The masters did this, and no one will investigate because it is just one of the slaves who has died. Justice must be served.'

'The Emperor judges us all in time,' Yakov replied instinctively. He pointed out of the window. 'And He'll be judging some of them this evening if you let this foolishness continue. Damn your souls to Chaos. Don't you care that they'll die?'

'Better to die fighting,' Lathesia whispered back, 'than on our knees begging for scraps and offal.'

The preacher snarled wordlessly and hurried out through the chapel into the street. As he rounded the corner he was met by the mutant mob, their faces twisted in anger, their raucous, raging cries springing to life as they saw him. Menevon was at their head, holding a burning brand high in the air, the embodiment of the revolutionary ringleader. Only he wasn't, Yakov thought bitterly; that honour belonged to the manipulative, headstrong teenage girl back in his room.

'What in the name of the Emperor do you think you are doing?' demanded Yakov, his deep voice rising to a deafening shout over the din of the mob. They ignored him and Menevon pushed him aside as the crowd swept along the street. The preacher recognised many faces in the torchlight as the mob passed by, some of them children. He felt someone step up beside him, and he turned and saw Lathesia watching the mutants marching past, her face triumphant.

'How did one so young become so bloodthirsty?' muttered Yakov, directing a venomous glare at her before setting off after the mutants. They were moving at some speed and Yakov had to force his way through the crowd with long strides, pulling and elbowing aside mutants to get to the front. As they neared the edge of the ghetto the crowd began to slow and he broke through to the front of the mob, where he saw what had stalled their advance. Across the main thoroughfare stood a small detachment of the SSA, their grey and black uniforms dark against the glare of a troop transport's searchlamp behind them. Each cradled a shotgun in their hands, their visored helms reflecting the flames of the torches. Yakov stopped and let the mutants swirl around him, his mouth dry with fear. Next to him the pretty young girl, Katinia, was staring at the SSA officers. She seemed to notice Yakov suddenly and looked up at the preacher with a small, uncertain smile. He didn't smile back, but focused his attention on the law enforcers ahead.

'Turn back now! You are in violation of the Slave Encampment Laws,' screeched a voice over a loudhailer.

'No more!' shouted Menevon, hurling his torch at the security agents, his cry voiced by others. Stones and torches rattled off the cobbles and walls of the street and one of the officers went down to a thrown bottle that smashed across his darkened helmet.

'You were warned, mutant scum,' snarled the SSA officer's voice over the hailer. At some unheard command the agents raised their shotguns. Yakov hurled himself across Katinia just as gunfire exploded all around him. There were sudden screams and shouts; a wail of agony shrieked from his left as he and the girl rolled to the ground. He felt something pluck at his robes as another salvo roared out. The mutants were fleeing, disorder reigned as they scrabbled and tore at one another to fight their way clear. Bare and booted feet stamped on Yakov's fingers as he held himself over Katinia, who was mewling and sobbing beneath him. Biting back a yell of pain as a heel crushed his left thumb between two cobbles, Yakov forced himself upright. Within moments he and the girl were alone in the street.

The boulevard was littered with dead and wounded mutants. Limbs, bodies and pools of blood were scattered over the cobblestones, a few conscious mutants groaned or sobbed. To his right, a couple he had wed just after arriving were on their knees, hugging each other, wailing over the nearly unrecognisable corpse of their son. Wherever he looked, lifeless eyes stared back at him in the harsh glare of the searchlight. The SSA were picking their way through the mounds of bodies, kicking over corpses and peering at faces.

Yakov heard the girl give a ragged gasp and he looked down. Half her mother's face lay on the road almost within reach. He bent and gathered the girl up in his left arm, and she buried her face in his robes, weeping uncontrollably. It was then he noticed the silver helmet of a sergeant as he clambered down from the turret of the armoured car.

'You!' bellowed Yakov, pointing with his free hand at the SSA man, his anger welling up inside him. 'Come here now!'

The officer gave a start and hurried over. His face was hidden by the visor of his helmet, but he seemed to be trembling.

'Take off your helmet,' Yakov commanded, and he did so, letting it drop from quivering fingers. The man's eyes were wide with fear as he looked up at the tall preacher. Yakov felt himself getting even angrier and he grabbed the man by the throat, his long, strong fingers tightening on the sergeant's windpipe. The man gave a choked cough as Yakov used all of the leverage afforded by his height to push him down to his knees.

'You have fired on a member of the Ministorum, sergeant,' Yakov hissed. The man began to stammer something but a quick tightening of Yakov's grip silenced him. Releasing his hold, Yakov moved his hand to the top of the sergeant's head, forcing him to bow forward.

'Pray for forgiveness,' whispered Yakov, his voice as sharp as razor. The other agents had stopped the search and helmets bobbed left and right as they exchanged glances. He heard someone swearing from the crackling intercom inside the sergeant's helmet on the floor.

'Pray to the Emperor to forgive this most grievous of sins,' Yakov repeated. The sergeant started praying, his voice spilling almost incoherently from his lips, his tears splashing down his cheeks into the blood slicking the cobbles.

'Forgive me, almighty Emperor, forgive me!' pleaded the man, looking up at Yakov as he released his hold, his cheeks streaked with tears, his face a mask of terror.

'One hour's prayer every sunrise for the rest of your life,' Yakov pronounced his judgement. As he looked again at the bloodied remnants of the massacred mutants and felt Katinia's tears soaking through his tattered priestly robes, he added, 'And one day's physical penance a week for the next five years.'

As he turned away from the horrific scene Yakov heard the sergeant retching and vomiting. Five years of self-flagellation would teach him not to fire on a preacher, Yakov thought grimly as he stepped numbly through the blood and gore.

YAKOV WAS TIRED and even more irritable than normal when the sun rose the next day. He had taken Katinia back to her home, where her brother was in a fitful, nightmare-laden sleep, and then returned to the site of the cold-blooded execution to identify the dead. Some of the mutants he did not recognise from his congregation, and he assumed they were more of Lathesia's misguided freedom fighters.

When he finally returned to the shanty town, the preacher saw several dozen SSA standing guard throughout the ghetto, each carrying a heavy pistol and a charged shock maul. As he dragged himself wearily up the steps to the chapel, a familiar face was waiting for him. Just outside the curtained portal stood Sparcek, the oldest mutant he knew and informal mayor-cum-judge of the ghetto.

Yakov delved into his last reserves of energy as the old mutant met him halfway, his twisted, crippled body making hard work of the shallow steps.

'A grim night, preacher,' said Sparcek in his broken, hoarse voice. Yakov noticed the man's left arm was splinted and bound with bandages and he held it across his chest as much as his deformed shoulder and elbow allowed.

'You were up there?' Yakov asked, pointing limply at Sparcek's broken arm.

'This?' Sparcek glanced down and then shook his head sadly. 'No, the SSA broke into my home just after, accused me of being the leader. I said they couldn't prove that and they did this, saying they needed no proof.'

'Your people need you now, before they...' Yakov's voice trailed off as his befuddled mind tried to tell him something. 'What did you just say?'

'I said they couldn't prove anything...' he started.

'That's it!' snapped Yakov, startling the old mutant.

'What? Talk sense, you're tired,' Sparcek snapped back, obviously annoyed at the preacher's outburst.'

'Nothing for you to worry about,' Yakov tried to calm him with a waved hand. 'Now, I am about to ask you something, and whether you answer me or not, I need your promise that you will never tell another living soul what it is.'

'You can trust me. Did I not help you when you first arrived, did I not tell you about your congregation, their secrets and traits?' Sparcek assured him.

'I need to speak to Lathesia, and quickly,' Yakov said, bending close so that he could whisper.

'The rebel leader?' Sparcek whispered back, clearly amazed. He thought for a moment before continuing. 'I cannot promise anything but I may be able to send her word that you wish to see her.'

'Do it, and do it quickly!' insisted Yakov, laying a gentle hand on the mutant's good arm. 'With all of these trigger happy agents around, she's bound to do something reckless and get more of your people killed. If I can speak to her, I may be able to avoid more bloodshed.'

'I will do as you ask, preacher,' Sparcek nodded as he spoke, almost to himself.

THE DANK SEWERS resounded with running water and constant dripping, punctuated by the odd splash as Yakov placed a booted foot in a puddle or a rat scurried past through the rivulets seeping through the worn brick walls. Ahead, the glowlamp of Byzanthus bobbed and weaved in the mutant's raised hand as he led the way to Lathesia's hidden lair. Though one of the larger drainage systems, the tunnel was still cramped for the tall preacher and his neck was sore from half an hour's constant stooping. His nose had become more accustomed to the noxious smell which had assaulted his nostrils when the grey-skinned mutant had first opened the storm drain cover, and his eyes were now used to the dim, blue glow of the lantern. He was thoroughly lost, he was sure of that, and he half-suspected this was the point of the drawn out journey. They must have been walking in circles, otherwise they would be beyond the boundaries of the mutant encampment in the city proper, or out in the fields.

After several more minutes of back-breaking walking, Byzanthus finally stopped beside an access door in the sewer wall. He banged four times, paused, then banged twice more. Rusted locks squealed and the door opened a moment later on shrieking hinges.

'You should loot some oil,' Yakov couldn't stop himself from saying, earning himself a cheerless smile from Byzanthus, who waved him inside with the lantern.

There was no sign of the doorkeeper, but as Yakov preceded Byzanthus up the wooden steps just inside the door he heard it noisily swinging shut again.

'Shy?' Yakov asked, looking at Byzanthus over his shoulder as he climbed the stairwell.

'Suspicious of you,' the mutant replied bluntly, giving him a hard stare.

The steps led them into a small hallway, decorated with flaking murals on the walls, they were obviously inside one of the abandoned buildings of the royal district.

'Second door on the left,' Byzanthus said curtly, indicating the room with a nod of his head as he extinguished the lamp.

Yakov strode down the corridor quickly, his hard-soled boots clacking on the cracked tiles. Just as he reached the door, it opened to reveal Lathesia, dressed in ill-fitting SSA combat fatigues.

'Come in, make yourself at home,' she said as she stepped back and took in the room with a wide sweep of her arm. The small chamber was bare except for a couple of straw pallets and a rickety table strewn with scatters of parchment and what looked like a schematic of the sewer system. The frescoes had been all but obliterated by crudely daubed black paint, which had puddled on the scuffed wooden floor. The remnants of a fire smouldered in one corner, the smoke drifting lazily out of a cracked window.

'We had to burn the carpet last winter,' Lathesia said apologetically, noting the direction of his gaze.

'And the walls?' Yakov asked, dropping his haversack onto the bare floor.

'Byzanthus in a fit of pique when he heard we'd been found guilty of treason,' she explained hurriedly, moving over to drop down on one of the mattresses.

'You share the same room?' Yakov asked, recoiling from her in disgust. 'Out of wedlock?'

'What of it?' she replied, genuinely perplexed.

'Is there no sin you are not guilty of?' he demanded hotly, regretting his decision to have anything to do with the wayward mutant. He fancied he could feel the fires of Chaos burning his soul as he stood there. It would take many weeks of repentance to atone for even coming here.

'Better that than freezing because we only have enough fuel to heat a few rooms,' she told him plainly before a smile broke over her pretty face. 'You think that Byzanthus and I... Oh, Yakov, please, allow me some standards.'

'I'm sure he doesn't see it that way,' Yakov pointed out to her with a meaningful look. 'I saw the way he looked at you in my bedchamber last night.'

'Enough of this!' Lathesia snapped back petulantly. 'I didn't ask you to come here to preach to me. You wanted to see me!'

'Yes, you are right, I did,' Yakov admitted, collecting his thoughts before continuing. 'Have you any other trouble planned for tonight?'

'What concern is it of yours, preacher?' she asked, her black eyes narrowing with suspicion.

'You must not do anything. The SSA will retaliate with even more brutal force than last time,' he warned her.

'Actually, we were thinking of killing some of them, strutting around with their bludgeons and pistols as if their laws apply here,' she replied venomously, her cracked hands balling into fists.

Yakov went over and sat down beside her slowly, meeting her gaze firmly.

'Do you trust me?' he asked gently.

'No, why should I?' she asked, surprised.

'Why did you come to me before, to ask the cardinal for help?' he countered, leaning back on one hand but keeping his eyes on hers.

'Because... It was... I was desperate, it was foolish of me, I shouldn't have,' she mumbled back, turning her gaze away.

'You are nothing more than a child. Let me help you,' Yakov persisted, feeling his soul starting to roast at the edges even as he said it.

'Stop it!' she wailed suddenly, springing to her feet and backing away. 'If I don't do this, no one will help us!'

'Have it your way,' sighed Yakov, sitting upright again. 'There is more to this than the casual murder of Menevon's brother. I do not yet know what, but I need your help to find out.'

'Why do you think so?' she asked, her defiance forgotten as curiosity took over.

'You say his throat was slit?' Yakov asked and she nodded. 'Why? Any court on Karis Cephalon will order a mutant hung on the word of a citizen, so why the murder? It must be because nobody could know who was involved, or why he died. I think he saw something or someone and was murdered so he couldn't talk.'

'But that means, if a master didn't do it...' Lathesia started before her eyes widened in realisation. 'One of us did this? No, I won't believe it!'

'You might not have to,' Yakov countered quickly, raising his hand to calm her. 'In fact it's unlikely. The only way we can find out is to go to where Menevon's brother died, and see what we can find.'

'He worked in one of the cemeteries not far from here, just outside the encampment boundary,' she told the preacher. 'We'll take you there.'

She half-ran, half-skipped to the open door and called through excitedly, 'Byzanthus! Byzanthus, fetch Odrik and Klain. We're going on an expedition tonight!'

THE FUNCTIONAL FERROCRETE tombstones had little grandeur about them, merely rectangular slabs plainly inscribed with the name of the family. The moon was riding high in the sky as Yakov, Lathesia and the other mutants searched the graveyard for any sign of what had happened. Yakov entered the small wooden shack that served as the gravedigger's shelter, finding various picks and shovels stacked neatly in one corner. There was an unmistakable red stain on the unfinished planks of the floor, which to Yakov's untrained eye seemed to have spread from near the doorway. He stood there for a moment, gazing out into the cemetery to see what was in view. It was Byzanthus who caught his attention with a waved arm, and they all gathered on him. He pointed to a grave, which was covered with a tarpaulin weighted with rocks. Lathesia gave Byzanthus a nod and he pulled back the sheeting.

The grave was deep and long, perhaps three metres from end to end and two metres down. Inside was a plain metal casket, wrapped in heavy chains from which hung numerous padlocks.

'Why would anyone want to lock up a coffin?' asked Lathesia, looking at Yakov.

YAKOV STOOD IN one of the rooms just down the hall from where he had met Lathesia, gazing at the strange casket. The mutant leader was beside him looking at it too, a small frown creasing her forehead.

'What do you…' she started to ask before a loud boom reverberated across the building. Shouts and gunshots rang out along the corridor as the two of them dashed from the room. Byzanthus came tearing into view from the doors at the far end, a smoking shotgun grasped in his clawed hands.

'The SSA!' he shouted to them as he ran up the corridor.

'How?' Lathesia asked, but Yakov ignored her and ducked back into the room to snatch up his satchel. More gunfire rattled from nearby, punctuated by a low bellowing of pain. As the preacher returned to the corridor Byzanthus smashed him across the jaw with the butt of the shotgun, sending Yakov sprawling over the tiled floor.

'You betrayed us, governor's lapdog!' the mutant hissed, pushing the shotgun barrel into Yakov's chest.

'Emperor forgive you!' spat the preacher, sweeping a booted foot into one of Byzanthus's knees, which cracked audibly as his legs folded under him. Yakov pounced forward and wrestled the shotgun from his grip, turning it on Lathesia as she stepped towards him.

'Believe me, this was not my doing,' he told her, backing away. 'Save yourselves!'

He took another step back and then threw the shotgun to Lathesia. Sweeping up his bag, Yakov shouldered his way through the doorway that led to the sewer stairs as she was distracted. Yakov's heart was hammering as he pounded down the steps three at a time, almost losing his footing in his haste. At the bottom someone stepped in front of him and he lashed out with his fist, feeling it connect with a cheekbone. He spun the lockwheel on the door and splashed out into the sewers, cursing himself for ever getting involved in this mess. Two hundred years of penance wouldn't atone for what he had done. As the sounds of fighting grew closer he hurried off through the drips and puddles with long strides.

YAKOV SAT ON his plain bed in a grim mood, brooding over the previous night's and day's events. He had spent the whole day a hostage to himself in the chapel, not daring to go out into the light, where some roving SSA man might recognise him from the raid on the rebels' hideout.

He had prayed for hours on end, tears in his eyes as he asked the Emperor for guidance. He had allowed himself to get involved in something beyond him. He was a simple preacher, he had no right to interfere in such matters. As his guilt-wracked day passed into evening, Yakov began to calm down. His dealings with the mutants may have been sinful, but he had discovered something strange. The chained coffin, and the murder of the mutant for what he knew about it, was at the heart of it. But what could he do? He had just decided to confess all to Prelate Kodaczka when footsteps out in the chapel attracted his attention.

Stepping into the shrine, he saw a figure kneeling before the altar, head bowed. It was Lathesia, and as he approached she looked up at him, her eyes red-rimmed from weeping.

'Byzanthus is dead, hung an hour ago,' she said dully, the black orbs of her eyes catching the light of the candle on the altar. 'He held off the agents to make sure I escaped. None of the others got out.'

'I did not betray you,' Yakov told her, kneeling beside her.

'I know,' she said, turning to him and laying a hand on his knee.

'I want to find out what is in that coffin,' Yakov said after a few moments of silence between them. 'Will you help me?'

'I watched them; they didn't take it anywhere,' she replied distractedly, wiping at a tear forming in her eye.

'Then will you go back there with me?' he asked, standing up again and reaching a hand down to help her up.

'Yes, I will,' she answered quietly. 'I want to know why they died.'

THEY TOOK THE overground route to the old aristocratic household, Lathesia leading him up a fire escape ladder onto a neighbouring rooftop.

From there they could see two SSA stationed at the front entrance and another at the tradesman's entrance to the rear. She showed him the rope-line hung between the buildings, tied there for escape rather than entry, but suitable all the same. Yakov kept his gaze firmly on his hands as he pulled himself along the rope behind the lithe young rebel leader, trying not to think of the ten metre drop to the hard road beneath him. As she helped him onto the rooftop of her one-time lair, a gentle cough from the darkness made them freeze. Out of the shadows strolled a man swathed in a heavy coat, his breath carving mist into the chill evening air.

'A strange pastime for a preacher,' he said as he stepped towards them, hands in the pockets of his trenchcoat.

'Who are you?' demanded Lathesia, her hand straying to the revolver wedged into the waistband of her trousers at the small of her back.

'Please don't try and shoot me,' he replied calmly. 'You'll attract some unwanted attention.'

'Who are you?' Yakov repeated the question, stepping between the stranger and Lathesia.

'An investigator, for the Inquisition,' he told them stopping a couple of paces away.

'An inquisitor?' Lathesia hissed, panic in her eyes.

'Don't worry, your little rebellion doesn't concern me tonight,' he assured her, pulling his hands free from the coat and crossing his arms. 'And I didn't say I was an inquisitor.'

'You are after the casket as well?' Yakov guessed, and the man nodded slightly.

'Shall we go and find it, then?' the investigator invited them, turning and walking away.

THE SCENE BEFORE Yakov could have been taken straight from a drawing in the Liber Heresius. Twelve robed and masked figures knelt in a circle around the coffin, five braziers set at the points of a star drawn around the casket. The air was filled with acrid smoke and the sonorous chanting of the cultists filled the room. One of them stood and pulled back his hood, and Yakov almost gasped out loud when he recognised the face of the governor. Holding his arms wide, he chanted louder, the words a meaningless jumble of syllables to the preacher.

'I think we've seen enough,' the investigator said, crouching beside Yakov and Lathesia on the patio outside the room. He drew two long laspistols from holsters inside his coat and offered one to Yakov. Yakov shook his head.

'Surely you're not opposed to righteous violence, preacher,' the stranger said with a raised eyebrow.

'No,' Yakov replied. Pulling his rucksack off, the preacher delved inside and a moment later pulled out a black enamelled pistol. With a deftness that betrayed years of practice he slipped home the magazine and cocked the gun. 'I just prefer to use my own weapon.'

Lathesia gasped in astonishment.

'What?' asked Yakov, annoyed. 'You think they call us the Defenders of the Faith just because it sounds good?'

'Shoot to kill!' rasped the stranger as he stood up.

He fired both pistols, shattering the windows and spraying glass shards into the room. A couple of the cultists pulled wicked-looking knives from their rope belts and leapt at them; the governor dived behind the casket shrieking madly.

Yakov's first shot took a charging cultist in the chest, punching him off his feet. His second blew the kneecap off another, his third taking him in the forehead as he collapsed. The investigator's laspistols spat bolts of light into the cultists fleeing for the door, while the boom of Lathesia's heavy pistol echoed off the walls. As Yakov stepped into the room, one of the cultists pushed over a brazier and he jumped to his right to avoid the flaming coals. A las-bolt took the traitor in the eye, vaporising half his face.

In a few moments the one-sided fight was over, all the cultists were dead, their blood soaking into the bare boards. Suddenly, the governor burst from his hiding place and bolted for the door, but Lathesia was quicker, tackling him to the ground. He thrashed for a moment before she smashed him across the temple with the grip of her revolver. She was about to pistol-whip him again but the stranger grabbed her wrist in mid-swing.

'My masters would prefer he survived for interrogation,' he told the girl, letting go of her arm and stepping back.

Lathesia hesitated for a moment before standing. She delivered a sharp kick to the governor's midriff before stalking away, emptying spent casings from her gun.

'I have no idea what is going on here,' Yakov confessed, sliding the safety into place on his own pistol.

'No reason you should,' the man assured him. 'I suppose I do owe you an explanation though.'

Slipping his laspistols back into his coat, the man leant back on the wall. 'The plague has been engineered by the governor and his allies,' the investigator told him. 'He wanted the mutants to rebel, to try to overthrow him. While Karis Cephalon remains relatively peaceful, the Imperial authorities and the Inquisition are content to ignore the more-or-less tolerant attitude to mutants found here. But should they threaten the stability of this world, they would be swift and ruthless in their response.'

The man glanced over his shoulder at Lathesia, who was studying the casket intently, then looked Yakov squarely in the eye before continuing quietly. 'But that's not the whole of it. So the mutants are wiped out, that's really no concern of the Inquisition. But the governor's motives are what concerns us. I, that is we, believe that he has made some kind of pact with a dark force, some kind of unholy elevation. His side of the deal was the delivery of a massive sacrifice, a whole population, genocide of the mutants. But he couldn't just have them culled; the entire economy of Karis Cephalon is based on mutant labour and no one would allow such a direct action to threaten their prosperity. So, he imported a virus which feeds on mutants. It's called Aether Mortandis and costs a lot of money to acquire from the Mechanicus.'

'And the coffin?' Yakov asked. 'Where does that fit in?'

'It doesn't, not at all!' the stranger laughed bitterly. 'I was hiding it when the gravedigger saw me. I killed him, but unfortunately before I had time to finish the burial, his cries brought an SSA patrol and I had to leave. It's just coincidence.'

'So what's so important about it then?' Yakov eyed the casket with suspicion. Lathesia was toying with one of the locks, a thoughtful look on her face.

'I wouldn't open that if I were you,' the stranger spoke up, startling the girl, who dropped the padlock and stepped back. The investigator put an arm around Yakov's shoulders and pulled him close, his voice dropping to a conspiratorial whisper.

'The reason the governor has acted now is because of a convergence of energies on Karis Cephalon,' the man told Yakov slowly. 'Mystical forces, astrological conjunctions are forming, with Karis Cephalon at its centre. For five years, the barrier between our world and the hell of Chaos will grow thinner and thinner. Entities will be able to break through, aliens will be drawn here, and death and disaster will plague this world on an unparalleled scale. It will be hell incarnate. If you wish, for your help today I can arrange a transfer to a parish on another world, get you way from here.'

Yakov looked at the man for a minute, searching his own soul.

'If what you say is true,' he said eventually, 'then I respectfully decline the offer. It seems men of faith will be a commodity in much need over the coming years.'

He looked up at Lathesia, who was looking at them from across the room.

'And,' Yakov finished, 'my parishioners will need me more than ever.'

THE LIVES OF FERAG LION-WOLF

Barrington J Bayley

FERAG LION-WOLF, CHAMPION of Tzeentch, ruler of five worlds, rose from the slab of sparkling white alabaster on which he slept and prepared to receive his honoured visitor. Young maidens bathed him, anointing his body with pleasant-smelling oils so that he gave off an enchanting aroma. The same slave-girls dressed him in garments of shimmering heliotrope silk, decorated all over with the sinuous symbols of the greatest of the gods, and accoutred him with his weapons.

When they had finished, an officer wearing the uniform designed for the palace staff by Ferag himself entered and bowed, waiting for permission to speak.

'The chariot of Lord Quillilil has been sighted entering our planetary system, my great and gracious lord,' the officer announced, once Ferag had impatiently signalled him to continue. 'It will arrive within the hour.'

'And is everything ready?'

'All has been made ready, my great and gracious lord.'

'Good...' Ferag purred.

He dismissed the officer and then turned to examine himself in a full-length mirror. He could not help but be pleased with what he saw. Ferag Lion-Wolf had always been a striking figure, even before he found favour with the Changer of the Ways, to give the great god Tzeentch just one of his many titles. Rugged, strong and handsome, Ferag had earned the admiration of all on his home world, as well as on the many worlds where he had fought and adventured before becoming a champion of Chaos.

But now! Ferag was almost beside himself as he beheld the magnificent transformation wrought on him by the Great Conspirator's marks of favour. In place of his left arm was a powerful, flexing tentacle with twice the reach. His right foot was a scrabbling claw, particularly exciting to behold as it so much resembled the claw of a Chi'khami'tzann Tsunoi or Feathered Lord, the rank of daemon closest to Tzeentch himself! An extra pair of eyes was set in his forehead, above the others but closer together, giving his face a curiously watchful appearance, like the face of a lurking spider. Those eyes could look into someone's mind and see if plots were being laid there. They could also kill with a single baleful glance. His mouth was also changed. It could pucker into a long tube, half the length of his arm, with which to suck pure magical energy from the souls of others. Tzeentch had given him power and change! And this was not the end of the rewards he was to receive...

Ferag made a magical sign, causing a shimmering oval surface to appear in the air, looking like a vertical pool of water or maybe quicksilver. With his forefinger he traced runes in the Dark Tongue, which could only be spoken in the warp. The runes spelled out his Chaos name, so recently bestowed upon him by his greater daemon patron.

With another gesture he dissolved the writing screen.

And now to welcome Quillilil!

Ferag strode from the lofty-ceilinged chamber and on to the spacious balcony overlooking the extensive palace, looking around him and, as always, taking immense satisfaction in his accomplishments. He was ruler of an entire planetary system within the Imperium of Chaos, called by outsiders the Eye of Terror. Five of the system's eight planets were inhabited. Several billion beings all lived in dread, in obedience, in utmost respect and adoration, of Ferag Lion-Wolf.

Ferag had designed his palace to resemble what he imagined the heavenly palaces of Tzeentch and his Feathered Lords to be like. Tier upon tier of terraces rose to the cloud layer, sparkling and glowing in iridescent colours. Towers and minarets and convoluted galleries twisted and twined like snakes. But none of it, of course, was restricted by gravity. The towers and galleries jutted out at crazy angles, as if they had been constructed in space or – as was the impression Ferag had striven to create – the vast unknowable reaches of the warp.

His aides and guards gathered around him. It was time for Quillilil's chariot to arrive. A magnifier had been set up on the balcony. Through it, events in the upper atmosphere became visible as though they were only a short distance away. So they were able to watch as the chariot from the neighbouring planetary system, an elaborate, burnished affair decorated with gold and silver curlicues, appeared in the lemon-yellow sky and swooped through the upper air. Diving for the cloud layer, it descended towards the palace.

Ferag and his aides carefully watched the surrounding countryside, dotted with towns and villages whose privilege it was to share a landscape with their mighty ruler. Yes, there it was! The plot was afoot! Shark-like craft were hurtling over the horizon, three altogether, coming from different directions. In addition, from hidden places nearer at hand, a dozen wild-looking figures mounted on flying discs were soaring upwards, long hair flying behind them, waving weapons.

There was magic at work, or those discs would not have been able to fly here. They were K'echi'tsonae, steeds of Tzeentch, and their proper medium was the warp. Peering closely at the magnifier, Ferag could see the rows of teeth around their rims.

Both shark-craft and riders were converging on the interstellar chariot. Ferag had a consummate sense of timing. He raised a hand, staying his aides who were ready to release a barrage and destroy the raiders. Instead, he allowed the raiders to get closer to their prey.

'Let me deal with this,' Ferag murmured in his melodious baritone voice.

When it seemed there could be no help for the descending foreign vessel on its state visit, he pointed with all five fingers of his right hand. The air became charged with power. It crackled. All present felt the waves of prickling sensations over their entire bodies. And from the fingers of master magician Ferag Lion-Wolf there issued streams of raw magic, crossing the intervening miles instantaneously, sizzling, swaying, touching all three shark-craft and the dozen disc raiders.

For a brief moment the great stream of energy flickered around them, and then, in that same moment, they shivered and were gone.

Ferag Lion-Wolf smiled knowingly. Lord Quillilil's chariot settled itself onto a marbled landing bay further down the terrace. Ferag and his party had already made their way there when the ornate door of the chariot swung open. Flamboyantly clad guards emerged and took up station on either side, glancing nervously around them.

Lord-Commander Quillilil stepped down from the threshold. Unlike Ferag, he had never been a Space Marine, and so was much shorter in stature than the hulking Lion-Wolf. He wore a cloak of brilliant blue. His hands were small, with a shrivelled, talon-like look. In place of a mouth, he had a compact, curved beak, turquoise in colour. A straw-coloured plume sprouted from the top of his otherwise bald pate. His eyes were round and unblinking, and seemed unable to stare in any direction but straight ahead, so that he looked about him continually with sudden nervous movements.

'My Lord-Commander Quillilil!' Ferag greeted breezily, spreading arm and tentacle in welcome.

'My Lord-Commander Ferag!'

Quillilil's voice was high and chirping. He allowed Ferag to embrace him briefly, then stepped back to gaze at the palace around him. He was clearly impressed.

'I am happy to have been able to protect you, my lord Quillilil,' Ferag said. 'It appears some of your enemies have gathered here.'

Twittering laughter rose from Quillilil's throat. His eyes glittered. 'Yes! Subversives from my own planet who fled here some time ago. I knew my visit would flush them out! Why do you think I came here? You should be flattered, my lord Ferag, at the trust I have placed in you. My chariot is unarmed!'

'I, too, have used the occasion to my benefit,' Ferag told him. 'Your renegades could not have acted without help from some of my own subjects. They are now paying the penalty for their disloyalty.' He glanced at the surrounding countryside, taking pleasure in knowing of the death and torture being inflicted there.

'I have prepared a banquet for tonight,' he continued to tell his guest. 'You are particularly partial to human flesh, I believe?'

Quillilil clacked his beak rapidly, in eager affirmation.

'Skinned specimens have been marinading in spices for the past week. Tonight they will be roasted for your delectation. Tomorrow we will discuss a treaty between us. For the present, though, allow me to show you round my palace. But first—'

Ferag raised arm and tentacle and swept them through the air, making magical passes. There came an immense rumbling sound. The huge edifice all around them was coming apart. Towers, terraces, galleries, halls, all separated and began gyrating in the air, performing a gigantic dance. The landing bay on which they stood also took part in the display, whirling lazily through a cloud and back again.

Then, with meticulous precision, everything came together again. Stone block met stone block in silent harmony, mortared together as before. In seconds the palace had reassembled itself.

Quillilil trilled in feigned pleasure. 'Most impressive, my lord Ferag! And if you will allow me in return...'

He too made an elaborate sign with his hand. Further along the terrace, a jutting arcade detached itself, floated a short distance away into the ether and then began spinning at speed.

Quillilil made delicate pulling motions with his fingers. The minaret ceased spinning and returned to its place with a deep grinding of stone upon stone. There was a gentle murmur of approval from the assembled aides and retainers.

It was common for Tzeentchian magicians to show off to one another on first meeting. But for all his chirpiness, the visitor could not hide the fact that he had been bettered by his host.

Surreptitiously, Ferag cast his guest a passing glance with his upper pair of eyes, not wanting Quillilil to see the dark flash that would show he was looking into his mind. It was as he had expected. Quillilil was not happy at being ruler of a mere one-planet system. He envied Ferag his domains.

The visit was but the first step in an elaborate, convoluted plan to take his place, stretching far into the future. Quillilil's brain was a maze of plot and counter-plot, intricate to the point of madness.

Which was as it should be in a champion of Tzeentch, the Great Conspirator and Master of Fortune. Quillilil would not, however, see his plans come to fruition. Ferag had laid a strategy to add his guest's planet to his own dominion. As for Quillilil himself, he would be disposed of as easily as one of the feeble humans he was about to feast upon.

Ushering his visitor from the landing bay, Ferag began conducting him through the great vaulted halls of the palace, pointing out feature after feature. But his mind was not on the task of being a tour guide. The promise made to him by his greater daemon patron recently – given to him at the same time as his Chaos name – had left Ferag in a state of pure exultation. It was not long, therefore, before he began talking instead of himself.

'Know, my friend, that I have lived a most eventful life, even for one of our kind,' he said seriously to Quillilil as they strode. 'Have you wondered at my name? Its meaning can tell you much about me. I was born on a primitive planet in the Imperium, outside of our Chaos realm. Life there was dangerous. What few human beings there were knew only how to make tools and weapons of stone, and they had it hard. Among my people one did not receive a permanent name at birth. One had to earn it as one grew to manhood. Now the lion-wolf is the most fierce animal on that planet. Standing twice the height of a human, with jaws that can crush a horse, able to outpace the fastest runner – it would take twenty armed warriors to defeat it! When I was eight years old, one of these beasts killed my father...'

THE REMINISCENCE TOOK his mind back. He was a naked boy, standing on the dusty scrubland of the world of his birth. In the sky was the looming globe of its smouldering red sun.

And barely ten paces away, the lifeless body of his father was being tossed back and forth in the jaws of a lion-wolf! When the beast had come loping across the landscape towards them, they had both run for the protection of a rocky tor. But when he heard his father's stout timber spear clattering to the ground behind him, he had turned to witness the dreadful sight.

The boy hesitated. While the beast devoured its prey he could, perhaps, gain the summit of the tor and the fearsome animal might forget him.

But it had killed his father!

A screaming rage gripped him. He ran back and laid his hands on the spear. It was almost too heavy for him to lift, but he raised its fire-hardened point and yelled at the fearsome lion-wolf for all he was worth.

'You killed my father!'

The creature dropped the torn, mauled body and turned its massive face towards him, sniffing the air. He could smell its shaggy coat as it came towards him to investigate. He made jabbing motions with the spear, yelling and retreating. He was at the bottom of the tor now.

The lion-wolf gathered itself together and leaped!

The boy stood his ground, determined to gain revenge for the death of his father. He jammed the butt of the spear in a crevice in the rock and aimed the spearpoint at the gaping jaws of the lion-wolf as it sprang.

The lion-wolf had intended to bite off his head with one snap of its great teeth. Instead, the spear rammed itself down the beast's throat and bore the full impact of that huge body's momentum. Sprawled on the scrubland, the lion-wolf struggled to extract the offending shaft, coughing up great gouts of blood. The boy gave it no chance to do so. On he came, pushing with all his might – pushing the spear down and down, until he came within reach of those deadly claws! But by then it was too late for the animal. The spear had entered its heart.

Even so, the end was long coming. The lion-wolf did not die easily. It writhed and thrashed as its lifeblood poured from its mouth, watched by the fascinated, exultant, grieving eight-year-old...

'SO THEN THE tribe gave me my permanent name,' Lord-Commander Ferag said to his guest. 'In my native tongue "Ferag" means "killer", so I was known as "Killer of the Lion-Wolf". I have retained the first word out of respect for my original people.

'No other warrior had ever borne such a name, for no one else had killed a lion-wolf single-handed, and probably has not even now.'

'A stirring tale!' Lord Quillilil chirruped. 'When did you become inducted into the Adeptus Astartes?'

'No more than forty days later, a squad of Purple Stars Space Marines landed near our village. They were told of my courage with the lion-wolf. They tested me in every way, then took me back with them to their monastery.

'I served the Purple Stars for the next twenty years, learning all their ways, going on their campaigns as a scout, as a messenger and in countless other roles. At the end of that time I was judged fit to be transformed into a Space Marine. I was given the extra organs, the progenoid glands, the sacred gene-seed. For two hundred years I served with the Purple Stars, and saw more action than I could hope to relate, eventually rising to the rank of company commander. I particularly distinguished myself in a raid on a tyranid hive ship...'

ONCE AGAIN FERAG Lion-Wolf found his mind regressing to the far past. A squad of Purple Stars Space Marines was cutting a way through the shell of a vast, snail-like form, its motive power crippled by laser fire so that it had become separated from the hive fleet. None of them knew what to expect on the inside, and what they did find was nothing they could have expected.

They were in a round tunnel which pulsed and throbbed like a living organ, branching at irregular intervals. A huge thumping sound was all around them, like the beating of a gigantic heart. The light was dim, blood-red, and seemed to seep from out of the very walls themselves.

Then, scrabbling down the tunnels which were scarcely large enough to contain them, came the tyranid warriors, huge bossed beasts, six-limbed, worse than the worst nightmare, each head a mass of razor-sharp teeth, each front pair of limbs whirling twin swords that could cut straight through a Space Marine's armour!

With horror Ferag saw his bolter shots bounce off the tyranids' armour while his men were butchered around him. There was no chance of retreating to the assault craft.

Then his mind flashed to the time he had fought the lion-wolf as a boy, and he took heart at the memory. He drew his chain sword in his left gauntlet. Sparks flew as he parried the tyranid boneswords, as he later came to know them. This enabled him to get close in – and the muzzle of his bolter went straight between the tyranid's massed teeth!

The monster jumped then slumped as the bolt exploded inside its body. Ferag let out a roar of laughter. He barked into his communicator.

'That's the way to do it, men! That's the way to do it!'

THE HEROIC DEED faded as Ferag brought his mind back to the present. 'The tactics I developed on that day became standard for fighting the foul tyranids at close quarters,' he finished.

He paused for a moment. 'Most warriors would be satisfied with such a life, I dare say, but I was not. The Imperium began to seem too confined for me – I wanted something grander, something to give scope to my abilities! In secret I began to study the ways of magic. I knew, of course, that there had once been a great heretical war, when fully half the original Space Marine legions took refuge in our Imperium of Chaos. I became attracted to the study of Tzeentch. And eventually I did the unthinkable. I deserted my Chapter, and made my way here to devote myself to his service.' He grinned.

'And now I am his champion! Commander of five worlds! It has been a glorious time! I could not begin to regale you with my adventures, or say how long I have lived. In the Eye of Terror a day is a thousand years, a thousand years is but a day, and time means nothing, until death comes.'

'Your fame spreads far and wide, my dear lord commander,' his guest cooed.

'And so it should!' Ferag made a face. 'Do you know, my lord Quillilil, with what contempt I was treated at first? I am a Space Marine of the

Second Founding, raised after the Horus war. The Chaos Legionaries are all of the First Founding. They thought themselves harder, and me as soft and weak. Well, they soon learned their mistake.'

Ferag's hand slashed through the air. 'I have killed thirty-five Traitor Marines in hand-to-hand combat! Twenty of them followers of Khorne, the berserker Blood God! And a dozen of those World Eaters, the most feared of all! There is no greater warrior than Ferag Lion-Wolf!'

His voice dropped and became more conciliatory. 'Forgive my boasting, my lord, but I only speak the truth.'

Quillilil twittered flattering laughter. 'It is no boasting at all, my fellow champion. Why, you are too modest. You almost deprecate yourself. Everyone knows of your great victory on the bowl planet.'

'Yessss.' Ferag grinned. It was one of his most beloved memories, perhaps his greatest exploit since coming to the Eye of Terror.

A great army had been assembled, an unholy alliance between the forces of Khorne, the Blood God, and Nurgle, the Great Lord of Disease and Decay, also Tzeentch's most implacable enemy! The battle had been fought in a planet shaped like nothing so much as a shallow bowl, governed by its own special physical laws. It was, in fact, possible to fall off the rim of this bowl and into some inescapable hell.

Ferag had commanded a much smaller Tzeentch force. At first sight the twin hordes looked invincible. The Khorne core of Chaos Space Marines had drenched themselves in blood before the battle even began, butchering their own massed soldiery and driving them towards the enemy. As for the Nurgle horde… a vast, filthy Chaos daemon, a great unclean one, had been at its head, and he had come up with a special tactic. The millions-strong army had been rotted with amoeba plague. Its soldiery were no longer separate individuals, but combined into one sticky, putrid mass which came rolling on, engulfing everything in its path.

Against all this, Ferag had only the special strengths of Tzeentch: strategy and sorcery! It had been a battle of titanic proportions. The bowl world had glowed and seethed with magical forces for months. But in the end it was Ferag's tactical genius that had won the day. The vile hordes of Khorne and Nurgle had been driven over the planet's rim to go toppling into an eternal hell-world.

Ferag had gathered together what survived of the planet's original inhabitants and had given them a generations-long task – to erect in the middle of the bowl a monument to Tzeentch that towered above the rim itself.

It was no wonder, when he looked back over his life, that the Changer of the Ways appreciated his services. Further, was about to reward him with the greatest possible fulfilment. His greater daemon patron, appearing before him in person, had informed him that he was to receive the ultimate gift.

He was to become a daemon prince. He would be immortal, no longer subject to death, able to live forever in the heavens of the warp!

But there was still his guest. Almost reluctantly, Ferag Lion-Wolf returned his attention to the tour of inspection.

'Step this way, my lord Quillilil. There is a most delightful aerial esplanade through here.'

They walked under an ornate archway, through which shone the lemon-coloured sky. Ferag Lion-Wolf heard a grating sound overhead. Looking up, he saw that a block of stone had dislodged itself from the masonry and had begun to fall.

In that instant it occurred to him that perhaps this was the section of the palace upon which Quillilil had demonstrated his magic. But whether this was so or not, Ferag had no time to act. The stone block struck his head with great force, knocking him unconscious.

HE RECOVERED HIS senses in what seemed like a split second. He was standing on dusty scrubland, naked except for a rag made of woven grass tied loosely around his waist. A vast, murky red sun hovered near the horizon, producing a lurid sunset.

A circle of a dozen men stood around him. They were all looking at him with a sort of avid expectancy.

He looked back, searching one face after another, utterly bewildered.

Until the change came, sweeping through his mind in an unstoppable rush.

The memory of another life flooded into his mind. The life he had really lived. Not the life of the surgically adapted, battle-hardened ex-Space Marine he had thought himself to be, or of the glory-drenched champion of Tzeentch who for uncounted centuries had faithfully served his master.

He was not a warrior at all. He had never left his native planet. His name was not even Killer-of-the-Lion-Wolf. He never could have earned such a name, not even as a man, let alone as a boy! He was known as Ulf Dirt-Creeper, and he was acknowledged by all to be puny physically and a coward morally.

But he did belong to a Tzeentch coven. He had an aptitude for lying, cheating, and low cunning, for which the worshippers of the Change God found uses. Now, however he had been found wanting. It was a small matter, really – he had been sent to murder a man in his sleep, an enemy of the coven, also his sister's husband, and he had been unable to find the courage. Now he stood condemned.

Condemned to end his life as Chaos spawn.

But because he had been of service in the past, Tzeentch had rendered him a final gift. In the last instants before he descended into mindless-ness, he had been allowed to stand at the end of a completely different life, one of glory and power. Of course, he could not be allowed to retain the delusion to the end. That would be un-Tzeentchian. The cruel truth had to be revealed.

The coven leader was intoning a formula redolent of untold power in a high-pitched voice. Ulf Dirt-Creeper felt a horrid crawling sensation within him. He whimpered and flailed miserably. Despite himself, his body bent double. His hands touched the earth and became flat, flappy feet. He felt his face swelling into a round, ridiculous travesty of anything thought of as human. His mouth elongated into a long, narrow tube, not for drawing magical force out of his adversaries, but for sucking up the worms and grubs which were to be his only food from now on.

The awful mutation continued, playing out before the disgusted yet fascinated gazes of his fellow cult members. Then Ulf Dirt-Creeper recalled having heard, so long ago now, another name for Tzeentch: the Great Betrayer. Sometimes, instead of the promised spiritual reward, would come the greatest betrayal of all. Not daemon prince but...

A burning question seized his petrified mind in the scant moments before it descended into gibbering insanity. Who was he, really? Ulf Dirt-Creeper or Ferag Lion-Wolf?

Which one is true?

Which one is true?

PLAYING PATIENCE

A Ravenor story
Dan Abnett

I

WEST OF URBITANE, the slum-tracts begin, and one descends into a ragged wilderness of dispiriting ruins where the only signs of life are the armoured manses of the narcobarons, projecting like metal blisters above the endless rubble. This is a destitute realm, a great and shameful urban waste, stalked by the Pennyrakers and the Dolors and a myriad other gangs, where Imperial authority has only the most tenuous grip.

A foetid wind blows through the slum-tracts, exhaled like bad breath from the sumps and stacks of the massive city. This miasmal air whines through the rotting habitats and moans in the shadows.

And those shadows are permanent, for the flanks of Urbitane rise behind the tracts, eclipsing all daylight. Flecked with a billion lamps, the rockcrete stacks of the sweating hive-city ascend into the roiling clouds like the angular shoulders of some behemoth emerging from chthonic depths, and soar as a sheer cliff above the slums that litter the lightless ground at its foot.

Sub-orbitals cross the murky sky, their trace-lights blinking like cursors on a dark screen. Occasionally the slums tremble as a bulk-lifter passes particularly low overhead on its final approach into the canyons of the hive, the bass rumble of its engines shivering the air.

Where, in the west, the hive stacks come tumbling down to meet the slums, shelving like giant staircases in bad repair, there is a patched stonework tower that houses the Kindred Youth Scholam. It is a meagre place, supported by charitable works, teetering on the brink between city and slum. Humble, crumbling, it faces west, its many window-slits barred, for the safety of the pupils.

At the start of of the year 396 Imperial, there were, amongst the scholam's many inhabitants, three sisters called Prudence, Providence and Patience.

The night I arrived on Sameter, the rigorists had locked Patience in the scholam's oubliette.

II

SAMETER IS A dismal place, and its morose air matched our mood. A slovenly, declining agrochemical world in the heartlands of the Helican subsector, it had seen better days.

So had we. My companions and I were weary and dejected. Pain clung to us like a shroud, so tightly none of us could express our grief. It had been that way for six months, since Majeskus. The only thing that kept us together and moved us along was a basic desire for revenge.

We had been forced to make the voyage to Sameter aboard a privately hired transport. the *Hinterlight* was dry-docked for repairs half a subsector away, and its mistress, Cynia Preest, had pledged to rejoin us as soon as the work was done. But I knew she was rueing the day she had ever agreed to assist my mission. When I had last spoken with her, she had confided, bitterly, that another incident like Majeskus would surely make her break her compact with me and return to the life of a merchant rogue in the Grand Banks.

She blamed me. They all blamed me, and they were damn well right. I had underestimated Molotch. I had given him the opening. My blind confidence had led to the disaster. Throne, what a fool I had been! Molotch was the sort of enemy one should never underestimate. He was Cognitae, perhaps the brightest and best to emerge from that infernal institution, which took genius as a basic prerequisite.

Our lander skimmed down through the filthy air above the Urbitane isthmus, bumping in the crosswind chop, and cycled in towards one of the hive's private landing gantries on the north side of the city. As the breaking jets fired, sudden, intense gravity hung upon us. Even inside my suspensor field, I felt its weight. I had linked one of my chair's data cables to the lander's systems, and so saw everything that the shuttered cabin denied my friends. The looming piles of the hive, the shelf-like stacks, each one kilometres wide, the bristling lights, the smog. Hive towers rose up, as vast and impassive as tombstones, etched with lit windows. Chimneys exhaled skeins of black smoke. The lower airways buzzed with small fliers and ornithopters, like gnats swarming up on a summer evening. There, the spires of the Ecclesiarch Basilica, gilded like a crown; beyond, the huge glass roofs of the Northern Commercia, so high that the clouds of a microclimate weather system had formed beneath their vault. There, the Inner Consul, the radiating rings of the transit system, the wrought-iron pavilions of the Agriculture Guild.

We touched down at sunset. Great, shimmering doughnuts of gas-flame were issuing from the promethium refineries along the isthmus, bellying up like small, fireball suns against the curdled brown undercast.

The private landing gantry was high up in the twisted mass of the inner hive-towers. Leased by the local ordos to provide convenient access to the city, it was a creaking metal platform trembled by the windshear. Even so, exhaust vapour from our dented, scabby lander pooled in an acrid haze inside the rusting safety basket of the pad. The lander, a gross-utility vehicle three hundred years old, reclined on its pneumatic landing claws like a tailless lizard. It had been painted red, a long time ago, but the colour was only a memory now. Steam hissed from the rapidly cooling hydraulics, and a disturbing quantity of lubricant and system fluid gushed out of its underside from joints and cracks and fissures.

Without asking, Kara Swole took hold of my chair's handle and pushed me out down the open ramp. I could have done it myself but I sensed that Kara, like all of them, wanted something to do, just to keep busy. Harlon Nayl followed us out, and walked to the edge of the safety cage to stare out into the foggy depths of the hive. Carl Thonius lingered in the hatchway, paying the pilot his fee and tip and making arrangements for future services. Harlon and Kara were both dressed in bodygloves and heavy jackets, but Carl Thonius was, as ever, clad in exquisite, fashionable garments: buckled wedge shoes, black velvet pantaloons, a tailored jacket of grey damask tight around his thin ribs, a high collar tied with a silk bow and set with a golden pin. He was twenty-four years old, blond-haired, rather plain of face, but striking in his poise and manners. I had thought him too much of a dandy when the ordos first submitted him as a possible interrogator, but had quickly realised that behind the foppish, mannered exterior lay a quite brilliant analytical mind. His rank marked him out amongst my retainers. The others – Nayl and Kara, for example – were individuals I hired because of their skills and talents. But Carl was an inquisitor in training. One day, he would aspire to the office and signet of the sublime ordos. His service to me, as interrogator, was his apprenticeship, and every inquisitor took on at least one interrogator, training them for the duty ahead. I had been Gregor Eisenhorn's interrogator, and had learned an immeasurable amount from that great man. I had no doubt that, in a few years, Carl Thonius would be well on his way to that distinguished rank.

Of course, for reasons I could not have ever imagined, that would not be the case. Hindsight is a worthless toy.

Wystan Frauka emerged from the lander, lighting his latest lho-stick from the stub of the last. He had his limiter turned on, of course, and it would remain on until I told him otherwise. He looked bored, as usual, detached. He wandered over to where a servitor was unloading our luggage from the lander's aft belly-hatch and looked for his own belongings.

Harlon remained at the edge of the safety cage, deep in thought. A heavyset man, thick with corded muscle, his head shaved, he had a dominating presence. Born on Loki, he'd been a bounty-hunter for many years before gaining employment with my mentor Eisenhorn because of his skills. I had inherited him, so to speak. There was no man I would rather have at my side in a fight. But I wondered if Harlon Nayl *was* at my side any more. Not since… the event. I'd heard him talk about 'going back to the old game', his defeated tone the same as Cynia Preest's. If it came down to it, I would let him go.

But I would miss him.

Kara Swole trundled me over to the gantry edge until we were facing the safety basket too. We stared out across the city.

'See anything you like?' she asked. She was trying to be light and funny, but I could taste the pain in her voice.

'We'll find something here, I promise,' I said, my voice synthesised, expressionless, through the mechanical vox-ponder built into my support chair. I hadn't mind-talked to any of them for a long time now, not since Majeskus, probably. I despised the vox-ponder's menacing flatness, but telepathy seemed too intimate, too intrusive at a time when thoughts were raw and private.

'We'll find something here,' I repeated. 'Something worth finding.'

Kara managed a smile. It was the first I had seen her shape for months, and it warmed me briefly. She was trying. Kara Swole was a short, voluptuous redhead whose rounded build quite belied her acrobatic abilities. Like Harlon, I had inherited her from Eisenhorn. She was a true servant of the ordos, as hard as stone when she needed to be, but she possessed a gentleness as appealing and soft as her curves. For all her dexterity, her stealth, her confidence with weapons, I think it was that gentleness that I most valued her for.

Molotch had faded into the void after his crimes above Majeskus, leaving no trace. Sameter, benighted planet, offered us the vestige of a clue. Three of Molotch's hired guns, three of the men we had slain in the battle on the *Hinterlight*, had proved, under forensic examination, to have come from Sameter. From this very place, Urbitane, the planet's second city.

We would find their origins and their connections, and follow them through every tenuous twitch and turn, until we had Molotch's scent again.

And then…

Carl had finished his transactions with the lander pilot. As I turned, I saw the pilot looking at me, staring at me the same way he and the other crew members had stared since they had first seen me come aboard. I didn't have to reach out with my mind to understand his curiosity.

The wounds of Chaos had left me a mangled wreck, a disembodied soul locked forever within a grav-suspended, armoured support chair. I had no physical identity anymore. I was just a lump of floating metal, a mechanical container, inside which a fragment of organic material remained, kept vital and pulsing by complex bio-systems. I knew the very sight of me scared people, people like the pilot and the rest of his crew. I had no face to read, and people do so like a face.

I missed my face. I missed my limbs. Destiny had left me one virtue, my mind. Powerfully, alarmingly psychic, my mind was my one saving grace. It allowed me to carry on my work. It allowed me to transcend my pitiful state as a cripple in a metal box.

Molotch had a face. A handsome visor of flesh that was, in its way, as impassive as my sleek, matt-finished metal. The only expression it ever conveyed was a delight in cruelty. I would take great pleasure in burning it off his shattered skull.

'Do we have the names and physiologues?' I asked.

'Nayl's got them,' Kara replied.

'Harlon?'

He turned and walked over to join us, pulling a dataslate from the hip-pocket of his long, mesh-weave coat.

He flipped it on.

'Victor Zhan. Noble Soto. Goodman Frell. Biogs, traces, taints and histories. All present and correct.'

'Let's do what we came here to do,' I said.

III

OUBLIETTE. A PLACE where things or persons are put so that they may be forgotten about. Or, as Patience preferred to think, a place where one might sit awhile and forget.

The scholam's oubliette was a cavity under the lower hall, fitted with a bolted hatch. There was no light, and vermin scuttled around in the wet shadows. It was the punishment place, the area where those pupils who had committed the worst infractions were sent by the rigorists. But it was also one of the few places in the Kindred Youth Scholam where a pupil could enjoy some kind of privacy.

According to its register, the scholam was home to nine hundred and seventy-six young people, most of them slum orphans. There were thirty-two tutors, all privately employed, and another forty servants and ancillary staff, including a dozen men, all ex-Guard, known as the *rigorists*, whose duties were security and discipline.

Life in the scholam was austere. The old tower, built centuries earlier for some purpose no one could now remember, was chilly and damp. The tower itself clung for support to the side of a neighbouring stack, like a climbing plant against a wall. The floors of its many storeys were cold ouslite dressed with rush-fibre, the walls lime-washed and prone to trickles of condensation. A murmur from the lower levels reminded the inhabitants that there was a furnace plant working down there, but it was the only clue, for no heat ever issued from the thumping pipework or the corroded radiators.

The regime was strict. An early rise, prayers, and an hour of ritual examination before breakfast, which was taken at sunrise. The morning was spent performing the many chores of the scholam – scrubbing floors, washing laundry, helping in the kitchen – and the afternoon was filled with academic classes. After supper, more prayers, ablutions in the freezing wash-house, and then two hours of liturgical study by lamplight.

Occasionally, trusted older pupils were allowed to accompany tutors out of the tower on trips into the nearby regions of the hive, to help carry purchased food stocks, fabrics, ink, oil and all the other sundry materials necessary to keep the scholam running. They were a distinctive sight in the busy streets of the western stacks: a grim, robed tutor leading a silent, obedient train of uniformed scholars, each one laden down by bundles, bales, bags and cartons. Every pupil wore a uniform, a unisex design in drab grey with the initials of the scholam stitched onto the back.

Few pupils ever complained about the slender comfort of their lives, because almost all of them had volunteered for it. Strict it might be, but life in the Kindred Youth Scholam was preferable to the alternative outside in the tracts. Existence in the wastelands west of the hive offered a lean choice: scavenge like an animal, or bond into a gang. Either way, life expectancy was miserably low. Municipally-sponsored scholams, offering a bed, food and a basic education that emphasised the values of the Throne, represented an escape route. Reasonably healthy, lice-free, qualified youngsters could leave such institutions with a real prospect of securing an apprenticeship to one of the hive guilds, a journeyship, or at least a decent indenture.

Patience had been at the scholam for twelve years, which meant she was twenty-two or twenty-three years old and by far the oldest pupil registered at that time. Most pupils left the care of the charity around their majority, when their age gave them a legal identity in the eyes of the guilds. But Patience had stayed on because of her sisters. Twins, Providence and Prudence were fifteen, and Patience had promised them she would stay and look after them until they turned eighteen. It was a promise she'd made to her sisters, and to her dying mother, the day their mother had brought the three of them to the scholam and asked the tutors to take them in.

Patience was not her birth name, no more than Prudence's was Prudence or Providence's Providence. They were scholam names, given to each pupil at their induction, symbolic of the fresh start they were making.

Except for Patience, few pupils were made to suffer the oubliette. She had now been in there nineteen times.

On this occasion, she was in for breaking the nose of Tutor Abelard. She'd punched the odious creep for criticising her work in the laundry. The crack of cartilage and the puff of blood had been very satisfying.

Cooling down, in the dark, Patience recognised that it had been foolish to strike the tutor. Just another mark against her record. For this, she was missing the graduation supper taking place in the vaults many floors up. There was an event like it every few months, when distinguished men of consequence – guild masters, merchants, manufactory directors and mill owners – came to the scholam to meet and examine the older pupils, making selections from the best and contracting apprenticeships. By morning, Patience knew, many of her long-term friends would have left the scholam forever to begin new lives in the teeming stacks of Urbitane.

The fact was, she'd been there too long. She was too old to be contained by the scholam, even by the hardline rigorists, and that was why she kept running into trouble. If it hadn't been for her promise, and her two, beloved sisters, she'd have been apprenticed to a hive mill long since.

Something bristly and locomoting on more than four legs scuttled across her bare hand. With a twitch of her gift, she hurled it away into the dark.

Her gift. Only she had it. Her sisters showed no sign of it. Patience never used her gift in front of the tutors, and she was fairly certain they knew nothing about it.

It was a mind thing. She could move things by thinking about them. She'd discovered she could do it the day her mother left them at the scholam gates. Patience had been practising ever since.

In the dark of the black stone cell, Patience tried to picture her mother's face, but couldn't. She could remember a warm smell, slightly unwashed but reassuring, a strong embrace, a hacking cough that presaged mortality.

The face, though, the face…

It had been a long time. Unable to form the image in her head, Patience turned her mind to something else. Her name. Not Patience. Her real name. The tutors had tried to rid her of it, forcing her to change her identity, but she still hung on to it. It was the one private piece of her that nothing and no one could ever steal. Her true name.

It kept her alive. The very thought of it kept her going.

The irony was, she could leave the oubliette whenever she chose. A simple flick of her gift would throw back the bolt and allow her to lift the trapdoor. But that would give her away, convince the tutors she was abnormal.

Patience reined her mind in and sat still in the darkness.

Someone was coming. Coming to let her out.

IV

HARLON NAYL's EYES didn't so much as blink as the fist came at him. His left hand went out, tilting inwards, captured the man's arm neatly around the inside of the wrist, and wrenched it right round through two hundred degrees. A bone may have snapped, but if it did, the sound was masked by the man's strangled squeal, a noise which ended suddenly as Nayl's other hand connected with his face.

The man – a thickset lhotas-eater with a mucus problem – shivered the deck as he hit it. Nayl kept hold of his wrist, pulling the man's arm straight and tight while he stood firmly on his armpit. This position allowed for significant leverage, and Nayl made use of it. Harlon was in a take-no-prisoners mood, I sensed, which was hardly useful given our objective.

A little leverage and rotation. A ghastly scream, vocalised through a face spattered with blood.

'What do you reckon?' asked Nayl, twisting a little more and increasing the pitch. 'Do you think I can get top C out of him?'

'Should I care?' replied Morpal Who Moves with mannered disinterest. 'You can twist Manx's arm right off and beat him round the head with it, he still won't tell you what you want. He's a lho-brow. He knows nothing.'

Nayl smiled, twisted, got another shriek. 'Of course he is. I worked that much out from his scintillating conversation. But one of you does. One of you knows the answer I want. Sooner or later his screams will aggravate you so much you'll tell me.'

Morpal Who Moves had a face like a crushed walnut. He sat back in his satin-upholstered buoy-chair and fiddled with a golden rind-shriver, a delicate tool that glittered between his bony fingers. He was weighing up what to say. I could read the alternatives in his forebrain like the label on a jar.

'This is not good for business–'

'Sir, this is my place of business, and I don't take kindly to–'

'Throne of Earth, who the frig d'you think you are–'

Morpal's place was a four-hectacre loading dock of iron, stock-brick and timber hinged out over the vast canyon gulf of the West Descent, an aerial thoroughfare formed by the gap between two of the hive's most colossal stacks. Beneath the reinforced platform and the gothic buttresses that supported it, space dropped away for almost a vertical kilometre to the base of the stacks. Ostensibly, this was a ledge where cargo-flitters and load-transporters – and many thousands of these craft plied the airways of the West Descent – could drop in for repairs, fuel, or whatever else the pilots needed. But Morpal was a fence and racketeer, and the transience of the dock's traffic gave him ample opportunity to steal, replace, backhand, smuggle and otherwise run his lucrative trade.

More than twenty men stood in a loose group around Harlon. Most were stevedores and dock labourers in Morpal's employ. The others were flit-pilots, gig-men, hoy-drivers and riggers who'd stopped in for caffeine, fuel and a game of cards, many of them regulars who were into Morpal for more than a year's salary each.

All this and more was visible from their collective thoughts, which swirled around the loading dock like a fog. I was five kilometres away, in a room in a low-rent hotel. But it was all clear enough. I knew what Mingus Futir had eaten for breakfast, what Fancyman D'cree had stolen the night before, the lie Gert Gerity had told his wife. I knew all about the thing Erik Klass didn't want to tell Morpal.

Wystan Frauka sat beside me, smoking a lho-stick, his limiter activated. He was reading a tremendously tedious erotic novel on his slate.

Surface was easy. Deep mind was harder. Morpal Who Moves and his cronies were well-used to concealing their secrets.

That was why Harlon had gone in first.

Morpal finally arrived at a decision. He had determined, I sensed, to take the moral high ground. 'This is not how things are done on my platform,' he told Harlon. 'This is a respectable establishment.'

'Yeah, right,' snorted Nayl. 'One last time. What can you tell me about Victor Zhan? He worked here once, before he went off planet. I know he worked here, because I had the records checked out. So tell me about Victor.'

'Victor Zahn hasn't been around in five years,' Morpal said.

'Tell me about him anyway,' Nayl snapped.

'I really don't see any reason to do that.'

'I'll show you one.' Nayl reached his free hand into his hip pocket, took something out and threw it down onto the cup-ringed, grimy tabletop. His badge of authority. The signet crest of the Inquisition.

Immediately all the men took a step beck, alarmed. I felt Morpal's mind start in dismay. This was the kind of trouble no one wanted.

Unless...

'Damn it,' I said.

Frauka looked up from the midst of his book's latest loveless tryst. 'What's up?'

'Morpal Who Moves is about to make a miscalculation.'

'Oh dear,' said Frauka, and turned back to his novel.

Morpal had run the dock for forty-six years. For all his misdeeds and misdemeanours, some of them serious, he'd never run foul of the law, apart from the odd fine or reprimand. He actually thought he could deal with this and get away with it.

+Harlon. Morpal's signal will be a double finger-click. Your immediate threat is the grey-haired gig-man to your left, who has a dart-knife. To his right, in the leather apron, the rigger has a pivot-gun, but he will not be able to draw it as fast. The flit-pilot in green wants to prove himself to Morpal, and he won't hesitate. His friend, the one with the obscura-tinted eyes, is less confident, but he has a boomgun in his cab.+

'Well?' Harlon Nayl asked.

Morpal Who Moves clicked both middle fingers.

I flinched at the sudden flare of adrenaline and aggression. A great part of it came from Nayl.

The rigger in the leather apron had drawn his pivot-gun, but Nayl had already stoved the table in with the face of the grey-haired gig-man and relieved him of his dart-knife. Nayl threw himself around as the pilot in green lunged forward, and slam-kicked him in the throat. The pilot went down, choking, his larynx crushed, as the pivot-gun finally boomed. The home-made round whipped high over Nayl's head as he rolled and triggered the dart-knife. The spring-propelled blade speared the rigger through the centre of his leather apron, and he fell over on his back, clawing at his belly.

Others ploughed in, one striking Nayl in the ribs with an eight wrench. 'Ow!' Nayl grunted, and laid the man out. The obscura fiend was running across the platform towards his hoy. Nayl threw another man aside, and grabbed the edges of Morpal's buoy-chair. The Mover yelled in dismay as Nayl slung the frictionless chair sideways. It sped across the platform like a quoit, knocking two of the stevedores over, and slammed hard against the dock's restraining rail. The serious impact dazed Morpal. He slumped forward.

Nayl backfisted a man in the nose, and then punched out another who was trying to flee anyway. Two front teeth flew into the air. The obscura fiend had his hoy's door open, reaching in.

A stevedore with a hatchet swung at Nayl, forcing him to jump back. Nayl blocked the next swing with his forearm, fractured the man's sternum with a jab, and threw him with a crash into the nearby row of porcelain samovars.

The obscura addict turned from his cab and racked the grip of his boomgun. He brought it up to fire.

Nayl slid the Hecuter 10 from his bodyglove and calmly shot him through the head at fifteen metres.

Blood splashed up the rusted fender of the hoy. The man cannoned backwards, dropping the boomgun from dead fingers.

The rest of them scattered.

Kara ran onto the platform, her weapon raised. It had taken her just thirty seconds to move out of cover at my command to back up Nayl, but the fight was already done.

'Don't leave any for me, then,' she complained.

'You should have been here,' Nayl said. He walked over to the rig and picked up the fallen boomgun, examining it.

'Nice,' he said.

+Harlon...+

Nayl looked over at Morpal, who was just coming round, the back of his buoy-chair rammed against the platform's rail. He saw Nayl, saw him aiming the weapon...

+Harlon! No!+

But Nayl's blood was up. The need for vengeance, suppressed for so long, was finally finding an outlet.

Nayl fired. Morpal had ducked. The shot exploded the seat-back above him, and the rail behind. The force of the impact drove the buoy-chair backwards.

Intact, unscathed, but still sitting in his chair, Morpal Who Moves went backwards, toppled, and fell into the inter-stack gulf.

'Well, damn,' Nayl hissed.

+For Throne's sake, Nayl! I told you not to–+

Thonius had just walked into the hotel room behind me.

'Good book?' he asked Frauka.

'Saucy,' Frauka replied, not looking up.

+Nayl's just ruined our lead.+

'Never mind,' Thonius grinned, a smug satisfaction on his face. 'It was pointless anyway. I've found a much better one.'

V

SHE KNEW FOR certain it was Rigorist Knill even before he opened the oubliette hatch. Just part of her gift, the same thing that allowed her to win at cards or guess which hand a coin was in.

'Come, you,' he said. A glow-globe coded to Knill's bio-trace bobbed at his shoulder and cast its cheap yellow light into the cell.

Patience got up and stepped out into the hallway, making a big show of dusting down her garments.

'They'll be dirtier yet,' Knill remarked, closing the heavy, black iron door. 'The dinner's over, and the Prefect wants the pots doing.' Knill chuckled and pushed her on down the hallway. The glowglobe followed obediently.

There was little to like about Rigorist Knill. In his days as an Imperial Guardsman, he had been big and powerful, but age and a lack of exercise had sunk his muscles into slabby fat, hunching him over. His teeth were black pegs, and a scarred, concave section of his skull explained both the end of his soldiering career and his simpleton's nature. Knill was proud of his past, and still wore his medal on his chest. He liked to regale the pupils with accounts of the glorious actions he had seen, and got angry when they mocked him and pointed out inconsistencies in his stories. But he wasn't the worst by a long way. Skinny Rigorist Souzerin had such a short temper and love of the flail that the pupils believed he had once been a commissar. Rigorist Ocwell was rather too fond of the younger girls. And then there was Rigorist Ide, of course.

'So I'm to wash pots?' Patience asked.

'Get on,' Knill grumbled, and gave her a cuff. Like all the rigorists, Knill wore a knotted leather flail and a longer wooden baton suspended from his wide leather belt. The flail was for minor punishments, the baton a more serious disciplinary tool. Knill, who trusted his fists, seldom used either. Many of Prefect Cyrus's long morning sermons revolved around the symbology of the rigorists' twin instruments, likening them to the paired heads of the holy aquila, voices of different pitch and measure through which the dogmas of the Golden Throne might be communicated in complementary ways. In the Kindred Youth Scholam, most lessons seemed to require some corporal component.

They ascended the draughty stone stairs, and passed through the unlit lesson halls of the seventh remove. The narrow hallways between class-rooms were formed by partly-glazed wooden partitions. The glass in the frames was stained the colour of tobacco by the passage of the years.

Then Knill unlocked the door to the next ascent.

'I thought I was wanted for scullion duties,' Patience said.

'The Prefect would clap eyes on you first,' replied Knill, and jerked his head upwards.

Patience sighed, and began to trudge up the winding stairs ahead of Knill's light. She knew what that meant. A quiz from the Prefect on the error of her ways. If she was lucky, she'd get away with an apology to Tutor Abelard, and a few *Lachrymose Mea* in the chapel under the Prefect's instruction before she spent the night in the potroom, freezing her hands in the greasy sop-tubs.

If she was unlucky, there would be Souzerin and his flail. Or Ide.

It took them over twenty minutes to climb the meandering tower to the upper vaults. In the main chamber there, servants and a few chosen pupils were clearing the last dregs of the feast. The air was still warm, and scented with rich cooking smells. Prefect Cyrus did not stint when important visitors came to the scholam. He even provided wine and amasec, and did not complain when manufactory directors lit up pipes and lho-sticks. Patience could smell the spicy smoke lingering in the long room. Two young pupils form the sixth remove were team-folding the white cloths from the feast tables. A tutor, Runciman, was supervising them, and explaining the geometry of the correct fold-angles.

'Wait,' Knill told her, and left her in the doorway. He shambled off down the length of the long, beamed hall, his light tagging along after him like a willowisp. Patience waited, edgy, arms folded. Three young children ran out past her, their arms full of candlesticks, napkin rings threaded around their tiny wrists. One glanced up at her, eyes wide.

Knill reached the far end of the room. Prefect Cyrus was sitting at the high table still, a swell-glass in his hand, talking quietly with a stranger in a dark red robe. One of the night's visitors, a guilder or a mill owner per-haps. Clearly a man of wealth and breeding, well-groomed. He was listening to the Prefect intently, sipping something from a tall crystal beaker. To his left, apart from the conversation, sat another man, another stranger. This man was short, but powerfully made, his cropped hair ginger in the lamplight, his bodyglove traced with silver. He was smoking a lho-stick, and gazing with half-interest at the ancient, flaking murals on the chamber walls. From her vantage point, Patience could see the ginger-haired man wore an empty holster on his hip. Prefect Cyrus did not permit firearms inside the scholam, but that holster suggested the ginger-haired man was a bodyguard, a paid protector. The man in red was evidently even more important than she had first suspected, if he could afford his own muscle.

Then Patience saw Ide. The rigorist was standing at the far end of the chamber, waiting. He was staring right at her. She shuddered. Tall, strong, Ide was a brute. His eyes were always half-open, and he wore his white-blond hair in a long, shaggy mane, secured at the nape by a silver buckle. Ide was the only rigorist who never bragged about his Guard days. Patience had a nasty idea why.

Knill spoke briefly to the prefect, who excused himself to the man in red, and walked down to the centre of the hall, Knill at his heels. The Prefect gestured that Patience should come join him. She approached obediently, until they were face to face.

Prefect Cyrus was anything between forty and four hundred. Slim and well-made, he had undergone many programs of juvenat work, making his flesh over-tight and his skin hideously smooth and pink. His eyes were violet and, Patience believed, deliberately sculpted by the augchemists to appear kind and fatherly. His blue robes were perfectly pressed and starched. When he smiled, his implanted teeth were as white as ice.

He was smiling now.

'Patience,' he whispered. She could smell the oil of cloves he wore to scent his body.

'My Prefect,' she answered with effort.

'You flinch. Why do you flinch?'

She could not say it was because Rigorist Ide had just taken the first few steps on his way to join them. 'I broke the rules, and committed an affront to the person of Tutor Abelard. I flinch as I await my punishment.'

'Patience,' the Prefect said. 'Your punishment is over. You've been set in the oubliette, have you not?' He looked round at Knill. 'She has been in the oubliette all night, hasn't she, Knill?'

'That is so, Prefect,' replied Knill with a nod.

'All done, then. No need to flinch.'

'Then why am I here?' Patience asked.

'I have good news,' the prefect said, 'and I wanted to share it with you as soon as possible. Good, good news, that I'm sure will lift your heart as surely as it has lifted mine.'

'What is it?'

'Patience, places have been secured this night for your dear sisters. Serving in the hall this evening, they so won the admiration of a merchant lord, one of our guests, he offered them indenture on the spot.'

Patience blinked. 'My sisters?'

'Have taken wing at last, Patience. Their particulars are all signed and contracted. Their new life has already begun.'

'No. That's not right,' Patience said sharply. 'They're too young. They haven't yet reached majority. I won't allow it.'

'It is already done,' the Prefect said, his face showing no sign of annoyance.

'Then undo it,' Patience said. 'Right now! Undo it! I should've been consulted! They are in my charge!'

'Patience, you were detained in the oubliette, for your own wrongdoings. I decided the matter. Your sisters are already long departed, and I trust you will wish them well in your prayers this night.'

'No!' she shouted.

'Shut your hole!' warned Knill, stepping forward, his light bobbing after him.

'No need for that, Knill,' said Cyrus. The Prefect gazed at Patience. 'I am rather surprised by your response, Patience. I had thought you would be pleased.'

She glowered at him. 'You cheated me. You knew I wasn't around to object. This is wrong! They are too young–'

'I tire of this, Patience. There is no rule or law that says girls of your sisters' age may not be contracted. Such an agreement is in my power.'

'It isn't! You can only authorise a contract of employ in the case of an orphan lacking the appropriate blood-kin! That's the law! I've only stayed here this long to supervise their well-being! You bastard!'

'Take her away, Knill,' said the Prefect.

'Don't even think about it, Knill,' Patience warned. 'I want his name, Cyrus. The name of this man who has taken my sisters.'

'Oh, and for what good?'

'I am of majority. I can leave this stinking tower whenever I choose. Give me the name… now! I will find him and secure the release of my sisters!'

Prefect Cyrus turned to Knill. 'Another period in the oubliette, I feel.'

'Yes, sir.'

'Oh, no,' said Patience, backing away. 'You can't touch me now. Not now. I've stuck by the scholam's frigging rules this long, one way or another, for the good of my sisters, but you have no hold on me! I am an adult, with the rights of an adult! Go frig yourself, Cyrus, I'm leaving!'

'Double the period for that vile language!' Cyrus barked.

'Double this, stink-breath!' Patience cried, making a gesture one of the pot-boys had taught her.

Knill lunged at her, arms wide. She ducked sideways, putting a little of her gift into the kick she slammed at the old soldier's belly. Knill lurched away and crashed into a table, knocking pewterware onto the floor, anxiously steadying himself against the table's edge in surprise.

Somehow, Ide had got behind her. The blow from his baton, swung two-handed, caught her across the back of the skull and dropped her to her hands and knees. Patience blacked out for a brief moment, and blood streamed out down her nose onto the flagstones. She felt Ide's big hand crush her left shoulder as it grabbed her.

'Never did live up to your name,' she heard Ide murmur.

Her name. Her *name*. Not Patience. The one little piece of her life she still owned entirely.

Ide was swinging the baton down again to smack her shoulders. She froze his hand. Ide gasped, sweating, terrified, as an invisible force slowly pulled his powerful arm back and drew the baton away from her. She let it smash Ide in the face.

He staggered back with an anguished cry, blood spurting from his mangled nose. Then she was up, on her feet, flicking her head back hard so that the blood from her nose spattered out in a shower. Knill was coming for her. So was the Prefect. Someone was crying an alarm.

Patience looked at Knill and he flew backwards through the air, slamming into the table again so hard it went over with him. She looked at Cyrus, and snarled as she simultaneously burst all the blood-vessels in his face. He fell down on his knees, whimpering.

'You bastards!' she was screaming. 'My sisters, you bastards!'

Ide swung at her again. He was crazy-mad now, trying to kill her. Patience held out a hand and Ide went sprawling over on his back... and continued to slide down the length of the hallway until his skull crashed into the stone doorpost.

Rigorist Souzerin had appeared from somewhere, his flail raised as he ran at her. Knill was clambering to his feet.

Patience ducked Souzerin's first slash, then hurled him backwards a few steps with a twitch of her mind. She was getting tired now. Knill thundered forward.

'I'll take that,' Patience said, and ripped the medal from Knill's tunic with a mental flick. She slapped her outspread palms against Knill's dented skull and blasted him away into the murals. The ancient plasterwork cracked under the heavy impact and Knill fell limp onto the floor.

Souzerin came in again. Knill's medal was still hanging in the air. Patience whipped it around and buried it in Souzerin's cheek. He fell down with a wail of pain, blood pouring from the long gouge.

'I've seen enough,' said the man in the red robe.

The ginger-haired man rose to his feet and turned off his limiter.

Patience shrieked as her gift went away completely. It was as if her strength had been shut off. A hard vacuum formed and popped in her soul. She had never met an untouchable before.

Staggering, she turned. The ginger-haired man came towards her, his hands open and loose.

'Let's go, darling,' he said.

She threw a punch at him. She felt so weak.

He caught it, and hit her in the face.

The blow seemed effortless, but she fell hard, barely conscious. The ginger-haired man leaned over and pinched a nerve point that left her paralysed.

Blind, helpless, she heard Prefect Cyrus being helped back onto his feet.

'You were right, Cyrus,' she heard the man in red say. 'An excellent subject. An unformed telekine. The gamers will pay well for this. I have no objection to meeting your price of ten thousand.'

'Agreed, Loketter,' the Prefect sniffed. 'Just… just get her out of my sight.'

VI

CARL THONIUS WAS patently pleased with himself. 'Consider the names again. Victor Zhan. Noble Soto. Goodman Frell. The forenames are all names, yes, but they're also all simple, virtuous. The sort of solid, strong, aspirational names a highborn master, for example, might give to his slaves.'

'These men were slaves?' Kara asked.

'Not exactly,' said Carl. 'But I think they're all *given* names. Not birth names.'

Carl had a particular talent in the use of cogitators and logic engines. Since our arrival, he had spent many hours in the census archives of Urbitane. 'I've been tracing the file records of all three men. It's laborious work, and the records are, no tittering at the back, incomplete. The names are officially logged and genuine, but they are not connected to any local bloodlines. Soto, Zhan and Frell are all common names here on Sameter, but there is no link between any of these men and any family or families carrying those names. In other words, I believe they chose the surnames themselves. They chose common local surnames.'

'Fake identities,' Nayl shrugged. 'Not much of a lead then.'

'Says the man who pushed our last decent lead off a kilometre high ledge,' Carl mocked. Nayl gave him a threatening look, and the interrogator shrugged. 'No, not fake identities. The evidence points to the fact that all three men were orphans, probably from the slums. They were raised in a poorhouse or maybe a charitable institution, where they were given their virtuous forenames. On leaving the poorhouse, as young adults, they were obliged to choose and adopt surnames so that they could be registered on the citizenry roll and be legally recognised.'

'Odd that he employed three men with the same background,' Kara said. She could not bring herself to utter Molotch's name.

'Curious indeed,' I agreed. 'Carl, I don't suppose you managed to identify the institutions that raised them?'

'Throne, you don't want much do you?' Carl laughed. He beamed, like a conjuror showing off a sleight-of-hand marvel. 'Of course I did. And they all came from the same one. A darling little place called the Kindred Youth Scholam.'

Nayl left the hotel room almost immediately and headed off to scare up some transport for us. For the first time in months, I felt my team moving with a sense of focus, so refreshingly different from the blunt-edged vengeance that had spurred them since Majeskus. Carl deserved praise. He had diligently uncovered a trail that gave us refined purpose once again.

We had been so squarely and murderously outplayed by the heretic Zygmunt Molotch. I had been pursuing him for a long time, but at Majeskus, he stopped running and turned to face me.

The ensuing clash, most of which took place aboard my chartered starship, The *Hinterlight*, left over half the crew dead. Amongst them, trapped by Molotch's malicious evil, were three of my oldest, most trusted retainers: Will Tallowhand, Norah Santjack and Eleena Koi. Badged with their blood, triumphant, the bastard Molotch had escaped.

I had lost friends before. We all had. Serving the ordos of the Holy Inquisition was a dangerous and often violent calling. I myself, more than most, can vouch for the cost to life and limb.

But Majeskus was somehow a particularly searing blow. Molotch's assault had been ingeniously vicious and astoundingly callous, even by the standards of such vermin. It was as if he had a special genius for spite. I had vowed not to rest until I had found him again and exacted retribution in full.

In truth, when I came to Sameter, I do not think I was an Imperial inquisitor at all. I am not ashamed to admit that for a brief while, my duty to the God-Emperor had retreated somewhat, replaced by a more personal fire. I was Gideon Ravenor, burning to avenge his friends.

The same, I knew, was true of my four companions. Harlon and Kara had known Eleena Koi since their days together in the employ of my former master Eisenhorn. Harlon had also formed a particular bond of friendship with the mercurial Will Tallowhand. In Norah Santjack, Thonius had enjoyed the stimulating company of a mind as quick and clever as his own. There would be no more devilish games of regicide, no more late-night debates on the respective merits of the later Helican poets. And Thonius was yet young. These were the first comrades he had lost in the line of duty.

Even Wystan Frauka was in mourning. Louche and taciturn, Frauka was an unloved, unlovely man who made no friends because of his untouchable curse. But Eleena Koi had been an untouchable too, one of nature's rare psychic blanks and the last of Eisenhorn's Distaff. There had been a relationship there, one neither of them ever chose to disclose, presumably a mutual need created by their shared status as outsiders, pariahs. He missed her. In the weeks after Majeskus, he said less than usual, and smoked all the time, gazing into distances and shadows.

Aboard the hired transport – a small, grey cargo-gig with whistling fan-cell engines – we moved west through the hive-city. Carl linked his dataslate to my chair's input and I reviewed his information concerning the scholam.

It had been running for many years, ostensibly a worthy charity school struggling to provide housing and basic levels of education for the most neglected section of Urbitane's demographic. There were millions, nay billions, of institutions like it all across the Imperium, wherever hives rose and gross poverty loomed. Many were run by the Ecclesiarchy, or tied to some scheme of work by the Departmento Munitorum or the Imperial Guard itself. Some were missionary endeavours established by zealous social reformers, some political initiatives, some just good, four-square community efforts to assist the downtrodden and underprivileged.

And some were none of those things. Carl and I inspected the records of the Kindred Youth Scholam carefully. On the surface, it was respectable enough. Its register audits were a matter of public record, and it applied for and received the right grants and welfare support annually, which meant that the Administratum subjected it to regular inspection. It was approved by the Munitorum, and held all the appropriate stamps and marques of a legitimate charitable institution. It had an impressive portfolio of recommendations and references from many of Urbitane's worthies and nobles. It had even won several rosettes of distinction from the Missionaria.

But scratch any surface…

'You'll like this,' said Carl. 'The Prefect, he's one Berto Cyrus. His official file is spotless and perfectly in order. But I think it's a graft.'

A graft. A legitimate dossier that has been expertly designed to overfit previous records and eclipse them. Done well – and this had been done brilliantly – a graft would be more than adequate to bypass the Administratum. But we servants of the holy ordos had greater and more refined tools of scrutiny to bring to bear. Carl showed me the loose ends and rough edges that had been tucked away to conceal the basic deception, the long, tortuous strands of inconsistency that no one but the Inquisition would ever think to check, for the effort would be too labour-intensive. That was ever the failing of the Imperium's monumental Administratum. Overseeing hives the size of Urbitane, even an efficient and ordered division of the

Administratum could only hope to keep up with day to day processing. There was no time for deeper insight. If one wanted to hide something from the Imperial Administratum, one simply had to place it at the end of a long line of diversions and feints, so far removed from basic inspections that no Administry clerk would ever notice it.

'He's older than he pretends to be,' said Carl. 'Far older. Here's the give-away. Three digits different in his twelve digit citizenry numeric, but changed here, at birth-registry date, where no one would ever go back to look. Berto Cyrus was actually a stillborn infant. The Prefect took over the identity.'

'Which makes him?'

'Which makes him eighty-eight years older than his record states. And therefore makes him, in fact, Ludovic Kyro, a cognitae-schooled heretic wanted on five worlds.'

'Cognitae? Throne of Earth!'

'I said you'd like it,' Carl smiled, 'and here's the other thing. Its implications are not very pleasant.'

'Go on.'

'Given the scholam's throughput of pupils over the years, very, very few are still evident in the city records.'

'They've disappeared?'

'That's too strong a word. *Not accounted for* would be a better term. The ex-pupils have dropped off the record after their time at the scholam, so there's no reason anyone scrutinising the school's register in an official capacity should question it. Pupils leave, sign up indentures, contracts, hold-employs, but then these documents lead nowhere.'

'From which you deduce what?' I asked, though I could see Carl had the answer ready in the front of his mind.

'The scholam is a front. It's... laundering children and young adults. Raising them, training them, nurturing them, and then moving them as a commodity into other hands. The fact that the pupils are known only by their scholam names means that they can be slipped away unnoticed. It's quite brilliant.'

'Because they take in anonymous children, give them new identities to provide them with legal status, and then sell them on under cover of perfectly correct and perfectly untraceable paperwork?'

'Just so,' said Carl.

'What do they do with them?' I wondered.

'Whatever they like, would be my guess,' said Wystan, glancing up from his tawdry book. I hadn't even realised he'd been listening. 'Those three we're tracking, they ended up as hired guns, probably because they were handy in that regard. Strong guys get muscle work. Pretty girls...'

'Whatever else we do,' I said, 'we're closing that place down.'

* * *

VII

THE CELL WAS a metal box and smelled of piss. The ginger-haired man opened the hatch and dragged Patience out. She tried to resist, but her limbs were weak and her mind muddy. The ginger-haired man still had his limiter off.

His name was DaRolle, that much she had learned, and he worked for a man called Loketter.

'On your feet, darling,' DaRolle said. 'They're waiting for you.' He prodded her along the dim hallway. Patience didn't know where she was, but she knew it was at least a day since she had been taken from the scholam by these men.

'It's Patience, right?' the ginger-haired man said. 'Your trophy name?'

'My what?'

'Trophy name. The scholam gives you all trophy names, ready for the game. And yours is Patience, isn't it?'

'Where are my sisters?' she asked.

'Forget you ever had any.'

Loketter, the man in red, was waiting for them in a richly appointed salon at the end of the hallway. There were other men with him, all distinguished older males just like him, sitting around on couches and buoy-chairs, smoking lho and sipping amasec. Patience had seen their type so many times before at graduation suppers. Men of wealth and status – mill owners and merchants, shipmasters and guilders – and Patience had dreamed of the day when one of them would select her for service, employment, a future.

How hollow that seemed now. For all their grooming, for all their fine clothes and fancy manners, these men were predators. The scholam which she had trusted for so long had simply been their feeding ground.

'Here she is,' smiled Loketter. The men applauded lazily.

'Still in her scholam clothes,' a fat man in green said with relish. 'A nice touch, Loketter.'

'I know you like them fresh, Boroth. Her name is Patience, and she is a telekine. I'm not sure if she realises she is a telekine, actually. Do you, my dear? Do you know what you are?'

Loketter addressed the last part of his question at her. Patience flushed.

'I know what I am,' she said.

'And what is that?'

'Trapped amongst a bunch of perverts,' she said.

The men laughed.

'Oh, such spirit!' said Boroth.

'And pretty green eyes too!' said another man, swathed in orange furs.

'The wager is seven thousand crowns per half hour of survival,' Loketter announced.

'Very high,' said the man in furs. 'What is the area, and the jeopardy?'

'Low Tenalt,' replied Loketter, and several of the men laughed. 'Low Tenalt,' Loketter repeated. 'And the jeopardy is the Dolors. Although, if she's nimble, she might make it to Pennyraker territory, in which case the wager increases by another hundred and fifty.'

'How many pawns?' asked a tall, bearded man in a selpic blue doublet.

'Standard rules, Vevian. One per player. Open choice. Body weapons only, although I'll allow a gun per pawn for jeopardy work. Guns are not to be used for taking the quarry, as I have no need to remind you. Gunshot death or disintegration voids the game and the pot goes to the house.'

'Observation?' asked a thin man in grey robes.

'Servo-skull picter, as standard. House will supply eight. You'll each be allowed two of your own.'

'Will she be armed?' Boroth asked.

'I don't know. Would you care to chose a weapon?' Loketter asked Patience.

'What is the game?' she replied.

More laughter.

'Life, of course,' Loketter said. 'A weapon, Patience? DaRolle, show her.'

The ginger-haired man walked over to a varnished hardwood case set on a side table, opened it and revealed the numerous polished blades and exotic killing devices laid out on the velvet cushion.

'Choose, darling,' he said.

Patience shook her head. 'I'm not a fighter. Not a killer.'

'Darling, if you're going to live for even ten minutes, you'll have to be both.'

'I refuse,' said Patience. 'Frig you very much, "darling".'

DaRolle tutted and closed the case.

'Unarmed?' Boroth said. 'I'll take the wager, Loketter. In fact, I'll double you.'

'Fourteen taken and offered,' Loketter announced.

'Taken,' said a man in pink suede.

'I'm in,' said the bearded man Loketter had called Vevian.

Four of the others agreed too, opening money belts and casket bands and tossing piles of cash on the low, dished table at Loketter's feet. In ten seconds there was a thousand times more money in that baize bowl than Patience had ever even imagined.

'Begin, ' Loketter said, rising to his feet. 'Pawns to the outer door for inspection and preparation. Drones will be scanned prior to release. I know your tricks, Boroth.'

Boroth chuckled and waved a pudgy hand.

'The game will commence in thirty minutes.' Loketter walked over to face Patience. 'I have great faith in your abilities, Patience. Don't let me down. Don't lose me money.'

She spat in his face.

Loketter smiled. 'That's exactly what I was looking for. DaRolle?'

The ginger-haired man grabbed Patience by the arms and marched her out of the room. They went down a maze of long, brass tunnels and finally up some iron steps into what seemed like a loading dock or an air-gate.

'Go stand by the doors, darling,' he said.

'What happens now?' Patience asked.

'Now you run for your life until they get you,' DaRolle said.

Patience put her hands against the rusted hatchway, and then pulled them away as the hatch rumbled open.

She didn't know what to expect when she looked out. Beyond the hatchway, the shadowy wastes of the slum-tracts stretched away into the distance.

'I won't go out there,' she growled.

DaRolle came up behind her and shoved her outside. Patience fell into the dirt.

'Word of advice,' called the ginger-haired man. 'If you want it, anyway. Watch for the Dolors. They use the shadow. Don't trust black.'

'I don't t–' Patience began.

But the hatch slammed shut.

Patience got to her feet. Gloom surrounded her. A hot, stinking wind blew in through the nearby ruins, smelling of garbage and city rot.

Somewhere, something whooped gleefully in the darkness. A lifter rumbled overhead, its lights flashing. When she turned, she saw the immensity of the hive filling the sky behind her like a cliff, extending up as far as she could see.

She started to run.

VIII

THERE WAS SOMETHING wrong with Prefect Cyrus's face: a blush of burst blood vessels that even careful treatment with a medicae's dermo-wand had failed to conceal. He was trying to be civil, and was clearly impressed by his visitor's apparel, but he was also put out.

'This is irregular, I'm afraid,' he fussed as he led them into a waiting room where Imperial teachings were writ in gold leaf on the darkwood panels. 'There are appointed times for inspection, and also for appren-ticeship dealings. Take a seat, won't you?'

'I apologise for the difficulties I'm causing,' Carl replied. 'But time is rather pressing, and you came highly recommended.'

'I see,' said Cyrus.

'And I have… resources to make it worth your while.'

'Indeed,' smiled Cyrus. 'And your name is?'

'I'd prefer not to deal in names,' Carl smiled.

'Then perhaps I should show you out, sir. This is a respectable academy.'

Sitting cross-legged on the old couch, his fur-trimmed mantle turned back over his shoulder to expose the crimson falchapetta lining, Carl Thonius beckoned with one gloved hand to Kara, who stood waiting in the doorway. Kara was robed and cowled like some dumb servitor, and carried a heavy casket. As she approached, Carl leaned over and flipped the casket lid open.

'Lutillium. Twenty ingots, each of a weight of one eighth. I'll leave it to you to calculate the market price, Prefect.'

Cyrus licked his lips slightly. 'I, ah… what is it you want, sir?'

'Two boys, two girls. No younger than eleven, no older than thirteen. Healthy. Fit. Comely. Clean.'

'This is, ah…'

'I'm sorry, I'm being very direct,' said Carl. 'I should have said this before. This is a matter of *the most pleasant fraternal confidence.*'

'I see,' said Cyrus. Carl had just used one of the cognitae's private recognition codes, by which one graduate knew another. 'I'll just see what's taking those refreshments so long to arrive.'

The Prefect bustled out of the room and hurried down a gloomy hallway to where Ide was waiting.

'Bring the others in,' Cyrus whispered to him. 'Do it quickly. If this is on the level, we look to earn well. But I have a feeling.'

Ide nodded.

In the waiting room, Carl sat back and winked at Kara.

+The Prefect's suspicious.+

'Really?' Carl said softly. 'And I thought I was bringing such veracity to the part.'

+Get ready. Nayl?+

Harlon Nayl grunted as he drove another crampon into the crumbling outer brick of the tower's side, and played out his line to bring him closer to a ninth floor window. A terrible updraft from the stack-chasm below tugged at his clothing.

'Ready enough,' he replied.

+Harlon's in position. Carl? You can do the honours.+

'Thank you, sir,' he whispered. 'It'll be a pleasure.'

Cyrus came back into the room, smiling broadly. 'Caffeine and cusp cake is just on its way. The cake is very fine, very gingery.'

'I can't wait,' Carl said.

+They're closing in. Four now arriving at the west door. Three on the stairs behind Kara. Two more approaching from the floor above. All ex-Guard. Armed with batons. And I read at least one firearm.+

Carl rose to his feet. 'Oh, Prefect? There is one other thing I did want to say.'

'And that is?' asked Cyrus.

Carl smiled his toothiest smile. 'In the name of the Holy Inquisition, you motherless wretch, surrender now.'

Cyrus gasped and began to back away. 'Ide! Ide!' he screamed.

Kara hurled the casket and it slammed into Cyrus's midsection, felling him hard. He grunted in pain and several of the heavy ingots scattered across the floor.

+Move!+

Kara threw off her drab robe and flew forward as the first rigorist came in through the doorway. Guns were forbidden in the scholam, but that didn't prevent this man from carrying one. Weapon scanners around the entry gate screened visitors for firearms. But lutillium, apart from its monetary worth, had value as a substance opaque to scanners.

Rigorist Ide raised his handgun as he came in. Kara, on her knees, reached into the fallen casket and produced the Tronsvasse compact hidden between the layers of ingots.

'Surprise,' she said, and buried a caseless round in his forehead. The rear part of Ide's skull burst like a squeezed pimple and he fell on his back.

She got up, shot the sprawled Cyrus once through the back of the thigh to make sure he wasn't going anywhere, and swung to face the door. The next two rigorists burst in on Ide's heels, batons raised, and she shot out their knees. Thonius winced and covered his ears.

In the hall outside, the other rigorists backed in terror from the sound of gunfire. Then a shaped charge blew out the casement behind them in a blizzard of glass and leading, and Harlon Nayl swung into the hallway. He had a large automatic pistol in his left fist.

'Any takers?' he asked.

One ran, and Nayl shot him through the heel. The others sank to their knees, hands to their heads.

'Good lads,' Nayl said. He took a neural disruptor from his belt in his right hand and walked over to them, cracking each one comatose with a fierce zap from the blunt device.

In the waiting room, the air threaded with gun-smoke, Kara turned to face the opposite doors as other alerted rigorists crashed in from the stairs. Knill led them, and didn't even blink at the sight of the small woman with the handgun. He flew at her.

'Ninker!' she complained, and shot him. The round penetrated his torso and didn't slow him. He crashed into her and knocked her flat.

Souzerin and another rigorist named Fewik were right behind Knill. Fewik knocked Carl over with a blow from his baton, and Souzerin raised the battered bolt pistol that he carried since his days in the commissariat. He fired at Kara, but managed only to blow off Knill's left foot and his left arm at the elbow.

Nayl appeared at the opposite door and yelled a warning that Souzerin answered by lifting his aim and blasting at the doorway. Brick chips and wooden splinters exploded from the jamb. Kara reached out from under Knill's deadweight and shot Souzerin up through the chin. The rigorist left the ground for a moment, then crashed back down dead. Nayl reappeared and put a round through Fewik's back as he turned to flee.

Nayl helped Kara out from under the half-dead brute.

'Nobody help me up then,' Carl complained.

Panic had seized the scholam. I could feel it, breathe it. Hundreds of children and young adults, terrified by the explosions and gunshots. And a deeper panic, a deeper dread, that emanated from the minds of the rigorists and tutors.

I hovered towards the main gate, Wystan at my side, and ripped the ancient doors off their hinges with a brisk nudge of my mind. Inside the entrance way, half a dozen tutors and rigorists were running towards us, hoping for a speedy exit.

+I am Inquisitor Ravenor of the holy ordos! Remain where you are!+

I don't think they understood the manner of the command, though several involuntarily defecated in fear as the telepathic burst hit them. All they saw was a lone man approaching beside a strange, covered chair.

+Now!+

My psi-wave threw them all backwards violently, like the pressure blast of a hurricane. Windows shattered. They tumbled over, robes shredding, flying like dolls or desperately trying to grip onto the floor.

Wystan lit a lho-stick. 'What I like about you,' he said, 'is that you don't muck around.'

'Thank you.'

I had switched to vox-ponder and now I activated my built in voxcaster. 'This is Ravenor to Magistratum Fairwing. Your officers may now move in and secure the building as instructed.'

'Yes, inquisitor.'

'Do not harm any of the children.'

IX

I HAD EXPECTED to find many things within the scholam: evidence of abuse and cruelty certainly, damaged souls, perhaps even answers, if I was lucky.

I had not expected to find traces of psyker activity.

'What's the matter?' Kara asked me.

+I'm not sure.+

We moved down the long hallways, past the frightened faces of pupils herded along by the Magistratum officers, past whimpering tutors spread against the old walls as they were patted down for concealed weapons. The traces were slight, ephemeral, fading, like strands of gossamer clinging to the brickwork. But they were there.

+There was a psyker here.+

Kara stiffened.

+Relax. He... no, I believe it was a she. She's not here anymore. But she was here for a long time and she left only recently.+

'When you say a long time, you mean?'

+Years.+

'And when you say recently..?'

+Days, maybe less.+

We explored the tower. For Kara, this was a curious process. She could not see or feel, taste or smell the traces that were so evident to me. She just followed me around, one empty room after another. I could sense her boredom and her frustration. She wanted to be with the others, active, rounding up the last of the scholam's inhabitants.

'Sorry. This must be tedious for you,' I said.

'It's fine,' she replied. 'Take your time. I can be patient. Patience is a virtue.'

'Indeed.' We entered a large dining hall in the upper reaches of the tower. The traces were strongest and freshest there.

'Telekine,' I said. 'I'm in no doubt. A telekine, raw but potentially strong.'

'We have to find her,' Kara said. 'If this damn place really was grooming subjects for the cognitae, she could be a lead. A direct connection to a cognitae procurer.'

Kara was right. Amongst their many crimes, the cognitae prided themselves on recruiting and retaining unlicenced psykers for their own purposes.

'Go and find Carl for me, Kara,' I requested. 'I want to get him working on discovering who this psyker was and where she might have gone.'

'Because of the cognitae link,' she nodded.

'Yes, because of that,' I replied. 'But even if no link exists, we still have to find her. An unsanctioned psyker, lose on Sameter. That cannot be permitted. We must track her down. And dispose of her.'

X

'I'M SORRY,' CARL Thonius said. 'Sir, I'm very sorry.'

The device was very small, no larger than a hearing aid implant.

'I should have searched him right there, but with all the shooting and screaming.'

'Don't worry about it, Carl,' I said.

'I think I will, sir. Everything's blanked.'

The device was a trigger switch, coded to Cyrus's thumb print. An advanced piece of tech. Down on the floor, helpless from the wound Kara had delivered to his leg, Cyrus had plucked this device from his pocket and activated it. And the scholam's entire data archive had been erased.

'Can you recover anything?' I asked.

'It's a fairly comprehensive wipe. I might be able to recode the last few days worth of material. The stuff most recently processed might still exist in the codification buffer.'

'Do what you can,' I advised. Privately, I was annoyed with his lapse. But we had, with the assistance of local law-enforcement, rounded up dozens of tutors and scholam elders, including Cyrus himself. And who could say what the poor pupils themselves might be able to tell us?

Besides, it was hardly surprising. Carl was so poor in circumstances of violence. I don't believe he had ever fired a shot in anger, though he performed well enough in weapons drill.

'I'll get to work, sir,' Carl said. 'I'm so very sorry–'

'So you bloody should be,' Nayl snorted.

'Enough, Harlon!' I rebuked. 'Carl is my interrogator and you will address him with respect.'

'I'll do that,' Nayl replied, 'when he earns it.'

'Do what you can, Carl,' I said. 'But remember, your priority is to find out all there is to know about the unsanctioned psyker they had here. Who she was, where she went. She has to be found and dealt with, quickly.'

'Yes, sir.'

As Carl moved away, the senior magistratum approached. His enforcement officers, clad in black and silver, were still clearing the scholam floor by floor. I could sense his unease. He was an experienced criminologist, but he'd never had his entire station house requisitioned to assist the Inquisition before. He was terrified of screwing up. He was terrified of me.

'Problems?' I asked.

'A few scuffles, sir. You'd rather taken the wind out of their sails.'

'I want all the children to be given medical checks, and then safe-housed until statements can be taken from them all. Inform the Administration that welfare assistance will be required, but not yet. No one is to be rehoused or re-homed unless they've been examined. Why do you frown?'

The magistratum started a little. 'There are over nine hundred children, sir...' he began.

'Improvise. Ask the local temples for alms and shelter.'

'Yes, sir. May I ask... is this an abuse case, sir?'

'Indirectly. I can't say more. The staff I'll interview here, now. I'll need some of your men to assist in guarding them while the interrogations are underway. Once I'm done, I will file charges, and you can begin to process them.'

'Yes, sir.'

'I'll start with the Prefect.'

A magistratum first-aider had patched Cyrus's leg wound, and they'd shackled him to a chair in one of the refectories. He was in pain, and very frightened, which would make it easier to extract information.

Cyrus stared at me as I rolled in to face him. Nayl followed me in, but sat his ominous bulk down at the far end of the long table from Cyrus, a threat waiting to happen.

'I... I have rights,' Cyrus began. 'In the eyes of Imperial Law, I have–'

'Nothing. You are a prisoner of the Inquisition. Do not ask for or expect anything.'

'Then I'll tell you nothing.'

'Again, you are mistaken. You will tell me everything I ask you to tell me. Harlon?'

From the far end of the table, Nayl began to speak. 'His name is Ludovic Kyro, Cognitae-trained, wanted on five worlds for counts of heresy and sedition...'

Cyrus closed his eyes as the words came out. We already knew his true identity. What else did we have?

'Tell me about Victor Zahn.'

Cyrus frowned. 'I don't know a Victor Zhan...' I was watching his mind. It wasn't the truth, but it wasn't an outright lie either. Cyrus didn't immediately recognise the name.

+Tell me about Victor Zahn.+

Cyrus blinked as the telepathy slapped him. My interrogative was accompanied by an image of Zahn's corpse in the *Hinterlight's* morgue which I dropped into his mind like a slide into a magic lantern.

'Oh Throne!' he murmured.

'You know him, then?'

'He was a pupil here, years ago.'

+And Goodman Frell? And Noble Soto?+

Two more graphic images.

'Oh, Holy! They were pupils too. This was years ago. Five or more.'

'And you groomed them,' said Nayl. 'You and your staff. Groomed them like you groom all the poor strays who wind up here. Sold them on.'

'No, this is a respectable place and–'

'So respectable,' I said, 'that you wipe all your records so we can't see them.'

Cyrus bit his lip.

'Zahn. Frell. Soto. Who did you sell them too?'

'T-to a merchant, as I remember.'

Lie. Bald and heavy. And well formed, not just vocally, but mentally too. A layer of mendacity cloaked Cyrus's thoughts, like a cake of dried mud. A mind-trick, one of the many taught by the Cognitae. I had been expecting as much. For all his fear, Cyrus was still a product of that heretical institution, and therefore had to be unlocked with precision. If I'd just burst into his mind telepathically from the outset, I might have damaged or destroyed many of his locked engrams. But now I had a solid lie out of him, and that lie revealed the way his mind-shields worked: their focus, their strengths, their inclination.

'Who did you sell them too?'

'I told you, a merchant. A free trader.'

+Who?+

He squealed as the psi-jab rattled his mind. He was utterly unprepared for the sharpness of it.

'That was a demonstration of how things will be if you resist,' I said. 'Now I'm going to ask the question once more...'

XI

PATIENCE HEARD THE buzzing, not with her ears but with her mind, and slid into cover behind a crumbling rockcrete wall. Moments later, a varnished human skull hovered past through the gloom. Tech implants decorated the back of its cranium, and lights shone in its hollow orbits. A sensor drone, sweeping for her. She'd heard the bastards talking about them before her release. This was the first physical proof that men were actually after her.

Men. Hunters. Killers.

The skull hovered on the spot for a moment, circled once, and then sped away into the shadows. Patience stayed low. After another minute, a second drone – this one built around the skull of a dog or cat – skimmed past and made off in another direction.

She slowed her breathing, and deliberately encouraged her mind to do the sort of tricks that usually happened unbidden. She reached out. She could feel the area around her in a radius of ten metres, forty, sixty. The shape of the geography: the sloping trench to her left, the broken columns ahead, the line of burned-out habs to her right. Behind her, the sewer outfall pouring sludge into a cracked storm drain. She sensed bright sparks of mental energy, but they were just rats scuttling in the ruins.

Then she sensed one that wasn't.

This spark was bigger, human, very controlled and intense. Right ahead, beyond the columns, moving forward.

Moving slowly so as not to dislodge any loose stones, she turned and began to creep away around the storm-drain chute towards a jumble of plasteel ruins. Her left toe kicked a rock and it rolled away off the drain's edge and started to fall. Patience caught it neatly with her mind and lifted it up into the silence of her hand.

The brief delay had been to her advantage. Now she sensed three or four human mind-traces in the ruins ahead of her. Not focused like the other one, feral. In the shadows.

Don't trust the black, that's what DaRolle had said to her. Trouble was, could she trust DaRolle's advice?

She crouched low, and stayed there until she could see them. Ragged human shapes, barely visible, moving like animals through the ruins.

632 Let the Galaxy Burn

Gangers, members of the notorious Dolor clan. She could see three, but was sure there were more. The hunter was closing from the right, now almost at the rockcrete wall.

Patience lifted the rock in her hand and threw it, sending it far further than her arm alone could have managed. It landed in the trench with a loud clatter.

The hunter turned and made for it immediately. She got a glimpse of a man in an armoured jack and high boots scurrying towards the lip of the trench.

Then the Dolors saw him too.

A pivot-gun roared and the hunter was knocked off his feet. The gangers rushed forward at once, baying and yelling, crude blade weapons flashing in their dirty hands.

The hunter's jack had stopped the worst of the ball round. He leapt back up, and shot the closest Dolor through the neck with his handgun. The savage figure spasmed and went down thrashing. Then the others cannoned into the hunter and they all went over into the trench.

Patience started to run. She heard another shot behind her. A scream.

She scrambled over a rusted length of vent-ducting, and dropped into the cavity of a roofless hab…

…where a man was waiting for her.

Patience gasped. There had been no spark off him at all. Either he was shielded, or his mind just did not register to her gift like regular human minds.

He was tall and thin, clothed head to foot in a matt-black, skin-tight body suit. Only his eyes were visible through a slit in the tight mask, but she saw the way the fabric beneath them stretched to betray the smile that had just crossed his face. He held a long, slender spike-knife in each hand.

Patience stretched out with her mind, hoping to push him away, but the tendrils of her gift slipped off his black suit, unable to purchase. He lunged at her, the twin blades extended, and she was forced to dive side-ways, grazing her palms and knees on the rough ground. She started to roll, but he was on her at once, the tip of one blade slicing through the flesh of her left shoulder.

Patience cried out, but the pain gave her strength. She kicked out, and as the man jumped back, she flipped onto her feet. She backed as he cir-cled again. She could hear him chuckle, feel the blood running down her arm.

He lunged again, leading with his right-hand blade. She ducked it, and came out under his arm, but the other blade raked across the back of her right hand as she tried to fend him off. She punched at him. He struck her in the side of the head with the ball of his right hand and knocked her onto the ground.

There was a rushing sound in her head. She thought of her sisters, and the mother she could no longer picture. In desperation, she lashed out with her gift, but the killer's black skin-suit again rendered him proof against her power. It was too slippery. She couldn't get hold of anything except–

The man stumbled backwards in surprise as the knives flew out of his hands. He might have been armoured against a telekine, head to toe, but his blades were good, old-fashioned solid objects.

Patience pulled them both in until they were slowly orbiting her body as she rose. It would the matter of a moment to toss them both away out of the hunter's reach.

But she had a much better idea.

With a bark of effort, she drove them point-first towards his eye-slit and nailed his skull against the back wall of the hab.

XII

CARL THONIUS KNOCKED on the refectory door and waited for a response. From inside, the oddly modulated screams and yelps of Prefect Cyrus shivered the air. As he waited, Carl glanced round at the four magistratum troopers guarding the hallway. They were clearly unnerved by the strange sounds of human pain echoing from the refectory. Carl smiled breezily, but got no response. He knocked again.

The screams ebbed for a moment, and the door flew open. Nayl peered out.

'What?' he spat.

'I need a word, dear fellow. With the boss.'

'Don't "dear fellow" me, frig-face. Is this important? He's busy!'

'Well,' Carl stammered. He was always edgy when he had to deal with the big ex-bounty hunter. 'It is, sort of.'

Nayl sneered. 'Sort of doesn't cut it.' He slammed the door in Carl's face.

Carl cursed and knocked again. Nayl threw the door back open.

'Don't do that,' Carl snapped. 'Don't treat me like that–'

'Oh, go away you frig-wipe…'

Carl looked Nayl in the eyes. 'Know your place, Nayl. You may not like me, but I am his interrogator. I want to see him now.'

Nayl looked Thonius up and down. 'Balls after all,' he said, grudgingly. 'Okay.'

Carl walked into the room. Cyrus was slumped forward in his chains, wheezing, blood leaking from his tearducts. Kara sat on a chair just inside the door, her face grim.

'Carl?' I said softly. 'This isn't really time for an interruption.'

'Sir, I've been trying to recover the lost data. The erased data. There's really not much to get back, I'm afraid. I doubt we'll ever find out what happened to most of the poor children laundered through this place.'

'Your incompetence could have waited,' Nayl said.

'Stop ragging on him, Nayl,' Kara hissed.

Carl shot Nayl a dark look. I could tell there was something more.

'I told you I might be able to recode the last few days worth of material. Uh, recently processed material still existing in the codification buffer.'

'Yes, Carl.'

He cleared his throat. 'There was one item there. A record of a transaction made two nights ago. An older female pupil named Patience. Groomed by these bastards partly because of her spirit, and mostly because she was a latent telekine.'

I swung round to face him. 'Are you sure?'

'Yes, sir.'

'A telekine?'

He nodded. 'The recoding is pretty clear. I think she was the psyker you were looking for.'

'Did you say her name was Patience?' Kara asked quietly.

'Yes, why?' Carl replied. She shrugged. She was holding something back.

'Kara?' I nudged.

'It's nothing,' she said. 'Just, when you were looking around, for traces of her, you thought I was bored and I said–'

'Patience is a virtue,' I finished.

Kara nodded. 'Yeah, Patience is a virtue. Spooky.'

'Coincidence,' Nayl muttered.

'Believe me, Harlon,' I said, 'in the length and breadth of this great Imperium of Man, there is no such thing as coincidence. Not where psyk is involved.'

'Duly noted,' he replied, not caring or believing.

'Where did this Patience go, Carl?' I asked.

'She was sold for ten thousand to a narcobaron cartel who purchased her for use in a game they like to play.'

'A game?' I asked.

'The record implies this is not the first subject the scholam has sold to the cartel for this purpose. I say game, it's more sport. They release the purchased child into the slum-tracts and then... then they gamble on how long he or she will survive. Once they send their hunters out.'

'So what?' asked Nayl. 'They'll clean up our little psyk-witch loose end without us having to break a sweat. '

'If the records are true,' I warned. 'Consider this. There might be a game. There might be a narcobaron with a taste for barbaric gladiatorial sport. On the other hand, all those things might be a substitution code to conceal an act of purchase to a Cognitae procurer.'

'I actually don't know which would be worse,' Kara said.

I turned back to Cyrus. He whined as my mind re-entered his. He was still weak and reeling from our initial session, and by rights I should have left him a while to be sure of getting accurate responses. But there was no time. An unsanctioned menace was loose somewhere, or already leaving the planet under close watch.

I tried a few key phrases – 'the psyker', 'the telekine', 'Patience' – pushing them at his mind in the way a child rams shaped blocks at a box, hoping to find the right hole to fit. He responded with various recurring words: *Loketter, the game, trophy worth…*

I wasn't sure how hard to push. I wasn't sure if I was slamming him back against the limits of truth, where there is nowhere left for sanity to go, or simply meeting some form of substitution. Substitution was another standard Cognitae mind ploy. Anticipating psychic interrogation, the brotherhood mnemonically learned to replace the details of true memories with engrammatic euphemisms. *Narcobaron*, for example, could stand for *procurer*. *Game* might stand for *purpose*. It was a simple but almost unbreakable deceit. Well-schooled, a Cognitae brother could mask memories with metaphors. He could not be caught out in a lie, because he wasn't lying. The truth had been erased and replaced with other facts. Using such techniques, a member of the brotherhood might withstand the most serious psyk-scrutiny, because the truth was no longer there to uncover.

'He's giving me nothing,' I cursed, turning away. 'Unless it is the truth. Do you have an active lead, Carl?'

Thonius nodded.

Kara got to her feet. 'Let's go and find her,' she said. 'If the story's real, I mean if there is this frigging barbaric game actually going on, there's a girl out there who really, really needs help right now.'

'Throne! Let her die!' Nayl barked. 'Frigging psyker! What? What?' Kara and Thonius were already heading for the door.

'One life, Harlon,' I said as I slid past him. 'I learned many things from Eisenhorn, but ruthlessness was not one of them. Thousands may die, millions even, unless Molotch is found and brought to justice. But any count of a million starts with one, and to ignore one life when there is still a chance of saving it, well, one might as well give up on the other nine hundred and ninety-nine thousand nine hundred and ninety-nine as well.'

'Whatever,' said Nayl.

'Thank you for your vote of confidence,' I said. 'Kara, inform the magistratum that these interviews are suspended until we return.'

XIII

THE ARMOURED MANSE did indeed belong to the man named Loketter, and nineteen counts of narco-traffic were outstanding on his name. The manse was a brass mushroom that dominated a long slope of rubble scree above the shadowland of the slum-tracts. Down here, with the monolithic bulk of Urbitane behind us, the immensity of the urban squalor and ruin was shocking to see.

The manse was ferro-armoured, and shielded, but our scanners lit with the buzz of electromag activity inside.

'Signals!' Kara reported. 'They're running drones out into the slum.'

'Can you track them?' I asked.

'Working…' She adjusted some dials. 'I've got a lock on nine. Covering a hex-grid twelve by ten. Map comparison… Throne, these archives are so old! Here we go. An area known as Low Tenalt.'

'Details?'

'Serious slum-land,' Carl said, speed-viewing the data on his codifier. 'Basically wreckage. High probability of gang activity. Territorially, the gangs are the Dolors and, to the west, the ruin-burbs are run by the so-called Pennyrakers. Magistratum advice is to avoid this area.'

'Really?'

Carl shrugged. 'Magistratum advice is a blanket "avoid the slum-tracts", so what the hey?'

'How far?' I asked.

At the helm of the cargo-gig, Nayl consulted the gyro-nav built into the stick. 'Eight spans to the Low Tenalt area from here, on boost.'

'Do it,' I said.

'You don't want to level this manse first?' Nayl asked.

'They can wait. This girl can't.'

Nayl nodded reluctantly, and hit the boosters. He wasn't in this like the rest of us were. Running low, like a pond-fly skating the surface, we zipped through the ruined landscape, skipping rubble heaps, ducking under shattered transit bridges, running fast and low along the brick-waste gouges that had once been hab-streets.

Everything was a grey gloom, caught in the immense shadow of the city. Such ruin, such endless ruin…

'Coming up, point three,' reported Nayl, hauling on the stick. The engines whined shrill. 'Two… one… setting down.'

The gig thumped and slithered as it settled on the loose brick.

Carl, Nayl and Kara were already up, arming weapons.

'Sit down, Carl,' I said. 'I need you to run scope from here.'

'Oh,' he said.

'I want full scanner input,' I said as I hovered towards the opening hatch behind Kara and Harlon. 'Wystan can watch your back.'

'You're going yourself?' Wystan asked, surprised. It was one of the few times I'd ever heard emotion in his voice.

'Yes,' I said.

Kara and Harlon looked at me.

'Yes, I'm coming with you,' I said. 'Have you got a problem with that?'

'It's just–' Kara began.

'You don't usually…' Nayl finished.

'This isn't usually,' I said, and powered out past them into the chilly gloom.

Nayl leapt out after me, his Urdeshi-made assault gun cinched high around his broad frame. Kara paused and looked back at Wystan and Thonius. 'Lock the door,' she grinned. 'And don't open it unless you know it's us. Even then, keep your powder dry.'

She jumped out, raised her Manumet 90 riot gun, and ran to join us.

Carl swallowed. Wystan Frauka got up, and locked the hatch shut. He looked at Carl, lit yet another lho-stick and patted the handgun tucked into his belt. 'I got your back, Carly,' he said.

'Great,' said Thonius. He turned to regard the sweeping screens of the scanner and adjusted his vox mic.

'Getting this?' he called.

'Loud and obnoxiously clear,' Nayl crackled back.

'A ha ha. Funny. Not. Move west, two hundred metres, then head north along the axis of the old fuel store. The drones seem to be gathering there.'

'Thank you, Carl,' I responded.

We moved through the wasteland. It was one of the few times my state allowed me speedier and quieter access than my able-bodied friends. Nayl and Kara followed, clambering over the dunes of rubble.

'See anything you like?' Kara said.

'I don't frigging believe we're doing this,' Nayl grumbled.

'Move left. Left!' Carl's voice rasped over the vox. 'I've got drones moving now. Gunshots.'

'I heard them,' Nayl said, and started away to the left.

'Flank him wide, Kara,' I said, and she moved away in the opposite direction.

'Throne,' I heard Carl say. 'I think we were right. I think this is some kind of frigging game.'

I propelled myself forward. Both Kara and Harlon were out of sight now, though I could sense them just fifty metres away, each side of me.

The twisted ruins of the tracts rose up on left and right. I tasted life-signs.

'Hello?' I transponded.

The Dolors appeared out of the gloom. Ragged, emaciated, filthy, feral. There were twenty of them.

Blackened teeth bared in wild grins. They raised their cudgels and spears and charged.

'Your mistake,' I said.

* * *

XIV

THE BARONS WERE laughing. Most of them were drunk, or out of their heads on lhotas and obscura.

DaRolle looked up from the drone relay.

'Have we got the bitch yet?' Boroth demanded.

'You wish,' DaRolle said. He walked across the lounge and crouched down beside Loketter.

'What?'asked the man in red.

'New players just entered the game,' DaRolle said.

Loketter sat up. 'Show me.'

DaRolle held out his data-slate. 'Three on the ground. A gig too, grounded there.'

'What the hell is this?'

'Problem, Loketter?' asked Vevian.

Loketter rose and smiled. 'Not a problem, but a bonus element to our game today. Look at your scans. See? Newcomers.'

'Who the frig are they?' Gandinsky blurted.

'Interlopers,' Loketter said. 'House will pay two thousand for each one killed. Firearms permitted.'

The intoxicated crowd applauded this energetically.

Loketter looked at DaRolle. 'The ones on the ground I can get these fools to mess with,' he whispered. 'You go and fry up this gig.'

'Yeah?'

'Yeah. Find out who these fools are. Then burn it and every one on it.'

DaRolle nodded. 'Pleasure,' he said.

XV

PATIENCE WAS STILL running. The Dolors, invisible in the shadows but everywhere now, were jeering and caterwauling, their strangled cries echoing around the ragged walls and shattered windows.

They were calling out to her, taunting her, abusing her with obscene words and suggestions, many of which, thankfully, were so choked by the gang-argot they made no sense.

Occasionally, stones or pieces of trash came flying out of the darkness at her, and she deflected all those she could. Some found her, especially the stinging stone bullets launched from catapults and slings.

Her instinct was to head back towards the colossal city, but no matter how much ground she managed to cover, it seemed not to get any closer. Its sheer scale made the distance hard to judge. It was probably kilometres away still.

She reached the ruins of a manufactory, its ply-steel roof collapsed. Seas of garbage and rubble spread out from its eastern side, and she began to pick her way across the weed-choked waste. Behind her, she could hear the gangers scurrying through the manufactory ruins. A few missiles flew out after her.

A figure suddenly appeared ahead of her, across the sea of trash. A small male, or perhaps a female, who'd been down in cover behind the remains of a yard wall, hidden by a chameleon cloak. Glancing up, Patience cursed as she saw a hunter drone that had obviously been shadowing her for several minutes.

Patience changed course, and began to run away from the figure. She ran wide across the overgrown trash. The figure started to follow, trying to cut her off, running hard, but neither made particularly good going. The trash and rubble was so uneven, so treacherous. Patience kept tripping, stumbling, turning her ankles.

As soon as the hunter appeared, the jeering from the invisible Dolors grew more ferocious. Catapult missiles and even the occasional arrow whipped out from the manufactory at the hunter.

The hunter – and it was clearly a female – stopped in her tracks, and produced an autopistol. She slammed in a clip and fired three times at the manufactory.

The shells must have been high-ex, because each impact went up like a grenade. Sections of the manufactory ruin blew in, and the Dolors went very quiet suddenly.

Patience was still running. The hunter put the gun away and resumed the chase.

A second drone zoomed into view suddenly, circled Patience once and then headed for the hunter. The woman stopped again, looking round frantically as she reached for her sidearm. Patience half-heard her shout a question into her vox-set.

There was a loud crack, a peripheral flash of light, and the female hunter jolted suddenly as a las-round went clean through her torso. She crumpled without a sound.

Her killer appeared, directly ahead of Patience. She skidded to a halt. He was big, and wore segmented plating over a coat of green hide. A glowing augmetic implant covered one eye. He had a las-carbine in his hands.

He stared at Patience for a moment, then put the carbine away in the leather boot over his shoulders. Then he drew a large dagger with a twisted black blade and took a step towards her.

'Make it easy now, and I promise you won't feel nothing,' he said.

Patience was breathing hard from the running. It made it easier some-how to summon up her gift. The man thought the first couple of stones that came flying at him were from the gangers, but then more came, and more, larger rocks, pieces of trash, chunks of garbage. Debris started showering off the ground all around her, whipping at him.

He cried out, shielding his face with his hands, and backed away. She heard him cry again, in pain, as a greasy lump of broken-off machinery hit him in the chest. He staggered, trying to fend the blizzard away. Then a piece of cinder block caromed off the side of his head, and he fell down on his knees, holding his head. Two more large rocks struck his face and forehead, and he slumped over entirely.

Patience sighed, and the rain of trash subsided, pieces bouncing off the ground as they landed. Silence.

She gave the body one last look, and started to run again. Behind her, in the manufactory, and all along the outer fence line, the invisible gangers started to whoop and holler again.

XVI

I HAD JUST seen off a second assault by the slum-gangers when I felt the telekinetic burst. Fierce, unfocused, not too far away.

'Turn west,' I voxed.

'Understood,' Kara responded.

'I read that,' came Nayl. 'I just heard bolter fire from that direction too.'

I slid through the ruins, my mind wide open. There were psi-traces all around me, at least a dozen as close as fifty metres. Most were the feral impulses of the hidden Dolors. But there. One other. Harder.

Two las-rounds struck the front of my chair and fizzled off harmlessly. I found the hunter as he was about to fire again, and picked him up. He yelled in fear as he left the ground, dragged up into the air ten metres, twenty. Then I let him go.

I didn't even bother to watch him land. The sharp light of his mind went out abruptly.

'I heard shots,' Kara voxed. 'Are you all right?'

'Fine,' I replied. 'Kara, it is a game. An obscene hunting game. We have to find this girl, whatever she is, before they do.'

'Understood. Absolutely.'

Kara was about a third of a kilometre away to my right.

'I've got a drone active in your vicinity,' Carl told her over the link.

Kara acknowledged, and glanced around. That was when the two hunters, twins clad in silver-grey skin sleeves, pounced. One pinned her arms from behind, the other came at her with a chain-fist. She rolled her body back, using the man pinning her as a back-brace, and bicycle-kicked the other in the face. He went over in the rubble, rolling.

But the man pinning Kara from behind rammed forward and head-butted her in the back of the skull.

+Kara!+

Even at that distance, I felt her pain and sensed that she had blacked out. They'd have her gutted before she could come round.

I knew I had no choice. I had to ware her. It wasn't something she – or anyone else I knew – enjoyed, but it was necessary. Besides, we had trained for this. Kara Swole was a particularly receptive candidate.

The wraithbone pendant around her neck lit up with psychic-energy. Kara's body suddenly animated again, but it was me moving her. I had taken her physical form over, put it on like a suit of clothes.

Blank-eyed, Kara's body twisted hard and broke the pinning hold. She tore clear, landed well, and swept out the legs of the hunter with the chain-fist so he went over on his backside.

Then she turned, raising a forearm block against the other's attack, following the block with two rapid jabs to his face and a side-stamp that caught and dislocated his right knee.

He howled in pain. Kara/I grabbed his flailing arms and swung him bodily around right into his partner, who was returning to the fight for the second time.

The partner's forward-thrust chain-fist, which had been sweeping at Kara/me met the ribs of his fellow hunter instead. The whirring bite-blades of the gauntlet weapon punched clean through the man's side in a shocking welter of blood and torn tissue. He screamed as he died, his whole body quivering in time to the rending vibrations of the glove's cycling blades.

His partner and accidental killer screamed too: in outrage and horror at what he had just done. He wrenched the glove out, but it was too late. His twin, a huge and awful excavation yawning in the side of his torso, stopped quivering and dropped. A film of blood covered everything in a five metre radius.

Berserk, the remaining hunter hurled himself at Kara/me. We leapt, boosted by a touch of telekinesis, and executed a perfect somersault over his head.

He swung around. But by then Kara/I had grabbed up her fallen riot gun. Her puppet hand racked the slide. A single, booming shot blew the hunter backwards eight metres.

We heard a sound behind us, and turned, bringing the pumpgun up.

'Steady!' Nayl warned.

'What are you doing here?' Kara/I demanded.

'You were in trouble, Kara!' he said. 'I heard it over the vox. I came as fast as I could.'

'What about the girl? What about the girl we're looking for?'

Nayl shrugged. 'Kara?'

'No, it's me, dammit!' I said with Kara's voice. 'Catch her for Throne's sake, I'm coming out.'

Nayl hurried forward and took Kara's limp form into his arms as I ceased waring her. She was semiconscious, and the trauma of being a ware subject would leave her disorientated and sick for a good while.

+Guard her, Harlon. In fact, get her back to the transport.+

'Where are you going?' he asked the empty air.

+To find the girl.+

* * *

CLOSED BACK INTO the womb-like nowhere of my support chair, I impelled it forward again, trying to reacquire the raw psychic-pulse I'd felt before. I felt edgy. Having to ware someone was a curious thing to deal with, and the feelings always left me conflicted. I was aware that the subject loathed the sensation, and it was also most usually done in moments of extremis, involving violence and furious levels of adrenaline. But for me it was a brief delicious escape, a cruel reminder of what I had lost. I despised myself for deriving pleasure from such painful, demeaning moments.

+Carl?+

'Yes, sir?'

+Do you have a fix on me?+

'Yes, sir. I've got two more drone tracks about half a kilometre ahead, converging. Please hurry, sir.'

+I'm hurrying.+

Back in the gig, Carl looked up from his scanner displays, fidgeting with his cuffs nervously. He looked at Wystan, who was reading his dataslate again.

'Don't you care?' Carl asked.

The untouchable nodded at his book 'It's just getting interesting.'

Outside, DaRolle scurried forward, keeping low behind a half-fallen wall. He checked the area, unshipped his laspistol, and deactivated his limiter.

Then he began to run, head down, towards the parked transport.

XVII

HER BREATHING WAS coming in short, sharp bursts. Patience had run as hard and as fast as she could. There was at least one person very close to her now, but the psychic-trace was faint and hard to place. She was worn out, exhausted, and her gift was weak from over use.

She clambered down into a cavity behind a ruined pumping station, crawling into a cave formed by the overhang of the fallen roof. She curled up against the back wall, her arms around her knees. Outside, the Dolors were still jeering and shouting, but it was more distant now.

She'd gone as far as she could. Now it was just a matter of waiting. Waiting for the end.

+Patience.+

She started, and looked around, not daring to speak.

+Patience. Stay calm. Stay where you are. I'm coming to help you. I want to help you.+

'Where are you?' she hissed in fear.

+Don't speak. They'll hear you. Think your answers.+

'What do you mean? Where the frig are you?'

+Don't be scared. Try not to speak aloud. They'll hear you.+

'This is another trick. You're one of them! One of the frigging hunters!'

+No. Patience, my name is Gideon. I swear by the God-Emperor himself I mean you no harm. I'm trying to help you. You're hearing me because I am speaking directly to your mind, psychically.+

'You lie!'

+Try me. Think of something I couldn't know.+

Patience closed her eyes and moaned softly.

+Prudence. And Providence.+

She gasped.

+Your sisters. You're worried about them. They were taken… wait… yes, they were taken from the scholam. Without your consent.+

'Just kill me, you bastard, or leave me alone!'

+Please, Patience, don't speak. They'll hear you.+

I was moving fast now. The jagged ruins of the slum-tracts slid by me on either side. Rocks and catapult bullets occasionally clattered off my chair's armour. Where was she? Where was she?

+Patience? Can you still hear me?+

'Leave me alone!' she sobbed, crawling deeper into the damp cavity. 'I can't do this! I can't do this any more!'

+Yes, you can! Just keep it together! Focus! Focus on something!+

Patience twisted in panic, clawing at the sides of her head. I was scaring her. My voice. Something about my voice. Not just the fact that it was coming, disembodied, into her mind. Something else.

What?

As I steered my chair out across a long sea of trash and debris, I gently peered into her mind, into the panic and turmoil. Into the fear.

I saw it. It was my voice itself. I sounded like a middle-aged, well-educated male. Reasonable, polite, refined. Exactly the sort of man who had betrayed her entire life, her fellow pupils, her sisters. I saw she had formed a picture of me already. It was part Cyrus, part Ide, part Loketter, part some ginger-haired man. It was all of these, blended into one monster.

Immediately, I switched the focus of my telepathy.

+Kara?+

I found her at once, bleary and sick. Nayl was helping her along a rubble ledge back towards the gig.

'What?' she asked.

+I'm sorry, Kara, but I need to ware you again.+

'Throne, no!' she whimpered.

'She's had enough, boss,' Nayl said.

+It's important. Really important. I need her voice.+

Kara looked at Nayl and nodded wearily. He caught her as her wraithbone pendant flashed and she fell.

I left her body limp in Nayl's arms, and put on her personality like a skin-suit. My psychic-voice became Kara Swole's soft, reassuring tones.

+Patience?+

'What? What?'

+Patience, my name is Kara. My good friend Gideon has asked me to talk to you. Time is very short, Patience, and you need to listen to me if you want to stay alive. Trust Gideon. Do exactly as I say.+

I could feel the girl giving way to panic.

+Patience, focus! Hold on! There must be something you can hold onto! Something you can hold onto so you can keep going! Your sisters, maybe? Your mother? Patience?+

She had found it at last. It was something so small and dark and hard in her mind that even my telepathy could not unlock it. She held onto it, tight, tight, as the dark closed in.

Her panic waned. Her breathing slowed. I was close now. I could reach her.

Patience opened her eyes. A skull, eyes bright, hovered at arm's reach in front of her, gazing at her. A drone.

I was too late. She had made too much noise.

The hunters had found her.

XVIII

'THRONE!' CRIED CARL, leaning back from his auspex station in alarm. 'What the hell did you do?'

'I might have broken wind,' admitted Wystan Frauka. 'Sorry.' He turned back to his book.

'Check your limiter, dear boy,' Thonius demanded.

'Why?'

'Why? I was just listening in, and Ravenor suddenly went off-line!'

'The vox?'

'The vox is still live! I mean his telepathic link just scrambled! Was that you?'

Wystan Frauka frowned and put down his data-slate. He checked his device. 'No, it's on. I'm blocked.'

'Then what?'

'Relax, Carly. I'll take a look.'

'Please–' Carl began

Frauka patted the handgun in his belt again. 'I told you, I've got your back.'

'No, it's just… could you not call me "Carly"?'

Frauka frowned. 'Okay. What about "Thony" then?'

'No!'

Frauka held up his hands. 'All right. Throne! I was just being pally. The boss said I was too aloof. Too aloof, can you believe it? He suggested I should try being more friendly. He said it would help with team building, and–'

'Frigging hell, Frauka!'

'What? Emperor's tits, you guys are so uptight! I'll go look! I'll go look! I got your back, remember?'

Frauka turned. DaRolle's laspistol was aimed directly at his face. The ginger-haired killer grinned.

'On a side note,' Frauka said, 'it would have been nice if you'd got my back too, Carly.'

XIX

'OUT!' SAID THE hunter in grey-scale armour. He gestured with his double-bladed harn knife. Patience got up, and slowly came out of the pumping station cavity. The hunter's drone circled her, purring softly.

'Gonna fight?' he asked.

She shook her head.

'Good girl. Step out here.'

She came out.

The hunter keyed his vox-link. 'This is Greyde. I've got her. Game's done. Tell Loketter that my master Vevian will want his winnings in small bills, so he can pay me off nice and handsome.'

The hunter looked at Patience. 'Why are you smiling?'

'No reason.'

He settled his grip on the alien blade. 'Sure you're not thinking of trying something dumb? I'd hate that. It'd make me take a lot longer with you.'

'I won't fight,' Patience said.

'Good.'

'Because Kara told me I didn't have to any more.'

'Who? Who's Kara?'

'The girl who told me her friend was coming. She told me to have patience, because patience is a virtue.'

The hunter, Greyde, looked around edgily. 'No one here but us, girl. No sign of any friend of yours.'

Patience shrugged. 'He's coming.'

A wind picked up, stirring the dust and the grit around them, billowing the filth up in swirling clouds. Like an exhalation from the sumps of the towering city.

Except it wasn't.

Larger pieces of trash lifted and fluttered through the air. Pebbles rolled on the ground. It was like a hurricane was gathering over the slums.

No hurricane.

Alarmed, Greyde grabbed the girl, viced her neck with one powerful arm, and raised the harn blade to deliver the kill-stab.

+Kuming Greyde. I know you. I know everything about you. I know the nine counts of murder that you are wanted for, and the fifty-seven other killings you have on your clammy soul. I know you killed your own father. I know you understand only hard cash and killing.+

'What? What?' the hunter wailed in terror as the tempest of wind engulfed him and his prey.

+I don't carry cash. No pockets. I guess it's going to be killing then.+

I turned on my chairs stablights, so I became visible as I ploughed in through the tumult of dirt and dust. The hunter screamed, but the dust choked him. Gagging, he threw Patience aside, and drew his Etva c.II plasma cannon, a pistol-sized weapon more than capable of burning clean through my armoured chair.

Staggering, half-blinded, he aimed it at me.

With a simple tap of my mind, I fired my chair's psi-cannon. The hunter's corpse slammed back through the wall of the pumping station. Even before it had hit the wall, every bone in that body had been pulped by concussive force, every organ exploded.

The wind dropped. Grit pattered off the sealed body of my chair.

+Patience?+

She got up. I wasn't using Kara Swole's voice any more.

+Are you all right?+

She nodded. She was singularly beautiful, despite the dirt caking her and the tears in her clothing. Tall, slender, black-haired, her eyes a piercing green.

'Are you Kara's friend?' she asked.

+Yes.+

'Are you Gideon?'

+Yes.+

She stepped forward, and placed her right hand flat on the warm canopy of my support chair. 'Good. You don't look anything like I imagined.'

XX

'So, WE'RE DEAD? Yeah, of course we are,' Frauka said softly.

'You'd be dead already,' replied DaRolle. 'I just wanted to find out which bastard was running you. Who is it? Finxster? Rotash? That'd be right. Rotash always wants a slice of the boss's game-play.'

'Neither, actually,' Frauka smiled.

'Frauka…' Carl began, terrified. He'd backed away as far as the gig's scan-console would allow, and even then knew there was no hope. This killer had them both cold. Carl wondered where he'd left his weapon. The answer – 'in the cabin lockers' – did not cheer him up.

'Who, then?'

'You won't know him. His name's Ravenor.'

DaRolle sniffed. 'Never heard of the frig.'

'Untouchable?' Frauka asked, casually indicating the limiter around DaRolle's throat.

'Uh huh. You too?'

Frauka smiled. 'Made that way, so help me. Still, the pay's decent. Always someone who needs a good blunter, right?'

'I hear that,' DaRolle grinned.

'Oh well,' Frauka sighed. 'Do me a favour, okay? Make it clean and quick. Back of the head, no warning.'

'Sure.'

'I mean, one blunter doing a favour for another? We gotta stick together, right, even if we are working for rival crews?'

'No problem,' said DaRolle.

'Okay,' Frauka said, and turned his back. 'Any time you like.'

DaRolle aimed his pistol again.

'I don't suppose...' Frauka began. Then he shook his head. 'No, I'm taking the piss now.'

'What?' asked DaRolle.

'Yeah, what?' Carl squeaked in frozen terror.

'One last stick? For a condemned man?'

DaRolle shrugged. 'Go on.'

Frauka took out his lack, set a lho-stick to his lips and lit it with his igniter. He breathed in the smoke and smiled. 'Oh, tastes good. Real mellow. Want one?'

'No,' said DaRolle.

'Real smooth,' said Frauka, inhaling a long drag. 'These things'll kill you, you know.'

'I wouldn't worry about that,' DaRolle smiled.

'I don't frigging believe this!' Carl whined.

'Hey,' said Frauka, glancing over his shoulder. 'Why don't you do him now while I'm smoking this baby? Save time. I never did like him.'

'Oh Throne!' Carl cried out and fell into a foetal position under the console.

'Frig, what a baby!' DaRolle laughed.

'Tell me about it,' Frauka said. He stubbed out his smoke. 'Okay, ready.' He held up the squashed butt. 'Know what that was, my friend?'

'Don't tell me,' smirked DaRolle. 'Best smoke of your life?'

'No,' said Frauka quietly. 'It was delaying tactics.'

DaRolle swung round. The hulking shape of Harlon Nayl filled the hatch behind him. Nayl's Hecuter 10 boomed once.

'Everyone alive?' Nayl asked, stepping in over the twisted body of the ginger-haired man.

'Saw you approaching on the scanners,' Frauka said. 'Thought I'd keep him talking.'

Carl Thonius got to his feet, shivering with anger and fright. 'You're unbelievable, Frauka,' he hissed.

'Thank you, Carl,' Frauka smiled, and sat down with his book again. 'See? Now you're team building too.'

* * *

XXI

I LED THE girl back to the gig, where the others were waiting.

'Hello, Patience, I'm Kara,' Kara said.

'Good to know you,' Patience replied.

By the time we raided Loketter's manse, backed up by a full squad of magistratum troopers, the narcobaron and his cronies had cleared out. There are warrants out for all of them. I understand Loketter is still on the run.

We returned to the Kindred Youth Scholam, and resumed the interrogations. It took several weeks, but by the end of it, I'd wrung some precious facts out of Cyrus and his staff.

There wasn't much. No, that's a lie. There was enough to ensure that Cyrus would face further interrogation at the Inquisition facility on Thracian Primaris, and enough to make sure the scholam's tutors and rigorists would remain incarcerated in the penitentiaries of Urbitane for the rest of their natural lives.

And a lead. Not much, but a start. From Cyrus, just before his mind finally snapped, I learned that Molotch was heading for the outworlds. Sleef, perhaps. Maybe even deeper than that. I instructed Nayl and Kara to provision for what could be a long, dangerous pursuit.

The day before we were due to leave Sameter, I met with Carl in one of the scholam's old, faded classrooms. Most of the staff had been shipped out by then, in magistratum custody.

'Did you trace what I wanted?' I asked.

He nodded. 'It's very little. With the records wiped–'

'What have you got?'

'Pupils Prudence and Providence were sold to a free trader who called himself Vinquies. The name was false, of course. No other records remain, and the name doesn't match any excise log I can get from Sameter Out Traffic.'

'The man himself?'

'There was a picture in Cyrus's mind, and in the minds of several of the other tutors present at the supper, but they're not reliable. I've fed them through both the local magistratum files and the officio itself. Nothing.'

'So… so, they're lost?'

Carl nodded sadly. 'I suppose, if we dedicated the rest of our careers to trying to find them, we might turn up some clue. But in all reality, they're long gone.'

'I'll tell her,' I said, and slid out of the room.

Patience was in the oubliette. By choice. The hatch was open. She sat inside, in the semi-dark, sliding her hands over the stones. She was still wearing her torn and filthy uniform. She'd refused to take it off.

'Patience?'

She stared out at me. 'You can't find them, can you?'

I thought for a moment, and decided it was better to lie. Better a lie now than a lifetime of hopeless yearning.

'Yes, Patience, I found them.'

'They're dead, aren't they?'

'Yes.'

She coiled up, and I felt her hold onto that small black nugget in her mind again.

+Patience.+

'Yes, Gideon?'

+I'm sorry. I truly am. We have to leave soon. I'd like you to come with us.+

'With you? Why?'

+I'll be honest. I can't leave you here. You know about your gift? What it means?+

'Yes.'

+You're a psyker. A telekine. You can't be allowed to remain in public. But I can look after you. I can train you. You could come to serve the God-Emperor of Mankind at my side. Would you like that?+

'Better than an apprenticeship to a mill,' she said. 'Will Kara be there?'

+Yes, Patience.+

'All right then,' she said, and stepped out of the oubliette to join me.

+If you follow me, it will be hard at times. I will demand a lot of you. I will need to know everything about you. What do you think to that?+

'That's fine, Gideon.'

+I'll be asking you questions, probing you, training your gift, unwrapping who you are.+

'I understand.'

+Do you? Here's a test question, the sort of thing I'll be asking you. What was it that you held on to? When the hunters were closing. I felt it as a dark secret part of you, something you wouldn't let go.+

'It was my name, Gideon,' she said. 'My true name, my real name. It was always the single thing my mother gave me that I didn't ever give away to the bastards in this place.'

+I see. That makes sense. Good, thank you for being so honest.+

+Gideon, do you want me to tell you my real name? I will, if you want.+

'No,' I said. 'No, not now, not ever. I want you to hold onto it. It's your secret. Keep it safe and it will keep you sane. It'll remind you what you've come through. Promise me you'll keep it safe.'

+I will.+

'Patience is a fine name. I'll call you that.'

'All right,' she replied, and started to walk down the hallway at my side.

'I'll need a surname, though,' she said at length.

'Choose one,' I replied.

She looked down at the monogram embroidered on her ragged scholam-issue clothes.

'Kys?' she suggested. 'I'll be Patience Kys.'

KILL THEM ALL!

SNARES & DELUSIONS

Matthew Farrer

THE TOWN SURROUNDS the obscenity, and the obscenity is eating the town. It has no name, this elegant pattern of buildings spread out beneath the wind on the dusty green hills. It is an oddity on this world, this town of dove-grey walls which seem to flow up out of the ground, their smooth lines and gentle angles forcing the eye to look in vain for any tool-marks or signs of shaping. Simplicity of shape and complexity of detail, like out-crops growing unworked from the soil, but natural rock could never grow in the delicate mandala of streets and paths, flowing across the hillside in a design so subtle that the eye can take it in for hours before it begins to understand how much the pattern delights.

Even the violence with which the obscenity has torn its way into the heart of the town has not eclipsed the art of its building, not yet. Despite the craters blasted into the buildings, the smoke in the streets, the dead scattered upon the ground, despite whatever invisible thing it is that is withering the grass and trees and silencing the song of the insects – the place still holds scraps of its beauty, for now.

The town has never needed a name. The Exodites speak of it as they ride their fierce dragons to and fro over the steppes and prairies, but they bring its uniqueness to mind without the coining of a label to go on a sign. For all that they are a warrior race of beast-riding and beast-hunting tribes, their language is the silky melody of all eldar and they are able to speak of the one little town on their world, its historians and artisans and seers, without its ever needing a name.

The obscenity is different. It drives its way out of the ground like the head of a murderous giant buried too shallow, buttresses bulging out from its walls like tendons pulled rigid on a neck as the head is thrown back to scream. Black iron gates gape and steel spines give an idiot glint from the parapets and niches. They are not there to defend. The thing leers and swaggers against the landscape in its power, sure that it is above attack. The spikes are there for cruelty, for execution and display. The obscenity is being built not for subjugating but for the pleasure of the subjugation.

It is growing. As small bands of figures grow from dots across the prairie, advance and join up and form into a procession through streets choked with the stink of death, they can see where buildings are being torn down and the earth beneath them ripped up to furnish more rock for the obscenity. There are rough patches, cavities along the side where new chambers and wings will be added, and the procession – the armoured figures gripping the chains, and the slim cloaked shapes staggering beneath the weight of them – passes the crowds of slaves, toiling in the dust, crying and groaning as the obscenity creeps outward and grows ever taller beneath their hands.

The town does not have a name, but the obscenity does. There is no eldar word for this red-black spear of rock, eating the town from within like a cancer, but it bears a name in the hacking, cawing language of the once-human creatures who drive the slaves ever harder to build it. It is called the Cathedral of the Fifth Blessing, and in its sick, buried heart its master is at prayers.

The air in the Deepmost Chapel was torn this way and that by the screams of the thralls, but Chaplain De Haan paid them no mind. The patterns on the warp-carved obelisk seemed to writhe, the lines and angles impossible by any sane geometry, and De Haan's eyes and brain shuddered as he tried to follow them. There had been times when he had relished or loathed the sensation in turn, even times when he had screamed when he looked at the pillar just as their mortal serfs were screaming now. That had been in the early days, when the Word Bearers had taken up the banner of Horus himself and Lorgar had still been crafting the great laws of faith in the Pentadict. Those laws had commanded contemplation of the work of Chaos as part of the Ritual of Turning, and now De Haan was calm as he felt the carvings send ripples though his sanity. *A lesson in self-disgust and abasement,* he had learned in his noviciate. *Realise that your mind is but a breath of mist in the face of the gale that is Chaos Undivided.* It was a useful lesson.

The time for contemplation was at an end, and he rose. The screams from the chapel floor, beneath the gallery where the Word Bearers themselves sat, went on. Although their mortal thralls were being herded out perhaps a dozen remained, those whose minds had not withstood the gaze at the column, who had begun to convulse on the floor and mutilate themselves. The slave-masters began to drag them toward the torturing pens; they would be adequate as sacrifices later. De Haan walked forward to the pulpit, turned to face the ranks of wine-dark armour and horned helms to begin his first sermon on this new world.

The cycle of worship laid down in the Pentadict decreed that sermon and prayers for that hour were to be about hate. There was a certain expectation in the air that plucked a little chord of pleasure at the base of the Chaplain's spine. Of all Lorgar's virtues hatred was the one De Haan prized most, the sea in which his soul swam, the light with which he saw the world. Some of his most beautiful blasphemies had been done in the name of hate. He knew he was revered as a scholar in the field.

The Sacristans moved to the dais below him and reached into the brocaded satchels they carried. They began to array objects on the dais: a banner of purple-and-gold silk tattered and scorched by gunfire in places; a slender eldar helmet and gauntlet in the same colours were set atop it. At the other end of the dais, a delicate crystal mask and a slender sword seemingly made from feather-light, smoky glass, a single pale gem set into the pommel. And beside them, carefully set exactly between the rest, a fist-sized stone, smooth and hard, that shone like a phoenix egg even in the dimness of the chapel. De Haan looked at them, heard the words in his mind: *All will be at an end.*

An exquisite shudder went through his body. He unclenched his right hand from the pulpit rail, gripped his crozius in his left and opened his mouth to preach. And something happened to the Revered Chaplain De Haan that had never happened to him in his millennia as a Word Bearer: he found himself mute.

HIGH CLOUDS HAD turned the sky dull and cool as De Haan stood on the jutting rampart outside his war room. His eyes narrowed behind his faceplate as if he were trying to stare through the curve of the planet itself.

'This race has been allowed to *go on*, Meer. It has been allowed to spread itself. They drink their wine on their craftworlds and stand under the sky on worlds like this. They crept out across the galaxy like the glint of mildew.'

Meer, chief among his lieutenants, knew better than to respond. He stood at the door which led out onto the rampart, hands folded respectfully before him. He had heard De Haan talk about the eldar many times.

'Not even the whining Emperor's puppies are like this. Nor the mangy orks. Tyranids, feh, beneath our dignity. But these things, these are an *affront*. To be assailed by them – ah! It gnaws at my pride.' His hand squeezed the haft of his crozius and the weapon's daemon-head hissed and cursed and spat its displeasure. Only during the rituals would the thing keep quiet. De Haan twisted it around and held it at a more dignified angle. It was a symbol of his office, a chaplaincy in the only Traitor Legion to remember and revere the importance of Chaplains. It did not do to show it disrespect.

De Haan wondered why he had not been able to speak like this in the chapel, why he had stood grasping for words, trying to force thoughts to his lips. A sermon on hate, no less, and yet he had stumbled over the words, choked on maddening distractions, images, snatches of voices, the swirl of memories he was normally able to leave behind at prayer.

'The eyes of our Dark Master see far, Meer, and who am I to set myself up beside them?' Meer remained silent, but De Haan was speaking half to himself. 'The words fled me. My throat was dry and empty. I am wondering, Meer, was it an omen? Do they prey on my mind because they are so near? There was a… a feel to this world, something in the words of our prisoners and spies. Perhaps the Great Conspirator planned from the start that it would end here. To end here, Meer, to bring the sacrament into full flower! Imagine that.'

'I know you believe your enemy is here, revered,' came Meer's careful voice from behind him, 'but my counsel, and Traika's, is still that the time was not ripe for you to join us here.'

De Haan's fist tightened around the crozius again, and the head – now a fanged mouth and eye-stalk; it was always different each time he looked at it – yapped and spat again.

'The fortifications are still not complete, revered, and only threescore of our own brethren are in this citadel. The battle tanks and Dreadnoughts are still being readied, and the dissonance in this world's aura has made auguries hard. We still cannot scry far beyond what our own eyes could see. Our bridgehead is not secure, revered. Do you believe this is worth the risk? The reports we had of eldar here seem only to mean these savages, or perhaps mere pirates. We cannot be sure Varantha has passed near this system. We have seen no craftworld eldar here, or–'

De Haan spun around. 'And I told you, Meer, that it is not suspicions and rumours which have drawn us here this time. I could feel the slippery eldar filth singing to me when I first heard the reports. I saw their faces dancing in the clouds when I looked from the bridge of our ship. What could this psychic "dissonance" you complain of be, but the cowards trying to fog our minds and cover their tracks?'

'These eldar savages keep a thing called a world-spirit, revered. They–'

'I *know* what is a world-spirit – and what is the stink of a farseer!' De Haan's voice did not quite go all the way to a roar, but it did not have to. There was a jitter in his vision and a rustle far off in his hearing as the systems in his armour, long since come to a Chaotic life of their own, tried to recoil from his anger. 'You were not given the sacrament, Meer! You do not carry the Fifth Blessing! I do, and I command you with it. I tell you that Varantha is here, and this is our doorway to it! I have known it in my soul since we broke from the warp!'

Meer bowed, accepting the rebuke, and De Haan slowly, deliberately turned his back. High in his vision he could see a point of light, visible even while the sun was up: their orbiting battle-barge. A space hulk full of Chaos Marines and their slaves and thralls, cultists doped with Frenzon with their explosive suicide collars clamped to their necks, mutants and beastfolk from the Eye of Terror and traitors of every stripe. Seeing it focused his thoughts again.

'We shall bring down our brethren soon enough. The engines and Dreadnoughts too. For now, fetch Nessun. And have the latest prisoner train brought before me.'

There was a scrape of ceramite on stone as Meer bowed again and turned to go, and by the time Meer had reached the bottom of the stairs De Haan was sinking back into reverie.

HE WAS THINKING of the cramped, fetid tunnels within the walls of the giant canal-cities of Sahch-V, where he and Meer and Alaema and barely a half-dozen Word Bearer squads had lived like rats in burrows for nearly two years, as around them their covert missionaries moved out through the cities and along the canals which brought life to the basalt plains, beginning their quiet preaching, their mission schools with their drugs and brainwashing rooms. He remembered the small chamber beneath the thermic pumps outside Vana City where the three of them had listened to their agents' reports and pored over their ever-spreading web of traitors and catspaws.

He remembered cries in the tunnels, in particular the voice of Belg, the scrawny cleft-chinned cult emissary loud in the coffin-like burrows as he shouted down the passages: 'We are lost! The missions are dying. Our rebellion is clipped before it begins!' Someone had shot Belg down in a fury before De Haan had had a chance to hear more, but he remembered the word that had gone flying through the base as the reports began to come in.

Eldar!

And the second, the three syllables that had not yet – he could barely remember the feeling – become sweet poison in his brain, not yet become the black-burning obsession hanging in front of his eyes, the name they had not heard until the Warp Spiders had begun to hunt them through their chambers and drove them out to where the rest of the eldar lay waiting with shuriken and plasma-shot, fusion-beam and wraithcannon. Alaema had gone down with a lightning-wrapped witchblade through his gut, and De Haan had barely managed to drag himself and Meer away to the teleport point.

Varantha.

Oh, he remembered. Twenty-one centuries of remembering.

He remembered the sick anger that had seized him when he first spoke to the Imperial scholar they had captured as the wretch thrashed on the torture rack. Varantha meant 'Crown of our Steadfast Hopes'. Human traders spoke in awe of the gems it crafted, the rare flowers it bred, the beautiful metals its artisans worked. Varantha that passed through the western galactic margins, scraping the borders of the Halo where not even the Traitor Legions went, Varantha that was supposed to have passed through Hydraphur itself, the home of the Imperial Battlefleet Pacificus, coasting through the system's intricate double-ecliptic and away again before the whey-faced Imperials had even a suspicion it had been there.

Varantha that hated Chaos with a white heat. Varantha that had held off Karlsen of the Night Lords in his raids on the Clavian Belt until the Ultramarines had arrived, Varantha whose farseers had tricked and feinted to lure the orks of Waaagh-Chobog into falling on the Iron Hands' fortresses on Taira-Shodan instead of the Imperial and Exodite worlds around them, Varantha whose warriors had driven Arhendros the Silken Whisper off the three worlds he had claimed for Slaanesh.

And Varantha that had balked the Word Bearers on Sahch-V, had unravelled their plans and made sure the great citadels and halls they would have built could never be. A Varantha witch blade had cut down De Haan's mentor, Varantha wraithships had driven their battle-barges and strikers out of the system. And when they had broken free of the warp outside the Cadian Gate, ready for their final jump back to the Eye of Terror and sanctuary, it had been Varantha craft which had led the fleets of Ulthwe and Cadia, driving into the Chaos fleet like a bullet tearing into flesh.

Fighting Varantha, stalking the craftworld through a quarter of the galaxy, De Haan had discovered a capacity for hate he had never realised that even a Traitor Marine could possess. Every battle against the craftworld had been like a stroke of the bellows, fanning it ever hotter. The orbital refineries at Rhea, where the eldar had lured De Haan and his warband in – then disappeared, leaving the Word Bearers in the abandoned, genestealer-infested satellite compounds. The island chains of Herano's World where their Doomblaster had smashed the eldar psykers into the ocean at the campaign's opening, and De Haan had led a joyous hunt through the jungles, mopping up the scattered and leaderless Guardians.

And at the last, the farseer, staggering beneath the red-black clouds of Iante as artillery flashed and boomed across the distant horizon, watching De Haan as he circled it, stepping over its dead bodyguard. The calm resignation in its stance and the cold precision of its voice.

'So tell me then. What do you see for us, little insect?' De Haan had taunted.

'Why, you will set your eyes on the heart of Varantha, and all will come to an end,' it had replied, before a howling stroke of De Haan's crozius had torn it in half. He had felt the spirit stone shudder and pulse as he tore it free of the thing's breastplate with a sound like cracking bone, and he wondered every so often if the creature's soul was aware of who owned its stone now. He hoped it was.

It had not been long after that that he had been called to receive his sacrament, the Sacrament of the Fifth Blessing. The highest priests of his Chapter had recognised the depth of his spite and had praised him for it: the Fifth Blessing was hate, and the sacrament had appointed De Haan a holy vessel, freed him from his duties in order to lead a crusade that he might express that hate to the utmost, a great hymn to Lorgar carved across the galaxy in Varantha's wake. He could never think back on his sacrament without the hot red flames of pride flaring deep in what he thought was his soul.

He walked to the edge of his rampart and watched the slaves toiling at the walls far below. His arms convulsed, as though he could already feel eldar souls pulsing and struggling in his fingers, and the wave of malice which surged up his spine made him almost giddy.

'Revered?'

De Haan started at the voice and spun around. His crozius head, now some kind of grotesque insect, chittered something that sounded almost like words. He ignored it and found his concentration again.

'What have the threads of Fate brought us, Nessun?'

The other Marine hesitated. Nessun was no full-fledged sorcerer as the adepts of the Thousand Sons were, but by Lorgar's grace he had developed a spirit sight that could scry almost as well as the eldar warlocks they hunted. The mutation that had given him his warp eye had pushed it far out and up onto his brow, making an ungainly lump of his head. The ceramite of his armour had turned glass-clear over it, but De Haan and the others had long ago become used to the way the great milky eyeball pulsed and rolled between the horns of Nessun's helm.

'In the way of eldar, revered, there is little I can say for definite. I see shadows at the corners of my vision and echoes that I must interpret. You know that nothing is certain with these creatures.'

'Describe these shadows and echoes, Nessun. I am patient.'

'I have kept my gaze on the tribes here in the days since our first landing, revered, and watched as they fought our thralls and Brother Traika's vanguard force. There is a... texture to them that I have taught myself to recognise, by Lorgar's grace. But I have caught ripples, something dancing out of sight. I am not sure how I can explain it, revered. Imagine a figure standing just beyond the reach of light from a fire, so that sometimes its shape is touched by the firelight...'

'I think I understand.' De Haan wasn't aware that he had tensed until he felt his armour, alive like his helmet systems, shiver and creak as it tried to find a comfortable position.

'Revered, I am abased and humble before the foul glory of Chaos, but I must venture the guess that craftworld eldar may be here. Here on this world. I have dimly seen the patterns that the minds of farseers form when they assemble, and I have felt... gaps in my vision that I believe are warp gates, webway gates here and in orbit beyond the planet from our own ship, that have opened and closed and that they have not been able to hide…' He stopped short as De Haan drove gauntlet into fist, hissing with triumph, sending his armour shivering and flexing from the blow.

'An omen! My voice was bound in the chapel as an omen!' And he was about to speak again when Meer called from the war room.

'Most revered lord, the prisoners await you.'

There was something in Meer's voice that made De Haan almost run for the doorway.

TWO ELDAR STOOD in the great hall, heads bowed as De Haan strode to his throne and sat down, crozius across his knees. The arm of one hung brokenly; blood matted the other's hair. Both were dressed in rough cloth and hide tunics, and their lasers, the power chambers smashed, had been hung around their necks. Traika, the commander of their vanguard and Raptors, bowed to De Haan and made the sign of the Eightfold Arrow with the hand that had fused to his chainsword. Traika's legs had warped and lengthened too, now bending backward like an insect's, the armour over them lumpy and stretched. It had made him fleet of foot but gave him an odd, tilted way of standing.

'We found these in the south-west quarter where the hills steepen. We thought we had cleansed the area, revered, but these were part of an ambush on one of our scouring forces. The fight was fierce but we carried the day.'

'Praise Lorgar's dark light and the great will of Chaos,' De Haan intoned, and the two were led away into the cathedral's cells. Traika gestured and a third alien was dragged up the steps, limping and tripping. The thrall holding its chains tossed a dead power-lance and a tall bone helm onto the floor. The prisoner did not react, standing slumped with its hair in its face, its long cloak of golden-scaled hide hanging limply around it.

'The last survivor of a group of Dragon Knights we believe were scouting the northern border of our controlled zone. I will attend the tormenting of this one personally, revered. I had felt sure that our deep raids had gutted the last of the Exodite resistance on the prairies. We must find out how this new raid was organised so soon.' The thrall began to drag the knight out, and Meer walked over to stand beside the throne.

'Revered, this is the final prisoner. It was badly wounded, and did not survive the journey back to be brought before you, but we believed you would want to see it. The Raptors brought it down in the river-valley to the south and our bikers brought it here with all haste.'

With a scraping groan of wheels the thralls pushed forward an iron frame with a figure stretched in it, a figure whose rich purple and gold armour caught the sunlight coming through the still-unglazed windows and gave off a burnished glow. Behind it four more – strong beastfolk these, whose muscles rippled and corded with their burden – dragged something into view and dropped it crashing to the floor, stirring the rock-dust that still coated the hall from its building. A jet-bike, its canopy cracked open by bolt shells, the drive smashed and burnt from its crash, but the pennons hanging from its vanes perfectly clear: the stylised crown-and-starburst of Varantha.

For a long moment, De Haan was silent. Then he threw his arms wide as though he were about to embrace the corpse, and gave a bellow that echoed through the length of the hall.

'All will come to an end! Horus's eye, but the filthy little creature spoke the truth. The craftworld's heart! It is here! The sacrament ends here, my brethren! I will end it here!'

'Revered!' De Haan did not look back. His stride had lengthened as his pace had picked up, and he was practically jogging through the halls to the Deepmost Chapel, Meer and Nessun shouldering one another aside to keep up. The air in the fortress shivered as the great gongs they had hung over the barracks rang out again and again. Under the sound De Haan left a trail of angry murmurs in the air, curses and threats and dark prayers. Every so often he would slash his crozius viciously around him as if to knock the air itself out of his path.

He knew what Meer would be saying. More weak-spirited yapping, more about caution and rashness and the trickery of the eldar. But the warp gate was close. Varantha was close. The time when the heads of Varantha's farseers were set on spikes atop his Land Raider was a breath away.

Why, you will set your eyes on the heart of Varantha, and all will come to an end.

The heart of the craftworld, the very heart of Varantha! He wondered how it would feel, walking from the webway gate into Varantha itself. The domes where the most ancient of their farseers sat, their flesh crystallised and gleaming like diamond, waiting for the blow of an armoured fist that would send their souls screaming into the warp. The Grove of New Songs, that was what they called the forest-hall deep in Varantha where the few eldar children were born and weaned. De Haan had spent a hundred weeks agonising over whether he would kill the children or take them as slaves after he had poisoned and burned the trees. The infinity circuit, the wraithbone core which held the spirits of a billion dead eldar, had shone through his dreams like a galaxy aflame. Oh, to crack its lattice with his crozius and watch the warp tides pour in! It would need a special ceremony, the culmination of his crusade and sacrament, something he would have to plan.

And was Varantha possessed of engines, a world that could control its drift and sweep through space? He had never been able to discover that, but he began turning the idea over feverishly as he strode down the hallway to the chapel. To take command of Varantha, hollow out its core of eldar souls and fill them with sacrifices and the cries of daemons, to sail the fallen craftworld to the Eye of Terror itself! His head swam with the audacity: a world that would put their daemon-world fortresses and the asteroid seminaries at Milarro to shame. A corrupted world that would carry them through the galaxy, a great blight that would stand as a testament to their faith, their hate, their spite, their unholiness.

The rest of the Traitor Marines began to file in and take their places, and the slave-choir in their cells beneath the chapel floor raised a hymn of howls and cries as the choir-masters puffed drugs into their faces and yanked on the needles in their flesh. De Haan closed his eyes and could see the conquered Varantha still, a great twisted flower of black and crimson, sprawled against the stars. The shapes of the spires and walls, great plazas where the zealous would come to plead for the favour of Chaos, the cells and scriptoria where Lorgar's holy Pentadict would be copied and studied, the fighting pits where generations of new Word Bearers would be initiated. There would be pillars and statues greater than those they had raised after driving the White Scars from the island chains of Morag's World. There would be chamber after chamber of altars more richly decorated than those they had seized when they had sacked the treasury of Kintarre. There would be the slaughtering pens for the worship of Khorne, great libraries and chambers for meditating upon the lore of Tzeentch. There would be palaces of incense and music dedicated to Slaanesh, and cess-pits for the rituals of self-defilement dedicated to Nurgle. And all just parts, even as the Chaos Gods were just facets, all parts of the great treacherous hymn, an obscene prayer in wraithbone and carved ceramite. The Sacred City of Chaos Undivided.

De Haan cradled his vision lovingly in his mind, and saw that it was good.

'Lorgar is with us, Chaos is within us, damnation clothes us and none can stand against us.' Voices around the chapel echoed the blessing as De Haan held his rosarius aloft and made the sign of the Eightfold Arrow. For the second time that day he looked out over ranks of helms, leaned forward to look down at the bright eyes of the cultists and beastfolk crowded below him. But this time, his thoughts and his words were clear.

'Be it known to you, most devout of my comrades in Lorgar's footsteps, that we are gathered here once again in the observance of the Fifth Blessing of Lorgar, the blessing of hate. Bring your thoughts to the sacrament granted to me by the most high of our order, that I might light a dark beacon of spite for all the cosmos to see.' He paused, looked down again. The eldar artefacts had gone from the dais, locked away again by the Sacristans. It was not important – he did not need them now.

'Hatred earned me the great and honoured sacrament. Hatred has pleased the beautiful abomination of Chaos Undivided, and shone a light through the warp to Varantha. My beautiful hatred has brought us to their scent. After more than two millennia, the fulfilment of our sacred charter is near.' The memory of the Varantha Guardian, the knowledge of what they had found here, surged through him afresh: his head spun, his joints felt weak with exhilaration. His crozius head as he raised it was now a contorted nightmare-face, grimacing as if in ecstasy, mirroring his feelings.

'Soon we will be joined by our brothers, our fellow warriors and bearers of Lorgar's words. Even now the order goes out to land our machines of war, our bound Dreadnoughts. Within the week, my congregation, this world will have felt the full fury of our crusade and when the Exodites are scoured from it we shall march through the warp gate into the craftworld itself! Hone yourselves, my acolytes, hone your spite and fan your hate to the hottest, most bitter flame. None shall pass us in our devotion, none are as steeped in poisoned thoughts as we!' His voice hammered out and boomed against the walls of the chapel, intoxicating even with the power of its echoes. De Haan fought back an urge to laugh – this felt so right.

'In the beginning, even in the days before my pursuit earned me the sacrament, I had spoken to one of the degenerate farseers the eldar claim to revere. At its death the maggot spoke a prophecy that the blessed oracles of our high temples have sworn to be true. Brethren, as I lead you to battle I will set my eyes on the heart of Varantha and then all will come to an end. I will cut down their last farseer, I will break open the seals of their infinity circuit, I will shatter the heart and eye of their home!' His voice had risen to a roar. 'All will come to an end! Our crusade, our sacrament fulfilled! The eldar themselves have sworn it will be so. What honours, what glories we will build!'

Above him the gong rang again, and De Haan opened his eyes and leaned forward.

'Look to your weapons, brothers. I will lead you now in the Martio Imprimis. I tell you this: by the end of even this day we will be at war!'

THE CHANT OF the Martio Imprimis was an old song and a good one, crafted by Lorgar himself in the days before the Emperor had turned on his Word Bearers and when even De Haan had been only a youngblood initiate. The words were strange and their meanings almost lost, but they filled him with a beautiful, electric energy. It rang in De Haan's blood even now. The service in the Deepmost Chapel had been over for an hour but the Word Bearers had caught something of their chaplain's mood and as the teleport beam sent thundercracks and sickly shimmers of light through the citadel's hangar, the Marines chanted still as they selected weapons and directed the thralls in moving the crates and engines away.

'Duxhai!' The crusade's chief artisan, still swaying a little from his teleport, turned as De Haan called him. He stepped back into a deep kneeling bow as De Haan strode across the hangar floor and left the moving of the icon-encrusted Razorback tanks to his seconds.

'Is it true, revered lord? I was told you have received omens and that Varantha itself is in our grip. They are singing hymns in all the halls and chambers of our fortress. Look!' The old Marine pointed to the nearest tank's turret, where splashes of blood glistened. 'They have already made sacrifices over our wargear.'

'It is true, Duxhai, and it is fitting that our brethren in orbit are making their thanks and obeisances. Lorgar has exalted us. I have been shown the way.'

Duxhai had worked on his armour himself over the centuries, making it a glorious construction of red and gold. Chaos had worked on it too: the studs and rivets on its carapace had all turned to eyes, yellow slit-pupilled eyes, which stared at De Haan now but rolled forward to watch Meer walk into the hangar. De Haan pointed to the Razorbacks.

'Give praise, Meer! See how Brother Duxhai's skills have transformed these? Captured barely a year ago, and already adorned and consecrated for service! These will carry Traika's vanguard squads into the teeth of the Varantha lines!'

'Our revered chaplain's own Land Raider will be brought down next,' put in Duxhai, 'and the transports are being readied to bring down the Dreadnoughts and Rhinos. We will be ready to move soon.'

'A dark blessing on you, brother, and thanks to the great foulness of Chaos. Revered, I must make a report.'

'Well?' De Haan was becoming nettled by Meer's manner, his shifty-eyed caution. He could see in the corner of his eyes that Duxhai had registered the offhand greeting also.

'Revered, we have lost contact with our patrols at the furthest sweep of the contested zone. I had our adepts move the communicators onto the outer balconies but there is still no way to raise them. The Raptors who went out to counterstrike at the areas where our own forces were ambushed cannot be reached either, and the bike squadron was due two hours ago but cannot be seen. The psychic haze has thickened, and Nessun's warp eye is almost blind. He reports a presence like a light through fog, but he cannot pinpoint it.'

'I will come to the war room, Meer. Wait for me there.' His lieutenant backed away, bowed and departed. 'Something in the air on this world turns my warriors to water, Duxhai. They whimper to me of "caution" and "fortification". Meer is a good warrior, but I should have made you my lieutenant for this world. I need your ferocity by me here.'

Duxhai bowed. 'I am honoured, revered. Lieutenant or no, I will gladly fight by your side. Allow me to prepare my weapons and I will meet you in the war room.'

De Haan nodded and waited a moment more, allowing the chanting of the Traitor Marines to soothe his ruffled nerves, before he strode away.

NESSUN WAS STANDING quietly in the war room when De Haan entered, head bowed, warp eye clouded. Meer and Traika were pacing, almost circling each other, clearly at odds. De Haan ordered them to report.

'Something is coming, revered!' Meer began. 'The slaves are restless, there have been revolts on the building crews! The eldar know something! We must prepare for assault!'

'We must make the assault!' Traika's rasping voice. 'We are Word Bearers, not Iron Warriors! We do not skulk behind walls. We take Lorgar's blessing to our enemies, His blessings of hate and fire and blood and agony!' The obscenely long fingers of Traika's left hand flexed and clenched, as if to claw the tension out of the air.

Listening to them, De Haan hesitated. For the first time he felt a tug, a tilt at the back of his mind that he could not identify. He could not see with Nessun's precision, no seer he, but ten thousand years in the Eye of Terror had tuned him to the coarser ebbs and flows as it had them all. Something was near. He raised his crozius for silence – its crown a snarling hound's head now – and looked to Nessun.

'Speak, Nessun! Stare through these walls. Tell me what you see!'

'Revered, I... am not sure. There are patterns, something moving... a ring, a wall... closing or opening, I cannot say... a mind... shapes, silent... rushing air...' His voice was becoming ragged, and De Haan cut him off.

'It's clear enough. Meer, Traika: you are both right. The eldar know of us.' He fought back a chuckle. 'And they fear us. Catch us off-guard, would they? A quick strike at the head, was it? Drive me off their trail?' And now he did laugh, feeling the tension lifting from his back.

'Time for our sortie, my brothers! Have the Razorbacks lowered to the ramp. Traika, assemble your veteran squads! Meer, have our space command ready a bombardment for when we–'

That was when the first plasma blast hit the side of the cathedral with a sound like the sky being torn apart. The thunderous roar died away amid vast dust clouds, the groan of masonry, frenzied shouts from up and down the halls. De Haan stared straight ahead for one speechless moment, then hurled himself to the balcony, the others behind him. And then they could only stand and watch.

The world had filled with enemies. Sleek eldar jet-bikes arrowed down from the sky to whip past the walls of the cathedral, and high above De Haan could hear the rumble of sonic booms as squadrons of larger alien assault craft criss-crossed over their heads. With sickening speed each distant blur in the air would grow and resolve into a raptor-sleek grav-tank, arcing in silently to spill a knot of infantry into the town before they rose and banked away again. In what seemed like a matter of heartbeats the fortress was ringed by a sea of advancing Guardians, their ranks dotted with gliding gun-platforms and dancing war-walkers, and the air swarmed with the eldar craft.

The aliens' assault started to be answered. Thumps and cracks came from the walls as the Word Bearers brought heavy weapons to bear and threads of tracer fire began reaching out to the purple-and-gold shapes that danced past on the wind. De Haan pushed to the edge of the balcony, heedless of the shapes above him and greedy for the sight of fireballs and smoke-trails, but he had time for no more than a glance before Meer and Traika pulled him away from the edge.

'Revered! With us! You must lead us. We cannot stay!' He cursed and almost raised his crozius to Meer, but the first laser beams had begun sweeping the balcony, carving at the rock and sending molten dribbles down the walls behind them. He nodded grimly and led them inside.

In the debris-swathed halls all was din and confusion. The slave-masters bellowed and flailed with their barbed whips, but their charges would not be ordered. De Haan realised someone had set off the Frenzon too early. Their thralls ran to and fro, shrieking and swinging their clubs, pistols spitting and making the stone chambers a hell of sparks and ricochets. Bullets spanged off De Haan's armour as he shouldered his way through the crowd of naked, bleeding berserkers.

'To me! They are upon us, we will cut them down here! To me!' and De Haan began the chant of the Martio Secundus. All around him Word Bearers turned and began to fall in behind him, dark red helms bearing down on him above the sea of bobbing cultist heads. Roars and growls began to mix with the cries of the mortals; the beastfolk were following too. De Haan gave a snarling grin behind his faceplate. *In Lorgar's name, we will make a fight of this yet.*

Reaching the great stair, they found that a whole part of the wall had gone, simply vanished leaving smooth stone edges where a piece had been erased. A distort-cannon crater – and the ceiling above it was already beginning to groan and send down streams of dust. He ignored the danger, sent his chant ringing out again and charged through the crater to the hall beyond; the hangar and teleport dais were close.

Then, swooping and darting though the breaches their cannon had made, came the eldar, Aspect Warriors all in blue, thrumming wings spreading from their shoulders. Lasers stabbed down into the throng underneath them and grenades fell from their hands like petals.

'Fight!' De Haan bellowed, and now that he was in battle he roared the Martio Tertius and sent a fan of bolt shells screaming through the squadron, smashing two Hawks backwards into the wall in clouds of smoke. His crozius, twisted into the head of a one-eyed bull, was belching streams of red plasma that hung in the air when he moved it; it had not boasted the blue power-field of the Imperial croziae for eight thousand years.

The remaining Hawks tumbled gracefully in the air and glided towards the ruined wall, now with other shots chasing them, but then the braying of the beastfolk changed note. De Haan whirled to see three of them, firing wildly, looking about them in panic, caught in a silvery mist. All three seemed to twitch and heave and fall oddly out of shape before they collapsed into piles of filth on the stone floor. Beyond them, the two Warp Spider warriors sucked the filament clouds back into the muzzles of their weapons. While shells from De Haan and Meer took one apart, the other stepped back. With a gesture, the air flowed around it like water and it was gone.

Down the hall and up the broad stairs, running hard, Duxhai came pounding out of the smoke, plasma gun clutched in his hands. The hangar was filled with smoke and flashes of light.

'The hangar is gone, lord, taken. We opened the gates to take the tanks down the ramp to the ground, but they drove us back with their strange weapons, and their heavy tanks are bombarding us. The teleport platform is destroyed. I have said the Martio Quartus for our fallen, and my brothers have dug in to hold them at bay. But we cannot stay here.'

De Haan almost groaned aloud. 'I will not be driven like an animal! This is my fortress, I will stand to defend it!' But his soldier's instincts had taken charge and were giving the lie to his words: he was already moving back down the stairs to meet the last of the Marines and a gaggle of thralls struggling up to meet him. He looked at them for a moment, and did not flinch as a Fire Prism fired through the hangar doors, opened a dazzling sphere of yellow-white fire over their heads.

'The Deepmost Chapel, then, and the Great Hall. We will cut them down as they enter, until our brothers can land. When the transports land the rest of our crusade the battle will turn soon enough.'

They hammered down the stairs. Beside them a glare came through the window-slits and then the rock wall flashed red-hot and crumbled as the Marines next to it hurled themselves away. The sleek alien tank which had opened the breach rose out of sight and the jet-bikes behind it – no Guardian craft these but the smoky grey-green and bright silver of the Shining Spears – threw a delicate cat's cradle of lasers through the opening. Thralls yowled and fell, while the beastfolk sent bullets and shot blasting out of the opening as the jet-bikes peeled off and rose out of sight.

Then the Word Bearers were in the chapel, the shadowy space and echoes calming De Haan, the familiar shape of the warp obelisk giving him strength. They fanned out into the chamber, around the upper gallery and the floor itself, needing no orders: within seconds the doors were covered. The pack of thralls and beastfolk huddled and muttered in the centre of the chamber, clutching weapons.

'Revered, we… we are beset on every side.' Nessun's voice was flat and hoarse with anger. 'I feel them at the gates, fighting our brothers and slaves. But they are above us too, they are breaching the upper walls and stepping onto the balconies from their grav-sleds. And, and… most revered lord…'

Suddenly Nessun's voice was drenched with misery, and even the heads of the warriors around him were turning. 'Our battle-barge. Our fortress. I see it reeling in space, revered… it is ringed by the enemy… their ships dance away from our guns… our brothers were preparing their landing, the shields had been lowered for the teleport to work. The eldar are tearing at it… my vision is dimming…'

There was silence in the chapel for a moment after Nessun's voice died away. De Haan thought of trying to reach the sensoria array in the spires above them, then pushed the useless thought away. The upper levels would be full of eldar scum by now, and by the time they could fight their way there his ship would indeed have been blasted from the sky.

He looked around. 'Alone, then. Alone with our hatred. I will hear no talk of flight. They will break against us as a wave against a cliff.'

'Lorgar is with us, Chaos is within us, damnation clothes us and none can stand against us.'

As they all said the blessing De Haan's eyes moved from one to the next. Meer cradling his bolter, seemingly deep in thought, Duxhai standing haughtily with plasma-gun held at arms, Traika glaring about him for any sign of weakness in the others, chainsword starting to flex and rev. De Haan raised his crozius and strode from the chapel, the others following, and as if on a signal they heard the bombardment outside begin again.

IT WAS ONLY fitting that De Haan and his retinue marched into the north end of the ruined Great Hall at the same time that the eldar filled its south. They had blown in the walls and shot the bronze doors apart and were fanning out through the ruins. De Haan leapt down the steps into the hall, letting the dust and smoke blur his outline as shots clipped the columns around him and his men returned fire from the archway. A plasma grenade exploded nearby, an instant of scorching whiteness that betrayed the eldar: in the instant that it blinded them the Word Bearers had launched their own advance, scrambling and vaulting over the rubble. There were insect-quick movements ahead and De Haan fired by reflex, plucking the Guardians out of their positions before he had consciously registered their location. The soft thrum of shuriken guns was drowned out by the hammer-and-yowl of the Word Bearers' bolt shells.

A stream of white energy flashed by De Haan's shoulder as Duxhai felled two more eldar, but there were Dire Avengers in the eldar positions now, with quicker reflexes and a hawk-eye aim to catch Duxhai before he could move again. The shuriken were monomolecular, too fast and thin to properly see, but the air around Duxhai seemed to shimmer and flash. Blood and ceramite gouted from his back as his torso flew apart, the eyes on his armour glazing over. He staggered back and De Haan jinked around him, launching himself into battle.

A grenade went off somewhere to his left and shrapnel clipped his armour. The Word Bearer felt the moist embrace of the plates around his body jump and twitch with the pain. He brought his crozius up and over, its wolf's head yowling with both joy and pain and belching thick red plasma. It caught the Avenger square on its jutting helmet and the creature twitched for a moment only before the glowing crimson mist ate it down to the bone. His bolt pistol hammered in his hand and two more eldar crashed backward, twitching and tumbling. Just beyond them, Traika cleared a fallen column in a great leap and landed among yellow-armoured Striking Scorpions whose chainswords sang and sparked against his own. In the rubble, Meer led the others in laying down a crossfire that strewed alien corpses across a third of the hall.

De Haan sang the Martio Tertius in a clear, strong voice and shot the nearest Scorpion in the back. Traika screamed laughter and swung at another, but as it back-pedalled another Scorpion, in the heavy intricate armour of an exarch, glided forward and whirled a many-chained crystalline flail in an intricate figure that smashed both Traika's shoulders and left him standing, astonished and motionless, for a blow that stove in his helm and sent ceramite splinters flying. De Haan bellowed a battle-curse and his crozius head became a snake that lashed and hissed. Two short steps forward and he lunged, feinted and struck the flail out of the creature's hand. It reeled back into Meer's sights, the plasma eating at it even as shells riddled it, but in the time it took for De Haan to strike down the last Scorpion the hall was alive with eldar again, and Meer and Nessun were forced back and away from him by a shower of grenades and sighing filament webs as the blast from a distort-cannon scraped the roof off the hall and let in the raging sky.

Even as De Haan charged, fired and struck again and again, some distant part of him groaned. Faint, maddening alien thoughts brushed his own like spider-silk in the dark, and shadows danced at the upper edge of his vision as jet-bikes and Vypers circled. The air around him was alive with shuriken fire and energy bolts. The eldar melted away as he struck this way and that. Ancient stone burst into hot shards as he swung his crozius, but rage had taken his discipline and, like a man trying to snatch smoke in his fingers, he found himself standing and roaring wordlessly as the hall emptied once more and the shots died away.

* * *

THERE WERE NO voices, no cries from his companions. De Haan did not have to turn to look to know that this last assault had taken them all. Meer and Nessun were dead, and behind him he could hear the boom of masonry as his citadel began to crumble. The Prayer of Sacrifice and the Martio Quartus would not come to his numb lips, and he nodded to himself. Why should not his rites unravel along with everything else? The Chaos star set in his rosarius was dead, lacklustre. He looked at it dully, and that was when he began to feel something tugging at his mind.

It was like an electrical tingle, or the distant sound of crickets; the way the air feels before a storm, or the thrum of distant war-machines. De Haan's warp-tuned mind rang with the nearby song of power. He remembered Nessun speaking of the pattern that farseers' minds made when they assembled.

You will set your eyes…

Suddenly he was running again. No screams now, just a low moan in his throat, a tangle of savage emotions he could not have put a name to if he had tried. Blood trickled from his lips and his crozius thrummed and crackled. The gates of the cathedral hung like broken wings. He ducked between them to stand on the broad black steps of his dying fortress.

…on the heart of Varantha…

His crozius's head had fallen silent, and he looked at it in puzzlement. It had formed itself into a human face, mouth gaping, eyes wide. A face that De Haan recognised as his own, from back in the days before his helm had sealed itself to him.

Turn, De Haan. Turn And Face Me.

The voice did not come through his ears, but seemed to resonate out of the air and throughout his bones and brain. It was measured, almost sombre, but its simple force almost shook him to his knees. Slowly, he raised his head.

…and all will come to an end.

More than twice De Haan's height, the immense figure stood with its spear at rest. It took a step forward out of the smoke that had wreathed it, to the centre of the plaza. De Haan watched the blood drip from its hand and stain the grey stones on the ground. It stood and regarded him, and there was none of the expected madness or fury in the white-hot pits of its baleful eyes, only a brooding patience that was far more terrifying.

He took a step forward. All the fury had gone like the snuffing of a candle: now there was just wrenching despair which drove everything else from his mind. He wondered how long ago Varantha's farseers had realised he was hunting them, how long ago they had begun cultivating his hate, how long ago they had begun to set this trap for him. He wondered if the farseer whose prophecy he had thought to fulfil was laughing at him from within its spirit stone.

He stood alone on the steps, and the air was silent but for the hiss of heat from incandescent iron skin and the faint keening from the weapon in one giant hand.

Then the lines from the Pentadict danced through his mind, the lines with which Lorgar had closed his testament as his own death came upon him.

Pride and defiant hate, spite and harsh oblivion. Let the great jewelled knot of the cosmos unravel in the dust.

He looked up again, his mind suddenly clear and calm. He raised his crozius, but the salute was not returned. No matter. He took a pace forward and down the steps, that volcanic gaze on him all the time. He walked faster, now jogging. He worked the action on his pistol with the heel of his hand. Running, its eyes on him.

Charging now, feet hammering, voice found at last in a wail of defiance, Chaplain De Haan ran like a daemon across his last battlefield to where the Avatar of Kaela-Mensha-Khaine stood, its smoking, shrieking spear in its vast hands, waiting for him.

APOTHECARY'S HONOUR
Simon Jowett

'APOTHECARY!' THE CRY crackled over the transceiver in Korpus's battered helmet, then vanished beneath a searing wave of static. Mid-stride, Korpus paused. A wheeze escaped from the joints of his armour, as if the suit he had worn since planetfall on Antillis IV was itself grateful for a moment's respite. The craggy uplands upon which the Avenging Sons had set their base camp were unforgiving of flesh and bone and power-assisted ceramite alike.

Korpus turned one way then the other, searching for the signal. The wind had changed direction and with it the currents of unholy energy which had been unleashed upon the planet, casting a blanket of infuriating static across every transmission. The last communication from the Scout Squad that had accompanied the Avenging Sons' Second Company onto Antillis IV had been swamped by one such obliterating wave. Nothing more had been heard from the squad in almost thirty hours. Every remaining Space Marine silently commended their soul to the Emperor.

Eddies of pale grey ash swirled about Korpus as he continued his sweep. The remains of much of Antillis IV's civilian population, it clogged the joints of every Space Marine's armour and cast a dense pall across his visor. Korpus automatically ran a gloved hand across his eye-plates, clearing away the soft, greasy veil which had collected there. The mud and ash swathed landscape around him jumped into sharper focus. Dispatched to support the beleaguered Imperial Garrison, the Avenging Sons had found themselves immured in a daemon's dream of winter: blizzards of human ash driven by winds that howled with the voices of souls lost to Chaos.

'Apothecary!'

The signal broke through the wail and hiss of static, stronger and more urgent than before. Korpus turned his face away from the steep, broken incline he had been climbing and began to negotiate a downwards path. Automatically, he checked the load in his bolt pistol and activated his power fist. In his heart he would rather have continued upwards, in order to stand beside his commander in the vanguard of the next assault. But he was an Apothecary, and not once in the years since he had first donned the white armour had he ever ignored the call of an injured Space Marine.

It was a matter of pride. It was a matter of honour.

'AVENGING SON!' KORPUS prayed that his own transmission was able to pierce the blizzard of ash and static.

He stepped over the last of the trail of black-armoured corpses that had led him down this narrow defile. Though of similar design to the armour worn by the Avenging Sons, the garish sigils scrawled across its midnight-black surface declared its wearer's true allegiance: to the Dark Gods of the warp. To Chaos.

He kicked aside an abandoned skull-helm and noticed with grim satisfaction the bloody stump of a truncated neck which lolled into view as it rolled away. Among the scattered corpses and their now-redundant weaponry, Korpus had noted the presence of a boltgun and bolt pistol, both sanctified with the sigil of the Avenging Sons, both discarded. Both empty.

'Apothecary?'

The strained query came from an inky, shadow-cast niche in the gully wall. Korpus restrained his desire to hurry into the darkness, well aware of the tricks that the servants of the warp could play on a man's mind, and edged forward.

The Space Marine lay propped against the rear of the niche, his lower body obscured by what Korpus thought, at first, to be an errant shadow, but quickly realised was another corpse. The Avenging Son's breastplate was scorched by bolter fire and cracked in several places. The blood of his many victims shone blackly in the dim light. One of his arms hung loosely to the side, the elbow bent at an unnatural angle. The other still clutched the handle of the chainsword he had driven between the plates of his opponent's armour.

'It's me, Korpus.' Holstering his bolt pistol and disconnecting his power fist, the Apothecary knelt beside his battle-brother. With practised ease he released the catches of the cracked and dented helmet and lifted it away.

'Pereus!' Korpus had stood beside the veteran sergeant on many worlds. 'You must have killed a battalion of the daemon-spawn.'

'And they me,' Pereus's words came in gasps, his normally rich, deep voice cracking with the effort. He glanced downwards, indicating something. Korpus followed his gaze, then rolled away the body of the sergeant's last kill.

The warp-forged chainsword had been driven through the lower plates of Pereus's armour, deep enough so that only its hilt remained visible, perhaps at the same moment that Pereus had struck his own fatal blow.

'Legs gone. No feeling,' Pereus croaked. 'My service to the Emperor ends here.'

As Pereus spoke, Korpus swiftly removed his own helmet. The ritual he was about to perform did not require that both participants be bare-headed, but Korpus believed it to be more fitting.

'Man is born alone,' Korpus intoned, removing his armoured gloves. The wind struck cold against his exposed, sweat-slickened hands.

'And so he dies,' Pereus answered in a halting voice. Reaching forward, Korpus began to release the catches of the sergeant's upper armour.

'You serve the Emperor?' Korpus continued, stripping the plates from Pereus's body, exposing the blood-soaked robe beneath.

'And I die in his service.' Pereus shuddered at the wind's chill kiss.

'You are content?' Korpus asked. In a single swift motion, Korpus sliced through the sodden, sticky robe, using a scalpel he had drawn from an instrument pack bolted to his forearm.

'I am content,' Pereus gave the final answer, his voice barely a whisper. Korpus parted the fabric to lay Pereus bare from waist to throat. 'Work fast, Apothecary,' Pereus whispered. 'There will more of these warp-spawned whoresons come to avenge their brothers.' His face and throat convulsed, as if he was trying to swallow an unpalatable morsel. His head rocked forward and his jaw dropped slackly open. A thick stream of blood ran over his lower lip.

Placing a hand under Pereus's chin, Korpus tilted it back upon the now nerveless neck, exposing the full length of the throat. There: a slight bulge resting atop the sternum. Korpus's first target. Replacing the first scalpel in the instrument pack, he selected a second, whose tapered, hair-thin blade was intended for one purpose only: the excision of a Space Marine's progenoid glands.

'When they come, I pray that I will face them as bravely as you,' Korpus told the unhearing sergeant. He watched as a flake of pale ash settled slowly on the pupil of Pereus's unseeing right eye, then set to work.

'THE PROGENOID GLANDS are the future of our Chapter!' Apothecary Lorus's barking tone echoed around the small room set at the centre of the Apothecarion. The tang of chemical preservatives hung in the air. Seated before him in the cold room, banked with glass phials and porcelain specimen dishes, sat the five candidates chosen to undergo training in the sacred rituals and duties of a Space Marine Medic.

'The Avenging Sons' survival as an arm of the Emperor's will is dependent upon the survival of the glands,' Lorus continued. 'And the survival of the glands will depend upon you.'

Lorus stood behind a gurney which had been wheeled into the room by a servitor, one of the small army of the mechanically enhanced wretches who moved tirelessly through the corridors of the Apothecarion, ferrying wounded Space Marines between wards, preparing beds for new occupants or removing the dead to the Chapel of Martyrs. The gurney's cargo was covered by a grey sheet.

Korpus's eyes kept flickering impatiently between the sallow, sharp-featured face of the instructor and the shape under the sheet. Neither he nor any of his fellow candidates were under any illusion about what lay under there. Their instruction in the other aspects of battlefield medicine was already well under way. Now they were to receive induction into the last and most vital of the Apothecarion's mysteries.

'All men die,' Lorus's tone had taken on a flat, liturgical air, his words echoing the Rite of Extreme Unction that Korpus and his fellows had already committed to memory and upon which they were expected to meditate each night before retiring. 'But, in death, an Avenging Son carries within him the means of ensuring that the Emperor's crusade against the tide of Chaos continues.

'Each gland is grown from the seed provided by the gland that came before it and that gland from a similar seed, in an unbroken chain which lies within every Space Marine of the Adeptus Astartes, until the point of death. At the end of a Space Marine's life, it is the duty of an Apothecary to remove the glands and see that they return here to provide seed for the future.

'Without it, there can be no more of us. Without it, the Emperor's crusade ends. Without it, Chaos has free rein.'

Lorus drew back the sheet, revealing the naked corpse of an Avenging Son, whose journey to the Chapel of Martyrs had been delayed for the sake of this demonstration. Korpus's gaze lingered for a moment on the dead man's face as he wondered what battles he had seen in the life of righteous conflict that had led him here. By the time the young apprentice medic looked back at his instructor, the old man had drawn a scalpel, longer and much thinner than those Korpus had seen thus far, from a stiff leather pouch strapped to his forearm. Lorus cast his eyes across the five who sat before him.

'Now you will learn what it truly means to be an Apothecary.'

THE LONG-DEAD instructor's words always echoed in Korpus's memory while performing an Excision. The ghost of the preservatives' tang pricked the back of his throat as he carved the tiny, delicate vesicles from the base of the throat and deep within the chest. Had the wind that howled along the gully not increased while he worked on Pereus, the scent memory would have been augmented by the more powerful odour of the fresh fluid in the phials he unlatched from the storage bays set beneath his armour's thigh-plates. Each of the pair of glands was deposited in a phial, their tops sealed and then replaced in their sheaths.

Korpus secured the catches on the plates of double-thickness ceramite, intended to shield the precious cargo from damage that would doubtless blow the rest of Korpus to the winds of space. Replacing the scalpel in the instrument pack and donning his gloves, he prepared to leave. But there was one last ritual to perform.

'You are a martyr to the Emperor's will,' he intoned over Pereus's eviscerated remains.

The dead man would have met the Apothecary's gaze, had not a dense layer of ash settled across his face, covering it completely.

'You shall be remembered. You shall be avenged.'

'APOTHECARY!' COMMANDER SELLEUS's voice rang in Korpus's ears during a sudden lull in the static.

'Apothecary Korpus reporting, praise His name,' he replied. Having worked his way out of the defile, Korpus was retracing his steps up the long, rocky incline, heading once more towards the base camp. The number of loaded phials he had been carrying, excised from the bodies of Avenging Sons who had fallen in the battle to hold the perimeter, had prompted his initial decision to return, to place the glands in more permanent storage to be returned via Thunderhawk to the Avenging Son's Chapter ship. Pereus's glands had filled the last of the bays and made his return all the more imperative.

'The order to regroup went out an hour past,' Selleus said. 'Where are you?'

'Incoming, my lord.' Korpus lifted his visored gaze. There, visible through the ash-storm, sat the fortified chateau from which Selleus spoke. In his mind's eye, he saw the remaining Avenging Sons, gathered around their commander, preparing themselves for the assault that would inevitably follow the regrouping. Longing to join them, to feel the holy fire of battle leap within him, he increased his pace over the uneven ground.

'Pereus fell. Excision was required,' he continued. 'Your order did not reach me. This damnable static…'

As if summoned by his words, a fresh wave of storm-generated interference engulfed much of Selleus's reply.

'…new incursion…'

Korpus slammed an armoured fist against the side of his helmet. As if mocking his frustration, the static rose in volume. The import of the commander's words was not lost on Korpus: yet more Chaos Marines had landed on Antillis IV.

'Cognis dead…'

The glands which resided within the Company Librarian were of especial value. Implanted in the correct candidate, they would provide the Chapter with a replacement for the veteran psyker, whose reading of the Emperor's Tarot and subtle awareness of the aetheric shifts that heralded the arrival of daemonic forces had turned the tide of battle against greater numbers than had thus far been encountered on Antillis IV. However, the idea of a psychic shock wave powerful enough to end Cognis's long and loyal service almost beggared the imagination. The odds against the Avenging Sons had, it seemed, become much worse.

The hiss and crackle faded and Korpus grabbed the opportunity to reply. 'I am almost with you, sir. I will perform the excision on Cognis and be ready to stand with you...'

'NO!' Selleus cut vehemently across his Apothecary's transmission. He spoke quickly, obviously mindful of possible interference. 'Your orders are to quit the planet, taking all excised glands with you. If that proves to be impossible, you are to destroy them all, including your own. Do you understand?'

For a heartbeat, Korpus struggled to digest the message. Quit the planet? That was not the way of the Avenging Sons. Fight, yes. Die, if necessary. But run?

'Apothecary, respond,' came Selleus's voice. 'Did you receive my last transmission?' A faint crackle had begun to edge his words.

'Transmission received, commander.' Korpus forced his reply from between numb lips. 'But not understood. I can store the glands on my return to base. Surely we can fight on?' Korpus glanced up at the chateau, still maddeningly far above him.

'Negative.' A susurrating hiss washed over Selleus's words, growing steadily in volume. 'Cognis's last message was clear... Outer wall breached... compound overrun... Imperative... all viable glands... out of enemy hands... Imperative!... We embrace... Mercy's Kiss.'

Mercy's Kiss: the name given to the small pistol which hung at Korpus's belt – and the belt of every Apothecary. With it, Korpus would ease the pain of the fatally wounded, thus buying his patient an easier demise and himself more time to perform an Excision. The message in Selleus's use of the name was clear.

The commander's voice erupted into a series of howling whoops and squeals – interference caused by the close proximity of a large concentration of warp energy. The picture in Korpus's mind's eye changed from one of his company preparing to take the war to the enemy, to one of a beleaguered outpost fighting a last-ditch battle against the warp hordes.

'Message received and understood!' Korpus shouted his reply in the hope that it might reach his commander. 'You shall be remem–'

Before he could complete the litany, the distant chateau dissolved in a series of explosions. Gouts of rock and ash flew into the air. A multiple concussion swept down the hillside, pushing a roiling cloud of ash before it. Korpus dropped to the ground, curled so as to present his back to the avalanche and protect the phials loaded in his thigh-packs.

For what seemed like an eternity, the falling debris beat a relentless tattoo against Korpus's ceramite carapace. As he lay there, his commander's last words rang in his ears – and with it, the questions he longed to ask: how had the situation become so dire that his entire company would choose suicide over continued resistance? Why was it so important for the glands in his care to be taken off-world or destroyed?

Eventually the rock fall subsided and Korpus climbed to his feet, ash falling from his shoulders like snow. Looking up at the smoking remains of the chateau, reduced to a ragged collection of charred fragments by the detonation of the company's entire store of munitions, he completed the ritual. Never before had he said the words with such fury and such determination: 'You shall be avenged!'

GUIDED BY THE advice of Tiresias, the Company Astropath, Selleus had ordered the Avenging Sons' Thunderhawk gunships to make landfall at the edge of the greatest concentration of warp energy. Never one to waste time picking a way through the opposition's perimeter, he preferred to strike at the enemy's heart. The reports received from Antillis IV's Imperial garrison upon their company ship's shift out of warp made it clear that any such tactical niceties were already redundant. The planet's Imperial Governor had waited too long before sending a request for help – whether this was due to misplaced confidence or sheer incompetence no longer mattered. The Avenging Sons would have to drive straight for the centre of the enemy's forces, or all was lost.

But all, it seemed, was lost. Korpus's mind nagged at the fact as he made his way towards the drop zone: a garrison airfield still several hours distant. Defended by a unit of Imperial Guardsmen, the Thunderhawks offered his only chance of obeying his commander's final order.

Turning his back on the rocky outcrop which now bore only the smouldering remains of his brothers, Korpus forged across a landscape littered with evidence of Antillis IV's damnation: shattered hulks of Chimera troop carriers, their tracks blown from under them while attempting a strategic withdrawal. A Leman Russ tank, presumably the troop carriers' escort, had been tossed aside like a discarded toy, its armour plating shredded, its crew reduced to bloody daubs. Korpus picked his way between the hulks, wary in case the Chaos-inspired troops that had inflicted such damage had posted a rearguard.

'Apothecary!' The faint plea drifted across the field of static that filled his transceiver's earplug and was gone so quickly that Korpus couldn't be sure it had come from beyond the confines of his own skull. Perhaps it was just a memory of cries he had heard on many battlefields on many worlds. He shivered, then picked up his pace, heading for a stand of flash-blasted trees, the ash-blizzard howling at his back.

Just inside the tree line, Korpus found more wreckage: a battery of Basilisks, reduced to so much scrap, their crews torn to pieces. As he surveyed the organic detritus that lay, draped across the remains of the artillery pieces, the cry came again.

'Apothecary!'

'An echo, nothing more,' he told himself, though he could not suppress the shiver that ran through him. The call of a wounded Space Marine, broadcast hours ago, bouncing back to the planet's surface from the warp-clogged troposphere. The rest of his company had answered the order to regroup and died beside their commander. Korpus was the last of them.

'And you have your orders,' he reminded himself, his voice sounding dead and flat inside his helmet. He should have been with them to meet that last assault. Selleus's last transmission made no sense. The righteous determination with which he had promised his commander vengeance had faded, leaving only questions and confusion.

'Confusion is the seed-bed of Chaos,' Korpus intoned, remembering an aphorism from the Avenging Sons' Chapter Book as he marched on through the trees. Their branches had been stripped and blackened in the wake of the Chaos army's progress. Massive boles had been overturned; wind-blown ash now gathered among their roots.

'Uproot it, in the Emperor's name,' he continued. *If only it were that simple.*

HOURS PASSED, EVERY one of them eating up the distance between Korpus and the airfield. Rugged, mountainous countryside gave way to flat plains and occasional patches of woodland. By nightfall, the Apothecary could see the gap-toothed outline of a city on the horizon, backlit by a dull reddish glow, which could mean only one thing: the forces of Chaos had reached the city. The firelight would be the result of the massive pyres built from the corpses of the city's inhabitants, gouting oily smoke and adding to the ash storms which continued to swirl about him as he marched.

The Thunderhawks' drop zone was located on the outskirts of the city. Had the Imperial troops left to guard the attack ships been able to hold off their attackers, then Korpus would be able to fulfil his commander's orders. If not...

'We may yet meet in the Book of Martyrs, Pereus,' Korpus muttered grimly as he strode on, step after tireless, servo-assisted step.

The night passed in a barely-remembered monotony of motion. Implanted in the early stages of a Space Marine's genetic conditioning, the Catalepsian Node allowed such a warrior to reduce all non-essential mental processes to a minimum, mimicking the effects of sleep, yet retain full awareness of his surroundings and objectives.

Korpus returned to full wakefulness as the first rays of the Antillis system's bloated sun rose between the buildings that now towered above him. He had reached the outskirts of the city and now marched along its cracked and buckled highways, still heading towards the airstrip. The ruins of what had once been an industrial area flanked the highway with shattered factories and storage yards.

As he marched, Korpus recited the Morning Prayer of the Avenging Sons: 'If this day be my last, I shall spend it in the service of your will, Emperor, Saviour, Last Hope of Mankind.' Light years away, aboard the vast, cathedral-like Chapter ship that was the home of the Avenging Sons, the morning bell would be tolling. Every Avenging Son not on assignment would be gathered in the Great Chapel, reciting the same prayer as if with one voice. 'For I am an instrument of your will, a scourge of your enemies. I am an…'

The voice that burst from his transceiver stopped Korpus in his tracks, the remainder of the Morning Prayer unspoken. The voice was high and clear, uttering a battle cry he never expected to hear again.

'Avenging Sons!'

'AVENGING SONS!' SCOUT Vaelus swung his bolter left and right, pumping bolt after bolt into the Traitor Marines which advanced towards him between the high towers of containerised foodstuffs that would now never leave this storage yard for other star systems.

'Avenging Sons!' Scout Salvus, to Vaelus's right, took up the war cry, as did Scout Marus, to his left. Their bolters spat explosive death into the faces of the servants of the warp, vaporising heads, severing limbs – but it was not enough.

Their black-armoured opponents seemed not to feel the pain of their injuries. Shrieking with daemonic laughter and crying, 'Khorne! Khorne!' even as another bolt detonated against their armour, they pressed forward. And there were so many of them, jostling with one another to be the first to taste the flesh of a fledgling Space Marine. So many…

Something slammed against Vaelus's back. Scout Tallis, flanked by Scouts Orris and Flavus, forced back by the Khorne-inspired berserkers that advanced towards them, equally as heedless of the cannonade of bolter fire that was being pumped into their midst, now stood back-to-back with their battle-brothers.

'For the Emperor!' Vaelus cried. They might fall here today, but their enemy would know in whose name they died.

'For the Emperor!' came the unexpected reply, moments before Vaelus heard the muffled crack of a bolt pistol being discharged against an armoured body from closer than the two arms-lengths which separated the Scouts and their attackers. The concussive report sounded again and again, counterpointed by the high-pitched crackling whine of a power fist at full charge. High-voltage detonations punctuated the whine as it connected with armour. The copper tang of boiling blood reached Vaelus as he caught his first glimpse of the figure that was cutting a swathe through the berserkers, fighting with an almost equally mindless fury: a figure whose armour bore the insignia of the Avenging Sons. A figure in white.

'FOR THE EMPEROR!' Korpus's blood sang as he parried the downward sweep of a chainsword with his power fist. The whirring blade shattered against the glove's energy field. Korpus slammed his bolt pistol against the black, sigil-etched breastplate of his attacker and pulled the trigger twice. Still laughing, the berserker fell back, his chest a smoking ruin. Stepping past him, Korpus placed the open palm of his power fist against the back of another skull-helmed traitor. The Chaos Marine, still too mindlessly intent on reaching the Scouts to react to the new threat, stiffened as his armour's servos went into spasm.

'Vengeance!' Korpus breathed, and closed his fist.

MINDS LOST TO the berserker fury of the Blood God, the Chaos Marines reacted with fatal slowness to the whirlwind of death that had appeared in their midst. Pressed close in their desire to reach the Scouts, they found turning to meet the white-armoured killer difficult: ablative plates snagged and took valuable seconds to disengage, seconds that allowed Korpus to step close, press the muzzle of his bolt pistol against the grinning, fanged skull of a face plate and pull the trigger.

Seeing this, Vaelus closed the gap between himself and the nearest Chaos Marine – and was almost decapitated by his intended target's chainsword. Dropping to one knee to avoid the chattering blade, the Scout pressed his bolter against the nearest of the Chaos Marine's knee joints and fired. Rising as the crippled berserker fell, Vaelus fired again, three times, vaporising the traitor's head.

'Forward, Avenging Sons!' Vaelus cried. 'The day can still be ours!' He turned, searching for a new target, and found himself visor-to-visor with the Scouts' white-armoured saviour. Without a word, the Apothecary stepped past him, heading for the line of Chaos Marines which had closed upon the three Scouts at Vaelus's back and now threatened to overwhelm them.

Before turning to follow Korpus, Vaelus glanced along the narrow passage-way between the containers. Moments before, there had been a seething mass of black armour and grinning skulls. Now a tangled carpet of shattered, smoking corpses lay before him.

'Emperor be praised. He has delivered us!' Vaelus breathed, then hurried to join the battle that still raged.

* * *

'ALL OF THEM?' Salvus's voice betrayed the mixture of disbelief, confusion and fear felt by all of the Scouts as they listened to Korpus's account of the last hours of the Second Company.

'The entire Second Company, yes,' Korpus, helmetless, replied as he worked on the stump of Marus's right arm, using a long-needled syringe to inject unguents into the raw pink flesh. The Scout's genetically-altered blood had already clotted, sealing the wound, but necrotising infections were still a risk to one who had yet to complete the full course of enhancements that would elevate him to Space Marine status.

'Time is a factor here,' Korpus said, after binding Marus's arm and re-securing his helmet. 'This world is lost. My orders are to save the glands in my keeping. There will be other traitorous abominations such as these who will try to stop me. I may require an escort.'

'We stand ready,' Vaelus declared. At his words, the Scouts snapped to attention. Korpus surveyed them and nodded approvingly. Of the five survivors who stood before him, only Marus had suffered serious injury.

'Then we move,' he said. 'Bring his weapons.' He gestured to the body which lay against one wall of the container-canyon – Flavus, his torso all but bisected by a berserker's chain-axe – then stabbed a finger first at Salvus, then Tallis, both busily donning their helmets while Orris clipped Flavus's bolt pistol and chainsword to his equipment belt. 'You take point. You guard the rear.'

As Korpus expected, decisive orders served to ease the Scouts' disquiet. Since the death of their sergeant, incinerated by a Chaos Marine's melta while leading them in a probing mission beyond the Avenging Sons' former perimeter, the Scouts had been playing a deadly game of cat-and-mouse with the enemy, zig-zagging across the battlefield in the hope of re-locating the Second Company. Bearings lost, communications frustrated by the blizzard of ash and static, they had sought shelter in this vast container yard, believing that they had shaken off their pursuers, only to find themselves trapped by a pincer attack.

'The Emperor sent you,' Vaelus had told Korpus. 'We were daemon-fodder, but for your arrival.'

'The Emperor watches over us all,' Korpus had replied automatically. His blood was still singing in his ears, the urge to rend and kill without thought, without emotion had yet to subside – and, in truth, he wished that it never would. The killing rage – the 'Vengeful Heart' as it had been dubbed, centuries ago – was the state aspired to by every Avenging Son. A unit of Avenging Sons in such a condition was all but unstoppable on the battlefield; their only desire was to move forward through whatever enemy stood before them, their only desire to kill.

Which is what made Selleus's last act so incomprehensible. As an Apothecary, Korpus understood that he should temper his own Vengeful Heart in order to perform his duties. It was an honour and he accepted it as the Emperor's will. But for Selleus to deliberately extinguish the hearts of his entire company...

Such doubts had crept back as the killing rage subsided. To quiet them once again, Korpus turned his mind to his new role as leader of the Scout Squad. But deep within the cage of his soul, his Vengeful Heart beat strong, demanding to be heard.

'THERE'S MOVEMENT,' VAELUS reported as he peered through the ocularius. He adjusted the focusing dials. Lenses spun within the brass casing, allowing him a greater depth of field. 'Possibly human.'

'Doubtful,' Korpus said. He and the Scout crouched behind a pile of discarded aero-engines at the edge of the airfield. Warehouses and hangars curved away to either side, many of them punctured by heavy cannon and las-fire. The field itself was pock-marked with craters, dotted with the remains of commercial and military aircraft. When their dropships had landed, both the aircraft and the buildings had been intact.

'The Thunderhawks?' he asked. Vaelus adjusted the dials again.

'Not good,' the Scout reported. 'Two are complete wrecks. The other three have all taken a pounding. There's no way to tell if any can fly.'

'We only need one,' Korpus replied, all too aware of the irony of his words, but determined to remain focused on the mission.

The sudden cough of bolter fire from the rear drew their attention from the attack ships. Vaelus stowed the ocularius and followed Korpus, who was already running towards the nearest hangar.

They arrived to find the other Scouts standing over the bodies of three Imperial Guardsman, members of the unit assigned to guard the Thunderhawks. Their bodies bore the marks of impacts both old and new, but also the buboes and other malformations that spoke of only one thing.

'Necromancy,' Korpus stated flatly. 'This world is now securely in Chaos's grasp. Time is short. Soon even the living will be unable to resist its influence.'

As if to underline his words, one of the corpses began to twitch. Impossibly, it raised itself on one shattered arm, opened its exploded eyes...

Tallis's chainsword sliced through the ex-Guardsman's head, rupturing it like an overripe fruit. Its brains, turned black and fluid by the same necromantic power which had re-animated its hours-dead corpse, splashed across the ground. A rank sewer-stench filled the air.

'Any sentient being in the vicinity will know we're here by now,' said Korpus. 'Make for the nearest Thunderhawk. Stay tight and stay alert.'

Korpus led the Scouts from the cover of the hangar, jogging swiftly across the open ground between it and the attack craft. The closer they got the worse the situation looked. Even the three Thunderhawks which remained upright on their landing skids looked ready for the reclamation plants of the Adeptus Mechanicus.

Bolter fire sounded from his left. He turned. Orris had dispatched another re-animated Guardsman.

'Head shots are not enough,' he reminded the Scout. 'Dismemberment is the only way to ensure they don't come after you again.'

'Understood,' Orris replied and set about the corpse with his chainsword. More gunfire erupted from the far side of the group of Thunderhawks. Tallis and Marus had encountered more of the foul things.

'Who here has received flight training?' Korpus demanded. 'I need someone to check the instrumentation.'

'Salvus!' Vaelus called. The Scout had stayed close to the Apothecary, adopting the role of aide-de-camp. Salvus ran back between two of the Thunderhawks, ducking to avoid the blackened and twisted remains of a sensor array.

'We need to know which of these can fly, if any,' Korpus told him. 'They may look like wrecks, but I've known them to take off in a worse state than this.' As Salvus ran up the ramp into the belly of the nearest craft, Korpus offered up a silent prayer that his words would prove to be more than a mere panacea.

The bark of Imperial-issue munitions echoed from the interior of the Thunderhawk. Both Korpus and Vaelus turned, stepped onto the drop-ramp, then dodged the selection of body parts that flew from the hatch, accompanied by a chainsword's chattering.

'Best check the others,' Salvus called out from the belly of the ship. Before Korpus could issue an order, Vaelus was already halfway up the ramp of the neighbouring craft.

Good soldiers, Korpus thought. For the first time, he dared believe that they might escape this doomed world and reach the Chapter ship, where the Scouts would undergo implantation of the gene seed from the glands that he carried in his armour. Perhaps they might form the basis for a new Second Company. If so, they would bring honour to the memory of the corpses they would leave on Antillis IV.

'Pressurising,' Salvus's voice crackled over Korpus's transceiver. He and Orris had spent the last hour jury-rigging the seal around the main hatch, using parts from interior hatches, making frequent reference to the Adeptus Mechanicus Prayer Book he had found in a locker on the flight deck.

Korpus stood outside the hatch, listening to the hiss and pop as the seal closed. After checking over each of the three Thunderhawks, Salvus had declared the first one to be the most spaceworthy. While he and Orris worked, the others continued to prowl the airfield, using bolter and chainsword to dispatch the necromantically resurrected.

On the flight deck, Salvus watched the icons on the control board. Several relating to non-essential systems were dead; others – including the weapons board – glowed red, indicating failure, but they too should not prevent spaceflight. Salvus narrowed his eyes, concentrating on the set of icons that related to the craft's internal environment. They showed green – for the moment.

Long moments passed. Through the gunship's view-screens, Korpus scanned the edge of the airfield. It was a miracle that they had been allowed so much time, that the Chaos Marines and the daemons that commanded them had not scented their presence here and closed in to finish them off.

'The Machine God is with us!' Salvus's relief-filled words jerked Korpus from his thoughts. Another hiss and pop, and the main hatch swung open. The smiling Scout stood in the doorway. 'With your permission, Apothecary, I could transfer the weapons system from Hawk Four…'

'No time,' Korpus interjected. 'Begin pre-flight rituals. We've been sitting around like targets on a shooting range for too long as it is.'

'Understood.' Salvus disappeared back into the craft.

Korpus strode up the ramp, following Salvus inside. While the Scout made for the raised flight deck, Korpus stooped to open a locker set into the wall beside the Navigator's chart table, which bore the seal of the Apothecarion. Removing his helmet and gloves, Korpus released the catches on the locker door and felt the gentle kiss of air as its vacuum seal was breached. The door swung open, revealing the racks of empty phial-holders within. Minutes later, all were full.

'Soon, my brothers. Be patient.' In his mind, Korpus addressed the Avenging Sons Scouts who, like those with him here on Antillis IV, were awaiting implantation of the gene-seed. The glands he had harvested – and which now floated before him, their preservative-filled phials nestling securely in the locker's racks – would help ensure that the Emperor's crusade would continue.

Korpus closed the locker door, secured its vacuum seal, then refastened the long ceramite thigh-plates over his suit's now empty storage bays. As he had placed each phial into the locker, he had felt a weight lift from his shoulders. Though he had performed this act on countless other worlds, never had the special duty of an Apothecary weighed so heavily upon him, nor had he felt such relief at its completion.

'Apothecary!' Vaelus stood at the Thunderhawk's main hatch. Korpus hurried the length of the craft's interior, re-attaching his gloves, automatically checking the load in his bolt pistol's magazine and the charge in his power fist.

'Report,' he demanded of the Scout, though the sound of bolter fire and a discordant, guttural chanting provided all the answer he needed.

'Brother, the enemy has found us!'

BEHIND THEM, THE Thunderhawk's engine ratcheted upwards in pitch. At Korpus's order, Salvus had rushed through the last verses of the pre-flight incantation. The engines didn't sound too healthy – what should have been a smooth rise in tone and volume was interrupted by coughs and judders that had more in common with a chronic chest infection – but the Scout remained confident that the craft would fly.

Korpus and Vaelus had paced away from the Thunderhawk, sheltering from the ash-storm kicked up by its back– and down-drafts under the fuselage of Hawk Four. Korpus held the Scout's ocularius to his eyes, scanning the perimeter of the airfield, while Vaelus continued his report. 'We made contact with their point men during a sweep of the southern perimeter. We hit them hard and fast – I don't think they had time to send out a warning. The others hung back. We still have a few frag mines. They were to lay the mines beyond the perimeter and then retreat. They should have been back by now.'

'Here they come,' Korpus said. 'And they are not alone.'

Through the lenses of the instrument, Korpus watched as the three Scouts raced through the ragged remains of the airfield's southern gate. Bolter fire chewed up the ash-covered ground all around them. A black-armoured horde was at their back, howling, scenting blood and one more victory in the name of their foul masters. From the unevenness of Tallis's stride, Korpus judged that he must have taken a serious hit to one leg. Shifting focus, he tried to assess the exact size of the threat they were facing, when his gaze fell upon a sight that could mean only disaster.

'Emperor's mercy!' he breathed as the vast, obscene bulk of a Dreadnought filled his view, towering over the troops around it, lurching as it stomped through the ash and mud. Its black armour was covered in twisted sigils proclaiming its daemonic allegiance, blasphemous verses in praise of the Dark Gods, and what looked like dolls hanging from chains attached to its carapace.

Despite his revulsion, Korpus adjusted the focusing dials again... Not dolls. Human corpses, some still wearing the tattered remains of Imperial Guard uniforms; faces bloated, limbs torn away, guts slit open and their contents hung like grotesque garlands around their necks. Final proof, if proof were needed, that Antillis IV had fallen.

'They need covering fire!' Korpus barked as he tore the ocularius from his eyes. His mind raced. Even if the jury-rigged Thunderhawk was airworthy, it would need time to achieve sufficient altitude to be out of range of the Chaos army's guns. He tried not to think of the range of the Dreadnought's cannon. It could swat the fleeing craft from the sky long after it had outdistanced the Chaos Marines' bolters.

'Hawk Four's weapons system is still operational,' he told Vaelus. 'Get to work.' With a nod, the Scout ran for the main hatch. Korpus donned and secured his helmet. By the time he spoke into his transceiver, he had come to a decision: 'Scout Salvus, immediate dust-off. Do you understand? Go. Now!'

'Apothecary, please repeat!' came the uncomprehending reply. 'Leave now? What about the others? Yourself? I cannot–'

'My job is done. The future of the Second Company is in your hands. We'll keep them busy until you're out of range. Tell our brothers that we took the Emperor's holy vengeance into the mouth of Hell. For are we not Avenging Sons?'

'Avenging Sons!' Salvus answered, his voice firm once again. 'Your name shall live forever in the Chapel of Martyrs, Apothecary Korpus!'

The engine's pitch changed again, rising to a scream as the control surfaces swung into the correct alignment. The landing skids groaned as the gunship's bulk began to shift.

'Avenging Sons!' Vaelus's voice echoed in the Apothecary's ears as the Scout fired a first volley from Hawk Four's lascannon into the approaching black horde. As he ran to meet the other Scouts, Korpus saw their impact: dark-armoured bodyparts flew in all directions like confetti, leaving holes in the oncoming line, which were quickly filled by more of their treacherous brethren. Vaelus fired again, punching more holes in the onrushing tide of Chaos. Behind him, the engines of Salvus's Thunderhawk had taken on the unmistakable tone of an airborne craft. His precious cargo was on its way home.

'Avenging Sons!' Korpus cried, his blood singing as he raced to battle. His last duty performed, he was an Apothecary no longer. Now he was just a warrior. A warrior with a Vengeful Heart.

KORPUS HIT THE Chaos line like a weapon wielded by the Emperor himself. Black-armoured abominations flew left and right, skull-helms shattered by close-quarters bolter fire and blows from his power fist at full discharge. To either side of him, Tallis, Orris and one-armed Marus carved sections from their enemy with their chainswords, blew away limbs and punctured breastplates with their bolters.

Marus was the first to fall. His bolter empty, he reached across his body to unhook his chainsword. In the few seconds it took for him to grasp the hilt of his weapon, a Khorne-chanting Chaos Marine tore his head from his shoulders with a chattering, sigil-etched chain-axe. Tallis returned the favour, severing the Chaos Marine's axe-arm with a well-placed sword-strike to its elbow, followed by a bolter volley in the face, but there was nothing to be done for Marus and no time to mourn. Tallis and Orris surged on, keeping pace with Korpus, cutting a gory swathe through the servants of the Outer Dark. The black tide closed behind them, still making for the Thunderhawks, some already wasting bolts in an attempt to bring down the accelerating Thunderhawk, already several hundred feet above them.

Korpus and the others ignored them. Vaelus, still at the weapons board of Hawk Four, scythed them down with the lascannon. Korpus had issued fresh orders as he ran, leading the Scouts into battle. They knew their target: the Dreadnought.

It already loomed above them, marching with implacable, earth-shaking strides to meet them. In one steel-clawed arm it held a mace the size of a man; its other upper limb had been replaced by a double-linked lascannon which was aimed far above the heads of the Marines. Korpus didn't need to turn to see its target. The half-dead, totally insane Chaos Marine encased within its inches-thick hide was drawing a bead on the fleeing Thunderhawk gunship.

Kicking aside the last, headless victim of his bolter, Korpus holstered the weapon and made an adjustment to his power fist. Already buzzing with energy, the glove began to emit a continuous high-pitched squeal. The plates of Korpus's battle suit rang with sympathetic vibrations. His teeth began to chatter insanely as the energy from the overloading glove hummed through his bones. His head felt as if it might explode within his helmet.

A single Chaos Marine stood between Korpus and the Dreadnought. Rapid fire from its bolter sprayed diagonally across the Apothecary's armour, knocking him back several steps, but the ceramite plates held. Korpus stepped up to his assailant and punched him squarely in the chest.

But for the lingering smell of ozone and the fragments of fused flesh and armour that lay scattered at Korpus's feet, the Chaos Marine might never have existed. For a heartbeat, the power fist was silent. Korpus feared that its power cell was already empty, that his plan would be undone by his unwise, pre-emptive strike. Then the glove resumed its ear-splitting squeal. Korpus smiled, then sprinted for the Dreadnought's nearest leg.

A VOLLEY OF las-fire arced up from the Dreadnought's cannon. Flashing across the intervening space, it missed the nose of the still-rising Thunderhawk by what felt like inches. The craft's superstructure groaned and creaked as it was buffeted by the shock-waves of super-heated air. As he jockeyed the flight controls, Salvus muttered a short prayer to the Machine God.

'Whatever you plan to do to that cursed thing, Apothecary,' Salvus added, sparing a thought for the comrades he was leaving behind, 'do it now!'

THE DREADNOUGHT PAUSED in its march to adjust its aim. Korpus knew that it would not miss a second time. Shucking his power fist, whose squeal had passed beyond the range of human hearing, he jammed it between the web of struts and power conduits that ran behind the unholy war machine's knee joint. Blue fire played across the surface of the glove. Tendrils of the barely-tamed lightning began to arc across the surface of the Dreadnought's lower extremities.

For a moment, Korpus stared, entranced by the sight. Orris's cry of pain as his armour was breached by bolter fire from a dozen attackers jerked him back to the deadly present. Spinning on his heel, Korpus made to rejoin the fray.

Orris lay where he had been defending the Apothecary's back, his chest a smoking ruin. One more son of the Emperor to be avenged. Tallis was nowhere to be seen; had he also fallen? Korpus noticed also that Hawk Four's lascannon had fallen silent. Was he the last Avenging Son alive on Antillis IV? If so the hordes of Chaos would remember his name.

'Avenging Son!' he bellowed, launching himself at the nearest of the surrounding Chaos-spawn, chainsword raised, bolter spitting death.

He never reached his target. The power fist detonated, vaporising the lower half of the Dreadnought. The corrupt war machine tumbled backwards, lascannon firing a wild, ineffectual volley into the sky. The shock wave from the blast slapped Korpus in the back, scattering him and the Chaos Marines around him like so many model soldiers, swept off a table at the end of a game. Ears ringing, Korpus momentarily lost consciousness.

Blinking back to awareness, Korpus found himself on his back, staring up at the sky. Above him arched a single vapour trail – the Thunderhawk, powering through the stratosphere, safe from attack.

His killing rage, his Vengeful Heart, had subsided. He felt a strange sense of peace, one borne of exhaustion and the knowledge that he had done his duty. He tried to move, to get to his feet, but his legs wouldn't respond. Something had been broken by the power fist's detonation. Was he dying? He thought briefly of Sergeant Pereus.

'Man is born alone,' he whispered. A grey mist edged his vision. He knew he should complete the Rite of Extreme Unction, but felt too tired to continue. The grey mist enveloped him.

'Apothecary!' It was the voice he had heard earlier, while marching alone across Antillis IV. He had thought it to be an echo, an old transmission bounced off the upper atmosphere. Now, undisguised by static, it sounded close to his ear. It was not the voice of any of the Second Company. It had a soft, unpleasant tone.

He tried to turn his head, open his eyes, see to whom the voice belonged. But his head wouldn't turn and his eyes wouldn't open.

The grey mist turned to black.

'Apothecary?'

Surprised that he was able to do so, Korpus opened his eyes. Rather than the sky above Antillis IV, or the ruins of the airfield, he found himself staring at the walls of what might have been a laboratory in the Avenging Sons' Apothecarion – might have been, were it not for the nightmarish collection of specimens that hung upon the walls and sat in clear jars of preserving fluid. The malformed limbs, misshapen heads and torsos bore no relation to humanity, but to the breeding grounds of the warp. In the shadows cast by the dull reddish light which illuminated the room, Korpus thought he saw movement. Narrowing his eyes, he saw that he was right. A collection of what resembled nothing so much as clawed, fanged foetuses thrashed against the glass of one large vessel.

'Apothecary!' The tone of the voice at his ear shifted from enquiry to satisfaction. Korpus tried to turn his head, move any of his limbs, but found that he could not. He was all but naked, stripped of his armour and robe, secured by metallic straps to a table of some kind, tilted at an angle close to the vertical. 'Of course,' the voice purred. 'You would like to see your saviour.'

A figure stepped into Korpus's field of view. Covered from throat to floor in a robe made from a slick, vulcanised fabric, he held in one hand a pair of gloves of the same material. The hand which held the gloves appeared normal, but the other was twisted, possessed of too many knuckle joints.

Noticing the direction of Korpus's gaze, the figure held up the hand – his left – and flexed the fingers before Korpus's eyes. The digits moved with an unnatural, insectile grace, each of the extra joints allowing the fingers a range of movement that Korpus, dedicated to the preservation of the human form, found appalling.

'One of my first refinements,' the vile figure said, proudly. 'I find it allows for a more subtle surgical approach.'

For the first time, Korpus focused on the stranger's face. With the bald pate, the sallow skin and sunken cheeks, Korpus might have been looking at his old instructor, Apothecary Lorus. But the skin was stretched too tightly over this man's skull, as if it had been removed, the fat scraped away from under the skin and then reapplied too closely. The black eyes shone out from under heavy brows. A warped intelligence, perhaps genius, danced in those eyes.

'It has been some time since I sought to preserve a human life,' the stranger continued. 'I am pleased that I have not forgotten how.'

Korpus tried to speak, but his throat was clogged as if from an unnaturally long sleep. He coughed, and tried again, his voice cracking. 'Who…?'

'Of course!' the stranger laughed. 'How impolite of me! It has also been some time since I received a guest schooled in simple social manners.

'I am Fabrikus. Apothecary Fabrikus.'

The words froze Korpus's heart. Fabrikus's name was a dark legend in the Apothecarion of every Space Marine Chapter. A brilliant man, he served with the First Company of the World Eaters, gaining distinction as a warrior and as a surgeon, before following Primarch Angron into the service of the Ruinous Powers. In the centuries since the Great Heresy, his name had become a byword for perverse experimentation.

Some said he was even behind many of the mutations undergone by Chaos Marines: the fusion of flesh to armour of the World Eaters, the hellish combination of near-dead warrior and implacable war machine that was a Chaos Dreadnought.

'I see you have heard of me,' Fabrikus smiled at the look of horror on Korpus's face. 'And I imagine you are wondering what my interest might be in a fallen Space Marine on a fallen world. The answer is simple: the gene-seed.'

Korpus's mind spun back in time, to his last communication with Commander Selleus. He heard again his words, obscured by the waves of static: 'New incursion... Cognis dead...'

'Your Librarian was a truly powerful psyker,' Fabrikus purred, as if reading his mind. 'Fortunately my... allies... were more than his equal. It seemed, however, that before his death he gleaned enough of our purpose in joining the assault on the planet you knew as Antillis IV to warn his commander. Their suicide destroyed all of our advance party. Had it not been for our interception of your leader's last transmission, we would have believed our cause was lost.'

'All viable glands... out of enemy hands...' Selleus's words rang in Korpus's memory.

'You see, my masters require more troops, more than can be provided by the harvest of the seed from those already serving their holy purpose. I have spent centuries experimenting with the other races available to me, but the seed refuses to take, or else it produces mutations that are... unhelpful,' Fabrikus's words carried a hint of frustration. As if hearing them, the fanged things thrashed against the confining glass walls of their preservative-filled prisons.

'Though I would never say this to my masters, I believe the warp causes problems with the seed from our own warriors, affects their potency. I have, therefore, decided to return to take up my earlier role and harvest glands from a more pure source, unaffected by the energies of my masters' home.' To hear Fabrikus speak, he and Korpus might have been fellow professionals, discussing the results of a failed experiment and the new measures that might be taken to ensure future success.

'I believe that the seed from those who continue to stubbornly serve the False Emperor might provide me with the material I need to create new types of warrior, loyal to the Dark Lords of the warp, unstoppable in battle.'

'You... you knew I had the glands,' Korpus whispered.

Fabrikus nodded. 'We tracked you across half the world,' he said, smiling. 'And we found you!'

Now it was Korpus's turn to smile. 'But I have them no longer! By the time I blew your Dreadnought to oblivion, they were already off-world! You have failed, Fabrikus! Failed!'

'By the time I found you, all the glands you carried so heroically were indeed off-world,' Fabrikus conceded, apparently unaffected by Korpus's mocking words. 'All of the glands – bar two.'

The import of his words crashed in on Korpus. Nestling at the base of his throat and deep within his naked chest, were the glands he had carried since the day of their implantation, the day that he truly became a Space Marine, a day of such pride, such honour.

'No!' he gasped, wide-eyed with horror. He had been so intent on vengeance, of dying as an Avenging Son should. Believing his duty as an Apothecary was complete, he had delivered the future of his breed, perhaps of the entire human race, into the hands of this monster, this twisted reflection of all he held dear.

'Oh, yes,' Fabrikus purred. Before Korpus's horrified gaze, the skin around his left eye began to bulge, the eye itself changing shape, elongating in an impossible manner, as if supplementary lenses were pushing forward from within the confines of his skull, improving his focus for the surgery to come.

He reached towards an instrument gurney set beside the table upon which Korpus now struggled vainly. The multi-jointed fingers of his left hand selected a scalpel. Longer and thinner than the others, it was designed for only one purpose: excision.

'I prefer to operate without analgesia,' he said, stepping up to the table. 'I think the absence of pain always dulls the experience, don't you?'

Apothecary Fabrikus set to work. His subject's screaming served only to excite the thrashing abominations within their tank into a frenzy, snapping and clawing at their fellows. Korpus cried out, not for himself, but for his honour, lost in the heat of battle. Lost forever.

UNTHINKING JUSTICE

Andras Millward

AND THOSE DEDICATED *to the Emperor's work will be beset upon all sides by ene-mies. Be vigilant, for they–*

The door signal sounded. Codicier Levi, of the Librarius of the Imperial Order of Black Consuls, sighed and ran a hand through his close-cropped dark hair. Reverentially, he closed his leather-bound copy of the Codex Astartes, stood up and walked to the window of his spartan quarters. The landing lights of one of the Chapter ship's shuttles briefly illuminated his angular, clean-shaven features.

'Enter.' Levi continued looking out of the window, contemplating the vast starry backcloth before him and the inauspicious verse he had read in the codex. He spoke again, softly, on hearing his visitor enter his quarters. 'A good day for the Emperor's work, standard bearer.'

A short laugh came from behind him. 'Your powers do you justice as always, Levi. But surely all days are fitting for His blessed work, brother-librarian. Or does your faith wane in these dark days?'

Levi turned to face his visitor. Brother Aeorum, standard bearer of the Black Consul's Third Company, stood smiling in the doorway. A powerfully built man, he was dressed as Levi was, in a black tunic edged with yellow. Levi gave a rare smile of his own. 'Aeorum, it's good to see you on this ill-omened day. Come in.'

Levi welcomed the unexpected appearance of the youthful standard bearer. He studied the broad face before him, the scar that ran across one cheekbone and the bridge of Aeorum's nose. The deep mark, left there long ago by a genestealer's claw, may have faded with time but the standard bearer had changed little since they had last met. Decades ago, Levi and Aeorum had served together in the Black Consuls' Scout Company, their friendship forged in tyranid blood during the bloody and costly battle for Manalar. While Levi's psychic powers had taken him to the Librarius, Aeorum's fearsome fighting ability had led to him being the youngest standard bearer in the Chapter's history. They met infrequently these days, but the inhuman terrors they had faced together ensured that the bond between them remained as strong as ever.

Aeorum sat down opposite Levi, his muscular bulk dwarfing the plain wooden chair. 'Ill-omened? So you've heard the news?'

'Heard what?' Levi asked. He'd already picked up enough warning tremors during the previous day's preparations, but had not heard anything concrete about their current objectives. The Second, Third and Fourth Companies had been mobilised, which suggested that the Imperium was responding to the gravest of threats.

'The Black Consuls have picked up a distress call from Suracto. Nearly half the planet has rebelled, brother. The Emperor's hold on the planet is threatened and we speed to answer their call. Captain Estrus will brief us later this morning.'

Levi nodded. 'So I understand. But this is grave news indeed, and explains the speed with which we were dispatched. Suracto has been a shining beacon against the encroaching darkness we face across the galaxy. An orderly, productive planet as I recall, unquestioningly loyal to the Emperor. We cannot let planets such as these slip from the Emperor's grasp.'

'You are not idle at the Librarius, I see,' Aeorum said, though there was little humour in his voice. 'Suracto has voluntarily yielded tithes a third higher than all other neighbouring planets in the system for the last five years. To see such a planet fall to disorder and disarray is a near-catastrophe for the Imperium.'

Levi nodded. 'What manner of heresy threatens the planet?'

'The rebels reject the Emperor's order and discipline. They claim His way is too harsh, too demanding. They seek a "more equitable and just way of life".' Aeorum laced his words with scorn. 'Their heretical ways threaten to snuff out your shining beacon, Brother Levi.'

'It shall not be so, Aeorum. Such a fundamental threat to the true order must be eradicated. Completely.' His words hung in the air. Abruptly, the codicier got up and extended his hand to Aeorum. 'In spite of the circumstances, I am pleased to see you, brother. As always, it will be a great honour to fight at your side.'

Levi sensed Captain Estrus struggling to dampen his annoyance with the newcomer. Less than an hour after the Black Consuls had made planetfall on Suracto, another ship had appeared from the warp, heading directly for the Space Marines' landing site, to the north of the hive city of Thuram.

The ship bore the markings of the Inquisition and immediately on landing an inquisitor, together with a small detachment of stony-faced
retainers, had presented himself to the captain, demanding that all the
loyal forces regroup with the Black Consuls in order to reassess the situation.

'Inquisitor Parax, I am simply not interested,' Captain Estrus was saying.
His irritation seemed to deepen every furrow on his already heavily lined,
tanned face. 'We have made planetfall, but over sixty minutes later we
have still not fully deployed.' Estrus fought to make himself heard over
the rumble of the Rhino engines revving behind him and the noise of a
nearby squad of Tech Marines and their blank-faced servitors loading
missiles onto the company's Whirlwinds.

Inquisitor Parax's lean face registered no emotion. A slightly built man,
clad only in his dark official robes, he struggled to maintain some semblance of authority next to the armoured Space Marine captain towering
above him. 'While I appreciate the subtler points of the codex, captain,
nevertheless–' he began, but the rest of his sentence was drowned by the
piercing noise of a Land Speeder squad roaring immediately overhead.

Once the craft had passed, Estrus spoke at once. 'With respect, inquisitor, the blessed codex is not in question here. However, your request to
re-group is. We must deploy and go to the aid of the loyalist Suractan
forces as soon as possible. Administrator Niall, assistant to Planetary Lord
Koln, will rendezvous with us in fifteen minutes and I am sure that he
will brief us all, in full. I am most grateful that…' Estrus paused, choosing an appropriate phrase. 'That your Eminence has chosen also to
respond to the distress call but we cannot afford to wait and give the
rebels any chance to gain the upper hand.'

Parax glanced at the closed faces of the half dozen members of his retinue who stood behind him, his dark eyes narrowing slightly. He gave
himself a moment to think, then turned back. 'Very well, Captain Estrus.
I accede. But I warn you that the Inquisition will frown upon any rash
decisions you may make.'

Estrus's face darkened. 'Inquisitor, I can assure you that the Black Consuls have never made any rash decisions. Company sergeants, prepare to
deploy.' He grabbed his helmet from a nearby Consul and strode towards
the Whirlwinds.

Levi watched as the inquisitor and his retinue returned to their shuttle.
An ill-omened day, indeed, he thought. The arrival of the inquisitor did
little to alleviate the sense of foreboding that hung heavy over him. He
hefted his chainsword, checked the armour diagnostic reading on his
viewer then turned to follow the captain.

HIS FACE A mask of hatred, the rebel soldier brought his lasgun to bear on
Levi. Reacting with preternatural speed, Levi stepped towards him and

brought his chainsword down. The sword's buzzing rose to a brief scream before the man's torso split apart, showering Levi with blood.

The faintest of sensations, at the back of the head.

Levi spun smoothly and squeezed off two bolter rounds. The two rebels behind him were hurled into the Rhino's sides, leaving a pair of dark smears on the vehicle's large white tactical arrow as their lifeless bodies slid to the ground. Catching a glimpse of the Consul's standard, he turned to see Aeorum, knee deep in rebel corpses, calmly aiming and firing his bolt pistol, felling an opponent with each shot. Like the old days, Levi thought, before taking aim with his own bolter.

The rebel ambush had caught the vanguard of the Black Consuls as it began to make its way to the rendezvous point, through the battle-scarred suburban wastes on the outskirts of Thuram City. The ferocity of the rebels had initially caught the Space Marines off-guard but very quickly the attack crumbled in the face of the Black Consuls' disciplined and dogged defence.

The attack was over in a few minutes, with no losses for the Consuls. As they re-grouped and prepared to move on, Levi studied the corpses at his feet. Strange how he could not feel any hate for these, the kind of heretical traitors that he had come to loathe during his decades as a Space Marine. He had come to expect feelings of justified anger when dealing with such traitorous vermin, but now those feelings were oddly absent. Distracted, he strode over to the command Rhino.

Captain Estrus was, once more, suppressing his irritation with the person on the other end of his comm-link. 'I don't care what you say, commander, we have fifty dead rebels at our feet. You will need to re-assess the territorial gains of the insurgent forces. No, it will not affect our ETA. Rendezvous in seven minutes.' Estrus pulled his helmet off as Levi approached and reached for an order scroll from the sergeant at his side.

'Brother codicier, you gave good account of yourself. I am pleased to see that your time at the Librarius honing your psychic skills has not softened your fighting prowess.' He glanced at the scroll in his hand, arching a dark eyebrow. 'I fear, however, that this rebellion has softened the brains of the loyalist commanders.'

Levi tilted his helmet to acknowledge the captain's remarks. 'I do only my duty as any Black Consul would, captain.' Distractedly, he looked over at a group of Black Consuls speaking to Aeorum. 'Yet, something troubles me.'

Estrus lowered the scroll, giving Levi his full attention. 'What's that, librarian? Are we to be beset by more foes before we meet Administrator Niall?'

'I apologise for troubling you, captain; I cannot pinpoint the source of my vexation.'

'Very well, librarian, but keep me informed. This disorderly planet also vexes me greatly and I do not wish for further surprises. Stay at my side.' Estrus's helmet-comm crackled into life once more and he flicked the speaker on with an armoured thumb and listened to the voice of Inquisitor Parax. He sighed. 'Yes, inquisitor, we proceed. No, remain in your vehicle...'

ADMINISTRATOR NIALL WAS an imposing figure, standing only a few inches shorter than the armoured figures of the Black Consuls nearby. His crimson cloak fluttered in the breeze that blew through the ruined town, the bright colour at odds with the sombre blacks and yellows of the Space Marines' armour. The distant sound of small arms fire and the more regular pounding of battle cannons drifted along the same breeze. Levi studied Niall's face as he spoke earnestly to Inquisitor Parax and Captain Estrus; the administrator's young face seemed at odds with the premature grey of his long hair and neatly trimmed beard.

'They must all be killed. Every one of them. Suracto has prided itself on its loyalty to the Imperium for decades and we must eradicate every last vestige of the smear that they have brought on our good name. I will not rest until I have personally overseen the execution of every last heretic.' He indicated the ruins around him. 'Every last soul in this town was put to death when we discovered the taint of heresy behind its closed doors.'

Parax smiled grimly, his face registering as little emotion as the action could allow. 'Admirable sentiments and noble actions, Administrator Niall, ones with which I concur wholeheartedly. The Inquisition commends your zeal and will seek to aid you in every way possible.'

'And commendable as these rousing speeches are, we do have the Emperor's work to do,' Levi said quietly. 'Let our actions speak first; self-congratulation you may indulge in later.' The three other men turned to look at him. Levi saw a flash of annoyance pass across the faces of both Niall and Parax. Captain Estrus's eyes blazed into life, stirred by his fellow Space Marine's discipline and dedication.

'Codicier Levi is right,' Estrus said. 'Pragmatism must be our watchword. We must act now, before the rebels can re-group. Administrator, what is the current situation?'

Niall continued to stare at Levi for a moment longer before turning to speak to Estrus. 'The main rebel force is on the other side of Thuram City. They have made some in-roads into the city itself but in the main the walls still hold. They are many, lightly armed save for a few battle cannons. However, their heretical vigour makes them formidable opponents.'

'We shall be the judge of that,' Estrus said. 'Let–'

'Let us use even greater force with which to crush them,' interrupted the inquisitor. 'Administrator Niall is right. Not one of them can be left standing.'

Estrus frowned. 'Inquisitor, I have warned you–'

'You dare to warn the Inquisition?'

'I have warned you that I will not brook any interference. We have the Emperor's work before us and by Guilliman, none will prevent us. Come, Administrator Niall, we have much to do.' Estrus led Niall away to the command Rhino.

Inquisitor Parax turned his thin face towards Levi. His dark eyes burned with anger for an instant, before he regained his composure. He appeared to want to speak, thought better of it, turned and walked over to his retinue, calling for his armour.

Levi turned to see Aeorum, helmet off, cleaning his bolter. The standard fluttered in the breeze an arm's length away from the standard bearer, planted in a small mound of rubble. Aeorum looked up, caught Levi's glance and raised his eyebrows. Levi nodded slowly, holding the standard bearer's gaze. Then, as if controlled by a single thought, both Space Marines abruptly looked away and went about their own tasks.

THE BLACK CONSULS were soon where they liked to be: in the thick of the battle, spilling the blood of heretics. The Second and Third Companies had each advanced around a side of the city, whilst the Fourth had moved to bolster the beleaguered loyal forces in the city itself. Beset on both sides by Space Marines, the rebels' siege was beginning to crumble.

A thick layer of battle-smoke hung over the southern outskirts of Thuram. The air was filled with a confusion of bolter and lasgun fire, the explosion of artillery rounds and the screams of the wounded and dying. Out of the smoky unknown, four lasgun rounds hit Levi in rapid succession, scoring the ceramite plates of his armour and singeing his over-tunic, but failing to penetrate further. He checked his IR scanner, found the sources of the shots and fired his bolter into the drifting pall of smoke. He heard the sound of the two bolter shells detonating as his infrared imaging showed him that they had found their mark – and that more rebels were closing on him from the right.

Three figures emerged from the smoke: lightly armoured men, their pale faces haggard with fatigue. The first was no match for Levi's reactions and barely had an opportunity to register the codicier's chainsword before it parted his head from his shoulders. The second man, frozen in horror at his comrade's sudden death was himself torn apart by a bolter round. The third man paused, lasgun hanging slackly at his side, gazing at his own reflection in Levi's helmet. Levi paused, dimly aware of the buzzing of the chainsword in his own hand. A distant part of his mind admired the bravery of this rebel, fearlessly squaring up to an Imperial Space Marine. His sword began to describe an arc towards the man.

'In the Emperor's name, brother.' Levi's sword arm froze. The man had not opened his mouth to speak yet Levi had heard the words as clearly as the sound of the chainsword and the battle around him. He probed with his own mind. A psyker! He felt the man's mind coil, gathering momentum for a psychic blast. Instinctively, Levi unleashed a pummelling mental attack of his own, tearing the man's neurons apart. A small trickle of blood began to run from the man's nose before he fell to his knees in front of the Space Marine, his mind destroyed. Levi despatched him with a single thrust, before powering down the chainsword.

As he stepped over the corpse, Levi became aware of the stillness around him. In the far distance, towards the Second Company's positions, the battle still raged, but in his immediate vicinity, calm had descended. Brother Consuls emerged from the smoke, doffing helmets or re-loading weapons. A cry rang out some distance away. Moments later, an armoured apothecary sped past towards the sound of the cry. A single heavy pistol shot rang out.

Captain Estrus appeared at Levi's side, accompanied by his sergeant aide. 'This accursed smoke prevents us from assessing the situation, brother-librarian. We have lost two of our battle-brothers and three more are injured. Against a foe far more numerous, that is to be expected. But reports are fragmented and I cannot see the greater picture. What can you see?'

Levi reached up for his helmet. There was a sharp hiss as his helmet seals released. The sergeant stepped forward and took the ancient helm. Levi breathed deeply and reached out with his mind, probing tentatively at first, then moving further away, gathering impressions, visualising sights, sounds, smells. Satisfied, he moved his perceptions to the city.

'–rarian! Brother-librarian! What's wrong?'

Levi gradually became aware of the captain's voice once more. Even in his armour, Levi felt cold. He leaned on his chainsword for support as a momentary weakness passed through his body.

'Codicier? How do our battle-brothers fare?'

'Well enough, captain. The Second Company suffers but gains the upper hand. For now, the Fourth stand their ground. But I fear we have underestimated the rebels, captain. The city, captain…'

Estrus kept his voice calm. 'What of the city, codicier?'

'It lies in a dark shadow, brother-captain. The unmistakable shadow of Chaos.'

LEVI HEARD A bone crack as the inquisitor's finger jabbed one of the prisoners in the chest. Tied to a charred wooden chair, the rebel winced but continued to stare directly at Parax. His voice hoarse after nearly an hour of interrogation, the young man struggled to speak calmly to the armoured inquisitor. 'And I tell you that we fight for the Emperor, inquisitor. We are loyal to the Imperium. We are on your side. I can't say it any clearer.' The men huddled in the shadows behind him murmured in agreement. A glance from the Black Consul guard at their side silenced them.

Parax whirled and faced the others in the burnt out room where they had assembled half a dozen prisoners taken in that first exchange. Drawn and tired as they were, all the rebels had said the same thing: they were loyal to the Emperor and Chaos had taken a hold in Planetary Lord Koln's palace. Inquisitor Parax's impatience had long been exhausted and a barely-controlled rage tinged his voice as he spoke.

'Brother Space Marines, administrator: we can see clearly here how Chaos warps the mind and sullies the soul. They are compelled, against their wills perhaps, to utter these profanities and heresies, even when the truth of the matter is self-evident. Suracto's peril is grave indeed.' He paused and lowered his head, staring at the floor.

Much as he disliked the showy flamboyance and melodrama of the man, Levi felt that he had to agree with the inquisitor. Chaos had so warped the minds of these rebels that they must have had no shred of understanding left. A grave peril, indeed.

Before Parax could say anything further, the bound rebel spoke again. 'The biggest profanity is that Chaos walks Suracto, clothed in Imperial garb and–'

Before the noise of the autopistol shot had died away, a dozen servo-motors whirred into life as the Black Consuls instinctively targeted Administrator Niall. The administrator slowly lowered his pistol and at a sign from Estrus, Levi, Aeorum and the other Space Marines lowered their own weapons. The force of the shot, hitting the prisoner in the throat, had pushed the rebel's chair over and he had been dead before he landed at his horrified comrades' feet.

'Such heresy! I could not bear to hear it,' Niall said, returning the autopistol into the folds of his cloak. 'I have spent far too long building this administration for the greater glory of the Emperor to hear such filth spoken so brazenly.'

'You have my sympathy, administrator,' Parax said, gesturing discretely. Two of his stony-faced retainers appeared in the tattered doorway. 'Take these vermin away and dispose of them.' Using the ends of their lasguns to prod them along, the two retainers began to herd the rebels out of the door.

'Wait a moment.' Levi stepped forward, an unwelcome sense of unease playing in his mind. 'We must not be hasty–'

Parax squared up to the Librarian. 'You plead for these traitorous scum? Where do your loyalties lie, Consul? You do not–'

'His loyalties remain true, inquisitor!' Parax involuntarily stepped away from Levi as Estrus's iron voice cut him short. 'Doubt it not. But my brother-librarian is right. We may miss an opportunity to find out more about the deployment of the rebel forces if we–' A series of lasgun shots sounded outside. Estrus groaned. 'Inquisitor, we are on the same side, yet your rash behaviour threatens to disrupt our operations here.'

'Are you sure that we are on the same side, captain? Or has this cunning heresy affected you?'

As the captain's hand moved to his bolter, Levi sensed a strong psychic presence approach the ruin. He heard the crackle of Chaplain Mortem's crozius arcanum moments before the battle rod and the fully-armoured figure of his holy brother dwarfed the ruined doorway.

'Brothers, we must move out,' Mortem said breathlessly. 'The Second Company is overwhelmed. A counter-attack, brother-captain – and it seems like the entire planet is against us.'

A BARRAGE OF Whirlwind missiles roared overhead as the speeders of the Second Company's tenth squad screamed towards the heart of the rebel force. The rebel force had appeared unexpectedly from the south and was swarming towards a breach in the city walls. The missiles screamed into the distance; a series of explosions lit up the horizon. Satisfied that the rebels' artillery capability had been disposed of, Estrus ordered the Third Company to advance.

Aeorum, standard grasped in one hand and bolter in the other, led the first and second squads into the heart of the rebel counterattack. Possessed of an almost daemonic rage, rebels hurled themselves bodily at the Black Consuls but their attacks were in vain as black-armoured fists crushed skulls, bolter shells tore muscle and sinew apart, flamers and melta-guns incinerated skin and bone. Very soon, both squads struggled to make headway, their progress impeded by the waves of rebels dead at their feet.

Levi tore his chainsword free from a dead rebel and in one smooth movement turned and hammered the pommel into the face of his compatriot. The blow shattered the man's forehead with an audible crack, killing him before his limp body began its fall to the ground. Kicking the corpse to one side, Levi followed the men of the third and fourth squads towards Thuram's breached walls. How he wished he could take his helmet off so that he could spit out the growing feeling of the rebels' hatred, for it had become a vile taste in his mouth. The deadly hiss of a melta-gun made him glad he was still fully armoured. A wave of anguish washed over the librarian as the Black Consul next to him was reduced to dust. Levi scanned the enemy ranks for the weapon – there, less than twenty paces away, but there were too many of his brothers in the way. The melta-gun fired again and another Consul exploded into a super-heated ball of flame.

Time to fight fire with fire, Levi thought grimly.

'Brother Consuls, hold your positions, hold your positions!' Unquestioningly, the Space Marines heeded the codicier's order and stopped in their tracks. Muttering a short prayer to the Emperor, Levi focused his mental energies on the ground beneath the rebel melta-gunner. With no

further warning a white hot ball of flame erupted upwards from the
ground, exploding outwards, engulfing the melta-gunner and a dozen
men around him.

Seemingly unfazed by the unexpected loss of their comrades, the
remaining fifty rebels regrouped and charged both squads. A woman
brought her autorifle to bear on Levi, but hesitated before firing. 'Rot in
hell, spawn of Chaos!' she screamed. She opened fire, the gun on full
auto, spraying Levi with bullets. Levi advanced against the hail of bullets
that were bouncing ineffectually off his armour. Out of ammunition, the
rebel battered the librarian's chest with the butt of the gun. 'Die heretic!
D–' Her words were cut short as the chainsword sliced through her waist.

Levi stared at the bloody severed torso.

This is not right. It had felt so, so wrong to kill her. Absently he fired
his bolter at two men charging him down, felling both. Something
exploded a few metres away, throwing Levi backwards. He landed heavily. A stream of damage data ran up his helmet readout but all Levi could
see was the woman's face, distorted by rage and hatred.

'Brother, can you hear me?' Levi tried to focus on the distant voice as
a pair of armoured arms lifted him to a seated position. Apothecary Mor-
dinian fumbled with Levi's helmet seals and removed the helmet. His
lined face cracked into the briefest of smiles. 'Ah, thank Guilliman, you
are alive, brother-librarian. I took your silence for death. A frag
grenade…'

'What? No, I live, as you see.' Levi still felt dazed, unsure whether it was
the aftershock of the grenade blast or something else. 'How do we fare?'

'Well, librarian, well. We must have accounted for over three hundred
of the rebels.' He examined Levi as he spoke. 'The Second has regrouped
over there, and we await the order to – ah, you are wounded.' Levi
became dimly aware of a discomfort in his right leg as the apothecary
dressed the wound. He put the pain out of his mind as easily as if it was
any other emotion. The apothecary helped him to his feet. 'A few minutes and the dressing will begin to– Oh, I must tend to another. Go well,
brother.'

As the apothecary hurried away, Levi replaced his helmet before taking
in the scene around him for the first time. Black Consuls of the first to
sixth squads of the Third Company were coming together, within a few
hundred metres of the city walls, a black and yellow armoured mass in a
sea of torn and bloody rebel dead. He caught sight of Aeorum. The standard bearer was making his way over to him, pausing now and again to
speak a few words to squad members. Levi checked his viewscreen
reports before watching the fifth squad's sergeant reverently touching the
edge of the standard before turning to muster his men.

'Brother Aeorum, your inspiration gives us all courage. The Second
Company holds its position but the Fourth is beleaguered.'

'Yes, I saw the reports.' Aeorum glanced over his shoulder. 'We move to hold the breach soon. Brother Estrus awaits the word from Captain Vanem of the Fourth. Yet you seem… distracted, brother.'

'Chaos so twists these rebels that they accuse us of heresy, of being servants of the Darkness ourselves.' *Something close. The thought intruded abruptly.*

'I heard their blaspheming too,' Aeorum shrugged. 'But we must hold true and must not be swayed.'

Close. Aeorum's voice faded as Levi felt a large presence looming. He fought to pinpoint it. The clamour of human minds, beyond the rise towards the city walls. He opened a channel on his helmet-com. 'Brother-captain, we are coming under attack, six hundred paces due north-west. A large force, repeat, a large force.'

'Acknowledged, brother.' The rest of Captain Estrus's reply was drowned out by a booming barrage of bolters as the Black Consuls opened fire on the seething mass of rebels appearing over the rise. Aeorum raced to join the first squad, firing with deadly accuracy as he closed with the attackers. As the standard moved through their midst, a great roar rose from the ranks of the Black Consuls. Levi, powering up his chainsword, began to follow. The air was suddenly alive with sheets of electricity. Levi's helmet visors darkened instantly. *Teleport!* Raw discharges of energy crackled wildly as a new presence materialised amongst the rebels.

It seemed to Levi as if a gateway to his darkest nightmares had opened up on Suracto. A squad of Space Marines had materialised in the midst of the rebel force, but to call them by that name would be a blasphemy. Their archaic armour sported all manner of grisly and morbid decorations, borne of Chaos-twisted imaginations and depraved urges: belts made of skulls hung around one waist, a rotting long-haired scalp adorned another's helmet, razor-sharp spikes encrusted most shoulder pads. But on every suit of ancient armour there was a common symbol, the hateful many-headed hydra of the Alpha Legion. It was worse than even the inquisitor had suspected. The rebels were under the sway of these foul Tzeentchian warriors.

Levi and his brother Black Consuls took all this in at a glance before turning their firepower on the new arrivals. A deadly hail of bolter shells rained on the Alpha Legionaries but though the human rebels around them were ripped to shreds, only two of the Chaos Space Marines fell before they opened fire with their own weapons. The crest of the rise was consumed in primeval savagery as the Black Consuls vented their long-suppressed anger on the twisted representations of the Emperor's warriors that stood before them.

Levi hacked his way towards the Alpha Legion squad, a cold hatred coursing through his veins. He barely gave a second thought to the rebels he despatched to the Emperor's mercies… until the slow, terrifying realisation dawned upon him. The rebels were turning away from the Black Consuls and were also training their weapons on the Legionaries. Soon, both Black Consul and rebel alike were fighting a common enemy, the Alpha Legion. Levi tried to ignore his confusion as he fought to get closer to the middle of the fray but abruptly the fighting stopped. Only the rebels and the Black Consuls still stood.

Estrus stood amidst the carnage, a dying Alpha Legionary at his feet. The foul warrior's chest-plate had been torn open, exposing a tangled mess of charred flesh and ruined machinery. His hand twitched. Estrus calmly pointed his bolt pistol at the armoured head. As the shot rang out, Levi reached his captain's side. He looked at the grisly remains of the Legionary's head, made waste by the bolter shell.

'Captain, we have been misled.' Levi looked around, at the drawn, sallow faces of the rebels, at the Black Consuls, already beginning to round up the ragged bands, their anger spent. The harsh noise of battle sounded from beyond the city walls. 'Brother-captain, the rebel prisoners–'

Estrus raised a hand. 'I hear you, librarian. And I understand. We have been made unwitting pawns in a dark and disturbing game. I must signal the Fourth. I fear that Planetary Lord Koln's forces may be a graver danger to them than the rebels.' He signalled to a nearby Space Marine. 'Brother-sergeant, give me a casualty report and find me a representative from these rebels that I can speak to.'

'This is treachery!' Levi and Estrus span to see Administrator Niall striding towards them. The administrator flapped a hand at the stunned rebel force. 'They must be executed, every last man and woman. You heard what the inquisitor said!' His voice cracked as he shrieked the words.

Estrus's helmeted head turned smoothly towards the administrator. 'You saw for yourself what happened here, Administrator Niall?' Niall hesitated, then nodded briefly. 'Then you know the scourge of Chaos is upon your planet–'

'But can't you see what's going on?' Niall interrupted, exasperated. 'The rebels have conspired with the Alpha Legion –'

'But the Chaos scum fought rebel and Marine alike,' interrupted Levi.

'Yes, that's what I meant. I...' He rubbed a hand across his face.

He seemed suddenly older, somehow, thought Levi.

'You know your Codex, Space Marine,' said Niall. 'All those who stand with Chaos must be shown the Emperor's mercies.'

'All those who stand by Chaos must be given the opportunity to seek the Emperor's light or be shown the just and swift mercies of those who do His work. That is what the codex says.' So saying, Levi strode nearer to the administrator. Visibly shaken, Niall backed off a few paces. 'Administrator, how is it that you have knowledge of our blessed book?'

'It is simply something that I heard...' Niall backed further away, his voice faltering. 'Your duty is clear. You, you must–' The left side of Niall's head erupted outwards in a shower of blood and tissue.

The rebel holstered his autopistol and spat on the administrator's still-twitching body. 'I am Mitago,' he said, his sunken eyes burning in his ashen, unshaven face. 'I am leader of this detachment of my people. And I have heard enough lies and cant from this verminous servant of Chaos.'

As the rebel leader hurried over to talk further with Captain Estrus, Levi looked down on Administrator Niall's corpse and mused on another verse of the Codex. Swift unthinking justice profits you nothing. It shall bring only misery and the tears of the wronged.

He went to find Aeorum.

As THE THIRD Company approached the city walls, a cold and grim determination had descended upon the Black Consuls. The fourth squad had been lost completely, and but two men remained of the sixth. The loss weighed heavily on their surviving brother Consuls. Mitago, whose men now brought up the rear behind the company's Rhinos, had revealed the unthinkable truth.

'We had endured enough,' he had told Estrus. 'Koln simply asked too much. We worked hard, filled with a joyful love for the Emperor. But Koln would make speeches demanding more, telling us that the Imperium would be angry if we did not increase our planetary tithe.'

'Then,' he said, 'the purges began. Loyal citizens disappeared as Koln's arbitrators terrorised the planet. Criminals were executed for any crime, often on nothing more than an Arbitrator's whim. 'Heresy' was found everywhere, heretics were rooted out of every house and home.

'And we knew it was wrong,' continued Mitago. 'The Emperor's law is hard, but in its harshness it is just. There was no justice left on Suracto and in our hearts, we knew that Koln was not doing the Emperor's work. It left us no choice.' He indicated the dead Alpha Legionaries. 'We had no idea that the taint on his soul was this abominable.'

Mitago's words had stunned the listening Black Consuls into silence. Each one knew what the implications were, but Levi knew that each Space Marine would be true to his training and his order: there would be no regrets, no accusations, no guilt. They had done nothing other than follow the Codex, however misguidedly. With their customary discipline and self control, they would shift their attention to the true enemy, and the blessed book would surely guide them along the path of righteousness.

All such thoughts quickly faded as the Third Company approached Thuram City. The Second had lost over thirty men and their armoured vehicles had borne the brunt of rebel artillery before their own Whirlwinds had eliminated that threat. Both captains had agreed that the

Second should remain where they were to protect against any threat from outside the city.

Levi had joined Aeorum and the first squad as they crossed the field of rubble which marked where the city wall had been. Months of fighting had made jagged, burnt-out skeletons of the city's fine architecture. Hundreds of bodies lay strewn, blackened, bloodied and forgotten, along the pockmarked streets.

'They've made their own pretty hell here,' Aeorum muttered as they advanced up Thuram's central avenue, the valley floor of a blasted concrete canyon that stretched upwards to a sliver of skyline a kilometre above.

Levi merely nodded silently as he listened to the reports that streamed in. Things changed dramatically with each passing minute. Captain Estrus had signalled to Captain Vanem of the Fourth Company, who had made efforts to contact the rebels' leaders. They in turn had spoken to Vanem and had welcomed the new understanding – but not so the until-now loyal forces opposed to the rebellion. As soon as they had heard what was going on, they had turned on the Fourth Company.

As Levi calmly took in all that was happening, he realised that he had not seen Inquisitor Parax since the prisoners' interrogation. Parax's overzealous fanaticism meant that he had his own part in the Tzeentchian machinations that had entrapped them all. Were it not for the seal of the Inquisition, Levi would have suspected a darker motive for Parax's actions, Holy Throne forgive the thought–

Levi's train of thought was shattered as they drew near to a scene of horrific carnage. Hundreds of rebels and Suractan loyalist forces clashed in a sprawling street skirmish; the Fourth Company, an uneasy presence between both sides, fought stoically against the red-uniformed Suractans, but were being hampered by the berserk zeal of the rebels. Unarmed rebels leapt over their dead comrades to tear at the Suractans' faces with their bare hands.

'Codex preserve us!' Estrus barked. 'We must restore some order here!' He bellowed some orders and his squads went smoothly into action. The first and second squads broke off to attack a detachment of Suractan autoriflemen. Dozens of red uniforms were mown down as the Consuls' bolters took their toll. Levi felled two men with a single chainsword stroke as, all around him, fellow Black Consuls fought with a refreshed, vigorous spirit. This was more than battle. This was atonement.

'Librarian, they retreat!' At Aeorum's call, Levi looked over his shoulder to see several dozen Suractans breaking away.

'Second squad, hold!' ordered Levi. 'First squad, standard bearer, with me!' The first squad broke away in pursuit. A dark shape in his mind's eye. The vision disappeared from Levi's mind, but its meaning was clear enough. 'First squad, slow down. We must be vigilant.' The Consuls obediently slowed to a walk, the Suractans retreating from view. Advancing through the twilit streets, Levi noticed a change in the architecture around him. He turned to the sergeant. 'Brother, where are we?'

There was a pause as the Sergeant searched for the right information. 'In Planetary Lord Koln's palace complex, brother-librarian.'

'Then we have another purpose here,' said Levi. 'Squad, halt!'

Aeorum approached Levi. 'We have lost the loyalists. What's your plan, brother?'

Levi gave no answer but bowed his head as he sent his mind out into the dark buildings beyond. A dark cancerous presence remained. They had not left.

'The Alpha Legion is still here.'

A murmur ran through the Space Marines at the codicier's words and grips tightened instinctively around weapons. Levi focused on the presence, found a direction. 'This way, my brothers.'

The Consuls made their way, in silence save for the whirring of servo-motors and the echoes of their footsteps, into the labyrinth of corridors that ran within Koln's palace, allowing themselves to be guided by the codicier's psychic powers. Levi felt an icy rage rising within him, the rage he had felt when he first saw the Alpha Legionaries. He strove to control his feelings, even though he knew that his brother Consuls must also be feeling the same anger. He felt the presence of Chaos draw near: nothing must now dull his purpose.

'Librarian! Your arrival is timely.'

Levi signalled to his brother Marines to lower their weapons as Inquisitor Parax emerged from the shadows, accompanied by his ever-present retinue. 'What are you doing here?' Levi asked, uncomfortable that he had not sensed the inquisitor's presence.

'I fear that Lord Koln is held hostage by the Alpha Legion.'

'Hostage?' Levi asked. 'But Koln is himself a servant of Chaos.'

'Not so, librarian–'

'Brother-librarian, shuttle craft powering up.' The sergeant checked his scanners. 'Six hundred metres north-east.'

Levi glanced at his own readouts. 'I have it. First squad, standard bearer, with me. Inquisitor, do not impede us.' Parax nodded slowly and allowed the Black Consuls to pass. The Space Marines broke into a run, armoured feet pounding the floor as they strove to cover the distance. Levi checked his scans again: shuttle craft preparing for lift-off, twenty metres and closing.

The tunnels opened into a landing bay. The high-pitched whine of the shuttle craft's engines, bearing the Suractan standard, filled the cavernous room. At the foot of the shuttle's entry gantry a red-cloaked human argued vehemently with the two Alpha Legionaries that loomed over him. As Levi took aim with his bolter, one of the Legionaries lifted his hand and placed a large gun against the human's head. The plasma pistol flashed and the human was torn apart by a glowing ball of super-heated flame.

The Legionary seemed to look at the Black Consuls for an infinity.

You have failed, Consul.

Levi heard the words clearly over the clamour of the squad's firing. Aeorum had already covered half the distance between the entrance and the shuttle but the Alpha Legionaries turned and fled up the gantry, the shuttle already lifting off the ground, its engines screaming.

'Get down!' Levi shoulder charged the standard bearer, throwing him to the floor, pinning him down as a white-hot stream of plasma poured from the shuttle's engines, incinerating the spot where Aeorum had been a second earlier. Helmet screens darkened as the landing bay was bathed in a brilliant light. With a monstrous thunderclap the shuttle took off.

Levi got to his feet. 'Brother-sergeant, contact the Chapter ship. That shuttle must be intercepted!' He glanced at the faint human outline scorched into the landing bay's floor as Inquisitor Parax strode over. His psychic discomfort was reaching the level of pain. 'Lord Koln?' he asked the inquisitor.

The inquisitor nodded. 'Yes. Another dupe in this Tzeentchian horror.' He paused, staring at the remains of the planetary overlord. 'This is a grave matter, Consul. When heresy runs this deep, it must remain a matter for the Inquisition.'

'But what if this has happened on other planets, in other systems?' Aeorum asked, removing his helmet. 'The Codex binds us; we must seek out such heresy.'

'We cannot smoke them out too early,' Parax said. 'Swift unthinking justice shall profit you nothing, Consul.'

'Too... too early?' Levi asked, unnerved by the inquisitor's use of that particular Codex verse. He gave himself a moment to collect his thoughts, checking a report. The shuttle had outrun the Consuls' ship and jumped into the warp on Suracto's dark side. 'Do you have evidence of other plots like this?'

Parax glared at him. 'As I said, librarian, this is a matter for the Inquisition. Cross me at your peril.' Parax spun on his heels and walked away. Levi started to follow when an armoured hand came to rest on his shoulder. The librarian turned to face Aeorum. He released his helmet and looked around at his fellow Black Consuls, methodically checking and securing the landing bay.

'Brother Levi, we have done all we can. For now.' Aeorum indicated Koln's final resting place. 'It does seem that Koln may have been tricked, as we were. It may be the time for you to let the Inquisition do what it does best. We have freed Suracto, which is prize enough. And Captain Estrus will require a full report.' Aeorum gave a half-hearted smile.

'The Codex tells us to be vigilant, to actively seek out all manifestations of Chaos, wherever they may be. As codicier of the Imperial Order of Black Consuls, it is my solemn duty.' Levi looked up at the standard in his brother Consul's hand. 'I am not best pleased at this decision.' He sighed, conceding. 'But you may be right. We have done all we can, for now.'

As he made ready to signal Captain Estrus, Codicier Levi remembered the verse he had read that morning.

And those dedicated to the Emperor's work will be beset upon all sides by enemies. Be vigilant for they are everywhere and you may depend on none but your brothers in arms to carry out His blessed work.

Levi signalled the captain.

As THE DOOR of his cabin aboard the Inquisition ship closed silently behind him, Parax wearily began to take off his armour. This time, he had narrowly succeeded in doing his master's work, though he was long used to the arduous nature of his blessed task. But if the extent to which Chaos had pervaded Suracto were to have become more widely known … He sighed as he put his armour away. Perhaps the Exterminatus would have been his only remaining option.

He reached for his robe. For now, the Black Consuls had played their part, and order had been restored. The other planets in the system were safe. Absently, he rubbed the Tzeentchian tattoo on the inside of his forearm. Their time was yet to come.

BATTLE OF THE ARCHAEOSAURS

Barrington J Bayley

WITHIN ITS OVAL frame of enamelled copper, the holo-plate displayed the nearly perfect sphere of a planet fringed with cloud and shining seas. Fleet Captain Karlache slapped a knob, causing the image of the world to rotate at a faster rate.

'The mapping is incomplete, having been carried out from orbit by the first surveyor ship to arrive,' Karlache explained. He struck the knob again, making the image halt and then move around in small jerks until a pear-shaped continent became visible. He positioned an arrow in the middle of it. 'This is where the first landing was made, on the sole inhabited continent. The initial survey had reported a sparse human population which, like many settlements dating from the Dark Age of Technology, had lost the technical arts and degenerated to the Stone Age. As you know, Imperial policy in such circumstances is to land amid the populated area and take control immediately. A single battalion, lightly armed, was deemed more than sufficient to subdue a primitive people, establish a military base, and secure the planet for the Imperium. As you also know by now, it was wiped out almost immediately, without a single survivor.'

The captain looked around at his guests. They were seated in his private cabin – with its darkly gleaming panelled walls embellished with icons of the Emperor, and its ribbed and curved ceiling – aboard the troopship he commanded, the *Mobilitatum*. With a thousand troopers aboard, the *Mobilitatum* was approaching Planet ABL 1034, the planet on the screen, as was its sister ship, the *Straterium*. Some distance to their rear came two immense travel pods containing Warlord Titans, the *Lex et Annihilato* and the *Principio non Tactica*, two prime examples of the mightiest land-war machines ever to exist.

713

Their commanders, Princeps Gaerius and Princeps Efferim, sat across the cabin, men of stern appearance in their diamond-shaped peaked caps, skulls stitched onto their epaulets. Also present were Imperial Guard Colonel Costos and Commissar Henderak, both of the Fifth Helvetian Regiment.

It was most unusual for sealed orders to be entrusted to a fleet captain rather than to an Imperial Guard officer, but security was of the essence. Public morale dictated that as few as possible should know what had happened on Planet ABL l034. 'A stronger expedition equipped with Leman Russ battle tanks and Basilisk mobile artillery was then despatched to the same location. It met a similar fate. Messages despatched to the orbiting transports spoke of giant beasts which the natives were using as battle weapons. Only one brief visual transmission was received.'

Planet ABL l034 vanished from the holo-plate. A blurred, shaking picture replaced it, showing a huge shape looming over the camera. Colossus-like legs, a vast neck, jaws that could have swallowed the cabin in which the officers watched – then nothing. The screen went blank.

'Large animals have been trained for use in battle on many primitive planets, including on ancient Terra,' Captain Karlache continued. 'Such forms of warfare have never presented the least problem to the Imperial Guard. The difference here would appear to be one of size. The Imperium has simply not encountered beasts this huge before.'

Again the fleet captain manipulated the knobs in front of the enamel-decorated holo-plate. A procession of lumbering creatures crossed the visual area, some with long necks and thick tails. The outline of a man in the corner of the screen gave some idea as to their size, which was much larger than any living Terran animal. 'Genetors of the Adeptus Mechanicus, by studying fossil records, have established that beasts such as these lived on Earth a hundred million years ago. Similar animals are common throughout the galaxy but are too unmanageable to be trained for war. In any case, they could be downed with a single shot. How even larger beasts are able to be utilised on the target planet is a mystery. However, Mechanicus Genetors have named them "archaeosaurs" because of their resemblance to the ancient Earth animals.'

Again the scene on the holo-plate changed to show clouds and filaments formed of stars. An arrow picked out the star that warmed Planet ABL 1034. 'The archaeosaur planet has a strategic value, as you can see for yourselves. It guards the crossing point between no less than three star systems, all of them of interest to the Imperium. It has been ordered that the planet will not be permitted to be lost by default. It must be occupied. That is why two Warlord Titans have been assigned to the next landing, so that there may be no question of further defeat.'

Colonel Costos coughed softly. 'While not wishing to criticise command decisions, is it not an overreaction to call on the Adeptus Titanicus in this case? Our Fifth Helvetian Regiment is battle-hardened, down to less than half its original strength.' He made this last statement with pride. Imperial Guard regiments generally dwindled in proportion to the number of engagements they had fought, their final remnants eventually being absorbed elsewhere. A regiment at full strength meant an inexperienced regiment. The second landing was made by elements of the First Ixist, a newly raised regiment that had never seen an engagement before. It is certain the whole affair was carelessly executed, the natives underestimated. It is sometimes a fatal error to suppose that primitive people need not be taken seriously in military terms. I have known men armed with nothing but stone axes to overrun a Guard outpost in a sneak attack.'

Commissar Henderak nodded in judicious agreement. 'Either that, or the First Ixist had not enough faith in the Emperor!'

On hearing this, Princeps Gaerius looked askance at the commissar, disdain flitting across his face. The Adeptus Titanicus was an ancient order, predating the Ministorum which promulgated the Cult of the Emperor, and it was unique among the Imperium's fighting forces in coming under the Adeptus Mechanicus. Its officers mostly followed the Martian religion, worshipping the Emperor as the Machine God and Totality of All Knowledge. The icons on the bridge of Gaerius's Titan were quite different from the 'holy' images he saw here. Tech sigils and arcane formulae overlaid the Emperor's stern visage. In his eyes, Imperial Guard commissars, with their emotional ranting about faith, were little short of lunatics.

The look on Gaerius's face did not go unnoticed by Captain Karlache. Surreptitiously he studied the princeps. He was hook-nosed, a feature common among Titanicus officers – a consequence, no doubt, of the hereditary strain in the Adeptus. Privately, Karlache agreed with Colonel Costos that the mission was a trivial misuse of such extraordinary machines. He wondered if Gaerius and Efferim thought so too. Not that they would ever voice such an opinion. The discipline of Titan officers was legendary.

For the first time, Princeps Gaerius spoke, his voice dry and sardonic. 'There is little to go on, it seems. But no matter. We of the Adeptus, at any rate, have little to fear. Let us get down on-planet and bring this business to a speedy finish.'

LANDING A TITAN was not a simple matter. This was the time when the monstrous machines were most at risk. On the bridge of the *Lex et Annihilato*, Princeps Gaerius took the command seat. Beside him were his bridge officers: Tactical Officer Viridens, Weapons Moderati Knifesmith, and Chief Engineer Moriens. Down below, sweating with fear, huddled the Titan's five dozen ordinary crewmen. Command had been temporarily handed to the four-man landing-and-ascent crew of the transport pod, who now were seated before the command podium which in turn was hooked through to the pod's controls.

The conning plate currently showed the view outside the pod. Feet first, the Titan was lowering itself through Planet ABL 1034's atmosphere. In the distance, the pod carrying the *Principio non Tactica* with Princeps Efferim and his crew could be seen. Heated air flamed around it, turning the pod white-hot.

The Titans were to be the first to land. The Imperial Guard would arrive under their protection. Using consummate skill to keep the tall pod stable as it fell, the crew steered the *Lex et Annihilato* towards its designated landing place. Deceleration over, they soared over a landscape of mountains, valleys, and plains interspersed with dense forests. It appeared to be a fertile world, Princeps Gaerius thought. No wonder it had been colonised, long ago in the Dark Age of Technology. Now it would become more than just a strategic outpost. He could see it someday becoming a productive agricultural world, perhaps later even a forge world or a hive world. He leaned close to the conning plate with this thought in mind, imagining how the landscape would look in the future.

'What in the All-Knowing's Name is that?' The exclamation was torn from his throat. 'Steersman, take us back over that ridge!'

The pod officer glanced back at him nervously. 'That will be tricky, princeps.'

'Take us back, I say!'

Although technically Gaerius was not in command of the Titan at this moment, the pod officer dared not defy him. Instead, he muttered to the men on either side of him. Carefully, consulting continually with one another, they eased the pod back over to the other side of the ridge and hovered. Oaths now came involuntarily from the mouths of all Gaerius's officers.

Five huge hulks lay toppled on their sides in a broad fern-clad valley. They must have lain there for centuries, for they were rusting away, dissolving with age, riddled with holes and covered in lichen.

Had they been standing they would not have been as tall as the Warlord Titans, but they were broader, monstrous rotund shapes. Tactical Officer Viridens gasped out shocked words.

'Ork Gargants!'

It was indeed astonishing to see these mighty machines, the crude ork version of Titans, felled and abandoned on a primitive world. Gaerius looked thoughtfully on the scene. 'It seems the orks have also tried to take this world at some time in the past.'

'And they were defeated?' Weapons Moderati Knifesmith ground out. 'It's hardly credible!'

'Hardly defeated by the natives,' Gaerius told him confidently. 'Orks usually end up fighting among themselves. In any case, we have nothing to fear. Whenever a Titan has met a Gargant, the Titan has prevailed.'

Gargants were best described as caricatures of Titans. In place of power bundles, they were worked by clumsy, clanking beams and cogwheels. And they were steam-driven! In place of fission reactors, banks of furnaces were fed by teams of stokers!

But then, no one could build such superb machines as those of the Adeptus Titanicus. They were all thousands of years old, and even though continually repaired and renewed, they still retained the special occult qualities of the Dark Age of Technology. The Adeptus Mechanicus had tried to build brand-new Titans themselves, but the fruits of their efforts never performed nearly as well.

'Enough!' Gaerius said shortly. 'On, pilot.'

The great pod eased itself back over the ridge. Far in the distance, Gaerius saw what looked like a herd of animals, but there was no time now to magnify the image. The slow thunder of the landing engine faded as the pod was lowered gently onto a plain scattered about with overturned artillery, smashed tanks, and flattened drop shuttles. This was where the second expedition had met its grisly fate, and this was where the Imperium would now, finally, exert its will.

Planet ABL 1034 was a low-gravity planet, perfect for the operation of Titans, which originally had been designed for use on Mars. The huge pod opened up and trundled away over the moss. The *Lex et Annihilato* was revealed in all its prodigious glory, roughly the shape of a man and the height of a 12-storey building, bristling with armament. A kilometre away stood its match, the *Principio non Tactica*.

Princeps Gaerius smiled. Whenever he saw two Titans standing on the same landscape, twinned colossi, he felt an urge to engage in a duel, to have the machines striding towards one another with shoulder cannon blazing. He was sure that his colleague Princeps Efferim, on the bridge situated within the cranium of the *Principio non Tactica*, felt the same. It had never been his luck to engage with a Chaos Titan, possibly the only worthy opponent of the Adeptus. But one day...

The landing crew left the bridge. Chief Engineer Moriens left too, descending into the body of the Warlord to rally the cowering crewmen. Now the drop shuttles were coming in, Imperial Guard detachments piling out and setting up a perimeter around the watchful Titans. More shuttles landed and disgorged Basilisk artillery, Leman Russ tanks and Rhino armoured carriers.

For the third time, Planet ABL 1034 was claimed for the Imperium. For a while, the landing force would merely hold its ground, scanning the terrain from within the craniums of the Warlords, waiting to see if an attack would come. If it did not, the Titans would stride out to seek the Emperor's revenge.

* * *

GUARDSMAN LECHE AND Colour Sergeant Hangist were the last two left in the prisoner cage. In his tattered uniform, Osmin Leche – smeared with mud and pale of face – stared from between the rough-hewn timbers at the stone-age village which sprawled all round him.

He had always thought of stone-age humans as shambling and brutish, a picture reinforced by the pre-landing morale lectures. But the people he saw striding among the fern-thatched huts were nothing like that. They were tall, muscled men, proud of bearing. They were gracious, equally proud women. They were agile, healthy children. It was he, Osmin Leche, who felt like a frightened primitive. By contrast, the natives, who should have cowered in fear and awe at contact with the Imperium, had shown no fear at all.

And no wonder. Far off, the Guardsman could see one of the natives' battle beasts ambling across the horizon. It was like watching a mountain move, a mountain with a long neck carrying a huge head like a rock outcrop, and an impossibly long and massive tail. From where Leche cowered, the human beings which he knew swarmed over the beast were too small to be visible. He shuddered, remembering the attack which had killed most of his comrades.

Colour Sergeant Hangist squatted in a corner of the cage, his head in his hands. One thing was true about the stone age primitives, and that was their cruelty. There had been fifty captives in the cage to begin with. The villagers had been killing one per day, always by some different method. Their ingenuity seemed inexhaustible.

While the commissar had been alive, Leche had been able to keep his own spirits up to some extent. The commissar had exhorted them constantly to keep faith in the Emperor, and he had encouraged them to believe that rescue was possible. The villagers had seemed to be amused by his hectoring, though of course they could not understand it. They had kept him till nearly last. He had been killed the day before.

True, it had been inspiring to witness the commissar's grim fortitude as he was torn apart, limb by limb. Only at the very end did his torturers succeed in wringing cries of agony from him. But the spectacle had finally broken Colour Sergeant Hangist. And it had broken Guardsman Leche too.

Leche shivered. He trembled. The Imperium was far away. The Emperor was but a word.

He glanced again at the distant archaeosaur, to use the name given the beasts in the morale lectures. It had turned and was approaching the village.

Then a creaking sound from behind made him turn. The cage's gate was opening. Bronze-skinned stone-age men entered. They dragged out the whimpering, sobbing Emperor's Guardsmen to face their doom.

* * *

THERE WAS A peculiarity to Planet ABL 1034. Cloud formations were all of the same type, a series of evenly spaced ribs or striations high in the sky, stretching from horizon to horizon. No one in the expeditionary force asked himself what produced this phenomenon. That was a task for an adept, and to the military mind, planetary peculiarities were too numerous to be worth thinking about. But as the striped cloud cover raced across the sky, it broke up the light of the hard, white sun and produced a rippling effect on the ground below.

Princeps Gaerius found the rapidly shifting light and shade eerie but also restful. The expedition had not so far been challenged, and the officers were enjoying a meal in the open air. Artillery and tracked vehicles grumbled and clanked around them.

It was a traditional courtesy for a princeps to eat with Imperial Guard officers during a combined operation, though both Gaerius and Efferim would much have preferred to be with the rest of their bridge crews, supervising a meticulous checking of their Warlords. Commissar Henderak was consulting the Imperial Tarot. Reverently he unfolded the purple velvet cloth in which the deck was wrapped, pushed aside the remains of the meal and laid out three cards to form a triangle, tapping each in turn.

The surfaces of the cards glittered and swirled, flashing with colour. The card at the apex of the triangle was the Significator. It was the first to clear and form an image. The Emperor appeared, seated on a throne carved from a single gigantic diamond, glaring out at the beholder.

The card on the left was the next to stabilise. It showed Universal Force, a snake with its tail in its mouth, whirling endlessly against a background of receding galaxies. The final card cleared almost immediately after it to show The Galactic Realm, producing one of several images by which that card manifested itself. A maiden in a flowing gown stood on a landscape, star formations in the sky at her back, pouring multicoloured liquid from two large pitchers she held, one in each hand. The liquid flooded the landscape, carrying away cities and forests.

The commissar banged his fist on the table. 'The meaning is clear!' he intoned. 'Might will prevail!'

'Of course,' Princeps Efferim drawled, glancing casually at the triangle of images. 'What else could the cards show if they tell the truth?'

'Yes, what else?' Commissar Henderak said feverishly. 'Though the message contains an ambiguity. One must judge carefully, when interpreting the Emperor's Tarot. True, the presence of The Emperor as Significator confirms that the message relates to our current operation. But Universal Force does not necessarily refer to the forces of the Divine Emperor. Forces opposed to His Terribilitas could be implied. Also, the Galactic Realm...'

The commissar's eyes widened as he redirected his gaze back to the final card. The image was changing, the landscape writhing and rising up around the feet of the maiden, threatening to topple her.

'Imperator Divinitas!' he gasped in horror. 'We are undone!'

Gaerius's patience had reached its limit. With a grunt of disgust, he swept the cards from the table. 'Enough of your superstition, faith cultist,' he snarled. 'True holiness is the holiness of the machine. Suggest defeat for our Titans on a planet of animals, and you are ripe for reprocessing as a servitor!'

Commissar Henderak leapt to his feet, fury on his face. It was not that he heard the princeps's words as an insult to himself personally. He heard them as an insult to the Emperor. He made a sudden movement, as if reaching for his laspistol.

Colonel Costos was about to intervene, but excited shouting from the perimeter interrupted the exchange. A veteran sergeant ran up and saluted hastily.

'Native war-beasts advancing on the camp, colonel!'

Princeps Gaerius laughed, sounding like a drain emptying. 'Now you will see!'

'BRING THE TWO slaves forward!' The order was barked out by the clan hetman. He stood in the middle of the village compound, wavy blond hair flowing down his hard-muscled back, a stone axe thrust into his belt of woven fern leaves. Colour Sergeant Hangist and Guardsman Leche were flung at his feet, where they cringed like dogs, peering left and right.

'These are not warriors!' the hetman roared at the villagers who were gathered round him. 'These are slaves of the Giant Shining Men, the real warriors who have come again from the sky to do battle with us. That is why the gods gave us the Defenders: to help us fight the Giant Shining Warriors!'

Leche and Hangist could not, of course, understand a syllable of what the hetman was saying. All they understood by this time was that every second they remained alive and untortured was a miracle. At the same time, the knowledge that pain and death were coming closer second by second struck stark fear into their souls. Leche gibbered as he was once more wrenched to his feet. Hangist groaned with despair.

And then they saw them again. There were two of them, coming closer, pacing the plain one after the other, looming against the sky: archaeosaurs. They were like mottled grey and brown mountains with massive, reptilian heads on the end of long, sinuous necks, the weight balanced by enormous rippling tails as long as the bodies themselves.

This was the second time they had seen such monsters. The first time was when the beasts had destroyed the Imperial Guard camp. Leman Russ tanks had been unable to stop them. Basilisk artillery had been unable to stop them. They had trampled everything, moving surprisingly quickly on their eight sturdy legs, four on a side, thicker than any tree trunk. Guardsman Leche found it incredible, almost unimaginable, that there could be animals as huge as these.

Either one of the beasts could have trampled the village to dust by merely strolling through it, but instead they halted far outside its bounds, heads swaying. Despite their size, they looked placid enough for the moment. Leche knew that really massive animals would have to be plant-eaters, and there was no grass on this planet, only ferns and moss – endless fern forests and fern-covered plains. He could imagine the wide swathes the beasts would cut through such forests as they fed.

With whoops and shouts, the villagers dragged Leche and Hangist out of the village. Being sacrificed to the monsters would at least be quicker than the deaths suffered by many of his comrades, Leche thought. They came nearer, and now men could be seen crawling over the vast bodies as if on hillsides. The Guardsman could also see house-like structures erected on their backs, and – what seemed most weird – one such structure atop each massive head.

The steadily flickering daylight of Planet ABL 1034 gave the scene an unreal, disjointed appearance. Now Guardsman Leche could see how the tribesmen climbed onto the huge beasts. Rope ladders hung down from their sides and trailed over the ground. Leche found himself at the foot of one. A tribesman mounted a rung, seized hold of Leche by one arm, and jerked him upward. Haplessly the young man was hauled up the ladder, soon forced to assist in the climb or fall a lethal distance to the ground below.

Leche saw Colour Sergeant Hangist being dragged towards the second archaeosaur. Once the Guardsman passed the point where the ropes fell away from the beast's hide, he saw how easy it was to move about on top of the archaeosaur. The immensely thick and tough hide was corrugated. On the lower slopes of the animal-mountain, one could walk in these corrugations as though in a trough or trench. Scrambling over these, he and his captors came close to the gigantic spine, where the corrugations smoothed out somewhat and it was like making one's way on the top of a heaving hill.

Leche now realised that the beast's hide was in fact armoured. Up here it was like stepping on steel or adamantium. Tribesmen dotted the vast back. The hetman had made his way here already. He bellowed and gestured. Leche was propelled forward, towards the beast's head. Even facing certain death, Leche found time for a touch of pure curiosity about what was to happen. Certainly this was an unusual way to die, an adventure he would have enjoyed telling to his comrades of the First Ixist – if there had been any way he could have survived it.

The archaeosaur's neck, though long, was not all that lengthy as compared with the huge body. It had, after all, only to reach ground level in order to feed, so it was little longer than the eight comparatively stubby legs. Traversing it was like walking up a mountain trail. And there, set on top of the giant reptilian head, was a square hut or covered platform. It was open at the front and back, and three tribesmen squatted in it. Leche got an odd feeling. It was like looking at a primitive version of the bridge of some fearsome war machine!

Leche was pushed through the hut and out the other side. In passing, he saw what at first he took to be a dozen bony spines projecting from the top of the archaeosaur's skull, but then he realised that they were rudely shaped stone spikes hammered into the animal's head! Before he could wonder what these were for his fate was revealed to him. Forward of the hut, also mounted on the beast's head, not far behind the eyes, stood a timber X-shape. Guardsman Leche's captors fastened him to this, limbs spread, and left him there.

Leche could hear the beast's stertorous breathing. It sounded like nothing so much as the engine of a Leman Russ tank. Turning his head, he was soon able to see Colour Sergeant Hangist spread-eagled on an identical X-beam above the eyes of the second war-beast.

So here Guardsman Leche was: a mascot, an emblem, a figurehead, and perhaps a taunt to the enemy. The archaeosaurs were going into battle. Against another tribe? Or a third Imperial Guard expedition?

From behind him came banging, clinking noises. The Imperial Guard officers who had faced these war-beasts had been at a loss to know how the primitive tribesmen control-led them. Here was the answer, though Leche could not look around far enough to see it. The stone-age people had lived on Planet ABL 1034 for a long time, and they had learned much. The stone spikes had been driven through the archaeosaur's skull to precise points within the tiny brain. By banging the spikes with his stone hammer and making them vibrate, the mahout could stimulate nerve centres at will. One spike and the creature would advance. Another spike and it would retreat. Others, and it would turn left, turn right, fly into a rage, and attack. Another, and it would spew fire!

The hetman barked an order. The squatting mahout banged one spike, then another. The two archaeosaurs lumbered off, away from the village. Towards the Giant Shining Warriors.

'HERE THEY COME,' said Princeps Gaerius. 'Ready to move out!' The bridge crewmen of the *Lex et Annihilato* took up their positions, pulling down the control sets to link with the metal sockets set into their skulls.

As commander, only Gaerius himself was free of such an interface. Chief Engineer Moriens was most encumbered. His head almost disappeared amid a nest of pipes, tubes and leads. It was his responsibility to keep contact with the whole internal machinery of the Warlord, to supervise its running crew, and to keep everything functioning whatever the damage. Tactical Officer Viridens would actually guide the giant battle machine, moving it like his own body at Gaerius's orders, with a direct neural connection to the power bundles.

The chief engineer was also effectively blind, seeing nothing outside. Gaerius, Moriens and Weapons Moderati Knifesmith had access to the conning holos. Gaerius looked to the right, where the companion Warlord *Principio non Tactica* stood, also gearing itself up to move.

The *Lex et Annihilato* roared. Warlord Titans had the imprinted mental nature of the grizzly bear, a powerful bad-tempered animal native to Terra, and this sometimes made them difficult to handle. The *Principio non Tactica* also roared. At a word from Gaerius, they each took a gigantic step forward, carefully treading in the spaces cleared for them. A few steps more, and they were outside the camp and striding towards the horizon.

'There are only two of them,' Gaerius murmured. 'I had expected more.'

At first it was difficult to estimate the size of the archaeosaurs as they loped onward. It was the speed of their approach, perhaps, that made them seem not as large as they really were. Moving with a shuffling motion on their eight sturdy legs, they appeared to Gaerius's eye scarcely larger than Terran dinosaurs. He relaxed. This should take no more than moments, after which the natives were unlikely to have any stomach for further action.

Gaerius, as acting group commander, outranked Efferim for the duration of the engagement. He spoke briefly into his communicator, issuing orders to his fellow princeps. Fibre bundles humming like swarms of angry hornets, leg shanks clanging, the twin Titans strode out towards their primitive challengers.

And then Gaerius caught his breath in surprise. The brief blurred transmission from the destroyed second expedition had not prepared him for what he now saw. The archaeosaurs were enormous – bigger than he would have believed remotely possible for any land animal, even taking the low gravity into account. The monster's head, when raised, reared even higher than the Warlord's!

That was not the only comparison between the two. Behind the Titans, using them for protection like mice scurrying behind a man, came the Imperial Guard force: tanks, mobile artillery, and infantry. It was the same on the other side. A ragged column of at least a thousand nearly naked primitives, armed with spears and stone axes, trailed behind the archaeosaur, ready to take on whatever their battle-beasts left alive.

How did the creatures stand up? Their bones must be made of steel, he thought with incredulity – or adamantium. Still, they could not conceivably withstand the Titans' armament. He barked orders again. The Warlords angled out to approach the archaeosaurs from their flanks and get an easier target, then their huge legs pumped faster, propelling them almost at a run.

By now, Tactical Officer and Weapons Moderati had almost become a single personality, joined by the grizzly-bear-essence imprinted on the *Lex et Annihilato*. The shoulder cannon swivelled, aimed at the flank of one of the impossibly huge beasts, and opened up. A shattering noise echoed through the cranium of the Titan as a volley of shells went hurtling towards the defenceless target.

Disbelievingly, Princeps Gaerius watched as the entire volley bounced off the beast's armoured back. Some exploded in mid-air; others flew away and fell to the ground. The archaeosaur, however, seemed unhurt by the explosions. It lumbered around to face the Titan with its smouldering, yellow eyes. Now Gaerius saw that what he had taken to be a fringe or crest on the creature's skull was actually an artificial structure in the form of a covered platform, and within it squatted men. Did these men manage to control the animal? If so, how?

But there was something else. Set in front of the platform an X-beam had been erected. To this – uniform torn and ragged, face covered in dirt – was bound a Guardsman.

Up to now, Gaerius's feelings for the enemy – whom he had scarcely considered an enemy, so inferior were they – had been neutral. Now his heart filled with hatred.

'Poor wretch,' he muttered to himself. There was no way he could help the prisoner, who was sure to die along with the archaeosaur. He put him from his mind.

He doubted that Weapons Moderati Knifesmith's aim was good enough to hit the swaying head. 'Aim lower!' he ordered. 'The belly will have less armour!'

Again the shoulder cannon roared their ferocious violence. This time, several shells struck home, creating a brief smoke screen. When it cleared, Gaerius expected to see the smashed carcass of the archaeosaur lying on its side, twitching. He gaped with renewed astonishment to see the monster still standing. True, some of the shells had penetrated the hide and left deep gaping wounds. Yet the archaeosaur was unshaken. It was as if it did not even feel the torn flesh and flowing blood.

And it was still on the move, turning to face the Titan. Gaerius was about to order another volley, but first he glanced towards the *Principio non Tactica* and momentarily froze. The second archaeosaur, also dripping blood from a cannon volley, was charging towards the Warlord at a run. Suddenly its jaws gaped open, and from between its rows of teeth came a white-hot gout of fire which enveloped the upper part of the Principio.

To the astounded princeps, it looked just like a plasma weapon – something with which he had not thought to equip the Warlords. Who would have thought to need it on a world like this? He did not know of the archaeosaurs' prodigious digestive system with its twenty-three stomachs, building up acetylene gas at high pressure, or of the unusual metabolism which mixed pure phosphorus into that acetylene. When the archaeosaur belched, which it did when angry or when made to do so by a bang on the appropriate stone spike, the acetylene was squirted out and ignited by the phosphorus on contact with the air. Evolution had devised the phenomenon as a defence against predators. It was even more effective as a weapon.

The *Principio*'s bridge must have been completely blinded during the discharge, though the void shields would have protected the crew from the heat. But there was a second tactic to the archaeosaur's attack. It reared up on its four hind legs. It now towered over the Warlord. When Princeps Efferim's view cleared, he saw the vast beast come crashing down on his land-war machine in an attempt to topple it.

'Assist Principio!' Gaerius shouted. 'All weapons!'

The *Lex et Annihilato* swivelled. Moderati Knifesmith let loose with both shoulder cannon and the belly lasgun. The *Principio* staggered back, its own belly lasgun also opening up, trying desperately to keep its footing against the monstrous weight of the angry beast. It probably would have succeeded, but the archaeosaur had yet another trick. It turned aside. The vast tail came swinging round and crashed into the body of the Titan, where the power source and main engines were located. The carapace buckled.

Now a red steam obscured the view as *Principio*'s two heavy lasguns bit into the beast and vaporised huge amounts of its blood. Through Gaerius's communicator came a faint voice – that of Efferim's chief engineer

'Void shields down.'

Then, with utter horror, Princeps Gaerius saw the *Principio non Tactica* fall, first losing its balance, unable to correct the momentum imparted by the archaeosaur's tail, then one foot lifting off the ground, then the huge structure descending with slow majesty in the low gravity, until it smashed into the hard earth.

Once a Titan was toppled, there was virtually no chance of it getting to its feet again. Princeps Gaerius shrieked orders, turning his attention back to the archaeosaur threatening the *Annihilato*.

'The head! Aim for the head!'

Alert to the fate that had overtaken the sister Titan, Viridens backed away, jinking aside to prevent the creature mounting a similar assault, even though it was clear by now that the archaeosaurs were more agile than their bulk gave them any right to be. Shoulder cannon barked, and both missed the waving head as it turned on its sinuous neck to follow the Warlord. Gaerius was dimly aware of the other archaeosaur trampling the fallen *Principio non Tactica*, rending and splitting the defenceless carapace. Briefly the lasgun hissed out again, but it was unable to target the beast.

Then Gaerius glimpsed a final indignity. Men were spilling out of the cracks in the casing like maggots from a festering body. And he could see what they were fleeing from: a blinding-white, ravening glow in the interior. The Warlord's fission reactor was in meltdown, its fuel elements fused together by the force of the archaeosaur's trampling.

Now Gaerius knew what had happened to the Gargants. And now, its business finished, the second archaeosaur was coming to join its brother. It was frightening how the mountain of an animal was still able to move with great chunks torn out of it by four repeat shoulder cannon and two heavy lasguns. It seemed the monsters were unstoppable. The bones of the beast were even exposed, a lustrous grey in colour. Gaerius could well believe they were made of iron or even steel.

'Aim right, Moderati! Aim right! Look out for the tail!'

The warning came too late. The tail lashed out swifter than the eye could follow and struck the Titan on one knee. The Warlord juddered. A muffled battle report came from Chief Engineer Moriens.

'Left leg disabled.'

Despite himself terror struck into Princeps Gaerius's soul. His Titan had lost mobility. And two archaeosaurs were bent on toppling and trampling it.

'The brain!' he insisted. 'You must go for the brain!'

Weapons Moderati Knifesmith did not need urging. He was still trying to target the head on which Guardsman Leche was strapped like a sacrificial victim. It was easier as the beast came closer. With a feeling of desperation he watched shell after shell bounce off the giant skull. Was there any brain in it? Was it pure metal-laden bone through and through?

Tactical Officer Viridens shifted the Warlord's good leg, attempting as best he could to brace the Titan against the strain that was to come. Both archaeosaurs spewed streams of burning phosphorus-acetylene, temporarily blinding the bridge crew. When the white-hot fumes cleared they faced the dreadful sight of two battle-beasts rearing on their hind legs, blotting out the sky.

Moderati Knifesmith realised that everything now depended on him, and that it would all be over in the next few seconds. In an act of intense concentration, he divided his firepower. He aimed one shoulder cannon up at the lower jaw of the first archaeosaur. At the same time, he levelled the belly lasgun and the other shoulder cannon together at the same target: one of the deep wounds in the second, grievously injured animal.

The hiss and racket of the weapons was brief. A single shell passed through the archaeosaur's jaw and entered the skull to explode within it and blast it to pieces. Meantime both cannon shells and laser beam ate their way deep into the innards of the other beast, inflicting explosion after explosion at the centre of the massive body. The enormous spine shattered. Both beasts fell, one soundlessly, one with mangled roars, to lie writhing in its death throes.

Luckily neither had fallen against the Warlord. Princeps Gaerius breathed a sigh.

'Well done, Knifesmith!' He turned to the Chief Engineer. 'Moriens, effect repairs immediately.'

Muffled by the mask-like neural interface, Moriens replied. 'Yes, princeps.'

Imperial Guard units were already attacking the fleeing tribesmen, causing terrible carnage Guardsman Osmin Leche, having fainted with terror, had died without feeling anything. And no one had heard the death-scream of Colour Sergeant Hangist as he was carried falling to the ground.

THE FIRES IN the village burned low that night. Women keened for their lost men, children cried for their fathers and brothers. The new hetman spoke gravely.

'We have acted with honour,' he said. 'We sent only two Defenders to fight two Giant Shining Warriors. Now here is only one other course of action. We must use the whole herd.'

'But that is dishonour!' protested a young warrior, one of the few to survive.

'When we fight another tribe, then there is honour,' the hetman pronounced. 'Beast is pitted against beast. The vanquished grants the victor tribute of grazing, tools and women, and offers battle the following year. Here there is no honour. The Giant Shining Warriors from the sky have come to take our world. They must know they cannot.'

The men pondered his words, and could find no fault with them.

THE FLICKERING DAWN had come, and repairs to the *Lex et Annihilato* were complete, when the herd came loping over the horizon. Princeps Gaerius stared aghast. He had assumed from yesterday's battle that the archaeosaurs were rare. Yet here were a hundred animals at least. And they were running straight for the Imperial Guard camp.

He looked stony-faced at Knifesmith, Viridens and Moriens. Stricken, they glared back at him.

Using the conning magnifier, he saw that the onrushing animals were bare of artificial structures. They were not under anyone's direct control – except for four or five 'managed' beasts at the back, and these were driving the others on. The herd was being stampeded.

There was nothing for it but to go down fighting. No officer trained by the Collegio Titanicus would do anything else. Gaerius clenched his fists. 'Battle stations!'

His order went unquestioned. All three bridge officers pulled down their interfaces. Klaxons sounded in the body of the Titan. The ground was shaking. An enormous pounding, as though the planet was breaking up, could be heard even here in the bridge.

The Warlord strode out to its doom, lasgun zipping, shoulder cannon roaring until all magazines were empty. Not a single archaeosaur was downed, but the lasgun, powered by the fission reactor, kept firing until it was destroyed. When the Warlord was caught in the onrush, the press of the creature's steely flesh was so hard that it could not even fall but was instead ground between numerous immense bodies. By the time the herd had passed, the *Lex et Annihilato* was smashed to fragments. Only the cranium was still intact.

TWENTY LIGHT YEARS distant, the destruction of the third expedition to Planet ABL 1034 was evaluated almost immediately. A visual account of the initial battle, in which one Titan was destroyed, had been retrieved. In the final hour, Colonel Costos of the Fifth Helvetian, showing great bravery, had managed to send a shaky record of the final dreadful events.

The commission was broad-ranging. Imperial Guard Tactical Staff officers accompanied by the obligatory commissar, Collegio Titanicus staff officers, and a priest of the Adeptus Terra, sat round a varnished teak table. They had watched the visual records, including the bridge logs from the *Lex et Annihilato* and the *Principio non Tactica*. All had been shocked to see what a people who did not even know how to smelt metal could do.

'The planet cannot be abandoned,' the Adeptus Terra dignitary pronounced. 'It must be occupied, even if only to deny it to others. What are the options?'

The Collegio Titanicus officer spoke sadly. 'We should not send more of our Titans against those monsters. We cannot afford such losses.'

The commissar, present as a representative of the Ministorum, stirred. 'The Cult of the Emperor has succeeded in worse places. We can take the long approach. Infiltrate trained missionaries into the local culture. Given time, they will create a religion favourable to the Imperium. We can then move in and take over a friendly population.'

'No! We cannot risk it!'

The cry had come from the Collegio Titanicus officer. His face was pained. 'Don't you see? The archaeosaurs are a direct danger to us! Our Dark Age Titans constantly decrease in number, even though slowly. None that are vanquished can be replaced. But these archaeosaurs are animals! They breed! If they get loose into the galaxy, they can be bred without limit! What if the orks get hold of them?'

It must have been hard for a senior officer of the Adeptus Titanicus to speak so. His voice was anguished. 'With respect, the commissar's plan will take too long to execute. Meantime, there is always the risk of an alien race – such as the orks – stepping in, learning from the natives, and eventually deploying these beasts against us!'

'We could do the same,' the commissar pointed out smoothly.

The suggestion that archaeosaurs might supplant the Adeptus Titanicus plainly horrified the Collegio officer. He shook his head vigorously. 'It is far too dangerous. There is only one real option. Exterminatus!'

'That will deny us the use of the planet, too, for centuries to come,' the commissar said. 'I advocate the gentler course.'

They pondered. And then a shivering stillness seemed to come upon them. It was as though a ghostly presence had passed through the assembly. Several of those present looked up, softly murmuring the same word.

'Exterminatus.'

TIGHTLY BOUND TO an X-beam far above the ground, on the swaying head of a giant beast, Princeps Gaerius raged with shame and frustration. Colonel Costos had been right. Primitive peoples were not stupid. They were bright. How, by the Emperor, had they ever learned to bend the archaeosaurs to their will? Could the Adeptus Mechanicus have done any better? Could it have done as well?

Gaerius was forced to admit the natives' cleverness and courage. But they had destroyed his beloved *Annihilato*! They had humiliated the Adeptus Titanicus! For that, only hatred!

Half a kilometre to his right, Weapons Moderati Knifesmith swayed atop a second battle beast. Tactical Officer Viridens was on a third beast to his left. Chief Engineer Moriens was luckier. He had not survived the final fall of the *Lex et Annihilato*'s cranium.

Gaerius raised his face to the sky and cried out with all his soul, as though he could cast his cry through the warp. 'Exterminatus!' he pleaded. '*Exterminatus!*'

THE WRATH OF KHÂRN

William King

'BLOOD FOR THE Blood God!' bellowed Khârn the Betrayer, charging forward through the hail of bolter fire, towards the Temple of Superlative Indulgence. The bolter shells ricocheting off his breastplate did not even slow him down. The Chaos Space Marine smiled to himself. The ancient ceramite of his armour had protected him for over ten thousand years. He felt certain it would not let him down today. All around him warriors fell, clutching their wounds, crying in pain and fear.

More souls offered up on the altar of battle to the Supreme Lord of Carnage, Khârn thought and grinned maniacally. Surely the Blood God would be pleased this day.

Ahead of him, Khârn saw one of his fellow berzerkers fall, his body riddled with shells, his armour cracked and melted by plasma fire. The berzerker howled with rage and frustration, knowing that he was not going to be in at the kill, that he would give Khorne no more offerings on this or any other day. In frustration, the dying warrior set his chainsword to maximum power and took off his own head with one swift stroke. His blood rose in a red fountain to slake Khorne's thirst.

As he passed, Khârn kicked the fallen warrior's head, sending it flying over the defenders' parapet. At least this way his fallen comrade would witness Khârn slaughter the Slaanesh worshippers in the few delicious moments before he died. Under the circumstances, it was the least reward Khârn could grant such a devout warrior.

The Betrayer leapt over a pile of corpses, snapping off a shot with his plasma pistol. One of the Slaanesh cultists fell, clutching the ruins of his melted face. Gorechild, Khârn's daemonic axe, howled in his hands.

Khârn brandished it above his head and bellowed his challenge to the sick, yellow sky of the daemon world.

'Skulls for the skull throne!' Khârn howled. On every side, frothing Berzerkers echoed his cry. More shells whined all around him. He ignored them the way he would ignore the buzz of annoying insects. More of his fellows fell but Khârn stood untouched, secure in the blessing of the Blood God, knowing that it would not be his turn today.

All was going according to plan. A tide of Khorne's warriors flowed across the bomb-cratered plains towards the towering redoubt of the Slaanesh worshippers. Support fire from the Chaos Titan artillery had reduced most of the walls around the ancient temple complex to just so much rubble. The disgusting murals painted in fluorescent colours had been reduced to atoms. The obscene minarets that crowned the towers had been blasted into well-deserved oblivion. Lewd statues lay like colossal, limbless corpses, gazing at the sky with blank marble eyes.

Even as Khârn watched, missiles blazed down from the sky and smashed another section of the defensive wall to blood-covered fragments. Huge clouds of dust billowed. The ground shook. The explosions rumbled like distant thunder. Sick joy bubbled through Khârn's veins at the prospect of imminent violence.

This was what he lived for, these moments of action where he could once again prove his superiority to all other warriors in the service of his exalted lord. In all his ten thousand year existence, Khârn had found no joy to touch the joy of battle, no lust greater than his lust for blood. Here on the field of mortal combat, he was more than in his element, he was at the site of his heart's desire. It was the thing that had caused him to betray his oath of allegiance to the Emperor of Mankind, his genetic destiny as a Space Marine and even his old comrades in the World Eaters Legion. He had never regretted those decisions even for an instant. The bliss of battle was reward enough to stay any doubts.

He jumped the ditch before the parapet, ignoring the poisoned spikes which lined the pit bottom and promised an ecstatic death to any that fell upon them. He scrambled up the loose scree of the rock face and vaulted over the low wall, planting his boot firmly into the face of a defender as he did so. The man screamed and fell back, trying to stem the flow of blood from his broken nose. Khârn swung Gorechild and ended his whining forever.

'Death is upon you!' Khârn roared as he dived into a mass of depraved cultists. Gorechild lashed out. Its teeth bit into hardened ceramite, spraying sparks in all directions. The blow passed through the target's armour, opening its victim from stomach to sternum. The wretch fell back, clutching at his ropy entrails. Khârn despatched him with a backhand swipe and fell upon his fellows, slaying right and left, killing with every blow.

Frantically the cultists' leader bellowed orders, but it was too late. Khârn was among them, and no man had ever been able to boast of facing Khârn in close combat and living.

The numbers 2243, then 2244, blinked before his eyes. The ancient Gothic lettering of the digital death-counter, superimposed on Khârn's field of vision, incremented quickly. Khârn was proud of this archaic device, presented by Warmaster Horus himself in ancient times. Its like could not be made in this degenerate age. Khârn grinned proudly as his tally of offerings for this campaign continued to rise. He still had a long way to go to match his personal best but that was not going to stop him trying.

Men screamed and howled as they died. Khârn roared with pleasure, killing everything within his reach, revelling in the crunch of bone and the spray of blood. The rest of the Khornate force took advantage of the destruction the Betrayer had caused. They swarmed over the walls in a howling mass and dismembered the Slaanesh worshippers. Already demoralised by the death of their leader, not even these fanatical worshippers of the Lord of Pleasure could stand their ground. Their morale broken, they panicked and fled.

Such pathetic oafs were barely worth the killing, Khârn decided, lashing out reflexively and killing those Slaanesh worshippers who passed too close him as they fled. 2246, 2247, 2248 went the death counter. It was time to get on with his mission. It was time to find the thing he had come here to destroy – the ancient daemonic artefact known as the Heart of Desire.

'Attack!' Khârn bellowed and charged through the gaping mouth of the leering stone head that was the entrance to the main temple building.

INSIDE IT WAS quiet, as if the roar of battle could not penetrate the walls. The air stank of strange perfumes. The walls had a porous, fleshy look. The pink-tinged light was odd; it shimmered all around, coming from no discernible source. Khârn switched to the auto-sensor systems within his helm, just in case there was some trickery here.

Leather-clad priestesses, their faces domino-masked, emerged from padded doorways. They lashed at Khârn with whips that sent surges of pain and pleasure through his body. Another man, one less hardened than Khârn, might have been overwhelmed by the sensation but Khârn had spent millennia in the service of his god, and what passed through him now was but a pale shadow compared to the battle lust that mastered him. He chopped through the snake-like flesh of the living lash. Poison blood spurted forth. The woman screamed as if he had cut her. Looking closer he saw that she and the whip were one. A leering daemonic head tipped the weapon's handle and had buried its fangs into her wrist. Khârn's interest was sated. He killed the priestess with one back-handed swipe of Gorechild.

A strange, strangled cry of rage and hate warned him of a new threat. He turned and saw that one of the other Berzerkers, less spiritually pure than himself, had been overcome by the whip's evil. The man had torn off his helmet and his face was distorted by a sick and dreamy smile that had no place on the features of one chosen by Khorne. Like a sleepwalker he advanced on Khârn and lashed out with his chainsword. Khârn laughed as he parried the blow and killed the man with his return stroke.

A quick glance told him that all the priestesses were dead and that most of his followers had slain their drugged brethren. Good, thought Khârn, but part of him was disappointed. He had hoped that more of his fellows would be overcome by treachery. It was good to measure himself against true warriors, not these decadent worshippers of an effete god. Gorechild howled with frustrated bloodlust, writhing in his hand as if it would turn on him if he did not feed it more blood and sinew soon. Khârn knew how the axe felt. He turned, gestured for his companions to follow him and raced off down the corridor.

'Follow me,' he shouted. 'To the slaughter!'

Passing through a huge arch, the former Space Marines entered the inner sanctum of the temple and Khârn knew that they had found what they had come for. Light poured in through the stained glass ceiling. As he watched, Khârn realised that the light was not coming through the glass, but from the glass itself. The illustrations glowed with an eerie internal light and they moved. A riotous assembly of men and women, mutants and daemons enacted every foul deed that the depraved followers of a debauched god could imagine. And, Khârn noted, they could imagine quite a lot.

Khârn raised his pistol and opened fire, but the glass merely absorbed the weapon's energy. Something like a faint moan of pleasure filled the chamber and mocking laughter drew Khârn's attention to the throne which dominated the far end of the huge chamber. It was carved from a single gem that pulsed and changed colour, going from amber to lavender to pink to lime and then back through a flickering, random assortment of iridescent colours that made no sense and hurt the eye. Khârn knew without having to be told that this throne was the Heart of Desire. Senses honed by thousands of years of exposure to the stuff of Chaos told him that the thing fairly radiated power. Inside was the trapped essence of a daemon prince, held forever at the whim of Slaanesh as punishment for some ancient treachery. The man sitting so regally on the throne was merely a puppet and barely worth Khârn's notice, save as something to be squashed like a bug.

The man looked down on Khârn as if he had the temerity to feel the same way about Khorne's most devoted follower. His left hand stroked the hair of the leashed and naked woman who crouched like a pet at his feet. His right hand held an obscenely shaped runesword, which glowed with a blasphemous light.

Khârn strode forward to confront his new foe. The clatter of ceramite-encased feet on marble told him that his fellow berzerkers followed. In a matter of a hundred strides, Khârn found himself at the foot of the dais, and some odd, mystical force compelled him to stop and stare.

Khârn did not doubt that he was face-to-face with the cult leader. The man had the foul, debauched look of an ancient and immortal devotee of Slaanesh. His face was pale and gaunt; make-up concealed the dark shadows under his eyes. An obscene helmet covered the top of his head. As he stood, his pink and lime cloak billowed out behind him. Tight bands of studded leather armour girdled his naked chest, revealing lurid and disturbing tattoos.

'Welcome to the Heart of Desire,' the Slaanesh worshipper said in a soft, insinuating voice which somehow carried clearly across the chamber and compelled immediate, respectful attention. Khârn was instantly on his guard, sensing the magic within that voice, the persuasive power which could twist mortals to its owner's will. He struggled to keep the fury that burned eternally in his breast from subsiding under the influence of those slyly enthralling tones. 'What do you wish?'

'Your death!' the Betrayer roared, yet he felt his bloodlust being subdued by that oddly comforting voice.

The cult leader sighed. 'You worshippers of Khorne are so drearily predictable. Always the same tedious, unimaginative retort. I suppose it comes from following that mono-maniacal deity of yours. Still, you are hardly to be blamed for your god's dullness, I suppose.'

'When Khorne has devoured your soul, you will pay for such blasphemy!' Khârn shouted. His followers shouted their approval but with less enthusiasm than Khârn would have expected. For some reason, the man on the throne did not appear to be worried by the presence of so many armed men in his sanctum.

'Somehow I doubt it, old chap. You see, my soul has long been pledged to thrice-blessed Slaanesh, so unless Khorne wants to stick his talon down Slaanesh's throat or some other orifice, he'll have a hard time getting at it.'

'Enough of this prattle!' Khârn roared. 'Death is upon you!'

'Oh! Be sensible,' the cultist said, raising his hand. Khârn felt a tide of pleasure flow over him, like that he had felt from the whip earlier but a thousand times stronger. All around him he heard his men moan and gasp.

'Think! You can spend an eternity of pleasure being caressed by the power of Lord Slaanesh, while your soul slowly rots and sinks into his comforting embrace. Anything you want, anything you have ever desired, can be yours. All you have to do is swear allegiance to Slaanesh. Believe me, it's no trouble.'

As the cult leader spoke, images flickered through Khârn's mind. He saw visions of his youth and all the joys he had known, before the rebellion of Horus and the Battle for Terra. Somehow it all looked so clear and fresh and appealing, and it almost brought moisture to his tear ducts. He saw endless banquets of food and wine. For a moment, his palate was stimulated by all manner of strange and wonderful tastes, and his brain tingled with a myriad pleasures and stimulations. Visions of diaphanously clad maidens danced before his eyes, beckoning enticingly.

For a moment, despite himself, Khârn felt an almost unthinkable temptation to betray his ancient oath to the Blood God. This was powerful sorcery indeed! He shook his head and bit his lip until the blood flowed. 'No true warrior of Khorne would fall for this pitiful trick!' he bellowed.

'All hail Slaanesh!' one of his followers cried.

'Praise to the great Lord of Pleasure!' shouted another.

'Let us grovel and adore him,' a third said, as the whole force cast themselves down onto their knees.

Khârn turned to look at his men, disbelief and outrage filling his mind. It seemed that they did not possess his iron-willed belief in Khorne's power, that they were prepared to betray him for a few tawdry promises of pleasure. In every face, in every posture, he saw slack-jawed worship of the posturing peacock on the throne. He knew that there was only one thing to be done under the circumstances.

The Slaanesh leader obviously felt the same. 'Kill him!' he cried. 'Offer up his soul to Slaanesh and unspeakable ecstasy shall be your reward!'

The first of Khârn's comrades raised his bolt pistol and squeezed the trigger. Khârn threw himself to one side and the shell whipped past his head. The Betrayer rewarded the traitor with a taste of Gorechild. The chain-axe screeched as it bit through armour in a mighty sweep that clove him clean in two. The warrior gave a muted whine as his Slaanesh-corrupted soul went straight to the warp.

Suddenly the rest of the berzerkers were upon him. Khârn found himself fighting for his immortal life. These were no mere Slaanesh cultists. Newly tainted though they might be, they had once been worthy followers of Khorne, fierce, deadly and full of bloodlust. Mighty maces bludgeoned Khârn. Huge chainswords threatened to tear his rune-encrusted armour. Bolter shells tore chunks from his chest-plate. Khârn fought on, undismayed, filled with the joy of battle, taking fierce pleasure every time Gorechild took another life. At last, these were worthy foes! The body count swiftly ticked on to 2460 and continued to rise.

Instinctively Khârn side-stepped a blow that tore off one of the metal skulls which dangled from his belt. The Betrayer swore he would replace it with the attacker's own skull. His return stroke made good his vow. He whirled Gorechild in a great figure-of-eight and cleared a space all around him, sending two more traitors to make their excuses to the

Blood God. Insane bloodlust surged through him, overcoming even the soporific influence of the Heart of Desire and for a moment Khârn fought with his full unfettered power. He became transformed into an unstoppable engine of destruction and nothing could stand against him.

Khârn's heart pounded. The blood sang through his veins and the desire to kill made him howl uncontrollably. Bones crunched beneath his axe. His pistol blew away the life of its targets. He stamped on the heads of the fallen, crushing them to jelly. Khârn ignored pain, ignored any idea of self-preservation, and fought for the pure love of fighting. He killed and he killed.

ALL TOO SOON it was over, and Khârn stood alone in a circle of corpses. His breathing rasped from his chest. Blood seeped through a dozen small punctures in his armour. He felt like a rib might have been broken by that last blow of the mace but he was triumphant. His counter read 2485. He sensed the presence of one more victim and turned to confront the figure on the dais.

The cultists' leader stood looking down at him with a faint expression of mingled disbelief and distaste on his face. The naked girl had fled. The throne pulsed enticingly.

'It's true what they say,' the man said with a delicious sigh. 'If you want anything done properly, you have to do it yourself.'

The insinuating voice drove Khârn's fury from him, and left him feeling tired and spent. The cultist strode down from the dais. Khârn felt almost too weary to parry his blow. He knew he must throw off this enchantment quickly. The runesword bit into his armour and a wave of mingled pain and pleasure passed through Khârn like poison. Summoning his last reserves of rage, he threw himself into the attack. He would show this effete fop who was the true warrior here.

Khârn hacked. Gorechild bit into the tattoos of the man's wrist. Gobbets of flesh and droplets of blood whirled away from the axe's teeth. The rank smell of hot bone filled the air as the hand separated from the arm – and began to crawl away with a life of its own. Khârn stamped on it and a rictus of pain appeared on its owner's face, as if the hand was still attached.

Khârn swung. The cultist's head separated from its shoulders. The body swung its blade, a puppet still controlled by the strings of its master's will. It bit into Khârn and the wave of sensation almost drove him to his knees.

'Nice trick!' roared Khârn, feeling the hand squirm beneath his boot. 'But I've seen it before.'

He brought his chain-axe down on the head and clove it in two. The body fell to the ground, a puppet with its strings cut. 2486, Khârn thought with some satisfaction.

738   Let the Galaxy Burn

The Betrayer advanced upon the throne. It pulsed enticingly before him. Within its multiple facets he thought he saw the face of a beautiful woman, the most beautiful he had ever seen – and the most evil. Her hair was long and golden, and her eyes were blue. Her lips were full and red, and the small, white fangs that protruded from her mouth in no way marred her perfection. She looked at Khârn beseechingly, and he knew at once he was face to face with the Daemon trapped within the Heart of Desire.

Welcome, Khârn, a seductive voice said within his head. *I knew you would triumph. I knew you would be the conqueror. I knew you would be my new master.*

The voice was thrilling. By comparison, the cult leader's voice had been but a pale echo. But the voice was also deceptive. Proud as he was, mighty as he knew himself to be, Khârn knew that no man could truly be the master of a daemon, not even a fallen Space Marine like himself. He knew that his soul was once more in peril, that he should do something. But yet again he found himself enthralled by the persuasiveness of a Slaanesh worshipper's voice.

Be seated! Become the new ruler of this world, then go forth and blast those meddlesome interlopers from the face of your planet.

Khârn fought to hold himself steady while the throne pulsed hypnotically before him, and the smell of heavy musk filled his nostrils. He knew that once he sat he would be trapped, just as the daemon was trapped. He would become a slave to the thing imprisoned within the throne. His will would be drained and he would become a decadent and effete shadow of the Khârn he had once been. Yet his limbs began to move almost of their own accord, his feet slowly but surely carrying him towards the throne.

Once more, visions of an eternity of corrupt pleasure danced in Khârn's mind. Once more he saw himself indulging in every excess. The daemon promised him every ecstasy imaginable and it was well within its power to grant such pleasures. He knew it would be a simple thing for him to triumph on its behalf. All he had to do was step outside and announce that he had destroyed the Heart of Desire. He was Khârn. He would be believed, and after that it would be a simple matter to lure the Khorne worshippers to ecstatic servitude or joyful destruction.

And would they not deserve it? Already he was known as the Betrayer, when all he had done was be more loyal to his god than the spineless weaklings he had slaughtered. And with that the daemon's voice fell silent and the visions stopped, as if the thing in the throne realised its mistake, but too late.

For Khârn was loyal to Khorne and there was only room for that one thing within his savage heart. He had betrayed and killed his comrades in the World Eaters because they had not remained true to Khorne's ideals and would have fled from the field of battle without either conquering or being destroyed.

The reminder gave him strength. He turned and looked back at the room. The reek of blood and dismembered bodies filled his nostrils like perfume. He remembered the joy of the combat. The thrill of overcoming his former comrades. He looked out on a room filled with corpses and a floor carpeted with blood. He was the only living thing here and he had made it so. He realised that, compared to this pleasure, this sense of conquest and victory, what the daemon offered was only a pale shadow.

Khârn turned and brought Gorechild smashing down upon the foul throne. His axe howled thirstily as it drank deep of the ancient and corrupt soul imprisoned within. Once more he felt the thrill of victory, and knew no regrets for rejecting the daemon's offer.

2487. Life just doesn't get any better than this, Khârn thought.

INTO THE MAELSTROM

Chris Pramas

'WAKE UP, CORSAIR! We're almost there.'

Sartak snapped back to consciousness, only to find himself looking down the barrel of a bolter. Beyond it was the disapproving face of Arghun, a Space Marine of the White Scars. Although Arghun had not slept for days, his eyes were alert and his grip on the bolter firm.

'I am not a Corsair,' Sartak said with dignity, 'I am like you, a Space Marine, of the Astral Claws Chapter.'

Arghun reached down, grabbed Sartak's shoulder with his left hand and hauled him roughly to his feet. Forcing his bolter against the side of Sartak's head, the White Scar spat in disgust: 'You filth. The Astral Claws betrayed the Emperor! You lost the right to be called a Space Marine long ago. You're nothing but a reaver and a pirate.'

Sartak felt the cool metal of the bolter against his flesh, but somehow he remained calm. He knew the White Scar would not kill him now. There was too much at stake. 'I am here to restore the honour of the Astral Claws,' he said in a level voice. 'My reaving days are over.'

Arghun released Sartak from his grip, but kept the bolter handy. 'Yes,' the White Scar growled, 'so you said in your moving speech before Subatai Khan. After years as a murdering cur, you woke up one morning and realised you still loved the Emperor.' Arghun's voice dripped with scorn. 'And now you're going to help us kill Huron Blackheart...' The White Scar's laughter filled the cramped quarters of the smuggler's ship. 'I've heard more convincing lies from ogryns.'

'If you don't believe me,' Sartak said, flatly exasperated after days of such exchanges, 'then why in the Emperor's name are you here?'

'If you were a true Space Marine,' Arghun thundered, 'you wouldn't even have to ask me that question! I am here because I was ordered to be. That's all I need to know.'

'Arghun, I'm weary of fighting with you,' Sartak replied with a sigh. 'What I've told you is the truth. Huron Blackheart is planning a massive attack on an undefended Imperial world. If I can find my friend Lothar on Blackheart's flagship, he should be able to tell us where the attack will fall.' Sartak had told his story a dozen times, but it was plain from the look on Arghun's face that the White Scar didn't believe a word of it. Still, Sartak felt compelled to speak the words, hoping in his heart that they were true. 'Then,' the Astral Claw finished, 'we can signal the rest of your Chapter and bury Blackheart forever.'

He paused, before adding, 'If you ever take off this inhibitor, that is.' Almost unconsciously, Sartak ran his fingers over the heavy collar around his neck. As always, he could not find any kind of seam.

Watching with amusement, the White Scar laughed. 'What's wrong? Don't you like being Arghun's dog, Corsair? It's the only way to teach you discipline and obedience.' The smile left Arghun's lips as quickly as it had come. 'Besides, I couldn't risk you alerting your friends in the Red Corsairs before our arrival.

'Whatever, we are almost to the Maelstrom,' Arghun continued. 'You'll have your precious powers back soon enough.' The White Scar slung his bolter reluctantly, but kept his eyes on Sartak. 'Just try to remember what it really means to be a Space Marine and a codicier.'

Sartak locked eyes with Arghun. 'I swear before the Emperor to prove the truth of my words and restore the honour of the Astral Claws.'

'Then may the Emperor have mercy on your soul, Corsair.'

ARGHUN AND SARTAK stood in the vast, reeking metal belly of Huron Blackheart's great warship. Surrounded by the Red Corsairs, renegade Space Marines of a dozen Chapters, they awaited Blackheart himself. Arghun stood proud and upright, staring defiantly at his fallen brethren, while Sartak shifted uncomfortably, searching the crowd for a friendly face. A haze of torch and incense smoke hung over the bay, but could not obscure the leering gargoyles that adorned its walls. From here, amidst twisted iron sconces and blood-spattered altars, Huron Blackheart led the Red Corsairs in their depraved worship of the foul gods of Chaos. Sartak had heard the screams of countless victims in this dark temple, and the memories haunted him still.

Blackheart's men were just as Sartak remembered them. Once the Emperor's elite, full of honour and courage, these Marines had betrayed their oaths and followed Huron into heresy. Where they had once used their strength to protect the citizens of the Imperium, they now used that same savage power to offer up victims to their cruel gods. Blood, booty and terror were their masters now, and Sartak found it increasingly hard to believe that he had been one of them. Looking down at the fading Astral Claws markings on his power armour, now but a dim trace of their former glory, Sartak wondered if there was any honour left to salvage.

Unwilling to meet the eyes of any of his former comrades, Sartak scanned the great bay. His gaze came to rest on the prone forms of Huron's dreadnoughts. These massive machines of destruction stood chained amongst the broken pillars of the central temple, as if their life-less husks could be reanimated at any moment. But it was naught but an illusion, for the sarcophagi which housed the pilots that gave life to the stomping beasts were well away from the dreadnoughts. Sartak knew them to be housed behind the Great Seal, safely locked away in Huron's temple of temples. Although the Red Corsairs consigned the deranged and insane to lives of living torment inside the metal sarcophagi, they still treated the dreadnought pilots with an awed respect, perhaps because their irrational power reminded the Corsairs of their own inhuman gods.

A hush fell over the assembled Chaos Marines, and Sartak could hear Huron Blackheart approach. As long as he lived, he would never forget the peculiar rhythm of Huron's thumping footsteps, a product of the meltagun blast which had destroyed half of the man's body. The Red Corsairs parted before their master as he strode into view. Blackheart was a towering figure, half man and half machine. His massive armour, a corrupted mockery of that of the Space Marines, bristled with blades and saws. In place of his left arm, he had an enormous bionic claw that jerked open and closed spasmodically, so eager was it to rend the flesh of the living. Huron's wreck of a face radiated sheer menace, and his eyes burned with an unholy fire. Stopping his thundering advance only a few paces from the two Space Marines, the Blood Reaver sized up his new guests as a butcher might study cattle ready for slaughter.

'Sartak!' Huron boomed, 'I last saw you dead on the bridge of a White Scars' cruiser, yet here you stand. Tell me, how are you alive?'

'Great tyrant,' Sartak began, ' I was but knocked unconscious during that savage fight. The White Scars took me prisoner, but I would say nothing to them.' The Marine could feel his mouth getting drier as the well-prepared lies came to his lips. Hurriedly, he continued, trying to finish before his voice betrayed him. 'Arghun here helped me escape, and we hired a smuggler to bring us back to the Maelstrom. I told Arghun that you were always looking for men like him.'

Huron's twisted face betrayed nothing as his gaze swept to the White Scar. Sartak felt relieved to be out from his scrutiny. He only hoped the proud White Scar could feign the humility needed to win the tyrant's trust.

'And you, loyal White Scar,' Huron said, 'you betrayed your comrades to help Sartak escape. Why risk death to help this lowly sorcerer?'

'I care nothing for this wretch,' Arghun spat defiantly. 'I used him because I knew he could bring me to you.' The White Scar bowed his head ever so slightly, for the first time acknowledging the power of the Blood Reaver. 'And you, lord, are the only man that can offer me refuge from the wrath of my gutless brethren.'

Blackheart laughed. 'This one's got spirit.' He took two great strides over to Arghun and grabbed the White Scar's neck in his wicked claw. As blood trickled ever so slowly down the hungry pincer, the Blood Reaver continued, 'Tell me, White Scar, what did you do to earn the wrath of your Chapter?'

Arghun stood rock still, lest a sudden movement cause the claw to snap shut. 'Great tyrant,' he choked out, 'I killed my sergeant in battle because he ordered a retreat. Cowards like him deserve only death.'

Blackheart stood silently for a long moment, the only sound in the room Arghun's increasingly laboured breathing as the claw squeezed tighter. Then the claw snapped open and the Blood Reaver stepped back. Arghun sighed in relief and drew in great gulps of air.

Sartak also relaxed. The worst was over. He knew how merciless Huron could be with potential new recruits, but it seemed that Arghun had passed the test.

Huron strode over to Sartak and put his good hand on the Astral Claw's shoulder. 'Brother, you have done well. You know how few sorcerers I command and we had mourned your loss.' Sartak, wary of trickery, could detect no falsehood in the tyrant's words. 'I want to welcome you back to the Red Corsairs.' Blackheart's voice deepened as he continued, 'But first, you must do something for me.'

'Anything, great tyrant!' Sartak exclaimed, nodding his head.

Blackheart removed his hand from Sartak's shoulder, unholstered his bolt pistol, and held it out to the Astral Claw. 'Kill the White Scar.'

'But, great tyrant,' Sartak stammered, 'he, well, he helped me to escape.'

'He helped you to escape so you would bring him here,' Huron said matter of factly. 'He's a White Scar infiltrator, no doubt sent to kill me. Now take this and execute him!'

The tone of the Blood Reaver brooked no contradiction, not if Sartak wanted to live. The Marine took the pistol and walked slowly over to Arghun. He had no love for the uncompromising White Scar, but nor did he want to be his executioner. He raised the pistol and aimed for Arghun's temple. At least death would be quick.

'What are you waiting for?' roared the Blood Reaver. 'Kill him!'

'Kill the traitor!' the Red Corsairs howled in unison.

Arghun looked at the Astral Claw and Sartak saw no fear in his face. 'Go ahead, Corsair,' Arghun said calmly. 'I always knew you would kill me in the end.'

Sartak squeezed the trigger twice. The White Scar died without sound or complaint and fell with an echoing thud on to the metal floor of the great bay. Not for the last time innocent blood stained the unholy ground of Blackheart's temple.

Huron Blackheart smiled and his insane joy was almost as terrible as his anger. 'Welcome home, Sartak. You've been away too long.'

SARTAK MOVED QUICKLY amidst the twisting corridors of Huron's warship. It had been two days since his return and at last it seemed safe for him to move about freely. The Blood Reaver's small fleet was even now cruising through the Maelstrom, heading for an unknown destination. Excitement ran high amongst the Red Corsairs, for Huron Blackheart had promised them booty and blood aplenty. Sartak tried to appear calm as he searched the ship for Lothar. By now his friend should have discovered where the attack was to fall, for he had won a place amongst Huron's inner circle. But the man had not been in his quarters, nor was he in the galley. Now, Sartak was forced to roam the great ship almost at random, hoping to find his friend before it was too late.

The Astral Claw found himself heading deeper into the bowels of the labyrinthine ship. The corridors stank of stale blood and he began to see skulls and bones littering the grilled walkway. This was the part of the ship claimed by the followers of Khorne, and Sartak usually went out of his way to avoid it. But he must find Lothar and this was one of the few places he had not searched.

Sartak had seen no one for almost an hour, and this only added to his agitation. Something was going on, he could sense it. Then he heard distant howls from up ahead and his heart sank. As he approached, Sartak could hear the roar of a crowd and cries of 'Blood for the Blood God!' At last Sartak emerged into a wide cargo bay and stopped in alarm. All of Huron's Khornate followers were assembled in a circle of crimson and gold, surrounding two combatants. Even above the shrieks for blood, Sartak could hear the distinct whirr of a chain-axe. He knew with cold certainty that this was no ordinary combat.

Pushing himself through the frenzied warriors, Sartak finally got a view of the combatants and his worst fears were confirmed. At the centre of the circle was Lothar, stripped to the waist and armed with a chain sword. His opponent was Crassus, a renegade Ultramarine who was Khorne's chosen champion amongst the Red Corsairs. Dark and wiry, Lothar was an experienced fighter, true enough, but Crassus was a bloody-handed psychopath a full head taller than him, with few equals in hand-to-hand combat.

This is not a duel, Sartak thought grimly. This is slaughter.

'Khorne demands a sacrifice!' the berserkers chanted wildly. 'Blood! Blood for Khorne!'

'Lothar!' Sartak bellowed and tried to break through the ring of blood-hungry berserkers, but half a dozen arms held him back. Lothar caught sight of him but was fully engaged in trying to fend off Crassus. The chain-axe of the insane warrior hammered down upon Lothar's chainsword, driving the weary warrior back with every blow. Sartak could see that Lothar was bleeding from many wounds. Each time he parried, the Marine was just a little slower, while Crassus seemed to grow stronger with each blow. As the howls for blood reached a frenzied pitch, Crassus roared and smashed the chainsword from his opponent's hands, and in the same fluid movement buried the axe in Lothar's chest. The chewing blades of the chain-axe tore through Lothar's flesh and he screamed in pain as his hot life-blood gushed all over the crazed Berserker.

'Blood for the Blood God!' the mob roared, and then, bearing Khorne's chosen one aloft, 'Crassus! Crassus!'

'No!' Sartak screamed and ran where to his dying friend lay, forgotten. Lothar lay on his back, his chest a bloody ruin. Still, he yet lived.

Sartak knelt next to him. 'Forgive me, Lothar,' he said. 'I couldn't find you.'

'I was... discovered,' Lothar gasped, blood frothing on his lips. 'But the attack... the attack will fall on Razzia. Emperor... redeem us.' His ravaged body convulsed one last time and lay still. Around Sartak, the berserkers of Khorne howled in savage celebration. Soon they were fighting furiously amongst themselves, driven mad by the sight and smell of freshly spilled blood. Taking advantage of the mayhem, Sartak slipped back into the welcome darkness.

SARTAK SAT ALONE in his chambers, still covered with the blood of his only friend. Now Lothar and Arghun were both dead, and Sartak knew it was up to him to finish Huron Blackheart alone. The Astral Claw shook with barely repressed fury as he thought about the lifeless body of Lothar, and of his own fall from the Emperor's grace.

Sartak's blood burned for vengeance on Blackheart, but a small inner voice crooned to him to wait. A relic of his reaving days, or a clear sign of impending madness, the voice tempted and chided his soul. It would be so easy, the voice told him, to stay with Blackheart and maintain his loyalty.

Yes, so easy, Sartak reflected, but he had followed the easy path for far too many years. Sartak remembered those dark days on Badab, when Huron had poisoned the Astral Claws against the Emperor. Sartak, loyal to his Chapter Master, as a Space Marine should be, followed him into heresy. But the years of reaving had taken their toll on the once idealistic warrior. Like a sleeping man jarred to consciousness, Sartak had opened his eyes to the depravity and corruption of the man once known as the Tyrant of Badab. With this shocking awakening Sartak had realised that there was only one way to make good his betrayal of the Emperor.

'If I must add my own blood to that of Arghun and Lothar,' he snarled aloud, 'then let that be my penance.' Sartak drew in a deep breath and steadied his beating heart. Now, it was time to finish what he had started.

THE ASTRAL CLAW knelt on the floor and pulled a small cloth bag from between the folds of his bunk. Reaching inside, he pulled out the Imperial Tarot. The magical paraphernalia cluttered about his chamber was just for show, mere superstitious frippery. Huron was strangely proud of his 'sorcerers' and Sartak had been forced to act the part. Runic wands, talismanic skulls, and ancient icons lay strewn about haphazardly, the accoutrements of his obscene trade.

Now all Sartak needed was the purity of the Tarot to communicate with the White Scar ship which circled the Maelstrom in eager anticipation of his message. It was time for him to take on once again the mantle of Space Marine, librarian and Astral Claw.

Sartak knelt and shuffled the Tarot. Focusing his mind, he drew three cards from the top of the deck and placed them face down. Holding his breath, he flipped them over one by one. Horror! Revealed before him were the Emperor reversed, the Tower, and the Ecclesiarch reversed.

Sartak suppressed the shock of such an ill-omened hand, quickly reminding himself that he was not divining but reforging long broken lines of communication. Trying to forget the grim portents thus revealed, Sartak concentrated on the Tower. Chanting quietly, he envisioned the Tower in the distance, across the great tide of the warp. Casting his mind outward, Sartak fell into a deep trance.

Always he kept the Tower foremost in his mind, as he searched for the spirit of the White Scar librarian he knew to be waiting. The warp embraced him as it always did, comforting him like a mother as it tried to suck him to its womb. Further and further he reached, beyond the gibbering hordes of demonic creatures which implored him for his soul. Then, at the last, the jolt of contact. Across the warp, their minds came together and in an instant it was done. 'Razzia,' he intoned, 'the attack falls on Razzia.'

Information delivered, Sartak broke the contract and fled back across the void to the safety of his own body. It was finished.

BEFORE SARTAK COULD so much as stand, there was a rending crash as the door to his chamber was smashed open. Standing in the doorway was Huron Blackheart, flanked by the tall, cadaverous figure of Garlon Souleater, the tyrant's most potent sorcerer.

Sartak jumped to his feet, scattering the Imperial Tarot across the floor. 'Great tyrant, I had not expected you,' he stammered hastily, knowing with certainty that the Tarot had shown him the future after all.

'No, I don't suppose you did,' Huron laughed. The Chaos leader shrugged towards his twisted sorcerer. 'Garlon tells me that you have been communicating with the White Scars... and I wanted to come and thank you personally.'

'Th– thank me, lord?' Sartak let his hand rest on the hilt of his force sword, yet maintained a pretence of servitude a while longer.

'Yes, Astral Claw, most certainly.' The tyrant grinned maliciously. 'I wanted to thank you for telling the White Scars that I would be attacking Razzia,' Huron continued, his words dripping irony, 'A touching show of misplaced loyalty.' The Corsair's voice rose to a thundering growl and he stabbed his power claw at Sartak. 'Especially when you consider that I've changed my mind!'

'Changed your mind?' Sartak gasped, taken aback. 'Wha–'

Huron waved his hand dismissively. 'Well, no, I lie. I haven't changed my mind as such – we never were attacking Razzia.'

Sartak began to see the trap which had been set for him, and his grip was firm upon his force sword. 'You twisted, evil... what do you mean?'

The tyrant laughed widely at this show of bravado, and beside him Garlon clapped politely in mock applause.

'We are, in fact, headed for Santiago.' Blackheart paused to let the awful truth sink in. 'Thanks to you, however, the White Scars will be far away when the Red Corsairs sweep down on that helpless planet.' The tyrant grinned again, obviously delighted with the Astral Claw's terrified expression.

Sartak staggered backwards, overwhelmed by the enormity of what he had done. 'Santiago? But why?' he whispered, horrified. 'There's nothing to steal there, it's an agricultural world of no military significance at all.'

Garlon rubbed his bony hands together eagerly, his wet tongue licking his thin lips in anticipation of some future pleasure.

'Ah, but you are mistaken. There's one thing Santiago does have,' Huron gloated, clapping Garlon on the back. 'Santiago has millions upon millions of defenceless citizens.'

Garlon whinnied in helpless pleasure. The sorcerer's eyes rolled in his head and he silently mouthed the words: 'Blood and skulls...'

Huron laughed mockingly. Sartak felt cold fury burning in his soul. The tyrant continued, 'And what do you think would happen in the warp, my loyal little sorcerer, were I to offer up the blood of a billion victims on one night?'

'You butcher!' Sartak screamed. 'I followed you, I trusted you, and you led me straight to hell!' In his mind, he commended his soul to the Emperor. He knew what he must do. 'In the name of all that is holy, it stops here!' he yelled, dragging his force sword from its scabbard and charging the Blood Reaver, howling his fury.

Huron Blackheart met Sartak's charge with a cry of delight, parrying the force sword with his great metal claw. The sword, pulsing with psychic energy, sparked and shrieked as it strove to tear the claw asunder. But the forbidden technology powering the tyrant's claw proved too strong, and after long moments of straining sinew and muscle, Sartak was forced to pull his sword away.

Backing up as far as he could in the cramped confines of the chamber, Sartak quickly uttered a calming prayer, before focusing his mind and unleashing a psychic blast at Blackheart's diseased consciousness. The energy of righteousness roared within him, and the bolt flew clear and true.

But Garlon Souleater, soaked in the black energies of Chaos, deflected the blow with a casual flick of a skeletally thin wrist, all the while cackling with perverse pleasure. 'There'll be none of that, Sartak.' His voice oozed mockingly into the Marine's mind. 'Goodbye, our lovely traitor.'

The Blood Reaver closed on Sartak, even as Garlon's twisted laughter echoed inside his skull. There was no more time for psychic trickery.

As the Tyrant attacked with all the power at his disposal, it was all the Astral Claw could do to parry the whirling power axe and merciless claws. Sartak held his force sword in both hands, trying to keep Huron at bay with great sweeps of the deadly blade.

Huron would not be denied blood. With a scream of rage and bitter satisfaction, the Tyrant slammed Sartak's blade into the wall and pinned it there with his axe. The sword was motionless for just a few seconds, as Sartak tried in vain to wrench the glittering weapon free, but that was enough time for Blackheart to close his great claw over Sartak's exposed wrists.

With a wicked grin, the Blood Reaver snapped the claw shut with a sickening crunch. Howling in pain, Sartak fell to his knees, staring in horror at the bleeding stumps.

Huron stood over Sartak, looking with disdain at the wretch at his feet. 'You'd like to die now, wouldn't you, last of the Astral Claws?'

Sartak would not answer. He watched his lifeblood slowly pump away, knowing that he had failed utterly.

Blackheart walked around Sartak's prone form, crushing the Tarot cards that still lay on the floor. 'But a hero's death is not for you,' he taunted, as he brought his leering face close to Sartak's bloody countenance. Sartak groaned aloud, but he could not bring himself to meet the tyrant's gaze. 'No, there will be no redemption for you, Sartak.' The tyrant howled in glee. 'Instead, I will give you the greatest gift an Astral Claw could hope for.'

Laughing with delight, Huron Blackheart turned to the capering sorcerer. 'Take him away, Garlon, and make this sad wretch a hero to be proud of.'

Garlon's mind reached out and smashed through Sartak's weakened defences. The Astral Claw fell into blackness.

SARTAK AWOKE IN total, unutterable darkness. Surprised to be alive, he tried to get up, to move, but found that he could not. Straining his limbs, he slowly realised that needles invaded his body, and unknown wires were entwined around his limbs. Some kind of mask was clamped to his face. Sartak tried to talk, but he choked on the array of tubes that had been rammed down his throat. In panic, he tried to cast his mind into the warp, but found that his powers had been suppressed.

After what felt like long, desperate hours of thrashing blindly in the darkness, Sartak lay in the blackness and waited. Huron would come to taunt him soon enough. Sartak waited and waited, cut off from feeling and perhaps time itself. How long have I been so? he wondered. Hours? Days? Time had lost its meaning.

Still Huron did not come. What have you done to me? the panicked librarian screamed silently.

Have I been jettisoned into the emptiness of space, in an escape capsule? Will I fall forever through the void?

How would that make me a hero?

His mind cast about, trying to find an answer, but to no avail. Nothing made any sense at all.

In a flash of realisation it all became clear. Sartak remembered his one walk beyond the Great Seal. He remembered seeing the maddened members of the Red Corsairs encased forever in coffins of adamantium, sealed up in the Great Temple until battle called.

Sartak knew beyond doubt that the life support systems of a dreadnought could keep a man alive indefinitely. But what if the sarcophagus were never to be hooked into a dreadnought? What if a man was locked inside and left to rot for all eternity? What then?

Sartak tried desperately to think of another possible explanation for his plight, but the logic was cold and inescapable. The epiphany of horror crashed into his consciousness with unstoppable power. He could not even scream as sanity fled.

IN THE FRIGID darkness of the Maelstrom, the fleet of Huron Blackheart tore through space, destined for doomed Santiago. The Blood Reaver was on his way to offer up a billion souls to the Dark Gods of Chaos.

ABOUT THE AUTHORS

Dan Abnett
Dan Abnett lives in Kent, England. Well known for his comic work, he has written everything from the *Mr Men* to the *X-Men* in the last decade. His work for the Black Library includes the popular comic strips *Lone Wolves*, *Titan* and *Inquisitor Ascendant*, the best-selling Gaunt's Ghosts novels, and the acclaimed Inquisitor Eisenhorn trilogy.

Barrington J Bayley
Barrington J. Bayley has been known for many years as a writer of science fiction stories and wonderfully entertaining novels such as *The Soul of the Robot* and *The Zen Gun*.

Mark Brendan
Mark Brendan was immersed in his *Bumper Book of Black Magic* from an early age, and nowadays his writings are considered by many to be 'a shame, and a caution, and an eldritch horror'. He lives in Yorkshire.

Andy Chambers
Andy Chambers is best known as a games designer, having contributed heavily to the development of Warhammer 40,000, Battlefleet Gothic, Necromunda, Epic 40,000 and many other Games Workshop games and supplements. He has contributed two short stories to *Inferno!* magazine, and now works as a freelance writer.

Ben Counter
Ben Counter has made several contributions to the Black Library's *Inferno!* magazine, and has been published in *2000 AD* and the UK small press. An Ancient History graduate and avid miniature painter, he is also secretary of the Comics Creators Guild. He has written the popular Soul Drinkers novel series, and *Grey Knights* for the Black Library.

Jonathan Curran
Jonathan Curran left college with an English Literature degree. He got a job on a magazine, which wasn't as glamorous as he thought it would be, but also did a stint as a film reviewer, which was. He lives in London and has been writing fiction for as long as he can remember.

Robert Earl
Robert Earl graduated from Keele University in 1994, after which he started a career in sales. Three years later though, he'd had more than enough of that and since then he has been working, living and travelling in the Balkans and the Middle East. Robert currently lives in the UK.

Matthew Farrer
Born in 1970, Matthew Farrer lives in Canberra, Australia, and is a member of the Canberra Speculative Fiction Guild. He has been writing since his teens, and his first published story was in *Inferno!* magazine. Since then he has published several novels and a number of short stories. He was short-listed for an Aurealis Award in 2001.

CS Goto
C S Goto has published short fiction in *Inferno!* and elsewhere, and has written several novels for the Black Library. In his spare time he dreams about what he would do if he had more of it.

Jonathan Green
Jonathan Green has been a freelance writer for the last thirteen years. His work for the Black Library, to date, includes a string of short stories for *Inferno!* magazine and six novels. Jonathan works as a full-time teacher in West London.

Alex Hammond
Alex Hammond lives in Melbourne, Australia. He works as a graphic designer and editor, and studies Law. Alex has written several short stories for *Inferno!* magazine.

Simon Jowett
Simon Jowett writes children's novels, animation scripts and has completed his first movie assignment. He loves the novels of Jeff Noon, the wines of Spain and wears Paul Smith, Katherine Hamnett and party-girl Jenny as often as his busy schedule allows.

William King
William King was born in Stranraer, Scotland, in 1959. His short stories have appeared in *The Year's Best SF, Zenith, White Dwarf* and *Interzone*. He is also the author of seven Gotrek & Felix novels, four volumes chronicling the adventures of the Space Marine warrior, Ragnar Blackmane, as well as the Warhammer 40,000 novel *Farseer*. He currently lives in Prague.

Graham McNeill

Hailing from Scotland, Graham narrowly escaped a career in surveying to join Games Workshop's Games Development team, which, let's face it, sounds much more exciting. He's worked on many codexes since then, including *Codex: Space Marines*. As well as six novels, he's also written a host of short stories for *Inferno!* magazine.

Andras Millward

Andras Millward fled from West Wales to Bristol where he divides his time between writing, manic bursts of hyperactivity and playing guitar. Any time left over is allotted between listening to obscure hardcore and pop-punk bands and dabbling in soft comics and hard fanzines.

Chris Pramas

Chris Pramas is an award-winning game designer whose punk-fueled writing has infected the game industry for over a decade. He is the founder and president of Green Ronin, a leading publisher of roleplaying games. He is also the designer of the new edition of *Warhammer Fantasy Roleplay* and thus has spent far too much time in the dark streets and back alleys of the Old World.

Neil Rutledge

Neil Rutledge is a veteran of the Games Workshop universe (he still has some of his first Citadel miniatures, purchased at eighteen pence each!). He lives in Carlisle and lectures in science education.

Gav Thorpe

Gav Thorpe works for Games Workshop in his capacity as Lead Background Designer, overseeing and contributing to the Warhammer and Warhammer 40,000 worlds. He has a dozen or so short stories to his name and over half a dozen novels.

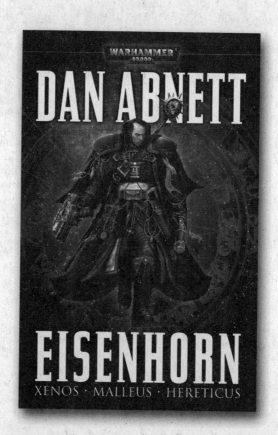

WARHAMMER
40,000

DAN ABNETT

EISENHORN

XENOS · MALLEUS · HERETICUS

More Warhammer 40,000 from the Black Library

EISENHORN

An extract from the anthology of *Xenos*, *Malleus* and *Hereticus*
by Dan Abnett

A cold coming.
Death in the dormant vaults.
Some puritanical reflections.

HUNTING THE RECIDIVIST Murdin Eyclone, I came to Hubris in the Dormant of 240.M41, as the Imperial sidereal calendar has it.

Dormant lasted eleven months of Hubris's twenty-nine month lunar year, and the only signs of life were the custodians with their lighted poles and heat-gowns, patrolling the precincts of the hibernation tombs.

Within those sulking basalt and ceramite vaults, the grandees of Hubris slept, dreaming in crypts of aching ice, awaiting Thaw, the middle season between Dormant and Vital.

Even the air was frigid. Frost encrusted the tombs, and a thick cake of ice covered the featureless land. Above, star patterns twinkled in the curious, permanent night. One of them was Hubris's sun, so far away now. Come Thaw, Hubris would spin into the warm embrace of its star again.

Then it would become a blazing globe. Now it was just a fuzz of light.

As my gun-cutter set down on the landing cross at Tomb Point, I had pulled on an internally heated bodyskin and swathes of sturdy, insulated foul weather gear, but still the perilous cold cut through me now. My eyes watered, and the tears froze on my lashes and cheeks. I remembered the details of the cultural brief my savant had prepared, and quickly lowered my frost visor, trembling as warm air began to circulate under the plastic mask.

Custodians, alerted to my arrival by astropathic hails, stood waiting for me at the base of the landing cross. Their lighted poles dipped in obeisance in the frozen night and the air steamed with the heat that bled from their cloaks. I nodded to them, showing their leader my badge of office. An ice-car awaited; a rust-coloured arrowhead twenty metres long, mounted on ski-blade runners and spiked tracks.

It carried me away from the landing cross and I left the winking signal lights and the serrated dagger-shape of my gun-cutter behind in the perpetual winter night.

The spiked tracks kicked up blizzards of rime behind us. Ahead, despite the lamps, the landscape was black and impenetrable. I rode with Lores Vibben and three custodians in a cabin lit only by the amber glow of the craft's control panel. Heating vents recessed in the leather seats breathed out warm, stale air.

A custodian handed back a data-slate to Vibben. She looked at it cursorily and passed it on to me. I realised my frost visor was still down. I raised it and began to search my pockets for my eye glasses.

With a smile, Vibben produced them from within her own swaddled, insulated garb. I nodded thanks, put them on my nose and began to read.

I was just calling up the last plates of text when the ice-car halted.

'Processional Two-Twelve,' announced one of the custodians.

We dismounted, sliding our visors down into place.

Jewels of frost-flakes fluttered in the blackness about us, sparkling as they crossed through the ice-car's lamp beams. I've heard of bitter cold. Emperor grace me I never feel it again. Biting, crippling, actually bitter to taste on the tongue. Every joint in my frame protested and creaked.

My hands and my mind were numb.

That was not good.

Processional Two-Twelve was a hibernation tomb at the west end of the great Imperial Avenue. It housed twelve thousand, one hundred and forty-two members of the Hubris ruling elite.

We approached the great monument, crunching up the black, frost-coated steps.

I halted. 'Where are the tomb's custodians?'

'Making their rounds,' I was told.

I glanced at Vibben and shook my head. She slid her hand into her fur-edged robes.

'Knowing we approach?' I urged, addressing the custodian again. 'Knowing we expect to meet them?'

'I will check,' said the custodian, the one who had circulated the slate. He pushed on up the steps, the phosphor light on his pole bobbing.

The other two seemed ill at ease.

I beckoned to Vibben, so she would follow me up after the leader.

We found him on a lower terrace, gazing at the strewn bodies of four custodians, their light poles fizzling out around them.

'H-how?' he stammered.

'Stay back,' Vibben told him and drew her weapon. Its tiny amber Armed rune glowed in the darkness.

I took out my blade, igniting it. It hummed.

The south entry of the tombs was open. Shafts of golden light shone out. All my fears were rapidly being confirmed.

We entered, Vibben sweeping the place from side to side with her hand-gun. The hall was narrow and high, lit by chemical glow-globes. Intruding frost was beginning to mark the polished basalt walls.

A few metres inside, another custodian lay dead in a stiffening mirror of blood. We stepped over him. To each side, hallways opened up, admitting us to the hibernation stacks. In every direction, rows and rows of ice-berths ranged down the smoothed basalt chambers.

It was like walking into the Imperium's grandest morgue.

Vibben swept soundlessly to the right and I went left.

I admit I was excited by now, eager to close and conclude a business that had lasted six years. Eyclone had evaded me for six whole years! I studied his methods every day and dreamed of him every night.

Now I could smell him.

I raised my visor.

Water was pattering from the roof. Thaw water. It was growing warmer in here. In their ice-berths, some of the dim figures were stirring.

Too early! Far too early!

Eyclone's first man came at me from the west as I crossed a trunk-junction corridor. I spun, the power sword in my hand, and cut through his neck before his ice-axe could land.

The second came from the south, the third from the east. And then more. More.

A blur.

As I fought, I heard furious shooting from the vaults away to my right. Vibben was in trouble.

I could hear her over the vox-link in our hoods: 'Eisenhorn! Eisenhorn!'

I wheeled and cut. My opponents were all dressed in heat-gowns, and carried ice-tools that made proficient weapons. Their eyes were dark and unforthcoming. Though they were fast, there was something in them that suggested they were doing this mindlessly, by order.

The power sword, an antique and graceful weapon, blessed by the Provost of Inx himself, spun in my hand. With five abrupt moves I made corpses out of them and left their blood vapour drifting in the air.

'Eisenhorn!'

I turned and ran. I splashed heavily down a corridor sluiced with melt water. More shots from ahead. A sucking cry.

I found Vibben face down across a freezer tube, frozen blood gluing her to the sub-zero plastic. Eight of Eyclone's servants lay sprawled around her. Her weapon lay just out of reach of her clawing hand, the spent cell ejected from the grip.

I am forty-two standard years old, in my prime by Imperial standards, young by those of the Inquisition. All my life, I have had a reputation for being cold, unfeeling. Some have called me heartless, ruthless, even cruel. I am not. I am not beyond emotional response or compassion. But I possess – and my masters count this as perhaps my paramount virtue – a singular force of will. Throughout my career it has served me well to draw on this facility and steel myself, unflinching, at all that this wretched galaxy can throw at me. To feel pain or fear or grief is to allow myself a luxury I cannot afford.

Lores Vibben had served with me for five and a half years. In that period she had saved my life twice. She saw herself as my aide and my bodyguard, yet in truth she was more a companion and a fellow warrior. When I recruited her from the clan-slums of Tornish, it was for her combat skills and brutal vigour. But I came to value her just as much for her sharp mind, soft wit and clear head.

I stared down at her body for a moment. I believe I may have uttered her name.

I EXTINGUISHED MY power sword and, sliding it into its scabbard, moved back into the shadows on the far side of the hibernation gallery. I could hear nothing except the increasingly persistent thaw-drip. Freeing my sidearm from its leather rig under my left armpit, I checked its load and opened a vox link. Eyclone was undoubtedly monitoring all traffic in and out of Processional Two-Twelve, so I used Glossia, an informal verbal cipher known only to myself and my immediate colleagues. Most inquisitors develop their own private languages for confidential communication, some more sophisticated than others. Glossia, the basics of which I had designed ten years before, was reasonably complex and had evolved, organically, with use.

'Thorn wishes aegis, rapturous beasts below.'

'Aegis, arising, the colours of space,' Betancore responded immediately and correctly.

'Rose thorn, abundant, by flame light crescent.'

A pause. 'By flame light crescent? Confirm.'

'Confirm.'

'Razor delphus pathway! Pattern ivory!'

'Pattern denied. Pattern crucible.'

'Aegis, arising.'

The link broke. He was on his way. He had taken the news of Vibben's death as hard as I expected. I trusted that would not affect his performance. Midas Betancore was a hot-blooded, impetuous man, which was partly why I liked him. And used him.

I moved out of the shadows again, my sidearm raised. A Scipio-pattern naval pistol, finished in dull chrome with inlaid ivory grips, it felt reassuringly heavy in my gloved hand. Ten rounds, every one a fat, blunt man-stopper, were spring-loaded into the slide inside the grip. I had four more armed slides just like it in my hip pocket.

I forget where I acquired the Scipio. It had been mine for a few years. One night, three years before, Vibben had prised off the ceramite grip plates with their touch-worn, machined-stamped engravings of the Imperial

Aquila and the Navy motto, and replaced them with ivory grips she had etched herself. A common practise on Tornish, she informed me, handing the weapon back the next day. The new grips were like crude scrimshaw, showing on each side a poorly executed human skull through which a thorny rose entwined, emerging through an eye socket, shedding cartoon droplets of blood. She'd inlaid carmine gems into the droplets to emphasise their nature. Below the skull, my name was scratched in a clumsy scroll.

I had laughed. There had been times when I'd almost been too embarrassed to draw the gang-marked weapon in a fight.

Now, now she was dead, I realise what an honour had been paid to me through that devoted work.

I made a promise to myself: I would kill Eyclone with this gun.

As a DEVOTED member of his high majesty the God-Emperor's Inquisition, I find my philosophy bends towards that of the Amalathians. To the outside galaxy, members of our orders appear much alike: an inquisitor is an inquisitor, a being of fear and persecution. It surprises many that internally, we are riven with clashing ideologies.

I know it surprised Vibben. I spent one long afternoon trying to explain the differences. I failed.

To express it in simple terms, some inquisitors are puritans and some are radicals. Puritans believe in and enforce the traditional station of the Inquisition, working to purge our galactic community of any criminal or malevolent element: the triumvirate of evil – alien, mutant and daemon. Anything that clashes with the pure rule of mankind, the preachings of the Ministorium and the letter of Imperial Law is subject to a puritan inquisitor's attention. Hard-line, traditional, merciless... that is the puritan way.

Radicals believe that any methods are allowable if they accomplish the Inquisitorial task. Some, as I understand it, actually embrace and use forbidden resources, such as the Warp itself, as weapons against the enemies of mankind.

I have heard the arguments often enough. They appal me. Radical belief is heretical.

I am a puritan by calling and an Amalathian by choice. The ferociously strict ways of the monodominant philosophy oft-times entices me, but there is precious little subtlety in their ways and thus it is not for me.

Amalathians take our name from the conclave at Mount Amalath. Our endeavour is to maintain the status quo of the Imperium, and we work to identify and destroy any persons or agencies that might destabilise the power of the Imperium from without or within. We believe in strength through unity. Change is the greatest enemy. We believe the God-Emperor has a divine plan, and we work to sustain the Imperium in stability until that plan is made known. We deplore factions and in-fighting... Indeed, it is sometimes a painful irony that our beliefs mark us as a faction within the political helix of the Inquisition.

We are the steadfast spine of the Imperium, its antibodies, fighting disease, insanity, injury, invasion.

I can think of no better way to serve, no better way to be an inquisitor.

So you have me then, pictured. Gregor Eisenhorn, inquisitor, puritan, Amalathian, forty-two years old standard, an inquisitor for the past eighteen years. I am tall and broad at the shoulders, strong, resolute. I have already told you of my force of will, and you will have noted my prowess with a blade.

What else is there? Am I clean-shaven? Yes! My eyes are dark, my hair darker and thick. These things matter little.

Come and let me show you how I killed Eyclone.

I CLUNG TO the shadows, moving through the great tomb as silently as I knew how. A terrible sound rolled through the thawing vaults of Processional Two-Twelve. Fists and palms beating at coffin hoods. Wailing. Gurgling.

The sleepers were waking, their frigid bodies, sore with hibernation sickness, trapped in their caskets. No honour guard of trained cryogeneers waited to unlock them, to sluice their organs with warming bio-fluids or inject stimulants or massage paralysed extremities.

Thanks to Eyclone's efforts, twelve thousand one hundred and forty-two members of the planet's ruling class were being roused early into the bitter season of Dormant, and roused without the necessary medical supervision.

I had no doubt that they would all suffocate in minutes.

My mind scrolled back through the details my savant had prepared for me. There was a central control room, where I could disengage the iceberth locks and at least free them all. But to what good? Without the resuscitation teams, they would fail and perish.

And if I hunted out the control room, Eyclone would have time to escape.

In Glossia code, I communicated this quandary to Betancore, and told him to alert the custodians. He informed me, after a pause, that crash-teams and relief crews were on their way.

But why? The question was still there. Why was Eyclone doing this?

A massed killing was nothing unusual for a follower of Chaos. But there had to be a point, above and beyond the deaths themselves.

I was pondering this as I crossed a hallway deep in the west wing of the Processional. Frantic beating sounds came from the berths all around, and a pungent mix of ice-water and bio-fluid spurted from the drain-taps and cascaded over the floor.

A shot rang out. A las-shot. It missed me by less than a hand's breadth and exploded through the headboard of an ice berth behind me. Immediately, the frantic hammering in that berth stopped, and the waters running out of its ducts were stained pink.

I fired the Scipio down the vault, startled by the noise it made.

Two more las-shots flicked down at me.

Taking cover behind a stone bulkhead, I emptied a clip down the length of the gallery, the spent shell cases smoking in the air as the pumping slide ejected them. A hot vapour of cordite blew back at me.

I swung back into cover, exchanging clips.

A few more spits of laser drizzled past me, then a voice.

'Eisenhorn? Gregor, is that you?'

Eyclone. I knew his thin voice at once. I didn't answer.

'You're dead, you know, Gregor. Dead like they all are. Dead, dead, dead. Step out and make it quick.'

He was good, I'll give him that. My legs actually twitched, actually started to walk me clear of cover into the open. Eyclone was infamous across a dozen settled systems for his mind powers and mesmeric tone. How else had he managed to get these dark-eyed fools to do his bidding?

But I have similar skills. And I have honed them well.

There is a time to use mind or voice tricks gently to draw out your target. And there are times to use them like a stub-gun at point blank range.

It was time for the latter.

I pitched my voice, balanced my mind and yelled: 'Show yourself first!'

Eyclone didn't succumb. I didn't expect him to. Like me, he had years of resilience training. But his two gunmen were easy meat.

The first strode directly out into the middle of the gallery hallway, dropping his lasgun with a clatter. The Scipio made a hole in the middle of his forehead and blew his brains out behind him in a grotesque pink mist. The other stumbled out on his heels, realised his mistake, and began firing.

One of his las-bolts scorched the sleeve of my jacket. I squeezed the pistol's trigger and the Scipio bucked and snarled in my tight grip.

The round penetrated his head under his nose, splintered on his upper teeth and blew the sides of his skull out. He staggered and fell, dead fingers firing his lasrifle again and again, blowing the fascias out of the hibernation stalls around him. Putrid water, bio-fluid and plastic fragments poured out, and some screams became louder.

I could hear footsteps above the screams. Eyclone was running.

I ran too, across the vaults, passing gallery after gallery.

The screaming, the pounding... God-Emperor help me I will never forget that. Thousands of frantic souls waking up to face an agonising death.

Damn Eyclone. Damn him to hell and back.

Crossing the third gallery, I saw him, running parallel to me. He saw me too. He wheeled, and fired.

I ducked back as the blasts of his laspistol shrieked past.

A glimpse was all I'd had: a short, wiry man, dressed in brown heat-robes, his goatee neatly trimmed, his eyes twinkling with malice.

I fired back, but he was running again.

I ran on, glimpsed him down the next gallery and fired again.

At the next gallery, nothing. I waited, and pulled off my outer robe. It was getting hot and damp in Processional Two-Twelve.

When another minute passed and there was still no sign, I began to edge down the gallery towards his last position, gun raised. I'd got ten paces when he swung out of hiding and blazed away at me.

I would have died right there, had not the joker-gods of fate and chance played their hand.

At the moment Eyclone fired, several cryo-tubes finally gave way and yowling, naked, blistered humans staggered out into the corridor, clawing with ice-webbed hands, mewling, vomiting, blind and ice-burned. Eyclone's shots tore three of them apart and hideously wounded a fourth. Had it not been for them, those las-shots would have finished me.

Footsteps, hurried. He was running again.

I pushed on down the gallery, stepping over the blasted ruins of the sleepers who had inadvertently spared me. The wounded one, a middle-aged female, compromised and naked as she lay in the melt-water, clutched at my leg, begging for salvation. Eyclone's gunfire had all but disembowelled her.

I hesitated. A merciful headshot now would spare her everything. But I could not. Once they were awake, the hierarchy of Hubris would not understand a mercy killing. I would be trapped here for years, fighting my case through every court in their legislature.

I shook off her desperate grip and moved on.

Do you think me weak, flawed? Do you hate me for setting my inquisitorial role above the needs of one agonised being?

If you do, I commend you. I think of that woman still, and hate the fact I left her to die slowly. But if you hate me, I know this about you… you are no inquisitor. You don't have the moral strength.

I could have finished her, and my soul might have been relieved. But that would have been an end to my work. And I always think of the thousands… millions perhaps… who would die worse deaths but for my actions.

Is that arrogance?

Perhaps… and perhaps arrogance is therefore a virtue of the Inquisition. I would gladly ignore one life in agony if I could save a hundred, a thousand, more…

Mankind must suffer so that mankind can survive. It's that simple. Ask Aemos. He knows.

Still, I dream of her and her bloody anguish. Pity me for that, at least.

I PRESSED ON through the tomb-vaults, and after another gallery or two, progress became slow. Hundreds of sleepers had now freed themselves, the hallways were jostling with their frantic, blind pain. I skirted those I could, staying out of the way of grasping hands, stepping over some who lay twitching and helpless on the floor. The collective sounds of their braying and whimpering were almost intolerable. There was a hot, fetid stench of decay and bio-waste. Several times I had to break free of hands that seized me.

Grotesquely, the horror made it easier to track Eyclone. Every few paces, another sleeper lay dead or dying, callously gunned down by murderers in desperate flight.

I found a service door forced open at the end of the next file, and entered a deep stairwell that wound up through the edifice. Chemical globes suspended in wall brackets lit the way. From far above, I heard shots, and I ascended, my pistol raised and braced, covering each turn of the staircase as Vibben had taught me.

I came up to what a wall-plaque told me was level eight. I could hear machine noise, industrial and heavy. Through another forced service door lay the walkways to the next galleries and a side access hatch of brushed grey adamite, which stencilled runes identified as the entrance to the main cryogenic generators. Smoke coughed and noise rolled from the hatch.

The cryogenerator chamber was vast, its roof reaching up into the pyramidal summit of Processional Two-Twelve. The rumbling equipment it contained was ancient and vast. The data-slate given to me in the ice-car had said that the cryogenerators that ran the hibernation tombs of Hubris had originally been constructed to equip the ark-fleet that carried the first colonists to the world. They had been cut and salvaged from the giant arks on arrival, and the stone tombs raised around them. A technomagos brotherhood, descended from the ark-fleet engineers, had kept the cryogenerators operating for thousands of years.

This cryogenerator was sixty metres tall and constructed from cast-iron and copper painted in matt-red lead paint. As it rose, it sprouted branches in the form of conduits and heat-exchangers that intertwined with the roof-vents. The hot air of the room vibrated with the noise of its operation. Smoke and steam wreathed the atmosphere and sweat broke out on my brow and back the moment I stepped through the hatchway.

I looked around and quickly noted where several inspection hatches had been levered away. The red paint was scored and scraped along each frame where a crow-bar had been forced in, and hundreds of years of sacred unguents and lexmechanical sigil-seals applied and tended by the technomagi had been broken.

I peered in through the open covers and saw rows of copper-wound cells, vibrating rack-frames wet with black lubricant, sooty ganglions of insulated electrical routing and dripping, lagged iron pipes. Sprung-jawed clips with biting metal teeth had been attached to some of the cells, and wiring from these clips trailed back to a small and obviously new ceramite module box taped inside the hatch frame. A digital runic display on the module flashed amber.

This was where Eyclone's men had artificially triggered the revival process. That meant he had either turned and recruited local technomagi or brought in experts from off-world. Either way, this signified considerable resources.

I moved on, and clambered up a ladder frame onto a raised platform of metal grille. There was something else here, a rectangular casket measuring about a metre and a half along its longest edge. It rested on four claw-like feet and had carrying handles built into its sides. The lid was open, and dozens of cables and leads snaked out, linking it to the cryo-generator's electromechanical guts, exposed by another prised-off hatch.

I looked into the casket, but could make little sense of what I saw there: circuit boards and complex mechanical elements linked by sheaves of cable. And there was a space, a padded recess in the heart of the casket's innards, clearly waiting to receive something the size of a clenched fist. Loose cable ends and plugs were taped in place, ready to be connected. But a key component of this mysterious device was evidently missing.

My vox-link chimed in my ear. It was Betancore. I could barely hear him over the noise of the cryogenerator as he made a quick report in Glossia.

'Aegis, heavens uplift, thrice-sevenfold, a crown with stars. Infamous angel without title, to Thorn by eight. Pattern?'

I considered. I was in no mood to take any more chances. 'Thorn, pattern hawk.'

'Pattern hawk acknowledged,' he said with relish.

I SAW MOVEMENT from the corner of my eye about a half-second after I broke the link with Betancore: another of Eyclone's black-eyed men, running in through the main hatch with an old-model laspistol raised in his hand.

His first shot, a twinkling ball of pink light, snapped the metal handrail of the platform I stood on with an explosive ping. His second and third passed over me as I dived down, and ricocheted off the cast-iron side of the cryogenerator with scorching crackles.

I returned fire, prone, but the angle was bad. Two more las-shots came my way, one cutting sideways into the edge of the platform deck and cutting a gouge through the grille. The gunman was nearly at the foot of the ladder-frame.

Now a second gunman entered the chamber, calling out after the first, a powerful autorifle in his hands. He saw me, and began to raise the weapon, but I had a cleaner angle on him, and dropped him quickly with two rounds through the upper torso.

The other was almost below me now, and fired a shot that punched clean through the grille just next to my right foot.

I didn't hesitate. I went up and over the rail and directly down onto him. We crashed onto the chamber floor, the powerful impact throwing the Scipio out of my grasp despite my efforts to hold onto it. The man was jabbering some insane nonsense into my face and had a good grip on the front of my tunic. I had him by the throat and by the wrist of his gun-hand, forcing the laspistol away. He fired it twice into the ceiling space above.

'Enough!' I commanded, modulating my tone to emphasise my will as I drove it into his mind. 'Drop it!'

He did, meekly, as if surprised. Psyker tricks of will often baffle those who find themselves compelled by them. As he faltered, I threw a punch that connected well and left him unconscious on the floor.

As I bent to recover the Scipio, Betancore voxed me again. 'Aegis, pattern hawk, infamous angel cast down.'

'Thorn acknowledged. Resume pattern crucible.'
I pushed on after my quarry.

EYCLONE MADE IT into the upper vaults and out onto a landing platform built into the sloping side of Processional Two-Twelve. The wind was fierce. Eyclone had eight of his cult with him and they were expecting an orbital pinnace that would carry them away to safety.

They had no way of knowing that, thanks to Betancore, their means of escape was now burning in a deep impact gouge in the permafrost about eight kilometres north.

What rose above the landing platform out of the blizzard night, its down thrusters wailing, was my gun-cutter. Four hundred and fifty tonnes of armoured alloy, eighty metres from barbed nose to raked stern, landing gear still lowered like spider-legs, it rose on the blue-hot downwash of angled jets. Banks of floodlights under its beak-nose cut on and bathed the deck and the cultists in fierce white light.

Panicking, some of them fired up at it.

That was all the cue Betancore needed. His temper was hot, his mind void of anything except the fact that Vibben was dead.

The gun-turrets in the ends of the stubby wings rotated and washed the platform with withering heavy fire. Stone splintered. Bodies were reduced to sprays of liquid.

Eyclone, more intelligent than his men, had sprinted off the platform to the hatch as the gun-cutter rose into view.

And that's where he ran into me.

He opened his mouth in shock and I pushed the muzzle of Vibben's gun into it. I'm sure he wanted to say something important. I didn't care what it was.

I punched the gun so hard into his mouth the trigger guard broke his lower teeth. He tried to reach for something on his belt.

I fired.

Having emptied his brain-case and shattered it into the bargain, the round still had so much force it crossed the deck and pinked off the armoured nose of the hovering gun-cutter, just below the cockpit window.

'Sorry,' I said.

'Don't worry about it,' Betancore crackled back over the vox-link.

The story continues in

EISENHORN

By Dan Abnett

Available now from *www.blacklibrary.com*

WARHAMMER
40,000

THE ULTRAMARINES
OMNIBUS

Buy these
omnibuses or read
a free extract at
www.blacklibrary.co

'Great characters, truck loads of intrigue and an amazing sense of pace.' **Enigma**

GRAHAM McNEILL
NIGHTBRINGER • WARRIORS OF ULTRAMAR • DEAD SKY BLACK SUN

WARHAMMER 40,000

THE SPACE WOLF

OMNIBUS

WILLIAM KING

SPACE WOLF • RAGNAR'S CLAW • GREY HUNTER

ISBN 978-1-84416-457-8

WARHAMMER 40,000

THE BLOOD ANGELS
OMNIBUS

Contains the
novels *Deus
Encarmine* and
Deus Sanguinius

'War-torn tales of loyalty and honour.' – SFX

JAMES SWALLOW

ISBN 978-1-84416-559-9